CRIMSON DEATH

Anita has never seen Damian, her vampire servant, in such a state. The rising sun doesn't usher in the peaceful death that he desperately needs. Instead, he's being bombarded with violent nightmares and blood sweats.

And now, with Damian at his most vulnerable, Anita needs him the most. The vampire who created him—who subjected him to centuries of torture—might be losing control, allowing rogue vampires to run wild and break one of their kind's few strict taboos.

Some say love is a great motivator, but hatred gets the job done, too. And when Anita joins forces with her friend Edward to stop the carnage, Damian will be at their side, even if it means traveling back to the land where all his nightmares spring from . . . a place that couldn't be less welcoming to a vampire, an assassin, and a necromancer.

Ireland.

PRAISE FOR *DEAD ICE*

"An absorbing plot and a tantalizing mystery."
—*St. Louis Post-Dispatch*

"A sex-positive, kick-ass female protagonist." —*Starburst*

"Hamilton spurs her readers on to an absorbing conclusion that will have you racing to the final page." —*RT Book Reviews*

Also by Laurell K. Hamilton

CRIMSON
DEATH

LAURELL K. HAMILTON

JOVE
New York

A JOVE BOOK
Published by Berkley
An imprint of Penguin Random House LLC
375 Hudson Street, New York, New York 10014

Copyright © 2016 by Laurell K. Hamilton
Penguin Random House supports copyright. Copyright fuels creativity, encourages
diverse voices, promotes free speech, and creates a vibrant culture. Thank you for buying
an authorized edition of this book and for complying with copyright laws by not
reproducing, scanning, or distributing any part of it in any form without permission.
You are supporting writers and allowing Penguin Random House to continue to
publish books for every reader.

A JOVE BOOK and BERKLEY are registered trademarks and the B colophon
is a trademark of Penguin Random House LLC.

ISBN: 9781101987742

Berkley hardcover edition / October 2016
Jove mass market edition / June 2017

Printed in the United States of America
1 3 5 7 9 10 8 6 4 2

Cover photographs: woman © Mimi Haddon/Photolibrary/Getty Images;
blood © worawut2524/Shutterstock.com;
wrought-iron fence © Macrovector/Shutterstock.com;
gritty background © Eky Studio/Shutterstock.com
Cover design by Judith Lagerman

This one has to be for Jonathon, Genevieve, and Spike. My husband, our girlfriend, and her husband, respectively. Here's to more love, less fighting, more joy, and less sorrow.

To Sasquatch, our beloved pug, who passed away just as I started writing this book. He was my constant writing companion for fourteen years, and I believe one of the reasons that this book took longer than normal to write is his loss. Apparently, I write better with a pug at my side.

ACKNOWLEDGMENTS

To Shawn, who is my three a.m. call, my wisdom check, best friend, and fellow outlaw. To Jess and Will, who are learning what it means to work for and with a writer. It's a magical experience!

1

I'D FALLEN ASLEEP cuddled between two of the men I
loved most, with one arm flung across their naked bodies so I
could touch the third. All three of them were warm when I fell
asleep, but when my phone woke me hours later, only two of
the bodies in the bed were still warm. The only vampire in the
bed had died when the sun came up a mile over our heads in
our nice safe cave of a bedroom. It was great for vampires, but
if you were afraid of the dark or didn't like the idea of tons of
stone pressing down on your head, well, you couldn't sleep
with us.

I scrambled over Nathaniel's almost fever-hot body for my
phone, which was plugged in on the bedside table, but when
the screen came on it was his phone, not mine, because his
lock screen was a picture of the three of us and mine was a
close-up of our hands entwined with the new engagement
rings. I finally got my phone and hit the button, but it had already gone to voice mail.

Micah asked in a voice thick with sleep, "Who was it?"

I squinted at the bright screen in the very dark room and
said, "I don't recognize the number, or hell, the area code. I
think it's international. Who the hell would be calling me
from out of the country?"

Nathaniel snuggled against the front of my body, burying
his face between my breasts, as he tucked himself lower under
the covers. He mumbled something, but since he was both the
heaviest sleeper and the most likely to talk in his sleep, I didn't
pay much attention.

"What time is it?" Micah asked, his voice less sleep-filled
and closer to awake.

"Five a.m.," I said. I clicked my phone to black and tried to put it back on the bedside table, but Nathaniel had pinned me and I couldn't quite reach.

"We've only been asleep for three hours," he said in a voice that was starting to sound aggrieved.

"I know," I said. I was still trying to push my phone back on the edge of the table with a now firmly asleep Nathaniel weighing me down.

Micah wrapped his arm around my waist and Nathaniel's back and pulled us both closer to him. "Sleep, must have more sleep," he said with his face buried between my shoulders. If I didn't slide down into the covers soon, they'd both be asleep and I'd be pinned with my arms and shoulders bared. The bedroom at night was about fifty degrees; I wanted my shoulders covered. I gave one last push to my phone, which fell to the floor, but it didn't light back up, which meant it was still plugged in, so I was good with it on the floor. Screw it, I was going back to sleep.

I had to force both men to give me enough room to slide down between them so we were all covered and warm again. I was just starting to drift back to sleep to the sounds of their even breathing when my phone rang again, but this time it played a different song, George Thorogood's "Bad to the Bone." It was the personalized ringtone for one of my best friends, Edward, assassin to the undead and fellow U.S. Marshal Ted Forrester. Interestingly, Edward and Ted were the same person; think Clark Kent and Superman.

I flung the covers off all of us and scrambled, falling to the floor and fumbling for the phone that was glowing in the pile of clothes beside the bed. I hit the button and said, "Here, I'm here!"

"Anita, are you all right?" Edward's voice was too cheerful, which was all the clue I needed that he was with other police officers who would be overhearing everything.

"Yeah, I'm good. You sound awfully chipper for five a.m.," I said, trying not to sound like I was already getting cold outside the body heat of the bed. I started to fumble in the clothes pile for something that was mine but kept coming up with just the guys' clothes.

"It's eleven a.m. here," he said.

He wasn't home in New Mexico, then, so I asked, "Where are you?"

"Dublin."

"Dublin what?"

"Ireland," he said.

I sat naked and shivering on the floor, scooping through the pile of clothes around me like a bird trying to make a nest, and tried to think. I failed, so I asked, "Why are you in Dublin, Ireland?"

"For the same reason I'm calling you, Anita."

"Which is?" I tried not to get irritated at him, because it usually amused him, and Ted usually took longer to tell anything. Edward was far more abrupt. Yes, they were the same person, but Edward was more of a method actor, and trying to get him to break character wasn't a good idea.

"Vampires."

"There aren't any vampires in Ireland. It's the only country in the world that doesn't have them."

"That's what we all thought until about six weeks ago."

"What happened six weeks ago?" I asked, trying to burrow myself into the clothes on the floor for warmth.

Someone from the bed above me threw my robe on top of me. I told whichever of my leopards had done it, "Thanks."

"They had their first vampire victim," Edward said.

I slipped into the robe, using my chin to hold the phone against my shoulder. The black silk robe was better than being naked, but silk isn't really very warm. I kept meaning to buy something with a little more heat retention, but it was hard to find sexy and warm at the same time. "Vampire victim, so dead?"

"No, just a little drained."

"Okay, if it was nonconsensual blood donation here in the States the vampire would be up on charges, but if it was consensual it's not even a crime."

"Vampire gaze wiped her memory of it," he said.

"If the vampire and blood donor had agreed that the vamp could use their gaze so the donor could get the whole vampire experience, then it's treated like you let someone drink too much at a party and then let them walk home drunk—again it's not even a crime here, just bad judgment."

"Vic can't remember, so we'll never know if consent was given or not."

"If they took a swab of the bite for genetics and he, or she, is in the system, they can find the vampire in question."

"Nobody believed it was a vampire bite, so they didn't treat it like an attack. They thought she'd been slipped a date-rape drug."

"The fang marks weren't a clue?" I asked.

"You said it yourself, Anita: There are no vampires in Ireland. In thousands of years of history, there's never been a vampire here. They noted the fang marks as possible needle marks for the drug they thought had been used on the vic; if they hadn't been hunting for needle marks and other signs of drug use, they wouldn't have even found them. They are some of the tiniest, neatest marks I've ever seen."

I sat up a little straighter, both to tie my robe tighter and because that meant something. "You've seen almost as many vampire bites as I have."

"Yep," he said in his best Ted Forrester drawl. He was probably playing the full American cowboy, accent and all, for the Irish police. He could be the ultimate undercover person and blend in damn near anywhere, but when he was Ted, it was like he enjoyed just how thick he could play the part. I wondered if he'd packed Ted's cowboy hat and brought it on the airplane. The thought of him wearing it in Ireland was either fun or cringeworthy. I wasn't sure which yet.

"How tiny? Do you think it's a child vampire?"

"I've seen female vamps that had a bite this small, but that one could be a child."

"What do you mean, that one?"

"We have at least three different bite radiuses."

"So three different vamps," I said.

"At the very least, maybe more."

"What do you mean, maybe more?"

"I've got permission to share photos with you if you can get to a computer."

"My phone is a computer. Can't you just text me?"

"I could, but you'll want a bigger screen to look at some of these."

"Okay, I . . . I can get to a computer. I just need someone to help me log on, or something."

"You have a secure email account, because I've sent you things to it before," he said.

"I know, I know. I just don't use the computers here much."

"Where are you?"

"Circus of the Damned."

"Tell Jean-Claude howdy for me?"

"Howdy? Even Ted doesn't say *Howdy*."

"I'm American, Anita. We're all cowboys; didn't you know that, darling?" he said in a drawl so thick it sounded like you should be able to do a Texas two-step on it.

"Yeah, like all the Irish are leprechauns and go around saying *Top of the morning to you*."

"If I had my way, you'd be here seeing all the leprechauns."

"What do you mean, if you had your way?"

"Go to the computer so you can see the pictures, Anita," and the out-West accent lost some of its thickness, fading into what was Edward's normal "middle of nowhere," maybe Midwestern accent. I'd known him for over six years before I'd learned that Theodore (Ted) Forrester was his actual birth name and the one that both the military and the Marshals Service knew him by. He'd just been Edward to me.

"Okay, but what did you mean, if you had your way?" I got to my feet and my lower body was instantly colder in just the silk robe without the nest of other clothes around me. I looked down at the bed, because both Micah and Nathaniel were better with the computers down the hallway than I was; hell, Nathaniel was still occasionally sneaking new ringtones for people into my phone. Some of them had been embarrassing when they sounded at work with the other marshals, but "Bad to the Bone" for Edward had worked so well, I kept it.

"When you're at the computer, call me back," he said, and hung up. That was more like Edward.

Once the phone screen stopped glowing, the room was pitch-black, cave dark, so that you could touch your own eyeball because you couldn't see your finger coming to flinch away. We usually left the bathroom door open, so the night-light inside could give some illumination, but whoever had gone in last had forgotten. The only thing that let me walk to the bathroom door without bumping anything was familiarity with the layout. I opened the door and it was so damn bright that for a second I thought the overhead lights had been left on; but as I blinked and adjusted to the glow, I realized it was just the night-light. It looked ungodly bright because my eyes had adjusted to the thick darkness of the other room, but as my eyes readjusted to the light it was just the night-light like normal.

I'd have liked to let the men in my life sleep, but I needed help with the computers. I was really going to have to take notes the next time someone showed me how to do all this because I never seemed to remember it the way that they did. I stared down at the bed. Nathaniel had curled down into the covers so that only the top of his head and the thick braid of his nearly ankle-length hair showed. The light was just bright enough to gleam red in the brown of his auburn hair. He was curled up on his side so that his broad shoulders rose like a hunky mountain above the rest of the bed. It was impossible to tell with him curled up like that, but he was five-nine. Micah lay just out of arm's reach from him; they were leaving my space in the middle of them empty, waiting for me to crawl back in and sleep, which I so wanted to do, but duty called. Micah's curls had spilled across his face so the most skin I saw was the darker skin of his slender shoulders and one arm that showed muscles, but he would never bulk up the way Nathaniel did. Genetics had made our very dominant and commanding Nimir-Raj, leopard king, my size, five-three. You couldn't see it under the covers, but he was built like a swimmer with that upside-down triangle of shoulders to slender waist and hips. Nathaniel was built not only more muscular but more lush, the man's version of curves. Jean-Claude lay on his back. He could sleep on his side but he preferred to sleep on his back, and since he died at dawn so he couldn't keep cuddling as we moved during our sleep, it wasn't as big a deal that he didn't spoon as well as the three of us, who were all side sleepers.

Jean-Claude was the tallest of us at six feet even. Lying on his back, he looked every inch of it. His long black curls fell almost to his waist now, as did mine. We both had truly black hair, me because my mother's family had been Mexican, and his because it just was; his skin was paler than mine, but not by much thanks to my German father. I was pretty sure that if Jean-Claude hadn't been a vampire I'd have been paler than he was, but no one is paler than a vampire. Even literally dead to the world he was still one of the most beautiful men I'd ever seen, and that was with Nathaniel and Micah to compare to, though admittedly both their faces were currently covered, but I knew what everyone looked like. I was told that I was beautiful and some days I believed it, but looking down at the three of them I was still amazed that everyone and everything in the bed was mine, and I was theirs. I caught a gleam in Micah's hair and realized it was his eyes open and watching me through the tangle of his rich brown curls.

I whispered, "Were you just pretending to sleep?"

He started to sit up and nodded.

I *tsk-tsk*ed at him. "It's police business."

"Then get a policeman to help you with the computer," he said, but he was already climbing out of the covers, carefully trying not to uncover the other two men.

"Get my gun," I whispered.

He reached into the specially made holster attached to the headboard and grabbed my Springfield EMP, and crawled to the foot of the bed to hand it to me so that he didn't cross Nathaniel's body with it. He was nowhere near the trigger, and he was being careful, but he knew the rules for gun safety. Treat every gun as if it's loaded and lethal, and never, ever cross someone's body with it unless you mean to shoot them. I took the gun and put it in my pocket, wondering if it would hold the weapon. The gun fit, but my robe was seriously hanging crooked from the weight. I tied the sash at my waist even tighter and tried to see if my hand would fit into the pocket well enough for me to draw the gun if I had to; it wasn't perfect, but it worked.

Micah crawled out of the bed with his own handgun. He was one of the few lycanthropes I knew who carried a gun and weren't professional bodyguards or mercenaries. He was not only the Nimir-Raj of our local wereleopard pard but also head of the Coalition for Better Understanding Between Human and Lycanthrope Communities. The Coalition was a national organization that was slowly but surely forging the country's different types of shapeshifters into a cohesive group with one voice, shared goals, and they looked to him to lead them toward those goals. Not everyone was happy that the infighting that had always divided the shapeshifter communities was being turned into something more cooperative. Some hate groups saw it as a danger to humanity. Some lycanthropes saw it as us forcing our rule onto them, even though the Coalition never entered another group's territory unless invited in to solve a problem they couldn't solve on their own. It was like people who called the police when they needed them and then got angry that the police found evidence of a crime while they were saving the phone caller and his or her family.

There'd been more than one death threat against Micah, so he had bodyguards when he traveled and carried his own gun when he could. Not all buildings and businesses would allow concealed carry on the premises, so sometimes he had to leave the gun behind and rely on the bodyguards, but he liked to be able to take care of himself, too. Just one more thing we agreed on.

Micah's robe was one that Jean-Claude had bought for him, or maybe had had made, because it looked like something from the Victorian era, deep forest green velvet covered in gold-and-green embroidery. The thick cuffs and the collar and lapels that swept from his neck to his waist were shiny gold with more of the brocade embroidery. The robe also fell exactly to his feet but was a fraction short enough that he never tripped on it or had to lift it up when he was walking on anything but stairs. Stairs were tricky with anything that went to your ankles. I knew that at least the robe had been tailored to fit him. He added dark green house slippers and he was ready to go.

I finally had house shoes, too, so that my feet were warm, and they stayed on rather than making me shuffle like the house slippers had done, but the silk robe . . . I needed something warmer. Especially now that we were here at least five nights a week. The two days in the Jefferson County house were mainly so we could get some sunlight. Except for Micah, we all worked almost exclusively nights, and after a while it was just depressing without some sunshine. I'd finally asked Jean-Claude if he missed it, and he'd said, "Very much, *ma petite*, much more than I thought I would when I agreed to become what I am."

Micah gathered his own phone and his eyeglasses from the bedside table on his and Jean-Claude's side of the bed. The glasses had green frames with gold accents to complement his green-gold leopard eyes. He'd been wearing prescription sunglasses for a long time without most of us being aware they were prescription. A very bad man had forced him to stay in leopard form until he hadn't been able to shift completely back to human form. He had his summer tan from running outside, so that the eyes looked incredibly exotic against the darker skin, but the serious downside to his having kitty-cat eyes was that cats are nearsighted. He'd also lost some of his color vision, though not as much as a real cat, as if something were more human about his leopard eyes. His optician had asked permission to write a paper on the difference in his vision and was cowriting the paper with a zoo veterinarian. Micah had worn the sunglasses to hide his eyes when he didn't want to stand out and because he'd worried that having less-than-perfect eyesight might be used against him in fights for dominance in the lycanthrope community, but finally he'd gotten glasses that helped him read more easily as well as see farther away. Cat eyes focused differently and had made him work harder to read than we'd realized. He had contact lenses, too, but here with us he didn't bother. I liked the way the dark frames bordered his eyes like they were works of art that finally had a frame worthy of them rather than being hidden away behind dark sunglasses.

We left Nathaniel deeply asleep nested in the covers and already wiggling a little closer to Jean-Claude. This bed was big enough that he might just wrap himself in covers before he reached the other man for cuddling, but Nathaniel was a cuddle-seeking sleeper more than any of the rest of us, and the rest of us were pretty cuddly.

Micah and I moved as quietly as we could toward the door, leaving our shared boy asleep and our shared master sleeping the sleep of the dead. We probably didn't have to move all that quietly, but it was just polite. Micah stopped me at the door and made motions for me to fluff my curls into place. I raised an eyebrow at him, and he mouthed, *Jean-Claude*. Which meant my vampy fiancé had requested that Micah remind me not to go out without tidying my hair a little. Since I was technically going to be queen of all the vampires once I married Jean-Claude, I guess a little decorum was called for, but it still irked me.

Micah actually finger-tamed his own curls, too, so at least it was evenhanded silliness. Jean-Claude had said that our appearance reflected on him, and vampires, especially the very old ones, could be exceedingly vain. It had been everything I could do not to say, *Vampires vain, you're joking*, but I didn't, since he rarely went anywhere when he wasn't perfect top to bottom. I didn't think of it as vanity, more just him, just Jean-Claude, and I loved him, so I did what men had done for centuries when they waited for their beauties to get ready for the night—waited patiently for the perfection that was worth waiting for. It had never occurred to me that he might start wanting me to do more perfection on myself as the wedding got closer. It was a trend I wasn't really enjoying, but I was letting it ride. One thing I'd learned was to pick my battles. I'd already lost on the size of the wedding; I was still hoping to win on the wedding dresses for the women, mine included.

Micah opened the outer door and the two guards went to attention, backs ramrod straight, shoulders back, arms at their sides as if they were still wearing a uniform that had a crease or stripe to follow.

I said, "At ease, guys. You're not in the Army anymore."

"I wasn't in the Army, Marshal Blake," the taller one said. His hair was still so short that I could see scalp through his nearly white-blond hair.

"It was a line of an old song, Milligan; I remember that it's 'Anchors Aweigh' for you."

The slightly shorter man, who was letting his brown hair grow out from the high and tight, gave a crooked smile and said, "Millie doesn't like the classics much."

I smiled back. "You need to broaden his horizons, Custer."

"Every time Pud tries to broaden my horizons, my wife

gets mad," Milligan said, smiling. I knew that *Pud* was the first syllable of *Pudding*, because they'd started calling Custer *Custard* as a nickname, but in that mysterious way of nicknames it had changed into *Pudding* and then *Pud*. How did I know? I asked.

Micah chuckled and shook his head. "Your wife made me promise that I wouldn't let Custer lead you astray when we traveled out of town."

"I know she talked to you, sir."

"It's just Micah, or Mr. Callahan—no *sir* needed."

"Are you serious? Your wife talked to Micah about me?" Custer asked.

Milligan nodded. "That last weekend trip, you almost cost me my marriage."

"I thought you were joking about that," Custer said.

His friend shook his head.

"Well, fuck, man, I'm sorry. I didn't mean that." Custer actually looked serious, which wasn't typical for him.

Milligan and Custer were part of a SEAL unit that had been attacked by a group of insurgents that thought being wereanimals made them a match for the SEALs. They'd been wrong, but the six-man unit had lost one of their own and the surviving five had all tested positive for lycanthropy, which meant an automatic medical discharge. We had other former military for similar reasons. One of them had brought the unit to our attention, and we'd offered them jobs.

Some of the private contractor firms would take shapeshifters, but they were all new enough shifters that full moons meant they were either in secure areas or with older, more experienced lycanthropes who babysat them as they learned to control their inner beasts. Until they got complete control of themselves they couldn't work for any of the private contractor firms, because their rule was that you had to be a lycanthrope for at least two years before you could apply. Some companies insisted on four years, and not all countries would allow lycanthropes across their borders. The former SEALs had less than a year of turning furry. When the time was over they might decide to go to the other firms, because the money was better, for some assignments a lot better, but the money here wasn't bad and the level of life-threatening danger was much lower.

Either way, they had good jobs with benefits for them and their families while they were deciding what to do next with a set of skills that was impressive as hell but of limited use in the civilian sector. So far their biggest complaint, and only from Custer and one other, was that there hadn't been enough excitement on the job.

Micah and I started down the hallway hand in hand. It meant one of us had to compromise a gun hand, but since we didn't expect to be attacked in our own inner sanctum, I figured we were safe. I even let him have my gun hand, even though I had better scores on the range. Custer said, "I'm not sure how this works, but we're on duty here to protect everyone in the room behind us, including the two of you."

"I'll go with them. You stay on the door," Milligan said.

Custer eased back to his post beside the door without an argument. You could always tell who outranked whom in the newly ex-military, because of moments like that. We'd only had one person at a time from a unit before this, never most of a group that had worked together for years and then lost their careers in the same fight. They were still very much together as a unit. In fact, Claudia, who was in charge of our guards overall but especially here at the Circus, had talked to me about whether we wanted to separate them for work. They needed to learn to work with the rest of our people and not just with one another, but so far it hadn't been an issue that anyone had complained about.

I honestly didn't think we needed a bodyguard here in the underground of the Circus, but I'd learned not to try to argue with some of the guards about where their duty lay. It just made me tired and didn't gain me much. I could have played the "I'm your boss" card, but I was also one of their protectees, so it was a gray area. If I was their boss, then I could tell them to take a flying leap and they had to listen, but if something happened and I got hurt on their watch . . . Like I said, it was a gray area, so Milligan trailed us toward the computer room. Though Jean-Claude had totally embraced the new technology, he didn't like everyone living on their phones and electronic devices instead of actually looking at and talking with the people around them, so he'd limited everything but smartphones to the one room. I happened to know that the other reason he'd done it was that some of the older vampires were a little intimidated by all the new tech. Besides, having to bring the wires and cables down this far through the rock hadn't been easy, and keeping the computers in one place helped make it just a little bit easier.

Milligan hurried forward and opened the door to the computer room for us. Micah and I both let him. The room was dim, lit only by the banks of computer screens that were still cycling through the images on their screens. Some had finally gone black and still for the night. We moved into the room and Milligan started to come in with us, but I said, "Sorry, Milligan, but I'm going to have to look at police evidence."

"I have to make sure the room is clear," he said.

Again, I could have argued with him, but I let him do his job, though again, I was pretty sure the two of us could take care of anything that might be lurking in the computer room down here. It wasn't that big a room and there was only one area that was actually out of sight of the door.

Milligan came back around the room after completing his circuit. "The room is clear, ma'am, sir."

"Then you can leave us," Micah said.

"You don't have to stay right by our sides," I said.

He hesitated, and you could almost watch the wheels turning as he weighed whom he was supposed to listen to and whom he could safely override. A lot of our new ex-military had issues with the new, less rigid chain of command.

"We're going to be talking police business, Milligan. You cannot be in here for it," I said.

Milligan nodded. "Okay, that makes sense." He went for the door.

"And don't stand just outside the door," Micah said.

Milligan turned. "Sir, I . . ."

"I know I could hear the conversation through the door, Milligan, which means so could you."

"Claudia will have my head if I don't wait for you."

"We're both armed, and we're standing in our own underground fortress," I said. "If we're not safe here, then we're in deeper shit than just one guard can handle."

Milligan got that arrogant look on his face, one I'd seen before from men with certain backgrounds.

"Even a former SEAL wouldn't be enough, Milligan. Now go back to Custer and guard Jean-Claude's door."

He tried to argue some more, but Micah said, "That's an order, Milligan. Anita and I both outrank Claudia."

He frowned, sighed, and said, "Yes, sir." He didn't question it again, just turned on his heel and went for the door.

I made sure Milligan walked down the hallway and then came back to Micah.

He sat down in the chair in front of the computer so he could type faster, and within a few minutes I was up and running. He didn't even have to ask for my password or username anymore, because he'd helped me too many times and had finally memorized it all. That probably wouldn't please the other officers if they knew, since he was a civilian, but I wouldn't tell if he didn't.

I called Edward back. He answered on the first ring. "Anita, are you online?" His voice was less Ted and more Edward, so I thought to ask, "Can you talk freely yet?"

"No." Edward's one-word answer rather than the longer way around the mountain that he sometimes took as Ted.

"While we wait for the email to come through, you said something about how if you had your way I'd be seeing more than pictures, or something."

"They don't like the fact that you're a necromancer." His voice held some of Ted's happy undertones, but there was also Edward's cold emptiness. He was not happy that they wouldn't let me come play.

I heard voices in the background. Edward said, "Sorry, Anita. I've just been corrected"—with more of Ted's accent this time—"because it would be against their own laws to deny someone entry to their country on the basis of the type of magic they could perform."

"I think of it as a psychic gift more than something mystical," I said.

"Their laws actually don't acknowledge a difference between psychic gifts and magic, only between magic and Church-sanctioned miracles."

"If they actually mention miracles in their laws, then that's a first outside of Rome that I'm aware of."

"Then be aware, Anita, because this is the second," he

said, and I could hear the smile in his voice, but it didn't match the words, as if he were having trouble staying Ted in front of the other cops. What had they done, or what had happened, between one phone call and the next to make him struggle with it?

"Are you okay, Ted?"

"I'm just dandy."

I let it go, because he either wouldn't talk about it or couldn't with all the other officers in the room. My email pinged. Micah helped me open the attachment on it, and we were suddenly looking at a throat with two delicate fang marks on it. It was a really small bite radius. It could be a child or a woman with a smaller-than-average mouth. The second neck wound had considerably bigger holes; no one was going to mistake them for hypodermic needle marks. These were definitely a different vampire.

"I'm going to put you on speakerphone, Anita. Tell us what you see." He didn't mean *tell us*; he meant *tell them*. I was pretty sure this was some kind of test. If I dazzled them, would they let me come play with Edward in Ireland? Did I want to go play in Ireland? I didn't want to do an international flight with my phobia of flying—that was for sure—but . . . I didn't like that they were all prejudiced against a psychic gift that I couldn't do anything about. Also, I was a wee bit competitive.

"Well, from the first two bite images you've got at least two different vampires. The first could be a child, or a grown woman with a small mouth, or a crowded one."

"This is Superintendent Pearson, Marshal Blake. What do you mean, *crowded*?" His voice sounded like I'd expected. Irish in that way that movies convince you must be real. It made me smile that he actually sounded like movie Irish; so many accents didn't match what you expected.

"Fang marks are just like human bite marks in one way, Superintendent Pearson. It's not always the size of the mouth that dictates how a bite mark looks; sometimes it's how the teeth are placed. Someone who has too many teeth for the size of their mouth can sometimes have teeth that are sort of crowded together, which will make the space between their canines much smaller than you'd expect for an adult."

Another man's voice said, "We don't care about canine teeth. We care about the fangs." His accent didn't match as well, as if he were from a different part of Ireland. It was the same idea as a Southern accent here, as compared to Northern, or Midwestern, though television and the Internet were erasing regional accents in a lot of places.

"The canine teeth are what become fangs after the person changes into a vampire," I said.

"That's Inspector Logan. Please ignore him, Marshal Blake."

I heard Logan make an unhappy noise, but he didn't make a second remark. Pearson outranked him, or someone else in the room did and had taken Pearson's side.

Edward said, in a much more cheerful version of Ted's voice, "Go to the next picture, Anita."

I did what he asked. The fang marks seemed bigger still, but the holes weren't as neat and tidy, so . . . "The marks look even bigger than the last set, but they're also less neat, as if the vampire used more force to bite down, or jerked out more when it stopped feeding, so it could be the same vamp as bite number two."

Pearson asked, "Do you think we can assume that vampire number two is an adult male?"

"With the spacing between fangs you'd probably be safe assuming that, but I've known a few women with exceptionally wide teeth spacing, so it's not a guarantee. The necks all look like women; is that correct?"

"Yes."

"Inspector Logan here . . ."

"Address her by her title," another voice said, and I thought it was a woman.

"Fine, Marshal Blake, this is Inspector Logan. The pictures don't show the Adam's apple; how did you know they were women?"

"I've spent a lot of years looking at fang marks on skin, Inspector Logan. After a while, you just know what you're looking at."

Edward said, "Is there anything else that makes you think male or female, Anita?"

"A lot of vamps prefer to take blood according to their

sexual preferences, so most males prefer to feed on women, and a lot of females feed on men, but some new vamps take any victim that they can, just like any other young predator on a learning curve."

"Detective Logan here, Marshal Blake." And there was something in the way he said my title and name that let me know he wasn't happy about it. Or maybe I was being overly sensitive.

Micah looked at me, and the look was enough; he thought the same thing about Logan. Maybe I wasn't being overly sensitive.

"Yes, Detective Logan?"

"Are you saying that gay vampires would feed on same-sex victims?"

"Possibly, but if you've never had vampires in Ireland before, then these may all be very new. So again, they're probably going after whatever victim is easiest. Some women feel safer feeding on other women, even though as a vampire they could beat the shit out of most human men. They never quite get rid of the idea that men are stronger and more dangerous than they are, so they feed almost exclusively on other women regardless of their sexual preference."

"So basically, you don't know anything about these vampires just from the pictures?" Logan said, and he made sure that I heard the disdain.

"I told you that Anita would be more useful in person, Logan," Edward said, holding on to the cheerful Ted voice with effort. Logan had already been a pain in the ass for his voice to struggle like that.

"I don't think we need to fly your girlfriend in, Forrester."

"Logan!" And now I was sure it was a woman.

"That's enough, Luke, and I mean it this time," Pearson said.

"Everyone knows . . ."

"No," Pearson said, and the Irish accent held anger just fine, "everyone does not know, and before you start spreading rumors about a fellow officer, you might want to make certain you know what you're talking about."

"That's how a lot of the rumors get started," I said.

"What, Marshal Blake?"

"One person says something that isn't true, but it's too scandalous not to repeat, and then the rumors feed on each other, and before you know it, everyone knows the truth, even when it's a lie."

"Well said. I'm Inspector Sheridan, Rachel Sheridan." The woman's voice again.

"Glad to almost meet you, Inspector Sheridan," I said.

"You would take her side," Logan said in his sour voice.

"Who got your panties in a twist about me? We've never even met," I said.

"It's me he's mad at," Edward said in a voice that was far more cheerful than the words warranted.

"Why in blazes would I be mad at you?" Logan asked.

"Because you're jealous," Edward said.

"Why would I be jealous of you, Forrester?"

"For the same reason you're going to be jealous of Marshal Anita Blake."

"And why is that?"

"Anita, look at the next picture."

I hesitated for a second, then thought, *Why the hell do I care if some cop in Ireland doesn't like me?* I moved to the next image and it was another set of fang marks like the last ones, bigger fangs, and this time rough enough that the wounds were jagged around the edges. It made me have to swallow hard and fight off an urge to rub at the scars over my collarbone at the bend of my left arm where the same vampire had worried at me like a dog with a bone. It had almost cost me the use of my arm, but serious physical therapy and devotion to the weight room in the gym had left me better than I had been even before the injury.

"A vampire tried to rip a little and wiggled its fangs in the flesh, deciding if it was going to try to take a bigger bite out of the neck. It looks like a man's neck this time, or a larger woman's."

"It's a different vampire," Logan said, his voice demanding that I believe him.

"Maybe, but I doubt it."

"It's a different style of attack," he said.

"A different style of biting doesn't mean a different vamp, Inspector. The vampire is experimenting, deciding what he prefers. This one was either hungrier with this kill, or he's beginning to like the potential violence of it."

"Potential violence, my arse. He's sinking teeth into their necks. How much more violent can it get?"

"A lot more," I said.

"Go to the next picture," Edward said. His voice was very still with that edge of coldness that was usually close to the surface for him.

I did what he asked, and this time the holes in the side of the neck were huge. I didn't even think fang marks, just holes, as if someone had taken an ice pick, or something like it, and just driven it into the neck as far as it would go.

Micah made a small exhale of breath and reached for my arm. I realized that he might never have seen a vampire attack this violent. He was always so strong, so certain, and dealt with the violence in his life and mine so calmly that sometimes I forgot he hadn't seen everything I had, or vice versa. I was pretty sure there were things happening on his out-of-town trips for the Coalition that would have scared the shit out of me, even if it was just me being scared because of the danger to him and other people I cared about.

I took Micah's hand in mine while I asked the next question. "Who figured out this was a vampire attack and not just a murder with something sharp and pointy?"

"We didn't think vampire, because Ireland doesn't have them," Pearson said.

"Exactly, but someone figured it out."

Edward said, "I did."

"This kind of damage isn't typical for vampires. A lot of police—even here where we know it's a possibility—might have missed this," I said.

"You don't have to be nice to us, Blake."

"I'm being nice to everyone else, Logan. You're just collateral kindness."

"What?"

"Let me just apologize for Logan for the rest of the conversation. It will save time," Sheridan said.

"I don't need you to apologize for me, Rachel."

"Oh, you're going to apologize for yourself. Good man, go ahead," she said, and I could hear the almost-laughter in her voice. Some people rubbed everyone the wrong way, and apparently Logan was one of those, because no one in the room seemed to like him. It made me feel better that he wasn't picking on Edward and me special; he just picked at everybody.

"Keep going through the pictures," Edward said, as if the others weren't really there. Ted played well with others; Edward didn't.

The next picture was worse, as if someone had torn the throat out but didn't quite know what they were doing, so there was a fang mark left to one side of the meat that had been someone's throat.

"The vamp is figuring out how strong they are, and what that strength can do to a human body," I said.

"He's getting a taste for it," Edward said.

"Was that supposed to be a pun?" Logan asked, his voice accusatory.

"No," Edward said, "just accurate. You should try it sometime."

"Try what?"

"Accuracy." That one word was low and cold with anger. What the hell had Logan done to earn that level of anger from Edward?

"Who the hell are you to come into our city and tell us that we aren't accurate enough for you?"

"I didn't say that everyone was inaccurate, Logan, just you."

"You bastard!"

"Please, pretty please," Edward said in a serious voice. He wanted Logan to take a swing at him. What the hell had happened in Ireland to make Edward as Ted fish that hard for a fight? It wasn't like him to mess around on the job like that. I was the one who usually mouthed off.

I did the only thing I could think of to help; I swiped to the next picture he'd sent me. There was another dainty bite on a neck, but on the opposite side of the same neck was the bigger set of bite marks, not the one that was messy, but the first one that I'd thought had degraded in the tearing-out of throats.

"Does this next victim have two bite marks on it from both

of our first vampires?" I asked. No one answered me, so I raised my voice. "Ted, talk to me!"

"Yes, the first two vamps seem to be working together."

"Did that victim die?"

"No," Sheridan answered. "He wandered into a hospital because his neck was bleeding, but he couldn't remember how he got injured."

"They're starting to figure out how to work together," I said.

Logan's voice was strident. "Some expert you are, Blake. You were wrong about the second vampire. It's not the one tearing out throats."

"You've got at least three vampires on your hands," I said.

"Did you hear me, Blake? You were wrong!"

"I heard you, Logan. I'm okay with being wrong if it gets us better information to catch the vampires that are doing this."

"Two of them haven't hurt anyone too badly," Sheridan said.

"Have any of the victims been attacked a second time?"

"No," Pearson said.

"I told them to put protection details on the earlier victims," Edward said.

"Did they do it?"

"They're having a little trouble convincing their bosses to approve the overtime."

"Jesus, don't they realize that the vampires can call their one-bite victims out again?"

"I explained it to them."

"What we have a hard time understanding is, if this is true, then why isn't America overrun with vampires? If one bite enslaves a person, then you should all be slaves by now. You yourself are engaged to a vampire, Marshal Blake. If it were that easy to be enslaved, I don't think you would still be trusted as a police officer," Pearson said.

"If you donate blood willingly without being completely bespelled by the vampire's gaze, then he can't enslave your mind and call you at his whim. Done willingly with the minimum of mind tricks, it's not much more than a hickey or a love bite."

"Do you donate blood to your fiancé?"

"I'll answer your question if you'll answer one of mine about your sex life," I said.

"I'm not asking about your sex life, Marshal."

"Yeah, you are."

Micah squeezed my hand and looked a caution at me. He was right; if I wasn't careful I'd be telling them more about my love life with Jean-Claude than I'd shared with my friends on the force here. Sometimes avoiding a question reveals more than just answering. I was sort of screwed on this one, very damned if you do and damned if you don't.

"They call it coffin bait in the States," Logan said.

"Coffin bait is the equivalent to a badge bunny, someone who will fuck any cop just because they're a cop. I'm actually only dating one vampire currently, so I don't qualify as coffin bait."

"How insulting a term is that considered to be in your country?" Pearson asked.

"He's basically called me a whore who will let any vampire both fuck me and bleed me, so pretty damned insulting."

Micah had let go of my hand so he could stand up and start massaging my shoulders through the robe, because I'd suddenly become very tense. Imagine that.

"I'll apologize on Logan's behalf and on behalf of all the Dublin Gardai."

"Gardai?" I made it a question with an uplift of the word.

"That's what the Irish police call themselves," Edward said. "Gardai is plural. Garda Síochána, literally Guardians of the Peace. Only between twenty and thirty percent of them are even trained with weapons."

"You're joking."

"No, I'm not."

"Wow, that's different from here."

"It only went over twenty percent because they had some foreign lycanthropes get out of hand about two years ago."

"It made the international news," I said. "Wasn't there a sorcerer involved, too? It was like a gang of preternatural criminals, right?"

"Not *like*, Marshal. It was," Pearson said.

"The sorcerer was homegrown, but the shapeshifters were immigrants, if I remember correctly."

"You remember correctly."

"And now you've got your first vampires. What's changed about your country in the last few years?"

"Nothing that I'm aware of," he said.

"Then why does Ireland suddenly have supernatural crime?"

"I don't know, but it's a good question."

"Do you have a good answer?" I asked.

"Not yet, but I may know who to ask for one now."

"We've all been trying to figure out why we have our first vampires," Logan said. "She hasn't told us anything that we didn't already know."

"She asked the question differently from anyone else; didn't you hear it?" Pearson asked.

"It's hard to hear anything when you have your head shoved that far up your own ass," Edward said.

"You won't always have other cops around you, Forrester."

"Is that a threat?"

"That would be illegal and I could jeopardize my career, so of course it's not a threat."

"Let's pretend it *is* a threat, because you need to understand that the other officers aren't keeping me safe from you; they're keeping you safe from me." His voice had started in Ted mode but had sunk all the way down to that cooler, slightly deeper Edward mode. What was it about Logan that made it so hard for him to stay in character? I'd been insulted worse than this before, and we'd both worked with bigger pains in the ass, so what had Logan done to get on Edward's serious shit list? Usually you had to be a bad guy to piss Edward off this badly.

"Enough out of both of you," Pearson said.

"I'll play nice if he does," Edward said.

"We're not playing here, Forrester. We're trying to catch these vampires before they kill more people. That's not a game."

"What good is playing if the stakes aren't high, Logan?"

"What does that even mean, Forrester?"

"It means that life and death are the ultimate stakes to play for."

"Ted, you might want to tone down the big-and-bad routine a little." It was the best I could do to warn him that he was being all too much Edward and not enough Ted. It was like Superman putting on Clark Kent's glasses but showing up to the *Daily Planet* in his super suit. If you're dressed up like Superman, the glasses aren't going to hide who you are.

"Yeah, Ted, tone it down for your girlfriend," Logan said.

"What are your rules on sexual harassment, Superintendent Pearson?"

"Why do you ask?"

"Logan just seems like he's going to keep pushing on this until it falls down around his ears."

"Nothing's going to be falling on me, Blake. This little problem goes one way, and that's your way."

"I'm glad we agree on something, Logan."

"What are you talking about?"

"You just said the problem is going to go my way; that means I win."

"That is not what I meant."

"Your language is imprecise, Logan. It has been the entire time I've been here," Edward said.

"Fuck you, Forrester."

"No, thanks."

"That is not what I meant, damn it, and you know that."

"I don't know anything about you, Logan, except you are an incredible pain in the ass," Edward said.

"If you can't work civilly with Marshal Forrester, then you may need off this case," Pearson said.

"I've been on this case from the beginning."

"We want the Americans to help us find and contain our vampires."

"We don't need some cowboy cop from the States to help us do our jobs," Logan said.

"I'll take all the help we can get. These vampires are killing innocent people, Logan, and all you can do is pick at Ted," Sheridan said.

"So it's Ted now, is it?"

I suddenly had a clue: Logan liked Sheridan, God help us

and her. She had reacted to Edward in such a way that Logan thought Sheridan liked Ted. We never really leave junior high and that he-likes-the-girl-who-likes-someone-else game, or reverse the sexes and get the same story. I wasn't a hundred percent sure I was right, but it was worth a try.

"How long have you been in Ireland?" I asked.

"A week."

"Donna and the kids must be missing you."

"I'm missing them, too."

"She must be frantic having you gone in the middle of all the wedding planning."

"Our wedding is just about finalized. It's your wedding that's taking forever to plan."

"The wedding has gotten huge," I said, and felt that familiar tightening of my stomach whenever I let myself think too hard about the size of the guest list.

"Looks like you'll be my best man before I get to be yours, at this rate."

"Wait. Did you say that Blake is going to be your best man?"

"Yep," Edward said, trying to get back into Ted-space, and failing worse than I'd ever seen him before. He was usually the master of disguise, but something about Logan just threw the hell out of his usual suave self.

"And your fiancée isn't bothered by Blake being in your wedding?"

"Donna encouraged it."

"Well, you know what they say: All the good ones are taken," Sheridan said, which meant she hadn't been subtle about being attracted to Edward. He was five-eight, blond, blue-eyed, naturally slender but in great shape, and, if you went by the reaction from other women, very attractive. I didn't see it, but then, he'd threatened to torture or kill me, which put a real damper on me seeing him as cute. Now we were so close as friends that it was almost an incest taboo.

I tried to swipe for more pictures on the computer, but we were done. "This can't be all the pictures, Ted."

"It's not, but it's the ones they'll let me share with you."

"Gentlemen and lady, are you really that prejudiced against my psychic gift?"

"It's nothing personal, Blake," Pearson said.

"The hell it's not."

"The hell it is," he said, and then he seemed to think about what he'd just said. "I'm having one of those flashbacks to that American cartoon where it's always duck season and never rabbit season."

"You're hunting vampires; my necromancy could help you do that."

"The dead do not walk in Ireland, except as ghosts, Marshal Blake."

"Bullshit, and you know it. You have a vampire problem."

"We concede that," he said.

"Then let Anita come in and help me help you," Edward said.

"Sorry, Forrester, and no insult meant to Blake here, but necromancy doesn't work here."

"Is it outlawed?" I asked.

"No, not exactly."

"Ireland is supposed to be one of the most magically tolerant countries in the world. I'm feeling seriously picked on," I said.

"It's nothing personal, Blake."

"I do not think that means what you think it means," I said.

He gave a small laugh. "Thanks, we needed that."

"Anita can help us," Edward said.

"Are you admitting that the high-and-mighty Ted Forrester, the one that the vampires have nicknamed Death, can't handle things here without his sidekick, the Executioner?"

"Death and the Executioner—has a nice ring to it," I said.

"So does Death and War," he said.

"That's catchy, too."

"*War* is Anita's newest nickname from the vampires and wereanimals," Edward explained.

"Why didn't you get a new nickname?" Sheridan asked.

"*Death* suits me," he said, and I could almost see him give her that terribly direct eye contact from his pale blue eyes. It was like having a winter sky stare at you.

I could hear the shiver in Sheridan's voice over the speakerphone when she said, "Yes. Yes, it does." Her tone told me that our bid to get her to back off the crush by talking about Donna and the wedding hadn't worked. Edward was handsome, but this level of persistence made me wonder what he'd done to impress her this much.

"Go back to sleep if you can, Anita."

"I don't feel like I've been that big a help."

"You've helped as much as you can when they won't let me share information with you freely."

"Yeah, because they wouldn't want the big bad necromancer to fuck up their case."

"There's no need for that, Marshal."

"What?"

"Cursing like that."

"Logan cursed."

"But he didn't say that."

I realized he was upset that I'd said *fuck*. "If you don't let me cuss when I talk, I may have to just smile and nod."

He laughed as if he thought it was a good joke. I hadn't been kidding, but since they didn't want me to help them any further I wouldn't have to shock them with my language anymore.

"Don't mind Pearson," Sheridan said. "The rest of us curse. He just doesn't like the F-word and we are having the meeting in his office."

"I'll try to be better if we talk again. Best of luck with your vampire problem."

"Thank you, Marshal. That's most kind," Pearson said.

"Don't mention it."

Edward picked up the phone and went off speaker so at least they couldn't hear my side of the conversation. "What did you do to cause Sheridan to have such a crush on you?"

"I don't know." I didn't press, because it was probably the truth. Since Edward could flirt and seduce to get information out of people without any emotional qualms, I knew he meant it.

"You just don't know how charming you are."

"I will try to use this superpower for good, or personal gain, or to hunt down my enemies and slaughter them so I can dance in their blood."

"You have the most cheerful analogies, Edward."

"We all have our strengths, Anita. Sleep well. I'll call you again if everyone will agree to it."

"Okay, be safe and watch your back like a motherfucker."

"I always do." He hung up. I hung up. We were done. We could go back to bed for a couple of hours.

I opened the door for Micah. He was one of the men in my life who didn't argue over which of us got the door. I valued that, because sometimes you just want to open the damn door. We were in the corridor and it was just as empty as it had been an hour and a half ago. We all mostly worked nights here, so six or seven a.m. wasn't a time that any of us expected to be awake to enjoy.

"Do you think the smallest bite is a child vampire?"

"I really hope not."

"Why?"

"I've told you this before. All the child vampires go crazy eventually. Jean-Claude says that some of them go nuts immediately after rising from the dead. They just never adjust to it."

We had a couple of child vamps that we'd inherited from Europe. They were both constant reminders of why it was a bad idea.

"At least Bartolome is old enough for everything to function like a grown-up," Micah said.

"Yeah, but he still looks eleven to twelve, a young twelve."

"Valentina is worse," he said.

I nodded. "Five to seven years old forever."

"Her mind isn't the mind of a child," he said.

"Just her body. I know."

"I know the other vampires killed the one who made Valentina, but it didn't really save her," he said.

I took his hand in mine and said, "I really hope that she's the youngest vamp I ever meet."

"She's older than Jean-Claude."

"Her body isn't," I said.

I prayed that the vampires in Ireland were just female with small bite radiuses. I prayed that no one was creating more child vampires, because if any vampires were damned, it was them. Please, God, no more.

2

WHEN WE WOKE for the night, Jean-Claude informed me that there had always been vampires in Ireland, and in fact we had a vampire from there in town. Which was why I was sitting in a very model of a modern business office waiting to talk to our Irish vampire, who wasn't actually Irish at all. He'd just died there. The office at Danse Macabre had once been Jean-Claude's; it had been black and white with an Oriental rug and a framed antique Japanese kimono on the wall. Jean-Claude's things left when he started to be too busy to manage all of his businesses. Damian became manager; he was good at it, but the office was so bland that I'd have never believed the person who decorated this room would be theatrical enough to run Danse Macabre, which showed what I understood about such things, or maybe Jean-Claude had spoiled me. He was theatrical about most things.

The office chairs matched the desk, all pale wood and neutral, as if they'd all been bought at the same time and were a matched set, which they had been and were, but somehow the red-haired, green-eyed vampire with his milk pale skin and six feet of ex–Viking warrior looked too exotic to be in this Office Depot–designed room. He needed Victorian furniture, antiques, rich dark colors to complement him, but instead the entire room was so normal it could have been any manager's office in almost any business across America, except for the vampire in the room and me. We were both too colorful for the beige walls and pale wood. Him in his green frock coat, skintight pants, and knee-high boots. Me in my royal-blue business skirt-suit, the skirt a little too short for a lot of businesses, but at five-three a longer skirt made me look even shorter. Besides, I had a date later with Jean-Claude and I might not have time to change before I had to meet everyone for the talky bit beforehand.

Damian had actually requested a meeting so we could talk about something that was bothering him before I knew he might have insight into the case Edward was working on in Ireland. I'd come prepared to hear his problem first, but he seemed reluctant to talk about whatever was bothering him. Fine, we'd talk about crime and vampires first, personal issues second.

"There have always been vampires in Ireland, Anita, or at least for the last thousand years, because that's when She-Who-Made-Me turned me into one, and she'd been there in her castle on the cliffs long before I tried to steal her gold and jewels."

"Then how come the humans didn't know about her?"

"You know as well as I do that if a vampire is careful, he can take a little blood from one person, and a little from another the next night. Our stomachs can't even hold the quantity of blood in an adult human being's body, so there's absolutely no reason to kill your blood donors."

"Unless you want to make them into vampires," I said.

"Or you're a sadistic serial killer who just happens to be a vampire," he said.

"You've told me that She-Who-Made-You is exactly that."

He nodded, staring at his hands where he'd spread them on the pale wood of his desk. "Yes."

"Then how did the human authorities miss a serial killer all that time?"

"You have to remember the times she began her . . . career in, Anita. People vanished all the time. They died young and tragically. Life expectancy was less than forty years and most died much younger than that. By forty, people were usually grandparents, or even great-grandparents."

"At forty?" I said.

He smiled. "The look on your face is priceless, and yes, at forty. Ireland has had a bloody history and a lot of battles fought especially since 1170 when the Normans invaded and stayed. It's so easy to disappear someone when there's a battle close at hand. Then there're displaced people trying to escape from the fighting. No one questions if they don't turn up at the next town, or a relative's house, or rather they assume that the enemy killed them or took them prisoner. It can be months or years before they finally learn that no one knows what happened to them, and by that time it's too late. The jail in the town was a place where people died of disease and starvation. No one ever questioned if they died a little quicker, and the jailer didn't give a damn as long as the dead prisoner was one of the ones who hadn't been able to pay him for better care."

"So you're saying I just don't understand how easy it was to kill people back in the day."

"Yes, that is exactly what I'm saying."

"But it's not the olden days now, Damian. How have she and her kiss of vampires gotten away with it in the twentieth and now twenty-first centuries? People freak out if someone is late sending them a text. It's not so easy to disappear a person now."

"It's harder now, much harder, but not impossible, Anita. You're a U.S. Marshal. You know better than I do how modern killers work. You've worked enough serial killer cases here in the United States to know just how good people can be at getting victims and hiding the bodies. And that's human serial killers. Think how much better they would get if they'd had centuries to perfect their techniques."

"I've worked cases where the perp wasn't human."

"I know that, but my point is still valid."

"How many vampires were there in your group?"

"It was small, but then, we were hiding. The more vampires you have, the harder it is to feed and stay undetected."

"I get that, but how small is small?"

"Never more than a dozen vampires, and usually less. We were harder to hide than the humans and shapeshifters that were part of her retinue."

"One of the reasons that vampires have human servants and *moitié bêtes,* beast halves, is that they can both move around better in daylight than their vampire master," I said.

"She-Who-Made-Me could walk in daylight."

"That's right. I'm sorry. It's such a rare ability that I forgot."

"Perrin and I were the only two of her vampires that were able to live in the light, even holding her hand. All the others that she'd tried to take for a walk in the sunlight had burst into flames and died, while she laughed at them. It was an envoy from the vampire council that suggested the evil thought that made her risk burning both of us alive."

I'd literally shared the memory with Damian once, and I didn't want to do it again, so I said the words. "He said, 'Perhaps the reason they can walk out with you in the sun is not you sharing power with them'"—and Damian joined his voice to mine, so we finished the speech together—"'but that they have gained power of their own, to sun-walk.'"

We looked at each other. "I really wish we didn't keep sharing the worst of each other's memories, Anita."

"Yeah, why can't either of us remember puppies and rainbows when we go all vampire and master?"

"I never owned a puppy," he said.

"I did."

"Oh right, the dog died when you were thirteen or fourteen, and then the dog rose from the dead and came home to crawl into bed with you."

"Okay, maybe not puppies, maybe just rainbows," I said.

"Sharing good memories would be better, but you're the master here, not me, so your wishes dictate the nature of our relationship."

"Are you saying if I can't find my happy thoughts, then none of us can?"

"When we share memories, apparently so."

"I'll talk to my therapist about trying for more cheerful memories."

"Is it helping? The therapist, I mean."

I thought about it, then nodded. "I think it is."

"What made you decide to finally see a full-fledged therapist? I know you were getting some informal counseling from the witch that works with the werewolf pack in Tennessee."

He was right. I'd been doing a little therapy while I was learning to control my metaphysical abilities with my magical mentor, Marianne. I was still seeing her from time to time. Nathaniel and Micah had both gone with me, because I wasn't the only one who needed to ask someone more knowledgeable about "magic," but real hard-core therapy wasn't Marianne's job.

"Oh, I don't know: my mother's death when I was eight; my

father's remarriage to a woman who had problems with me being half Mexican and ruining her blond, blue-eyed family picture."

"Which means you don't want to tell me, because you give almost no emotion to any of that," he said, looking at me very directly out of those greenest of green eyes. They really were the purest green eyes I'd ever seen in a human face. Hell, I'd only seen a few domestic cats with eyes that green. He swore they'd been the same color when he'd been alive.

"When I go too long without talking directly to you, I forget how impossibly green your eyes are."

"Which means you really don't want to tell me why you started therapy."

"What, I can't compliment you?"

"First, I'm not sure that was a compliment. Second, you almost never compliment me, so yes, it's a distraction technique for you, though your best distraction is what you started with: Trot out your tragic family history and most people would leave you alone about it."

I gave him an unfriendly look. "If you know I don't want to tell you, then why are you still pushing on it?"

"Maybe I'm thinking that if I understood why you went, I might go, too."

"Is that why you wanted to meet? To talk about going to therapy?" I didn't try to keep the surprise off my face.

"No, but it's not a bad idea."

"No, it's not. I think most people could use a little good therapy."

He nodded, but more because he thought he should than because he meant it, as if he was already thinking about something else.

"What's wrong, Damian? You asked for this meeting days before I knew I needed to ask you about Ireland."

"I'm having nightmares."

"Vampires don't have nightmares," I said.

"I know."

He blinked those impossibly green eyes at me, then tucked a strand of that equally impossibly red hair behind one ear. He was so nervous that it showed in the tightness of his muscles as he moved, or tried not to move and betray just how nervous he was. For once, I didn't need to sense anything from him to know exactly how he felt.

"How bad are the nightmares?" I asked.

"Bad enough."

"Are they memories?"

"Some, but most of them are modern-day, and I don't recognize most of the people in them."

"I've had dreams like that, where it's like you're guest-starring in someone else's dreams," I said.

He nodded. "Yes, but they are violent, awful dreams." He stared at his hands, shoulders slumping this time, as if he was beginning to hunch in upon himself. "I wake up and Cardinale is still dead, cool to the touch, and I'm burning up like a fever."

"Vampires are hard when you have daymares," I said.

He nodded. "I guess it is a daymare, not a nightmare."

"Either way, when your lover is cold to the touch, they can't hold you while you scream."

"No, she can't. She keeps saying, *Why aren't I enough for you?* But she doesn't understand."

"You need someone there who can wake you up, hold you, be warm for you," I said.

"Yes, I do, damn it. I do."

"What did Jean-Claude say when you told him?"

"He doesn't know."

"You're telling me first, before your king?"

"You're my master, Anita, not him. I'm supposed to tell you first."

"We'll debate that later. Are you dying at dawn?"

"Sometimes, but most of the time I curl up beside Cardinale and I sleep until the nightmares wake me."

"You should be dying at dawn, Damian."

"Don't you think I know that? When I woke this morning I had sweat blood, Anita. It's like I have a fever, a human fever, but I sweat blood. It's like I'm sick."

"Vampires don't get sick," I said.

"If I'm not ill, then what is it?"

"I don't know, but first we have to tell Jean-Claude," I said.

"And then?" He gave me a very direct look.

I met the look with one of my own. "What do you want me to say, Damian? We'll talk to Jean-Claude. Maybe I'll talk to my friend Marianne; she's a witch—maybe she'd have an idea about where to start."

"I think this is happening because you, Nathaniel, and I almost never see each other. You're a necromancer, I'm your vampire servant, and Nathaniel is your leopard to call, but the three of us have almost no relationship."

"You say that like it's normal for a necromancer to have a vampire servant the way a master vampire has a human servant, but it's a first in all of vampire history. The fact that I can make *moitié bêtes* like a master vampire is even weirder, because that has nothing to do with my necromancy."

"You gain power through Jean-Claude's vampire marks, through being his human servant."

"Yeah, but that doesn't explain everything I can do."

"You came with your own power, Anita."

"I'm sorry I accidentally bound you and Nathaniel into a triumvirate of power."

"You saved my life more than once with your power, Anita; I don't regret being bound to you. The only thing I regret is that you grew closer to Nathaniel than to me."

"You and your lady love, Cardinale, asked me to back off and let the two of you be monogamous together. I respected the request."

"You had already fallen in love with Nathaniel, and were so not in love with me. Don't blame that on Cardinale's relationship with me."

"I'm not, but we were lovers before you and she went monogamous."

"You slept with me less than you sleep with Richard now."

"Look, I'm sorry you're hurting, or scared, or sick, or whatever, but it wasn't just me that contributed to whatever is happening, or not happening, between us."

"I know that."

"Do you? Because you don't sound like you do."

"I could say you're my master, so responsibility ultimately lies with you, but that would piss you off and I don't want to do that."

"You're doing a damn good job, if that's not what you want,

and Cardinale hates me. I don't see her letting you and me get closer in any way."

"She's not happy about anyone being near me who isn't her, but I can't go on like this, Anita. You keep saying that vampires don't sleep, or have nightmares, and you're right, but vampires also don't have human masters, not even necromancers. I believe that whatever is happening to me is tied to the triumvirate not working the way it should."

"How do you envision it working?" I asked.

"More like the one that Jean-Claude has with you and Richard Zeeman, our local werewolf king."

"And that would mean what, exactly?"

"Don't be coy, Anita."

"I'm not being coy. I'm not good enough at it to try. I genuinely don't know what you're getting at, because Jean-Claude and I don't see Richard much at all anymore. He's dating other people, off trying to find someone to marry and do the white-picket-fence thing."

"You see him at least once a month."

"For sex and bondage, yes. Wait. Are you wanting to have sex with Nathaniel and me?"

"The look on your face, Anita. Is the thought of us being lovers again such a bad one?"

This was the guy version of the girl trap: a question where there either is no winning answer or one where you have only one answer that won't start a fight. This was one of those questions, but luckily I could answer truthfully and not hurt his feelings.

"No, it's not a bad thought. You're beautiful and you're good in bed; it's not that."

"Then what is it?"

"If you sleep with me, let alone with me and Nathaniel, it will cost you Cardinale, because she won't stand for it."

He nodded one more time. "I know, but I need to figure out what's happening to me, Anita, and for that I need you and Nathaniel to be closer to me. I need our triumvirate of power to work more like you, Jean-Claude, and Richard do."

"We don't always work that well," I said.

"Your triumvirate with them works better than the one you have with Nathaniel and me," he said.

I couldn't really argue with that, so I didn't try. "Okay, but before we do anything that would piss Cardinale off, we are going to talk to her first. If we can do this without it costing your relationship, then we will."

"Why do you care so much about my relationship with her?"

"I caught enough of your emotions to know you were in love with her; that's important, and I don't want to screw that up because the metaphysics between us has gotten weird."

"You really do want everyone around you to be happy, don't you?"

"Yeah, doesn't everyone want that for their friends?"

He smiled then, and shook his head. "No, Anita. No, they don't."

"If you really care for people, you want them to be happy, Damian; otherwise you don't actually care for them."

"You don't think like any other woman I've ever met."

"Oh, come on, in centuries of life you've never met another woman who thinks like I do?"

"I swear to you, Anita, you are unique in a lot of ways."

"*Unique* is usually a polite way of saying *weird*."

He grinned, gave a little laugh. "Well, that, too, but weird isn't always bad."

I smiled. "No. No, it's not; in fact, sometimes weird is exactly what you need."

"I'm a vampire and you're a necromancer. I think weird is where we start."

I laughed then, and debated how much of the case in Ireland I could share with him. One of the side effects he had from being my vampire servant was that if I told him not to tell anyone else what I told him, he couldn't. He couldn't seem to disobey a direct order from me, which wasn't typical for human servants. It certainly wasn't how I was with Jean-Claude.

"You're thinking something that's made you very serious."

"If I told you that there were vampires in Ireland that were taking victims and making no effort to hide them, what would you say?"

"I'd say it's not the work of the vampire that made me. She would never be so careless hiding bodies."

"I'm not sure how many we have dead so far; the others just wander the streets or take themselves to a hospital with complete amnesia about how they got hurt."

It was his turn to look serious. "She would never let people wander around like that. It would attract far too much attention. How many victims so far?"

"At least half a dozen."

"She would kill a vampire of her kiss that was so careless."

"So you're saying it's not your old group?"

He shook his head. "No, Anita, She-Who-Made-Me would never risk the humans knowing about us."

"Even in modern times when more countries are making you legal?"

"She's one of the old ones who don't believe the new attitudes will last. She said that staying hidden was the only true safety from the plague of humanity."

"She called us a plague, really?"

He nodded. "She didn't seem to like humans much. If she could have fed off something else and stayed alive as a vampire, I think she would have done so."

"A vampire that tries to feed on animals starts to rot," I said.

"I remember what Sabine looked like," Damian said, and shuddered. It had been worth a shudder or two.

"Yeah, and once a vampire gets damaged like that there's no healing it, so you guys have to feed on humans."

"She enjoyed tormenting humans and having sex with us if it suited her, but she didn't seem to actually like us, or maybe she didn't truly like anyone."

The timer on my phone sounded. I turned off the alarm and stood up. "Jean-Claude made me promise not to be late tonight, but is there anything you can tell me about vampires in Ireland that might help explain what's happening?"

"The only thing I can think of is that her power is finally fading enough that she has lost control of some of her vampires and they are mad with power now," he said, standing too.

"Why would she suddenly start to lose power after all this time?"

"I do not know. She was very in control of them when I left Ireland five years ago."

"Could it be vampires from out of the country that she doesn't control?"

"It is possible, I suppose."

"But you don't believe it," I said.

"No, I don't. She-Who-Made-Me is very covetous of her power and control. She would not allow some upstart vampires to come as near to her as Dublin and make her existence difficult without making their existence impossible."

"You mean she'd kill them."

"Oh yes, but you need to go. I will think upon what I know about my old mistress and her retinue, but this has to be someone or something new in Ireland. Within her fortress she was mad and capricious, but outside it she was very disciplined. Whatever is doing this doesn't seem very disciplined. In fact, I'd say it was new vampires learning how to control themselves, but she could hunt them down easily and destroy them, or 'invite' them to join her kiss." He made little air quotes around *invite*.

"Join us or die, huh?"

"Something like that. Jean-Claude cautioned me to make certain you leave by about now," he said, glancing at the wall clock.

I let the surprise show on my face. "I don't think he's ever talked to one of my other people before like that."

"He didn't want you to get distracted by me."

"Fine. I'll fill Jean-Claude and Nathaniel in on what's happening with you and we'll come up with a plan."

He offered his hand to me, as if it were any other meeting, and I took it the same way. We forgot that weird was where we started. Power jumped between our skin in a wash of heat, as if a sudden fever had gripped us both. The last time I'd touched him there'd been attraction, power, magic, but not like this heat wave.

I let go of his hand, but he held on, until I said, "Let go of me, Damian," and he had to let go, because I'd ordered him to do it.

Our hands parted, but it was like pulling our hands out of

some invisible taffy: sticky, sweet, and trying to hold on to both of us. We stood there staring at each other, both of us breathing fast, chests rising and falling with the need for air as if we'd been running.

"What the hell was that?" I gasped it, because I didn't have air for anything else. I was even sweating, just a little.

"I don't know," he whispered, and there was the faintest dew of sweat on his face. The sweat should have been pinkish with blood, but it was darker than that, more red than pink. One drop of that bloody sweat trailed down his face and took my gaze with it, to find more sweat down the middle of that bare line of chest, so that it looked like he was bleeding from a hundred tiny puncture wounds, except it was the fine pores of his skin. He wasn't wounded; he wasn't even truly bleeding; there was always a little blood in a vampire's sweat, enough to make the clear liquid slightly pink.

I watched Damian bleed down the paper whiteness of his skin, and knew something was wrong, as in call-a-doctor wrong, but who do you call when a vampire gets "sick"? Since they didn't get sick in any traditional sense, there weren't a lot of doctors that specialized.

Damian touched his fingers to his skin and stared at the blood on them. "What is happening to me, Anita?"

"I don't know," I said.

"You're a necromancer and my master; shouldn't you know something?"

I felt that little spurt of anger but pushed it down, because he was right. "Yeah, I should, but I don't. I'm sorry for that."

He got some Kleenex from his desk drawer and started dabbing at the bloody sweat. The tissues came away soaked. "I woke from the nightmares like this today, Anita, drenched in blood. I ruined the sheets and Cardinale just lay there in the bloody bed like the corpse she was."

I stared at him, because I'd never heard a vampire describe another vampire like that before. "Damian . . ." I reached out to touch him, comfort him, but stopped myself before I finished the gesture; shaking hands had been exciting enough.

"Whatever is wrong with me is getting worse, Anita." He threw the bloody Kleenex in the small office wastebasket.

"We'll talk to Jean-Claude first."

"And if he doesn't know what's wrong with me, what's second?"

"We'll cross that bridge when we come to it," I said.

"If Jean-Claude doesn't have an answer for this, Anita, then you and Nathaniel and I have to make our metaphysics work better."

"Even if it costs you Cardinale?"

He stripped off his coat and held it out by two fingers away from his body. Blood was still beading on the skin between his shoulder blades. Shouldn't it have soaked into the coat? He turned around and fresh blood was sweating onto his chest and forehead.

"Cardinale said she'd rather I keep having nightmares than have me sleep with someone else." He wiped at the fresh blood with more Kleenex, until it was all a bloody mess. "I can feel it dripping down my back," he said with distaste.

"It is, but I'm afraid to touch you again after the handshake," I said.

"Nothing personal, but I don't want to bleed more," he said.

"Maybe Jean-Claude can help us figure out why my touch made you do this," I said.

"The next time we touch he should be in the room."

"And Nathaniel," I said.

"And maybe some security guards," Damian said, as he threw more bloody tissues into the trash can.

"Why security?" I asked.

"The last time things went wrong with me, Anita, I killed innocent humans, just slaughtered them. I don't remember doing it, but I believe that I did. I was worse than a freshly risen vampire, more like one of the revenants that never regains its mind."

"You didn't have any of these symptoms before last time, did you?"

"No, no nightmares, no bloody sweats, no power jumps, just out of my head with bloodlust."

"That was different, then, Damian."

"Was it?"

"You said it yourself: The symptoms are different."

"I suppose."

"You just went crazy that time, Damian."

"No, I didn't just go crazy, Anita. You had cut me off from my connection to you and instead of dying finally and completely, I was old enough, or powerful enough, to go crazy."

"Damian . . ."

"I know you haven't cut me off from your power as my master this time, Anita, but you've still distanced yourself from me."

"Because you and Cardinale asked me to."

"We did, but I didn't understand how much I would miss interacting with you and Nathaniel."

"We were never that close, the three of us."

"No, but I feel the lack of you both, somehow."

Since Nathaniel had said almost the same thing about Damian a few months back, I wasn't sure what to say; I didn't seem to miss Damian as much as my other fiancé did. "I did what you asked, Damian."

"Maybe I'm unasking," he said.

"What does that mean?" I asked.

"It means that I'm lonely."

"You live and work with Cardinale, and you're in love with her."

"I know that."

I wanted to ask, *Then how can you be lonely?* But I wasn't sure how to say it. He said it for me. "I thought being in love meant you'd never be lonely again, that it would be like coming home in every sense of the word."

"It is like that," I said, and couldn't help but smile as I said it.

He shook his head. "That smile on your face, that's what I wanted to feel, but it's not like that with Cardinale, not anymore."

I didn't know what to say to that, so I said, "The bleeding has almost stopped."

"Oh good, I've stopped sweating blood for the second time today." He threw the last of the bloody Kleenex in the small trash can and turned to me with angry eyes. "Jean-Claude told me if I went mad again he might have to kill me."

"I remember," I said.

"You can't let me hurt innocent people again, Anita."

"I know," I said.

"I told Cardinale about the last time something went wrong with me, and I honestly think she'd prefer me dead than with someone else. How can that be love, Anita? How can she prefer me insane and having to be killed like an animal to me sleeping with other people?"

Again, I had no good answer, so I said nothing. I rarely got in trouble saying nothing.

"Answer me, Anita. How is that love?"

Of course, not everyone will let you say nothing; sometimes they demand more than that, even when there's nothing good to say. "I don't know, Damian."

"You don't know, or you know that isn't love—it's obsession?"

"Since I'm the other woman as far as Cardinale is concerned, I'd rather not comment."

"She-Who-Made-Me didn't understand love, but she understood being obsessed with someone. She'd find someone among the prisoners or the would-be treasure seekers who would come to the castle; like ordering pizza, the food comes to you." He laughed, but it was a bad sound, the kind of laughter that made you cringe or want to cry. "She'd pick one special person to tease and torment and maybe fuck. Sometimes they thought she loved them, but it was the kind of obsession that scientists feel for insects, so beautiful until you kill it, stuff it, and put a pin through it."

I fought not to point out that insects aren't stuffed, and not to ask if She-Who-Made-Him actually stuffed or pinned her victims. Neither comment would help the pain in his eyes, so I let them both go. I can be taught.

"You can't equate Cardinale with her," I said, finally.

"Why not? Maybe after so many centuries with She-Who-Made-Me, obsession is all I understand? What if that's what I saw in Cardinale? What if years of being tormented have made me mistake someone who wants to possess me for someone who wants to love me?"

"I don't even know what to say to that, Damian, except it's probably above my pay grade on the therapy scale and it sounds like a question for a real therapist."

He nodded. "Maybe it is."

"When do you get off work tonight?" I asked.

"Two hours before dawn."

"You and Cardinale live at the Circus, so you'll be heading that way anyway. We'll see you an hour before dawn."

"That won't give us much time."

"I'll fill Jean-Claude and Nathaniel in on everything, so we'll have less to explain."

"An hour is still not much time to solve the unsolvable," he said.

"Jean-Claude doesn't have to die at dawn, if I'm touching him, and you aren't dying at dawn. That gives us more time," I said.

He seemed to think about that, then nodded, putting his coat over the back of his chair so his hands were free. He stood there bare from the waist up, except for the blood that was beginning to dry on his back. "A bright side to this cursed sleep, then," he said.

"Most vampires are a little afraid of that moment when they die each day," I said.

"I think a part of me would be relieved to finally die for real."

"Are you thinking suicidal thoughts?" I asked, because you have to ask, or you won't know.

"No, I was raised to believe a death in battle meant a good afterlife, and I was fighting when She-Who-Made-Me took my life."

"You mean Valhalla and all that."

He grinned. "Yes, Valhalla and all that."

"So you count that moment as your death, and wouldn't count dying as a vampire now?" I asked, because it was me and I wanted to know.

He shook his head. "She-Who-Made-Me killed me, Anita. Make no mistake about that."

I wasn't sure I agreed with his definition of life and death and when he was killed, but if it gave him comfort, who was I to argue with it? I believed in heaven, and wasn't Valhalla just Damian's version of that? If it wasn't, the difference was a question for a priest and I wasn't one of those, so I let him take his comfort and I kept mine.

"I'll see you later tonight, then," I said.

"I can't go to work like this," he said. "I smell like fresh blood and sweat. It's disgusting."

"I haven't noticed you smelling bad; maybe just take a bird bath in the bathroom back here," I suggested.

"You haven't gotten close enough to smell my skin," he said.

"You just said you don't want me closer since you sweated blood from one touch."

He sighed. "Yes, I did."

"I'm heading to the Circus of the Damned, then. I've got people waiting for me."

"Can I catch a ride with you? I need a shower and clean clothes."

"You fly better than almost any vampire I know; you don't need a car."

"I don't feel myself tonight, Anita. I'd rather use a car."

"How did you get here tonight without one?"

"Cardinale and I carpool. You know that."

"Sorry. You're right. I do."

"Look, if you don't want to give me a ride, just say so."

"I'm not sure you and I in a car alone together is a good idea until we know why shaking hands made you bleed."

He took in a lot of air and let it out slow. Was he breathing more than normal for him, and for most of the vampires I knew, or was I just more aware of it? I almost asked, but then left it alone. I'd ask Jean-Claude later after he'd had time to watch Damian tonight.

"You're right," he said.

"Maybe you can drive the car to the Circus, shower, and come back for the big dance number at the end of the evening," I said.

"Sensible," he said.

"You sound like you'd rather I not be sensible."

"The urge to touch you is always there, Anita, even after what just happened."

Since I wasn't as drawn to him as he was to me, I kept quiet, because when a man tells you something like that it's just mean to tell him you don't feel the same. I did my best not to hurt anyone's feelings if I could help it.

"You're shielding so hard, Anita, harder than when you came through the door."

"We shook hands and you sweated blood, Damian, and I don't know if I caused it. So yes, I'm shielding as hard as I can from you right now."

"It's like you're not there at all now."

"You can see me," I said.

He shook his head. "It's not the same, Anita."

"I haven't cut our ties as master and servant. I know enough not to do that by accident now."

"You might as well be on the far side of the world for all the energy you're sharing with me."

"See my earlier statement, Damian."

"You're probably right to do it, but I feel worse, as if a little bit more of my air was cut off and I'm suffocating more quickly."

"You're a vampire. You don't have to breathe except to talk."

"I tell you how I feel, and you're going to argue semantics with me?"

It was my turn to take in a lot of air and let it out slow. I wanted to get impatient, maybe even angry, but I tried to do better. "You're allowed to feel the way you feel, Damian, but vampires can't suffocate. It was just odd phrasing."

"There's a lot odd about me lately, Anita."

"I'm going for my date now. You tell Cardinale why you're borrowing the car and missing part of your shift."

"I'll talk to Angel about working around me in the dances. We really need another male vampire that can take some of my performances, or hers. She's a great assistant manager, but we both need someone to take the dance floor for us sometimes so we can manage things."

"Mention it to Jean-Claude tonight. He'd probably know which of our people might be good at it."

"You know all our vampires, too, Anita."

"I can tell you which of them would be the best for security, or law enforcement backup, but I can't tell you who could dance some of the old routines you perform here at Danse every night."

"Nathaniel might know, too," Damian said.

"Yeah, or Jason," I said.

"I'll ask them, and could I find you after I shower and change to talk about everything?"

"Text me when you're done showering and changed. If we're at a stopping point, I'll text you back, but if I don't reply, then we'll talk an hour before dawn like we planned."

"Fair enough," he said, but he still stood there shirtless and looking lost. If I hadn't been afraid of touching him again, I'd have given him a hug. Since I couldn't do that, I went for the door. I had a rare night off and a date. There'd been a time when I would have allowed Damian's issues to derail the whole night, but there was always a fresh emergency, and there always would be. Police work had taught me that, and it had taught me something else: that if I wanted to have a life outside of the blood, death, and scary stuff, I had to fight for it. I had to protect my free time as fiercely as I did anything else in my life, because if I didn't, then my "life" would be another casualty as surely as any other crime victim.

I kept my metaphysical shields as tight as I could between me and the vampire behind me, because otherwise I'd have felt all the emotions that were making him look lost and I might not have been able to go for the door. I reached for the door, and it crashed open toward me. I jumped backward, pulling my gun as I moved, just automatic when a door opened with that much angry force. If it was someone who'd done it by accident, I'd apologize for scaring them, but I didn't have to apologize, because it was Cardinale and she hadn't come to be scared—she'd come to be scary.

In her stilettos she was over six feet tall, all thin bones and angles, the makeup that carved her face into model-perfect beauty floating on the white glow of her skin like water lilies on a pool. The cross inside my blouse was warm. I kept one hand very steady on the gun and used the other to drag the chain up and put the glowing cross on the outside of the silk. It wasn't glowing bright enough to burn flesh yet, but it could. Holy fire wasn't always careful what it burned when evil was in the room.

I could see the bones in Cardinale's skull as she turned to look at me, like shapes half seen under the glow of her flesh. I should have sensed her that deep in her power, so close, which meant I'd been shielding from Damian too hard to sense any other vampire.

"Don't shoot her, Anita!"

"I'd rather you shoot me than fuck him behind my back." She yelled it at me, her teeth and fangs moving almost like one of those X-ray short films they used to show in biology class, except this image glowed like light carved into a pretty monster. Her long red hair fanned around her glowing skull like airborne blood frozen in a cloud that would not fall to the floor; her eyes were like blue fire.

"I haven't touched Damian since you told me you were monogamous." I was having to squint against the growing glow of my own cross, like having a white star hanging around my neck; soon I'd be blind except for the light. I had to shoot her before that happened, or I wouldn't be able to see to aim. I hated to kill Cardinale over a jealous misunderstanding, but I'd hate her tearing my throat out even more.

"Tone the power down, Cardinale, or I will shoot you!"

"We were just talking about my illness, Cardinale."

"You stand there half naked with her bloody nail marks down your back and you were just talking!" She screamed it at him and moved toward him, which was better than her moving toward me.

"I started sweating blood again. I could not reach my back to clean it off."

The cross around my neck was filling the room with bright white light; it wasn't actually hot, like flame, and wouldn't be unless it touched vampiric flesh, or demon, or someone who had given their soul to evil, or . . . hell, it burned if evil with a capital *E* touched it. The glow of the cross was mingling with the glow of the vampire, so it seemed to be swallowing her to my sight, though I knew that wasn't it. She'd have to touch the cross to burn. The fact that she wasn't hiding her eyes from the glow was a bad sign. It meant she was more powerful than I'd given her credit for, or she was so pissed she didn't care yet.

I couldn't risk glancing at Damian to see if he was hiding his eyes from the glow; the room was too small, and Cardinale was too close to me. If I was going to have to shoot, it would be in the blink of an eye, and glancing anywhere but at the vampire that was menacing me would cost me that blink.

"I give you my word of honor, my heart, that I started to sweat blood again. I took the jacket off so it would not be ruined. My back is covered in the blood I could not reach."

The cross's glow was almost complete. I aimed at the glow of her blue eyes, set in the swimming blood of her hair, because that was all I could see past the white light. Take out the brain and all the monsters die.

"Cardinale!" I screamed her name, and my finger started to squeeze the trigger.

3

THE WHITE LIGHT died abruptly like someone had turned a switch. I took my finger off the trigger and pointed the gun in as neutral a direction as I could find. Cardinale stood there with her orange-red hair in careless curls around her shoulders, her blue eyes blinking at me in the careful makeup that made them look like a bright blue sky to match Damian's perfect summer green. My pulse was in my throat still; I hadn't even gone to the quiet place in my head where I normally went when I was going to shoot someone. Maybe I'd known she didn't mean it? Maybe I hadn't wanted to shoot her? My body felt so full of blood and heartbeat that I was shaking with it, which meant I'd have probably missed the shot anyway. Fuck.

Cardinale was very still as she looked at me. It wasn't just vampire stillness, though they could be statue still, but I think she was trying not to make any sudden moves. If she was trying not to spook me, she was a little late.

"Thank you for not shooting her," Damian said. I thought he was talking to just me, and then I saw the security guards in the doorway behind her. One had his gun out; the other one didn't. The fact that I hadn't realized they were there meant I was still shielding too tight not just against Damian, but vampires and apparently shapeshifters since both bodyguards were that, or maybe part of my metaphysical ability picked up normal humans, too, because as soon as I lowered my shields a fraction, I could feel more of the energy of the customers already out in the club beyond us.

It took me a second to adjust from almost no psychic input to having more, and in a shooting emergency that second could have cost me my life. I had to find a middle ground for shielding around Damian, damn it. But one problem at a time. "Where the fuck were you while all this was going on?" I asked.

The two men just inside the door glanced at each other, and then the one with the gun out, Ricky, said, "I didn't have a clear shot, Anita."

"I'm not mad that you didn't shoot Cardinale, Ricky," I said. I had my gun loose in my hand, but I still hadn't holstered it because once a vampire goes that apeshit around me, especially in a small room, I like my gun out.

"Then what are you mad about?" he asked, and he fought not to sound sullen. He was tall, dark, and handsome if you liked the standard Midwestern Romeo type who usually got the prom queen's virginity, or promised you the moon at the dance club with a few drinks, and meant none of it. I might be prejudiced; Ricky and I had had a serious misunderstanding the first time we met. He was still digging his way off my shit list, and I was still not his favorite boss. Fine with me; I wasn't here to win popularity contests. I was here to make sure everyone stayed safe and as happy as I could manage. Safe was easier than happy most nights.

The other guard was new, too, and I couldn't place his name. We had too many new people lately doing security; I should know the names of everyone that I might have to depend on for backing me in an emergency.

"What's your name?" I asked the other guard, who was standing there with no visible weapon and looking worriedly from me to Ricky and the vampires. God, he looked young, big and tough looking, but young.

"Roger, Roger Parks." Most shapeshifters didn't give their last name in introductions, which meant he was very new, maybe even to being a wereanimal. Great.

"Well, Roger, Roger Parks, what's the first thing you saw when you opened the door?"

He did that nervous glance around at all of us again, then said, "Light, white light."

"Is that all?" I asked.

"There were a red glow and a green-and-blue glow, which could have been either of the vampires."

"What alerted you that there was trouble?"

"Echo alerted us," Roger said.

I looked at Ricky. "Do I need to ask you the next question, or can you just answer it?"

He took in a lot of air and let it out slowly, licked his lips, and said, "We were told there was an issue in the manager's office, and that you and Damian were both in the room, and to be kept safe."

"What about me?" Cardinale asked; her voice was very careful as she asked, as if she didn't want to even raise her voice. She was being very careful now, which was good; she'd need to be very careful for a long time around me after this.

Ricky glanced at me, and I knew he was asking for guidance; he could be taught. I said, "You were endangering two of the principals that our security force is charged with keeping safe, Cardinale. That makes you a liability, not an asset."

"What does that even mean?" she asked, her voice holding more of that British Isles accent than her normal middle-of-nowhere one. It was like most of our British vamps had been given voice lessons to sound like all the announcers on the major news sources so that they blended in everywhere and nowhere.

Ricky looked at me again, and this time I just nodded.

"How blunt do you want me to be, boss lady?" Ricky asked.

"Tell her what you were told about your job," I said.

"Echo is head of security at Danse Macabre now, Anita."

"I'm aware of that."

"She uses pretty cold logic."

"That's fine. Just say it, Ricky. Maybe it'll help keep Cardinale alive."

He nodded, then looked back at Cardinale. "The job of security is to protect assets. Danse Macabre running smoothly and making money is an asset. Anita is one of the principal assets that we are all charged with keeping safe, and Damian is another asset both as the manager of the club and as Anita's servant. You are an employee here at Danse Macabre, but you are not one of the major dancers, or a headliner of any kind, nor do you have a direct metaphysical tie to any of our principal assets."

"What does all that mean?" she asked, her voice trying for neutral but holding the first hint of anger.

"It means you aren't a principal, so we don't have to protect you like you are one. You aren't an important financial asset either, so we have to put even less energy into protecting you, which means none of us has to put our body between you and a bullet, or whatever."

"So I'm not important at all," she said.

"You said it. I didn't," Ricky said.

"What are your orders when a principal is in danger?" I asked.

"To protect them at all costs and to take out the threat," Ricky said.

"Tonight that threat was you, Cardinale. If they'd come to the door before the light blinded us all you'd be shot, if not dead, so get jealous all you want, but don't do it on the clock where security is going to have to help deal with it, because it's going to get you dead."

"He was half naked and covered in blood down his back. How was I supposed to know that you hadn't already fucked each other?"

Damian spoke for the first time. "I have never cheated on you, Cardinale, never."

"But you were sleeping with her when you started sleeping with me." And she pointed a very accusing finger at me. I'd have said it was overly dramatic, but after all the glowing and holy objects, it wasn't that dramatic.

"I never lied about Anita or anyone else, Cardinale. I never lied to you about anything."

"I can't stand the thought that you want to be with other people."

"I don't want to be with other people."

"But you think Anita is beautiful, and you think Echo is beautiful, and you admire Fortune."

"I admire beautiful women with a look, or a glance, but that is all."

"That is not all you do with the customers that you take blood from."

"That is not all you do with the ones you drink from either."

"But I don't enjoy it; it is just food, and it is more than that to you."

I felt like we were in the middle of an old fight, and I was tired of it already.

"I've told you that feeding was all the softness I had in my existence for centuries, so it means more to me than simple food. It was all the kindness She-Who-Made-Me would allow me."

"Why am I not enough for you?" She yelled that part.

"Because I cannot feed on another vampire! Because it is my job to seduce the crowd and choose someone to feed upon. It is part of the show here, and it gains us money and more customers, which makes us more money, and that is what this club is supposed to do."

"I cannot watch you flirt with all the women night after night, and know that if I would allow it you would fuck them while you feed." She wasn't yelling, but her hands were in fists as she fought to keep her voice even.

"I would not have public sex with strangers, Cardinale. That is very different from feeding on blood in public," he said.

"But you'd fuck Anita in private if I allowed it, wouldn't you?"

"It's a girl trap," I said out loud.

Damian looked at me and said, "I know, but I don't care."

"Do not drag me into this further than I already am."

"I'm sorry, but you're already in it, because she won't let you out of it," he said.

"What's happening?" Roger the guard asked.

"He's about to tell the truth," Ricky said.

"Why is that bad?" Roger asked.

"It just is."

"Shut up," Cardinale said. "This is between Damian and me."

"Then have the conversation with just the two of you," I said, and started for the door. Surely with two security guards to back me up, I could get out of the office without Cardinale doing something we'd all regret.

"No, if he wants you that badly, I want you in the room when he says it."

Fuck, just fuck. "You know, this is your relationship, Cardinale, not mine, so I don't really care what you want. I've got a night off, and I'm going to go enjoy it while you let your jealousy issues wreck your relationship on your own damn time." I was at the door with Ricky and Roger parting the way, so I was in the doorway with them behind me, between me and Cardinale, the possible threat, like good bodyguards.

I was really hoping that Damian would let me get out of the room before he answered her, but I knew . . . Hell, I could feel that he'd reached a level of anger with the situation where he wanted it to blow up, to be done. I could feel his loneliness now; whereas before he just told me he was lonely, now I felt it. Loneliness, anger, frustration, and . . . need. A need beyond sex, or blood, or even love; there were so many reasons I shielded around Damian. Shit.

"I've already asked Anita to be my lover again, and if sleeping with her and Nathaniel will stop these nightmares, then I'll do that, too."

I hesitated between one step and another, then kept going. I wanted out of the room, out of the mess, out of their relationship, but more than that, I wanted away from Damian's emotions before he dragged me further into whatever was happening between them.

Cardinale yelled after me, and the door was open so some of the customers would likely hear it. "Are you and Nathaniel both going to fuck him now?"

Ricky and Roger had closed in behind me like a movable wall of security. I stopped walking so abruptly that Roger almost ran into me, but Ricky said, "Don't do it, boss."

"Do what?" Roger asked.

"Just walk away, boss," Ricky said.

Cardinale screamed, "Are you that much better in bed, Anita? Is that it? Is that why everyone wants you, because you just fuck so good?"

"Shit," Ricky said, softly under his breath.

Even Roger had caught up, because his eyes were wide and he asked, "Can we shoot her, or do we have to do nonlethal?"

"Nonlethal if you can," I said, and turned around to look back into the room. Cardinale's eyes were starting to gleam the way jewels do when light comes in behind them. My cross wasn't glowing yet because it might just be her anger showing. Damian stood by his desk, his pale upper body still smooth and bare with his long hair falling straight and crimson around all that white skin. Our eyes met, and the marks between us let me feel the defeat in him. He didn't know what to do with Cardinale anymore; it wasn't that he didn't love her, because he did, but he wasn't "in love" with her anymore, because she'd beaten that out of him with the constant jealousy, the recriminations, the accusations, and the lack of faith in him and their love.

Out loud I said, "What do you want me to do, Damian?" I felt so many emotions from him and knew he was deeply conflicted. Part of him would be relieved if it were over between them, but part of me—I mean, him—would miss her and what they had together. I looked at the tall woman standing there with her amazing cheekbones, knowing it wasn't from dieting but from starving most of her human life. She'd come to being a vampire partly so she'd never be hungry again and because she was beautiful enough for the Master of London to want her in his bed forever. But he'd never made her feel secure; she was just one lover among many. He'd never promised her otherwise, but she'd done the same thing to him she was doing to Damian, so that in the end, no matter how lovely she was to look at, the sex wasn't worth the emotional blowups. Damian knew all that about her, so suddenly, so did I. There was a long list of bad boyfriends in her human past who had taught her she was okay for a lark, a week, a month, months, but eventually there'd be someone else who caught their eye.

"Damian isn't like that." I said it out loud and hadn't meant to.

"He isn't like what?" Cardinale asked.

"He has been as loyal and faithful to you as any man could be to a woman."

"You would say that, since you're his mistress."

"I'm not his mistress. I'm his master, and there is a big difference between the two titles," I said.

"You don't have to fuck your master," Cardinale said.

I looked past her at Damian. "Do you want me to say it?"

"Say whatever you want, Anita."

I took in a lot of air, blew it out slow, then said, "The Master of the City of London brought you into his kiss with the understanding you'd have to fuck him to be one of his vampires, didn't he?"

She looked behind her at Damian. "How could you tell her that?"

"He didn't have to tell me anything, Cardinale. I'm his master. We have to work at not sharing thoughts and memories."

"It has never been like that with me and any master I have ever served."

"Damian is my vampire servant, as I am Jean-Claude's human servant. It's a different kind of master relationship, a deeper relationship than that between vampire and Master of the City."

She looked at me then, tears shining in her eyes. "So you have a deeper relationship with Damian than I do—is that what you're saying?"

"There's no way to win with you, is there?" I asked.

"I'm not a game to win, Anita. I'm a person with a heart and right now you're breaking it."

Shit.

"No," Damian said, "there's no way to win with Cardinale. She's a riddle with no answer."

"My answer is that I love you more than anything in the world," she said, turning toward him and starting to cry.

"You're a rigged game, Cardinale, because your rules make it impossible for Damian to convince you that he loves you enough."

"I'll love enough for both of us, then!" she said, reaching out to him. He didn't reach back; in fact, he'd done nothing to get closer to her physically since she walked into the room. It was a bad sign for any relationship.

"It doesn't work that way," Damian said. "You have to leave room for me to love you, too, and your issues don't leave any room for me. It's like you're fighting men from your past that I don't even know about, but I'm paying for their sins."

"I don't know what that means. I just know I love you more than life itself!" She moved toward him then, hands reaching for him.

His hands stayed at his sides as he said, "I can't fight ghosts from your past unless you help me, Cardinale."

"I don't know what you're talking about, Damian." She was crying now, softly.

"Would you be willing to see a couples therapist with me?"

"Why? There's nothing wrong with us except you're cheating on me."

He hung his head, and the wave of despair that washed over me was almost soul crushing, as if it would wash away all of me and leave nothing behind but a black loneliness that we'd lived with for so long before we came to St. Louis. I was choking on the utter isolation he'd endured when he was trapped in Ireland with the vampire that made him.

Again I spoke out loud without meaning to. "Why didn't you kill yourself?"

"I was too frightened to do the one thing that would kill me for certain," he said.

"What are the two of you talking about?" Cardinale asked.

"Sunlight," I said.

He nodded.

I had shared the memory of his best friend, his shield mate, brother-in-arms, his heterosexual life partner, being forced outside into the sunlight by She-Who-Made-Them, to punish them, yes, but mostly just to cause them both pain, because she could. She'd done a lot of things because she could, and there was no one to stop her; some people are only good because there are rules and punishments in place to make them be good. Take that away and it's amazing what people will do to one another if they think they can get away with it. I felt the weight of centuries of having no safety, no surety of what evil thing she'd do next, and still being forced to share her bed when she wanted it. I was impressed that Damian had been able to get it up for the evil bitch century after century.

"A man who couldn't service her was tortured to death, or mutilated and left alive. It gave us all a great incentive to rise to the occasion."

"Why are you talking about such horrible things?" Cardinale asked.

I felt the vampire behind me before she spoke, and knew it was Echo before I heard her voice. "They are speaking mind to mind, sharing emotions, memories, pieces of their heart and soul."

"No," Cardinale said, "no, no one gets a piece of his heart but me."

"You are only his love. She is his master. It is a closer bond."

I turned and looked at her then, because that last part was rubbing salt in Cardinale's wounds. Was my new head of security at Danse Macabre here to make things worse, or better?

Echo was shorter than me tonight, because I was wearing heels and she was in flat boots, but then, she was security tonight and I was hoping to have a date. Her hair was a brown so dark, it was almost black. It even looked black until you got her too close to Jean-Claude's hair, or mine, but whereas we were curly she had waves that helped hers fall in a more orderly fashion to her shoulders, framing one of the most delicate triangles of a face I'd ever seen. She was one of the few women who made me think *dainty*, but once you looked into her dark blue eyes you stopped thinking *dainty* and started thinking *dangerous*. She wore no makeup when she worked security, which would have made most women's faces look plain, but Echo's natural black lashes and brows framing deep, rich blue eyes, and all that dark hair, well . . . *plain* was just never a word you thought of when looking at her. *Beautiful* maybe, but never *plain*. She did her best to dress down for the job, with a looser black T-shirt over a tighter-fitting black tank top. I couldn't see the tank top under her T-shirt, but I knew it was there, because she didn't like the weapons at her waist digging into her bare skin, so there'd be a layer of clothing to protect her bare skin. She'd had a business jacket thrown over all that, so that she hid as much of the trim figure underneath as she could, but you never forgot that Echo was a beautiful woman for very long, no matter how she tried to hide it. Since I was sleeping with her, that should have been a good thing, but she made me strangely nervous, like I was fourteen again and had my first crush.

"You don't know anything! No bond is closer than true love! No bond!" Cardinale screamed it, and started walking stiffly toward us all.

"I think you are too emotionally overwrought to work tonight," Echo said, her voice very calm.

"That is not your decision. It's Damian's. He's the manager, not you!"

Echo looked past the tall, redheaded vampire who was still stalking toward us, to the tall redheaded vampire standing behind his desk, though since Ricky and Roger were the ones who would be in the line of her anger first, I guessed Echo and I could stay calm a little longer. I wasn't sure I was capable of calm with all of Damian's emotions boiling through my head. My mouth was dry, which meant his was, because he was afraid, so afraid. Afraid of losing Cardinale, afraid of not having enough of a relationship with me to take up the slack, afraid of giving up too much, to gain too little. I started to say aloud that he couldn't use me as his next relationship, that I was booked up, but Echo touched my arm as if she'd read my mind, or my heart, or my intentions. Whatever it was, that one slight touch on my arm kept me from saying that bit of truth, and the moment passed and we were on to other things.

"Damian is a fine manager, but I'm the head of security here, and if I think you're a danger to the peaceful workings of this club tonight, then you will not work tonight."

"You have no right to treat me like that!" She turned and looked at Damian. "Tell her that I'm working tonight. Tell her that you want me at your side in the dance tonight."

He looked at her, and then past her to Echo, and then at me. I felt his gaze like a weight, as if he'd touched me.

"Tell her, Damian! Tell her that she can't treat me this way!"

"Echo is head of security at Danse Macabre, Cardinale," he said, in a voice as empty and neutral as any I'd ever heard from him.

"But you're the manager."

"I am."

"Then tell her she's wrong. Tell her she can't send me home like a child." She was standing in front of him now, so tall that she blocked my view of Damian's face and most of his body, but I could still feel him. He wasn't sad anymore. He felt nothing, as if he'd locked all his emotions away along with his body movement; without seeing him clearly I knew he was standing there in that utter stillness that the older vampires could do. It was that stillness that made me want to stare at them harder, as if once I looked away they would just sink into that stillness and vanish. I'd thought it was a way of hiding what they were thinking, but now I could feel that it was more than that, that it was a way of being still all the way to the core of their being. It was like the quiet place I went in my head when I knew I had to pull the trigger and kill someone; in that moment, I felt nothing but the gun in my hand, thought about nothing but how best to use the gun and get the shot. It became very analytical, cold physical logic. I felt that from Damian now and knew either he was hiding away his feelings so the next few minutes wouldn't hurt that much, or he was hiding them away so he could do what needed doing, or maybe both?

"I've let my love for you interfere with my ability to manage the club, or at least my ability to treat you like an employee."

"I don't know what you're talking about, Damian. I love that we work together every night."

"You love keeping an eye on me at work, but you hate the job. You hate watching me flirt on the dance floor, and you hate having to dance with strangers. You've gone from being one of the top moneymakers on tips to making almost nothing, because you're so busy watching me with my partners that you don't pay enough attention to your own dance partners."

"I'll do better tonight," she said, touching his arm.

"People come here to dance with vampires and shapeshifters, Cardinale. They come for the illusion that they can have a romance with one of us. They come for someone to pay attention to them, to really look at them, talk to them, listen. If Guilty Pleasures is about lust and the possibility of sex, then

Danse Macabre is about romance and the possibility of a relationship."

"But you and I are each other's relationship," she said, a hand on both his arms as if she were trying to get him to look at her, or shake some sense into him.

"That's what I wanted more than anything else in the world, a real relationship with one person who truly loved me."

"I love you! I love you truly, madly, completely!"

"People come here to be listened to, to feel special, but you're so worried that I'm cheating on you that you don't have any room to even pretend for a few minutes."

"Pretend what?" She yelled it, even though they were inches apart. Her hands dug into his bare arms hard enough that she mottled his skin.

Roger said softly, "Do we need to be here?"

His whisper made Ricky and me jump, as if we'd been frozen by the emotions in the room.

"No," Echo said, stepping back and herding me ahead of her and both male guards, as she got us out of the office and into the corridor that led to the main part of the club. She wasn't leaving me alone with Cardinale, and I couldn't argue, because I wasn't worried about her hurting me anymore. I was more worried that she'd force me to kill her. If Cardinale wanted to do suicide by cop, she needed to find a different cop, someone who wasn't emotionally invested. Of course, that emotional investment had made me hesitate and not shoot her earlier. I couldn't remember the last time I'd let a vampire make my holy objects glow that much and not shot them. If she'd pulled this shit with a regular police officer they'd have shot her a long time before they were blinded by holy fire. I was glad I hadn't shot her, and that would make me hesitate the next time, if there was a next time.

Echo stayed a half step behind me, with Ricky behind her and to my other side. She'd sent Roger ahead to wait by the door at the end of the hallway. That she kept Ricky with her meant she had some faith in his skills, or maybe Roger was just that much worse. I owed him a thank-you for suggesting we leave before Damian finished his talk with Cardinale. One of the things I was working on in therapy was that I had trouble protecting my boundaries from the people I was close to, but apparently Roger was better at it. I could shoot and fight just fine, but if Roger, Roger Parks, was better at boundary issues, maybe I could just have him follow me around and get me out of awkward emotional conversations all night. It wasn't in security's job description, but it might be damn useful to me.

"If you are in a private area with Cardinale, you must have security personnel with you from this point on, Anita," Echo said.

"Okay," I said.

She gave me a sideways glance. "You aren't going to argue with me?"

"No. If she wants to suicide by cop, I don't want it to be me."

"Suicide by cop: When a person wants to commit suicide but is afraid to do the task themselves, so they threaten police or pose a threat to innocents so that police feel they must kill them to protect others or themselves. Yes?"

I nodded. "Yeah, that's it."

"Do you believe that was what Cardinale intended with you tonight?"

"No, at least not in the front of her head."

"Front of her head?"

"It was a subconscious thought, in the back of her head, not a conscious thought, which would be in the front of the head."

"Ah, I think much more happens in the back of people's heads than in the front."

"Ain't that the God's honest truth?" I said.

"Yes, I think it is," Echo said.

I could feel the bass beating through the still-closed door; I kept walking and Roger opened the door, so well-timed it was like an automatic door. I didn't even have to pause as we walked through. In fact, I hadn't been planning to pause. I was just so used to security opening doors for me I took it for granted now. When did that happen?

There had been a time when I would have known as much about Cardinale's background as possible by now, but I'd trusted that if Jean-Claude thought she was okay, then she was, but what a six-hundred-year-old vampire king would think was okay might not be okay to me. Was it a sign that I trusted Jean-Claude that much, or that I'd grown arrogant?

Echo paused with her hand on the door and turned to say, "I will make certain that Cardinale does nothing unfortunate tonight. If you can put this incident aside and be truly present for the date and its issues, I think that would be best. If you talk of all this first, it may spoil the mood."

"I was thinking the same thing."

She smiled, and it took her face from severe to truly beautiful. I understood why she didn't use that particular smile much at work. Customers would have begged her to dance with them, even as dressed down as she could manage. I basked in the warmth of that smile, because I was on a very short list of people who got to have it aimed at them. It made me smile back, and blush, which was a habit I couldn't seem to break entirely.

The blush made her smile broaden enough to flash a delicate hint of fang and show that there was a dimple in that classically beautiful face. She touched my face and leaned in for a very unprofessional kiss. I knew how to French-kiss a vampire without nicking myself on the fangs, but her mouth was smaller than that of anyone else I'd kissed so it was more of a challenge, but it was worth it. She drew back first, leaving me a little breathless.

"Enjoy as much of tonight as you can, Anita."

"It's Jean-Claude. What's not to enjoy?"

She smiled. "Very true. I look forward to the next time we can share our king."

I blushed and couldn't stop it. "Me, too."

She turned and looked at Ricky and Roger; I'd sort of forgotten about them. Echo could have that effect on me.

Roger was staring at the floor as hard as he could. Ricky was looking at us as if we were something to eat. I glared at him. "You got something to add?"

"You can't blame a man for enjoying the show."

"Yes, actually I can."

"I am your superior and she is your queen. Both are people you should not be leering at," Echo said.

"I can control what I say and what I do around beautiful women, but I can't control involuntary body responses."

"We don't care about your erection," Echo said. "It's not important to us."

His anger slid across my skin like the smell of well-cooked meat. I'd acquired the ability to feed on anger the way that Jean-Claude could feed on lust. He'd shared that ability with me, but so far siphoning off people's anger was something only I could do.

I sniffed the air, making a big deal out of it. "Calm the fuck down, Ricky. You're starting to smell like food: yummy, yummy anger."

"Fuck you."

"You wish."

"You just can't behave respectfully, can you?" Echo asked.

"Anita just seems to bring out the worst in me, I guess," Ricky said.

"You are officially on probation, Ricky," she said.

"That's not fair."

"Life isn't supposed to be fair."

"What does that mean?"

"It means that only children whine, *That's not fair.* Grown-ups understand that fairness is rare and good treatment must be earned."

"I'm good at my job."

"You are. That's why I'm not going to fire you tonight. But remember this, Ricky: If you disrespect Anita, or any of the female employees again, you will be out of a job."

"How can I not look at them and do my job?"

"You can look, but don't leer."

"I don't understand the difference."

She sighed. "I think you mean that." She frowned and turned to me. "Go to our king and shared lover. I will see that Cardinale does no harm and try to explain the difference between a look and a leer to this one."

"Good luck on that last part," I said.

"Perhaps I will enlist some of the other male guards to explain the masculine niceties of looking but not being lecherous."

"Good idea," I said.

She opened the door for me, and the music engulfed us so that I could barely hear her as she told me good-bye, with her face back to its super-serious head-of-security expression. I found myself a little sad to leave her without one more kiss. I'd had other female lovers, but never one that made me think words like *girlfriend*. Was Echo my girlfriend? I wasn't sure what to call her, but I was beginning to want to call her something. I'd never had a woman make me feel like I wanted to hang a title on her. I'd had one who had demanded it, but I hadn't wanted to call her my girlfriend. This time it would be my idea, and ironically, I wasn't sure Echo would want the title. She'd take it if I wanted to give it to her, but she didn't need it to feel secure, and maybe that was part of why I wanted to give it to her. Romance can be very confusing.

I left my girlfriend behind to make sure the live-in girlfriend of my ex-lover and current vampire servant didn't harm anyone, while I went to have a date with our shared lover. I would have said *shared boyfriend*, but Echo really only had one person she dated, and that was Fortune, the love of her life and afterlife. Fortune was my girlfriend's girlfriend, or maybe Fortune was my girlfriend, too. So did that make either of them my girlfriend's girlfriend or just my girlfriend? Was Jean-Claude their girlfriend's boyfriend? Or since everyone had at least occasional sex with one another, were words like *boyfriend* and *girlfriend* too old-fashioned to cover it? I was beginning to get a headache, and it wasn't from the dance music.

4

I CALLED EDWARD FROM my Jeep, because I'd finally figured out how to use the Bluetooth so that I could talk and drive at the same time. It was a little bit like being able to pat your head, rub your stomach, and jump on one foot at the same time while chewing gum, but much more useful and less silly looking.

The phone had rung three times before I realized I hadn't done the time zone math and it was probably the wee hours of the morning there. Had I learned anything that couldn't wait until he was awake? No. I hung up, hoping he'd slept through it. I wasn't used to Edward being half a world away from me. We'd never been more than about a five-hour plane ride from each other before. I guess Ireland wasn't that much longer actually, but the time difference made it feel like more.

I wasn't surprised when his ringtone filled the car just moments after I'd hung up. I'd have called him back, too. "Hey, Ed . . . Ted," I said.

"I'm in my room alone; you can call me whatever you want." His voice was thick and rough with sleep.

"I forgot the time change. Sorry."

"Just tell me you found out something that will help."

"Yes and no. There have always been vampires in Ireland, or at least for the last thousand years and change."

I heard the sheets move as he changed positions. "Say again."

I did.

"How do you know?"

"First Jean-Claude told me, and then we had one of the vamps from Ireland in town."

"I didn't know you had any Irish vampires in St. Louis."

"He doesn't consider himself Irish even though he was a vampire there for about a thousand years, give or take a few hundred."

"You don't have that many vampires that old, or you didn't. Is it one of the Harlequin?" See, he really did know most of my business.

"No, it's Damian."

"What? He doesn't sound Irish."

"Like I said, he doesn't consider himself Irish. He said, *I just died there*. He still thinks of himself as a Viking. He was what history calls a Danish Viking, and that's still how he thinks of himself."

"Even after a millennium in Ireland."

"Yep."

"Okay, I don't have to understand Damian's motives. What did you learn?"

"His old mistress, She-Who-Made-Him, literally, you can't say her name without risking her invading your mind. She can do some of the tricks that the Mother of All Darkness could do, and some of the old vampire council could do."

"He tell you, or you experience it?"

"She's visited us once. She caused fear in Damian and it spread to me and Nathaniel. It was pretty awful. I think that if Richard and Jean-Claude hadn't been able to lend a metaphysical hand, she could literally have killed us with fear."

I heard the sheets move again. I was betting he was sitting up against the headboard. "You mean scared to death, literally?"

"Yes."

"I know you've met other vampires that could cause fear like that."

"Night hags, yeah, but they were amateurs compared to She-Who-Made-Him."

"You really don't want to say her name out loud."

"No, I really don't."

"She spooked you."

"Let's just say that I don't want a revisit."

"You don't spook that easy," he said.

"Not normally, no."

"Why didn't the Irish know they had vampires?" he asked.

"Damian said that they kept their numbers small, a dozen at the most and usually fewer. They took a little blood here and there, and when they did kill it was easy to blame it on war, wild animals, just the violence of the day. He said there was usually some battle or something to blame disappearances on."

"That makes sense."

"He also said that the jail nearby didn't care if people died a little early as long as they weren't the ones who paid the jailer for better treatment."

"A thousand years ago jails and hospitals would have been perfect for a vampire to feed from, and he's right: no one would have given a second thought to a few more deaths."

"Most of the vampires I've known well wouldn't feed in jail or hospitals. It wasn't elegant enough victims, I guess. I know the vampire council didn't feed like that."

"They were aristocrats, Anita. They could prey on peasants and no one would question it, or no one that mattered. There were enough human nobles who used the common people like their personal hunting ground and no one questioned them either."

"The only two nobles I know that were ever brought up on charges were Elizabeth Báthory and Gilles de Rais, but at least Báthory was caught because she had the bad taste to use a minor noble's daughter as a victim. Only de Rais was actually put on trial without a noble victim."

"I always thought one of them must have had a vampire involved somewhere."

"The vampire community actually thinks that Gilles de Rais sold his soul to the devil after his friend Joan of Arc was burned alive. It sort of damaged his faith in God's goodness."

"I could see that," Edward said.

"You and I both know that even if the devil wanted his soul, the urges that made him a murdering pedophile had to be there all along."

"Yes, but he used his faith in God to not act on them. It was the theory that the Church used for centuries that you could pray yourself out of pedophilic urges, so become a priest."

"Yeah, ask the victims of pedophile priests and nuns how that's worked out."

"I didn't say I agreed with it."

"Sorry. Raised Catholic, so it's a sore point with me."

"Sometimes I forget that about you."

"What?"

"That once you were a good little Catholic schoolgirl."

"I actually didn't go to Catholic school."

"Really, so no little plaid skirt outfit?"

"No. Sorry to disappoint you."

"Schoolgirl really isn't my thing."

"Somehow I didn't think it would be."

I could almost hear the smile on the other end of the phone as he said, "I don't think either of us spends a lot of time wondering what each other's kinks are."

"Nope," I said.

"So why is She-Who-Must-Not-Be-Named suddenly going apeshit with her vampires?"

"Damian doesn't think it's her."

"Could it be some of her vampires without her knowledge?"

"He only left five years ago, Edward, and he says she'd kill any of her vamps that were this careless."

"Vampires are legal in more countries than ever before, Anita. Why is she still in hiding if she's not doing this?"

"Apparently, she's like a lot of the really old ones. She doesn't believe the new attitude will last and when the humans start killing vampires again, she'll still be hidden in her fortress in Ireland, untouched."

"Then Damian's old group isn't the only vampires in Ireland anymore."

"She was powerful enough to keep out other vampires for centuries. If she can't stop this new wave, then Damian thinks she's lost power."

"What would cause her to go from scary enough that you don't even want to speak her name to letting a bunch of new vampires run riot in Dublin?"

"Damian didn't have a guess on that."

"Do you?"

I thought about it as I drove through the night-dark neighborhoods, wending my way toward the old warehouse district that, thanks to the Circus of the Damned, had gotten gentrified into a tourist attraction area.

"Anita, you still there?"

"I'm here, Edward, just thinking. I don't know. Vampires either grow in power or fade. The force I felt a few years back wasn't going to fade away."

"If She-Who-Must-Not-Be-Named isn't causing this, but she can't stop it either, then what is going on?"

"It would almost have to be something more powerful than her that's just arrived in Ireland."

"What could be more powerful than a night hag that can throw fear halfway across the world?"

"I'd say the Mother of All Darkness, but she's dead."

"We killed her," he said.

"Yes, we did." I could have quibbled that the actual killing part was mostly me, but if Edward hadn't fought his way to me with reinforcements I'd have been dead instead of her, so "we" killed her. Striking the death blow without acknowledging all the people who helped you get in place to deliver it is just poor sportsmanship.

"Then what else, or who else, is tough enough to make She-Who-Must-Not-Be-Named back off?"

"You do know it's She-Who-Made-Him, right?"

"Yeah, but saying it the other way is more fun."

"I didn't know you were a Harry Potter fan."

"We took turns reading them to Becca when she was little. By the end of the series, she helped read it aloud to all of us."

"I can see why you like the books," I said.

"So, what's scary enough to make She-Who-Must-Not-Be-Named scared?"

"I didn't say she was scared, Edward."

"Scary people only back off for one reason, Anita."

"And that is?"

"That they meet someone scarier," he said.

"Or you reach an understanding like you and I did when we just worked together but weren't friends yet."

"True, but I don't think ancient vampires really have work friends."

"Not really," I said.

"How do I contact Damian's old master?"

"You don't."

"She has to know something about this, Anita."

"I've shared Damian's memories of this woman, this thing, and you do not want to be alone with her."

"I can take care of myself."

"I know that, but unless you're going to kill her, leave her alone."

"She really did scare you."

"Yes, Edward, she really did."

"I still need information from her, or one of her group."

"I'll talk to Jean-Claude and Damian, and the others. I'll see if I can find you someone to talk to without dealing directly with her."

"The last vampire you were this scared of was the Mother of All Darkness."

"Which should give you a clue why I don't want you messing with her while I'm half a world away."

"You think I need the backup?"

"I think anyone going up against her would need backup."

"I'll bear it in mind," he said, and I didn't like the way he said it.

"Promise me that you will wait until I get back to you to try to find her."

"People are dying here, Anita."

"But they're strangers to me. You aren't."

"You just don't want to explain to Donna and the kids why I'm not around anymore."

"Damn straight I don't, so don't get dead while I'm not there to watch your back."

"I'm trying to get them to invite you in on this, but they have a serious hard-on against necromancy here."

"The Irish are so welcoming to almost all kinds of magic, except mine. Peachy."

"I may have found a way around the mainstream police to bring you over."

"Do tell."

"No, I'll share when it's a reality, or I'll share when you tell me how to contact Damian's old master."

"Fine, keep your secrets. I've got a date to get to."

"Jean-Claude, or Micah and Nathaniel?" he asked.

"Some mix of those," I said.

"Do I want to know?"

"Probably not."

"Have fun, then, and don't do anything I wouldn't do."

"Edward, you're a heterosexual man. I plan to do all sorts of things that you wouldn't do."

He laughed then, and we hung up on the sound of laughter, which was a good way to end. I hoped Edward would keep his promise to leave Damian's old master alone. I was supposed to be his best man at his wedding to Donna. They were finally going to make it legal. I did not want to miss the wedding because the groom got killed in Ireland. I said a quick prayer that he'd be safe and that we'd find a way to stop the killings.

I saw the bright lights of the Circus of the Damned up ahead, turning the night into a carnival of color. I would avoid the bright front and the happy crowds and go in the back, where it was darker, less crowded, and far more romantic. Jean-Claude was waiting for me. It would be a good night.

5

JEAN-CLAUDE'S PLAN TO help Damian was to have him sleep over with us and Nathaniel. He agreed that the three of us needed to strengthen our metaphysical connections with one another. Micah agreed with it, too, which was good, because one of our rules was that the core group of us, the primaries for each other, had to be okay with anything that might affect the domestic arrangement, and adding sleepovers with Damian, even without sex, would change things if it became a regular thing. You don't think how important just sleeping together can be for pair bonding until you keep changing how you do it, and whom you do it with. Sex was so much easier than actually sleeping with your lovers.

It also helped that Micah had been asked to travel out of town to settle a dispute between two rival shapeshifter groups. They were afraid it would escalate to open war if they couldn't find someone to come in and help negotiate a settlement between them. Both group leaders had invited the Coalition in, so the chances were good that Micah wouldn't have to fight anyone to force the fighting to stop, which was great. It meant that when I kissed him good-bye, I worried less that I'd never see him again. After years of him kissing me good-bye when he didn't know if his badge-wearing fiancée was coming home safe, it was my turn. Let me just say that turnabout was not only not fair play, but it was downright scary.

He had bodyguards with him, and Rafael the Rat King was going with him for a show of solidarity even though neither group were wererats, because the rats were the largest and most powerful single lycanthrope group in the United States. Rafael had done the unprecedented and forged all the rat groups into one huge rodere with one king—him. His actions had been part of what inspired Micah to make the Coalition into a governing body of the groups that either wanted to join or were too dangerous to be left unsupervised.

I was standing beside the big bed in a blue silk robe that touched the floor when Damian came through the door. Jean-Claude was still in the bathroom cleaning up after our date. He'd even insisted on blow-drying my hair with a diffuser so that my hair would be dry before bed, and my curls would be intact. I hadn't been allowed to use a blow-dryer on my own hair since the infamous white man's 'fro incident. Thanks to Jean-Claude, I stood there with every curl in place; come to think of it, the blue silk robe had been a gift from him, so it was all his doing. He'd even managed to give me a moment alone with Damian. I suddenly felt stage-managed, but it wasn't the first time, and it wouldn't be the last. Jean-Claude had lived by his social wits for too many centuries to stop now.

Damian hesitated just inside the door. He was wearing a green velvet-and-brocade robe long enough to hide all but the tips of his slippers. They were new, but the robe was Victorian, as in he'd bought it during that time. It had rubbed spots where the velvet had worn away, and patches where it had been repaired like a child's much-loved stuffed toy. I knew it was something Damian wore when he was needing reassurance, like his version of our comfy clothes at the end of a hard day.

"How did Cardinale take the news of you sleeping over?" I asked, because I couldn't help myself.

"Badly, but Jean-Claude made it an order from him, so she couldn't refuse it, or I couldn't refuse. When your king summons, you go and do his bidding; that she understood."

"Okay," I said, not sure if I'd really gotten an answer, but I let it go. It was too confusing to do anything else with it.

"I like the robe," he said.

"Jean-Claude bought it for me." I touched the sash. "He said he wanted me to expand my color range for lingerie."

"Well, I approve, if my approval matters."

"I'm not sure what you mean by *if your approval matters*. You matter, and compliments are always welcome."

He smiled. "Good." He walked toward me and looked behind me. "I take it that it's Jean-Claude I hear in the bathroom."

I couldn't hear a thing from the bathroom, but I bowed to

his superior vampire hearing and said, "Yeah, he'll be joining us in a minute. Wait. How did you know it wasn't Nathaniel?"

"He hugged me in the hallway and said he'd be there as soon as he changed from work."

"There are going to be a lot of disappointed fans at Guilty Pleasures when they learn that he's not going onstage again tonight," I said, smiling.

"I'm sorry he had to cut his act short just for me," Damian said, not smiling.

"Nathaniel is thrilled that we're going to work on our triumvirate for a change."

"He seemed happy about it."

"He is happy about it."

"But are you?" he asked.

"Happy about it?" I asked. "Your girlfriend almost attacked me when I hadn't done more than shake your hand. I'm a little worried about her reaction tomorrow night."

"That's completely fair," he said.

"You look like you're about to bolt back out the door, Damian."

He came to me then, looking uncertain. "We're going to be sleeping together tonight, and we've been lovers, so why is this awkward?"

"Maybe because we were lovers, but now we're not and we're just sleeping together tonight and nothing else."

He smiled, a little sad around the edges. "I'd be willing to do more, but I know that it wouldn't be fair to you, or Cardinale, or maybe even to me."

"If you want a clean break from Cardinale, then do that, but I won't be the excuse for the big blowout fight. That's on you and her, not me."

"I said it wouldn't be fair to anyone."

"You did. I guess I'm just beating the point home."

"I appreciate you and Jean-Claude letting me sleep with you tonight. You are both good masters and try to take care of your people."

"Thanks. We do our best."

We stood there, close enough to touch, but not touching, and it was those last few empty inches that screamed awkwardness. The bathroom door opened behind us; Damian looked up, but I kept looking at him. Jean-Claude said, "Have you greeted each other at all?"

I turned and looked at him then. "We said hello."

"I know you do not kiss hello, but hugging must be allowed even by Cardinale."

"I think we've missed the window for hugging," I said, frowning at him.

"Do not frown at me, *ma petite*. It is you who is being silly. You have a Viking warrior in front of you, as striking and beautiful a man as Cardinale is a woman, and yet you refuse to touch him. Even friends touch more than the two of you." He strode farther into the room dressed in his own comfort robe, but it wasn't threadbare; it was as beautiful as all his other favorite clothes. The robe was black with more thick black fur at the lapels and sleeves. I knew the fur was even softer and more luxurious than it looked. I loved the way it framed a triangle of his chest, making it look even whiter and more perfect than it was. He'd tied the robe loosely so that it showed more of his chest, enough so the cross-shaped burn scar on his chest showed faint and darker against his skin. Some human had shoved a cross into him in a bid to survive, but I knew that long-ago person had failed. I had a cross-shaped burn scar on one arm; a vampire's human servant had branded me with it, thought it was funny that it would make me look like holy items burned me like a vampire. I'd killed him, before his master could kill me. Jean-Claude and I had done the same thing for the same reason: If something hurts you and tries to kill you, you fight back. If something tries to kill you, you try to kill it first. Sometimes life comes down to very simple rules.

I looked up at Jean-Claude as he stood there motioning at Damian. I looked up into those green eyes and that face that was more perfect now than when I'd met him, because something about becoming my servant had literally changed his bone structure so he was an even more perfect, more handsome, more sexy vamp than he'd been before. I hadn't done it consciously, but I had changed things about Damian that had been true for a thousand years, and yet I was nervous about giving him a hug. It was ridiculous when you thought about it.

I stepped forward and put my arms around his waist, feeling the harsher rub of the old velvet. Real velvet isn't like the modern version; it's not soft and squishy, more soft but rougher, but Damian was real and solid as I hugged him, and that was the point.

He hesitated a second, then put his arms around me. He seemed to like the way the silk slid under his hands. He looked down at me and smiled. "Greetings, my master."

"Hey, Damian."

We smiled at each other and hugged for real, then broke apart.

Jean-Claude threw his hands up at us. "You are exasperating, both of you, and where is our cat? We must to bed before dawn decides things for us."

He was right. I could feel the press of it in the air even deep underground where we were. It wasn't as easy to feel the pull of it, but sensing sunrise and sunset seemed to be a natural ability for most animators and necromancers. I'd fought many a night with dawn my only hope of surviving, and I'd had days when sunset meant the monsters would rise and eat me.

"We're less than two hours out," I said.

Damian shuddered.

I touched his arm. "It will be all right."

"Enough of this," Jean-Claude said, and took off his robe. His body looked incredibly white against the black of the robe, as if his skin were carved of marble, and he was absolutely nude. He looked like some Renaissance statue come to life, like a male version of Galatea come to make all your romantic wishes come true.

Damian looked at the floor as if the rug at the foot of the bed had suddenly gotten much more interesting. You'd think after a thousand years of "life" he'd be less embarrassed by nudity, or maybe it was the nudity in question. Jean-Claude could have that effect on people, or maybe it was the whole heterosexual-man-outside-the-locker-room thing.

"We're just sleeping with Damian, remember?" I said, half laughing.

"Since I am not sleeping beside Damian but on the other side of you, *ma petite*, I think my lack of clothing will not infringe upon his virtue."

Damian was so not looking at the other man in the room. I

tried not to laugh again at his discomfort because there'd been a time when I'd have been just as uncomfortable for other reasons. I'd tried so hard not to have sex with Jean-Claude, to not let him seduce me. For Damian, nudity just wasn't a thing that straight men did with other men much, at least not in the modern day, and Damian was very straight, much to Nathaniel's disappointment. My happily bisexual fiancé would have loved for Damian to be at least as friendly as Richard was with Jean-Claude. Oddly, Richard was just about as heterosexual as Damian, but he did bondage with us. There were needs we met in Richard's life and he in ours because of it. Damian was utterly vanilla—not a fault, but for the rest of us in these relationships it made it even more awkward, because we were so rocky road with extra cherries, gobs of whipped cream, and sprinkles on top.

Damian looked at me, and the look seemed to ask a question as I stood there in my blue robe.

"I'm wearing jammies, under my robe," I said.

Damian smiled. "Should I say *thank you*, or *aww*?"

That made me smile. "Either, neither, let's get some sleep."

"We are still waiting for Nathaniel," Jean-Claude said, "but we can get into bed while we wait." He walked to the side of the bed nearest the outer door, which had become his side. He flung the black coverlet aside to reveal sheets the same royal jewel-tone blue as my robe.

"You matched my lingerie to the sheets," I said.

He smiled, obviously pleased with himself, but it was as he swept back the blue sheets with a flamboyant gesture that I realized he was nervous. It had taken me years to figure out that though he could be flamboyant, it wasn't his preference, and when he was doing it when it wasn't necessary, it meant he was nervous. Why the nerves? I wondered, as he climbed between the sheets and lay down. His long black curls spread across the pillow perfectly so that they framed his face, caressed the pale spill of one shoulder and still managed to leave half his face almost bare of hair so that the royal blue pillowcase framed the perfect line of his cheek. It also brought the blue very close to his eyes so that they went from a blue so dark as to be almost navy to suddenly a brighter blue set off by the thick black lace of his eyelashes, the perfect arch of his eyebrows. It was the kind of show he'd put on for me when he was trying to convince me just how beautiful he was, except then he'd worn pajamas, because he'd known that him nude made me run for the hills in the early days.

Did he want Damian to see him as beautiful, or was one of the most gorgeous men on the planet needing reassurance that I still appreciated his beauty? If it was for Damian's benefit, that was a conversation for another night, but if it was for mine, that I could do something about. If it was something else altogether, I'd ask Jean-Claude later when we were alone. I smiled at him and let him see that I saw every bit of theatrical-worthy beauty on display in the bed. If we'd been willing to let down our metaphysical shields he could have felt exactly how much I admired the view, and I'd have known precisely what his motives were, but then, Damian was my servant, as I was to Jean-Claude, so maybe we'd all have gotten a peek into one another, and that might have made Damian run for the hills, depending on what we were all thinking and feeling.

"You do know that one of the reasons it took so long for you to seduce me is that I just couldn't believe that anyone as beautiful as you really wanted to date me, and not just make me another notch on their bedpost."

He smiled and some tension left him, so at least part of what was going on in his head was a need for reassurance from me. I'd come into this relationship believing that someone who had been a ladies' man for centuries wouldn't need any reassurance. Jean-Claude had taught me that everyone needed it.

"There are no notches on my bedposts, *ma petite*."

I grinned at him. "The bedposts couldn't survive all your conquests."

"There are not so many as that." And then he laughed.

I felt a bubble of eagerness in my stomach, like happy butterflies. It wasn't me. "Nathaniel is almost here," I said.

The bodyguards gave a businesslike knock and opened the door for our other half, or would it be our other third, or our fourth? Nathaniel walked in wearing a pair of silky lavender sleeping shorts that fit him very nicely, so nicely that the view from the front distracted me for a minute from the rest of him, but I recovered, because it was all a nice view. His shoulders were wide, his arms well muscled, his chest deep, and his stomach flat and fit. He'd started to get a six-pack of abs, but every time he got truly cut across his abs, he lost too much of that great ass of his, and Nathaniel just didn't look right below a certain weight. He had the Adonis belt where the line of his waist did that soft square line down along the hip, now hidden inside the silky shorts. The muscles of his thighs were impressive and so were his calves. He'd actually had to cut down on his weight lifting because he'd started to muscle up more than he wanted to for dancing onstage. Genetics would have let him muscle up in a way that the other two men in the room couldn't. Jean-Claude and Damian both looked great, and Jean-Claude hit the gym for the same reason Nathaniel did, so he'd look great taking his clothes off onstage, but he was built long and lean like a long-distance runner or a basketball player as opposed to a football player.

Damian didn't hit the gym as hard as the other two, but then, he got to keep all his clothes on at Danse Macabre when he danced with customers, or his dance partners. Knowing you're going to get nude in front of strangers was a great incentive for working out more.

Nathaniel's hair was still damp from the shower, so it was a darker brown than its true red auburn color. He'd tied it back in a braid still wet, because when your hair reaches to your calves you have to braid it to sleep or you strangle yourself and your partners by the end of the night. He had an even-better-than-normal smile, so for once that dominated his face rather than his eyes. His driver's license listed blue as his eye color, but that was only because they wouldn't let him put down lavender or purple. The normal color was pale like lilacs, but depending on his mood, the lighting, and the color near his face, they could darken to the true purple of violets. They were almost that dark now, which meant his emotions were running high, but happy; if they'd been grape dark it would have meant he was angry. His eyes rarely got that dark.

His happiness was contagious, or it was to me. I felt myself smiling back at him like a mirror, and maybe there was more to that analogy than I wanted to think about since he was my *moitié bête*, my animal to call. He nearly bounced across the room to wrap his arms around me and lay a very thorough kiss on my mouth. I responded to that eagerness with some of my own so that the kiss grew into my hands tracing the warm muscled smoothness of his back. His hands smoothed over the silk of my robe and pressed hard enough that he probably knew what I was wearing underneath it.

"I'll give you all a few minutes alone," Damian said, and started to move toward the door.

We broke from the kiss and Nathaniel said, "Why do you want to leave?"

"Not everyone is as comfortable with physical affection as you are, *notre minet*." Which meant "our kitty," or "pussycat." It was a term of endearment, though you had to be careful which French word you used for "cat," because some of them in French slang meant a very different kind of pussy.

"I thought you might want some privacy," Damian said.

Nathaniel looked genuinely puzzled.

"Nathaniel is an exhibitionist and a voyeur, Damian. He's not going to understand why the kiss made you uncomfortable."

Damian gave a smile that was more sad than happy. "I guess that's true, but if you want to have sex, then I can come back."

"I always want to have sex," Nathaniel said, laughing a little as he said it, because it was pretty much true, "but I can control myself even around Anita. We're here for you tonight, Damian, and what you need."

Damian smiled, then almost laughed, and shook his head. "That means a lot to me, Nathaniel, because I know you mean it."

Nathaniel stepped away from me, just trailing his hand down my arm so he kept our fingers entwined as he moved toward Damian, trailing me behind him by just our fingertips. "Of course I mean it, Damian. You're the other third of our triumvirate. Just tell me what I can do to help you feel better."

Damian gave a little laugh that seemed more nerves than anything. "If I asked you to wear something else to bed tonight, would you understand what I meant?"

I didn't have to see Nathaniel's face to know he was frowning. I could feel his confusion. "I can take off the shorts and sleep nude, but I thought you'd be more comfortable if I slept in something."

Damian shook his head and smiled. "That's not what I meant, Nathaniel. I don't want you to wear less to bed. I'd prefer if you wore more."

"More?" Nathaniel asked.

I wrapped my arms around his waist from behind so I could lay a light kiss on his bare back. "He means that he'd like you to wear more than just the shorts to bed tonight."

He turned in my arms so he could see my face, and his expression was completely *There must be some mistake.* When he realized I was serious, he turned back to Damian. "I'm sorry. I don't have anything that covers more of me that's pajamas."

"If you are protesting Nathaniel's shorts, then you must be deeply offended by what I am not wearing," Jean-Claude said from the bed, where he lounged like some sex god waiting for the cameras to roll. I'd have said that was just the fact that I was in love with him talking, but he really was as sexy as I thought, so said everyone else.

Nathaniel called out, "Jean-Claude," as if he'd just noticed him there. He let go of me and ran to the bed. He literally launched himself into the air and landed on top of Jean-Claude, catching himself on his hands and toes so that he didn't smack into the vampire, but was almost in a push-up over him. Only someone with Nathaniel's dexterity could have done it without the romantically exuberant gesture going horribly wrong. I couldn't have done it with practice runs.

I got to see Jean-Claude look genuinely surprised as he gazed up at Nathaniel. That alone made it worth it. "You look amazing tonight!"

Jean-Claude laughed, but it was a good laugh. "Thank you, pussycat. You look good enough to eat, as you always do."

"If you want to take a bite out of me, just ask." Nathaniel's face was serious, and why not? He had become one of the master vampire's regular feeds, just like I had. But this was the first time that Nathaniel had offered to feed him while he hovered just above the other man's body, their faces almost touching. Nathaniel's body was in what amounted to a plank like you did in gym, except he was doing it on a soft mattress, so that the muscles in his back, legs, and arms showed the strain of it. His ass was tight and firm, helping hold his body in place above Jean-Claude.

"We are supposed to be getting ready to sleep, pussycat. If I feed on you, it will not make me want to sleep."

Nathaniel smiled down at him. "I'll be good."

"Of that, I have no doubt," Jean-Claude said.

Nathaniel lowered his face just enough to kiss Jean-Claude. It was a chaste kiss compared to the one that he and I had just done, but there was something very erotic about them doing it with Nathaniel's body held just above the other man's. Jean-Claude raised a hand to caress the line of Nathaniel's bare back, tracing the muscles that kept him so still above him. Nathaniel rolled over to one side of the bed to lay his head against Jean-Claude's chest. The vampire did the natural movement that went with that, which was to put his arm around Nathaniel's shoulders and hold him. He cuddled closer to Jean-Claude, snuggling into the hug. I wasn't sure what had gotten into Nathaniel tonight. He was in a good mood, but it was mercurial, so that even I didn't know what was coming next.

"As I said, before I was so delightfully interrupted, I can wear more to bed if it will help your comfort level."

"If the king wants to wear nothing to bed, then that is the king's pleasure," Damian said, but he was uncomfortable with the pair of them cuddled up in the bed. It showed in the way he held his shoulders and how he didn't stare too long at them. Was Nathaniel trying to make our so-heterosexual vampire more uncomfortable? That didn't seem like something Nathaniel would do to Damian, unless I'd missed the redheaded vampire making Nathaniel uncomfortable elsewhere. Nathaniel was usually one of the nicest people you'd ever meet, but occasionally if something hit him wrong, his payback was very tit for tat. *You do this to me and I will do it to you in spades.* What had Damian done to make Nathaniel want to pull on this issue so hard?

"I do have pajamas if it would make you more comfortable tonight," Jean-Claude said, still holding Nathaniel in the crook of his arm.

"You said you were sleeping on the other side of Anita."

"I am."

"Then what you wear, or don't, isn't as . . . pressing," he said at last.

"They will be too long for him, but I could lend Nathaniel a pair of pajama bottoms," Jean-Claude said.

"I usually sleep nude," Nathaniel said, rubbing his cheek against Jean-Claude's bare chest like a cat scent-marking its person.

"We both do," I said.

"Show him what you are wearing, *ma petite*. Perhaps that will make our crimson-haired guest more willing to come to bed."

I didn't hesitate about it, because the way Damian was standing said in every line from shoulder to feet that he was debating leaving. I gave Damian all the eye contact I could as I dropped my robe beside Jean-Claude's and revealed a lacy blue camisole and boy shorts that were the same royal blue as the robe.

"Beautiful," Nathaniel said.

"Very nice," Damian said.

"Thanks. Jean-Claude picked it out," I said.

"I chose the color, but it is your body that turns a bit of silk and lace into something extraordinary," Jean-Claude said.

I turned and started walking toward the bed, and maybe I put a little extra sway to my hips in the lacy boy shorts. I wanted Damian to want to come to bed. The men were being strangely uncooperative about it, or seemed to want to feed his straight-guy nervousness about sharing a bed with extra men. I wanted to appeal to the part of him that wanted to crawl into bed beside me, regardless of what the men were doing.

I looked back at Damian and did my best to put the smile he wanted to see on my face. He looked stricken, as if I'd slapped him instead of just walked away in lacy pajamas. Apparently, I looked even better in the outfit than I'd thought, or at least my ass did. I grabbed hold of one of the bedposts to help me climb up on the tall mattress. I very deliberately crawled the long way across the bed toward the other two men so that Damian got a good view.

"Come to bed, Damian," I said, and turned to look over my

shoulder at him, and the look on his face was everything I'd wanted it to be. Was it unfair since we weren't going to have sex? Maybe, but if we were going to see if sleeping between Nathaniel and me could fix the whole sweating-blood-and-nightmares thing, Damian needed to get in bed with us and sleep.

Damian took off his robe last, laying it at the far foot of the bed, where we'd never accidentally touch it unless we grew several feet taller. When I say it's an orgy-size bed, I'm not joking.

Damian was wearing pajama bottoms that looked as silky as my robe, but they were a deep red and made his upper body look almost translucently pale, as if you should have been able to see his bones move as he walked, or as if the red brought out a shine to his skin that I hadn't noticed before.

"Nice color on you—the red, I mean."

"Thank you," he said.

"Come up on the bed so we can get some sleep," I said.

"I hope I don't sleep. I hope I just die at dawn," he said. I had a moment of wanting to ask if he meant die at dawn to wake the next night, or just die. He'd talked about it in his office, and that was never a good thing for a person to begin to speculate about. But I didn't ask, because some things you do not ask before bedtime, and you certainly don't ask about death and suicide when you're about to curl up between two walking corpses that may die with the rising of the sun.

Damian climbed tentatively onto the other side of the bed from us. He had to crawl a ways to reach us, and then we had another awkward moment as he stared at the three of us. The men were still cuddled up, but I was leaning against them almost like they were the back to a lounge.

Jean-Claude kissed Nathaniel on the forehead. "You need to sleep beside Damian, *mon minet*."

Nathaniel kissed just above his nipple, and for a moment I know he was debating whether to kiss on it, but he just came to his knees and kissed me lightly on the mouth and moved across the bed to make room for Damian.

I lay down next to Jean-Claude; this would be a sort of test for me, too, because I generally put one of the other men between me and the vampire. I loved Jean-Claude to pieces, but the fact that he did usually die at dawn was unnerving to me. His body cooled as the hours passed, and sometimes I would wake from nightmares of being trapped in coffins with other vampires. I'd been a little claustrophobic thanks to a diving accident, but that first time waking up trapped in a coffin built for one but holding two, one corpse and me trapped in the dark, the other body cold and dead, and knowing that if I screamed no one was coming to help me, and I'd screamed anyway, had put the scary cherry on my phobia. So I'd earned my issues about sleeping beside vampires, but Jean-Claude and I were going to get married, so I needed to try.

Jean-Claude kissed my cheek as I snuggled under the covers and up against his still very warm and wonderful body. "Thank you, *ma petite*. I know this is trying for you."

"I don't mean to be a burden," Damian said.

"It is not you that is a burden, Damian. It is any vampire that sleeps pressed against her. She finds it disturbing that we grow cooler as the hours pass until it is truly like sleeping beside the dead."

Damian climbed under the covers and settled down close, but not touching me. "I'm sorry. I didn't know that was an issue for you."

"You said you don't die at dawn now, so you won't be an issue," I said.

"Aren't we hoping that he does die at dawn and there are no nightmares because we're here with him?" Nathaniel asked.

"*Oui, mon minet*, but perhaps saying it out loud like that to *ma petite* was not diplomatic."

Nathaniel looked very sorry. I could feel his instant regret. "I'm so sorry, Anita. I wasn't thinking."

"It's okay, but please start thinking more." I wasn't really referring to what he'd said, but more how he'd acted as if he wanted to make Damian run away from us. Nathaniel had been asking for more up close and personal with Damian for months; I didn't understand why he wasn't helping more now that he had the chance.

There was another awkward moment as we all tried to settle into sleep, but Jean-Claude was there this time and didn't let the awkwardness grow.

"Damian, do you sleep on your side, your back, or your stomach?"

"My back, or sometimes my stomach," Damian answered.

"*Ma petite* and Nathaniel are side sleepers. I prefer my back but we will do what we can to compromise."

Jean-Claude turned off the bedside lamp and snuggled up against my back until I could feel his groin pressed against the silk-and-lace boy shorts so that I wiggled against him just a little. His upper body curled over me almost protectively, one arm holding me close against him. "It has been too long since I took blood, *ma petite*. You can writhe against me all you like, but I will be of no use to you."

Nathaniel was on his side on the other side of Damian, who was still sitting upright.

"Lie down, Damian, please," I said, and smoothed some of the covers near me.

He did what he was told, but he lay on his back with the arm closest to me across his stomach and the one beside Nathaniel straight at his side. Both arms were above the covers. Nathaniel and I looked across the vampire's body at each other. Nathaniel raised his eyebrows at me, as if asking, *What now?* We both had our arms underneath the covers, but Damian's arms now had them pinned so we couldn't reach under them toward each other.

Most of my lovers were side sleepers or had trained up to sleep on their side after a few months. Here was a new one to try to train all over again to sleep on his side so we could spoon while we slept. I freed a hand from the covers and laid it across his bare chest. He moved under my touch, but it was like he was as afraid to touch me now as when he first came into the room.

"At least put a hand or arm across her, Damian."

"I thought you might not want me to touch her, my king."

"If I did not want you to touch her, I would not have insisted you sleep with us today."

"I suppose not." And Damian touched my hand where it lay on his chest.

"You have to move this arm, Damian," Nathaniel said.

"Why?" he asked.

"Because you've trapped the covers, and I can't reach

across you and touch Anita without getting my arm out of the covers. I like under the covers when I sleep."

Damian sighed but turned onto his stomach, with one arm tucked up under his body and the other reaching over my side, but that had him touching Jean-Claude's bare side, and Damian pulled back.

"I gave you my word of honor when you first came here that I would never force myself on you. I have never given you a reason to doubt my word."

"You have been a man of your word, Jean-Claude."

"Then put your arm over *ma petite* and touch me, or not, but do not flinch every time you touch me accidentally or none of us will sleep tonight."

"I'm not comfortable yet," Nathaniel said.

"Then get comfortable, our pussycat."

Nathaniel slid an arm across Damian's back until he could touch me, and lightly Jean-Claude if he stretched.

"Damian, scoot closer to Anita, so we can all cuddle."

Damian drew a breath, as if to argue, then seemed to finally give in to the whole idea. He didn't say anything, but his arm went over me and across Jean-Claude, and then Damian snuggled in against me, pinning Jean-Claude's arm between us. Nathaniel snuggled in tighter on Damian's other side, throwing a leg across the other man's legs, which pressed his body tight against Jean-Claude's arm and Damian's side. Nathaniel stretched out his arm across Damian's back and finally must have put part of his shoulder on the other man's back, because he could reach not only me but enough of Jean-Claude so he was able to wrap his hand over the other vampire's side and hold him, too. Jean-Claude raised his arm and put it across Damian's back and Nathaniel's side. Now Damian could press himself closer against me. He turned a little bit on his side so that his arm and a bit of hip were propped up on me, which meant that Nathaniel pretty much rolled partially on top of him, but he didn't protest this time. It wasn't perfect with him on his stomach and me on my side, but as I let my hand and then my arm slide over his back, some tension in me eased. I was able to stroke Damian's back at the same time that I could caress Nathaniel's side, we were all so intertwined. It was always good to have Jean-Claude pressed in at my back, but there was a goodness to Damian's and Nathaniel's skin touching mine that wasn't about love, but almost about need, as if I'd been needing to touch both of them together for a very long time.

Was this how Jean-Claude felt about sleeping with me and Richard? If so, he'd been missing it lately. I'd ask Jean-Claude later, but right now I suddenly just wanted to sleep.

I heard Damian's breath go out with a long, almost contented sigh. I buried my face against his red hair and found it still damp near his scalp from the shower and smelling like clean herbs. I kept petting his back and playing along Nathaniel's side with the same gesture. Jean-Claude held us all, and somewhere in the warmth of skin, silk sheets, and clean, damp hair, we all fell asleep. We weren't thinking of nightmares, but that was okay, because the nightmares were thinking of us.

6

I WAS STANDING on a narrow cobblestone street. I'd have called it an alley, except cars were parked on it. It was after dark, but the streetlights kept it from being truly dark, so the light was electric-kissed and softened in a fine, misting rain that made halos around the lights as if angels had been beheaded and put up on poles as a warning.

Even in the dream I thought, *That's a weird thought*, and thinking it made me realize it was a dream. There was something lying in the shadows against the far wall, lost in a pool of blackness that all the light seemed to miss, as if the light were afraid of it or didn't want anyone to see it. I went forward, because I had to somehow, and as I reached out toward that darker shadow my hand was too big, too pale, a man's hand. Then it was mine, and then it wasn't, like a television channel that isn't steady so that it wavers between one show and another, until the dual images pile on top of each other and you can't tell what you're watching anymore. I/he got close enough to the shadowed heap, because it was a pile of something against the wall. There was a pool of dark water near it, was the first thought, but as the liquid crept around our shoes—my jogging shoes and his dress boots—we knew it wasn't water. We stood in a growing pool of blood, and the shadow lifted like a magician taking away a cloth, and . . .

The body lay crumpled on its side, one hand drawn up tight against its side as if it had tried to hold in some of what was spilling out of its stomach. Something had ripped it open—her, ripped her open, because the staring face was female. She looked young, maybe even pretty, but it was hard to tell now. The rain beaded on her skin like someone was sprinkling her. The head began to slide as if she were going to shake her head, but it was just her dead muscles giving up on holding her head in place. Her throat had been torn open like her stomach, so that the soft light glistened on her spine among all that red meat. I thought I saw teeth marks in her flesh, but I couldn't be sure because there were sirens in the night, but they didn't sound right. The man in my head turned to run and the corpse grabbed his/my ankle.

I woke sitting upright in the dark, my breathing ragged and panicked. Except it was as if I woke up twice—no, three times—and was sitting beside myself as we all fought not to scream. I managed to whisper, "Damian, Nathaniel, it's Anita."

Damian said, "Oh God, you saw, right? You saw the body."

"Yes." The bed felt soaked with sweat as if we'd been trapped in nightmares for too long.

"That didn't feel like any dream I've ever had," Nathaniel said, and he had reached through the dark so that we were holding hands across Damian.

Jean-Claude turned on the bedside light from where he was standing beside the bed, and the moment he did, I gasped, because it wasn't sweat that had soaked the bed; it was blood. Damian and Nathaniel were covered in it. Damian cried out, holding his hands in front of him. Guards came through the door without knocking, guns naked in their hands. They were both tall, in good shape, like most of the guards. They aimed at Damian, because you can't shoot your king, or his queen, or one of their main lovers.

"No, don't hurt him!" I called out.

Jean-Claude said, "It is Damian who is hurt, I think."

My blue nightie was purple with blood; half of Nathaniel's face and upper body were stained red, and his shorts were black with it, but Damian's pale skin was dotted and splotched with blood like castoff from some terrible crime. His red pajama bottoms were black from waist to ankle, the cloth wrapped tight to his legs with so much blood.

"What have I done?" he asked, hands held out toward us.

"Nothing, *mon ami*, it is you who have bled, not *ma petite*, or Nathaniel."

"Who hurt him?" I asked.

"No one. I believe it is sweat."

The guards, one brunette and the other with paler brown hair, aimed their guns at the floor but weren't leaving. I couldn't even blame them. The bed looked like a serial killer crime scene except everyone was alive. Damian began to check himself for wounds. Nathaniel and I helped, touching his back and places he couldn't reach, but once we wiped the blood away his skin seemed whole.

"I woke to *ma petite* struggling in the dark with a dream, but when I went to wake her, I realized all of you were dreaming. Damian began to sweat, and though we have some light color to our sweat, this was . . ." He gestured at the ruined bed. "I have never seen this before."

"What's happening to me?" Damian asked, and it was almost a yell, but the look on his blood-spattered face was a plea.

"I do not know," Jean-Claude said, and I got a quick flash of how worried he was, before he shut it down and pushed me further from his emotions, but that was okay because I was feeling enough from Damian. Nathaniel and I were both fighting to separate his terror from our unease. I wasn't afraid, not yet. I'd save being afraid for when there was something real in front of me to fight. Or that was what I told myself as I calmed the pulse that was trying to gallop out of my neck, as if I were choking on my own heart. God, Damian was so afraid.

Nathaniel looked at me from the other side of our vampire third, and he was as calm as I was; we were both working through our fears. No, we were both working through Damian's fears.

"First, the three of you need to clean up. I will have the bed stripped and see what can be done with it."

"How come you're not bloody?" the brunette guard asked.

"Because I noticed it starting and got out of the way."

"Why didn't you wake us?" I asked.

"I felt it was important to see it play out."

"Thanks a lot," I said, as I started crawling across the bloody sheets toward the edge of the bed. Nathaniel was crawling to join me.

"*Ma petite*, you are forgetting someone."

I stopped and looked where he was nodding. Damian was still staring at himself as if he were trapped in another nightmare, but this one he couldn't wake up from. I wanted to help him, but if I was choking on his fear from here, touching him would make it worse.

I said out loud, "If I touch him I'm not sure I can stop his fear from overwhelming me."

"Try. Just try, *ma petite*."

I swallowed hard, and so didn't want to, but Jean-Claude was right: I had to try. I crawled back to Damian and reached out to him. He jerked back from me. "No, don't. I'm unclean. Can't you see that there's something wrong with me?"

Nathaniel had crawled back with me. "You aren't unclean, Damian."

"We aren't vampires. We won't catch anything," I said, as I reached out slowly, the way you approach a skittish animal.

"Anita . . ."

"Let me try, Damian."

"Let us both try," Nathaniel said.

His eyes looked so green in their mask of blood, like a macabre Christmas image, but he sat still and let me touch his arm. The moment I did, my pulse slowed, and so did his. It was like touching him calmed us both. Nathaniel touched his

other arm and it was like a circuit completed; we'd plugged in
the last thing and with that sense of completion there was a
peacefulness that I hadn't thought possible while we were sitting in the blood-soaked sheets.

I looked back over my shoulder at Jean-Claude. "How did
you know that would happen?"

"I did not know for certain, but in the past Damian has
been your calm center in the midst of emotion. I thought it
might work both ways."

Damian took my hand in his and the last of the fear receded like the sea pulling back from the shore. He blinked at
me. "Thank you. Thank you both."

"What now?" I asked Jean-Claude.

"Now you need a shower. For such as this, the bathtub attached to this room will not do."

"I mean after the shower."

"Come back here and if the bed is fit to sleep on we will try.
If not, we will use one of the guest rooms for the rest of the
day."

"I don't want to sleep again," Damian said. "Did you see
the nightmare I shared with Anita and Nathaniel?"

"No," he said.

"Then you don't understand."

"I can see the aftermath of the dream, Damian. I understand that it was terrible enough to make you sweat blood."

I started pulling Damian by the hand toward the edge of
the bed. Nathaniel helped me tug him toward the edge of the
bed. "Let's clean up and then we'll talk about what comes
next," I said.

Jean-Claude took pictures of us with his cell phone before
we left to shower. "If we find a doctor to consult, we can show
them pictures of this," he'd said, and it made sense, though it
felt like being part of a crime scene evidence collection.

Jean-Claude sent with us the two guards who had come
through the door. "They are not to be left alone," were his
orders.

"What does that mean?" I asked, as I stood there holding
Damian's hand.

"It means we do not know what is happening, *ma petite*,
and it would be beyond careless of me to send you and Na-

thaniel off alone with Damian without other eyes to watch over you."

"You think I'm a danger to Anita?"

"Are you not ravenous?"

"Hungry, no."

"After losing so much blood, *mon ami*, you should be."

Damian nodded. "I learned to control all my needs centuries ago, Jean-Claude. She-Who-Made-Me used every need and want against us. It was better to feel nothing, want nothing, than to give her that opening."

"I have known very few vampires that could control their bloodlust to that degree."

"She would deny us blood until we felt crazed with the need for it. She liked letting the starved vampires free on prisoners. It was . . ." Damian shook his head. "I both witnessed such feedings and partook in them. I thought I had control of that part of me until a few years back when I lost myself and attacked those people."

I squeezed his hand. "That was my fault. I didn't know I was your master and if I did, I didn't understand what it meant."

"Your power being withdrawn from me drove me mad, yes, but it wasn't your teeth, your strength, that slaughtered that poor couple."

"I thought you did not remember what you had done, *mon ami*," Jean-Claude said.

"I still don't, but I believe you when you say I did it." He raised my hand back up, waving our clasped hands. "With Anita's hand in mine, I can control myself, and not be the beast that She-Who-Made-Me could reduce me to." He raised his other hand, where Nathaniel was still holding on. "With both their hands in mine, I can be more than I was."

"If I truly believed you dangerous, I would not allow them to leave this room with you, but I would like help to be there if something else unusual happens. That is all."

I wasn't sure I believed it either, but I took it at face value. Though I did ask, "Wait. Does not taking their eyes off us mean they have to watch us in the shower, or can they just stand outside the door?"

The guard with pale brown hair said, "We don't donate blood, or anything else. We just do our jobs."

"I was not volunteering you as food," Jean-Claude said.

"If they can wait outside the door, then it's not a problem," I said.

"I'd prefer a closer eye," Jean-Claude said.

"They can wait outside the showers. We'll be fine," I said, and we led Damian to the door, where one guard opened it and the other followed behind. I was calm enough now that I wasn't happy that Jean-Claude was casually encouraging strange men to watch me shower. Yes, they were shapeshifters, which meant nudity didn't mean much to them, but I wasn't a shapeshifter and I didn't want two new guards that I didn't know at all watching us in the showers. I wouldn't argue with Jean-Claude anymore, but once we were out of his sight, then I'd argue with the two guards he was sending with us. I had a much better chance of winning the argument with them than with Jean-Claude.

7

I'D MANAGED TO ask the two guards' names by the time we were walking past the group showers. Brunette was Barry, Barry the Brunette, and pale brown was Harris. I wasn't sure if it was his first or last name, and I didn't ask. They both felt like a lot of the new guards, interchangeable, as if someone had hired them from the same pool of tall, athletic, younger men, mostly white, though not all, and unfinished in a way that the guards that Rafael's people hired weren't. In an effort to get a greater variety of wereanimals into our personal guards, we'd let other groups besides the wererats offer up candidates for guard duty; so far no one was better than Rafael's rats, some of the werehyenas, and the Harlequin. They were the personal guards of the old queen of vampires and they were the best of the best, but then, they'd had hundreds, sometimes thousands of years to practice their skills. It was hard to compete with that when you were under thirty like most of the new guards; but still Barry and Harris didn't fill me with the same confidence that some of our longer-term guards did.

I had no intention of us using the group showers. We'd use the shower in the room that Nathaniel and I shared with Micah. We could hear the noise from the group showers down the hallway. Men laughing, calling out to one another, and just the energy of so many athletic and professionally competent violent men contained in good-natured rivalry, because that was always an underlying energy to the guards. The type of men who are good at the job description are always speculating who's the best, the fastest, the strongest; who will win. Add that they were all wereanimals, and the testosterone level could be enough to drown in; normally I was okay with that, but not today.

I felt Nathaniel flinch on the other side of Damian, and that was about how I felt, too. It was like it was too much energy to deal with while all three of us were still raw from the dream.

We were almost past the showers when I realized the noise inside was a lot less. It was reduced from a rollicking noise fest to almost silence. It was like being in the forest when the birds and crickets stop singing—you know something's wrong. I had left the bedroom with only my Browning in my hand, because lingerie sucks for places to put weapons. I fought the urge to point the gun at the door, and the fact that the two guards with us didn't react to the sudden silence made me take points away from them.

The guards inside the shower spilled out of the doorway in front of us, some low to the ground on their knees, others standing; some of them took cover around the edge of the doorway, and others just filled the hallway, weapons in hand and mostly nude. There was a moment when you almost felt them hesitate as they saw us, and then the weapons steadied— all pointing at Damian. It was interesting that they just assumed Nathaniel and I were innocent of whatever carnage had happened.

"Ease down," I said.

They all ignored me; not good.

"It's Damian's blood, not mine."

That made some of them glance at each other, as if looking for a clue, but most of them stayed with their guns nice and steady. One gun moved a fraction and was pointing at me; how could I tell? When you've had enough guns pointed directly at you, you get very sensitive to that kind of thing.

It was Ricky again. He'd used up all my goodwill at Danse Macabre last time I saw him. "Unless you're going to shoot me, move the gun off me, now," I said in a low voice.

"If that's Damian's blood, then you're more dangerous than he is." His voice was as steady as his hand, but there was an edge of anger to that calm.

One of the other guards, naked in the doorway, said, "Ricky, are you pointing your gun at one of our main protectees?"

Harris moved in front of us to act as a meat shield. Barry had his gun out, but neither of them wanted to draw down on this many of their fellow guards. I sympathized, but I also knew I'd be reporting their lack of enthusiasm for protecting my life. Since that was one of their main jobs, it wasn't reassuring.

I called out over the broad shoulders of my meat shield. "Ricky, the last time I saw you, Echo was telling you you'd fucked up, and now you've pointed a gun at me. You just don't want this job, do you?"

"You show up covered in blood and tell us it doesn't belong to the vampire—what are we supposed to think?" he asked. He even sounded like he might believe it. Maybe I had scared him more the first time we met than I realized. Sometimes, once you've used basically vampire powers on someone and let them keep the memory of what you did, they never get over it. I know I've held grudges against real vampires for shit like that.

I heard other sounds and knew the guards were closing around Ricky. They'd report what he'd done, because the only thing that hurts a bodyguard's reputation worse than having a client die on their watch is one of their own security specialists killing the client.

"You all smelled the fresh blood, but we were right on top of you before you reacted to it."

"Yeah." It was Bobby Lee wearing a pair of boxers and

holding a Smith & Wesson M&P loose in his hands. His body was lean and muscled in that way that long-distance runners get sometimes; there was almost no body fat to him, so he looked impressively cut, each muscle showing under his skin, but it was a little too lean, and I wondered if he was eating enough. Bobby Lee was one of the men most likely to be sent out of country on mercenary work for the wererats that had nothing to do with us, and everyone deals with the stress of that kind of work differently. His short blond hair was still on end, but his gold-framed glasses showed that his medium-brown eyes were steady. He was always steady, was Bobby Lee, but I'd be talking to some of the other guards I trusted to see if he was doing okay.

"I didn't make Damian bleed. I just woke up in the mess with him."

"Well, darlin', if you didn't hurt him, who did? Because this is too much blood to be losing." He always had a slight Southern accent, and every woman was *darlin'*; when he was under stress, the accent got thicker and he started adding *honey chile* and *sugar*.

"It's a long story, Bobby Lee, but if you want to help these two walk us to Nathaniel and Micah's room so we can use the shower, I'll fill you in."

"Happy to help, ma'am. Can you give me a minute to get dressed and rearmed?"

"Sure."

He smiled, and then his brown eyes swam to black. His rat eyes in his human face. "Just so you know, darlin', the blood doesn't smell like vampire. It smells warmer than that."

I felt the jump of energy through the guards as their beasts flashed through them. I was suddenly looking at amber, orange, red, brown, and more black—wolf, lion, hyena, rat. I fought with everything I had not to shiver or show any sign of fear. Damian had gone so still that if I hadn't been holding his hand I wouldn't have been able to feel him there at all. I felt more from Nathaniel on the other side of him, even though we were both holding hands with the vampire and not each other.

The guards' energy whispered through me and I could see my own beasts inside me the way you see dreams in your head. My wolf, my lion, my hyena, my leopard, and my newest beast, rat, all looked up and their energy ran over my skin and spilled out toward the energy in the hallway. I had enough control now to make sure that was all that happened, and I was happy for that as I looked at them all, because smelling like fresh blood around a bunch of wereanimals isn't always good for your health, even if you had your own monster to throw back at theirs.

"And just like that, we don't know whether to fight you, fuck you, or eat you." Ricky again, though he was unarmed now with other guards on either side of him in a way that they usually reserved for bad guys.

"Two out of three isn't happening, Ricky boy, but that first one, maybe we should meet on the practice mats and see what happens."

"And when I start to win, you'll use your magic and cheat."

"If we meet on the mats, I promise not to eat your anger, or raise the *ardeur*."

"You'd fight me fair?"

"You're six feet plus to my five-three, so I'm not sure there's any way to have a fair fight between us, but if you mean I won't use any preternatural abilities that we don't both have, then yeah—a fair fight."

"Yeah, I'd like that, a lot." He gave me a look that held something close to hate. I'd humiliated him the first time we met. Yes, he'd started it, but I might have taken it too far, and if I did, then his reaction to me today was my fault. I was supposed to be his boss, so I'd try to fix it the only way I knew how, by letting him win. He was a big guy, and he was training with our guards, so I didn't expect to win; and because I didn't expect it, losing in a match with someone to call it before he hurt me didn't risk any ego on my part, and it might restore some of his. But this was the last chance for Ricky; if he ever stepped out of line after I saw him on the practice mats, either he was gone or he'd keep pushing until he got dead, and that was about as gone as you could get. I felt vaguely like it was my fault for messing with him the first time, so I'd literally go to the mats with him.

"Let me get this thing with Damian fixed, and we'll set something up," I said.

"Tomorrow?" Ricky asked.

"I don't think my problem will fix that soon," Damian said, and he managed to sound disdainful and sad at the same time.

"No," Nathaniel said, "it won't be tomorrow."

Ricky frowned at us, and just like the first time I'd met him, I wasn't sure he was the brightest bulb in the box. It was one of the things that had contributed to our misunderstanding. I had overestimated how much he understood of what I was saying until it was too late.

"It may be a few days," I said, "but you'll get your chance on the practice mat with me."

"You promise?" he said.

"I already did."

Ricky nodded and for the first time I saw something on his face besides fear, or hatred. I wasn't sure that his being eager to beat the shit out of me was really an improvement, but some days you take what you can get.

8

BOBBY LEE CAME back out minutes later with his still-wet hair combed in place. He was all in black, which was the unofficial uniform for the guards. Fully armed, he had on a black T-shirt, black tactical pants, a good leather belt with a black-on-black buckle, and matching boots laced up so that his pants were inside the tops of them. Most former military I knew wore their pants that way. Hell, I had all the same clothes and had started wearing them when I was out in the field serving a warrant of execution with the Marshals Service. I'd never been in the military but a lot of my friends had been, and a lot of the police I worked with had been, and I was always willing to learn from other people's experience. I still wore jeans a lot, but more and more tactical pants were becoming my go-to. It was partially the extra pockets, so damn useful.

"How you doing, Bobby Lee?" I asked.

He gave me a look, and then he smiled; the smile lines around his eyes seemed deeper, but his brown eyes shone with humor. "Darlin', you are covered in blood, holding a naked gun in one hand and a blood-soaked vampire in the other one, with your blood-covered boyfriend holding the vampire's other hand. Shouldn't I be asking you that question?"

He had a point. I laughed. "I'll stop throwing stones at your glass house until I get mine in order. I get it."

His smile widened into a grin. "Thank you, sugar. Now, let's get you to some showers that aren't full of shapeshifters that think all this fresh blood makes you smell good enough to eat."

I frowned at him, studying his face. Bobby Lee never flirted with me, so either the double entendre was unintentional, or it was just a statement of fact. Looking into his eyes, I thought the latter. "I've been around most of the guards with blood on me, or they've been around each other when they've been hurt in practice. Why is this more of a temptation?"

"Let's walk and talk," he said, still smiling, but now it didn't reach his eyes. They looked tired suddenly, as if he couldn't hide it all.

I narrowed my eyes a little, but said, "Okay." I trusted him to explain later when we had more privacy.

He looked at Harris and Barry and nodded toward the hallway. "You need to report back to Claudia. She's got another assignment for you."

"Hey, we didn't do nothin' wrong," Barry the Brunette said.

"Nobody said you did." But something in the way that Bobby Lee looked at the other man made Barry flinch.

Harris touched his arm. "Come on, Barry, we've been ordered to report to Claudia, so that's what we do."

Barry glared at Bobby Lee, then visibly swallowed his anger and said, "Fine. Let's go report to the Amazon."

"That is not Claudia's name," I said.

Barry looked at me and he did that up-and-down look, not sexual, but disdainful. I was a short woman in a bloody nightie, holding another man's hand. Even the gun in my hand couldn't offset the rest, at least not for Barry.

"I know her name."

"Then use it," I said.

He sneered at me, raised his lip like he didn't care if I saw. "Fine. We'll go report to . . . Claudia for reassignment."

"Ma'am, or sir," I said.

"What?" he asked, frowning.

"Say *yes, ma'am*, or *yes, sir*, when you address me, Barry."

"I don't . . ."

Harris said, "Yes, ma'am, we will do so in the future. Come on, Barry, we gotta go."

Barry still looked sullen, but Harris looked worried. It made me think better of Harris. He was smart enough to be afraid for his future here; Barry wasn't. Barry needed to go, along with Ricky.

"You all the guard we need, Bobby Lee?" I asked.

"Compared to those two, I am an improvement."

"I hear that," I said.

"But no, I was going to include Kaazim."

As if his name had conjured him, Kaazim spilled around the corner of the door behind us like liquid made solid and alive. He was one of the most graceful men I'd ever seen when he moved. I knew and dated dancers, dancers who were were-animals, but none of them made me think of water poured from long-necked, widemouthed jars to spill and shape itself to everything, except for Kaazim.

He looked tall, dark, and slender until he stood beside Bobby Lee, and suddenly the illusion of height disappeared because you had Bobby Lee's height to compare to. Kaazim was five-six, or a smidgen under. He and I had been paired together on the practice mat more than once, because of our sizes. Like I'd told Ricky, size matters in a fight. Especially if it's a fight where we can't maim, cripple, or kill our opponent quickly. When you're equally well trained, the only hope a smaller person has is to end the fight as quickly and violently as possible. The rules that would keep Ricky from hurting me too badly in combat training also kept me from hurting him badly, and in a long fight, the bigger person usually wins.

"Kaazim," I said, and smiled.

He gave that faint smile of his, almost lost in the blackness of his facial hair and dark skin. His hair was the exact same color as his beard and mustache, and his skin so dark; even his eyes were a brown so dark they looked black most of the time. He was all monotone so that your eyes had trouble seeing details, and he always dressed in black, which contributed to the lack of contrasts in his coloring. There were sections of the world where he would have vanished into any crowd, the perfect spy, perfect assassin, because they wouldn't remember him. Here in St. Louis he stood out, because he was too far from the desert sands and the spired cities of his original homeland.

"Anita. Nathaniel. Damian." Almost any other guard would have at least remarked on Damian and me covered in blood, but he wouldn't ask. He was one of the least talkative people I'd ever been around, but his dark eyes seemed to see everything.

He was dressed in flowing robes, with loose, soft trousers underneath. It wasn't what he wore on duty, and he must have noticed me noticing, because he said, "I can change if you wish."

"One glance and you knew I was taking in the robes?"

He gave a small nod.

"As long as you can move and fight as well in the robes as you can in regular guard gear, I'm fine with it."

"I fight well no matter what I am wearing."

I grinned. "Of that, I have no doubt."

He flashed me a smile almost big enough to be called a grin, one that left his dark eyes shining.

Damian drew me in against his side. "Please, Anita, I need to get clean."

I looked up into those green eyes and saw the pain, so raw. Nathaniel and me touching him was helping him control it, but it was like water tension, and once that tension broke, the emotion was going to pour out; we needed to get cleaned up before that.

"Sorry, Damian. You're right. We'll use the shower in our room." I meant the room I shared with Micah and Nathaniel. It was funny that even after dating Jean-Claude for seven years, I still thought of his bedroom as his, but I thought of bedrooms with the other two men as ours. I wasn't sure why, but I knew it was true.

"There's a shower in my room," Damian said.

"Cardinale will be in there," I said.

"But she won't care, Anita. It's after dawn, so she'll be dead to the world."

"She will so care when she wakes for the night," I said.

Bobby Lee said, "Taking you three near Cardinale right now, like this, is against my job parameters."

"Cardinale is unstable and dangerous," Kaazim said, and for him to say anything at all let me know things were worse with Cardinale than even I knew.

"No, she won't care when she wakes up, because when I told her I was sleeping with you and Jean-Claude last night, she left me."

"What?" I said.

"You didn't tell us that," Nathaniel said.

"She said that if I wanted to sleep with other people she couldn't be with me anymore. That I had to choose."

"Did you tell her you were just sleeping, not having sex?" Nathaniel asked.

"Yes."

"What did she say to that?" I asked, because I had to ask.

"She didn't believe me, and she told me that if I was buggering Jean-Claude and Nathaniel and fucking you, she hated me and never wanted to speak to me again."

"That's not what she said. I mean, not really."

"No, but it's the cleaned-up version."

"If that's the cleaned-up version, I'm okay not hearing the other," I said.

"Are you sure Cardinale won't be in the room?" Bobby Lee asked.

"Even if she is, it's daylight. She'll be passed out."

"You aren't," Kaazim said.

"Neither is Jean-Claude," Damian said.

"Yes, just you and he of all the vampires are awake now," Kaazim said, and he was looking at Damian now, as if trying to see something in him that he'd missed.

I jiggled Damian's hand in mine and said, "He's with me, Kaazim."

"Of course," he said.

"Stop sizing him up for the kill, then."

He blinked and looked very steadily at me with his dark eyes. "You are very observant."

"Not as observant as you are."

He gave a small self-deprecating smile. "I have had more practice at it."

"Yeah, a few centuries more," I said.

"By the grace of my vampire master, I have lived long past my expected time."

"If we keep talking, we're going to use up all our time," Bobby Lee said. "Let's get moving."

It was unusually abrupt for him, but something about the way he gripped his AR and stood there in all his gear made me not argue with him. Whatever had happened on his last out-of-town assignment had been bad, because I'd never seen Bobby Lee like this when he got home.

"Let's move," I said.

Bobby Lee took point leading the way. Kaazim took rear guard. Damian, Nathaniel, and I stayed in the middle, where we belonged. I had my gun in my hand, but in that moment it didn't matter. Armed or unarmed, I was their protectee, and that was that; with Bobby Lee this high-strung, my best move was to let him do his job. Besides, I only had one gun; he had several.

I could feel tension starting in Damian again. It telegraphed through his hand into mine.

"You okay?"

"If Cardinale is dead to the world in our bed, then we still have a chance, but if she's not in there, then it's over. I can't live like this anymore."

Nathaniel touched his head against the other man's shoulder lightly as they moved. "I'm sorry, Damian."

We were still holding hands, but somehow I felt like I needed to touch him more, so I put my arm around his waist. It took a second for all of us to adjust our walking together, but we managed. "I'm sorry, too, Damian."

"So am I," he said, and we followed Bobby Lee's overly armored and armed back down the hallway. Bodyguards are great at saving your life, but they can't help at all when someone is trying to break your heart.

9

DAMIAN HAD WANTED to know if he was a suddenly single vampire or if he still had a relationship. He felt like he needed to know, so we went to his room first. If Cardinale was in the bed we'd go back to Nathaniel's and my room for showers. The five of us stood in Damian's room. A bedside lamp shone beside a perfectly made-up bed. It had a flowered coverlet, and lace draped from the bed frame. There was a large rug on the floor that was covered in huge daisylike flowers. There were pictures on the walls of flowers in vases, flower-filled meadows, a small girl holding flowers. In all that flower-filled, overly feminine room, there was no sign of Cardinale. I knew her coffin was in one of the coffin rooms, so there was no hidden place for her here. She was either in the bed, under the bed, or sleeping in the bathtub. No vampire I knew willingly slept in a tub, so . . . "I'm sorry, Damian." It seemed so inadequate, but it was all I could think to say.

Nathaniel hugged him and Damian hugged him back as if he wasn't really seeing him.

Bobby Lee and Kaazim just stood there, taking up positions in the room so they could watch the door. They were as empty as they could make themselves, taking themselves away from the emotion of the moment. Normally, Bobby Lee was more helpful, but I think he was full up on his own emotional shit, no energy left for anyone else.

I expected Damian to break down, or scream, or go looking for her, but he didn't do any of that. Instead he said, "I hate what she did to my room. I hate the bedspread." He stalked into the room and dragged it off the bed and threw it on the floor. "I hate these paintings!" He grabbed the one that looked like a bad imitation of Van Gogh's *Sunflowers* and threw it across the room like a Frisbee. "I hate these rugs!" He picked the biggest one up and pulled it behind him like the train on some impossible formal gown. He opened the door, shoved it through, and brought the bedspread out to join it. The sheets underneath were pink, but I refrained from saying anything that might add to the emotion of the moment.

He slammed the door behind him and ranted, "I hated the colors she chose, the mess she made of my closet, and how her clothes were more important than mine." He went for the closet in the far wall and slid the door open. I think he was going to throw her clothes out beside the rug and bedding, but when he got the door open, he froze in front of it.

"Oh God," he said.

I came to his side, wondering if he'd found Cardinale "asleep" in the closet. Maybe she'd just hidden to see what he'd do; I'd known humans who did stuff like that, so why not vampires? But when I could look into the closet, there was no body in it, but there weren't many clothes either. I realized her clothes were missing.

"She's really gone," he said, and the anger was replaced by sorrow, loss, remorse maybe, all those emotions that hit you after a breakup, especially right after a breakup. Though I guess this was in the middle of it.

"I'm sorry, Damian."

Nathaniel echoed me. "We're both sorry, Damian."

"So am I, but I really do hate what she's done to my room, my space. It's like it's all about her, and I didn't matter."

"You mattered to her, Damian."

"Would either of you have let anyone turn your bedroom into some flowered nightmare?" He looked at me when he asked, and his expression let me know that lying wasn't an option.

"No, I wouldn't have."

"When I was younger, I would have, but not now," Nathaniel said.

"So why did I let Cardinale do it?"

"I don't know."

"I don't either," he said, still staring into the nearly empty closet.

"Where are the rest of your clothes?" I asked.

"In a room further into the underground. I had to get dressed for work in a storage area, because she needed room for her things." He touched the empty hangers.

"We'll go wash up in our room. Give you some privacy."

"Don't, Anita."

"Don't what?"

"Don't go. Please don't go. It's daylight and I'm awake and I'm afraid to sleep again. I'm covered in my own blood, and . . . I'm afraid of what's happening to me. Even if Cardinale were here, she couldn't help me. That's why I went to you and Jean-Claude, because something is wrong with me, and if we don't figure out what it is soon, I'm afraid of what will happen."

Nathaniel hugged him first, but I came and added my arms to his. "I know you're afraid you'll lose control like you did before, but that time was my fault. I'll never cut you off from me metaphysically again, I promise."

"We're both here," Nathaniel said.

He grabbed our arms a little more forcibly than I'd touched him. "Last time I slaughtered innocent people. I don't remember doing it, but I remember being covered in blood like this, and I remember trying to kill people who were my friends. And now I'm covered in blood again, and I don't know why!"

"It will be all right, Damian," I said.

"You can't know that. Whatever this is, it's getting worse, Anita. I sweated enough blood to soak the bed. I've never heard of a vampire doing that." He shook me a little with his hands gripping us too tight.

I put my hands on his arms, partially just to touch him, and partially to try for some control. "We have a lot of old vampires with us now, Damian. One of them may know something."

Bobby Lee said, "Kaazim's not a vamp, but he's been with the vampires for centuries."

We both looked from Bobby Lee to Kaazim where he stood quietly near the door. Damian let go of us enough for me to turn toward the other man. "How about it, Kaazim? Have you ever heard of a vampire sweating this much blood?"

"From a nightmare, no."

"But from something else, yes?" I asked.

I think he smiled again, but it was hard to tell with him in the shadows. He'd picked the perfect place to stand to be as invisible as possible; he'd had centuries of practice. "Yes."

"Tell us," Damian said.

"I do not answer to the servant of my queen."

Damian frowned, and I felt his anger run through us both, and then he went cold, still, the emotion not so much shoved down but gone. I was never sure how he did that, but I knew why he did it. She-Who-Made-Him had used all emotions against people, so to survive he had learned to hide them under an icy calm that he'd shared with me. Sometimes I thought it was his calm that had helped me, as much as therapy.

"How about your queen's pet? Will you answer it for me?" Nathaniel said.

Kaazim smiled, just a little. "If that were all you were, then no, I would not answer you."

"Then answer to your queen," I said, but my voice showed some of my displeasure that he'd slighted the others. I wasn't as good at hiding my emotions.

He gave a small bow and said, "As my queen commands," but that was all he said.

"You're going to make me drag it out of you, aren't you?"

"I will answer any direct question you ask, my queen."

"I can't say it's Anita when we're working out in the gym and you just answer as a friend?"

I couldn't quite read his expression from the shadows. I just knew it was one I hadn't seen before. "You would call me friend?"

"I know we don't go drinking together, or see the same movies, but yes."

"We are not friends, Anita, not in that way."

I nodded. "Okay, then we're work friends."

He seemed to think about that for a minute, then said, "I know this term. It implies we are friends at work, but how can we be friends if I am your bodyguard?"

"I'm friends with a lot of my guards," I said.

He smiled wide enough that I saw the flash of it even in the shadows. "I do not think we will ever be that friendly."

I laughed with him. "I don't mean that kind of friendly. I

mean more like I am with Claudia, or Bobby Lee, or Fredo, or Lisandro, or Pepita, Pepe."

He nodded again. "Work friends." He said it softly.

"Yeah."

"As a queen I would have made you hunt and ask the right questions. It is what my master told me to do if you asked certain things."

"Why would Billie tell you to withhold things from me?" *Billie* was short for *Bilquees*, though she'd informed me that sometimes she went by *Queenie*. I liked *Billie* better.

"My master's reasons are her own."

Which probably meant he couldn't, or wouldn't, tell me her reasons. Fine. I moved on. "But if we are friends, then will you just help me help Damian?"

He nodded. "It is a long time since someone has asked me something in the name of friendship, Anita, a very long time."

"I'm sorry for that."

"Why are you sorry?"

"Because everyone should have friends."

He smiled again, but I couldn't see his eyes at all, so I didn't know if it was a happy smile or a hiding smile. "The Harlequin do not have friends, Anita. The animals of the Harlequin have even less than that."

"I've done my best to eradicate the double standard that the old vamps feel toward their animals to call."

"You and Jean-Claude have done much to help us."

Damian kept my hand in his, but he took a step toward the other man. "Help me, Kaazim. Help me because Anita is your friend, or your queen."

"You are a servant. I do not answer to servants."

"Kaazim, what is it with you and so many of the Harlequin? All of you seem to dislike Damian. Why?"

"I can answer that one," Bobby Lee said.

"Then answer it," I said.

"All the Harlequin are old vampires. That means they think that human servants are lesser beings, but Damian is a reminder that to you, they are the servants. They don't like that much."

"Okay, I get that, but why do Kaazim and the other shape-shifters have an issue?"

"They all treat any Harlequin human servant as a lesser being, because very few of them were ever good enough to fight at the skill level that the vampires and shapeshifters of the Harlequin did."

"I've noticed that almost none of the Harlequin vamps have human servants."

"Humans are too fragile for our world," Kaazim said.

"The world of the Harlequin, you mean?" I asked.

"Yes."

"Damian is a vampire servant, so the animals to call of the Harlequin have one vampire they can feel superior to," Bobby Lee said.

"That makes sense, I guess."

"Feel superior to me, then," Damian said, "but if you know anything that can explain what is happening to me, please share it."

Kaazim stepped out of the shadows enough so I could see the puzzlement on his face. "Doesn't it bother you that I think of you as less, because Anita has forced you to be her servant?"

"No."

"Because you do not care about my opinion." Kaazim sounded angry now. The first thread of his beast breathed through the room as if someone had opened a hot oven for a second.

"You are Harlequin. That means that you are a better warrior than I will ever be. That alone gives you reason to feel superior to me, but the vampire who made me tortured any pride out of me centuries ago. She made of me an empty vessel to fill as she saw fit. Empty vessels do not have pride, so I have no pride to be injured."

"We know of your creator."

"I always hoped that She-Who-Made-Me would finally do something so awful that the vampire council would send the Harlequin to slay her."

"If we had been sent to kill your master, we would not have left any vampires so old as you alive."

"Either way, I would have been free of her."

"You would have embraced death to be free of your master?"

"Oh, yes."

"Suicide would have freed you, too."

"But it might have denied me entrance to Valhalla. Death at the hands of the Harlequin would have been a glorious death."

"Do you still believe in your Valhalla after all these centuries?" Kaazim asked.

"Yes, I do."

"Most of us lose our faith under the power of the vampires."

"It was one thing she could not take from me."

Kaazim studied him, emotions playing over his dark face like cloud shadows on a windy day, too fast for me to understand, but it was more emotion than I'd ever seen him display. "If she left you your faith, then it was only because she could not understand it enough to tear it away from you."

"Yes, most likely."

"You are lucky that your master did not understand faith."

"I am."

"I was sent to spy on her once, your mistress. She was a terrible thing."

"Did you see me?"

"Yes."

"I did her bidding."

"I saw."

"I will not ask what you saw me do on her orders, because I do not want Anita to know the worst of me."

"You are her servant. She knows all your secrets."

"No, she leaves me space and privacy."

Kaazim looked surprised. "Why would she do that?"

"I don't want Damian to know all my secrets either. I don't want anyone that far inside my head."

"That is very you," Kaazim said.

"Yeah, it is. What do you know about what's happening to Damian?"

"Nothing," he said.

Bobby Lee said, "What do you know about a vampire with symptoms like Damian has?"

Kaazim smiled and nodded respect at the other guard. "Well worded, my friend."

"I've been in your part of the world a lot."

"It has been centuries since we have seen such symptoms."

"Symptoms of what?" I asked.

"Of having angered the Mother of All Darkness."

"I don't understand."

"Did the Mother ever visit your dreams, Anita?" he asked.

I nodded. "Yeah."

"Did you ever wake up in a cold sweat from it?"

I tried to think back to when Marmee Noir was trying to take me over. "I don't think so, but I'm not sure. I wasn't paying attention to how much I was sweating after she'd just been in my dreams."

"I understand," Kaazim said.

"Wait. Are you implying that the Mother of All Darkness is behind Damian's issues?"

"The last time I saw such symptoms, it was her."

I shook my head. "She's dead."

"She's a vampire, Anita. She started out dead."

I shook my head harder. "No, she is dead, completely, utterly, really, truly dead this time."

"How do you kill something that is only spirit, Anita?"

"I know that the Harlequin that witnessed her death were in contact with others. The Harlequin say they were witness to her death."

Kaazim nodded. "Indeed some of us were."

"Then answer your own question," I said.

"You absorbed her through the very skin of your body."

"Yeah, creepy as fuck, but yeah."

"How did it feel to devour the night, Anita? For she was that, the night made alive and real. How could one small human, even a necromancer, consume the night itself?"

"I learned how to take someone's energy from another vampire."

"Yes, Obsidian Butterfly, the Master of Albuquerque, New Mexico."

"If you know all the answers, why are you asking the questions?"

"I know what happened, but that is bare facts, and this was so much more than just facts."

"I don't even know what that means, Kaazim."

"You ate the living darkness, Anita. It has given your own necromancy a power jump of near-legendary proportions. You raised every cemetery and lone body in and around the city of Boulder, Colorado, last year, while you chased down the spirit of the Lover of Death, one of the last members of the now-disbanded vampire council who did not bend knee to Jean-Claude's rebellion."

"You say rebellion. I say killing crazy motherfuckers to save the world from their plans to spread vampirism and contagious zombie plague across the planet."

"It would have been an apocalypse for the human race."

"But not *the* apocalypse."

"You mean the biblical one?" he asked.

"Yeah, as in *the* apocalypse."

"You say that as if there is only one."

"There *is* only one."

"You have prevented two on your own. We have prevented more events that would have destroyed the planet, or at least the human population. Some of us lived through the last great extinction and the coming of the great winter."

"You mean the Ice Age, as in the real Ice Age."

He nodded.

I took in a deep breath, let it out slow, and said, "Okay, some of you guys are old as fuck. Make your point."

"My point, Anita, is that apocalypse as in the great devastation or second coming of some religious significance has happened before and will likely happen again."

"I'm not sure we're defining it the same way," I said.

"Perhaps not, but there really does need to be a plural for *apocalypse*."

"Fine. You've made your point. Now tie all that back to what's happening with Damian."

"You are so impatient for someone who will likely live to see centuries."

"It's not certain that I'm immortal, Kaazim, and besides, I've killed more supposedly immortal beings than anyone else I know, so who will live forever is really up for debate."

"Fair enough," he said, "but you absorbed the Mother of

All Darkness without having any idea how to control that much power."

"It's like eating steak; my body uses the energy of the food I eat automatically. I don't need to tell it to make bone, or more red blood vessels; it just does it."

"And whoever said that metaphysical food was the same as physical food, Anita?"

I stared at him, trying to reason my way through what he'd said. "I'm not sure I understand."

"He's saying that eating magic isn't the same as eating steak," Damian said.

I looked up at him, squeezing his hand. "Okay, maybe I'm being really slow, but I still don't get it."

"Did you really think you could consume the Mother of All Darkness, the one who created vampirekind, who gave us our civilization, our rules, our laws, and it would have no effect on you?"

"She was trying to do worse than kill me, Kaazim. She was trying to take over my body and use it for her house, car, whatever. She'd even tried to get me pregnant so she could transfer her spirit to my unborn baby, in case she couldn't take me. I had no choice but to kill her the only way I could. You said it: She was just spirit, untouchable, uncontainable, so I destroyed her the only way I could."

"By eating her," he said.

"Yeah, sort of."

"You gained a great deal of power, and Jean-Claude has used it well."

"Yeah, he has."

"But you were the power that consumed her, Anita, not Jean-Claude. You were the one who put your flesh against the body she was using and drank down the darkness between the stars."

I remembered the moment of it and how I'd thought the same thing: a darkness that had existed before the light found it, and would exist after the last star had burned out and the darkness took everything again. But I'd won. I'd defeated her. I'd saved myself and stopped all the evil she had planned for the rest of humanity, the rest of the vampires, and the shape-shifters—she'd been an equal-opportunity villain. She'd planned to take over all of us and make us her slaves, or puppets, or just die at her whim.

Nathaniel hugged me from behind, drawing me in against his body. He'd been tied to me metaphysically when I'd consumed the Mother of All Darkness. Part of what had helped me defeat her was my love and craving for him, and Jean-Claude, and all the men I loved. The Mother of All Darkness hadn't understood love.

"Say what you are thinking, Anita," Kaazim said.

"There was a moment when I thought I couldn't swallow the darkness, because it existed before the light, and would exist after the last star burned out. The darkness is always there. It always wins in the end."

"Yes, Anita, that is the truth."

"But I won."

"Did you?"

I frowned at him. "No more riddles, Kaazim. Just say it, whatever it is."

"The Mother would torment vampires she wanted to bend to her will. She haunted their dreams, and some bled out through their skin as Damian has today."

"Marmee Noir didn't do this, Kaazim, because she's dead."

"She's gone, but you are here."

"Yeah, that's what I said. I won, she lost. I'm alive, she's dead."

He sighed and shook his head. "You talk about her as if she were a body you could stab and watch die, Anita, but she was pure spirit. She housed herself in the bodies of her followers, but she did not have to use a body."

"Yeah, the Lover of Death was able to pull that trick off, too, but he had to keep his original body unharmed, just like the Traveller, one of your other council members."

"The Mother of All Darkness is not a council member, Anita."

"She was their queen, I know."

"No, you don't know. You absorbed her, drank her down, and perhaps she is dead, but her power is not, because you took it into yourself."

"We all know that Anita took the power into herself," Damian said.

"We don't all know any such thing," Bobby Lee said.

We looked at him. "Oh come on, Bobby Lee, don't tell me you didn't know."

"I did, but I don't want you all discussing this out of this room in front of everybody."

"Kaazim already knows."

"Still, one of the debates against Jean-Claude being king is that it was you who killed the big, bad not him."

"Whatever belongs to the servant belongs to the master," Kaazim said.

"Yes, but the vampires that are against Jean-Claude argue that it's the necromancer that's the master, not the vampire."

Kaazim nodded. "They use Damian as proof that Anita makes vampire servants."

"You mean some of the vamps think Jean-Claude is my servant, too?"

"Yes."

"A vampire can only have one servant at a time."

"As a vampire, you can only have one animal to call at a time, but you have nearly a dozen animals to call, so it is not a large stretch of logic to think you could have more than one vampire servant."

I wanted to argue with him, but I wasn't sure how. "Jean-Claude is not my servant."

"How can you be certain of that?"

"It's totally not how my power works with Damian, and he is my servant."

"As your connection is different with Nathaniel, your leopard to call, and Jason, your wolf to call, and all your tigers to call."

I opened my mouth, wanted to argue again, but wasn't sure I could work my way to a logical argument. I wrapped Nathaniel's arms tighter around me and squeezed Damian's hand. I knew it wasn't true about Jean-Claude, but I couldn't prove it by talking, only by how it felt, and feelings make piss-poor testimony.

"And what does any of that have to do with what's happening with Damian?" Bobby Lee asked, while I was trying to think my way through the logic maze that Kaazim had put me in.

"Anita absorbed the power of the Mother of Us All, but she is young and inexperienced. It is as if you gave a baby an AR rifle. It is a perfectly safe tool in the right hands, but in the wrong hands, it can do much harm."

"What?" I asked.

"What if you are causing Damian's problem, Anita? The power that is flowing through you, that you don't know how to control. He is your vampire servant and you have avoided him in nearly every way, but a vampire's power is drawn to its servants. You ignore him, but your power doesn't."

"I am not doing this to him."

"This doesn't feel like Anita's power," Damian said.

"Have you not listened to me? It is not Anita's power. It merely resides inside her, but it is not her."

"What are you talking about?" I asked.

"Wait," Damian said. "You're saying that the power is the Mother of All Darkness's power."

"Almost," Kaazim said.

"What do you mean, almost?" I asked.

"I'm not saying it's the Mother of All Darkness's power. I'm saying it *is* the Mother of All Darkness."

"No, she tried to take over my body, but I stopped her."

"Did you, or did you help her do the very thing she wanted to do?"

I shook my head. "She's dead."

"You ate her power, her magic, her spirit, and that was all she was, just spirit. Perhaps it didn't work the way she wanted it to, but she is inside you."

"She is not in control of me, and that's what she wanted."

"True, but if she's in there, Anita, she is trying to figure out how you work, like a new car. Maybe what is happening to Damian is her learning to use the gas pedal, or figuring out how to drift around a turn."

"No," I said, and sounded very sure of it.

"Then if it is not the Mother, it is her power, and by your not forging a tighter bond with Damian, that power is treating him like a runaway vampire."

"Runaway vampire, what the fuck does that mean?"

"When she was more physical and less spirit, sometimes vampires she wanted close to her would run away from her.

They would run as far away as they could go. She used to send us to fetch them, but then her power grew. She was able to hunt them in their dreams, to torment them until they did what she wished."

I thought about everything he'd said and finally asked, "What do I do to make him closer to me? I mean, he's right here, holding my hand."

"You are of Jean-Claude's bloodline, or your power is, which means lust is your coin to exchange for goods, Anita."

I looked at him.

"Why that look, Anita? You have had sex with Damian before, and he seems handsome enough for a man. Why do you run from him so?"

"I promised Cardinale and Damian that I would honor their monogamy."

"She took her clothes, Anita. I think they're done," Bobby Lee said.

I shook my head. "Cardinale is like the ultimate drama queen, an extreme girl."

"What does that mean?" Damian asked.

"That I wouldn't put it past her to move her stuff out as a sort of test to see how much you love her."

"You mean she wants me to see how much I'll miss her."

"Something like that."

He shook his head. "I spent centuries crawling for She-Who-Made-Me. I won't do it again." He motioned around the room, which looked like it belonged to anyone but him. "I've crawled enough for Cardinale already."

"If the relationship is at an end, then your promise to honor their monogamy is at an end," Kaazim said.

"I've felt how much you love her," I said.

"You're holding my hand. I'll lower my shields. You can feel exactly what I'm feeling."

"If you lower shields now, I'll feel it, too," Nathaniel said.

"I know," Damian said.

"Why do you want me to know how you feel about Cardinale?" I asked.

"Why are you nervous, Anita?" Kaazim asked.

"I'm not sure."

"If you don't want me, that is your right." Damian pulled

away from my hand and lost the physical connection to both of us. He was still covered in his own dried blood like an extra from a horror show. I guess all three of us looked like horror show escapees.

"It's not that I don't want you, Damian. You're beautiful."

"Then why do you hesitate?" Kaazim asked.

"This is really none of your business."

"When you asked for my help, you made it my business."

"Well, thank you, and now back off."

"You destroyed our queen, Anita. You ended our way of life and our reason for existence. Now you are our dark queen, and Jean-Claude is our king. We are your bodyguards. How can your well-being not be our business?"

When he put it that way, it was hard to bitch at him, but I so wanted to. "And how is who I have sex with your business?"

"If you were descended from a bloodline that thrived on violence, I would tell you to hurt him. If a bloodline of terror, I would say make him fear you. If anger, then rage at him. But it is lust that holds your power."

"I can feed on anger," I said.

"Then make him angry, and bind him to you with screams of rage. Perhaps hit him. It will give you more food to siphon out of him."

"If it's all the same to you, I'd rather just have sex," Damian said.

"I vote sex," Nathaniel said. I waited for Damian to protest that sex would include all three of us, but he just kept looking at me.

"Anita," Bobby Lee said, "why are you being weird about this?"

"I don't think avoiding adding another name to my list of regular lovers is weird. I think I'm over my limit for giving enough attention to the ones I have."

"If that's all that's worrying you, Anita, I'm a big, grown-up vampire. I'm not expecting hearts and flowers." Damian looked around the room at the decor and added, "I think I've actually had enough flowers for a while."

"I don't believe you."

He held out his hand. "Touch me, lower your shields and I'll prove it."

"Anita, just touch him and then we'll know how he really feels. No commitments, no promises, just touch him," Nathaniel said, hugging me close and saying the last almost against my cheek.

I sighed, then reached for Damian. His hand was strangely warm for his having lost so much blood and not having fed yet. We wrapped our hands together, looked into each other's eyes, and lowered our shields. Nathaniel held on to me but made no move to touch the vampire.

I was very carefully feeling nothing much, but Damian was feeling a lot of things. Sad, tired, angry, confused, but mostly tired. Cardinale had done what a lot of intensely jealous people do; she'd worn him down, worn him out emotionally. I tried to feel that love that I'd gotten a glimpse of just a few hours earlier in his office, but I couldn't find it. What did that even mean? That it hadn't been real, or that Cardinale had used up the last of it, as if love could be a cup that you both filled up with love, kindness, joy, sex, all the things that made you a couple, but if you could fill the cup up, you could also drain it dry with cruelty, sorrow, pain, jealousy, and anger.

"I'm so sorry, Damian," I said, finally.

"We're so sorry," Nathaniel said.

"I just feel used up. I can't do this anymore," he said.

"Do what?" I asked.

"Cardinale and me."

"You feel done."

He nodded. "I think I am."

"Okay, then, let's get cleaned up."

We were still hooked up emotionally so I felt the flash of hope, and then the desire right behind it. His need for sex with me was so intense that it made me catch my breath for a second. I slammed my shields back in place, and we were suddenly just holding hands. It was nice, but it wasn't the intimacy of a second before.

Nathaniel's body jerked against me as if my slamming the shields had actually hurt him. "Are you all right?" I asked.

"Warn me next time we're all hooked up before you do that, Anita; that fucking hurt."

"I'm sorry. I didn't mean to hurt anyone."

"I'm sorry that you felt my need, and it's made you uncomfortable," Damian said, and tried to take his hand from mine.

I held on and said, "The emotion was a little intense, but that's okay—you're entitled to feel what you feel."

"It didn't scare you away?"

"Everyone likes being wanted, and our metaphysics means that we are sort of bound to want each other; like Kaazim said, lust is the coin of my bloodline."

"I know it makes you uncomfortable, but I'm glad it's not terror, or rage, or so many other horrible things, Anita."

"I don't blame you, and honestly, sex isn't a fate worse than death, and I know that the Lover of Death could feed on each death he caused, which would be a pretty terrible bloodline to descend from. Jean-Claude's line is not the worst thing out there."

"No, it isn't."

"You have no idea how true that is," Kaazim said. The slightest of tremors ran down his body, and I realized that he had shivered. The Harlequin were mostly impervious to that much overt display of fear, so whatever he was remembering must have been truly awful. I didn't ask him what he'd remembered. I had enough of my own bad memories; I didn't need more.

"We'll shower, get this mess off us," I said, and started leading Damian toward the bathroom.

"Harris said his orders were not to leave the three of you unsupervised," Bobby Lee said.

"Yeah, I guess so."

"Then leave the door open."

"I'd like a little more privacy than that," I said.

"I know you would, darlin', and I'd love to give it to you, but if you close the door and something bad happens, I don't want to explain to Jean-Claude, or Micah, or any of your beaus how we let you get hurt because we were too delicate to make you keep the door open."

I sighed, but I guess I couldn't blame him. If positions were reversed I wouldn't have wanted to explain it either. "Fine, but stay back from the door; give me some illusion of privacy."

"Anything you say, darlin'."

"Bullshit on that, Bobby Lee."

He grinned. "Sorry about that."

"We were planning to have sex in the shower, once we're clean, and you being able to see is going to make Anita very uncomfortable," Nathaniel said.

"I don't remember agreeing to having sex in the shower," I said.

Nathaniel gave me his patient look. "Anita, we tried just sleeping with Damian and the nightmares and bloody sweats didn't get any better."

"They got worse," I said.

"The blood, yes, but not much more than last time. The nightmare was not as bad," Damian said.

"See?" Nathaniel said.

"I don't see why every problem is solved with sex."

"Not every problem. Sometimes we have to kill people. Would you prefer that as a solution?" Nathaniel asked.

"No," I said, sounding grumpy, even to myself.

"We'll avert our eyes if you start having sex in the shower," Bobby Lee said.

"I will not, for fear that I will look away at the wrong moment and Damian will harm them," Kaazim said.

"It was a polite fiction, Kaazim, to make Anita feel better."

"Oh, I'm sorry. Did I spoil it?"

"Never mind," I said.

Nathaniel started leading us both toward the bathroom again.

"Are you really planning on us having sex in the shower?" Damian asked, his voice low, though he knew that both shapeshifters would hear him; sometimes the illusion is all we have.

"Yes," Nathaniel said.

"No," I said.

"Good to know we've made a decision," he said, managing to sound sarcastic and a little bit like he was laughing at himself.

"And if not the shower, I was thinking we clean up and then use the bed, but now we have way more audience and Anita won't do it in front of Bobby Lee and Kaazim."

Damian glanced back at the two guards. "I'm not that fond of being watched either."

"I am, but I don't think either of them are voyeurs, and the two of you won't do it with them watching, so shower it is," he said.

Damian touched the drying blood on his face. "Whatever we do, I want this off me first."

"Don't worry," Nathaniel said. "Sex isn't happening until we get cleaned up."

"I haven't agreed to sex happening at all," I said.

"Clean first. Then we'll see," Nathaniel said, but he seemed way more cheerful about it than I was, or than Damian was for that matter. The vampire had gone strangely quiet once Nathaniel took his side of things. I wondered if Damian was worried that Nathaniel was after his virtue. He didn't have to worry about that; I knew that Nathaniel would have popped his cherry ages ago if he'd thought Damian wanted it. I didn't say that part out loud, but I might if Nathaniel kept pushing the whole sex thing.

10

DAMIAN STARTED TO turn on the shower, but I did the math in my head and said, "This is a regular-size shower. The three of us will never fit in here."

Damian looked at me, and he looked more woebegone than he might have with the blood drying on his face. "I can clean up here and the two of you can use your shower."

Nathaniel said, "Why don't the three of us go down to our shower since it's bigger?"

I nodded. "That was what I was trying to suggest."

"Was it really?" he asked.

"Yes, really; we've all three just had a horrible nightmare and some not-unhorrible side effects," I said, looking down at the blood that was beginning to stick more and more to the once very nice lingerie and to my skin. "I think none of us would want to be alone right now."

"I do not," Damian said.

"I almost never want to be alone," Nathaniel said, and grabbed Damian's hand and led him toward me. He pushed me ahead of them through the door to find Bobby Lee and Kaazim standing near the bed, where they could see into the bathroom and maybe sit down on the bed.

"Is something wrong?" Kaazim asked.

"The shower is too small," Nathaniel said, and continued to herd the two of us toward the door. Bobby Lee had to hurry to open it before we got there.

I started to laugh. "What's the rush?"

"Don't you want to clean the blood off you?" he asked.

"Yeah."

"Then no time like the present."

I frowned at him and glanced at Damian, who gave me a look that seemed to say he had no idea what the rush was either. Bobby Lee led the way back down the hallway to Nathaniel's, Micah's, and my room. Kaazim brought up the rear. We were suddenly back to the room that we had just passed by minutes before.

Bobby Lee opened the door, and Nathaniel led both of us through and damn near pulled us toward the bathroom. Our room was a mix of personalities; three walls were a pale green and the fourth was a dark lavender, almost a purple. It was the wall that the head of the bed sat up against. The king-size bed was covered in a green-and-purple paisley bedspread, which had been a compromise with the peacock-patterned one that Nathaniel had wanted. I'd thought the paisley would look terrible, but it actually looked nice. Purple, green, and teal pillows of various sizes were artfully tossed around the bed. A stuffed toy penguin sat amid the peacock-colored cushions. The toy didn't match the bed, but it was Sigmund who had been my comfort object long before I met any of the men in my life. There were more penguins in the far corner on and around a chair. It was half my penguin collection; the other half stayed in the house in Jefferson County. Sigmund was the only one that traveled back and forth with me from the Circus to the house. I rarely actually slept with him in the bed anymore, because with two or more people there just wasn't room for him, but I liked knowing he was wherever I was staying the night.

There was a collage of pictures up on one wall, because we had more wall space here than at the house. The pictures were mostly candid shots of all of us, and when I say all of us, I mean all. Almost everyone we were sleeping with or had a strong connection to was somewhere in the framed photos. There had been pictures of Micah's family on the wall, but I had protested that it felt weird having sex while his parents and siblings were looking at us, so he'd moved those to stand-up frames in the living room of the Jefferson County house. There were also pictures of the two of us as small children mixed in with his family there, and even a few of my own family, though those had been added under protest. Nathaniel had no family pictures to add, and no pictures of him as a child either. He'd run away from home with nothing but the clothes he was wearing. He'd been seven when his stepfather beat his older brother, Nicholas, to death in front of him. His brother's dying words were to tell Nathaniel to run, so he had. I knew he regretted not having a picture of his brother or his mother, who died of something that he thought had been cancer, but he'd been so little when it happened he wasn't sure. I knew he regretted not having childhood photos to add to the collections that had been his idea to put up in the first place.

There was a bookshelf underneath the pictures. It held mostly children's books, because that was what we read to one another most. We'd started reading to one another when Nathaniel had said that he'd never had anyone read him *Charlotte's Web*, which was one of my favorites, or *Peter Pan*, which had been one of Micah's. We'd since moved on to other things, adding a few adult mysteries like the Nero Wolfe books by Rex Stout, and the Spenser books by Robert B. Parker, and even a few Louis L'Amour Westerns, which had been a favorite of my father and Micah. We were currently reading *One Hundred and One Dalmatians* by Dodie Smith to one another. The book was much better than the movie, though Micah and I had been out of town so much lately that we might have to start over from the beginning, just to get the rhythm of the book again.

There was a small mostly teal rug just in front of the bookcase, and a much larger square rug across most of the middle part of the room that was all shades of purple with some black in it. The rug we were currently standing on was mostly green with purple here and there. I'd thought the different-colored rugs would have clashed, but it all worked together somehow. The color coordinating had all been Nathaniel. Micah was partially color-blind and I had no sense of how to mix patterns in a room.

"I bet your closet isn't just Anita's clothes," Damian said.

"We share the closet," I said.

"It is bigger than a normal one, though, so it's easier to share," Nathaniel said, and went across the room to open the door and show that we actually had a small walk-in closet, making ours one of the few rooms with one. Though we were negotiating with the same contractor to see if the stone walls in Jean-Claude's bedroom would stand up to being drilled out of the solid rock like this one had been.

"This is what a couple's room is supposed to be like; you can see bits of all three of you here."

I hadn't thought about it when we decided to change rooms and apparently neither had Nathaniel, because he hugged Damian, and he said, "You will never let another partner control you like that."

"I don't know how to interact with a woman who doesn't control me."

We looked at him, but he seemed to be serious. "So the fact that Anita doesn't want to control you must bother you, a lot," Nathaniel said.

"I think it does."

I glanced behind to find that Bobby Lee and Kaazim were finding places to stand that would let them see into the bathroom. We hadn't fixed my issues with being watched in the shower, but I was getting too tired to care as much. The nightmare had cut our sleep short by hours, and I was finally beginning to feel it. Raising zombies took energy and I hadn't eaten breakfast, not even coffee yet. I was suddenly hungry.

"I'm hungry."

"Showers, sex, feed the *ardeur*, and then we'll get real food," Nathaniel said.

"I'm not sure I agreed to actual sex," I said.

"You didn't feed the *ardeur* last night," Nathaniel said.

"Damn, I didn't. That's why I'm so hungry."

Bobby Lee said, "Are you really going to feed the *ardeur*, Anita?"

"I think I have to; it's like Jean-Claude's bloodlust, or your own hunger for flesh; if you feed it before it gets too bad you have more control over it. I don't think any of us want me losing control of the *ardeur*." It was the power that allowed Jean-Claude to feed off the lust of the customers at Guilty Pleasures, and to feed through actual sex when he was with his lovers, including me. It was part of the gift of his original bloodline from Belle Morte, but our version of it wasn't just lust but seemed to have more love mixed in with the lust than Belle did with hers. I'd inherited the power from Jean-Claude. Now when I didn't feed it often enough, my ability to heal most injuries began to go back to human-normal. My healing abilities had saved my life more than once.

"Then Kaazim and I will wait closer to the door."

"Jean-Claude was very clear that we are not to leave them unsupervised," Kaazim said.

"That was when they were just having sex. The *ardeur* can spread through a room unexpectedly. I don't want to be anyone's food."

"Nor anyone's sex slave," Kaazim added.

"I resent that. I do not make people into sex slaves."

"I don't know, Anita," Nathaniel said. "I crave your sex all the time."

"You crave sex all the time."

He smiled. "That, too, but my therapist says I'm officially not addicted to it anymore."

"Good to know and yay, you," I said, and meant it.

"I like sex a lot, but now I am a recovering addict. I thought sex was my only value to anyone, so I offered the only thing I thought I was good for, which was sex."

I touched the side of his face that wasn't covered in blood and smiled up at him. "You are so much more than just sex to me."

"I know that; that's part of what helped me figure it all out," he said, pressing his hand over mine.

"Once we feel the *ardeur* rise, we'll be outside the door," Bobby Lee said.

I looked at him and Kaazim. They both looked nervous. I would have said that nothing could have spooked the two of them, but this had. "You know that I can't really make anyone my sex slave, right?"

"Has anyone who has had sex with you wished to stop?" Kaazim asked.

"Yes."

"Since you acquired the *ardeur* as a power?"

I started to say *Sure*, then had to stop myself. Damn it, I thought he was right. "I don't know. I . . . I guess not."

"Then we will wait outside once you raise that particular power," he said.

I was out of arguments that made any sense, so I stopped trying to argue. A few years back I'd have argued until either we had a fight or the cows came home, but therapy had helped me realize that I could just let some things go. I let this go and let them stand by the door, which meant now they couldn't see in the bathroom at all. My modesty was saved.

11

THE SHOWER IN our room was big enough for all three of us with room to spare. It had multiple showerheads; in fact, water came from so many directions that if I was in it alone I only turned on part of them. Okay, I turned on one of them, but Nathaniel had a very different view of the shower. He liked all the showerheads and as much pounding, pouring water as possible. He opened the hinged glass door and walked inside so he could start turning on the water. He hadn't even bothered to take off his shorts. He adjusted the temperature dial a little cooler, then stood to one side so the initial cold burst of water wouldn't hit him. He let the water run while he came back out to us.

"We all have too many clothes on," he said.

"I think you're the only exhibitionist in the room," I said.

He shook his head. "Anita, this isn't about being an exhibitionist. It's just the three of us. It's okay if we see each other nude."

Damian's voice was soft and sort of sad as he said, "We haven't seen each other nude since the first night Anita bound us to her as her servants."

"That doesn't seem true," I said.

"You've seen Nathaniel nude a lot," Damian said, then smiled. "We've all seen him nude just walking around here."

"I'm a wereanimal; none of us like clothes."

"Micah wears clothes when he's outside the bedroom," I said.

"That's just polite," Nathaniel said with a smile and an eyebrow waggle.

I laughed, partially from his delivery and partly out of something close to happy embarrassment.

"The rest of us appreciate his consideration," Damian said.

I looked at him, expecting to see a smile, but he looked serious.

"Micah's well endowed, but he's not scary big."

Damian raised one pale eyebrow.

"Oh, come on," I said.

"Anita, if you don't think Micah is scary big, then the rumor about you liking really well-endowed men has to be true."

"Oh, it's not a rumor," Nathaniel said, smiling.

Damian nodded. "I figured as much." He looked way more unhappy than he should have from the news.

"I am not just a size queen," I said. "Skill counts, too."

"Yes, yes, it does," Nathaniel said, wrapping his arms around me so that our faces were almost close enough to kiss. It would have been more romantic if we hadn't both still been covered in blood, but staring into his eyes from inches away, it didn't matter as much as it might have. He smiled that certain smile that said he was thinking of naughty things to do with and to me. It made me smile back and give my own version of the look.

"I am sorry that I didn't measure up, Anita," Damian said.

It startled us both, and we turned to stare at him with our arms still around each other. "What do you mean?" I asked.

Nathaniel said, "If you mean you don't measure up to Micah, then none of us do, except maybe Richard."

"Trust me, Damian, there's more to what I like in the bedroom than just size."

He looked at the floor then and said, "Then I'm even sorrier that I disappointed you in other ways."

Nathaniel and I exchanged looks; he gave a little shrug and let me go, so I could move to stand in front of Damian. I touched his arm, and he flinched, as if I'd hurt him. "Damian, are you . . ." I tried to think how to say it, because if I was misunderstanding and said the wrong thing, then I could give him a complex where he hadn't had one.

Nathaniel helped me by saying, "Do you think the reason Anita hasn't been back for more sex is that she wasn't happy with you?"

Damian sort of nodded, still not making eye contact. His green eyes rolled up just enough to see my face, and whatever he saw there made him look at me a little harder. I must have looked as astonished as I felt. I finally found some words and said, "Damian, I swear to you that your skills, or lack, or anything about you was not why I didn't pursue you as a lover."

"She didn't mean you lack skills," Nathaniel added for me.

I glanced at him and then back to the vampire in front of me. "No, of course not."

"Then why did you cut me out of that part of your life after that?"

"I don't know, except it was pretty overwhelming finding out that I had a vampire servant, which was supposed to be impossible, and an animal to call, which should only work if I were a vampire."

"She didn't have sex with me at all that night, remember," Nathaniel said.

"You weren't my lover for months after that," I said.

"Almost a year," he said.

Damian looked shocked. "But you'd been living with Anita for months by then."

"In retrospect it seems silly, but I was determined not to make Nathaniel my boyfriend."

"Why?" Damian asked.

"It's hard to explain," I said, "but it made sense to me at the time."

"The fact that she let me move in and be part of her life without sex helped me start valuing myself as a person. Before Anita I thought that all I had to offer anyone was my skills in the bedroom and my beauty."

"Are you saying not having sex was a good thing?" Damian asked.

Nathaniel smiled. "At the time it drove me nuts, but in the long run, yes, because I could see that Anita valued me, cared for me without sex. It made me start to realize that maybe there was more to me than just sex and looking good when I took my clothes off."

Damian looked at me. "Okay, I'll ask what I've been afraid to ask: Why am I the only man you had sex with once and then never wanted it again?"

"You're not. I fed the *ardeur* on Byron just once!"

"Okay, why am I the only man who prefers women you've slept with just once?"

I tried to think what the answer was, because I didn't really have one. "I don't know."

Damian's face showed that he didn't believe me. "Every woman knows why she doesn't want a man."

"I fought not to sleep with anyone, remember? Not Jean-Claude, or Richard, or Nathaniel. I guess the only two men I've ever slept with the first time I met them and then continued to have sex with have been Micah and Nicky."

"You slept with Sin the first time you met him," Nathaniel said.

I shook my head. "That's different. The Mother of All Darkness mind-fucked us both and used him like the rest of the weretigers she chose as a sort of distraction to keep me from messing with her plans." Damian had asked me why I'd finally gone into real therapy; I hadn't wanted to answer, because I'd had all sorts of issues with Cynric—Sin. I'd thought it was his age, which had been sixteen when we met, and eighteen when he moved in with us, but I'd finally realized it wasn't the age difference. It was that I saw our first night together as rape. All the weretigers that had been part of that night were reminders that the Mother of All Darkness had basically raped us all. She'd used other bodies to do it, but it hadn't been consensual for any of us. Crispin and Domino were within a few years of my own age—one younger and the other older—but I hadn't made them part of my main lovers either. I'd fed the *ardeur* on them occasionally, but in the end they'd been painted with the same issue-heavy brush that Sin had been coated with; they all reminded me of that night. They reminded me of the loss of control, the lack of choice, of waking up the next morning in bed with strangers whose names I barely knew and realizing we'd had an orgy. Domino and Crispin had both found other interests, but Sin hadn't. He'd been the only one who persisted in trying to make his life with me even though I found reason after reason to reject him. He'd been sixteen and a virgin when Mommy Darkest had mind-fucked us both and used my body to be his first time. That gave me more issues than I knew what to do with about Cynric, and then he decided he would go by the nickname Sin. It was like rubbing salt in the wound.

"Whatever you're thinking can't be good," Damian said.

"You've been really honest with me, Damian, so I'll try to be the same. You asked why I finally got into therapy. The truth is that it was Cynric—Sin. I still see our first night together as rape. Our bodies were there, but it was like the Mother of All Darkness used both of us. One of the reasons I've managed to stay less attached to him, or keep breaking the attachment we have to each other, is that he reminds me of that night."

Damian opened his mouth as if to say something, closed it, and finally said, "That was honest."

"Too much honesty for you?"

"No, no, just I'm really sorry that you feel . . . victimized by that night. I didn't realize you saw it as . . . like that."

"You can say the word, Damian. You didn't realize I saw it as rape."

"I'm a man and I was a Viking when I was alive. I really can't throw that word around, Anita."

"I get the man part, but I hadn't thought about the other. I guess you didn't see it as wrong back then."

"I'm not sure right or wrong applies, but culturally we were raiders. We didn't just rape; we kidnapped them and brought them home with us, or sold them as slaves to other people, so other people could keep raping them. One of the hardest things about living in this century is looking back at some of the things I did hundreds of years ago and living with what I did."

"You didn't think it was wrong?"

"Not while I was doing it, no, and if you ask me to explain it, you won't like any of the answers. I know Cardinale didn't."

"I'm not her."

"No, but you're a modern woman who sees her body as hers. You don't see yourself as belonging to anybody but yourself, and certainly not to any man. You just can't understand how different most cultures were toward women a thousand years ago."

"I have some of Jean-Claude's memories from hundreds of years ago."

"But he was raised by his mother and sisters, and then a noblewoman chose him to come be a companion to her son and heir. He was part of Belle Morte's court for hundreds of years. She was very much her own woman. He spent centuries surrounded by strong women; I didn't, not until She-Who-Made-Me took me. She's evil and makes jealousy into a horror show, but she is ruler of everything around her."

"You're saying that Jean-Claude wasn't truly part of the prevailing attitude toward women, so he can't share it with me."

"Exactly."

"We're wasting all the hot water," Nathaniel said.

We looked at him, as if we'd forgotten where the hot steam was coming from.

"If we're going to keep talking, I'll turn it off and save it for actually getting clean," he said.

"We all need to clean up," I said.

"The two of you can clean up in here. I'll go back to my

room." He actually started to walk past us, but I caught his arm.

"Don't go, Damian."

He looked down at me, at my hand on his arm, then at my face. "Tell me why I should stay, Anita."

"Jean-Claude thinks that me keeping you at arm's length is why you're sick. That our triumvirate needs more up-close-and-personal time to be whole."

"It's like Kaazim said: Sex is the power from Jean-Claude's bloodline," Nathaniel said.

Damian looked at him. "We might have to negotiate exactly what sex for the three of us means."

Nathaniel flashed a grin that was part mischief and just a little touch something more. "Then let's negotiate while we shower the blood off. I'd like to use some of the hot water for the sex part."

Damian and I looked at each other. He looked a question at me from those green eyes set in their mask of blood. I shrugged. "It sounds like a plan."

He smiled. "You smooth-talking devil, you."

I frowned at him. "What does that mean?"

He squeezed my hand. "It means yes."

I took the yes and left the rest alone. One relationship hurdle at a time; if you try to jump them all at once you fall flat on your face and it all falls apart. We got into the shower together, all three of us trying very hard for it not to fall apart.

12

WHEN WE WERE clean, all our long hair plastered tight to our shoulders, though Nathaniel's hair was plastered down most of the back of his body, I released the *ardeur*. Kaazim had accused me of making people into my sex slaves. I didn't believe that, but this was the power that made him think it. I finally let myself concentrate on it, and the craving was there, like it nearly always was if I allowed myself to hear it. If the *ardeur* was well fed, then it was like needing another meal, a faint emptiness to be filled, but if I'd gone more than six hours it was like being truly hungry after you've missed several meals. I treated the *ardeur* the way I treated hunger for actual food, something to be forgotten about while I was doing other things, which meant I had eaten almost nothing last night and not fed the *ardeur* at all. The more real food I ate, the easier the *ardeur* was to control. I'd slept, but none of us had eaten breakfast. I was supposed to be Nathaniel and Damian's master. I was supposed to be in charge and in control, and I might have been if I'd eaten a real meal in the last sixteen hours, or fed the *ardeur* in the last twelve. I hadn't meant to forget to eat, and I rarely went that long without having sex with one of my lovers, but it had been a busy day. Micah had been called out of town on Coalition business and taken one of my main feeds with him. Damian had requested that there be no sex with him in the bed with Nathaniel, Jean-Claude, and me, so we'd missed that window for feeding me. Jean-Claude had taken blood, which was his main food source; sex was a supplement for him. It wasn't a supplement for me. It was what kept me from sharing his bloodlust or Richard's craving for flesh. It was what kept me from sharing Damian's bloodlust and Nathaniel's craving for flesh. It was what helped me keep all the beasts inside me quiet and controlled. It was what helped me not become a monster. Feeding the *ardeur* was like feeding the monster something safe when what it really wanted was to tear people's throats out.

I freed the *ardeur* and it roared over all of us, because I'd been arrogant and ignored most of my safety precautions. One minute the three of us were standing in the shower like reasonable naked adults and the next we were hands and mouths that just wanted to touch, kiss, suck, and bite each other. The water pouring over us from nearly every direction became part of the hot, pounding need. Damian was pressed against the back of my body as tight as he could make us, one arm around my waist, the other turning my head to the side to bare my neck. Nathaniel knelt in front of me, his fingers playing between my legs, his mouth kissing along my thigh. Damian's body was so

tight against me that I could feel him tucked up tight against
my ass, but he wasn't hard at all, because he hadn't fed either.
Until he took blood he couldn't feed my need.

Nathaniel stared up the line of my body; his eyes were the
darkest they had ever gone, true purple, and his fingers teased
between my legs. He licked water off my thigh, and just that
made me shiver. Damian's arm tightened across the front of
my body, pinning me against him, and just that much extra
force made me catch my breath.

"Pull her hair to hold her for your bite," Nathaniel said,
raising his mouth off my skin enough to speak.

Damian hesitated. I ground my ass against the front of him,
and said, "Please."

He grabbed a handful of my hair and used it to pull my
neck taut for him. I said, "Harder."

"Harder," Nathaniel said.

Damian hesitated.

"Do it!" I said.

He grabbed a bigger handful of my hair and pulled harder.
I made small happy noises for him.

"I'm going to bite her thigh when you bite her neck."

I had enough of myself to ask, "Where are you going to bite
me?"

He set his teeth lightly in my thigh, marking his spot.

"Yes," I whispered.

Damian's heat had cooled; he had such control of himself,
and that was part of the problem with him and me. We were
both so controlled that together we were more so, and it was
enough to help us climb back into our heads.

Nathaniel said, "No, not this time!" He bit me hard enough
that I screamed for him more from surprise than pain.

Damian still hesitated.

"God, please!" I cried out, shuddering from the feel of Nathaniel's teeth in my thigh. I looked down to find that his eyes
had bled to his pale, almost blue-gray leopard eyes. His beast
poured heat over me and over the vampire at my back. It was
enough. I felt Damian tense as Nathaniel growled around the
piece of me in his mouth. Damian bit me, driving his fangs
into my neck.

I screamed for him, then felt him beginning to suck. Nathaniel raised his mouth from my thigh, my blood decorating his lips. He growled up at me as he leaned over to lick between my legs. I both wanted him to and was afraid for him to; how much was his beast in control? How much of him was in there as he began to lick over that most intimate part of my body? He'd left a bloody imprint of his teeth on my thigh. I didn't want that there, but with Damian feeding at my neck it was like I couldn't talk, couldn't do anything but make small noises. Nathaniel loved me; he would never hurt me more than I wanted to be hurt. I trusted him. I trusted him. That's what I kept telling myself as he brought me writhing to my orgasm between them as the vampire drank me down, and the wereleopard licked the last bit of orgasm from between my legs and then grabbed more of me in his mouth, so I was like meat between his teeth, as he began to bite down.

13

NATHANIEL LET ME feel the grip of his teeth around the meat of me, his teeth pressing in slowly like a threat, or a promise. Damian's body was growing thicker against the back of me. He drew back from my neck and took a long, shuddering breath as if he'd come up for air. The feel of his body shuddering against me made me shudder in return, which moved the part of me between Nathaniel's teeth. It pulled more and it was all my fault. Nathaniel half growled and half laughed with me still in his mouth. I fought not to writhe from it while his teeth closed slowly down. It still didn't hurt, but the game was the promise of hurting to come without ever actually doing it. Damian tightened his hand in my hair and across my body, more reflex than choice as his body reacted to mine, but I liked it and let him know it, whispering, "Yes, Damian, yes."

Nathaniel bit down a little harder, and I said, "No, Nathaniel."

He bit down more.

It made me gasp, but I said, "Yellow," which meant to ease up.

He bit down even more.

I called, "Red!"

He stopped biting down and, with one more long lick across me, moved back to gaze up at me with flower-colored eyes, which tried for innocence but held too much evil mischief to be believed.

He stood up and I was suddenly sandwiched between both men. Nathaniel put his arms around both of us, encouraging Damian to push himself even tighter against the back of me and pulling himself as tight against the front of me. The combination made me writhe between them, which made them both harder and thicker, so hard that I wondered if it was painful to be that hard. If I remembered later I'd ask, but right that second the sensation of all that hardness pressed so tight against me was almost overwhelming. I cried out just from that.

Nathaniel licked my neck where Damian had bitten me. The vampire licked over it, and then they took turns licking over the wound, until I cried out half in protest and half that it felt good, but I wanted them to do other things.

Nathaniel leaned over my shoulder and it was Damian's body suddenly startling that helped me realize he'd kissed the vampire, before I turned my head to watch. In all the negotiating Damian had done, he hadn't mentioned kissing the other man as either a negative or a positive. Anything not talked about in detail gave you room to maneuver. Damian was immobile in the kiss but hadn't pulled back. I wasn't sure if he was enjoying it or so shocked he'd frozen.

Nathaniel took the lack of protest as consent and kissed him thoroughly, putting more lip action into it. He wasn't a mind reader, so until Damian said something he had no way of knowing that the other man's body had gone so still and that he was less happy to be pressed against me. I loved watching the two men kiss from inches away, while I was sandwiched between them! But was I supposed to tell Nathaniel that Damian might not be enjoying it, or was the vampire supposed to speak up for himself?

Jean-Claude's power whispered through my mind. "*Ma petite*, why have you not fed?"

"We're too controlled," I said out loud.

Nathaniel turned to me, kissing me with the taste of the other man still on his lips. He drew back enough to say, "I can fix that." He lowered his mouth to my breast and began to kiss and suck on it the same way he'd kissed my mouth, as if he wanted to lick the taste of every inch of me. It was the way he'd kissed Damian, so he could bring the scent and taste of his mouth to mine.

He drew my nipple out with his teeth in a line of flesh that felt so good, it was almost pain, almost but not quite. Damian's body was pressed tight against me again. I was making small, eager noises as Nathaniel sucked my breast, then turned to the other breast, whispering, "Oh, look, a second one."

"Be less controlled then, *ma petite*," Jean-Claude whispered through my head, as Nathaniel began to suck at my breast as if he were trying to feed from it. Since lycanthropes fed by biting off chunks of flesh I had to call, "Yellow." He eased down to a point where it felt good again, and I moaned for him. Damian pressed harder against my ass, and I rubbed against him, feeling him grow achingly hard. I wanted him inside me, wanted it so badly. It was as if all the months of avoiding each other, of letting him be with Cardinale and not us, were concentrated down to this one moment in time. Desire . . . It was as if desire were a drug that someone had injected straight into our bodies.

"Fuck me," I said.

"Fuck her," Nathaniel said.

"Please," I said.

"Fuck her," Nathaniel repeated, kneeling down in front of me, letting the water pound against the front of my body and pour over his head, plastering his hair against the back of his body like a second skin. He pushed his hands against my hips, driving me even harder against Damian's body.

Damian cried out, "Gods!"

"No more control," Nathaniel said, "no more waiting."

There were too many words in the sentence. I couldn't

think with Damian pressing against me, his hands cupping my breasts. Nathaniel's fingers digging into my hips, his body covered in water and the drowning color of his own hair. "What?" I asked.

Nathaniel stared up at me, and the lavender of his irises spilled out over his eyes, so that he stared up at me blind with his own power. "I want this," he said.

"I want this," Damian said. I turned to look over my shoulder to find that the vampire's eyes were a solid, shining green.

"We want this," they said, and their voices echoed each other just a second out of sync.

"We want this," I said, even as I knew that I wasn't a hundred percent sure that was true.

"Ma petite, *lower your shields and let them inside.*"

"I don't know how," I said.

"I do," Nathaniel said.

I stared down into his flower-colored eyes and said, "What?"

"Look at me," he said.

"Look at us," Damian said, but I couldn't look at both of them at the same time. I stared down into the drowning lavender of Nathaniel's eyes and couldn't look away. Jean-Claude couldn't capture me with his eyes—no vampire could—but staring down into Nathaniel's eyes I couldn't look away. I couldn't do anything but stare down as his eyes started to glow like that streak of lavender in a sunset. I fell into that glowing sunset as if the world had become light and all I could do was fall into the light and wait for something to catch me.

14

I WOKE IN a welter of sheets on the bed in our room. I didn't remember leaving the bathroom, or getting into the bed. Nathaniel's arm pinned me around the waist, his hair lying in a tangled mass as if he'd gone to sleep with it wet. Damian lay on the other side of him. He was on his back, his face peaceful with sleep. Nathaniel's other arm was flung across his waist, so he had gone to sleep hugging us both. I lay there trying to remember what had happened earlier. I remembered getting in the shower. I remembered some foreplay, and then . . . nothing.

My body was letting me know that we'd had sex, because what goes in has to come out eventually. From the feel of things we hadn't used condoms. I didn't use them with Nathaniel, but I would have with Damian. Had I? Had I just had multiple intercourse with Nathaniel and that was what I was feeling? I'd check the trash can in the bedroom and bathroom to make certain. If I didn't find a used condom in any of them, then I'd know we all forgot the most important safety rule of safe sex. I was on birth control and neither the vampire nor the lycanthrope could carry any sexually transmitted diseases, but still . . . what the fuck were we all thinking?

I tried to sit up, but Nathaniel snuggled tighter so that his arm pinned me to the bed and tight to his body. Damian hadn't moved at all. I looked at him and held my breath while I looked to see if he was breathing, but his chest never moved. Vampires didn't have to breathe. I stretched out a hand across Nathaniel's shoulders until I could touch Damian's arm. His skin was cool to the touch, and for the first time ever, I found my lover's flesh gone cold comforting. He'd died like a good vampire should. There'd be no nightmares for us the rest of today, so at least whatever we'd done had helped.

But what had we done to cure him? I couldn't remember a damned thing after we got in the shower. Okay, we got in the shower, and then . . . What?

I lay there with Nathaniel hugging us both while he slept, and there was something. A memory, a thought, a . . . something. It was like the harder I thought at it, the more my mind shied away from it. Sex, even sex with the *ardeur*, had never been like this unless something else was interfering with us. The Mother of All Darkness could cause blackouts, and so had Belle Morte and the Lover of Death. Two of the three were dead, because I'd helped kill them; that left Belle Morte, but this was too subtle for her. She liked you to know that she'd fucked you over. So if it wasn't another vampire, then why couldn't I remember what had happened?

I glanced at the bedside clock and had to do a double take. It said it was almost one p.m., which meant we'd been in here almost seven hours. That wasn't possible. The first trickle of fear tightened my stomach and made it a little harder to take a deep breath. The last time I'd lost this much time had been because of the vampire council, or Mommy Darkest. We'd destroyed the power of the first and killed the second. I remembered Kaazim's words, that the Mother's power was inside me, and that her power might be acting in ways that I didn't understand at all.

I tried to move and again Nathaniel's arm tightened around me, holding me in place, but this time it panicked me. I had one of those claustrophobic moments where I had to get out of the bed. I had to find out what had happened and how long we had really been in this room. I was able to sit up, but Nathaniel's arm squeezed around my waist, so that moving off the bed wasn't happening. Nothing was wrong, no one was hurting me, but I was suddenly choking on panic. I pushed at Nathaniel's shoulder hard enough that he raised his head and blinked at me groggily.

"Up!" I said, my voice strident.

"Up what?" he mumbled.

"I need up, out of bed."

He rose up on one elbow, letting me go and asking, "What's wrong?"

I looked down into his lavender eyes and I remembered his eyes glowing in the shower. I backed out of the bed so fast I half-fell to the floor. He came to the edge of the bed and looked down at me.

"Anita, what's wrong?"

"I don't know." But that was a lie. I did know, or thought I did. I just didn't want to say it out loud.

"Did you have a nightmare?" he asked.

I got to my feet and shook my head. "No. Did you?"

"No, I slept great. How about you?"

"I'm not sure."

"What do you mean, you're not sure?"

"What do you remember from after we got in the shower?" I asked.

He gave a very self-satisfied grin, like the proverbial cat that ate the canary. "Everything."

"Define everything."

"The sex was amazing, even for us."

"We had sex with Damian," I said.

Nathaniel's smile began to dim. "Are you saying you don't remember having sex with Damian?"

I shook my head.

He sat up in the bed, and without him to hold Damian in place the vampire slid down the pillows to lie awkward as a broken doll. The angle of his head alone let me know for certain that he was dead to the world, because asleep he'd have changed position. The angle of his neck was so awkward that it looked almost broken. If I could have changed it without getting back on the bed I'd have done it, but at that second nothing would have gotten me back on the bed. I was so scared my skin was cold.

My voice was only a little breathy as I said, "I don't remember the actual sex."

He frowned and sat up in bed, the sheets pooling behind him so that he was nude as he sat there looking concerned. "I don't understand."

"Neither do I," I said.

"You look scared."

I nodded.

"Are you scared of . . . me?"

"I'm scared of whatever made me not remember the last few hours."

"Are you seriously saying you don't remember any of the sex?"

"The last thing I remember was your eyes glowing and you said, *I want this*."

"Then we had amazing sex," he said.

"I don't remember that part, Nathaniel."

"You don't remember Damian fucking you?"

"No, I don't."

"Or me going down on him for the first time?"

"No."

"Or him taking blood from me so we could all keep having sex?" Nathaniel moved his tangled hair to one side so I could see the fang marks in his neck.

"I don't remember that."

"What's the last thing you do remember?"

"I told you, your eyes glowing, and Damian's eyes glowing."

"Your eyes glowed, too, Anita, like brown diamonds in the sun."

"I'll take your word for it, but I don't remember it."

"You should remember, Anita."

"I don't."

"Why don't you?"

"I don't know."

He glanced behind him at the other man lifeless in the bed. "I hope Damian remembers more of it than you do. We hit some serious firsts. It would be sad if I was the only one that remembered them."

"We need to talk to Jean-Claude," I said.

"Why?"

"Because I don't remember anything, Nathaniel. I mean, nothing after your eyes started to glow."

"Everyone's eyes glowed, Anita, not just mine."

"I'll take your word for it, but I honestly don't remember."

He slipped off the bed and I took a step back. He went very still, his face very serious. "You're not just afraid. You're afraid of me."

"I think so."

"Why? I would never hurt you, Anita."

"Logically I know that, but this isn't about logic."

"No, it's all about emotion for you. I can smell it."

"Smell what, my emotions?"

"Your fear," he said, his voice calm as if he didn't want to add any more emotion to the situation. It was usually the way that Micah talked to me when I was upset, but I guess we'd been dating enough so that we all knew how to handle one another now.

"Anita, I don't know what happened, or why you can't remember everything, but if we did get rolled by some bigger vampire, don't do to me what you've done to Sin, or Jean-Claude and Richard in the past."

"And what is that? What did I do to them?" I could hear the fear and edge of anger in my voice.

"Let your fear of what happened paint everyone involved with the same issues. It would break my heart if you treated me that way."

I stared into that handsome face and didn't know what to say.

"I don't think I'd deal as well with it as they do."

"What does that mean?" And my voice was still strident with the first stirrings of anger, because it would help chase away the fear.

"It means don't blame me, or Damian, when we got rolled, too."

"But you remember. If you'd been rolled, you wouldn't remember."

"I don't know why I remember, but you and Damian said yes to everything we did. I hate the idea that you don't remember saying yes, and hope like hell that Damian remembers later."

I glanced at the vampire lying broken-looking in the bed. "Can you change his position? He looks . . . broken."

"Can it really hurt him to lie like that?" he asked.

"No, but it just looks uncomfortable."

Nathaniel didn't argue, just climbed back onto the bed and moved the vampire until he was lying in a more normal sleeping position. His body moved as only the dead can, boneless and hard to keep where you put it, so that the head kept lolling to one side at that broken-neck angle. Nathaniel finally had to use the pillows to prop the vampire's head at an angle that made me happier.

"Let's go find Jean-Claude; he should be awake by now," I said.

"You'll want to at least finger-comb your hair," he said, smiling.

I frowned at him. "Do you really think I care how my hair looks right now?"

"No, but you might if you look in the mirror."

I half-smiled and shook my head. "For you to keep insisting, it must be bad."

"Pretty bad. I think we all forgot to put hair-care products and conditioner on after we finished the shower part."

"You never forget hair-care products," I said.

He frowned. "True."

"Are you sure you remember everything that happened?" I asked.

"I thought I did, but now I'm not sure."

I reached up and touched my hair, but just feeling it didn't seem so bad. I started to walk to the bathroom, but Nathaniel followed me, and I had to stop him. "I don't want to be in the bathroom with anyone but me right now, Nathaniel."

He looked so sad.

"I'm sorry, Nathaniel, but until we figure out what just happened I need a little space."

"Don't pull away, Anita."

"I want some privacy in the bathroom. I don't think that's asking too much," I said.

He nodded and let me walk away alone, but his shoulders slumped forward, every line of him sadder than a few seconds ago. I wanted to run and hug him close, erase all the sadness from him, but I had a right to go to the bathroom alone, damn it. I had a right to a little privacy, a little space, even with him.

I closed the door, but standing there in the room where I'd lost time wasn't good. I suddenly wanted out of the room as much as I'd wanted out of the bed. I opened the door and came to stand outside, breathing hard.

"Anita, are you okay? Did something happen in the room just now?"

I shook my head. "Going to leave the door open, okay?"

"Okay, I won't try to come in while you're in there."

"Thank you," I said.

"I don't know what's wrong, but I don't want to make it worse," he said.

"I know you don't." I moved back into the bathroom to look in the mirror and instantly understood why Nathaniel had said something. My curls didn't always look great after I slept on them wet, but this was spectacularly bad, even for me. It

looked like I had lopsided horns, along with other odd protu-
berances in between. Just sleeping on my hair wet wouldn't do
this; it was like we'd put in shampoo and just left it in, or gotten crazed with hair-care products but never smoothed the hair
into place. Once I saw my hair, I knew that Nathaniel didn't
remember everything either. He'd never have let me sleep with
this much stuff in my hair without helping me neaten it. Nathaniel thought he remembered the entire thing, but he didn't.

I did my best to splash water on it and try to help matters,
but I finally let Nathaniel in to try to help me. He finally ended
by braiding it close to my head with a promise to help me wash
it out later. He had to braid his own hair, too. We'd both have
to start over with our hair later, but there was no way I was
getting back into the shower until I'd spoken with Jean-Claude.
I needed to know who had rolled us, and why. Some older
vampires will fuck with you just to fuck with you, but most of
them have a purpose if they torment you; call it sadism with a
reason. I needed to know that reason, and Jean-Claude needed
to know there was still someone big and bad enough to roll me
that thoroughly, because if they could do that without alerting
him to it, then they were serious bad-asses. Every time we
destroyed the great evil, another one seemed to rise up in its
place like an evil version of "Nature abhors a vacuum." It was
almost like the Mother of All Darkness had kept the other bad
vampires in line, and now that she was gone, they were trying
their supervillain wings out. I was getting real tired of being
the target du jour for them.

15

"MA PETITE, I do not believe that it is an outside force that
has cost you time."

"Then what was it?" I demanded, as I paced the room. We
were back in his bedroom but had to sit in the chairs around

the faux fireplace, because the bed where he usually liked to lounge had been reduced to nothing but the bed frame. The custom-made mattress and bed frame were ruined by the blood that Damian had shed. The cleanup crew that was made up of our own people wouldn't guarantee that they could fix it. It would take weeks or even months to get a custom replacement.

He glanced at Nathaniel, who had curled up in front of the electric fire wearing nothing but a pair of silky black shorts and the long braid of his hair.

"Cats always find the warmest place in a room," Jean-Claude said.

"I wish you would let the electric fire run when we sleep in here," Nathaniel said.

"I cannot trust that it will not spark and catch fire while I am unable to save myself."

"Modern electricity is a lot safer than it used to be," Nathaniel said.

Jean-Claude nodded. "Logically, yes, but some worries are not about logic."

"We have another big bad vampire attacking us and you're worried about being warm while we sleep. If I were any warmer sleeping between you and Micah, I'd melt."

"I'm usually on the end, so warmer would be good for me," Nathaniel said.

"How can you be so calm?" I asked him.

He shrugged and stared at the flickering flames. "The *ardeur* was fed. We all feel better. Damian is even dead for the day. Nothing seems to be wrong; why aren't you calmer?" He looked up at me as I paced.

"Our pussycat is right about one thing, *ma petite*. There seems to be no harm done."

"This time, this time no harm is done, but one thing I've learned is that once one of these fuckers starts messing with us, they don't stop until they get bored, or hurt us."

"Do you agree, pussycat, that whoever did this will not stop until they are bored or hurt us?"

Nathaniel shook his head. "I don't think they'll get bored."

I looked from one to the other of them, because I realized

I was missing something. "What does everyone else in this room know that I don't?"

They exchanged a look, and Jean-Claude gave a small wave of his hand toward the other man. "Do I have to?" Nathaniel asked.

"Yes, *mon minet*, you do."

"What does Nathaniel have to do?" I asked.

"Tell you the truth."

"About what?" I asked.

Nathaniel hugged his knees to his chest and looked at the floor rather than at me. That was never good. "It wasn't a vampire that mind-rolled you."

"Then what was it?"

He glanced up. "Don't be mad. I didn't mean to. I didn't know I could."

"What are you talking about?" I asked.

"You were conflicted about feeding on Damian for the *ardeur*. You were conflicted about the three of us being together like you always are."

"So?"

"I'm not conflicted."

"I know that you'd love it if the three of us were a real threesome in a sexual way at least."

"I don't understand why you don't see Damian as yummier than you do."

"His conflicts and mine get in our way," I said.

"Mine don't get in my way."

"You don't have any conflicts about the three of us being closer," I said.

"Exactly."

I frowned at him.

"You must be more forthright with *ma petite*, Nathaniel. You know this."

Nathaniel sighed. "The two of you were letting it all get away from us again, and I wanted it to work, so I made it work."

I frowned harder. "I don't understand."

"It is not some outside force attacking us, *ma petite*, but those inside growing into their power."

"I still don't understand." And then suddenly I did understand, or thought I did. "Wait. You mean that Nathaniel mind-rolled me."

"I didn't mean to do that part, but I wanted you and Damian to be with me, for us all to be together."

"What did you do?" I asked, coming to stand in front of him.

He rounded his shoulders and hunched up. "You looming over me isn't helping."

"You're taller than I am."

"It is not about physical height, *ma petite*, and you know this."

"Fine," I said, and backed up so I wasn't looming. I stood there, arms crossed under my breasts, trying not to scowl at him and probably failing.

"I wanted it to work between us."

"Wait. I remember you saying something: *I want this,* you said."

"Yes."

"Your eyes were glowing lavender, so it was your power, not some interloper's, because then your eyes would have been the color of whoever was trying to take us over."

"Damian's eyes glowed his color, and yours glowed to your power. It was all us, just us."

I shook my head. "So why don't I remember?"

"This was his first time being in charge of your metaphysical union, *ma petite*. I believe he used more power than was needed, but he did not realize that until you had no memory of it."

"Did we all have unprotected sex? I mean, did you think to grab a condom for Damian?"

Nathaniel looked miserable. "No, I got carried away with it all. I'm sorry, truly sorry about that part."

"Normally I would be more angry about that," Jean-Claude said, "but *ma petite* is on birth control other than condoms. Damian is also older than even I am, so it is unlikely that he would be fertile. If you had to make that mistake with anyone, he is a good choice."

"Thank you for not being angry," Nathaniel said.

"He's not angry, but I am."

"I didn't know I could be in charge of us all. You both simply said yes to what I wanted. I asked for permission several times and you both said yes."

"Yes to what?" I asked.

"Let's just say that I hope Damian either remembers saying yes to me or doesn't remember anything at all."

I shook my head. "What did you do to our heterosexual vampire boy?"

"I didn't do anything to him, exactly."

"Then what exactly did you do to him?"

He turned his head to one side, and finally moved his braid to one side to expose more neat fang marks in the side of his neck. "He wanted to have sex again."

"So you supplied the blood for the next go-round," I said.

He let his braid fall back over it. "For round two, yes."

"How many rounds were there?" I asked suspiciously.

He grinned, but the look that went with it said he was far too pleased with himself.

"How many, Nathaniel?"

He opened his knees and moved his shorts out of the way to show another neat bite on his inner thigh.

I reached down toward my leg. "I didn't notice one when I got dressed."

"You were pretty upset when you dressed," he said, giving a small smile. He was trying not to look happy, but failing. I appreciated the effort not to piss me off more. It wasn't working, but I appreciated the effort.

"Four times, really? Four times with no condom—that's upping the odds a little too much, Nathaniel," I said. I let the frown go to the scowl I'd been wanting to have for the last fifteen minutes.

"It didn't up your chances four times, and I don't have to worry about getting pregnant."

"What does that mean?" I asked.

Jean-Claude laughed, loud and long, head back, mouth so wide-open that he was flashing not just his fangs but almost every sparkling tooth in his head.

I turned the scowl on him. "What is so fucking funny?"

"*Ma petite*, Nathaniel was gallant enough to use his body to protect yours."

"What?" I asked.

"You and Damian kept saying yes. How was I supposed to know that you weren't sober enough to give permission?"

I'd been slow on the uptake, because I was angry and it was easier to just be angry instead of listening, but Nathaniel deserved better than that from me. I loved him, was in love with him, would have married him if I could have married more than just one man.

I took in a deep breath and let it out slow, counting my breaths, calming my body to calm the rest of me. Anger and blaming everyone else were easy. It had kept me emotionally safe for years, and emotionally isolated. I'd made the choice that I didn't want to do that anymore, which meant I had to choose something else to do. I'd decided what didn't work in my life; I was still working at what to put in its place that did work.

"Are you well, *ma petite*?"

I nodded. "I'm trying to be." I went to Nathaniel and offered him my hand. He looked up at me, then took my hand.

"I'm really sorry, Anita. I swear to you that I thought you and Damian were enjoying everything as much as I was."

"I believe you."

He smiled and squeezed my hand. "I love you."

"I love you more."

"I love you most," he said.

"I love you mostest," I said, smiling. Usually Micah was there to help us finish the litany, but it worked for just the two of us.

"I don't know what Damian will think when he wakes up for the night, but I'm okay."

"I think, *ma petite*, *mon minet*, it will depend on whether Damian received or gave attention."

"I received," Nathaniel said. "A lot of heterosexual men are willing to do it, but being on the other side of things weirds them out more. I didn't push."

"It can be difficult to tell the difference between normal persuasion and vampiric powers at first," Jean-Claude said.

"I didn't expect to have vampiric powers," Nathaniel said. "I thought only Anita and Damian had 'powers.'" He made air quotes with his free hand when he said *powers*.

"Richard is stronger for being a part of our triumvirate," Jean-Claude said.

"He's the leader of the local werewolves. He started stronger," Nathaniel said.

"Do not underestimate yourself, Nathaniel. There are different kinds of power. You have done something that Richard has never managed to do."

"He's tried to bespell me before," I said.

"But never successfully, and this was very successful," Jean-Claude said.

"I hope that Damian agrees with the successful part when he wakes up," Nathaniel said.

"One problem at a time, pussycat."

My phone rang and it was Edward's ringtone.

Nathaniel squeezed my hand and said, "It's Edward. Take it."

I pulled out my phone and said, "I'm here . . . Ted."

"We don't have to pretend right now," he said.

"Okay, what's up, Edward?"

"I told the police you had a vampire that knows the older vampires here."

"And?"

"If you bring him to help us talk to them, the police would agree to you coming in to consult."

"I can't agree to Damian coming back into Ireland, Edward. He feels like he barely escaped the first time."

"This time we know the vampires are here and real. Damian can come in with the full protection of the police."

"You don't know what you're asking, Edward."

"I know people are dying, Anita. I know more are going to die if we don't figure out how to stop this."

"It's just a bunch of vampires, Edward. You know how to kill vampires. Kill them and get out of there."

"The local police aren't letting me off leash much."

"What's that mean?"

"It means that the Irish are having trouble deciding how to deal with the vampires."

"Have you found the vampires that are doing this?"

"Not yet, but when we do the Irish still don't have a death penalty."

"Wait. Are you seriously telling me that when you finally trace these bastards down, the locals aren't going to kill them?"

"You know better than I do that vampires can become good little citizens, Anita."

"Not if they're doing this kind of shit, Edward."

"I'll bet if you ask your fiancé what he did when he first rose from the grave it won't be any worse than this."

Jean-Claude had heard both ends of the conversation, of course. He said, "When the bloodlust first rises we all do horrible things, unless our masters lock us away for those first nights."

I looked at him while I said to Edward, "No one's innocent, I guess, but whoever is doing this in Ireland is killing people now, not hundreds of years ago."

"I guess that does make it worse," he said, his voice very dry.

"I can't ask Damian to go back to Ireland."

"Anita, his old master was so scary that she spooked you, but just a few years later she's lost enough power that she can't control a bunch of new vampires. What changed?"

"Damian won't know the answer to that."

"No, but he will know more about the local vampires than anyone else here, because he was one of them."

"I can't promise that he'll agree to come, Edward."

"Aren't you his master?"

"I won't force him, Edward."

"I don't ask for help often, Anita, but I'm asking now."

"Has something else happened, Edward?"

"Two more bodies."

"You've seen dead bodies before, Edward."

"I'd rather stop seeing them here, Anita."

"What aren't you telling me, Edward?"

"Are kid vampires more likely to attack other children?"

"Sometimes. It's easier for them to subdue them physically. Even modern kids who are warned against pedophiles trust other kids. Crap, the last two victims were kids."

"Yes."

"Kids are always hard."

"You don't have kids of your own yet, Anita; once you do you'll understand."

"I'm not planning to ever have kids, Edward."

"Neither was I."

"I think I can avoid dating people who already have a family," I said.

"That's what I thought, too."

"I'll talk to Damian when he wakes up for the night, but don't hold your breath."

"I can send you the latest pictures, Anita. It might change his mind."

"I doubt it."

"It might change yours."

"Me coming was always on the table."

"I've been trying to find the older vamps, Anita. It's like they aren't here."

"They're there, Edward. I promise you that."

"Then help me find them."

"Damian won't be awake for hours yet."

"Let me know when he wakes up. Maybe I can help persuade him."

"Have you and Damian ever had a conversation?"

"No."

"Then what makes you think you can be more persuasive than I can?"

"Desperation."

"You don't get desperate easily, Edward; what aren't you telling me?"

"I have that feeling, Anita. That feeling that says things are going to get worse."

It wasn't like him to be this spooked. "Guard your ass."

"Don't I always?"

"Yeah, you do, but I feel like you're leaving stuff out."

"Don't I always?" he said.

"Yeah, you do." I sighed.

"Call me with Damian's answer," he said. He hung up.

"Fuck," I said to the phone.

"What's wrong?" Nathaniel asked.

"More dead in Ireland. Apparently one of the vampires has a taste for kids."

"I didn't think vampires attacked children that often," Nathaniel said.

"We do not," Jean-Claude said.

"Their throats are so tiny that a good bite can close down the blood supply, so why attack them?" I asked.

"Ask Edward to send you photos of the new victims. If their throats are intact and the bites dainty enough, then the new Irish vampires may be breaking one of our few strict taboos."

"You mean they're making new child vampires," I said.

Jean-Claude gave a small nod. He didn't try to hide the anger on his face. "I am only king of America, but if they are doing this, then they must be stopped. It is forbidden to bring children over for a reason."

"As king of America you have no authority outside this country, right?"

"The only authority in Ireland was Damian's old master. If she cannot police her country's newest members better than this, then something has gone very wrong."

"What could have damaged her power this badly in just a few years?" I asked.

"You have felt her power from a distance, *ma petite*, Nathaniel. I have felt her power in person. I can conceive of nothing that could leave her toothless and powerless before any foe, save for the Mother herself."

"This feels like new monsters, not old ones," I said.

"Agreed, *ma petite*, but powerful new ones."

"It doesn't matter if it's old power or new," Nathaniel said. "We need to stop whoever is doing this."

"Yeah, we do," I said.

"We are agreed," Jean-Claude said.

We were all agreed, and that was great, but what we needed was a plan. Edward was asking for help. He almost never asked for help. One of the scariest vampires around seemed powerless in the face of whatever was happening in her country, or maybe she just didn't care.

I asked Jean-Claude, "Could She-Who-Made-Damian just not give a damn?"

"What do you mean, *ma petite*?"

"Could she just not care enough to police the new vampires?"

"Do you mean, has she given up?"

"I mean, is she old enough that she just isn't moving with the times? Some of them do that, right? They just refuse to accept change and sort of hide from it all."

"It has happened, but in the past the council did not allow it to disrupt business as usual."

"You mean that the Mother of All Darkness would send the Harlequin out to see what was wrong and fix it."

"*Oui*, that is what I mean."

"We killed the Mother of All Darkness, and most of the Harlequin work for us now."

"That is true, *ma petite*."

Nathaniel looked from one to the other of us. "Were they doing something that we aren't doing now?"

"What do you mean?" I asked.

"Jean-Claude is in charge of the new power structure, but it's not like the old one. It's mostly just us here in America. The old council ran things differently, right?" Nathaniel said.

"They were concerned with more of the world than we are," Jean-Claude said.

"Have we dropped a ball here, Jean-Claude? Were the Mother and the Harlequin or the old council doing things to keep Ireland moving safely along, and now that we've destroyed their power did we cause this somehow?" I said.

He went very still. I knew it meant he was either thinking, or hiding what he was thinking. "I do not believe so, but if we wish to know what the council was doing to maintain the status quo in Ireland, we have people here to ask."

"The Harlequin," I said.

"Our guards now," he said.

"Wouldn't the Harlequin have told you if there was something important that needed to keep being done?" Nathaniel asked.

"All the Harlequin are older than I am, and there is something about being a certain age that gives you a longer view of things."

"Which means what?" I asked.

"They might not see it as important enough to share until it became a problem."

"Even if it cost lives?" I asked.

"The vampires of the Harlequin are thousands of years

old, *ma petite*. They may not consider human life as valuable as we do."

"Then their attitude needs to change," I said.

"I would settle for their sharing any important secrets before they become an issue."

"We don't know that they hid anything about Ireland," I said.

"No, that is true, but the old council is disbanded. Their power is destroyed and incorporated into our power base, and suddenly a country that has run seamlessly for thousands of years is in turmoil. At the very least, we should question the coincidence."

"If it is a coincidence," I said.

"Do not borrow trouble, *ma petite*. Not everything that goes wrong in the world is our doing."

"True, but if we're only in charge of American vampires, who's in charge of Europe now?"

"If I try to spread our power over the rest of the world, we will have more battles on our hands. One of the reasons it has gone so smoothly is that I have not fought to rule the world, as it were."

"I don't want the equivalent of a vampire world war, but someone needs to be in charge of you guys."

"We have been in charge of ourselves longer than humans have known there was a world to rule."

"But all that time the Mother of All Darkness was in charge of all of you, right?"

"Oui."

"Now she's not, because we killed her."

"You are wondering what the vampiric mice are doing now that the cat is dead—is that it, *ma petite*?"

"Yeah, that," I said.

"They're doing what the mice always do when the cat's gone," Nathaniel said.

We looked at him.

"And that would be what, our pussycat?"

"Destroy everything they can before a new cat comes along."

"And we're the new cat," I said.

"Perhaps, *ma petite*, *mon minet*, or perhaps we need to find another cat to rule Europe."

"Who?" I asked.

"I do not know, but I know that I do not wish to rule the world. America is enough for me."

"Have we let the monsters loose in Ireland, Jean-Claude?"

"Let us ask the Harlequin that we trust most. If there is a secret to Ireland's vampire past, they will know it."

"Who do we ask first?"

"Magda," Nathaniel said.

We looked at him.

"She's one of our lovers and she's so blunt, it's painful. If there's something she knows, she'll share it. If we ask her without Giacomo at her side."

"Are you saying she would obey her vampire master before her vampire king?" Jean-Claude asked.

"Let's not make her choose," Nathaniel said. "Let's just ask her now while she's awake and her master is still dead to the world."

"You are growing craftier, *mon minet*."

"I had to get smarter sometime," he said.

"No, sadly, some people live for centuries and never become wiser."

I was pretty sure we were all thinking about the same person, but none of us said his name. Asher had been Jean-Claude's on-again, off-again love of his afterlife for centuries. They'd loved and lost the same woman, Asher's human servant Julianna, and neither of them had stopped mourning her. They say love heals all wounds, but if Jean-Claude and Asher were any judge, maybe not. Asher's jealousy issues had led him to make some seriously bad political choices that had almost started a war here in St. Louis between us and the local werehyenas. That final stupidity had been enough even for Jean-Claude and all of us to dump him. Asher, our golden-haired and sadistic beauty, was now trying to be monogamous with the one lover he had left, Kane. None of us liked Kane, and he returned the sentiment. We all missed parts of Asher when he was behaving himself, but none of us missed those parts enough to forgive this last near-disastrous choice. A war among the preternatural set here in St. Louis just as Jean-Claude was being the very public face for vampires as good citizens could have lost the vampires so much, like the new voting rights that grandfathered in all vampires regardless of how long they'd been dead. Less than fifteen years ago a vampire could be killed on sight just for being a vampire, no questions asked. There were still laws in some Western states that allowed lycanthropes to be killed like varmint coyotes, or rats. You could kill someone and as long as their blood tests came back positive for lycanthropy you were justified. One of the things that the Coalition was trying to get changed was laws like that. We were so not free and clear in this country, or anywhere in the world. Asher had risked so much more than just us when he'd made his last bad decisions. In the end, that level of carelessness was what we couldn't forgive.

Nathaniel sighed. "I'll admit it, if neither of you will."

"Admit what?" I asked.

"I miss Asher topping me in the dungeon. I even miss sex with him."

"If I did not miss sex with *mon chardonneret*, my goldfinch, I would have been done with him centuries sooner."

"Fine, fine. I miss him in the bedroom and the dungeon."

"What we miss is that we can't find anyone else who tops us like he does," Nathaniel said.

Since I was still working through my issues about the whole bondage and submission being an ongoing part of my sexuality, I wasn't sure what to say to that.

"The only one I have ever known as talented with such things as Asher is Belle Morte," Jean-Claude said.

"I know she tried to contact you and come here after the vampire council fell and she had to flee France," I said.

"She seemed most confused that I would not allow her sanctuary in my lands."

"She thought you'd take her back," Nathaniel said.

"She offered that the three of us could be together as of old."

"You, Asher, and her?" Nathaniel asked.

"Yes." He looked out into the room, but I was pretty sure he wasn't seeing anything in front of him.

I moved to make sure I blocked his line of sight. He looked

up at me; his blue eyes looked as black as his hair and the robe he was wearing in the dim light, so that only the paleness of his face and that triangle of chest relieved the darkness of him.

I held my hand down and he took it lightly with just his long, slender fingers. "I never asked you at the time: Were you tempted?"

His lips moved, and it wasn't quite a smile, more like he thought about smiling. "What she offered was a lie, *ma petite*, as it was always a lie."

"You and Asher were her main boys for centuries."

"We were her favorite pawns, or perhaps tools. Yes, we were her favorite tools, or weapons to be aimed at whoever she wished us to seduce, or embarrass, or help her manipulate for her schemes. Belle almost ruled all of Europe once, the true power behind many thrones. The two of us helped her seduce a great deal of the nobility, church officials, anyone in a position of power that she wished to control."

"I've been inside your head when you have memories of those days, Jean-Claude; you loved her. You were in love with her."

"I was, but she was never in love with me, or Asher. If she was ever able to love anyone, it was not us."

"So you weren't tempted?"

"For a moment, perhaps, but it is like being tempted by a dream. It is not real."

"But while you're dreaming it, it can feel real," I said.

"She kept us all like addicts, *ma petite*. We were addicted to her charms. We competed for her love, but as you have said before of others in our lives, it is a rigged game. There is only one winner in any game involving Belle Morte, and that is Belle Morte."

Nathaniel unfolded from beside the fire and walked on two legs, but there was something about the way he moved that was very catlike, as if his human body were remembering a lighter grace and it was all there as he came to take my other hand and look down at Jean-Claude.

"We are a game you can win," he said.

Jean-Claude smiled then, and offered his other hand to him. Nathaniel took it, smiling back. "Oh pussycat, pussycat, you are right, because all of us are willing to talk about what is true and what we need, or want, or cannot live without. We do not—what is the phrase?—game each other."

"You don't game the people you love," I said.

He sat up very straight in the chair, still holding our hands, while we held each other's. "You are quite right, *ma petite*. Now, let us follow the recommendation of our clever cat and find Magda before her master wakes for the day and she becomes more clever."

"She's not stupid," Nathaniel said.

"No, but she is not a deep thinker either."

"Her body awareness and physical intelligence are amazing," I said.

"That makes her an excellent warrior," Jean-Claude said.

"And a really physical lover," Nathaniel said.

I felt the first heat of the blush that was creeping up my face. I didn't blush as often anymore, but occasionally . . . Jean-Claude laughed and kissed my hand. "Oh, *ma petite*, you never grow jaded. It is one of your many charms."

"Dating women is new, okay?"

"We don't date Magda," Nathaniel said. "She's more a bodyguard with benefits."

I drew him into a hug and put my arm across Jean-Claude's shoulders, bringing us into a sort of group huddle. "I'm dating as many people as I can do justice to; 'with benefits' is okay."

We all agreed with that; though I hated the concept of "with benefits," sometimes it was all I had to offer. If someone didn't think that was enough, they were free to stop being part of our poly group. I'd finally realized that I didn't have unlimited time and energy to date this many people. We were looking at closing our circle and making it closed poly, which meant eventually we'd start saying no. The trick was to figure out who was a yes before the door of possibilities closed, but right now, we needed to figure out what had gone wrong with the vampires in Ireland. Once, I'd thought that Damian's master was so powerful and evil that she should be destroyed, and now I was worried about why she wasn't powerful enough to protect her turf. Sometimes evil was in the eye of the beholder, right along with beauty.

16

JEAN-CLAUDE HAD to take a business call, because though he was now head of all the vampires in the country, he was still running his own businesses and finances. Sometimes I forgot that part of what had led him to become king was his ability to do business, but he didn't. It was part of our power base that I was no help at all with; my idea of investments was my 401(k) plan at work. Nathaniel and I went to find Magda to ask about Ireland, because we could handle that part while Jean-Claude did things only he could do. It was delegation at its best, though usually Nathaniel didn't go with me when I was working on crime busting, but then, this really wasn't about the police work; it was more about trying to figure out why a country that had worked fine for eons was suddenly going apeshit. Had Jean-Claude and I done something to fuck it all up? If we had, how did we fix it? If we hadn't, then what had changed in Ireland?

Before we could find Magda, Nicky found us. He was tall, blond, blue-eyed, and so in shape it was almost intimidating. He wasn't the tallest person in my life, but as he strode toward us down the hallway he seemed like he was; it was part attitude and part that his shoulders were almost as wide as I was tall. His biceps strained against the sleeves of his black workout shirt. He was wearing the new shorts that were split up the outer thighs to accommodate men who had awesome muscled thighs like Nicky, so they'd have full range of movement in the octagon during MMA—mixed martial arts—matches. I'd seen them first on a pay-per-view match that I'd watched with Nicky and other friends among the guards.

My happy-to-see-you smile faded when I saw the outfit. Saturday morning was an informal fight practice. Sometimes there weren't enough people showing up for it and those of us who did drag our asses out of bed for it ended up just hitting the weight room or the track. There was no reason I knew of for Nicky to be wasting some of the new fancy shorts on a Saturday workout.

Nathaniel saved me from having to ask. "Why are you dressed for a serious fight workout?"

"I'm one of the instructors today. Why are you awake this early?" Nicky said with a smile.

Nathaniel smiled back, and said, "Hey, I don't sleep all day."

"I thought you'd be tucked into bed between Jean-Claude and Damian for a few more hours at least."

"We had enough sleep," I said.

"Speak for yourself," Nathaniel said.

"You would sleep all day," Nicky said, grinning.

I led Nathaniel forward until I was close enough to touch the other man. He looked down at me with one blue eye and the other covered by a black eye patch that had a white skull embroidered in the center of it. I let go of Nathaniel's hand so I could reach up and touch the long, thin braid on the right side of his face. It was the side of his bangs that fell in a long triangle down his face so that his own hair hid the missing eye. It was how he had kept enemies from realizing he was completely blind on that side for real fighting. Werelions fought to the death more than most lycanthropes when they met other groups of their own kind. In fact, they were the animal group most likely to fight savagely within their own group. Every other kind of lycanthrope I knew had traditions that limited serious fighting among themselves. The lions had one of the most vicious cultures of any group, so being a lion who had a blind side was a serious problem.

I touched the side of his face, smiling up at him. "God, you're handsome."

He smiled but shook his head. "I'm good-looking, but I have Nathaniel, Jean-Claude, Micah, and even Dev to compare to and they're all prettier than I am."

"Well," Nathaniel said, "I am prettier, but that doesn't mean you aren't handsome." He flashed that grin, the one that held so much mischief. "You know I'm sad you're not more bisexual, Nicky, and I only do gorgeous men."

Nicky smiled and shook his head. "You and I don't think of each other that way, but if I did you'd be too pretty for me. I like my men more guy-guy. You're prettier than most of the women that I've fucked."

"Oh, Nicky, you always know just what to say to flatter a girl," I said.

His eye widened, and his other eyebrow rose, too, even though there was no eye to widen behind the piratical-looking eye patch. "You know I didn't mean you, Anita."

I smiled up at him. "You're my Bride, Nicky. You're meta-physically compelled to keep me happy, so that could be a complete lie so I won't be upset."

His face started to show him trying to think his way through what I'd just said, and then he gave me a more typical cynical look. He put his arms around me and drew me into a hug. I didn't fight him, just wrapped my arms around his slender waist. "I can feel your emotions, remember?"

"I remember," I said, smiling.

"Then I know that you are happy with me and enjoying being in my arms, so you're teasing me." He'd started smiling as he said the "in my arms" part.

"Sometimes I wish I could feel your emotions like I could feel Nathaniel's if I lowered my shields and we wanted to share."

"I'm a sociopath, Anita. You wouldn't want to read my emotions, or my thoughts, most of the time."

"You told me that I was your conscience."

"You are. Your magic keeps me tame, because a Bride is designed to do anything to keep their master happy. Acting like I have a conscience pleases you."

"It does." I hugged him around the waist and he flexed his arms just a bit, letting me feel the strength in all those muscles. He could have crushed me easily. If he'd been just human and this in shape, he could have broken my spine in half with little effort, but being a lycanthrope on top of that meant he literally could have crushed me, or torn me to pieces, and that was with-out changing form to have claws and fangs. He tightened his arms around me so that he compromised my rib cage and it was hard to draw a full breath. Nicky liked breath play and he'd taught me to enjoy it, too, but we'd never done it this way.

"I'm in love with you, and that makes any man want to keep a woman happy," he said.

My words were careful, because I had to concentrate to breathe enough to talk normally, as I said, "And I'm in love with you, which makes me want to let you make me happy, and to return the favor."

His smile changed to that certain one that was part happiness and part evil, or maybe evilly happy. I knew what he was going to do a second before he tightened his arms and I suddenly had to struggle to breathe. I had enough breath to use my safeword and stop the whole thing, but I didn't. With most people I'd have told them to stop and been figuring out how to reach my gun, but Nicky was my bit of rough sex and bondage, and I was his, which meant that the sensation of being trapped and fighting to breathe excited me. It made me want to ask him to squeeze tighter, but if I did that I might not be able to say my safeword, and then I'd be at Nicky's mercy, but like he'd said, he could feel what I was feeling. It literally seemed to cause him pain for me to be unhappy with him, so he would feel if I wanted him to stop.

Hands touched my back underneath where Nicky's arms squeezed around my ribs, and I knew it was Nathaniel. His hands caressed their way down my body until he could trace the swell of my hips and ass. It made me have to close my eyes and shudder with that first faint preamble to the possibility of an orgasm. It was like the scent of rain on the wind, even though the sun was out. It promised you'd get wet, but the wind could change. But the one and only time I'd allowed the two of them to use a gag while they double-teamed me, Nathaniel had bitten me much harder than I'd been happy with and he'd absolutely known it when he did it. We now had a hand signal for me to use in case I had trouble talking, but still . . . Nathaniel pressed the front of his silky shorts against my ass and even through the jeans I could feel that he was happy to be there. It made me shudder again in equally happy anticipation.

"God, Anita, you have the fastest windup of any woman I've ever met and I love it, but Jake is expecting me at the practice. I'm supposed to be helping him instruct the class."

Nathaniel leaned his forehead against my hair, moving his

hips back enough so he wasn't pressed against me. "Please tell me that we can do this later."

"Oh yeah," Nicky said.

"Maybe," I said, my voice raspy and almost painful to hear, though it didn't hurt me. I wanted the sex with them, but I wasn't completely sold on doing breath play with my chest being squeezed. I was harder to hurt than a normal human, but I wasn't as indestructible as a lycanthrope. I'd hate to crack a rib because we were doing rough sex and I just didn't understand what Nicky was doing well enough to understand when to call it for sure. We'd need a lot more negotiating and information sharing before we did anything like this for real.

Nicky gave me a look. He stopped squeezing me, and my voice was almost normal as I answered that look. "I want the sex with both of you, but I'm not sure about having my rib cage compressed while we do it."

"Fair enough," he said.

"Even I've never had anyone compress my chest for breath play," Nathaniel said.

"It would almost be worth it to do something as a bottom in the bedroom that you haven't done," I said, turning my head so that I could offer him a kiss, which he took.

"I've been bottoming in the dungeon and bedroom a lot longer than you have," he said, smiling.

"I didn't even know I liked bondage and submission, or rough sex, until the last few years."

"I've always known that I liked bottoming in the dungeon, but I didn't know that I enjoyed topping until you came into my life," he said, and kissed me again.

"Do you know where Magda is?" I asked.

"In the gym. I saw her go in as I went to change."

"Can you give me fifteen minutes?"

"Why?"

"I'll change and come to practice. There's a chance I may be going out of the country on a job, and I never know when I'll get to work out while I'm hunting bad guys."

"I'll change, too," Nathaniel said.

We looked at him.

"What? I work out and you've been forcing me to take at least one fight practice a week."

"Fighting is my version of your kitchen," Nicky said.

"You're my brother-husband; of course I know fighting is your version of my kitchen. You're the best sous chef I've got."

Nicky grinned. "Well, we wouldn't want you cooking dinner for everyone all by yourself."

"Or worse yet, with only Anita to help me."

"Hey," I said.

Nathaniel hugged me. "I'm sorry, but you really can't cook."

"Maybe I just don't want to cook," I said.

Nicky hugged us both. "So cute," he said.

"I am not cute," I said.

"Yes, you are," Nathaniel said. "You just hate being called cute."

"Short, delicate-looking people don't like being called cute."

"Micah hates it, too," Nathaniel said.

Nicky hugged us both and kissed the top of my head, then turned and kissed Nathaniel on the forehead. It made him laugh. "You're the one who says we don't think of each other that way."

"We don't, but you hate being left out when the physical affection is being passed around."

Nathaniel just smiled, because he couldn't disagree.

"My love, and my brother, if you're going to change for practice do it quick. This is the first time Jake has asked a non-Harlequin to help instruct. Don't want him to regret it."

We went to our room for our exercise clothes. I wondered how the other Harlequin would feel about Jake choosing Nicky over one of them. Some of them had serious issues with anyone that wasn't Harlequin. The only saving grace was it was still too early for most of the vampires to be awake. The Harlequin wereanimals were proud, but the vampires were just downright superior to everyone. They wouldn't take well to anyone making them question that superiority. It promised to be an interesting fight practice.

17

NICKY WENT AHEAD so he wouldn't keep Jake waiting, but he agreed to wait for us to get there before the actual practice began, if we hurried. Nathaniel and I changed into clothes that we could wear on the practice mat. The braid that he'd done to help me cope with my hair's lack of product, and fuzziness, was perfect for working out. Magda was at the gym with her blond hair tied back in a tight ponytail; she was wearing a sports bra and a pair of jogging shorts that would have made Nathaniel happy, which meant that she was wearing very little. I admit to being a little distracted by the way her breasts mounded at the edges of the sports bra, and the way the tiny shorts fit as she stretched over the long legs that made up most of her five-ten height. I don't think I'd ever been so distracted by a woman in the gym, but then, I'd never been lovers with one who worked out like I did. Something about all that tall Valkyrie genetics made her muscle up even better than I did, but you'd never mistake her for a man as she stretched out over first one long leg and then the other. In the right clothes she could dress up and pass for a man, but the clothes that would have allowed that needed layers to hide the curves. Without makeup her face could be stark, her gray-blue eyes cold, and that was enough to make some people think masculine for a woman, especially a tall woman, but those were people who looked on the surface of things, and that wasn't how I saw most people, and it certainly wasn't how I saw Magda anymore.

Cynric was beside her stretching out. His forehead touched his knee, all that long torso bending over the even longer legs. He was six-three now; when I met him he'd been ten inches shorter, but then he'd been sixteen and now he was nineteen. His hair looked black in the gym lights, but in brighter light, it was shades of dark blue from navy to cobalt. He got people asking him where he'd gotten such an amazing dye job, but it was his natural color. It was back in a tight ponytail for the workout; he still hadn't figured out how to braid his own hair because it, like the rest of him, had been shorter once. Usually one of us braided it for him, but this morning he'd woken up on his own in his bedroom down the hallway from ours.

His ass looked as nice in his little shorts as Magda's did, but he'd added a pair of compression shorts and a loose-fitting tank top to cover most of his chest, so only the muscled arms and shoulders gave a hint of how nice the rest of the view would be.

There were only a few other people stretching out for the workout. The early-morning Saturday class was just whoever showed up and wanted to work on things. It meant that you'd have people working hand-to-hand or weapons drill; it all depended on what they thought they needed to work on most, or what they could get someone to help them work on. But today there were enough people for a full class.

Nathaniel and I joined the stretching group. If there'd been room we'd have gone to Magda and Cynric, and used the preparation before class to ask her the preliminary questions about Ireland, but there wasn't room without making people move, and that just seemed rude. I tried not to pull the boss card more than I had to, and I could move us up beside Magda and Cynric when we all lined the edges for drill practice. It wasn't worth making a half dozen guards stop stretching and move out of our way to do it minutes earlier.

Nathaniel didn't like fight practice of any kind, but he'd started coming at least once a week after I insisted. I insisted after he'd ended up having to wrestle a bomber who had planned to kill him, me, and several others we loved. I didn't want him to just rely on his otherworldly speed, strength, and dexterity. I wanted him to have actual fighting skills if he ever needed them again. Wisely, he hadn't argued, just found time in his schedule to do it. He wasn't great at it. It was one of the very few physical activities that he wasn't a natural at. Claudia, who taught the main hand-to-hand class and made Magda and most of the men look tiny, said it wasn't natural skill that Nathaniel lacked; it was the will to win. He just didn't like being that forceful in practice, and nothing she'd been able to figure out seemed to get him out of his own way. He practiced and he improved, but he didn't come to win.

Cynric—Sin—wanted to win, but he was usually up against one of the professional guards and that meant he wasn't going to win, no matter how hard he tried, but he kept trying, and in the end, that's what counts. I didn't win much either. The fact that I won occasionally still bothered some of the guards, especially if I was winning against someone who was more than a foot taller than me and outweighed me by a hundred pounds of muscle. Magda wasn't one of the people I won against, but a slender figure only a few inches taller than me was stretching out on the mat, too; she was a different story. Pierette looked almost delicate as she stretched out in the nearly knee-length compression shorts and short-sleeved T-shirt. She never showed much skin in the gym, or elsewhere. She was also one of the few of the Harlequin who used the name of her alter ego that used to come with a mask and an outfit that hid everything. The idea behind the Harlequin had been that they were sexless, formless almost, and their outfits had reflected that from capes to clothing that wrapped around, or slid into, the next piece, sleeve into glove, pants into boot, scarf or balaclava on the face so the mask that hid the middle part, covered the last bit of them. Only their eyes had shone out and some of the Harlequin had gone modern and put mesh or reflective surfaces in the eyeholes so that even the color of their eyes had been a mystery. Most of them, including Magda, had gone back to the names they'd had centuries before, their birth names, or nicknames, but Pierette was now simply Pierette, in workout clothes or her assassination getup. She hadn't been the first Pierette among the Harlequin; she had only replaced one who had died. The names didn't change, only the people who bore them.

Her dark hair was cut very short and the strands clung to her triangular face in an almost delicate lace. I was never sure how she got her hair to do something so perfect, and since her hair was baby fine and utterly straight, whatever worked on hers wouldn't work on mine anyway. The fact that she'd styled her hair and put on makeup before coming to fight practice puzzled me, but maybe it made her feel better.

Sin had spotted us and wasted a very nice smile our way. He'd been so unfinished when I met him, and now he was all handsome and sexy. I still hadn't made the transition to what box he was in in my head, or at least not a graceful one. He put a little more heat into the smile he directed at me, as he moved his clasped hands behind his back in a shoulder stretch that didn't actually go as far as mine did. I bowed my head so he couldn't see the blush that crawled up my face at that last smile from him. He was over a decade younger than me, but that didn't mean he was more flexible. He was more flexible than he'd be when he was older unless he kept working at it, but even being a weretiger didn't make him more flexible than I was, let alone Nathaniel. If he wasn't careful he'd turn into one of those big men who lose flexibility as they gain muscle strength. At nineteen it wasn't an issue, but in five years it could be, depending on the training he did. He'd been a track star and quarterback in high school, but with college coming up he'd had to choose between his sports. Football was winning out, because it opened up more chances for scholarships and professional money later. He'd been offered scholarships for track, but not as many and nothing as close to home as football had offered. I thought he'd go off to college somewhere and this heat between us might cool. Maybe he'd find a nice girl his own age, but he'd made it clear that wasn't part of his plans. The fact that I thought he didn't have a big enough piece of my life to make him happy was my issue, not his, or so Sin had told me recently.

Nicky and Jake walked out of the side room that was both a snack room and a place for the instructors to plan. They were almost the same height, just under six feet. Jake looked shorter, because he usually rounded his shoulders and just held himself in such a way that he tried not to stand out. His hair was brown, neither too dark nor too light, not too straight, but not exactly curly, cut short so that it was in a hairstyle that had been in style for decades and would probably still be in style decades from now. His eyes were a brown that was, again, not too dark, not too light, just medium brown. Even his skin tone was medium; in fact everything about Jake was medium. He was one of the Harlequin who most made me remember they were the ultimate spies, as well as the ultimate assassins. Jake didn't even look all that perfectly Caucasian. We had Hispanic guards from some of the South American countries and parts of Spain who were as pale as he was, and who probably wouldn't tan any darker. He was the man from nowhere and most-wheres. Jake always made me think he was what James Bond was supposed to be, a man who could walk into most places and go unnoticed, while his stalking horse asked for his martini to be shaken and not stirred.

If Jake was the antithesis of Bond, James Bond, Nicky looked like he would have made a great Bond villain with all that muscle on display and the skull eye patch. It was a touch of theatricality that seemed very much like a movie bad guy. I guess if you're as muscled as Nicky you can't exactly hide that you're a bad-ass, so why try? He could have calmer energy more like Jake was giving off in nearly peaceful waves. In fact, Nicky could be nearly neutral, like a good bodyguard that could sink into the background until they were needed, but he wasn't trying to hide today. He radiated attitude that said clearly he was the biggest, baddest thing in the room, period, end of story. It was the same kind of posturing that dogs will do either as a warning to the other dog or as a way to start the fight. He'd had that attitude when I first met him; it hadn't impressed me then, and it didn't really impress me now, but then, I knew he was out of my weight class. The display wasn't for me, or any woman in the room. It was aimed at the other men. If you think that's sexist, you're right, but it's still the truth. Men do not see women as physical competition, with rare exceptions. Magda was one exception, but she was the only one in the room; even Pierette, who was fast enough to hit almost anyone twice before they could touch her once, wouldn't make Nicky posture like this. It was almost as if something about teaching with Jake had freed my big werelion to be as masculine as he wanted to be with no apologies. It made me wonder just how much my attitude dampened down this part of him.

We all moved our stretching to the edges of the mat, so that Jake and Nicky had the center of the mat. Nathaniel and I moved to Magda and Sin, and he happily helped us make sure we were all sitting together. Some of the other people in the room had just stopped stretching to watch our two instructors. Jake smiled out at everyone.

"We're going to spar today."

"I hate sparring," Nathaniel whispered.

I glanced at his suddenly unhappy face. His lack of aggression in practice meant that he was really bad at sparring.

"I love sparring," Sin said.

There were a few others who made noises against it like Nathaniel, but not many. Sparring was a safe-ish way to learn how to fight in the real world, or to find what you needed to work on the most. Almost everyone in the room made their living from some form of violence, which meant we all needed to be better at it, or at least better than whoever was trying to hurt us. Even Sin used aggression to help him focus and be better on the football field; only Nathaniel had a job that fight practice probably wouldn't help him be better at. If he had needed to be in better shape for taking his clothes off onstage, then MMA would have been a great workout for him, but Nathaniel was in fabulous shape already.

Magda wasn't one of the people who groaned. She was like me; we came to the gym to work out, not whine. Besides, we were women, and there's only one way to be successful in martial arts, or combatives, and that's to be as tough as the men, or tougher. Is it fair? No. Is it still true? Yep.

"You are improving on sparring, but your groundwork needs more attention," Magda said.

"And if someone throws me, then I'll get to work on my grappling and groundwork," Sin said; he wanted to get better at anything he tried to do physically.

Nathaniel sighed, heavily. This was the first physical thing where he whined and complained. He really did hate it, but my life was too dangerous to have someone in it who couldn't do the minimum in self-defense.

Jake motioned Scaramouche to come join them in the center of the mat. Scaramouche stood up, his long black hair in a tight bun at the nape of his neck. He always looked tall, and in regular clothes he looked slender, almost delicate, and always elegant like he was some maharaja's son gone off to the West to dress in designer clothes and forget everything he owed his family in India. Shirtless, wearing nothing except workout shorts with all that medium-brown skin showing, he looked lean, muscled, and much more warrior than spoiled prince. He walked onto the practice mat like he had springs in his feet and legs. He still looked delicate compared to Nicky, but he also looked fast and strong, and was giving off his own version of *come and get some* energy. When he bowed to Jake, muscles played in his back and across his shoulders. He didn't have Nicky's bulk, but it would be a mistake to think he was weak.

Jake bowed back as a sign of respect, but he was careful to keep his gaze on the other man. I knew Scaramouche had done the same thing when he bowed without having seen his face. It didn't take long for you to learn that taking your eyes off any potential opponent on the practice mat, at the dojo, was a mistake.

Nicky and Scaramouche put on pads, shin guards, and fight gloves. The gloves were padded on the front of the hand, but with bare fingers so the men could grab and hold on, but not tear their hands up as badly as they would without protection. They bowed to each other and this time I could watch them watching each other.

I felt Nathaniel tense beside me. He leaned in just enough for his bare shoulder to touch my arm. Now that he wasn't having to worry about sparring himself, he was worried about Nicky. I was a little surprised that Jake had let his teaching assistant spar with anyone rather than just instruct. That must have meant something was up. Maybe there'd been more than one reason for Jake to tag Nicky to help him today.

I looked around and realized that there were more Harlequin here than normal, and most of them were ones like Scaramouche and Pierette, who had made it known that they weren't entirely content here in St. Louis. Hortensio, the animal half to his vampire master, Magnifico, was sitting near Pierette, much as we'd moved closer to Magda and Sin. Some of the Harlequin had been given their names by their dead queen, but others had chosen their names with permission of their queen. Magnifico was one of those, so I guess if that's the name you choose, your ego is going to be large enough that you are going to be a problem. Hortensio reflected his master's attitudes in almost every way, which made him seriously irritating without his master's suave and debonair manners to offset it. Funny how most of the Harlequin who had kept the names of their masked alter egos, the names they killed under, were all pains in our asses.

Nicky and Scaramouche both dropped into a fighting stance, but it wasn't the same one. I knew Nicky didn't always telegraph his fighting style like that, but the two men had fought before and had watched each other spar with other guards. They had no deep, dark fighting secrets from each other. It was a plus to know your fellow soldiers' strengths and weaknesses, but it was anything but if you actually had to fight against them and not with them. Nicky knew that, so he wasn't trying to be coy.

Nicky feinted a kick at Scaramouche's leg, and the wererat returned the favor, but neither of them put much power behind it. The wererat feinted a punch at Nicky's face. He bobbed to the side, letting it go past, and then Scaramouche moved in a blur of speed with his other hand. Nicky's arm was just in front of his face, blocking the other man's fist. I hadn't even seen him move to block; it was like magic. Scaramouche tried to follow with a punch to Nicky's ribs, but the werelion blocked with his elbow and moved just enough, so that missed, too.

Scaramouche gave himself some distance from the other man, hands still raised up protecting his face, elbows tight in over his ribs. "You should not be that much faster than I am, lion."

"I'm Rex of our pride, rat."

"It doesn't matter. You are not Harlequin. You should not be faster than me."

Nicky faced him with his own arms up, elbows tucked tight against the side of his body; he was on the balls of his feet, almost bouncing in place. Someone his size shouldn't have bounced like that either; he'd always been more agile than he looked, but I agreed with Scaramouche on the new speed. I'd never seen Nicky move like that.

"Don't you mean that you shouldn't be this slow?" Nicky said; his voice already held an edge of growling to it.

"Yes, that is exactly what I mean, lion. Only the Harlequin

are so swift that another wereanimal cannot see them move."
Scaramouche kicked at him, but Nicky moved out of the way
of it, no need to block. Scaramouche moved in suddenly with
a rain of blows and kicks that were just a blur of motion. I
couldn't follow it all, but it was as if Nicky's hands, arms, and
legs were just there, where they needed to be. Scaramouche
was a dark blur, but Nicky was so fast my eyes couldn't even
see the blur of his motion. The last time I'd seen anyone that
fast, it had been some of the Harlequin before we killed their
dark queen. All but one of those particular Harlequin had died
rather horrible deaths, so the preternatural wonder speed
hadn't helped them all that much, but I'd never seen one of our
people be this fast.

Frustration in a fight can lead to four things: You give up,
you fight harder, you fight worse, or you cheat. Scaramouche
was Harlequin; they didn't give up. He fought harder, but
when that didn't get him past Nicky's guard, his arm swung a
little too wide. Nicky landed a fist on the exposed ribs.

I felt the warm rush of power, and for the first time, it was
my inner rat that responded to the energy as Scaramouche
lashed out. Nicky rocked back and his cheek was bleeding, but
Scaramouche hadn't hit him. I'd have seen that.

Jake was between them, moving so fast, it was as if he'd
just appeared to separate them.

"No claws—you know that, Scaramouche."

I saw the claws curling from the fingers of his gloves now;
both hands had sprouted claws, which meant he was powerful
enough to shift just that much and no more. Micah could do it,
but he was Nimir-Raj; Nicky couldn't do it, and he was Rex.
Nicky touched fingertips to the small cuts on his face. He'd
kept the claws from doing much more than touching his skin.

Jake started to stop the fight, but Nicky said, "Let's do
this."

"No claws, no shifting," Jake said.

"Only because the Rex is not powerful enough to do a par-
tial shift."

"And you aren't good enough to beat me without shifting,"
Nicky said.

Scaramouche made a low evil sound that I think was a rat

equivalent of a growl, because again a small, dark-furred shape inside me reacted to his beast. Rafael had shared his beast on purpose with me, but it was still new.

"I can defeat you without changing form."

"Prove it," Nicky said.

Jake made the wererat show his hands, making sure his fingers were just human digits again.

"Are you certain you both want to do this?" Jake asked.

"Oh yeah," Nicky said.

"Very much so," Scaramouche said.

"If you bring out your beast again, I will finish the fight in Nicky's place. Is that clear, Scaramouche?"

The wererat's eyes widened a little, but he bounced in place to loosen his body up and said, "I will defeat the lion fairly."

"Scaramouche," Pierette said, but he ignored her as if she had not spoken.

Nicky did his own bounce. Jake stepped back and said, "Fight."

They took Jake at his word; even blocking the punches and kicks had force to it. They both made harsh involuntary noises, but there was none of the yelling that they teach you in some martial arts classes. Yelling when you didn't have to was for show. The two men weren't putting on a display. This was a fight, a real fight. Only their combined skill kept it from being even more violent because neither was able to get through the other's guard. They were both so fast, I couldn't follow all of it.

Nicky's fist came through all Scaramouche's punches and caught him in the mouth. It staggered the wererat, and I saw blood. Nicky followed it up with a hook to the ribs that he blocked, but Nicky landed a knee to the other man's thigh. Scaramouche covered up as much of himself as he could as Nicky blew into him, raining punches, kicks, and elbows down on him.

People were looking at Jake to step in and call it, but he didn't.

Scaramouche came up under everything that Nicky was throwing at him and hit him with an uppercut right on the chin. He'd taken the damage until Nicky got carried away and gave an opening, and then he'd gone for it. It staggered Nicky and rang his bell hard. If it had been a real UFC fight they might have called a knockout, because his one blue eye was not focusing. He was still standing.

Scaramouche came up and around with a roundhouse kick aimed at the side of Nicky's head. Nathaniel's hand squeezed mine tight. Sin gasped. Nicky's hand was there just in time to keep the kick from connecting and to grab the leg and get a joint lock on the knee. Scaramouche dropped to the ground trying to unbalance Nicky, but the werelion had more mass and stayed firm. Scaramouche ended up with his hands on the mat as he swung his other long leg up in a kick for Nicky's face. Nicky didn't try to block it; he finished the joint lock. I heard the wet, meaty pop. Scaramouche screamed, even as his kick bloodied Nicky's mouth.

Jake stepped in then and stopped the fight. He helped Nicky lay Scaramouche on the mat. His leg was bent in a way that legs aren't meant to bend. Scaramouche was trying not to writhe in agony. He looked green with pain and was probably trying not to throw up.

Pierette knelt beside him. Hortensio stood glaring at Jake and Nicky. "What was that supposed to be?"

"That was not sparring," Pierette said from where she knelt.

"No, it was a lesson," Jake said, and his voice was as cold and threatening as I'd ever heard it.

"A lesson about what?" she demanded, holding Scaramouche's hand.

"That the Harlequin must learn to respect our new comrades in arms," he said.

Scaramouche's voice was strained with pain. "They have not spent centuries earning our respect."

Nicky took out his bloody mouth guard and said, "I'm fine with earning your respect by beating the shit out of you."

"You are not king over me, lion," he said between gritted teeth.

I'd walked out on the mat with Nathaniel shadowing me, though I'd made him drop my hand. Tempers were high, and I wanted both my hands free just in case. Magda and Sin were at my back. I wasn't sure how much help Sin would be, but the lioness at my back would make them think twice before doing something stupid in our direction. I'd have liked to think that

I'd give them pause, but I knew better. Most of them considered me a poor substitute for their lost queen; no matter what my title was, I was just not good enough for some of the Harlequin.

"How about me? I'm supposed to be your queen," I said.

"You are Jean-Claude's fiancée, but you are not a vampire. How can you rule us as one?"

"Anita is Nimir-Ra, to the wereleopards, too," Nathaniel said. "She is Queen to Micah's Nimir-Raj."

"She does not shift into leopard form; I will not acknowledge a Nimir-Ra who is trapped in human form," Pierette said.

"She may not change shape, but she is still a necromancer and our new dark queen," Jake said.

"No. No, she is not. She is not our dark mistress. It was luck that allowed her to drink down the power that was ours, and now she has given it to him." She pointed a dramatic finger at Nicky.

"Not just him," Magda said, in a low voice.

"No, all the Harlequin that sleep with you and Jean-Claude have kept their powers, or regained them," Pierette said.

Hortensio made a sound that was half laugh and half snarl. "Scaramouche wanted to be your *moitié bête*, your rat to call, and your lover. He said he would show you what a true *moitié bête* can do for a queen. That boast is why your Bride crippled him."

I glanced from Nicky to Jake. Nicky said, "Scaramouche bloodied me first. I just ended it." I looked at Nicky for a minute. "Do you want him to think he can win you like a prize?"

I turned back to Scaramouche. "I'm sorry you're hurt, but even if you managed to take the crown from Rafael, your rat king, I would not make you my beast half, or my lover. If what you want is to be closer to Jean-Claude's throne and me, then hurting my lovers gains you nothing."

Green with pain, his leg bent damn near backward, he glared up at me from his dark brown eyes with more anger than pain, and more arrogance than I'd have been able to manage if it had been me. "I would make a better king for the rats, and do not turn down what you have not tasted, for I know that what I would serve you would be far sweeter than anything you have had before."

"Wow," Sin said, "with four of us standing right here and you're going to insult all of us."

"I know my worth," Scaramouche said.

Hortensio said to Sin, "You are a boy. He"—motioning at Nathaniel—"is a catamount more skilled with men than women. The Rex is as brutal in bed as he is in the ring. No woman wants that kind of brutality."

Nathaniel, Sin, and Nicky all laughed at the same time. I said, "You've got to know your audience, and you obviously don't."

"What about me?" Magda asked.

"You are a woman," Hortensio said. "You are not competition in this arena."

I felt the warm rush of energy from her before the low, soft growl trickled from between her human lips. "You have always been a fool."

Hortensio took a step toward her, which put him closer to me, but he was looking over my head at Magda. "Back up," I said. He ignored me. I hit him with a short jab in the solar plexus. He'd been totally unprepared, so it took all the wind out of him and doubled him over. I grabbed the back of his head and pulled it down as I drove my knee up as fast and hard and as many times as I could. I'd caught him completely by surprise, so he never even tried to fight back. When I saw blood pouring over my leg and onto the mat, I shoved him away from me and he crumpled to his side on the floor. He didn't move. His lower face was a mass of blood so thick that I wasn't even sure how much damage I'd done. I knew his nose was broken. His eyes were open, but like after the punch that had staggered Nicky, they weren't focusing.

Pierette looked pale and a little less sure of herself. Scaramouche still looked angry and arrogant, in pain and nauseous, but there was something new in his dark eyes. I think it was uncertainty. He'd made his plans on the idea that I wouldn't be able to fight back. I think he was reevaluating that. Good.

"I am your queen, Hortensio; that means when I say back up, you back the fuck up!"

"I don't think he can hear you," Sin said.

"Then Pierette and Scaramouche can repeat it to him later, right?" I said, looking at Pierette mostly.

She let go of Scaramouche's hand and knelt in front of me, putting her head to the floor in front of my feet; it was about as low a bow as she could make. Her hands were politely back near her shoulders so that her head was the only thing near my feet. It was the real deal, but then, she'd had centuries to practice bowing in all sorts of ways.

"She'll stay like that until you tell her to rise," Jake said.

"That sort of works for me right now," I said.

Jake made a little movement with his mouth like I'd surprised him but pleased him at the same time. "You are the queen."

"That's right, I am, and the next time one of you forgets that, it won't be my knee that I use to bloody you. Is that clear, Scaramouche?"

"Are you saying you will kill us yourself?"

"No, that is not what she is saying," Jake said, quickly.

"I don't want to kill you, damn it. It's a waste of centuries of talent and power, but if you force me to make the decision, I will."

"I believe you," Scaramouche said.

Pierette's voice was muffled against the floor as she said, "Yes, my queen."

"Get up, Pierette."

She raised her head slowly, cautiously. "Do you wish me to stand, my queen?"

"Stay with Scaramouche, or stand. I don't care; just don't do anything stupid."

"Yes, my queen."

"You have tamed another leopard, Anita," Scaramouche said.

"How about you, Hortensio? Are you still going to be a pain in my ass, or have I made myself clear?"

He had his hands pressed gingerly over his nose. It made his voice sound odd, but it was understandable as he said, "Very clear, my queen."

I looked down. "And you, Scaramouche? Are you tamed?"

"I will never be tamed by anyone save my master."

"Then are we clear?"

He wasted a serious hate-filled look at Nicky, then looked back at me. "You and your Bride have been most clear."

"Great, then we won't have any more problems between us."

"We will not disrespect you, but we have a problem, our queen."

"And what would that be?" I asked.

"That the people you are having sex with have acquired our old speed and skills, or regained them in the case of Magda and other Harlequin in your bed, while those of us not in your graces continue to lose both skills and power."

I opened my mouth, closed it, and looked at Jake. "Is he right?"

Jake sighed, shrugged, and then said, "It is not a hundred percent certain, but as a hypothesis it has unfortunate merit."

"Well, fuck," I said.

"Not enough," Scaramouche said.

"We can't fuck everyone."

"If I cannot regain my former glory with a plan worthy of a warrior and a king, then I would agree to whatever arrangement Jean-Claude wishes."

I stared at the wererat. "Do you understand what you're saying?"

"Or is the pain speaking for you?" Jake added.

"I know what I am saying, and for the return of my power, I would be whatever Jean-Claude needed me to be," Scaramouche said.

Pierette just shook her head and looked scared. She wasn't willing to be whatever was needed, and I didn't blame her. That was too much carte blanche to give anyone.

"I will not be Jean-Claude's catamite," Hortensio said; his voice sounded worse as his nose continued to swell. He coughed and started to choke, having to struggle to sit up enough to throw up blood on the mat, which made his face hurt so that he moaned with the pain.

"We need to get them to medical," Jake said.

"Yeah," Nicky said, "they're bleeding all over the mat."

I looked to see if he was making a joke. His mouth was still bleeding enough that he was having to dab at it with the back of his hand. He'd taken off his gloves sometime during all of this. If he was being sarcastic his face didn't show it. The marks on his cheek weren't nearly as bad as his mouth.

"Or everybody could shapeshift and heal themselves," I said.

"They'll get goopy stuff all over the mats," Sin said. "Claudia has told us we aren't allowed to shift in the gymnasium."

"Fine. The hallway will work."

"I dare not, my queen," Scaramouche said.

"It's a dislocated knee. Shifting should heal it."

"Yes, but in my beast form I would need food to regain the energy I expended in the rapid healing."

"Yeah, so you walk down to the area where the live food is kept."

"No, my queen. If I shifted form, I could not guarantee that I would not see you and others as food for my beast."

"Are you saying that you wouldn't have enough control of your animal form to keep from attacking us?" I asked.

"I am ashamed to admit it, but it is true."

"You are the Harlequin, the ultimate spies and assassins. That means you have ultimate control over yourself, or that's what I thought it meant."

"Once, that was exactly what it meant, but when our powers began to fade, so did our control of our inner demons."

I looked from him to the other two troublemakers. Pierette bowed her head and wouldn't meet my gaze. Hortensio was rolling around in fresh pain; apparently he'd squeezed his nose too hard.

"Are you saying that none of you can control your beast half?"

"When we first turn, we must eat flesh. Once we have eaten, we come back to ourselves and can control the beast, but until that first feeding we are mindless and will attack as if we are new lycanthropes who have not gained control of ourselves yet."

I looked at Jake and Magda. "Is this true of all of you?"

"I have not diminished in my abilities," she said.

"Because you are sleeping with them," Pierette said, her voice bitter. She stared down at the floor as soon as she said it, as if afraid of her own reaction.

Jake's face was as blank and unreadable as he could make it. "I have retained my abilities as well, and I am not sleeping with our new leaders. Kaazim is also fine and not their lover."

"Wait, Jake, Magda. Are you saying that neither of you knew about this either?" I asked.

"I did not know," he said.

Magda just shook her head.

"You guys are supposed to report to Jake," I said, looking down at the others.

"He is one of the ones who betrayed our Dark Mother," Scaramouche said.

Hortensio found his voice again, though it was thick and harder to understand as his nose continued to swell. "He helped hide the golden tigers from us. If they had been killed as the Mother of All Darkness commanded, then you would never have been able to rise to power. You had to possess the power of the Father of Tigers and become the new Father of Dawn, and for that you needed the gold cats."

Scaramouche said, "Jake and Kaazim were both part of the traitors who knew the gold tigers had not been slaughtered, and now that they have won they still have their powers, while those of us who were ignorant of their plot do not."

"So maybe it's more than just sex with Jean-Claude and the rest of us," I said.

"Perhaps," he said, but not like he believed it, or maybe he didn't want to believe it, because if sex wouldn't fix the problem, then they were screwed in more ways than one.

"Does Micah know about this?"

Scaramouche and Pierette shook their heads. "We have told no one of our shame," he said.

"If we had decided to send you out on a mission like Kaazim just came back from, would you have told anyone then?" Nicky asked.

"We don't owe you an answer, Bride," Hortensio said.

"Then pretend I asked it, because it's a good question and I want the answer."

"None of the leaders here trust us enough to send us out," he said.

"We are trapped here in this small city when we had the world to travel for centuries," Pierette said, and she looked—grief-stricken was the only word I had for the sudden haggard look on her eternally youthful face.

"I guess it is a change," I said.

"If they cannot shapeshift safely, then we need to get them to the infirmary," Magda said. If she felt pity for her fellow warriors' plight, it didn't show.

"I would request a stretcher, for I cannot walk," Scaramouche said.

"What have you done to deserve a stretcher?" Nicky asked.

"Nothing, but I would humbly ask of my queen and her princes that they be magnanimous and show mercy."

"I'm not big on mercy," Nicky said.

"Nor I, especially for warriors who keep forgetting about me," Magda said.

Scaramouche swallowed hard enough that I heard it, and he said, "My queen, her princes, and her princess, I beg for mercy and to be allowed a stretcher."

I wasn't sure Magda was my princess, but I let it go. We were winning; never quibble when you're winning. We let him have a stretcher. What the hell? We'd made our point.

18

THE MEDICS INSISTED on Nicky going to the hospital in the underground along with the rest of the wounded. He insisted he was fine. "My mouth has stopped bleeding."

"You could have a concussion," the doctor said.

"Can we get concussions?" Sin asked.

The doctor assured us it was possible, though unlikely, which meant Nicky got to go to the hospital, too.

"I can shift to animal form and heal myself without endangering anyone else," Nicky said.

"But if the concussion is severe enough, the shift won't heal everything. Let's do some tests before you change form and confuse the issue," the doctor said.

Reluctantly Nicky agreed. The four of us were going with

him, but my phone rang and it was Edward's ringtone. He was the reason that I'd had my phone with me in the gym in the first place.

"Hey, Edward."

"Pack your bags for Ireland."

"You got them to agree to bring me in on the case?"

"You and some of your preternatural friends," he said, and sounded pleased with himself.

"Take the call," Nicky said, and started to walk away.

"Hang on a second, Edward." I caught up with Nicky, touching his arm so he turned toward me. I'd wanted to kiss him good-bye, but his chin and lower lip were still smeared with blood; the blood combined with the pirate eye patch made him look even more like a Bond villain, but he was my villain, or maybe my henchman.

He smiled down at me and leaned down to offer his cheek for a kiss, which I gave him. "I take it your mouth is hurting too much for a kiss right now."

"I like dishing out pain, not taking it," he said with a grin.

"Don't I know it," I said.

"We can go with Nicky to the hospital so you can talk business," Sin said. I wasn't sure who the "we" included, and apparently neither were Nathaniel and Magda, because they looked at each other.

Nathaniel said, "I know some of the details of the case already, and it may have something to do with what's happening with Damian."

"He's part of your triumvirate, I understand," Magda said. "Stay. I'll go with Sin and Nicky."

"Thank you," Nathaniel said.

"It is not often that you ask for something like this. I am glad to see the three of you working things out," she said, and moved off to go with Nicky.

It was Nathaniel who remembered to ask, "Magda, did you go to Ireland on Harlequin business?"

"No, they were very isolationist for most of their history, and my master, Giacomo, could not pass for one of them."

I felt stupid once she said it, because Giacomo was the exception to the rule about the Harlequin. He went by the name he'd used as an assassin, but he wasn't a pain in the ass. He had been a Mongol, from what would now be considered Mongolia. He lived there when being in a Mongol horde meant that you rode the steppes, conquering or killing everything you met. If you didn't know his ethnic background you'd still never mistake him for Irish; Chinese maybe, or Korean, or maybe even from some island in the Pacific, but he definitely looked Asian and not European. He was also almost as broad through the shoulders as Nicky, and it wasn't from weight lifting. Giacomo's basic framework was just that big.

"That makes sense," Nathaniel said.

"Do you know if any of the Harlequin traveled to Ireland regularly, or at all?" I asked.

"Pierette and her master traveled there more than anyone else that I am aware of." And Magda said it like that because they were spies, which meant that they didn't all know what the rest of them were doing. Spies mean secrets, and the fewer people who know a secret, the easier it is to keep. Only the Queen of All Darkness had been given all the reports, and when she fell into her centuries of sleep, or hibernation, or Sleeping Beauty curse, or whatever it had been, then they reported to the vampire council. They had given reports to different council members depending on what they were reporting on, which made sense but didn't help us. Pierette hadn't liked us before today's "lesson"; I doubted that watching her friends get beaten up had made her like us better.

"Of course it would be Pierette who knows Ireland better than anyone else; perfect," I said.

"Do you have another vampire who knows Ireland?" Edward asked on the phone.

"Wereleopard, but who knows if she'll talk to us after we just beat the hell out of her friends?"

"Why did you beat up her friends?" he asked.

"Long story."

"Order her to tell you, Anita, and she is oath bound to do so," Magda said.

"You're the queen, Anita; act like it. Demand the information," Edward said.

It was a little unnerving that I was getting stereo advice from Edward and Magda, but I guess not surprising. They were both very practical most of the time.

I shook my head. "She's part of the world's oldest and maybe best spy ring ever; if she wants to lie to me, she can."

"You can all control your breathing and heart rate," Sin said, "but I swear that some of you can control your scent, so it doesn't change when you lie."

"Some of us can."

"If we get Pierette alone we can scare her into telling us about Ireland," Nicky said.

"We must do it before her master wakes for the night, because once Pierrot is with his Pierette she will no longer scare so easily," Magda said.

"She's probably still in the hospital area holding Scaramouche's hand," Sin said.

"And the doctor did say I needed to go to the hospital," Nicky said.

Sin smiled. "Can I help?"

"Can you be scary?" Nicky asked.

Sin seemed to think about it. "Yes, but scary enough to intimidate one of the Harlequin? Probably not. Can I watch the two of you intimidate Pierette?"

Magda clapped him on the shoulder hard enough to stagger him a little. "Come watch; maybe we can teach you how to be scarier."

"I'm not sure he needs that kind of skill set," I said.

Nicky gave me a look I couldn't quite read. "It's always good to be scary, Anita; you know that."

"I don't think that's true in the real world for most people," I said.

"We don't live in that world and we aren't most people," he said. I'd have liked to argue with him, but I couldn't.

"If they can learn anything that will help us solve the vampire problem here in Ireland," Edward said, "let them scare the fuck out of her, Anita."

"Do you want me to talk to you, or go help them be scary?"

"I heard Nicky's voice, right?"

"Yep."

"He doesn't need help being scary, and you and I need to start planning your trip to the Emerald Isle."

Sin came back while the others started toward the far tunnel entrance. "My mouth isn't too sore for a kiss," he said.

I frowned at him.

"Stop being a hard-ass and just kiss me."

The comment made me smile, and just like that all my grumpy street cred went out the window. "Hold on for just another minute, Edward."

"Who's asking for a kiss? I don't recognize the voice."

"Cynric," I said.

"My, my, he sounds all grown-up."

"I'm putting you on hold, just so you know."

"I wasn't going to critique the kiss over the phone, Anita."

"Putting you on hold now, Edward." I turned back to Sin, standing so tall, and older just like the deeper voice that had made Edward not recognize him over the phone.

Magda called to him from the hallway. "Nicky says if you're late we start the intimidation without you."

"I'm coming," Sin called back. He turned to me and leaned down for his kiss. I went up on tiptoe to meet all that six-foot-plus height halfway. His lips were soft, gentle, but his hands where he gripped my arms weren't. He squeezed just enough for me to feel the strength in his hands, which could throw a football far enough and well enough for colleges to scout him. Some combination of his hands and the kiss made me a little breathless as he pulled away. He grinned at the look on my face, and he knew he'd made my pulse speed up. He was a weretiger; he could taste my heartbeat on his tongue.

He jogged off after the others. He didn't want to miss learning to be scarier.

19

"YOU BETTER TAKE Edward off hold," Nathaniel said.

"Oh, right."

Nathaniel grinned. "I like that little brother can make you forget yourself like that."

"You calling him *little brother* doesn't help me with the age gap issues, Nathaniel. Just saying. But let's go into the break room for the call, in case someone wants to use the gym."

"He is my brother of choice, and he is younger," Nathaniel said as he walked toward the small room that Nicky and Jake had come out of less than an hour ago. It had been a busy hour.

"He's your brother-husband. There's a difference," I said.

He held the door for me as I hit the button to take Edward off hold.

"I said kiss the boy, not make out with him," Edward said.

"I'm frowning at the phone, just so you know."

He chuckled; I think I was one of five people on the planet who got to hear that sound from him. "I'm putting you on speakerphone, Edward," I said. I sat down at the four-seater table so we could lay the phone on the table and both of us sit near the phone.

"Who's listening with you?" he asked.

"Nathaniel."

"Since when do you include him on our phone calls?"

I had a moment of not knowing what to say, but Nathaniel leaned into the phone and said, "Are you still wanting Damian to come to Ireland to help you?"

"Yes," Edward said, and that one word was very clipped and not exactly friendly.

"He's still out for the day, so I'm listening for his benefit, so he can make an informed decision."

"Don't you trust me to tell Damian the truth?" I asked.

"You'll tell him your truth, the cop truth. I love you, Anita, but you'll have solving the case as your primary focus."

"Are you saying I'd manipulate Damian to get him to come to Ireland just so I could solve the case?"

"Not in the front of your head, but in the back of your head, yes."

"You're saying I value the case over Damian's well-being?"

"If you can convince yourself that he won't be in that much danger, or that it would be good for him to confront his fears and he can help you stop the killings in Ireland, yes, absolutely."

Edward laughed, and it was a real laugh, the one that said he was truly amused.

"*Et tu*, Edward?" I said.

His voice still held an edge of laughter as he said, "We're both good at finding reasons to make people do what we want them to do, Anita. He's right on that."

"Maybe. Are you okay with him listening in?"

"If you are," he said, and him taking it so calmly surprised me.

"Yeah, I'm okay with it."

"Fine. Then I'll talk to you like Nathaniel isn't standing right there, and he can interject."

"Interject?" I said.

"I've been helping Peter fill out applications for college," he said.

"So he's not going into the military right away?"

"His mother and I persuaded him to try a year of college. If he doesn't like it he can still join up."

I was pretty sure that Donna had done more of the persuading than Edward had, but I let that go. I actually agreed with Donna on this one. "I'm glad to hear that. It's easier to try college and then sign up for the military than the other way around."

"Which is one of the reasons I sided with Donna on this." Something about the way he said it made me let the topic drop.

"Have you done any college visits? We did some with Sin," Nathaniel said. He didn't know Edward's tone of voice the way I did, so he'd missed the "this topic is closed" inflection.

"A few, but let's save Old Home Week for later," Edward said.

Nathaniel started to say something, but I shook my head at him. He took the hint and let it go.

"You said something about getting me and my preternatural friends into Ireland; what did you mean by that?" I asked.

"You can bring your deputies like you did on the case in Washington state."

I said, "Outside of special circumstances, in the Preternatural Branch of the U.S. Marshals Service I can't even deputize civilians in the country. How the hell did you get it to work in Ireland?"

"You can't call them deputies here, but you can still bring them."

"To Ireland?"

"Yes."

Nathaniel gave me wide eyes, because I'd discussed with him that no one wanted me to come play.

"How? I wasn't sure you'd get me into the country, let alone me and extra people."

"First, the Irish police are interested in seeing how well the shapeshifters work with us, and them. Bring Socrates unless you think he won't work well with the rest of the group."

"Because he's an ex-cop," I said.

"Yes, I'd go with more ex-military and police if possible."

"I'll do what I can. Will the guards who helped us out in Washington state be okay by you?"

"They'll do, and Nicky can always come play with us."

"He's so not ex-cop, or military anything," I said.

"No, but he's good enough that I'd take him for backup even if you couldn't come with him."

"Wow, that is high praise coming from you."

"Just truth."

I'd have to remember to tell Nicky later, though he would probably just shrug it off and say, *Of course*, or say nothing. I might not even be able to tell if it pleased him. It had tickled the hell out of me when Edward told me I was good enough for backup, but of course my background and Nicky's were vastly different, and so were our reactions to certain things.

"Okay, Socrates and Nicky. Any other requests?"

"Lisandro, Claudia, Bobby Lee."

"Claudia doesn't travel out of town with me, but the other two, check."

"She came to Colorado."

"She came with Jean-Claude, not me."

"Okay, whatever, you can explain to me why that matters later, but right now just bring a small group that would play well enough with police and military to not make them regret the decision to let us come play."

But Nathaniel felt compelled to answer the Claudia question. "Claudia doesn't want the *ardeur* to rise with her alone with Anita. That's why she won't travel out of town with her."

I gave him the look that oversharing deserved. It was not a friendly look.

He shrugged and said, "What?"

"I'm beginning to like having Nathaniel on this call," Edward said.

I frowned harder at Nathaniel and then aimed it at the phone, too, as if Edward could see it. Truth was, he wouldn't have been bothered if he'd been there for me to glare at.

"Let's concentrate on business, shall we?"

"I'm all about business, Anita; you know that."

"I don't know how the hell you pulled this off, Edward."

"We got lucky; they're thinking about putting their own preternatural unit together, but they don't want to simply duplicate the British unit. They weren't entirely happy with how the Brits handled the last time they had to call them for help."

"Didn't they fight to get free of British control for a long time?"

"Yeah, so having to call in the Brits for help the last time they had a preternatural citizen go rogue on them didn't sit well with the government, or the popular vote."

"Ah, I hear elections coming," I said.

"It's not just the politicians, Anita. You have to know more of the history of the country to understand just how desperate they were to turn to their nearest neighbors for help."

"Why didn't they ask Interpol for help?" I asked.

"Interpol's preternatural unit was tied up elsewhere and couldn't get there as quickly as the Brits could. To save Irish lives they let their old conquerors into their country again. The president of Ireland and his party lost the next election because of it."

"Wait. This is like a footnote in something else I read. It was a mixed group of lycanthropes, a human sorcerer, a couple of witches, and some fairies—I mean, Fey, or whatever."

"Important safety tip in Ireland: Don't call them fairies."

"I know that, Edward, honest."

"Just a reminder. Tell all your people to remember it, too."

"Why can't we call them fairies?" Nathaniel asked.

"In old-world Fey it's the equivalent of calling someone who's African-American the N-word, except that Fey have magic to punish you for the insult."

"Wow, really, it's that big an insult?"

"To some of the older Fey in the Old World, yes," I said.

"What do we call them instead?" he asked.

Edward answered, "Fey, the gentle folk, the kindly ones; *little people* has fallen out of favor, but some old-timers still use it."

"*The hidden folk* is another one," I said.

"*Fey* is shorter and more common among the police in most countries," Edward said.

"I know that Ireland has kept the highest concentration of Fey in the world," I said.

"But most of the wee folk are good citizens, or they just want to be left alone to do what they've done for the last thousand years."

"Bullshit, there are still Unseelie Fey over there, and they've always been prone to do bad things."

"They don't see it that way, Anita. They think they're neutral like nature."

"Yeah, nature is neutral, but a blizzard will still kill you, and there are a few types of gentle folk that really do like to hurt people."

"But they don't, because they don't want to be deported," he said.

"I still remember reading in college about what it took for some of the European countries to deport the gentle folk. Massive magic, because they are tied to the land; you remove some of the folk and the land can actually start to die."

"That would complicate things."

"They didn't know it would kill the land back in the day, and they didn't understand that Fey that weren't tied to their land could go rogue in a big way, or the British didn't know. Apparently Ireland's Fey population was more wild and even more closely connected to the land than their British Isles counterparts."

"And you remember all this from college?"

"Enough that I looked it up online briefly after you told me Ireland was a possibility."

"You, on a computer willingly?"

"Anita's gotten much better with all the tech," Nathaniel said.

"Hey, I've totally been won over to my smartphone, and it's a little computer."

Edward chuckled. "Fair enough."

"I wanted to refresh myself on some of what I remembered after I talked to you the first time. Some of the Irish believe that the great potato famine and the British occupation not only lost them artists and writers, but their native-born psychics and witches, so they're pretty welcoming to anyone who's talented, except necromancers, apparently. Back when they let writers out of income tax, they did the same thing for anyone with a demonstrable psychic or magical ability."

"That last is news to me."

"It wasn't pertinent to you, personally, and except for me I'm not sure you even work with people who are gifted enough to care."

"True."

"Marshal Kirkland raises the dead, too," Nathaniel said.

"Larry and I are two of the very few with any demonstrable psychic talent."

"I know your gifts help you survive and be better at your job. How do the rest survive without any psychic gifts?" Nathaniel asked.

"We manage," Edward said dryly.

"I didn't mean you. You're Edward."

I actually understood what he meant by that. "You know he's right; you are Edward and that's better than magic any day."

"I just always assumed that Edward was just bad-ass enough not to need magic, but that everyone else had some."

"Nope," I said. "There're me, Larry, and Denis-Luc St. John, Manny before he retired, a couple on the West Coast and one on the East Coast, but everyone else is psychic free."

"Seems like it should be the other way around," Nathaniel said.

"People didn't trust psychics when the business started," Edward said. "It was too close to being a witch, and a lot of the old-time vampire hunters hunted witches, too."

"We had a coven that went rogue a few years back here in St. Louis. They didn't have an order of execution on them, but the police called me in to consult anyway."

"When the preternatural citizens go off the reservation, who you gonna call?" Edward asked.

"Us."

"Us," he said.

"So the Irish want us to bring preternaturals over so they can see if they want to integrate them into their new home-grown unit—is that it?"

"Something like that," he said. I would remember later how he said it, and that I didn't question it at the time.

"This seems almost too good to be true, Edward. It gets us around the no-guns rule, the badges being American. Are they really going to let us bring in a bunch of nonpolice armed for big bad vampires?"

"That's the deal, though I did have to promise them we wouldn't make too big of a public mess."

"If it goes well, no one will know we were there," I said.

"That's what I told them."

"You said you had some contacts in Ireland. This is a hell of a lot more than just 'some contacts,' Edward."

"I told you, we got lucky. One of the men in charge of putting the new unit together owed me a favor."

I had a moment to think about what it took to owe Edward a favor. I'd owed him one once upon a time, and he'd called me to New Mexico to hunt a monster that was doing worse than just killing people. He and I had both almost died that time.

"What kind of favor did he owe you?"

"You know I won't answer that."

"If it's just because I'm standing here, I can put my fingers in my ears and hum," Nathaniel said.

"It's not because you're standing there," Edward said.

"He's not going to tell me," I said.

"If you knew that, why did you ask?" Nathaniel asked.

"I keep hoping he'll get chatty."

"When have I ever been chatty?" Edward said.

"Did the man who owed you a favor know you in the military, or after you got out?"

"No comment."

"Okay, I know you keep a secret better than almost any human being I know."

"Almost?" He made it a question.

I smiled, though he couldn't see it. "Okay, you are the human champ of secret keeping."

"Just human?"

"Vampires keep secrets better than anyone I know."

"Is Tall, Not So Dark, and Handsome hiding things from you while you plan the wedding?"

"He's over six hundred years old, Edward. I'll never know all his secrets, but no, I wasn't thinking of Jean-Claude, just vamps in general."

"And I'll let that go, because you've told me all you're going to tell me," he said.

I laughed. "Hey, I learned from the best how to keep a secret."

"So I'm getting my own back—is that it?"

"Yeah."

"We got lucky, but we also have something that our Irish counterparts need."

"What exactly is that?"

"A mixed group of preternaturals who have worked with the police, or been police before."

"How much does your old friend know about me and my people?"

"He's not my friend, more a work acquaintance."

"Okay, so you didn't tell him much."

"The minimum."

"Which would be what?"

"You know how there's a certain group of military and

covert operations that knows more about you than either of us is comfortable with?"

"You mean Van Cleef."

"Did you really want to say that name in front of Nathaniel?"

"I've heard the name before," he said.

"Donna doesn't know that name," Edward said.

"Nathaniel was with us in Colorado when the name came up last."

"When you told the story it was just you and Micah in the room when his father dropped the name."

"Micah and I thought it would be safer if Nathaniel knew the name."

"I haven't told Peter either."

"You like to keep secrets, Edward. I prefer to share information more than you do."

"I know Nicky learned it in Colorado. Who else did you tell?"

"I was careful."

"Who did you tell?"

"You tell me to stay away from any hint of Van Cleef. Are you telling me that he's involved with the new unit in Ireland?"

"Not him personally, but people like him. They're all interested in the fact that you seem to have all the benefits of being a lycanthrope without the side effect of changing shape."

"Yeah, I keep being told that the military complex—not the military itself, but some mysterious powers that be—is fascinated with the possibility of super-soldiers with some of my abilities."

"Mainstream military has nothing to do with the idea, Anita."

"I know they're still giving people medical discharges if they catch lycanthropy on the job."

"But some of the firms that are more private security are very interested."

"I thought your acquaintance was Irish police."

"He is, but he wasn't always."

"Military?" I asked.

"Yes."

"Private security firm?"

"Yes."

"I didn't think the regular military or PD liked you much after you were private security."

"He's a native-born son of Ireland come back with new skills and new money to throw at a project that the government wants done."

"Money. Wait. Is he funding this thing himself?"

"No, but he's helping outfit it, hoping to prove the worth of the new weapons to the government so they'll order up his new gadgets."

"A government contract would be a lot of money down the road," I said.

"It would be, but that's down the road. Right now he's spending a lot of his backers' money as an investment that may or may not pan out."

"So it's a big gamble," I said.

"Yes."

"And we're going to help him win his bet."

"Yes."

"Is your . . . I can't keep calling him your acquaintance."

"Brian."

"Brian. Really? How . . . Irish."

"It's still his name."

"Okay, is Brian planning on following us around while we hunt the bad vamps?"

"He's planning to help us."

"Can we kill the bad vamps when we find them?"

"I've got you in the country armed, Anita—one problem at a time."

"Wait," Nathaniel said. "Are you saying that Anita can't kill the vampires when you find them?"

"We think the vampires that are giving us issues in Dublin are the newly dead. We have some disappearances, but no one has been declared dead, so they're still legal citizens with all the rights of the living. Irish law doesn't cover vampires. Doesn't even mention them."

"What are we supposed to do when we find the bad guys, Edward, arm-wrestle them?"

"Humans, even ones with vampire bites, are to be treated

like regular humans, unless they are actively trying to kill us; then they become targets of opportunity."

"What about the vampires themselves? Have they made up their minds what they're going to do when they find them if they don't kill them?"

"No."

"That's insane," Nathaniel said.

"The Irish cops really want to save the vampires that are murdering their kids?" I asked.

"The Irish are very serious about not taking life."

"Figure out something lethal before we land, Edward. I'm not bringing over my people to be killed because someone in power flinches."

"I'll do my best, but the local police take the whole peace-keeping thing seriously."

"They can't have ever seen what vampires are capable of," Nathaniel said.

"Most of them haven't, except for Brian."

"There will be no peaceful end with these killers, Edward."

"I'm not arguing that, Anita, but your reputation for necromancy isn't the only thing that the Irish have reservations about."

"What else don't they like about me?" I asked.

"Your reputation for violence."

"Yours isn't any better."

"Actually, you've still got the highest kill count, so I'm less bloodthirsty than you are."

"Great, so I'm the big bad whatever."

"They're talking about putting a human officer with your preternatural friends while they're in Ireland."

"A guard on my guards?"

"Think of it as more a battle buddy. If one of your shape-shifters does something unfortunate, the officer with them will be in trouble, too, so they'll be motivated to keep everyone on the straight and narrow."

"The way to heaven is straight and narrow, Edward. We aren't going that way."

"Brian's been to hell, Anita. He'll be fine."

"You and he have served together."

"I didn't say that."

"Fought together, then."

"I didn't say that either."

"Fine, damn black ops, but if you tell me that you've seen Brian handle himself, I'll believe you."

"I trust Brian to hold up his end of any operation, but I don't know his men. I trust him to pick good people, but he's working with the government."

"Which means what?" I asked.

"Which means that he may not have been able to pick his entire team, so be careful until we know they're as good as Brian."

"I'll pass that word on to my people here."

"Do that."

"I'll finalize my team here, and tell them the good news that we can bring our guns."

"No explosives. If we need those, Brian's people will supply them."

"I don't think I've ever traveled with explosives; that's your gig."

"You used phosphorus grenades on ghouls and other undead."

"Fine. I'll leave them at home. Besides, the European grenades you had in Colorado were a hell of a lot more destructive."

"If we need them, Brian will get us some."

"Good to know."

"Pack and get in the air as soon as you can, Anita. I'll meet you on the ground in Ireland."

"This would be so much easier if I weren't still afraid of flying."

"I keep forgetting you're phobic of flying. I should take you up one day and get you over it."

"Can you fly? I mean, are you a pilot?"

"I'll see you in the Emerald Isle, Anita."

"Damn it, Edward."

"Yes?"

"Nothing. Just keep your secrets and be all mysterious. You keep telling me I'm your best friend. You know, people don't keep this many secrets from their best friends."

"I do," he said. "See you across the pond, Anita."

"See you there, Edward."

"Good-bye, Nathaniel."

"Bye, Edward."

"You didn't tell me not to endanger Anita."

"I know what Anita does for a living and I know that she trusts you at her back more than anyone else. I trust her judgment."

"That is not how my fiancée would have taken this conversation."

"Donna knows what you do for a living, too," Nathaniel said.

"She knows some of what I do for a living, but she doesn't want to know all of it."

"Maybe, but Peter does."

"He told me you and he have been talking on the phone," Edward said.

"He's wanting help putting together the bachelor party."

"I'm your best man. Shouldn't I be planning that?" I asked.

"Do you really want to be planning my bachelor party?"

"No, but I'm not sure I want your nineteen-year-old son planning it either."

"He asked to do it," Edward said.

"He's doing fine with the planning," Nathaniel said.

"I admit I was a little worried how much you and Peter were talking," Edward said.

"Why worried?" I asked.

"You think I'm a bad influence on him?" Nathaniel asked.

"No, according to Anita, that's my job."

"I just don't think him going into the family business is the best thing," I said.

"Before we got grandfathered into the Marshal Program he was going to be a vampire executioner, but now he'd have to go through the new training program. He's too young to go straight into it, so he's rethinking his options."

"Does that mean he's not going into the other side of the family business either?" I asked.

"Not now, Anita."

"You don't have to be afraid to talk around me, Edward. I know what you do, or did, before you put on a badge," Nathaniel said.

"Do you?"

"Yes, Donna asked me to help talk to Peter about college."

"So you were just pretending not to know that he'd agreed to try college?"

"I wasn't lying. I just didn't know Peter had made up his mind. He was still debating the last time we talked."

"I didn't know you and Peter were such good buddies." Edward's voice was not happy. It was a tone that would have made me afraid for Nathaniel once, but I knew that Edward would never do anything to endanger my domestic happiness, just like I would never do anything to endanger his; we'd both worked too hard to find people to love to screw it up now.

"We're not."

"He seems to talk to you more than any of his friends here."

"He doesn't talk to me more, but he talks to me about the things he can't discuss with his friends from high school. I already know the deep dark secrets that even his mother doesn't know. You've put Peter in a position where he can't talk to his mother, his sister, his therapist, or his best friends there in New Mexico, because it would be betraying your secrets. It's like he knows his stepdad is Batman, but he has to pretend he only knows Bruce Wayne. He can't talk about it with anyone."

"He can talk to me about it," Edward said.

"You can't talk to Bruce Wayne about Batman if you know they're the same person."

"I know where all the bodies are buried," I said. "He could talk to me without telling me anything I don't already know."

"You're a woman, a beautiful woman who is tough enough to go out hunting monsters with Batman. You're also Edward's best friend. How can Peter talk to you without wondering if you'll tell Edward?"

"Point made," I said.

"Peter needed someone to talk to who already knew your secret identity. Trust me, if he'd had someone else he'd have talked to them."

"Why did you say it like that?" I asked.

"He wouldn't have confided in one of your boyfriends if he'd had anyone else."

"What does you being my boyfriend have to do with it?"

"We talked about this, Anita," Edward said.

"I know, I know. I rescued him and he's bonded to me like a baby duck."

Nathaniel looked angry then, his beast's energy trickling out. "Don't do that, Anita. Don't make less of it than it is."

"I don't know what you mean."

"I hope you don't mean that, because it's one of Peter's most important truths."

I shook my head. "I don't know what you mean about his truth."

"Fine. Here's the truth. You're right. He did fixate on you, but how could he not? He was kidnapped and they tortured him sexually. It was scary and horrible, but it was his first sexual experience and then Anita shows up and saves him. Then you're with him when he killed the woman who had fucked with him. It was you who grabbed him off her body and shoved him up against a wall and told him that she was dead, that he had killed her, and that was as good as revenge got."

"I know Anita didn't tell you all that," Edward said, and his voice wasn't neutral or angry now.

"Peter needed someone he could tell the whole truth to, and you've set him up so he can't tell anyone else."

"He hasn't even told me all the details, and I already know them," Edward said.

"He hinted and I told him about my background. Once he knew that I'd been abused and raped, too, he was pretty sure I wouldn't judge him for what happened to him. It's hard for men to admit they were victims. I invited him up to our men's group here, but he's not ready to talk in group yet."

"You have a group?" Edward asked.

"There are more men with stories like Peter's and mine than you think."

"It's not that . . . I'm sorry, Nathaniel. I didn't know that you were . . . helping Peter. Thank you for being there for him when I couldn't be."

The anger just leaked away from Nathaniel. He looked surprised. "You're welcome. He's a decent person, confused, a little broken, but strong and trying to figure out if he's Robin to your Batman, or something else."

"Did he talk to you about some of his . . . girlfriends?"

"Yes."

"And?"

"And Peter asked my advice on a few things. He wanted to know that he wasn't a freak for enjoying what he enjoyed."

"What did you tell him?" Edward asked.

"That he's not a freak. He just has to make sure that it's all safe, sane, and consensual. He and I have talked a lot about consent."

"I tried to talk to him about sex," Edward said.

"I know, but he couldn't talk to you about some of it. You're his dad, and you're more vanilla than he is."

Somehow *vanilla* was not a word I would have used for Edward, ever, but then, he and I didn't discuss his sex life. I just gave him the benefit of the doubt that he wasn't pure vanilla.

"I don't understand some of the things that Peter . . . wants."

"He knows that, and he knows you tried to understand, but his kinks are not your kinks, and you sent him to a therapist who treated his interest in bondage and submission as a part of his brokenness."

"His therapist feels that Peter is acting out about his own abuse and anger from it in the bondage and rough sex."

"Some, but whether it's from the abuse or was inside him waiting to be part of his sexuality doesn't really matter."

"Of course it matters."

"No, Edward, it really doesn't. What matters is that Peter doesn't feel like a freak or a monster but understands that his sexuality is okay. I stressed that he has to negotiate any scene play, so that his partner knows exactly what's going to happen and agrees to it all. I also told him that just because he fantasizes about something doesn't mean he'll enjoy it in reality, and that some fantasies must always remain as just that, fantasies."

"Has he told you his fantasies?"

"Some."

"I won't ask you to tell me."

"Good, because I wouldn't betray his trust like that."

"Can I ask you something, with you promising not to tell Peter?"

"Depending on what it is. I can't promise blindly."

"I guess that's fair. I told Anita that I was worried Peter was going to be an abuser, because of what happened to him."

"He could be, but he doesn't want to be, and sometimes when things like this happen to you, just deciding not to become the monster is enough to avoid it."

"He's a predator like I'm a predator, and that's not just from what happened to him at fourteen," Edward said.

"No, it's not," Nathaniel said.

"I told Anita that I was afraid Peter would take it that extra step and be more of a predator than I am; do you understand?"

"You're worried that the fact that he likes it rough, even violent, in the bedroom means he's going to turn into a serial killer."

"I told you I didn't think that was true of Peter, when you asked me, Edward," I said.

"But he hasn't talked in detail to you like he has to Nathaniel."

"You don't just become a serial killer, Edward," Nathaniel said, "not without long-term and systematic abuse, which is not what happened to Peter."

"You can be born one," Edward said.

"Edward," I said, "Nathaniel's right. You don't just become a serial killer without more damage than Peter has had in his life."

Nathaniel said, "Was Peter a bed-wetter when he was younger?"

"No."

"Does he have a history of starting fires?"

"No."

"Torturing animals?"

"No," and that last *no* sounded more relaxed than the first two.

"Peter is missing the serial killer trifecta, so he's not a born serial anything. He saw a werewolf kill his father in front of him when he was eight, and he picked up the gun his father dropped and killed the beast, saving his mother and baby sister. That's traumatic, but it was also brave and heroic. Maybe it made him more prone to violence in other parts of his life, or maybe the violence was always in there; maybe that's what helped him be able to pick the gun up and use it to kill the monster that killed his father. Being good at violence isn't always a negative. You should know that better than most people."

"You're right. I should, but it's always different when it's your kid."

"I hope to find out how different someday," Nathaniel said, then turned to give me a look that was far too serious.

"Don't look at me. I'm not planning on breeding, thanks."

"Kids are great, Anita," Edward said.

"Don't you start."

"I can't imagine you pregnant and doing our job, but I can't imagine you never wanting kids either."

"I really thought you'd be on my side on this one, Edward."

"I'm not on anyone's side. I just want my best friend happy, whatever that means for her."

Nathaniel smiled at me.

I pointed a finger at him. "We are not having this talk again. Especially not while we're planning the big wedding to Jean-Claude and an only slightly smaller ceremony with you and Micah."

"I'm helping plan both of those, plus helping Donna with her and Edward's wedding, but I'm not complaining."

"Bully for you, but I mean it, Nathaniel. The baby talk is shelved until we've survived all the nuptial bliss."

"Fine. Babies are shelved until after all three of the weddings are over."

"That is not what I said."

"It sort of is," Edward said.

"Damn it, you are on his side."

"I'm not. I mean, if you got pregnant, who would come play cops and robbers with me?"

I rolled my eyes, which made Nathaniel smile, but it was lost on Edward. "Yeah, you'd lose me as a playmate."

"You and I play the best games together."

"No," Nathaniel said. "Anita and I play the best games together."

"And we're done," I said. "The two of you are not comparing notes on anything like that."

"Would we do that, Anita?" Edward said, his voice teasing.

"I'm not finding out, because this conversation is over."

Edward laughed, Nathaniel joined in, and after a minute of trying to pout at them both, I gave up and joined them. When the laughter stopped, Edward asked again for Damian to come to Ireland and help find the vampires that were plaguing Dublin. Nathaniel asked more questions then, because he'd want to give as much information as possible to the vampire when he finally woke for the day.

"He's your vampire servant. Just order him to come with you to Ireland," Edward said.

"You know I won't do that, Edward."

"You complicate your life, Anita."

"If I didn't complicate my life none of the men I love would be in it, and that includes Nathaniel."

Edward couldn't argue with that, so he didn't try. "If we have a vampire who knows the city, it could make all the difference, Anita."

"I know, Edward."

Nathaniel said, "What haven't you told us?"

"Anita has more details about the actual murders."

"What about your mysterious friend Brian, and where you met?"

"No."

"What about the person behind the new project who isn't Van Cleef, but is like Van Cleef? Who is he? How dangerous is he to Anita?"

"If I thought he was dangerous to her, I wouldn't ask her to come."

Nathaniel tried a few more questions. I knew better. Once Edward had decided the amount of information he would share, then he was done.

We left it like that, because being besties with Edward meant I had to be all right with the fact that I might never know everything about his past. I could live with that, and so could Edward. I suspected that he had some secrets that if he shared them with me, we might not be able to live with them, because someone would find us and make sure we didn't. Maybe it would just be jail time in a government facility, but I was betting that the mysterious Van Cleef was more a final-solution type of guy, and nothing says final like being dead.

20

I PICKED MY phone up and looked at Nathaniel across the small table. "I didn't know you'd been talking to Peter in that much detail."

"Donna and Edward—Ted—suggested Peter call me for help planning the bachelor party. We talked about things for the party that helped him know I wasn't embarrassed by certain topics and he started talking to me."

"You never mentioned it to me."

"Peter spoke to me in confidence."

"I get that, but still it feels like I missed something important."

He smiled. "You didn't miss anything you'd want to know."

I puzzled through that for a second and then shrugged. "I don't understand what that means, Nathaniel."

"It means that he confided in me and he talked to me about things that would embarrass you coming from Peter. You've known him since he was thirteen or fourteen, so to you he's a little kid. What he needed help with was grown-up stuff that he couldn't have talked about with any woman, let alone you."

"Okay, what does that mean?"

The smile faded around the edges and he shook his head. "I am not going to talk to you about what Peter and I discussed. It's private and it would bother him a lot if I broke his confidence to you."

"And what does that mean?"

"It means the topic is closed, because I am not going to let you ask questions until you figure out things from my answers. We're done talking about Peter."

"So serious all of a sudden."

He raised both eyebrows and looked at me very steadily.

"What?" I asked.

He pushed his chair back, stood, and offered me his hand. "Let's go find Sin and the rest and find out if Pierette knows as much about Ireland as Damian does."

"You really don't want him to go with me."

"Damian feels he barely escaped She-Who-Made-Him once. Sending him back where she could physically touch him again seems like a bad idea."

"He didn't escape. She let him go, because she was done with him. If he'd escaped, I wouldn't take him back there."

"I still hope Pierette can give you intel about Ireland so you can leave Damian at home." He waggled his hand at me.

After a moment's hesitation I took his hand in mine. Yes, I did think about not taking it, but that would have been childish. I was trying to be better than that. We walked through the door together this time. The gym was still empty and seemed very quiet without all the hustle and bustle of other people.

"Edward may talk to Peter about what you said," I said.

"No, he won't," Nathaniel said.

"How do you know that he won't?"

"Because he's relieved that Peter has someone to talk to about this stuff."

"If he tells Donna, she'll pester Peter about it."

"If he tells her."

"You think he won't?"

"I think Edward will do what he thinks is best for Peter."

"And you think that doesn't include telling his mother that you're his confidant?"

"Don't you?" Nathaniel asked.

I thought about it for a minute and then nodded. "Donna wouldn't be able to leave it alone. It would bug her that her son is able to confide in you more than in her."

"Even though the topics he's needed help with would have been wildly inappropriate for a mother/son talk?" Nathaniel asked.

"You've talked to Donna enough on the phone and via Skype while you've been helping with the wedding; what do you think?"

It was his turn to think, and he finally said, "You're right. She would have to poke at it."

"So you're right. Edward won't mention it to her, because

he'd know better than we do that she wouldn't be able to leave it alone."

We walked into the hallway outside the gym area, and it felt like a tunnel after the wide-open spaces of the gym. I heard Sin's voice, though I couldn't pick out the actual words. A woman's voice answered him, but it wasn't until they came into sight that I could see it was Sin and Pierette. Nicky and Magda were nowhere in sight. Pierette was talking earnestly to him. He nodded as if encouraging her to go on. All the anger seemed to have seeped away from her; what the hell had Sin said to Pierette to get her so eager to tell all?

She saw us first and almost startled, standing taller, as if she were coming to attention. "My queen," she said, and bowed.

Nathaniel and I exchanged a look. If I hadn't known she would hear me, I'd have suggested it was pod people, because Pierette's entire attitude had changed in just minutes. Sin could be charming, but he was a twenty-year-old man; he hadn't had enough life experience to be this charming. Hell, Jean-Claude couldn't have pulled this off without using vampire mind powers on her.

"Pierette," I said, and inclined my head to her, though honestly I never knew what to do when someone referred to me as their queen. I let them use the title because that had been the Mother of All Darkness's title, and it was very much a case of "The queen is dead. Long live the queen."

Sin glanced back at us with a smile. "Pierette has been telling me about all her travels around the world with her master, Pierrot."

"Are any of those adventures set in Ireland?" I asked.

"Yes, my queen," she said.

"Ireland was one of the places that Pierette and Pierrot policed for the old vampire council," Sin said.

"Police arrest people. They save lives. Did you arrest people, Pierette?"

"There was only one punishment for vampires who had overstepped themselves, my queen."

"And that was?" I asked.

"The same as it is now: death." I couldn't really argue with her reasoning. I was a U.S. Marshal, but really my job description hadn't changed. I was still a legal executioner with a badge.

"Did you ever kill anyone in Ireland?" I asked.

"No, M'Lady took care of such things herself."

"M'Lady? I've never heard her called that before." We were up even with them now, so I got the full weight of her large brown eyes.

"Even we of the Harlequin with the strength of the Mother of All Darkness behind us dared not speak her true names, for it called her attention to us, so we christened her M'Lady, for it was the name she forced her pets to call her."

"Pets. Do you mean her animals to call?" Sin asked.

She turned that delicate face with its large dark eyes up to his face. "No, my prince. Though she made some wereanimals into pets, most were vampires like the queen's servant, Damian."

"What do you mean, Damian was her pet? I don't understand what the word means in this context."

"They were her sexual partners, but to call them lovers suggested an emotion that M'Lady did not seem to exhibit. She was as likely to torture them as share pleasure with them. They were at the mercy of her whims and she was . . . very whimsical."

"I thought *whimsical* meant fun and lighthearted," I said.

"Then I have misspoken, because M'Lady was not prone to fun, and if she had a heart in the sense that you mean, there was nothing light about it. She forced them to call her M'Lady much as the way a slave in the bondage-and-submission community will call their dominant *master*, except that title is usually earned and freely given, and nothing was free of cost between M'Lady and her pets, or slaves."

"Calling someone *master* is a term of endearment and respect in the BDSM community," Nathaniel said.

"Then again, I have misspoken, because it was a demand, a title like *queen*, or *king*, with nothing endearing about it."

"Didn't it bother you to use the same name she forced her pets to use?" I asked.

"Somewhat, yes, but what else were we to call her?"

"*Wicked Bitch of Ireland*'s been working for me."

Pierette looked shocked for a moment, and then she laughed, but it was laughter you make when someone surprises or shocks you, more than amuses you. "If you have the misfortune to see her, my queen, please do not call her that to her face. I do not want to lose another dark queen in less than two years."

"What if I told you that M'Lady is allowing vampires that aren't hers to terrorize a city in Ireland?"

"I would say that it isn't true. She holds absolute sway over the vampires in Ireland, because they can only rise through her bite, her line. She is her own *sourdre de sang,* fountain of blood, just as Jean-Claude has become, as Belle Morte and the Dragon have been for centuries. Only her power has been great enough to overcome the reluctance of the land to give up its dead."

"What do you mean about the land?" I asked.

"The wild magic of the Fey is stronger in Ireland than anywhere else remaining in the world. Even if someone dies by vampire bite with the three bites and the right amount of blood taken in the last feeding, most bodies do not rise in Ireland. They are simply dead and begin to rot. Only someone who was their own bloodline could have any hope of creating vampires in Ireland."

"So, a vampire that was a fountain of blood would be able to raise vampires there, but no one else?" I asked.

"Even then it wouldn't be a given. We have seen M'Lady try to create vampires and the bodies remain inert. She was enraged by her failures, and they were not infrequent. The land's magic is too alive for any kind of death magic to work well there."

"Then why do the Irish not like necromancers?"

"True necromancers are so rare throughout history that I would not think they had a policy for or against," Pierette said.

"Another Marshal has been trying to get permission for me to come to Ireland and help him on a case, but they didn't want to let a necromancer into their country."

"That surprises me, my queen. They are one of the most welcoming countries in the world to all magics."

I shrugged. "All I can tell you is that they didn't want to let me in at first."

"He did say your reputation for violence was part of the reason," Nathaniel said.

I frowned at him. "Okay. Well, yeah."

"I can see them protesting that, but not your magic," she said.

"It's what I was told."

"Maybe it's that you're a true necromancer," Sin said.

"What do you mean?"

"You killed the Mother of All Darkness, Anita; that's like a step up from normal necromancy," Nathaniel said.

"There is no normal necromancy," Pierette said. "There have only been a handful of necromancers worthy of the name in the last thousand years, and we killed them before they could grow into their full powers."

"And yet everyone's afraid of us," I said.

"They're afraid of people like your coworkers who raise and control zombies. They have no idea what a true necromancer could do."

"There are videos all over the Internet showing the zombies in Boulder, Colorado, last year," Sin said.

Pierette nodded. "Some show Anita surrounded by her own army of zombies. Yes, that might give the Irish authorities pause."

I hadn't thought about it like that. "But wait. Shouldn't the magic of the land keep me from raising zombies there?"

"It should, but there shouldn't be a case involving vampires there either," Pierette said.

"Why couldn't M'Lady have gone crazy and attacked people?" Sin asked.

"She is too controlled and far too old to risk everything for such indulgence."

"What would cause new vampires to rise in one of the cities there?"

"Nothing," she said, and seemed very certain.

"I need your word that you won't share anything I am about to tell you with anyone, Pierette," I said.

"I cannot keep any secrets from my master, for when he wakes he will know everything that I have experienced while he slept."

"Okay, then I need your word and his that this goes no further."

"You have my word, and my word is his, as is his to me."

I was a little puzzled by her sentence, but I accepted it. "I have your word of honor?"

"You have it."

One of the good things about the older vampires was that their word of honor really was good, because they still believed it really was their honor at stake, and that meant something to them. I told her as little as possible, but enough to let her know there were new vampires rising in Dublin nearly every night.

"That should not be possible," she said, and she looked perplexed as if she was thinking very hard.

"But it is what appears to be happening."

"If she did not create them, then that would be more true, but even vampires not of her making should be subject to her power."

"Is she lying?" Sin asked.

Pierette glanced at him and then down. "I do not know, but if she is not lying, then something has gone very wrong."

"What could that be?" I asked.

"When you slew the Mother of All Darkness, there were vampires that went to sleep at dawn that never woke that night. She was their power source and once that was gone they could not rise from the dead again. I would have thought M'Lady as her own bloodline would have been safe from any diminishment of power, but it is one possibility."

"We didn't have anyone that didn't rise here in St. Louis," I said.

"You and Jean-Claude are here. It is your seat of power and all the vampires blood-oathed to him would have gained in power from you eating the Dark Mother, but power comes from somewhere, Anita. You took it from the Mother of All Darkness and gave it to your vampires, your animal allies, but it cost others dearly to be disconnected from their power source."

"Why didn't they just keep going with Jean-Claude and Anita as their power source?" Sin asked.

"I do not know, but I have never seen a master vampire that

was their own bloodline slain without costing the lives of some of their vampires, even when a new master has taken over the territory. The move from one source of life to another is never as neat and clean as modern vampires believe."

"Older master vamps still tell their little vampires that if the master dies, they won't wake up the next night, but I've proved that's not true."

"For a simple master vampire it is not, but Masters of the City can take some of their lesser vamps with them to the grave, and a *sourdre de sang* can take many of their creations down to death with them. When you slew the Lover of Death for well and good last year, many of his children died with him."

"I didn't know that," I said.

"Would you have cared if you had known?"

"Maybe, but we're not talking about vampires dying and not rising from their coffins. We're talking about more new little vampires rising," I said.

"The magic of the land itself should prevent such a plague of vampires in Ireland."

"According to the police there are more attacks every night," I said.

Pierette frowned and looked at the floor again, which apparently was what she did when she was thinking hard. "Are there any attacks outside the city?" she asked at last.

"Not that's been mentioned to me."

"If it's only happening in the city and not the countryside, then it could be that the wild fairy magic itself is beginning to wane. It's happened nearly everywhere else in the world, and it would start in the city if that was the reason. The countryside without all of mankind's technology and metal would retain its magic longer."

"How would they check to see if that's what's happening?" I asked.

"Ask the little people—they're still there and they deal with the humans. Ask the Fairy Doctors—they'll know."

"Literally fairy doctors?" I asked.

She gave a small smile. "No, they are humans who either gain their magic through the gentle folk, or are beloved by the Fey in some way. The Irish call them Fairy Doctors because in past times they would cure ill livestock or people like a doctor, but they did it through fairy magic, not medical science."

"Are they still allowed to use magic to cure people?" Nathaniel asked.

Pierette didn't seem to hear him.

"I'd think modern medicine would have done away with them," I said.

"They are not allowed to act as doctors, but they are still valued as a type of psychic ability," she said.

"Can they cure things that modern medicine can't?" Nathaniel asked.

Again, Pierette ignored him.

"Nathaniel asked you a question," I said.

She looked at me. "You are our queen and our conqueror. Sin is the young prince and is treated as such by our new king. But he"—and she pointed at Nathaniel—"is nothing to us. Not king, not prince, not Nimir-Raj, not Rex, not Ulfric, not a leader of any group. Why should I answer his questions?"

"He's my fiancé," I said.

"No, Jean-Claude is your fiancé. Nathaniel is someone that you will do an unofficial ceremony with that even your own laws do not recognize as a legally binding contract."

"The same is true of Micah and me."

"He is a king in his own right both of the leopards and of the Coalition," she said.

"I'm not a prince in my own right," Sin said. "I'm only that because Jean-Claude says so."

"And you are in the bed of the queen."

"So is Nathaniel," he said.

Pierette shook her head. "It is not the same."

"She's putting a ring on his finger, not on mine."

She shook her head stubbornly. "You act as a true *moitié bête*. He does not."

"Nathaniel is part of my triumvirate of power with Damian; why doesn't that give him more status?"

"Jean-Claude gains power through his triumvirate, but you seem to gain none through yours. He chose the most powerful necromancer since the Mother of All Darkness herself as his human servant, and the Ulfric of the local werewolf pack as his *moitié bête*. Nathaniel is one of the weakest of the wereleopards in the local pard, and Damian was one of the weakest of M'Lady's vampires."

"So you don't respect Damian either," Sin said.

"I pity him for what I saw him endure over the centuries, but no, I do not respect him. The Harlequin do not respect weakness."

"I'm in love with Nathaniel and would marry him, Micah, and Jean-Claude legally if I could."

"Which is more than she'd do with me if she could," Sin said. He didn't sound bitter, or angry; he was just stating fact.

"None of the other men see you as their catamount, my prince. You cannot marry Anita, because none of the other men see you romantically."

"Nathaniel and I actively share Anita."

"But you do not share each other," she said.

Sin glanced at the other man. "Help me out here, Nathaniel."

"I don't think I can, Sin. Pierette is right. I'm not a king or a prince."

"Some of the guards called you and Micah both my princes," I said.

"Not since Micah made the Coalition a power to be reckoned with, and Sin became the young prince."

"So unless someone is a leader, you discount them?" I asked.

"Not discount, but if they are not in charge of anything else, then they cannot be in charge of the Harlequin," she said. She said it like it was just a fact of life, a given.

"Nicky is in charge of the local lions, but you don't respect him as much as Micah, or Sin," I said.

"Scaramouche should not have used his claws today," she said.

"But in everyday dealings, you don't treat Nicky as well as you do me," Sin said.

She sighed. "I do not wish to insult anyone."

"Just tell us, Pierette," I said.

She nodded, but it was more like a bow from the neck. "If my queen commands."

"Yeah, I command."

"Nicky could have fought his way to be Rex of your local pride, but he could not have maintained the leadership without your backing. Everyone knows that if they challenge him, the might of you and Jean-Claude will be with him. If he did not have the other two male lions to help him run the lions, even that might not be enough. He is a good warrior, but not a good leader, and he is your Bride, which is less than an animal to call, or even a human servant. No disrespect meant to you, my queen, but Brides aren't meant to be kept this long. They are designed to please their Groom and be sacrificed for his or her safety as needed."

"No disrespect meant, but huh? You and your other two playmates that got beat up aren't usually this respectful even to me. What changed?"

"You showed that you noticed us and did not approve of our behavior."

I frowned at her. "Magda said almost the same thing when I got her to stop picking fights with some of the other lionesses, that I'd noticed her efforts or something like that."

"We need our queen, or our king, to rule us, Anita."

"What does that mean exactly?"

"It means exactly what I said."

I was pretty sure that the phrasing meant more than I understood, but I wasn't sure how to ask the right question to get an explanation that would make sense to me.

Nathaniel said, "Maybe they're like people who push until someone pushes back, because they need to know the rules, or maybe they need to have rules."

"You mean, like Nicky beat the shit out of them and suddenly Scaramouche is offering to do Jean-Claude, or let Jean-Claude do him."

"Yes."

"So if they can't have good treatment they'll misbehave until they get bad treatment—is that it?" I asked.

"I think so," Nathaniel said.

Pierette was watching us talk as if she were memorizing the conversation, and maybe she was so she could repeat it back to her fellow Harlequin.

"Is that it, Pierette?" I asked. "Is any attention better than no attention?"

"I do not understand the question."

"Magda was picking fights with one of the local lionesses until I slept with her the first time. She literally said that now that I'd noticed her efforts, she would leave the other lionesses alone. Scaramouche is a pain in our asses, until we have Nicky punch him out, and now he's willing to cooperate with us. Magda got positive attention and behaved better. Scaramouche and you get negative attention and you behave better, so it doesn't seem to matter what kind of attention you get as long as it's some attention from me. I guess Jean-Claude's attention would serve just as well, but do you understand the point we're trying to make now?"

She thought about it, staring at the floor while she did it again. She looked up before she said, "I believe so, and it may be accurate. I would want my master to hear your words, before I answer for certain."

"Fair enough," I said.

Sin said, "What Nathaniel did just now is one of his purposes in Anita's life."

"I do not understand, my prince," Pierette said.

"He helps her think better."

"Ah, yes, I see. Then he may be more her *moitié bête* than we thought, but he is still weak both as a leader and a warrior."

"But he's very strong in my heart," I said, and reached out to hold Nathaniel's hand.

"We have no doubt you love him, my queen, but love is not enough to set someone as king above us."

"It's okay, Anita. Concentrate on Ireland," Nathaniel said.

"It's not okay that they disrespect you."

"No, but save lives first. The rest can wait."

"Even you?"

He smiled. "Even me."

"Okay, Pierette, do you think that M'Lady lost enough power when Mommy Darkness died that she can't stop a new vampire from populating Dublin with new vamps? Is that really possible?"

"Many things are possible, my queen, but likely, no."

"Why would the fairy magic be diminishing, then?"

"I do not know. I have no dealings with the gentle folk.

They do not like vampires or those who associate with them. They tolerated M'Lady because she had the power to force them to deal with her. Perhaps the Fey magic was more important to her own powers than we understand, and it is the failure of that magic which is weakening M'Lady."

"So it's not that M'Lady lost power when Mommy Darkest died, but the fairy magic fading that's hurting her power levels?"

Again Pierette stared at the floor while she thought about what I'd said. "That could be the case."

"So whoever is in the city doing all this is a new player in the country?"

"A new vampire, yes," she said.

"Why would fairy magic fading cause M'Lady's power to fade?" Sin asked.

"Because it is a part of her, as is the very soil of Ireland itself."

"Is that where the myth about needing to lie in their native soil comes from?"

"Some very weak vampires do need to lie in their original soil, or they will die and never waken again."

"It's certainly not true for any of you. You've traveled the globe," I said.

"We had the Mother of All Darkness to power us on our travels. We knew she would sustain us."

"Are you saying that without her power to back you, if you travel to another country you won't wake again?"

"My master has not been on his native soil for centuries, and he sustains me."

"If you didn't die with him, what would happen to you?" Sin asked.

"No one knows, for when one half dies the other follows."

"You guys always die with your masters?" I asked.

"Yes, but then, most *moitié bêtes* will die with their masters, for it is their power that sustains us."

I squeezed Nathaniel's hand and touched Sin's arm. He smiled down at me and put an arm across my shoulders. "It's okay, Anita."

"You didn't ask to be my animal to call."

"I was pretty much begging for it," Nathaniel said, smiling.

"You wanted anything that got you closer to me," I said, bumping my head gently against his shoulder.

"I still do," he said, and kissed me ever so gently.

Pierette tried to keep her face blank but couldn't quite manage it.

"You don't approve?" I asked.

"It is not for me to approve or disapprove."

Sin put his other arm around both me and Nathaniel, so that we were in a group hug. Touching both of them like that made my skin run warm with power. The rush of it made me close my eyes for a moment. It felt so good.

"And that is why we do not tell you how to run your power, my queen, for just that extra touch has made the three of you burn brighter."

"We all love each other," Sin said.

I looked up at him.

He smiled down at my upturned face. "Don't look so surprised, Anita. That talk we had recently about how I could be content with only having part of your life, well, one of the reasons it works is Nathaniel, and Nicky, and Micah. They are my brothers."

"Most brothers don't share their girlfriends," I said.

"Brother-husbands, then, but you're just trying to dissect it like you always do. Just accept the fact that we love each other, that the three of us love each other. Our own magic tells you it's true." He tightened his hug around us and Nathaniel hugged him back and I was held between the two of them. It felt warm and safe and good. I finally let myself lean my head against Sin's chest, and something hard and tight inside me let go as he and Nathaniel held me. The power was gentler than the *ardeur*, but it still spilled over us, around us.

"Is this what love feels like?" Pierette asked in a soft voice.

I looked up to see her touching the air in front of her. I think she was caressing the power that was rolling around us. I concentrated for a moment and felt her fingertips almost as if the power she was touching were a part of my skin.

"Yes," Sin said, "that's what love feels like."

"It is warm and safe, but it feels like power, too." She looked startled and drew her hand back. "Your power doesn't just feed on lust; it feeds on love."

I nodded. "Yeah."

"Some of us think you spend too much time with the emotions of your lovers, when all you need is the sex, but we did not understand that you feed on love and not just lust. Love strengthens you, literally."

"I think love strengthens everyone, literally," I said.

"Oh no, my queen, love can be a terrible weakness."

"Or a great strength," I said.

Pierette did her floor-gazing routine again as she thought. "Perhaps it is both."

Sin leaned over closer to me. "There is nothing stronger than love." He whispered it as he leaned further, and I came up on tiptoe to meet his lips with mine. Nathaniel closed the small space that my going up on tiptoe had made in our hug so that he was holding us even tighter while we kissed. He kissed my shoulder while Sin kissed my lips. It reminded me of all the times they'd shared me between them, and the memory was enough to make me shiver between them.

Sin drew back from the kiss enough to say, "Keep doing that and I'll forget everything but you."

Nathaniel bit gently on my shoulder, which made me not just shiver but writhe a little bit.

"No fair," I said.

"Very fair," Nathaniel said.

"Unless we can actually have sex, no fair," Sin said.

I don't know what we would have said next, because energy rolled off Pierette like the first rush of cold air in front of a rainstorm. We all turned and looked at her. Her eyes weren't brown anymore; they were a rich gray like rain clouds just before the sky opens up and tries to drown the world.

Nathaniel tensed beside me, and I felt Damian wake on the bed in our room. His moment of disoriented panic was enough to let me know that he didn't remember last night either. I shut down the link between us enough not to get distracted by his emotions, because we had other problems right in front of us.

"Well, what a pretty sight to wake up to." Pierette's mouth said the words, but the intonation and pitch were not hers. All the rest of the vampires were awake for the night.

"Pierrot," I said.

The gray eyes fluttered almost like Pierette would faint,

though her body stayed rock steady. "My queen, I see that much has happened while I slept."

"It's been a busy day," I said.

"So Pierette has told me." It wasn't just the voice; even her facial expressions were no longer hers. It was like she'd become some living ventriloquist's dummy. I'd seen vampires do similar things before, but it never ceased to creep me out.

The men had opened up our hug enough so we could move if we had to, which meant they saw this new mix of personalities as more of a threat than Pierette on her own. Good that we all agreed.

"Jean-Claude has treated us as if we were like you, some sort of metaphysical policemen. He has chosen to isolate and worry only for his adopted country and allow the rest of the world to go to hell."

"The European vampires said they'd go to war against us if we tried to rule all the vampires as the old vampire council had done, but you know that. You and Pierette helped bring their messages to us."

"We did, my queen, but I never dreamed Jean-Claude would agree to their blackmail. He had us, the Harlequin, at his beck and call. At his command, we would have chosen targets and rid him of his enemies. He could have ruled the world as king of all vampires. It is what we had done for the old council for centuries."

"Jean-Claude didn't want his reign to begin with more bloodshed," I said.

"But there has been bloodshed, Anita, so many vampires killed across the world in a fight to rule their small piece of it. We would have killed with precision like a surgeon cuts away diseased flesh to make the body whole again. Instead he has let the disease spread across the world."

"What disease?" Sin asked.

"Freedom, my prince. Vampires cannot be allowed this much freedom unless he wishes anarchy to rule the rest of the world while he sits comfortably in America."

"If you had foreseen what is happening in Ireland, you'd have used that as a bargaining point when we were discussing how to handle the new council setup," I said.

"I did not see this particular problem, because I thought if anyone could keep her kingdom safe it would have been M'Lady. That she has lost control and power is most worrisome."

"Because she was a fountain of blood, her own bloodline," I said.

"Exactement, Ma Reine." He pronounced the last word like the bird, *wren*, though I knew it didn't sound exactly—oh I mean *exactement*—the same. I didn't even have to borrow Jean-Claude's memories to know that Pierrot had said, *Exactly, my queen.*

"Do you really think the Wicked Bitch of Ireland has been weakened by Marmee Noir's death?"

"I can think of no other explanation," he said, though it was still Pierette's body doing the talking.

"There are always other explanations," I said.

"But this is the most likely."

"Pierette thought that Fey magic finally fading in Ireland might do it."

He shook her head. *"Non,* my queen. It is the death of our creator that has spread chaos over Ireland."

"You don't know that for certain."

"If you are going to Ireland, you will need us."

"We'll see."

"No one knows the country and the vampires in it better than we do."

"I can think of someone who knows the vampires better than either of you."

Pierette's delicate face made an expression I'd only seen on Pierrot's face before; he was disgusted at the thought. "You cannot compare the aid you would gain from Damian to what we could do for you."

"He is my vampire servant and the third of my triumvirate of power; that makes him pretty helpful."

"Pierette has already made our views clear on the uselessness of your triumvirate. Our weapons skills alone would be of more help than either Damian or Nathaniel."

"I don't know about that," Nathaniel said, but his voice didn't sound right, and when I turned to look at him his eyes weren't lavender anymore. They were green.

21

NATHANIEL'S EYES HAD changed back to lavender by the time we got to our bedroom and the freshly showered, though very pissed-off vampire. He was pacing the room, but it was a little hard for Nathaniel and me to take the anger seriously since he was wearing nothing but a towel wrapped around his waist. He'd forget and try to gesture angrily with both hands, the towel would start to slip and he'd have to grab it to save his modesty, and whatever outrage he'd managed to work up was lost on both of us.

I finally said out loud, "If you really want to make your point, you need more clothes."

He stopped pacing and turned to face us, one hand clutching the side of the towel. "Are you saying you haven't been paying attention to anything I said, because I'm wearing a towel?"

"No, I'm saying I can't concentrate on what you're saying, because you're mostly naked and wearing a towel that keeps slipping every few sentences."

"That's great, just great. I finally speak up for myself and you ignore me." He was almost yelling.

"We're not ignoring you, Damian. If anything, we're paying too much attention to you."

"To my body, but not what I'm saying!"

"Isn't that what you wanted?" Nathaniel asked.

"What, to have two more people ignore what I want and what I need so they can get what they need instead?" He stalked to the foot of the bed, where Nathaniel was sitting and I was standing.

"You said that what you wanted was to be desired, wanted, the way that Anita and I desire each other and Micah."

Damian frowned as if he were trying to think and couldn't.

"I don't remember that. I don't remember much." He pointed at me, very dramatically. "You rolled me! You mind-fucked me!"

"Uh-uh, this isn't my doing. When I first woke up and couldn't remember anything I thought you'd rolled me."

That stopped him. He looked at me, frowning, trying to remember through the haze of his damaged memory. I hadn't tried yet, because I'd been mind-fucked before. I knew that if the memories came back they'd come back slowly on their own, or not at all. Usually something would remind you of what had happened and you'd get a brief glimpse of what had happened, but it would come in its own time. You could do things to force it, but they all came with a price.

"I thought Jean-Claude couldn't mind-roll you, because you were his human servant and a necromancer."

"I didn't say it was Jean-Claude. I said I thought it was you when I first woke up and couldn't remember anything."

"But I can't remember anything either, so it wasn't me."

"No, it wasn't you."

"And it wasn't you," he said.

"Nope."

"And it wasn't Jean-Claude," he said.

"Nope."

He frowned harder, rubbing one hand against his temple while the other kept clutching at his misbehaving towel. "Then what happened to us?"

"I'm sitting right here and you've totally ignored me," Nathaniel said.

Damian shook his head. "I'm not ignoring you."

"You haven't even asked me if I remember anything."

"If Anita and I don't remember anything, then you won't remember either."

"Really?" Nathaniel was finally getting angry, and I guess I couldn't blame him. In a way I'd done the same thing, assumed that it couldn't be him. That he couldn't have taken control of the power we raised and used it against us. I realized, watching Damian make the same mistake, that we both discounted Nathaniel. I was in love with him, but I didn't see him as a threat. He was five-nine, a man, in really good shape, and a wereleopard. He could have been a physical threat if he'd wanted to be, but none of us saw him that way. He was the only man in my life who had picked up a dropped gun and used it to kill someone to save me. Until Nicky had started going monster hunting with me, Nathaniel had been the only man in my life who had killed to save me. Yet I still hadn't thought he'd been the one who took charge between the three of us. Shame on me.

"What if I told you I do remember?" Nathaniel asked, and his voice held a hint of warmth to it that prickled along my skin and not in a good, foreplay kind of way. It was more like a mix of standing too close to an open oven and a dance of electricity down the side of my body nearest him. His beast was beginning to answer to his anger.

I took a small step away from him so my beasts didn't start rising to his.

"What do you remember?" Damian asked.

"All of it."

Damian shook his head. "I don't believe that."

"Why not?" Nathaniel stood up then, and I was suddenly very aware that he was only three inches shorter than the vampire. It didn't seem like nearly the size difference it usually did.

"What's wrong with you?" Damian asked.

"Maybe I'm tired of being discounted in this relationship."

"What relationship? I don't even have a relationship with Anita."

"And if you don't have a relationship with the girl, then you can't have a relationship with the guy—is that it?" He had moved forward so that he was invading Damian's personal space.

Damian backed up from him; I wasn't even sure he realized he'd done it. "What are you talking about, Nathaniel?"

"This. I'm talking about this." And he took his shirt off in one smooth motion, baring all that muscular and well-toned chest. It made Damian take another step back. He looked startled this time and knew he'd given ground, but he didn't care and gave more as Nathaniel turned his back on him and swept his braid to one side.

Damian didn't seem to understand at first and neither did I, but then I saw the vampire's face grow pale, which was a trick since his skin was paper white, pale even for a vampire. "What . . . what is that?"

"You know what it is," Nathaniel said, and his voice still held anger. He was glaring at me as if I were included in his anger with Damian.

Damian stopped backing up and took a step toward the other man. He took another step forward and put his hand out toward Nathaniel's bare back. His hand was shaking as he reached out, but didn't quite touch, as if he couldn't make himself close those last three inches.

It was too much; I had to know what was spooking him so badly. I started walking to them with Nathaniel glaring at me; his eyes had gone from their usual lavender past lilac to almost a grape purple. I wasn't sure I'd ever seen his eyes that dark with anger.

He bent forward so I could see better, rolling his right shoulder down and a little more out of reach of Damian's hand, but the vampire wasn't trying to finish the gesture. He seemed frozen in midmotion. What the hell was it?

I put a hand on Nathaniel's arm to steady myself as I went up on tiptoe to look at his back, and there it was, a neat vampire bite, not on his neck, but on his back. One higher up near the shoulder and the other lower down nearer the shoulder blade. There was no reason to bite there for blood; it wasn't a good place to feed. There were only two reasons to bite there: for torture or for pleasure. I was pretty sure which Nathaniel had thought it was at the time. He was a happy little pain slut when sex was involved.

"Are you saying I did that?" Damian asked.

"And this." Nathaniel showed the bite on the other side of his neck.

"I've got one of those, too," I said.

Damian looked from one to the other of us. "I asked for more blood, so we could keep having sex. Didn't I? Didn't I?"

"Yes," Nathaniel said, standing upright. His anger was beginning to fade. He always had a hard time holding on to a fight. I guess that helped balance out my own temper.

"But the bites on your back—that wasn't so I could feed."

"I asked you to bite me," Nathaniel said, turning around so he could see the other man's face.

Damian was frowning hard. He was lucky he was eternally youthful or he'd have ended up with permanent creases between his eyes if he kept doing that often. "When? I mean, what were we doing that I'd bite you there?"

"Do you remember biting me here?" Nathaniel turned his leg to one side to expose the inside of his thigh. He moved the leg of his workout shorts to show the bite on his thigh.

"I've got one of those, too," I said, and this time I moved the legs of my shorts until I found the bite very high up on my thigh. If we'd worked out for real today I'd have felt that.

"How many times did we . . . do it?" Damian asked.

I answered, "Four."

"One per bite," he said, "except not the back."

"You still don't remember, do you?" Nathaniel asked, and he looked sad.

"I remember you kissing me." I could see Damian struggling to remember, chasing the memory, but sometimes the harder you chase, the faster it runs away.

"That's right. We kissed."

Damian looked at me. "Do you remember everything?"

I shook my head.

He frowned and looked at Nathaniel. "Do you remember?"

"More than Anita remembers."

Damian rubbed his forehead. "Why can't I remember?"

Nathaniel sighed, and started to say something, but I interrupted. "We raised more power between the three of us than we ever had before."

"So why don't I remember? Why don't you? Why does Nathaniel remember more?"

"Jean-Claude thinks it's because you and I are conflicted about the three of us and Nathaniel isn't conflicted."

"So because Nathaniel is all right with anything the three of us do, he remembers what we've done?"

"Something like that," I said.

Nathaniel looked at me, his face soft. He held his hand out to me and I took it. We'd raised the most power ever between us, and were closer to being a real triumvirate of power than ever before, and it wasn't my doing, or Damian's; it was Nathaniel's. Maybe every triad needed someone who wasn't afraid to grab the power and run the metaphysical bus. Jean-

Claude drove the bus for his own triumvirate with Richard Zeeman and me, because Jean-Claude was the only one of us who wasn't conflicted six ways to Sunday.

"What do you think would have happened to Jean-Claude's triumvirate with Richard and me if it had been up to the Ulfric and me to control things?"

Damian frowned, but said, "It wouldn't have worked, not even as well as it works now."

"Why, or why not?"

"Richard hates being a werewolf, hates being attracted to Jean-Claude, hates that he loves rough sex and bondage."

"And I used to be as conflicted as Richard about most of the same things," I said.

Damian nodded. "If you had been less conflicted about you and me . . ." He shook his head and ended with, "That's not fair, or maybe it's just useless. You didn't want me enough and you did want Nathaniel enough."

"I found a way to fit into Anita's life, and Micah was willing to open his life up enough to love us as a threesome."

Damian blinked those big green eyes of his and said, "Threesome, we were a threesome. We didn't just take turns having sex with Anita, did we?"

Damian stared at us, a look of soft horror on his face. "You rolled us. You said, *I want this*, and your eyes glowed."

"You said the same thing, Damian. I remember hearing you say it, which is almost the last clear memory I have," I said.

"I asked both of you every step of the way, and you said yes. I didn't know that I could roll both your minds. I didn't know I could roll anyone's mind. I'm not supposed to have those kinds of powers as a wereleopard."

Damian put his hands over his face and mumbled something.

"What?" I asked.

He spoke up but kept his eyes covered as if he couldn't bear to look at us. "I asked you to go down on me, because Cardinale couldn't because of the fangs. I don't like pain and the fangs make it hard to do without it hurting."

"Yes," Nathaniel said.

"I asked for it, but I didn't ask Anita to do it. I just said, go down on me. I remember both of you . . . taking turns." He lowered his hands, and he still looked horrified, but he said, "It had been so long for me and it felt so good."

"I swear to you, Damian, that if you had told me to stop, I would have," Nathaniel said.

"I didn't tell you no. I remember that now. I remember the first time I rolled someone's mind that completely. I didn't know exactly what I had done. I thought the woman wanted me. I didn't understand until the second night, when I tried to see her again and she didn't remember me at all."

"You're not mad?" Nathaniel asked.

"No, I remember what it's like when the mind powers first happen. It's heady stuff. I'm the vampire. I should have been the one helping you learn, but I was too worried about you being a man and . . . Oh gods, I remember when I bit your back." He put his hand over his mouth. I couldn't read the look in his eyes, but it wasn't anything good. We could have all dropped our shielding and felt everything between the three of us emotionally, but we were all too afraid to do it. No, we were all fairly sure that we wouldn't like what the other ones were feeling.

I got a glimpse, a memory of Nathaniel on top of me, inside me, and then Damian's face over his shoulder. The vampire's eyes had been full of green fire, his own power, not Nathaniel's.

"I thought you were enjoying yourself," Nathaniel said, at last. The anger was gone and now so was the contented happiness he'd woken up with. Fuck.

Damian took a deep breath and let it out very slowly. "I like giving . . . anal, and I haven't been with many women who enjoy it."

"What are you saying?" I asked.

"If you were both women I'd have had a very good time. My only objection is that Nathaniel is male and I don't like men, but I like someone going down on me, and I enjoy doing anal to someone else. We didn't do anything that I couldn't have done with two women, so why should I be freaking out about it?"

"I don't know," Nathaniel said.

"You have some of the same issues with men that I had with other women," I said.

"But you've got three, or is it four, female lovers now?" Damian asked.

"It was four before I decided Jade had more issues than I could deal with in bed with another woman, so three."

"How did you . . . How are you okay with it now?"

"I was bound metaphysically to Jade without meaning to be, and you're always attracted to your animals to call. If she and I had matched up better in the bedroom she might have been my only-ever girlfriend, but she likes almost the opposite of what I enjoy for sex. But it finally made me realize what a good sport all the men have been with the other men. Nathaniel is the only truly bisexual boyfriend I have. Even Jean-Claude is more into women than men."

"Most people wouldn't think that about him," Damian said.

"I'm in his head. I know what he's attracted to most. He likes men—don't get me wrong—but not to the degree he's demonstrated to keep me happy. It just seemed fair to try to bring in women who would be more into all my lovers and not just me."

"You have that with Dev, too," Damian said.

Nathaniel grinned. "He's as bi as I am."

"But a lot more vanilla," I said.

"Rocky road, maybe."

I nodded. "I'll give you that."

"It's like I'm horrified by what we did, but not. It's almost as if I think I should be upset, but I'm not as upset as I . . . Why aren't I more upset?"

"I think Nathaniel was driving our little threesome and he has no conflicts about what happened."

"He's shared that with us?" Damian asked.

"Maybe."

"I remember both your eyes glowing."

"I remember your eyes like green fire."

"I wanted to be desired the way that you and Nathaniel want each other. I remember thinking that."

"I heard you think it, and I gave you what you were wishing for," Nathaniel said.

"Our flavor of Jean-Claude's bloodline gives a person their heart's desire," I said.

"I wanted to be desired the way the two of you are about each other, so the two of you desired me together."

"Something like that," I said.

"Yes," Nathaniel said.

"Now what?" Damian asked.

"If you aren't mad at me, I'd really like a hug," Nathaniel said.

Damian smiled. "I'm not mad. Part of me thinks I should be, but most of me is just happy for anyone to want me. I think that was the hardest part of being gone from She-Who-Made-Me. She was a sadistic bitch and she tortured me, but she wanted me the way a woman wants a man. She made me feel desired more than anyone ever had before in a sick, twisted, and totally serial killer way, but she told me I was her favorite toy and I believed her. I think she only let me go to Jean-Claude because she was finally growing bored with me. I think she was worried she would finally destroy me and . . . part of her didn't want to do that."

"Are you saying she let Jean-Claude bargain you away from her because she cared for you and was worried she'd finally hurt you permanently?" I asked.

"Yes," he said, and it was almost a whisper. "I was so glad to be free of her, but I've never had anyone desire me so much. That sounds so sick, doesn't it?"

"It sounds a little like Stockholm syndrome," I said.

"I understand," Nathaniel said. "When I was on the streets and selling myself, I thought being desired was the same thing as love. I know that's not true now, but if someone doesn't desire me, then I don't feel loved."

Damian nodded. "Yes, yes. Cardinale loved me, but after a few months, she didn't desire me in bed anymore, or if she did it was full of questions about who I was fantasizing about. Was I thinking about that one customer I'd danced with, or the one I'd taken blood from? It felt like she didn't want me so much as she didn't want anyone else to have me. But even her level of obsession with me wasn't close to the obsession of She-Who-Made-Me when she was with me."

"Everyone wants to be wanted," Nathaniel said.

"Just not always in the same way," I said.

"I just want to be desired without being tortured at the same time."

His hand was still clutching the towel around his waist, but the towel had slid down one side to expose more of his hip than he probably wanted.

"Would it help for me to say that part of me wishes you'd drop the towel?"

"You want to see me naked?" he said, smiling and trying to make a joke of it.

"Yes," I said.

"Yes," Nathaniel echoed.

Damian looked from one to the other of us.

"You really do need to start being more specific about which of us you're talking to," I said.

Damian laughed. "I guess I do. I'm not sure how I feel about all this, but with everything I've just remembered, what the hell?" He let the towel fall to the floor and stood there pale and perfect with the only splashes of color against the pure white of his skin being the searing crimson of his hair and the grass green of his eyes. He lowered his gaze as if he couldn't look at us while he stood there nude.

"God, you're beautiful," I said.

He looked up then and smiled. "You've never told me that before."

"If I haven't, then I'm a fool."

Damian looked at the other man in the room and said, "What do you have to say for yourself, Nathaniel?"

He gave a nervous laugh and said, "I think what I want to say wouldn't make you happy with me, and this is going way better than I thought it would, so let me admire the view and not say much."

"Say what you're thinking."

Nathaniel shook his head. "No."

"Please."

He sighed and glanced at me. "Is this a trap, like a girl trap, but a guy version?"

"I don't know."

He looked back at Damian. "Okay, but if this gets me in trouble I won't be this honest again."

"I understand," Damian said.

Nathaniel sighed, and said, "I want to offer you the other side of my neck so we can go down on you again until you tell us to stop, or you come, and you don't want to go that way. You want to fuck us."

"I did say that, didn't I?"

Nathaniel nodded.

"You'd just finished licking my dick, both of you. One of you on either side like it was a Popsicle you were sharing." His eyes fluttered shut and he shivered hard enough for certain parts of his anatomy to shake and distract the hell out of both of us.

"Wow," I said, "I don't know what's changed, but da-amn."

"What she said," Nathaniel said.

Damian smiled. "I don't know what's changed either, but I like that you're looking at me like I'm one of the best things you've ever seen. I've seen you look at each other and Micah that way, but never me." He started walking toward us all nude and tempting.

"I hate to ruin the mood—God knows I do—but I have to get ready for a plane ride to Ireland. Edward needs my help."

The happiness was suddenly gone from Damian's face. He was as unreadable and distant as if he'd been turned into a marble statue, white and perfect, but not very alive. "What's happened now?"

Nathaniel sighed. "I know you have to tell him, but I'm allowed to be disappointed."

"Hell, I'm disappointed, but I need to get over there ASAP."

"Tell me," Damian said.

"Put your towel back on and I'll be able to concentrate enough to tell you," I said.

That made him smile again. "I like that I can distract you."

"Towel back on so we can talk about vampires in Dublin."

He went back for his towel and bent down to pick it up. Nathaniel and I both turned our heads as he moved so our view was as good as possible. When we caught each other doing it, we giggled like we were thirteen and had been caught looking at nude photos online.

"What's so funny?" Damian asked.

"Just admiring the view," I said.

"What she said," Nathaniel said again.

Damian smiled. "I love that you both want me, and I think that means that whatever Nathaniel did to us all is still working. Even the thought that my old mistress is doing awful things back in Ireland doesn't change that I'm happy you both want me." He frowned.

"If you're happy, you're supposed to smile," I said.

"Does it make any sense to say that I'm not sure I'm supposed to be happy about this?"

"Oh yeah, I totally get that," I said.

"Then can you explain it to me?"

I laughed. "Sorry, Damian, but it doesn't make sense to me when I do it either. If something makes you happy you should just enjoy it and embrace it, but I've got a whole list of things that make me happy and I fought like hell not to enjoy them, not to want them, not to do them, because they didn't match who I thought I was, or who I thought I should be."

"Are you saying, I think I shouldn't enjoy the two of you looking at me like that, but I do, so I'm trying to make myself miserable about it, even though it actually makes me happy?"

"That is exactly what I'm saying."

"Fuck that. Just tell me what she's done, Anita. That should be awful enough to help us appreciate whatever happiness we can find."

I couldn't argue with him. I didn't even want to. We sat down on the edge of the bed, because there weren't enough chairs, and I told him what was happening in Dublin. He was right. It was awful, but it didn't make us want to stop enjoying the happiness we'd just found together. It just made us sad, and then I asked him to come to Ireland with us, and that made him scared. Nathaniel didn't want him to go either. I suggested that Pierette and Pierrot could act as our guides to the local vampires, and Damian liked that even less. He hated them both for having watched him and other vampires being tortured over the centuries but never lifting a hand to help any of them. He hated them enough to be willing to go back to Ireland and help me solve the mystery. They say love is a powerful motivator, and it is, but sometimes hatred gets the job done, too. Love or hate, I'd take the help.

22

DAMIAN PUT HIS towel back on so Nathaniel and I could focus. I called Jean-Claude to ask if I could use his private jet to fly to Ireland or if we'd have to find a commercial flight. Micah and Rafael were going to be at least a few more days on the West Coast, so, yes, the jet was free to take us to Ireland. I did a group text to Bobby Lee, Claudia, and Fredo about a need for guards who could work with the police in Ireland. Which was a polite way of saying, *Avoid anyone with a criminal background*. We had a few who had started life as muscle for gangsters or had juvenile records with gangs. I didn't want that to make things in Ireland more complicated. We needed simpler, not harder. What I didn't realize was that harder was still in the bedroom with me, and I didn't mean that in any fun, literal way.

"I should go with you," Nathaniel said.

Damian smiled. "I'd like that."

I looked from one to the other of them as they sat beside me on the bed, and I said, "No."

They both looked at me and said in unison, "Why not?" Since I was sitting in the middle it was like stereo.

"There's no reason for Nathaniel to go with us," I said.

"I'm part of your triumvirate," he said.

"Which doesn't work well enough to gain us anything on this trip," I said.

"Nathaniel made it work yesterday," Damian said.

"And you're okay with the way he made it work?" I asked.

"Anita, are you trying to make Damian upset with me?"

I looked at Nathaniel and wanted to say no, but I tried for honest instead. "Not in the front of my head."

Nathaniel gave me the look the comment deserved.

"I'm sorry, but I really don't want you to come to Ireland with us."

"Why not?"

"It's a murder investigation for one thing, and that's not the part of my life that you help with."

"I helped in Colorado," he said.

"You did, but the initial trip was to see Micah's family. It didn't turn into a police case until after we got there."

"Funny how many of your out-of-town trips turn into cases," Damian said.

It made me look at him. "What do I say, that it's not my fault?"

"Just an observation," he said, putting his hands out in a show of innocence.

"I helped you find some of the people that the vampires kidnapped," Nathaniel said.

"You changed into your leopard form and tracked them for me, and it was helpful, but Micah's family was well-known in the area. I'm not sure we'll have that kind of connection in Ireland, so you shapeshifting will probably not be a great idea there."

"You're concentrating on the details and ignoring the fact that I have helped, which is more than Damian has done."

"You've had more opportunities because you live and travel with her," Damian said, smoothing back a strand of still-wet hair.

"That's true," Nathaniel said.

"I keep waiting for you to argue, but you don't if it's true."

"Why should I argue if it's true?"

"Cardinale argued about everything, almost."

"We're not her," Nathaniel said.

I didn't like the way he said it, as if we were taking the place in Damian's life that Cardinale had. I didn't have room in my life for another romantic triangle. Wisely, I kept my mouth shut. He'd just broken up with Cardinale yesterday and had his first sex with both of us since we formed our triad by accident years ago. I'd had enough therapy to know not to push, especially since I wanted him to travel with me to the place he probably feared most on the planet. Then I thought about being trapped in Ireland with Damian freshly broken up from Cardinale without Nathaniel to help me balance things. Crap.

"You know how people in romances say, *but no one is me*, or *no one is you*?" Damian asked.

"Yeah," Nathaniel said.

"That can be a positive and a negative. No one will ever be the good things that Cardinale was to me, but the bad things were pretty bad and I never want those again."

"I hear that," I said.

"Me, too," Nathaniel said.

I patted Damian on the back and Nathaniel reached around me and patted his leg. We all had our bad relationships.

Nathaniel sat back on his side of the bed and said, "You're going in as a consultant, not a Marshal, and they want Damian to come and help them. Just tell them he wouldn't come without me."

"And how do I do that without explaining that I'm a sort of living vampire and he's my vampire servant and you're my animal to call?"

"The police in Ireland have less experience with vampires than the ones here," Damian said. "It won't occur to them to ask those kinds of questions, Anita."

Nathaniel said, "If they ask, just tell them that I'm Damian's animal to call."

"Damian's not a master vampire."

"The police won't know that."

"I can't do my job if I'm worried about your safety."

"But it's okay to endanger me?" Damian asked.

"I didn't mean it like that."

"I know you're not in love with me, Anita, but seriously, if it's too dangerous for Nathaniel to go, then why isn't it too dangerous for me to go?"

The first answer that came to mind wasn't something to say out loud, because it was basically that I needed Damian to help us with the vampires in Ireland. I didn't need Nathaniel. I was willing to endanger Damian to help save lives and solve the case. Nathaniel didn't need to come to help solve the case, or that was how I saw it, so any risk to him had no payoff. Police work was often about risk assessment and gain versus loss. Probably M'Lady was now scrambling to shore up her own power base, so she wouldn't be a threat to any of us, and I wouldn't be taking Damian with me when we finally hunted the rogues, so he wasn't going to be in the line of fire either way. If I'd thought otherwise I wouldn't have taken him, so why was it different adding Nathaniel? The only truthful answer was that I valued him over Damian, and that was something better not shared.

"If I really thought you would be in serious danger, I wouldn't take you either, Damian, but you have information about the local vampires that might help us figure out what is happening. You could help us save lives, and that's worth a little risk for both of us. Nathaniel hasn't even been to Ireland, so he can't help us. There's no cost benefit to him possibly risking himself by coming with us to Ireland."

"I'm coming with you, Anita," Nathaniel said.

"No."

"I'm not asking your permission, Anita."

"Excuse me?"

"I'm not asking permission. I'm telling you I'm coming."

"It's my case. If I say no, then it's no."

"I was able to take control of the power between us and make it work, which is something that neither one of you has managed to do. Don't you think that it might be useful to have a working triumvirate of power in Ireland when you're up against rogue vampires?"

"I'm already part of a working triumvirate."

"Richard's doubts cripple Jean-Claude and you, too."

"Jean-Claude and I work just fine, and it's helped make Richard Ulfric here in St. Louis."

"I'm not sure it's been your trio so much as the fact that you ended up being so fucking powerful, and that fed into Jean-Claude and Richard. I think if you'd just been a normal animator and not a true necromancer, or if you hadn't gotten contaminated with one of the rarest types of lycanthropy on the planet, that having your first triumvirate crippled could have gotten all three of you killed by some ambitious master vampire years ago."

I stared at Nathaniel. It was like he was somebody else suddenly. Someone more serious and more . . . Was it wiser? I didn't want it to be true, because I didn't like what he'd said, but he was right in one thing. Richard's reluctance to fully be with Jean-Claude and me had damaged the power the three of us could have had, but luckily for Jean-Claude I had become a metaphysical miracle.

"I think he's right."

I glared at Damian. "Don't help."

"I thought you wanted me to help by going back to the one country I most want to avoid. She let me go once, Anita, but part of me worries that if I get this close to her again physically, she'll find enough power to steal me from you forever."

"You're my vampire servant and in a triumvirate with Nathaniel and me. Your metaphysical dance card is all filled up."

"She won't know that."

"She will if she tries to break you free of me."

"She almost killed me once from a distance, remember?"

I did remember.

Nathaniel said, "We remember."

"I always wondered why she didn't try to take you again. Maybe this is why," I said.

"What do you mean?"

"Maybe something about the Mother of All Darkness waking up and then getting killed damaged She-Who-Made-You's power."

"If she's allowing lesser vampires to invade Dublin, then she's lost power. She would never have allowed that many new vampires to just happen that close to her."

"The Harlequin think that the magic that kept her, or any vampire, from creating too many vampires in Ireland is fading."

"What do you mean, the magic that kept the vampires from being created? She-Who-Made-Me kept our numbers low to help us hide."

"According to the Harlequin, the Fey magic of Ireland itself makes the land so alive that the dead don't rise easily."

"Are you saying that She-Who-Made-Me didn't keep our numbers low because she wanted to, but because she had no choice?"

"If Pierette and Pierrot are correct, yeah."

"If that is true, then she lied so we wouldn't realize her power had limits."

"What did that gain her?" I asked.

"She's controlling us all through fear of her power. If we'd known that power had limits, we might have pushed back more. Hell, Anita, she had some pretty powerful people under her power. If they had known the land itself was fighting back, it might have made them fight harder to be free. Her animal to call is seal, so she can call the Roane, or Selkies."

"I thought they were considered a type of fairy creature, not a shapeshifter," I said.

"I know that's what folklore says, but from my experience they reacted to her the same way that the wolves react to Jean-Claude, or the tigers interact with you. She can call real seals to do her bidding and their half-human counterparts the same way that I've seen other master vampires call their natural animals and their preternatural ones."

Nathaniel said, "Maybe folklore thinks they're fairy creatures, because they didn't know what else to call them?"

"Maybe," I said.

"Knowing the land itself was fighting her might have been enough to get the Selkies to fight harder for their freedom. The rest of us were created by her, part of her bloodline, but the Selkies are born free folk. Only her magic, or the theft of their sealskin, could bind them to someone on land as a slave."

"Like the stories of the seal maidens where fishermen stole their skins and forced them to be their wives," I said.

"Yes."

"Some of those legends are supposed to be romantic stories," I said.

"There's nothing romantic about a man stealing something of yours and then blackmailing you into his bed or forcing you to marry him, Anita."

"When you say it like that, no," I said.

"Remember that the romantic versions of these stories were told in centuries when women didn't always have a lot of freedom to choose a husband. Ancient Ireland had some of the best laws for women when it came to marriage, but overall marriage was less about romance and more about land, wealth, safety, and procreation. I mean inheritance and the safety of land and even countries. The idea that marriage is about romance and love is such a new idea."

"Curse those French troubadours," I said.

He smiled. "The British troubadours helped spread the new ideas, too."

"I guess when singing and poetry were your major entertainment, that was the way new ideas traveled."

"A good singing voice, someone who could play an instrument or recite poetry and tell a good story—they were so important that some rulers would compete to have the great bards under their roofs. A good jester wasn't just to amuse the king but to help the rest of the court while away the formal feasts. Traveling theatrical troupes were welcome in all the major cities of Europe, and the small ones, though actors were usually paid better in larger cities."

"You were a young Viking before you became a vampire. How do you know all that?"

"She brought over an actor and a few of his troupe to entertain us. She pretended at the time that she thought making them all vampires would endanger our hiding places, but now I know that she couldn't raise them all. She wasn't strong enough. Gods, just saying that is frightening and thrilling at the same time."

"Why frightening and thrilling?" Nathaniel asked.

"Because to question her meant punishment. I left Ireland believing that she was all-powerful. To know that she's not is exciting, because that means that maybe I could rescue the ones I left behind."

"I didn't know you left anyone behind," I said.

"Not in the way you mean, probably, but you spend centuries with anyone and you become something to each other."

"Friends?" Nathaniel asked.

"True friendship was not encouraged, and in fact any relationship that didn't revolve around her was actively discouraged."

"How actively?" I asked.

"Not as actively as a lover that you might prefer to her. I mean, she wouldn't kill someone that you were just friendly with, but actively enough that she made certain you'd remember the lesson."

"So if not a lover or a friend, who did you leave behind?" I asked.

"You can't actually keep people from being friends, Anita. There are people that I would rescue from her slavery if I could without risking falling back into it myself. I hate myself for saying it that way, but it's the truth. One of the things I had to understand about myself was that I wasn't that brave. In battle, sure, that's easy, but everyday torture and torment . . . I'm not that kind of brave."

"Everyone breaks, Damian," I said.

He looked at me. "No, Anita, not everyone."

"Edward told me that everyone breaks eventually. Maybe the people you're thinking of just haven't hit their *eventually* yet."

Damian looked down at his hands where he was still holding the towel across his lap. "How many centuries does someone have to stand up to torment before you call them unbreakable?"

"I don't know what to say to that, Damian."

"How many centuries are we talking about?" Nathaniel asked.

"Eight hundred years."

"That's a very long time," Nathaniel said, raising his eyebrows to go with the comment.

"Eight hundred years, okay; how about we call him hard to break?" I said.

Damian looked at me. "You believe that everyone has their *eventually*, don't you?"

"I do."

"But you still want me to go back to Ireland and give her another chance at me."

"No, I want you to go back to Ireland and help us stop a bunch of murdering vampires from killing people. Police and our own guards will be with you."

"Will I have to talk to her?"

"I doubt it, but even if you do, you'll be guarded by our people and the police."

"And Anita and I will both be there," Nathaniel said.

I shook my head. "No."

"You just said it yourself: We'll have our own guards and the police. I'm not going out hunting vampires with you. I'll just be there to make sure Damian has all the power our triad can give him."

"We're not taking him back to challenge his old mistress to a duel, Nathaniel."

"I know that, but we have more power together than apart."

"More power would be good," Damian said.

"Jean-Claude does just fine without Richard at our side all the time," I said.

"Let's ask him," Nathaniel said.

"And if he says what you want him to say, then what?"

"Then we all go to Ireland."

"And if I keep saying no?"

"You wouldn't tell Micah no, or Jean-Claude."

"That's different."

"How?"

"It just is." And yes, I heard that it sounded lame.

"Yes, neither of them would help me have more power, because they aren't part of my triumvirate," Damian said.

"You both keep saying that we raised more power than ever before with Nathaniel leading the way, but how do we know we raised any power? All we really know for certain is that the three of us had sex without you and me angsting about it and getting in each other's way. The two of us don't even remember much of it."

The two men looked around me at each other. "I feel more energized," Nathaniel said.

"So do I, but maybe that's just the rush after sex," Damian said.

"I can't afford to have Nathaniel roll me while I'm working the case. I mean, how would the Irish police react if their two vampire experts got mind-fucked by their leopard and lost hours while they were supposed to be crime busting?"

"I didn't mean to make us lose hours," Nathaniel said.

"I know, but when the metaphysics first come online like this, there's always a learning curve. I don't want that curve to be when the police or Edward needs me most, needs us most."

"I thought I knew exactly what had happened and what needed to happen. I felt so certain that I should stay with you and Damian, that you'd need me there. He'd need me there.

Am I wrong? Am I just wanting our triumvirate to work that way?"

"What way?" I asked.

"So that I'm essential, and that the three of us being together does raise power and strength for all of us."

"You're essential to me," I said, smiling, and rubbing my hand up and down his thigh.

He smiled and patted my hand where I touched him, but the smile didn't reach his eyes. They stayed serious and unhappy.

"Let's talk to Jean-Claude," Damian said.

"Why?" I asked.

"He knows more about controlling a triumvirate than we do. If anyone will know the answer to our questions, it's him."

I couldn't think of a better idea. I thought Damian would insist on getting clothes, but he didn't. He seemed just fine with tightening the towel around his waist and padding barefoot up the hallway to Jean-Claude's room. Nathaniel would have been fine with it, but it wasn't like Damian at all. Nathaniel gave me a sad look and mouthed, *I'm sorry.*

I shrugged, because maybe it was temporary.

Damian looked back at us; his longer legs had taken him effortlessly ahead of us down the hallway. He flashed a grin so big it showed off the dainty points of his fangs. I could count on one hand the number of times that he had done that when he was in his right mind. Crap. Then he waited for us to catch up with him, and he took Nathaniel's hand in his and we went hand in hand down the corridor. He started humming under his breath. I wasn't sure I'd ever seen him so relaxed and happy before. Nathaniel and I exchanged a look.

"Don't be gloomy," Damian said to us both. "I remember now what else I was thinking: that I wanted to be happy." He swung Nathaniel's hand in his as if he were about to start skipping down the hallway. "I am happy. I feel happy, just happy with no guilt, no fear. We'll go to Ireland and it will be all right. Now that the human police know about her and the rest of us, doesn't she fall under human law just like the little people who deal with the human authorities?"

"Yes, it should work that way," I said.

"Then she's holding people against their will, and that's illegal, right?"

"Yes," I said, studying his happy face.

"Then the police will help us free the people I left behind."

"Theoretically," I said.

He shook his head, and his hair was still so wet it clung to his neck and shoulders rather than moving with the gesture. "Or maybe just telling the Roane that She-Who-Made-Us has lost control of the city and can't stop an invasion of foreign vampires will be enough."

"Enough for what?" Nathaniel asked.

"Only fear of her power and obedience to their ruler keep the seal folk from fighting against their enslavement."

"You think once you tell them she's losing power, that will change," I said.

The happiness in his eyes changed to something closer to rage. It flashed in green fire for a moment deep in his eyes, and then he was smiling again. "Yes, yes, they will rise up if they think they can win."

"You seem very certain," I said.

He swung Nathaniel's hand again. "I feel very certain of a lot of things today. I didn't when I first woke up for the night. I didn't when you came to talk to me, but somewhere in all the talking I just started feeling better and better. I think it's seeing the two of you." He actually raised Nathaniel's hand as if he meant to kiss it, then stopped himself with a bemused smile on his face. "This isn't like me at all, is it?"

"Nope," I said.

"No," Nathaniel said.

He looked lost for a moment and then laid his lips gently to the back of the other man's hand. He rose back up and started walking down the hallway with us, still hand in hand. "I don't care. I feel . . . hopeful for the first time in centuries. We can do this."

"Do what?" I asked.

"Stop the vampires in Dublin and rescue everyone that I left behind." He sounded so certain. Nathaniel looked at me and I gave a small head shake. We'd let Damian have his moment. Who were we to rain on someone's moment of unadulterated happiness, hope, and certainty of victory? Moments like that were too rare to spoil. Usually they came with good antidepressants, or alcohol, that rush after great sex, or the first blush of being in love when all things seem possible, and apparently, vampire mind tricks. Who knew?

23

DAMIAN LOUNGED IN the second big chair by the electric fire in Jean-Claude's room. He was still smiling, happy, and relaxed. He sat in the chair wearing nothing but the towel and even his mannerisms were more like Nathaniel's, or maybe Jason's, or even Jean-Claude's if he was trying for nonchalant. Either this was a part of Damian that I'd never seen, or he was being seriously impacted by whatever Nathaniel had done to him.

Jean-Claude sat in the other big chair across from him and asked, "Is this a problem, or a desired result, *ma petite, mon minou*?"

Nathaniel and I exchanged a look. He gave a small shrug. I answered, "Sort of both."

"Explain, please," he said.

"Damian was wishing that Anita and I would desire him the way we desire Micah."

"Not as you desire me?" Jean-Claude asked.

I don't know what Nathaniel would have said, because Damian said, "I could never be you, Jean-Claude. No one is you."

Jean-Claude gave a small bow that seemed to involve just his neck and barely his shoulders. He made it look utterly graceful. I'd have looked like I was having a spasm in my neck. "A pretty compliment from a pretty man."

I waited for Damian to get stiff and vaguely offended, but he laughed, damn near giggled, and did a bow from his waist while sitting down, and damn me if it wasn't graceful and very sexy. That might have been helped along by the fact that he let go of his towel to sweep his hand out and down as if he were holding a hat to touch to his chest, so the towel slid into his lap, leaving the tops of his hips bare. The towel covered the tops of his thighs and the critical area of his lap, but not much else as he settled back into the chair.

"You have never taken a compliment of that nature from me with such grace, Damian," Jean-Claude said.

The other vampire smiled. "I am sorry for that, Jean-Claude, truly."

"You are comfortable with me saying you are pretty, attractive even?"

"You are one of the most beautiful people I have ever seen. Why would it not be a compliment coming from you? Most people live their whole lives waiting for someone like you to want them."

Jean-Claude narrowed his eyes and took in a long breath, and let it out even slower. "I do see your problem, my pretties."

"I did not mean to do this," Nathaniel said.

"It's like he's drunk," I said.

"Not drunk, *ma petite*, but freed of his usual doubts and personal issues. You have had our werewolf, Richard, almost this relaxed through my powers."

I thought about it, and finally nodded. "I have, but it didn't last like this, or get . . . stronger."

"Is he getting more at ease as time goes on?"

Nathaniel and I both nodded.

"That is interesting. I offered the ability to be at ease to Richard and he agreed, but he could not let himself sink into it completely. He fought against it, because so much of what vexes him are lines that he does not wish to cross."

"Richard would so do you, if he could get out of his own way," Damian said, and he laughed again.

"Bluntly put, but I believe he would have done so at least once by now if his issues were not entrenched so deeply in his psyche."

"What man doesn't like dishing it out?" Damian said.

"He does seem intoxicated," Jean-Claude said, looking at us.

"Why is it just Damian and not all three of us?" I asked.

"Nathaniel was in control. In effect he played master so he would not be . . . intoxicated."

"Okay, why isn't it hitting me?"

"For the same reason that my powers do not intoxicate you."

"And that reason would be?" I asked.

"You are a master in your own right, as is Richard."

"So we're powerful enough to fight off the effects?" I asked.

"And I believe that neither of you wishes the effects to be permanent."

"You are too far away," Damian said, holding his hands out to the room.

"Whom are you addressing?" Jean-Claude asked.

Damian blinked and seemed to have to think harder than the question warranted. "No offense, Jean-Claude, but I was addressing Anita or Nathaniel."

"Do you have a preference for which of them comes to hold your hand?"

Again it seemed to require more thinking than it should have, but finally Damian said, "I don't . . . I don't think so, but I very much want to touch one of them."

"He was himself when we first got to the room after he woke up," I said.

"Go hold his hand, *ma petite*. Let us see what happens."

I wasn't sure how much I liked being an experiment, but I went because Damian's face was losing that happy glow. It was almost as if sadness were seeping in as the happiness faded. Surely there had to be more than two choices for him. What had Nathaniel's mind-fuck done to Damian?

I took his outstretched hand in mine; there was a hum of power as our fingers touched, and as more of our hands touched, the power rose until when we settled our palms against each other's, it was like a jolt of electricity, except it didn't feel bad; it felt good. It sped my pulse until I had to fight not to pant as if I'd been kissing someone too long and too hard, and forgotten to take a deep enough breath.

"Wow," I said, "that's new."

"That was amazing," Damian said; his face was flushed as if he'd taken more blood from somewhere.

"What were you thinking when you touched him, *ma petite*?"

"Nothing. I mean that I didn't like being the experiment and that I didn't want him sad. I preferred him happy to sad, or something like that."

"And you, Damian, what were you thinking?"

"That I wanted the power to rise between us. I want what Nathaniel did to raise our power level."

"Why?" Jean-Claude asked.

"To have more power, of course." He started rubbing his thumb along my knuckles as he said it.

"Most vampires would mean that, but you do not. You said the expected. We want the truth."

"I . . ." He looked up at me, then at Nathaniel, who was still standing in front of the fireplace halfway between the two chairs. He held his hand out mutely for the other man.

Nathaniel moved toward us, but Jean-Claude said, "Let him answer the question first, *mon minou*."

I squeezed Damian's hand and said, "The truth, Damian, just tell us."

He swallowed hard enough that I could watch his throat work and see the pulse in the side of his neck. He was a vampire; they didn't always have a pulse, and they certainly didn't have such a rich, throbbing beat in the sides of their necks.

"If we truly raise power for each other, if Nathaniel has finally figured out how to get our triumvirate to work, then he will have to come with us to Ireland."

"Why do you wish him to come?" Jean-Claude asked.

Damian looked at the floor; as his happiness receded, so did the easy confidence. He kept one hand in mine, but the other pulled at the towel, trying to raise it higher up his body. The bold vampire who hadn't seemed to care if the towel stayed, or fell, was gone. This was the Damian I knew: not shy, but not comfortable with being nude in front of other men, or certain people in general. He saw nudity the way I saw it, as a type of vulnerability.

"I don't know," he said at last, but he stared at the floor as he said it. I don't think any of us believed him.

Jean-Claude motioned to Nathaniel, and he came to us, laying his hand on Damian's bare shoulder. It wasn't a lover's touch, just a friend's hand on your shoulder when you are feeling sad. Damian flinched and started to pull away from that friendly touch, and then he stopped. He didn't just stop moving away; he stopped moving in that way that the older vampires could. His energy, the flow and hum of him, was almost not there at all. His hand wasn't warm and alive in mine anymore; it was like trying to hold hands with a mannequin, or some kind of lifelike doll, but it wasn't alive. Whatever I was touching wasn't alive. I'd always hated it when Jean-Claude did it. I didn't like it any better now.

Nathaniel shook him by the shoulder. "Don't do this to us, Damian. Don't go away like this."

Damian looked up then, his eyes almost flat without the shine of living eyes. He'd said that She-Who-Made-Him had killed him in battle that night so long ago. In that moment I understood what he meant.

I tried to pull my hand out of his, but his fingers just stayed around mine; it was like holding a corpse's hand. "Either feel alive or let me go, Damian. I mean it."

"I still have to do whatever you order me to do," he said. It was like magic—his hand just felt alive again.

"Fine. Then why do you want Nathaniel to come with us to Ireland?" I asked.

He shook his head.

"Say his name, *ma petite*. You must be specific or he has room to wiggle."

"Damian, tell me why you want Nathaniel to come with us to Ireland. Tell me the true reason you want him to come with us."

He shook his head. "I don't . . ."

"Damian," Nathaniel said, "why do you want me to come with you to Ireland?"

The vampire sighed and again I was taken by the thick, beating pulse in the side of his neck. I wanted to lick the side of his neck and feel the beat of his life against my tongue.

"Now I have to obey both of you." He looked up at me and his green eyes were so alive and so angry. He turned the intensity of his gaze to Nathaniel. "I feel braver when you're with me. It takes everything for me to fight off the feeling of euphoria. I don't remember feeling this good, maybe ever." He put his hand up to cover Nathaniel's where he was still touching the vampire's shoulder. The towel began to slide back down to pool in his lap.

"I wanted someone to desire me the way you and Anita seem to want Micah, and you made that wish come true. You wanted me to want you the way I want Anita, and I can't seem to stop you from getting your wish either." He turned and looked at me. "What did you wish for, Anita? What did you want from us? What did you want the three of us to be?"

I thought about it for a minute. "I've thought life would be easier for a while if you were a little more bisexual."

Damian laughed then, and it was part amusement and part something that wasn't light or funny at all. It wasn't exactly bitterness, but if irony had a sound, that was it. "I don't think I'm bisexual, but I may be Nathaniel-sexual." He looked up at Nathaniel.

"You wanted to be desired. I wanted you happy and not sad about Cardinale. Did I do a bad thing to us?"

"I do not know, but I know that with you and Anita beside me I am brave enough to go back and face her."

"We are not going to face her, Damian. We don't have to face her."

"Maybe not to save the humans that are being killed, but once we have stopped the plague of vampires in Dublin, I want the human authorities to help us free the rest of the people she is holding captive, Anita." He turned back to give me the full weight of that emerald gaze of his, but there was a purpose in it that I hadn't seen before.

"Can we do that without messing things up for you with the European vampires?" I asked, looking at Jean-Claude.

"One of the Harlequin told us that what's happening in Ireland may be because we killed Marmee Noir, and we aren't sending them back out to spy on all the other vampires, so we don't know what's happening," Nathaniel said.

I asked Jean-Claude, "They said that some lesser vamps didn't wake up the night after we killed the Mother of All Darkness. Since no one here in St. Louis died, or for that matter no one I know of in this country, I didn't think about Europe. Did you know?"

"That some lesser vampires would die and not reawaken at dusk if we killed her? That was possible."

"You didn't tell me it was possible," I said, and felt that first flush of anger.

"*Ma petite*, you know that when masters are injured, they reach out to their servants and the vampires that are blood-oathed to them for power to heal themselves and stay alive."

"Yeah, so what?"

"What did you think the Mother of All Vampires would do when she felt herself fading, dying? Did you not think that she would reach out to her children and use them in an attempt to save herself?"

"I . . . No, I didn't," I said.

"I kept nothing from you, *ma petite*. You simply failed to want to understand what might happen. You had the same knowledge of her and vampires as I did. If you did not know that slaying her would kill some of her lesser children, it is because you did not wish to know."

"That's harsher than you usually talk to her," Nathaniel said.

"Perhaps I am angry with myself tonight? Perhaps seeing Damian holding your hand shows me yet again the mistakes I made with Richard in my attempt not to force myself on him."

Damian picked up Nathaniel's hand in his and brought our hands together in front of him so that he could lay a soft kiss on first my hand and then Nathaniel's. "No, Jean-Claude. Richard was brave when you met him. He knew who he was and what he wanted out of life. What bravery I had was used up centuries ago by her. I knew only I wished to be free of her, but beyond that I had lost everything I was, or wanted to be. I was directionless. Richard was never that, from what I know of him. Nathaniel has given me back my bearings. He has given me back a star to hang in the sky, a fixed mark that will guide me home." He kissed the back of Nathaniel's hand again. "He is my star."

"And what is Anita to you, Damian?" Jean-Claude asked.

"She is my master. She is wolf-kissed, beloved by the eagles."

"Very poetic," he said.

"It sounds pretty," I said, "but its meaning isn't."

Damian looked up at me. "It is the highest compliment for a warrior among my people."

"And an insult depending on how it was used."

"How do you know that, *ma petite*?"

"I'm not sure, but I know I'm right."

"Is she right, Viking?" Jean-Claude asked.

"We used to say of a great leader that the eagles must have cried out on the day he was born, for they knew he would feed them many corpses. The wolves must have howled with joy when you were born, because they knew you would feed them well."

"So wolf-kissed and beloved by eagles is a way of saying that Anita is a great leader and kills a lot of people?" Nathaniel asked.

"It is a great compliment," Damian said.

I smiled, almost laughed. "I guess I do rack up the body count."

"The vampires have given you two honor names, Anita. No other vampire hunter has ever been given two names by us."

"I've been the Executioner for a long time."

"But your other nickname among us is fresher, *ma petite*."

"Yeah," I said.

"War," he said.

"And Edward is Death," Nathaniel said.

"You are traveling to Ireland with two of the horsemen of the apocalypse," Jean-Claude said.

"Kaazim talked about the fact that there should be a plural for *apocalypse*, because the Harlequin have stopped so many of them," I said.

"To that, I cannot speak, but I know that you are sharing more memories with Damian, because you understood his compliments before he explained them."

"We are a triumvirate," I said.

"I think you are one, at long last in more than just name and metaphysics."

"What if Nathaniel rolls us again?" I asked.

"I think now that he knows he can, he will work harder not to bespell you. Won't you, *mon minou*?"

"I didn't mean to do it this time."

Damian said, "That's it. That's what you've done to me. You've bespelled me," and he wasn't looking at me or Jean-Claude when he said it.

24

NATHANIEL AND I were in our bedroom packing when Bobby Lee knocked at the door and asked to come in. He came to stand in the center of the room and was uneasy. That was the only word I had for it. It wasn't like him.

I turned and looked at him. "What's wrong?"

Nathaniel turned with the neatly folded clothes in his hands. I heard him sniff the air, and I was betting Bobby Lee smelled like anxiety. It had a scent, or so I was told by all my wereanimal friends.

"I can't go with you to Ireland."

"I'm sorry for that. Edward requested you specifically," I said.

"None of the wererats can go with you."

"Excuse me. Repeat that, because I could not have heard you right."

Bobby Lee sighed, then said, "Rafael says that you had an agreement that if you tested positive for rat lycanthropy, he would be your beast half."

"Yeah. So what?"

"You just tested positive last week. You and he haven't had time to formalize it."

"We'll worry about that when I come back from Ireland."

Bobby Lee shook his head. He took off his wire-frame glasses and rubbed the bridge of his nose like he was tired. His eyes without the glasses showed the tired more. "In an emergency you reach out to anyone close to you, Anita. You've tied more animals to call to you accidentally than on purpose, right?"

"I guess."

He put his glasses back on and looked at Nathaniel. "Help me out here."

Nathaniel shook his head. "I'm going with Anita to Ireland. You've just told us that some of our best people can't come with us. Since you're potentially endangering both of us, why should I want to help you?"

"There are good people for this job who aren't rats," Bobby Lee said.

"Like who?" I asked.

"Nicky for one."

"Nicky was going with us anyway. Name someone else."

"Wait," Nathaniel said. "Why can't the wererats go with us?"

"Can we all agree that Anita has tied more of her animal halves to her through metaphysical emergencies than on purpose?" he asked.

Nathaniel and I exchanged a look, and finally we both shrugged. "Sure, I concede that."

"Okay, then, Rafael says that we can't travel with you just in case you accidentally turn to one of us. He is our king and it's either him as your rat, or no one."

"I've been carrying hyena lycanthropy for months now and I haven't accidentally made one of them my beastie. I'm even taking Socrates with me and Narcissus is cool with it."

"You've already made it clear to Narcissus that he has no chance of being your hyena half. You could do worse than Socrates."

"I'll be sure and tell him you said that."

"Anita, please, this is an order from my king. I can't disobey it, or him." He clenched his jaw and looked like he might even be grinding his teeth.

"Fine. Besides Nicky, who else do you trust to replace you?"

"Kaazim and Jake are going," he said.

"That's a good start," I said.

"You need guards who can double as food, and none of us qualifies since Rafael dictated that he's the only wererat you feed on."

"I'm aware of that, which is why Fortune and Echo are going, along with Magda and her master, Giacomo."

"And you're taking Damian and Nathaniel," he said.

"Yes, but we're not going as just food," Nathaniel said.

Bobby Lee looked surprised, before he could stop himself. He went back to a neutral expression, but the damage was done. "I know you're one of Anita's fiancés."

Nathaniel's energy whispered across my skin like a warm wind.

Bobby Lee must have felt it, too, because he said, "I know you're one of Anita's fiancés, and that makes you more than just food."

The wind felt hotter, more summer than spring, as Nathaniel said, "I'm Anita's leopard to call, and part of her triumvirate of power."

"I know that," Bobby Lee said.

"Do you?" Nathaniel said, and his power didn't just bleed over onto me and whisper sweet nothings to my inner leopard. It spilled out into the room in a way that I'd never felt his power do before; it was closer to how Richard's energy worked when he was upset.

Bobby Lee's hands clenched. I watched the tension in his shoulders and arms as he fought to relax.

Nathaniel's power swirled through the room deeper, warmer, hot and aimed not at me but at the wererat. He wasn't attacking him, but he was letting him know to be careful. It was a type of metaphysical posturing, and totally not how Nathaniel usually acted around anyone, let alone Bobby Lee.

The wererat took a deep breath and let it out slow. He was still fighting the tension in his own body, because a display like what Nathaniel was doing could be a precursor to a fight. It was certainly a metaphysical slap in the face to a wereanimal as dominant as Bobby Lee.

I said, "Nathaniel, I don't know what you're trying to prove, but . . ."

"No, Anita, he doesn't get to dismiss me like that."

"Be careful, Nathaniel. You don't want a new power level to make you forget," Bobby Lee said.

"Forget what?" Nathaniel said, and his voice held a purring edge to it.

"That I'm dominant to you, and I teach some of the fight classes you take."

Nathaniel's power flexed; that was the only word I had for the sensation of the heat expanding and contracting as if the energy were trying to wrap around us.

I looked at my calm boy, the one who never made trouble like this. "Don't do this," I said.

"This is your last warning. I don't care if you are Anita's fiancé."

"I don't want to fight, Bobby Lee, but I'm beyond tired of everyone discounting me and Damian."

"You don't want to fight? Ya coulda fooled me," Bobby Lee said.

"I'm going to have to second that," I said.

"I've tried just being nice, but that doesn't get you respected by people like him."

"People like me? What's that supposed to mean?" Bobby Lee asked.

"The big athletic guys who have been big and athletic for most of their lives. The ones who played sports. The natural athletes. Military. Police. All the guy-guys. I can't win points with any of you for cooking, cleaning, because that's wimmin's work."

I was staring at Nathaniel as if I'd never seen him before, and I hadn't seen this side of him. I knew that guy-guys confused him and he'd never fit into their world, but this level of bitterness was a surprise to me.

"You're a dancer. That's athletic," Bobby Lee said.

"But it's not football, is it?" Nathaniel shook his head, his power so thick in the room now it was hard to breathe past it. It wasn't calling my inner beasts like most of the wereanimals did when they started doing shit like this; it was almost more like warm vampire power than wereanimal energy. It was too warm, too alive, to be vampire, but it just felt like power. The kind that vamps threw around to impress or attack one another, and to torment the lesser beings.

"Back down, Nathaniel," I demanded.

"Him first."

"If you hadn't noticed, Bobby Lee is doing his best not to throw more energy onto this little fire. His control is admirable, which is more than I can say for yours."

"You heard him, Anita. He doesn't count our triumvirate as important."

"Until right now, only Anita had gained power, and she's gotten the respect that deserved."

"And now?" Nathaniel asked, his voice purring along my skin as if his breath had touched me for real. It made me shiver and have to catch my breath. It was something Jean-Claude would do, but not Nathaniel.

"What are you trying to prove, Nathaniel?" I asked, rubbing my hands along my arms.

"Now you're proving that the only reason you've been nice up to now is that you didn't have enough power to be mean," Bobby Lee said.

The power from Nathaniel faltered as if magic could trip over its own feet.

The door opened without a knock. It was Damian. "What are you doing in here?"

It was while Nathaniel and I looked at the door that Bobby Lee proved that he was as fast as Nicky had been in practice. He went from standing still to being up against Nathaniel with a naked blade against his neck.

We all froze, because any movement could make things worse, so best to think carefully before you act. Honestly, I froze because it was just so damned unexpected that I didn't know what to do. Bobby Lee wasn't a bad guy. He wasn't even one of the guards who were a pain in my ass. Until this moment I'd have trusted him damn near implicitly.

His voice came low and careful. "Power is like strength. It means nothing if you don't know what to do with it."

"You've made your point, Bobby Lee," I said.

Damian started walking farther into the room.

"Have I made my point, Nathaniel?"

Nathaniel spoke carefully with the blade against his neck. "Powers down."

"You powered down because I startled you, not on purpose. It takes time to learn how to use magic, just like muscles." He started to ease the knife back from Nathaniel, then pushed it in tighter.

"Bobby Lee," I said.

"Tell your other man to back off."

I looked at Damian, and he was behind the wererat with a blade in his hand. I'd never seen Damian carry a knife; a sword, but not a knife. "What the hell are you doing?"

"Defending us."

"I'm not the enemy," Bobby Lee said.

"You have a knife at my friend's neck."

"I'm teaching a lesson."

"What lesson?" Damian asked.

"The next person he throws that kind of power at won't be teaching, or playing; they'll just kill him."

"We get it; now everyone back down," I said.

"Tell your vampire to back off first."

"Damian."

"Tell him to take the blade away from Nathaniel's neck."

"Bobby Lee."

"He backs up first."

"Damian, put the knife up," I ordered. He should have just done what I said, but for the first time ever he didn't. What the hell was happening? I tried again. "Damian, put up your knife, now!"

"I don't seem to have to." He sounded puzzled, as if he wasn't sure what to do with the fact.

The door opened; I had a glimpse of black-and-white curls and knew it was Domino. He held his hands up to show that he meant no harm. His voice sounded more than just regular normal—it was that false cheerful voice you use when trying to de-escalate, rather than push things further. "Who's throwing all the magic around?" he asked.

"Nathaniel," I said.

He didn't look surprised, just took it in stride. "What's up, Bobby Lee?"

"Nothing much. You?" His voice sounded perfectly ordinary, as if he weren't holding a blade to the neck of someone he was supposed to be protecting.

"You know that Nathaniel wouldn't really hurt you. He's just a little drunk on the new magic," Domino said.

"He doesn't know how to use it as an offensive weapon yet."

"Then why are you holding a knife to him?"

"To prove to him that power won't keep him safe from a trained attacker."

"I think you've made your point," Domino said; he was walking farther into the room as he talked. He was close enough now that I could see his guns clearly against the black-on-black clothing. Some of the guards carried knives; he didn't like blades, but I knew he had a collapsible baton, an ASP, on him somewhere. I could see his fire-colored eyes; of all the clan tigers, the black and red had the most inhuman-looking eyes. He was part black tiger and his eyes and black curls showed that. The white tiger part of his mixed heritage only showed in the few white curls scattered through the black.

"Now I'm doing it because his friend's behind me with a knife."

"Damian, would you really stab him?" Domino asked.

"If he hurts Nathaniel, yes."

"Are you really going to hurt Nathaniel, Bobby Lee?"

"I guess not."

"Then everyone put their knives up," Domino said.

"Yeah, what he said," I said, because I had no idea how things had gotten so out of hand. Normally I'd have picked someone to take out and de-escalate without needing help, but it was Nathaniel and Bobby Lee. One I didn't want to hurt, and the other one I didn't want to throw down on, because I wasn't sure I'd win. They were usually two of my most dependable and reasonable people. Damian was usually reasonable, too, and usually had to obey any direct order I gave him. What the hell was wrong with all of them?

"If Damian puts his knife up, I'll be happy to," Bobby Lee said.

Domino was standing nearly beside the vampire as he said, "How about it, Damian?"

He stared down at the knife in his hand, as if he'd just seen it. "I don't know why I did that."

Nathaniel's voice was very careful, and suddenly I could

feel the press of the blade against his throat as if it were mine. "I think it was my fault."

"First, Damian puts his knife away, and then Bobby Lee is going to take the knife away from Nathaniel's throat, and then we're going to talk about what just happened and try to figure out why," I said; my voice wasn't as steady as Domino's, but it was clear and understandable.

"I don't have to obey you anymore," Damian said, and he sounded almost befuddled, not himself.

"I'm not telling you as your master vampire. I'm telling you to put the knife up as your queen, your boss, or your boss's wife. I don't care, but I know that I have more authority in this room than anybody else, and we are not going to be this stupid. Put the fucking knife up, now!" My anger came fresh and hot and my beasts coiled around it as if they were warming their hands on it. They threw little bits of their own frustration, trying to make it blaze higher. *Trapped. We're trapped. We need out. How dare they threaten our mate? How dare they threaten us? How dare they . . .*

I must have lost a few minutes fighting for control, because when I could "see" the room again Nathaniel and Bobby Lee were standing beside each other, not fighting. Damian must have handed his blade over to Domino, because he was holding a naked blade, and he had a gun still nicely holstered and visible.

Damian said, his voice calm and even, the way you talk someone down off a ledge, "I don't know what made me draw my knife on Bobby Lee, so I gave it to Domino until we figure this out."

I nodded, and let out a long, slow breath. My beasts were still huddled around my anger, eager to make it worse, so they could come out to play. The newest beast, the rat with its black eyes shining in the dark, wasn't getting along well with everyone else. Rats would eat anything, including people, but they were prey animals, too. My beasts didn't like having food inside with them, especially food that they couldn't rend and tear and eat.

We'd wanted to give me a beast that could come and help me in its natural form if I lost all my guards, but no one had asked how my inner leopard, wolf, lion, hyena, and rainbow of tigers felt about adding a new beast. It had never occurred to me to go into meditation as I'd been taught by my spiritual mentor, Marianne, and get everyone else's furry opinion. This was the first time I'd taken a new beast on voluntarily, and could have asked first. It had never occurred to me to ask until this moment when they exploited a weakness of mine to be loud enough to demand to be heard. Fuck.

"What's wrong, Anita?" Nathaniel asked, and his voice sounded like him again. He was part of my calm center again.

I shook my head. "One problem at a time. What did you mean about Damian and all this being your fault?" I asked.

"I was angry, but part of me knew that Bobby Lee is better than I am at fighting, so I was scared and angry."

"I felt that," Damian said, "and I knew I needed to protect you." He sounded like he was repeating a memory, not something that had just happened.

"And the anger may have been me," I said. They all looked at me. "The emotions just now stripped some of my control away and let my beasts talk to me."

All the wereanimals in the room said in unison, "Talk to you?"

"I translate it to words, but I'm not sure . . . Anyway, they're upset about the newest addition."

"What do you mean, the newest addition?" Damian asked.

"You mean the rat?" Bobby Lee asked.

"Yes, apparently they see it as prey and it's just one more thing that they can't do. They can't come out of my body and be whole, and now they're trapped inside me with a prey animal that they're not supposed to eat."

"I don't understand," Damian said.

"That would be very frustrating," Bobby Lee said.

"Did they complain about the rat before you did it?" Nathaniel asked.

"My control is really good now," I said.

Nathaniel looked at me. "Anita?"

Domino came to stand in front of me. "You didn't talk to them first, did you? You ignored them."

I opened my mouth, closed it, and shrugged.

Nathaniel said, "Marianne taught you how to meditate and

communicate with your beasts. I thought you were doing that regularly. I thought that was part of your new uber-control over them."

"If I said *I'm sorry*, would that help?"

"Are you saying that your inner beasts' anger transferred to Nathaniel and Damian?" Bobby Lee asked.

"Maybe."

Nathaniel paced away from me, then back. "Anita, you can't keep pretending that you don't carry the beasts inside you."

"I don't pretend . . ."

"Control doesn't mean you ignore your beasts. Control means you make peace, or something, with them. It's a cooperation, not a dictatorship."

I shrugged again. "I'm powerful enough that most of the time I can dictate."

"Losing control once a month or more isn't a curse, Anita. It's a release," he said.

I shook my head. "I don't like losing control."

"Well, that's an understatement," Bobby Lee said.

I frowned at him.

"Don't give me grief when you just fucked up your inner menagerie."

"They didn't complain when I caught the hyena."

"That was another predator and an accident. You let Rafael cut you up in rat-man form, hoping to catch what we have."

"I didn't think they'd see a difference."

"You mean your beasts wouldn't see it as different?"

"Yeah."

"Why wouldn't they see the difference between an accident and a deliberate act?" Bobby Lee asked.

I didn't want to say it out loud, because even in my head it sounded condescending and stupid. But sometimes if you're thinking loud enough, the people tied to you metaphysically can hear you thinking. I thought I had control of that, too, but I was going to be wrong again.

Nathaniel stared at me. "You didn't think they'd know the difference. Even a real leopard knows what an accident is, Anita." His face let me see just how disappointed he was in me.

"That's pretty species-ist, Anita," Domino remarked.

"No, it's human-centric," Bobby Lee corrected. "She still thinks of herself as human first."

"No," Damian said, "I can feel . . . She thinks of herself as human, period."

"Just because you don't shift into animal form doesn't make you human," Nathaniel said.

"I think it does."

"So the fact that I shift to leopard means I'm less than human?" And there was the anger again, him speaking for my beasts, or maybe just for part of me that I couldn't accept.

"No, of course not," I said.

"But being human is better," he said.

"I didn't say that. I would never say that."

"You're still relieved that you don't shift," he said, and his lavender eyes stared into me as if he saw my thoughts and feelings laid bare, because he was right. I was relieved that I didn't change form. I did think it was better. Did that make me the species equivalent of a racist? Did it make me human-centric? Maybe it did.

"Wow, okay," Domino said, "that's a lot of truth to share all at once."

"Can you feel what she's feeling, too?" Nathaniel asked.

"I hear her thoughts more than her feelings."

Nathaniel turned to Damian. "Are you her thoughts, or her feelings?"

"Her thoughts, your emotions, I think. This level of contact is new, so I'm not positive which way it runs."

"As the only person in this room not tied to you intimately, I'll say this: You have to consider your beasts as a real part of you, Anita. You are one of the most powerful metaphysics I've ever met, but eventually you'll need to become whole, and that means embracing all of yourself, including the parts that want to turn furry once a month," Domino said sternly.

"Even if they don't turn furry once a month?"

"Maybe especially then, because contacting them through meditation and magic is the only way you can communicate with them."

I didn't know what to say to that. "It's a little late to apologize."

"Apologize to who? Your beasts, Nathaniel and Damian, Bobby Lee?" Domino asked.

"All of the above," I said.

"That's a start," he said.

Bobby Lee said, "You asked me who else goes to Ireland. How about Domino? He de-escalated this nicely."

"Yeah, thanks for the help, Domino."

"It's my job. Besides, this is nothing next to some of the fights Max and Bibiana used to get into in Vegas. When your Master of the City and the queen of your clan go at it, you've got serious trouble."

I laughed. "I bet they have real doozies."

"They're powerful enough to destroy each other. Instead they've been married for over seventy years. As bodyguards, part of our job is to see trouble and head it off."

"The three of you are going to be on a learning curve with this new power level. Looks like Domino can help with that," Bobby Lee said.

I nodded. "Agreed."

"And no offense meant, but he can act as food for the *ardeur* if needed."

"No offense taken," I said.

"I'm actually off the menu," he said.

Bobby Lee looked from one of us to the other. "I'd heard Anita was shortening her list of lovers."

"I'm sorry, Domino, but there just isn't enough of me to go around to this many people. I can't date a dozen people. No one can."

"I remember our talk, Anita." He only sounded a little bitter.

"I'm not going to apologize again."

"No one's asking you to."

"Enough," Bobby Lee said. "Domino only goes if it's going to make things better, not worse."

"I can handle myself and it's like any breakup; you heal in stages," he said.

I tried very hard not to think that it didn't feel like a breakup to me, because we hadn't had a relationship; we'd had sex on a semiregular basis, but for whatever reason it had never clicked emotionally between us like it had between Nathaniel and me. Hell, it had never clicked between the wereleopard and the vampire until this last literally magical moment. Domino had never crossed the emotional divide for me, or not enough. I understood that it was Nathaniel's emotions that were making Damian more than he had been, but even knowing that, I couldn't seem to separate it out into his, my, and Damian's feelings. Lucky for me none of my other animals to call had a vampire to back them up, and I wasn't tied to any other vampires except for Jean-Claude and Damian. I'd almost married Richard once, thanks in part to the vampire marks that Jean-Claude had on both of us.

I looked from Nathaniel to Damian, and for the first time my gaze lingered over both of them. I suddenly wished Micah or Jean-Claude could come with us to Ireland—not for solving crime, or physical safety, but for emotional safety. It probably wasn't a great idea to go to Ireland without either of the other two that I wanted to marry. I needed someone else who would help Nathaniel not obsess about the new relationship parameters with Damian, because his obsession could so easily become mine. I was taking the two women that we shared with us, but one was more a fuck buddy for all of us and the other had a primary in her vampire master, who was the love of her life. If I was looking at Damian like he was way more to me than he had been, than I knew Nathaniel was, we needed a buffer.

I was pretty sure I knew who to take to help me hold on to my heart, but we needed someone to help Nathaniel, too. I looked at Domino and knew another weretiger who might be just the ticket.

25

I FINALLY GOT Micah on the phone between peace negotiations. "How are the negotiations going?" I asked.

"We haven't had to fight anyone yet. Everyone is still talking about a resolution that may actually be bloodless."

"That's great. You know I worry when you go out to these peace talks."

"Because before they'll settle for peace, they usually want a little war," he said, and his voice held laughter, but it was too close to true for me to find it funny.

"Ironic that I don't like the shoe being on the other foot for the dangerous stuff," I said.

"You're very good about not saying the worry out loud."

"Thanks. You've been such a good sport about all the crime fighting over the years that it would just be bad form for me to bitch now."

He did laugh then. "Since when is being part of a couple fair?"

"Since I try to be," I said, and I gave him a little laugh, because that was what he was wanting.

"We all try to be fair," he said.

"We really do."

"So Edward found a way to bring you in as a consultant to Ireland."

"Yeah, but not just me. I can bring some of the guards with me."

"Really? How did he manage that?"

"It's Edward. He's like the go-to guy for the nearly impossible stuff."

"Who are you taking with you?" he asked.

"That's what I wanted you to know before we left."

"Uh-oh," he said.

"What uh-oh?"

"You don't expect me to be happy about some of the people you're taking with you."

"How do you know that?"

"Your voice just now told me."

"I love that you know me so well, and sometimes it's a little unsettling."

"That's better than *creepy*, which is what you thought all of this interpersonal couple stuff was once."

"I wasn't that bad," I said.

"Do you really want to have this debate now? I only have a few minutes before I have to go back inside and play referee for more negotiations."

"Point made," I said, and tried to explain how I'd ended up going to Ireland with not just Nathaniel, but every lover he had. Jean-Claude was staying home, but he and Micah weren't lovers, contrary to the rumor mill.

He was quiet for a minute, then said slowly, as if he were choosing his words, "So let me test my understanding—you're taking Nathaniel because he finally figured out how to control your triumvirate with Damian, which gives you a power boost and makes Damian feel safer going back to the country he escaped from?"

"He didn't escape. His old master let him go."

"After torturing him for centuries, she just let him go?"

"Yes."

"Why?"

"He thinks in her own twisted way she cared for him and was afraid she would finally kill him."

"You mean she sent him away to save him?" Micah sounded dubious. I couldn't really blame him.

"That's what Damian said."

"What do you think?"

"I think we'll have guards and the police, plus a paramilitary unit, looking after our safety. I don't think we'll be seeing Damian's old master in person."

"And you really think that the death of Marmee Noir lost his old master that much power?"

"It's possible."

"A lot of things are possible, Anita. Explain to me again why you and Nathaniel are suddenly more attracted to Damian."

"You know how your wish was to find a safe haven, a home, for you and your wereleopards when you met me, and my wish was to find a true partner, so the *ardeur* gave us both our hearts' desires?"

"Yes."

"Damian wanted us, someone, to desire him the way we desire you. Nathaniel wanted Damian to want him and be a real lover to him. He's tired of so many men being afraid of guy-on-guy stuff."

"He's been very patient with me; it's one of the reasons I love him."

"I wasn't hinting about you, Micah."

"Maybe I just feel guilty that I made Nathaniel feel rejected for so long."

"That's your issue in your head. I did not think it or imply it, and wasn't trying to."

"That's fair," he said. "What did you want when the power rose, Anita?"

"I remember thinking life would be easier if more of the men were actually bisexual."

"And you say Damian took it well? I mean, he's truly homophobic. I just wasn't into guys before Nathaniel."

"He seems fine, in fact eerily so. Jean-Claude thinks that Nathaniel literally bespelled him."

"And you, because you lost time, too."

"I know."

"How did the spell work on you?"

"I told you I'm more attracted to Damian than I ever have been."

"So much so that you're taking other lovers to make sure you and Nathaniel don't get carried away romantically with him." Micah's voice was a little dry.

"Yeah," I said.

"Fortune, Echo, and Magda—I understand they're all Harlequin and your lovers."

"Hey, you're lovers with all the women, too."

"You don't need to get defensive on my part, Anita. I'm not criticizing."

"Sorry. I think I feel bad that I'm taking all your lovers out of town."

"Don't. You explained why you can't take any of the rats and you need people you can feed the *ardeur* on anyway. With Magda you also get her master, Giacomo, and they are some of the toughest warriors we have. I like you taking good people with you and Nathaniel."

"We'll have Nicky, too. He'll keep us safe."

"I never doubt Nicky. He'd give his life for you and Nathaniel, so I'm good with him going, too."

"Jake and Kaazim, Pride, Dev, Domino, Socrates, and probably Ethan."

"We don't have any bad people working security for us,

Anita, and you've got to weight the list toward ones who would be willing to feed you and the vampires that will be traveling with you. What's bothering you that you feel like you have to explain it all to me? Usually you just grab your choice of backup and go. You take Nicky the way I take Bram, but other than that we both pick the people best for the job."

"You told me that you had an issue with Dev."

"No, I have an issue with me that I didn't realize until Dev started dating Nathaniel, you, and Jean-Claude."

"Dev and I don't really date."

"He dates both the men."

I nodded, realized he couldn't see it, and said, "Yes, he does."

"He's also completely and comfortably bisexual with both of them and I'm not."

"You and Nathaniel are lovers, and you're . . . more than just friends with Jean-Claude."

"There are still things I don't do with Nathaniel that he misses. It's one of the reasons I agreed to Dev dating him. We're polyamorous, not monogamous, so it seemed logical and fair that he have another man in his life who could give him what I couldn't."

"Anytime you make romantic decisions that are logical and fair, they usually end up making someone feel that they are very illogical and unfair," I said.

"Now you tell me." He tried to make it a joke, but it didn't quite work.

"Jean-Claude still won't be in bed with Dev and Nathaniel without at least you or me."

"He won't be with Nathaniel without you in bed with them. Jean-Claude wasn't meeting all of Nathaniel's guy-on-guy needs any more than I was."

"You told me that you were having issues with Nathaniel getting more serious with Dev than you expected, or something like that."

"Yeah, something like that. I totally underestimated how much it would mean to the man I love to have a man in his bed who was happy to do everything possible with him."

"And Dev is frustrated that Jean-Claude isn't responding to his charms with as much enthusiasm as Nathaniel," I said.

"I don't think Jean-Claude is as into men as either of them."

"He likes men," I said.

"I just said he doesn't like men as much as Dev and Nathaniel."

"Nathaniel is one of the most evenly bisexual people I've ever met, and Dev is a close second."

"He leans a little bit more to the guy side," Micah said.

"Probably, but it's hard for me to judge, being a woman."

"Fair enough. Where would you put Jean-Claude on the Kinsey scale?"

"Wherever he wants to be."

"That's probably truer than we understand about him."

"I said it. Maybe I do understand him."

"You've known him longer than I have."

"I'm taking Dev specifically to help me buffer Nathaniel from falling too much in love with Damian. That's the part I'm not sure you'll like."

"When you know that I'm a little worried that Nathaniel is already too in love with Dev for my comfort."

"Yes," I said.

"Dev is your golden tiger to call, and that is an amazing power boost for you and for me as your Nimir-Raj. A combination of your panwere lycanthropy and his power as gold tiger helped me find a second form as a black tiger. Being able to shift into a second beast has helped me win fights I might have lost, and just plain scared some of the shapeshifters who would have fought us on these trips. A panwere is the rarest form of lycanthropy. They're almost legend among us. The extra power I've gained through our ties to Dev has saved my blood and body more than once."

"And that makes me very happy," I said.

"Me, too," he said, and there was that edge of a smile in his voice that I loved to hear.

"You told Dev if he gave you enough power to do exactly what you just said, that you'd put a ring on it, on him."

"He wants to be the weretiger in the commitment ceremony with you and the men you choose."

"If I could I'd just marry you, Nathaniel, and Jean-Claude."

"Legally you can only marry Jean-Claude, and if you can only marry one of us it has to be the vampire king."

"You're the leopard king."

"Of St. Louis, not the whole country."

"I'd still marry the three of you legally if I could."

"I know, and I appreciate that."

I was quiet for a second and almost didn't say it, but finally I had to. "You know it's not the boy-on-boy sex that's made Dev move up in Nathaniel's estimation, right?"

He sighed heavily. "I know I was stupid. I know I'm being stupid."

"I didn't say that."

"I didn't expect Nathaniel to propose to me that he and I get married for real the way you and Jean-Claude are going to."

"You proposed to both of us once, Micah. You said you'd marry us both if you could."

"I meant I'd marry both of you, not just one of you."

"Micah, be honest. You'd marry just me if you could, so you can't blame Nathaniel for being hurt that you won't marry just him."

"I told you I was being stupid. It's just he's the first boy-friend I've ever had. If I got married I just always saw myself with a woman."

"A lot of us get stuck on what we think we should have, should love, should want, should lust after. Therapy helped me get over my white-picket-fence fantasy, because it so wasn't going to work for my life."

"Fine. I feel threatened by Dev, because he would marry Nathaniel."

"I don't think they would work as each other's primary partner," I said.

"They don't have to, Anita. That's what makes the thought of Dev putting a legal ring on Nathaniel's finger so possible. They both want to get married. Nathaniel asked me and I'm hesitating. Dev proposed to Asher and got turned down flat."

"Asher was a shit about it. We all broke up with him be-cause he's such a shit," I said.

"I didn't break up with Asher. I do not see what any of you see in him."

"You don't like bondage and rough sex enough to appreci-ate Asher's finer qualities."

"I know he's really good at being mean both for pretend in

the dungeon and in real life. The last part sort of makes the first part not work for me."

"You don't like the first part," I said.

"You don't like the second part," he said.

"None of us do, which is why Jean-Claude, Nathaniel, Richard, and I all broke up with him."

"From all accounts he's miserable with just Kane as his lover and *moitié bête*," Micah said.

"Asher is one of the least monogamous people I know and one of the kinkiest. He's now stuck being monogamous with Kane, who is totally vanilla and doesn't do kink at all. Of course Asher is miserable. He's created his own living hell."

"Some people would say that homosexuality is a type of kink," Micah said.

"Then *some people* haven't been around enough homosexuals, because they can be every bit as conservative and narrow-minded as any heterosexual."

"My experience is limited, and most of the bisexuals I know are also kinky."

"Bisexuals seem to have a higher kink level than either end of the scale," I said.

"At least the ones we know," he said.

"Fair enough, so do you want me to leave Dev at home?"

"You'd really do that just because I'm blaming him for something that is my fault?"

"No, because Dev is charming and I don't want to make this problem between Nathaniel and you worse. I don't know if I want Dev living with us constantly. He doesn't work with our entire poly group as well as some of the others do."

"Nicky works great, but neither Jean-Claude nor I will do a commitment ceremony with him. Sin works great, but neither you, I, or Jean-Claude will commit to him."

"He's a nephew to Jean-Claude and a brother-husband to the rest of you."

"I'll call Sin that, but not Nicky."

"Nicky is only a lion, so he doesn't help us over the whole tiger issue anyway," I said.

"I know that the tiger clan leaders won't rest until you're married off to one of the clan tigers."

"Legend says that if I don't marry a tiger, the Mother of All Darkness will return from the dead and destroy the world."

"Nice to know they backed off on the tiger being your legal spouse and are content with a commitment ceremony," he said.

"Yeah, it was big of them."

"You're being sarcastic, but it really was a compromise for them."

"So we need a tiger as part of the commitment ceremony that we're all willing to live with, and the group of us can't agree on one."

"Welcome to one of the serious downsides of polyamory when everyone has veto power over everyone else's lovers," Micah said.

"Lovers, schmovers, it's the living-with part that's making the choice impossible."

"Agreed. I'm being signaled that it's time to talk some more here. Have a safe flight. I wish I were able to go with you and help keep Nathaniel's and your minds off Damian."

"Me, too."

"I love you, Anita Blake."

"I love you more, Micah Callahan."

"I love you most."

"I love you mostest."

"I've got to go make sure they don't start trying to kill each other."

"And I've got to go to Ireland and stop them from killing each other."

I heard a voice on his end, someone talking low to him. He had to go, and so did I. Both of our jobs saved lives, and both of us would take a life if we thought it would save more lives down the road. Most of the time I did it with the legal blessing of my country. When Micah killed someone in a duel it was never legal, because duels were illegal no matter if you were human or more than human.

26

I FOUND NATHANIEL and Damian back in Damian's bedroom. I almost didn't recognize the room. There was a large mirror that covered the half wall that held the bathroom door. The mirror had a heavy antique-looking frame and the glass would reflect anything happening on the bed. Nathaniel was both a serious voyeur and exhibitionist; mirrors seemed to satisfy both needs for him. He'd been asking Micah and me to put one in our shared bedroom, but we'd been resisting. I didn't want to sit up in bed and see my reflection every morning, or in the middle of the night when I was half asleep. There'd been an incident on an out-of-town business trip where I'd damn near shot the full-length mirror in the hotel room, because I thought it was an intruder. That had been years ago when I was new to hunting killers and carrying a gun, but the moment had stayed with me. Micah didn't really want the mirror either, but obviously Nathaniel did, and Damian had let him do something that his two fiancées had refused him for years.

The bed was now covered in a very dark green bedspread with pillows in browns, dark purples, and a shade of orange that had brown undertones so it all matched. If you'd set me loose in a store with this as a color scheme, it would have looked like it had been put together by a partially color-blind lover of autumn, but this was magazine perfect. The brown and orange were a new addition, but they echoed the purple and green of our own room, though our shades were brighter, shinier, more vibrant, and this was muted, more autumn leaves than summer flowers. It still had Nathaniel's touch everywhere.

It had taken months of negotiations for Nathaniel to do our room; this had to have happened in less than two hours. Either

Damian was more bespelled than I was, or he was always this easy a touch for a lover to control the decorating. Maybe it hadn't been all Cardinale's fault that the room had reflected mostly her, which said something important about Damian. I just didn't know exactly what.

They were sitting on the bed, their heads together over Nathaniel's iPad. He looked up, smiling. "We're looking online for new towels for the bathroom, so we can get rid of all the pink ones."

"Nothing wrong with pink if you like the color," I said.

"I don't," Damian said, looking up.

Their faces were very close together, the bright green eyes and the lavender ones, milk pale skin and the darker pale that let you know Nathaniel might tan if he ever tried. His face was wider through the cheekbones, Damian's longer and narrower. Was Nathaniel more beautiful? Yes, but it was like saying a rose is more beautiful than a lily. They were both beautiful flowers. It just depended on whether you wanted something rounder, fuller, more lush, or if you wanted something leaner, taller, more careless summer garden instead of formal rose garden. I preferred roses to lilies, but they grew well next to each other if you were willing to have your rose garden a little less formal and a little more cottage.

Nathaniel put the iPad down on the bedspread and met my eyes with his; he knew how distracted I suddenly was, because he'd watched himself affect me like that for years. It was closer to the way I got distracted with Jean-Claude and Asher, back when he was in our bed. Did Micah and Nathaniel together make me this stupid-faced? Maybe. It was like I couldn't remember, which let me know that I needed to walk out of the room and find Jean-Claude, or find a phone and talk to Micah—again. But I didn't. I stood there and drank in the beauty of them, the possibility of them.

I couldn't seem to leave the room, but I found my voice. "You couldn't have ordered the bedspread and pillows online. There hasn't been time for them to ship." My voice sounded a little hoarse, so I cleared my throat, trying to sound and feel more like myself.

"No, we ran out and picked up a few things," Nathaniel said.

"We? You and Damian went out during the day just to shop?" I asked.

"Sunlight doesn't burn me anymore," Damian said, studying me with those pure green eyes of his.

"I know, but you still don't like going out in it."

"Nathaniel was with me," he said.

"And that made you feel safer," I said.

He put an arm around the other man's shoulders. Nathaniel put his head a little to the side so his auburn hair and Damian's red intermingled like two streams of some blood-colored sea where the tides meet. It was like Damian's eyes were the color of leaves to complement Nathaniel's flower-colored ones.

I shook my head forcefully and looked at the floor. The carpet was new, too. It was dark brown with a pattern of green leaves and autumn-colored flowers on it. I wondered if Damian realized he'd just given up one color of flower for another.

I heard the bed move before Nathaniel crawled into sight, gazing up at me from the ground so I couldn't hide behind the thick fall of my hair. He gazed up at me with those large lilac-colored eyes. He was improbable, too beautiful, but it was his eyes that tipped the scale from beautiful to something exotic and unreal, like an orchid grown in some hothouse. I could almost feel the heat and humidity of it. I closed my eyes so I couldn't see him, and it was better. The air was less close. I should have started backing out of the room and run for it, but I just closed my eyes, as if that would save me. That hadn't been a good strategy since I was five and I believed that if I couldn't see the monster under the bed he couldn't get me. If there'd really been something under my bed it wouldn't have worked then, either.

Nathaniel traced his fingers along my arm, the lightest of touches, but it was enough to make me open my eyes and drown in that violet gaze. I was better than this, damn it! I knew how to escape vampire gaze, but then, he wasn't really a vampire and I'd never met a wereleopard who could capture me with his eyes.

I squeezed my eyes shut tight and shook my head, trying to clear my thoughts. He caressed my arm again, but I was able to keep my eyes closed this time. I'd played this game with

Jean-Claude for years. Of course, that had been back when he wasn't sure I wouldn't tell him to go to hell and mean it. It had limited what he would risk, how far he would push. Nathaniel didn't have those kinds of doubts. Nothing gives you courage like believing someone loves you absolutely.

He ran his fingers along my arm again, and another hand echoed him on the other side of me. It made me open my eyes. Nathaniel was still kneeling in front of me, but Damian was kneeling beside him now. It was his hand caressing my right arm, while Nathaniel stroked the left. I opened my mouth to protest, but I wasn't sure what I was protesting. We were all lovers already, and the pilot had informed Jean-Claude, who had informed me, that we had a couple of hours more before we could take off.

As if he'd read my thoughts, Nathaniel said, "We have at least two more hours before we need to be at the plane. We had sex, but you didn't feed the *ardeur*, because I didn't know how."

I had to cough to clear my voice before I could say, "Jean-Claude wishes Rafael were here so I could feed on all the rats through him before we leave."

"Rafael won't get back in time to feed you," he said, rising higher on his knees so he could bring his face closer to mine.

I straightened up so that I wasn't half-bending over toward him.

Damian leaned in to lay the brush of his lips against my arm, too delicate to even be called a kiss. It made me shiver and wrap both my arms around myself as if I were cold, but it wasn't cold that had made me shiver. I should walk out, leave . . . now.

"Let us be your food," Damian said, and I was suddenly staring into the green of his eyes as if I'd never seen them before, never realized how fair of face, how . . .

I shook my head a little more forcefully and took two steps back so I wasn't between the two of them. "I'm going to . . . go somewhere . . . else."

"Why?" Nathaniel asked.

"I . . . You're trying to bespell me again."

"We're engaged. We'd marry if you could legally take more

than one spouse. I'm not trying to force you to do anything we haven't already done. You have to feed the *ardeur* before we get on the plane. You can't risk feeding hundreds of miles in the air."

"I'd be too nervous," I said.

"That means it's more likely to get out of control, not less."

"What's that supposed to mean?" I tried to call up some anger to protect me from his so-reasonable voice and the two of them kneeling so close to me.

"What if you lost control on the plane and it spread to everyone?"

"I've only lost control like that once, and that was because the old vampire council was fucking with us."

"Emergencies happen, Anita; let's not make the *ardeur* one of them."

"This doesn't even sound like you, Nathaniel."

"Maybe it sounds like me," Damian said. "I'm afraid to go back to Ireland, but I'll do it for you."

"You're not doing it for me. You're doing it to help the police save lives."

"You can believe what you want, but if it had just been Edward asking me, I wouldn't be going. I'm going because my master wants me to go and my leopard is going with me to hold my hand. I want to help save lives and make up for some of the things I've done in my existence, but I am going for you, Anita."

I wanted to say, *Don't go for me. Go for yourself*, but I was afraid he'd change his mind, and we needed him. "I don't know what to say to that, Damian."

"Say you'll make love to us. Say you'll let us be your food."

They were right about one thing—I did need to feed before I got on the plane, but I was forgetting something. It was something important. Nathaniel's fingers played with the edge of his T-shirt, and began to slowly lift the cloth to bare the flatness of his abs an inch at a time.

I backed up a step. If I was going, it was time to leave, but why did I want to go? I loved Nathaniel. We had sex on a regular basis. There was no reason to run away, so why was I wanting to run? It was like I was forgetting something that I really needed to remember. Whatever I had forgotten was the reason why this wasn't a good idea, but for the life of me I couldn't think of it, just this nagging feeling that there was something.

I closed my eyes and turned around so I couldn't watch them slowly taking their shirts off. "There's something we're forgetting," I managed to say, "something important."

"You're missing the show that we're putting on just for you," Nathaniel said, in a voice that had more honey in it than I ever remembered, as if his words could drip down my skin in thick, sweet lines.

"This is wrong. It's the power talking. It's making us forget something important. A reason that we shouldn't feed now," I said.

Nathaniel said, "Turn around, Anita, please."

I started to do it, and had to catch myself, clenching my hands into fists.

"No, Nathaniel, she's right. We're both drunk on the new power. It's like when you're first in love. It makes you forget things."

"What sort of things?" Nathaniel asked, his voice sounding more normal.

"All sorts of things," I said.

"Important things," Damian said.

I opened my eyes and turned cautiously to them. They were both shirtless, which wasn't helpful, so I closed my eyes again. All I wanted to do was go to them and start touching all that bare skin.

"Everyone take a deep breath and ground and center," I said with my eyes still closed. I tried to follow my own advice, and found it much harder than it should have been. I knew how to control my breathing, and once you controlled that your pulse and heart had to follow. Either everything sped up, or nothing did. I knew all that, but I could still feel my pulse in my throat.

"We're going with you to Ireland," Damian said.

"That's the plan," I said in a voice that was still slightly breathless.

"Then you'll need to keep us for food there. If you feed on us now, we won't be any good to you for at least twenty-four hours, maybe forty-eight. Two days where you'll have to find other food."

"We're taking Nicky," Nathaniel said.

"He can't feed her for two days by himself without compromising his ability to fight."

"We're taking Domino."

"He's emergency food only. He's not one of my lovers anymore, remember?" I said.

"Fortune, Echo, and Magda are going," Nathaniel said.

"Well, that's true," Damian said, and sounded less certain.

"I'm thinking of taking Dev, too," I said.

"See? She'll have plenty of food," Nathaniel said.

"But you weren't thinking that when you started us taking off our shirts."

The energy in the room was calmer now; I could think again. Whatever Nathaniel was doing had stopped. Damian had made him think too much about other things. It was hard to keep your concentration pure enough to do magic when you were having to think about relationship issues. Maybe that's why so many major witches and wizards throughout history never married?

"I'm sorry, Anita. Damian. You're right. If we'd been the only two lovers going to Ireland, I'd have still wanted the three of us to make love and feed the *ardeur* together. We've never done that before, and I know it's a rush when Anita and I do it with another person."

"I look forward to it," Damian said, "but not tonight. She should feed off someone who isn't traveling with us."

I looked at them and they were still yummy to see all shirtless and, well, just handsome as hell, or maybe handsome as heaven—yeah, that sounded better—but they weren't so overwhelmingly beautiful that I had to have them now, right now. The compulsion was gone, replaced by my usual desire for Nathaniel, which was a near-constant like breathing, and there was a new spark when I looked at Damian that wasn't as strong, but it was most definitely there.

"I've never gotten this much power before. If I'm not careful I'll want to use it all the time." Nathaniel was frowning.

"I told you, it's like being in love, that new-relationship energy that almost overwhelms you, but feels so good."

"So instead of NRE it's NME?" I asked.

"I know NRE is new-relationship energy, but what's NME?" Nathaniel asked.

"New metaphysical energy," I said.

He grinned. "I like it, and it's accurate, especially because my new magic seems to be based on sex and love, but I like New Magical Energy, instead of Metaphysical."

"Lust and love are what Belle Morte's bloodline does best," Damian said.

"Lust is Belle Morte's line," I said. "Love is what Jean-Claude's power added to it when he became powerful enough to be his own bloodline."

Damian nodded. "It's true. There is a softer power to this energy than anything Belle Morte ever offered."

"Is love softer energy than lust?" I asked.

He thought about it and finally smiled. "No, no, I suppose it's not."

"Love is the hardest thing of all," Nathaniel said. "Just sex is so much easier."

I gave him a look.

He smiled at me. "It's like the difference between sleeping with someone and really sleeping with them. Having sex is easy compared to trying to learn to sleep with someone."

I laughed. "God, that is the truth."

"Love is even harder than sleeping overnight in the same bed for the first few times. They're both worth the effort, but you still have to work at it."

"You have to work at sex, too," I said.

It was his turn to give me a look.

"I mean, we all get better at it with each other, because we know what everyone enjoys and who has what skill set."

"I don't think I had to work on much," he said.

I laughed again. "I can't really argue about the actual skills. It was the emotional issues that kept stopping us."

He nodded, no longer smiling.

"I don't think I've been with either of you enough to know what you enjoy," Damian said.

Nathaniel looked at him. "We'll fix that."

Damian started to be embarrassed, and then a calmness

came over him. He seemed to steady, and held out his hand to Nathaniel. "Yes, we will."

"You just helped him be calmer about it all, didn't you?"

Nathaniel nodded and took the vampire's hand in his. "Just like he helped me get over my power trip just now."

"We're supposed to help each other," Damian said.

"We're supposed to be stronger together," Nathaniel said.

I looked at them, holding hands, and waited for Damian to protest, but he looked . . . content.

"Stronger together is the ideal," I said.

"We are that now," Nathaniel said.

"We are," Damian said, smiling at him.

"I guess we are," I said.

Nathaniel looked at me and his face had a new resolve that I'd never seen before. It reminded me of one of my expressions. One thing you did with a triumvirate was share bits of one another's talents, memories, and personality. It had never worked quite that way between the three of us before, but it had always worked that way with Jean-Claude, Richard, and me. Richard had inherited my temper, Jean-Claude my ruthlessness; I'd gotten Jean-Claude's blood hunger and Richard's craving for flesh. I really didn't want to go through all that again, but I wasn't sure that what I wanted was really going to matter.

"Go find someone to feed the *ardeur*, Anita. We'll keep shopping for towels. If we put an order in they should be here by the time we get back from Ireland," Nathaniel said.

I left them shopping for linens on the Internet, and I went to find someone to have sex with and feed the metaphysical hunger that could only be satisfied by some very up-close-and-personal interactions. The *ardeur* was the other thing I'd inherited from Jean-Claude. He was an incubus, not demonic, just a vampire who could feed off lust as well as blood. I was a succubus to his incubus now. No, I really didn't want to inherit any more metaphysical surprises from anyone again.

27

NOW THAT I wasn't drunk on metaphysics I went to find Jean-Claude. I wanted to tell him what had happened, and if I was having a last hurrah with anyone I was leaving at home, I wanted it to be him. He was in his bedroom talking to a man I didn't know. The man was in a regular brown business suit with a clipboard and a pen in his hands. At first glance Jean-Claude seemed to be in a white button-up business shirt and black slacks, except that the slacks fit well enough and tight enough to his body to fit seamlessly into knee-high black boots. He held his hand out to me with a smile. "*Ma petite*, I have organized a temporary bed until the custom mattress can be remade and shipped to us."

I took his hand in mine and let him draw me in against his body so that we could kiss. I went up on tiptoe, my free hand steadying me against his stomach, which gave me an excuse to pet down the line of buttons on his shirt. The buttons were covered in platinum and sapphires almost as dark as his eyes, so that the jewels looked bright blue one moment and black the next. The first time I'd seen the shirt I'd thought they were the buttons, but they were button covers, so he could change them out with ones he'd had made in ruby and gold. The button covers weren't the only change to the business suit look. The shirt's French cuffs were very wide and turned back thick and crisp, far more cuff than any fashion I was aware of, but they had to be wide enough to accommodate the cuff links with sapphires as big as his thumb set in glittering platinum and diamonds. Yes, he had a set of ruby-and-gold cuff links to match the other button covers.

He introduced me briefly to the man with the clipboard, who promised to bring in two king-size beds ASAP. They shook hands; he never offered me a hand to shake, but the days when that would bug me were past. Besides, my hands were busy around Jean-Claude's waist; my hands had to go somewhere during all the business hand shaking.

A guard at the door saw the man out, then closed the door behind them without being asked. The new guys were training up better and better. We had some who were great at the fighting-and-protecting part, but had been lost about the niceties of how to escort someone in and out of the house who was just there to fix the plumbing, or whatever. Being a good bodyguard for us was closer to being a bouncer in some ways; you had to know how to work the door, too.

I wrapped my arms around him a little tighter, smiled up into those deep blue eyes, and said, "I'd like 'Good-bye, I'm going to another country' sex, please."

He laughed, that surprised bleat of sound that I so rarely got from him, which was why I made the effort for it. He hugged me close, petting my hair as he held my cheek in against his chest.

"*Ma petite*, how could I turn down such a charming proposal?"

I moved my head enough so I could see his face again. His face was still alight with the edge of laughter, which made me smile even more. "I'm going to miss you."

His face sobered almost as slowly as a human's would have, but honestly, the older vampires have trouble holding on to surprised expressions. They tend to go back to whatever they've trained themselves is their neutral expression. I'd been puzzled by that until I met enough of the vampires who used to be in power over them all. Any emotion could be used against them, and likely would be. Cops had a neutral face that they hid behind. No one did that kind of hiding as well as older vampires, but then, they'd had more practice than most human cops.

"I will miss you, too, *ma petite*." He bent down and had to loosen his arms so that I could rise up enough to meet the kiss. I tried to put more body language into the kiss, but he drew back before I could get us too distracted. "I have not fed yet today, *ma petite*."

"Me either," I said, and tried to go back to kissing him.

He raised his head out of reach and said, "I must take blood before I can make love to you."

"You taking blood can be part of the foreplay. We enjoy that."

He smiled, then shook his head. "Alas, *ma petite*, I believe you should conserve your precious blood for the three vampires who will be traveling with you. They cannot afford to feed on the Irish during such a case."

"That's almost exactly what Damian said."

"He has grown wise."

I sighed and suddenly wasn't feeling half as sexy. "Actually, yes and no."

He gave a small frown. "What does that mean in this instance, yes and no?"

I started to tell him what had happened, then realized I was wasting time. I opened the link between us a little wider; if I thought of the memories, he could just remember with me. When we'd first started doing this kind of thing, I hadn't been good enough to give selected memories, but practice makes better. What would have taken minutes took only seconds.

"It seems our kitten has become a cat," he said.

"You mean Nathaniel?"

"Oui."

I nodded. "You could say that."

"Damian will help you control the new powers."

"Yeah, and Nathaniel will be more cautious with them from this point on, I think."

"I believe you are correct."

I studied his face. "You're not entirely sure, or you wouldn't have shut the marks down tight again. You don't want me to know what you're thinking."

"If you are asking if I am concerned that Nathaniel will let the new magic go to his head, of course I am, but we must trust each other, for we are built link by link into a chain that is stronger together than as a pile of individual links."

"You know what they say: The chain is only as strong as its weakest link."

"Do you believe that Nathaniel is our weak link?"

I thought about it for a second, then shook my head. "No. No, I don't."

He smiled. "Good. Do not doubt our cat now that he has grown claws, but rejoice in the extra power it will bring to us all."

"Just because something brings us more power, does that make it all right?"

"Not always, but power is often a balance between benefits gained and danger risked."

"I get that."

"Good, but you do need to feed the *ardeur* before you board the plane, *ma petite*."

"If I can't donate blood, can you catch some fast food?"

His smile brightened. "I have not had to catch my food for a very long time, *ma petite*."

I frowned, couldn't hold it, and smiled again. "You know what I mean."

"I do, but anyone who offers their life's blood to me deserves to be treated as far more than fast food."

"Agreed, but I don't want to lose the chance of making love with you before I leave."

"Nor do I, but the answer is simple: We include a blood donor who can be part of our foreplay, so that the feeding is still part of the sex."

"So someone to donate blood to you and feed the *ardeur* for me?"

"*Oui.*"

"Who'd you have in mind?"

28

HE HAD NICKY in mind; that worked for me, so we sent one of the guards off to find him. I then realized that we had cell phones. He asked, "What are you doing, *ma petite*?"

"Texting Nicky."

"*Non, ma petite*, for something as delicate as this it should be in person."

"Nicky isn't that formal a guy," I said.

"He is in love with you, *ma petite*, but he is not with me. He is also a very recent volunteer for donating blood to me. I would rather be overly solicitous than give offense."

I frowned at him. "Either that all means you like Nicky more than I think you do, so you don't want to blow it, or you're afraid of offending him for a different reason."

He smiled. "You are in love with him, *ma petite*, and yet he has not demanded to be included in the larger commitment ceremony with all of us. I value very much that Nicky is not being difficult about that."

"You mean like most of the weretigers?" I asked.

"I do."

I sighed twice like I was trying to get enough air to swim a sprint. "The problem is that we can't all agree on a weretiger to include."

"Mephistopheles is proving most amiable."

"Yeah, Dev gets along with everyone better than anybody else."

"You do not sound convinced, *ma petite*."

I broke from the hug, because it was hard to think sometimes when I was too close to him. I started pacing the room a little as I tried to explain. "Mephistopheles—Dev—is great in a lot of ways. I know you value that he actually is bisexual, so he's your lover and mine."

"He is also in Nathaniel's bed."

"Yeah, and he does everything with him, including things that Micah still can't quite wrap his head around."

"Micah has never had a male lover before, *ma petite*. It can take some adjustment."

"I know it does for me with the women." Then I realized that he might have said more than I'd understood, so I asked him, "You weren't always bisexual, were you?"

"There had been drunken explorations, but I believe that I would now call that heteroflexible."

"Did you cross the line with another man before you were taken to Belle Morte's court?"

"No, I did not."

I blinked at him. "Fuck, Asher was your first man, male lover, wasn't he?"

Jean-Claude nodded, then looked away so I couldn't see his face, which meant he didn't trust himself to be able to control his expression. It was incredibly rare for him to be unable to control himself like that.

"God, Jean-Claude, I'm sorry. I didn't know."

He spoke with his face still turned away. "Why should you be sorry, *ma petite*?"

"It explains a lot about why you were willing to put up with Asher's jealousy and temper tantrums over the centuries. It also explains . . . Your first lover gets a piece of your heart until you have enough therapy to take it back."

He laughed then. "Ah, *ma petite*, such a mix of romance and practicality—I value it a great deal that you do both equally well."

"I share enough of your memories to know that Belle was very good at both, too."

"But she was never in love with me, as you are. To find a second woman who could be everything I wished in the bedroom and in the boardroom was more than I thought I would ever find."

"I'm also better in an actual physical fight than Belle."

He turned and smiled at me; whatever emotion he'd been trying to hide, he'd managed. "Belle was powerful enough that she did not resort to fisticuffs."

"I'm a double threat. I'll kick your ass with metaphysics and then I'll just plain kick your ass."

He laughed, but it was his controlled laugh, the one that I'd thought was his real laugh for a long time. Now I knew that it was a sort of practiced laughter, one that showed joy, or humor, but he could trot it out at will, even if he didn't get the joke. To be part of Belle Morte's court he'd had to laugh at the jokes and not show disgust at other things.

"It is true: You are the first warrior I have ever fallen in love with, *ma petite*."

"I've seen you and Asher do sword practice. Doesn't that count?"

"He is good at the sort of practice one does to impress a

lady, or a lad, but in a real fight he tends to let his emotions overwhelm his knowledge, and blade work is about precision and control."

"All fighting is about precision and control," I said.

He nodded. "I concede that is true of most fighting, but not all. I have seen battles won through sheer uncontrollable rage. At the right moment it can turn the tide of battle and renew the bravery of those around the warrior who can show strength when all around him have given up."

"Agreed, though actual battle, I don't think what I've done qualifies as actual battle yet."

"That is for you to define, *ma petite*, but Asher's temper always unmanned him in a fight. He was much better at being a lover than a fighter."

"He's great in bed, but he sucks at the relationship part."

"He does not suck, as you say, at all the relationship part, but I understand you have not seen the parts he is good at as much as I have."

"I've never been on a single date with him."

"You have been on dates with us both."

"Please, never take me to the opera again."

He laughed, but again it was that careful laugh, delightful to hear, but it was still camouflage.

"Asher does like what is now called highbrow culture more than you do."

"The complete Tchaikovsky *Sleeping Beauty* made me want to hurt myself, and I thought I liked ballet."

"Most people like selections of the well-known ballets but have no idea how much has been cut for time."

I might have had to admit I was totally uncultured, but a knock at the door saved me. I started to ask who it was, but just thinking about asking, I could feel Nicky on the other side of the door, and . . . Cynric.

"Why is Sin with him?" I asked out loud.

"I do not know," Jean-Claude said, and called, "Come in, Nicholas."

The door opened and Nicky's broad shoulders filled it as he walked through, but there were a few inches of dark hair over his head, because Sin was the taller of the two.

"I've told you before, Jean-Claude, it's just Nicky. It's not short for anything."

"I am sorry, Nicky, but it seems too little a name for the man you have become."

He shrugged as much as his shoulder muscles would allow. "My maternal grandfather's name was Nicholas, the bitch who called herself my mother was named Nicole after him, and I was named Nicky after both of them. Let me just say while we're on the topic that I know that Nathaniel wants to name a boy Nicholas, after his dead brother, but I'd rather not."

"What boy are we naming?" I asked.

"Now you've done it," Cynric said.

"Sin, it is always lovely to see you, but we have personal matters to discuss with Nicky," Jean-Claude said.

"Are you saying that Nathaniel is picking out baby names?" I asked.

"You know he has baby fever," Nicky said.

"Picking out names is a little more than baby fever," I said.

"Nathaniel wants a family, Anita—you know that," Sin said.

"Yeah, and if he could get pregnant we could talk about it, but since I'm the only womb in the relationship it's not happening."

"You aren't the only girl anymore," Sin said.

I looked at him, ready to be mad at Nathaniel for picking out names for a baby I hadn't agreed to have, but any target would do. "What's that supposed to mean?"

"It means that when Nathaniel talked about wanting a baby, Fortune was there last time and said she might be willing."

"To have Nathaniel's baby?" I asked.

"It didn't get that far, but she's never had a baby, and if she and Echo feel safe enough she might consider it, that's all." Sin held his hands out in a little push-away gesture.

"I guess I'll talk to her on the plane about babies," I said, and I was really angry and some other emotion was in there. I realized that the thought of Nathaniel having a baby with another woman bothered me, a lot. Damn it, I was not breeding!

"I didn't mean to start a fight, Anita. You made it sound

like your objection to babies is getting pregnant. I thought knowing that one of the other women in our poly group was willing to get pregnant would solve things, not make you mad," Sin said.

"Well, it didn't solve things," I said, and I sounded pissed. Damn it.

"*Ma petite*, we do not have time for an argument if you are to feed before you get on the plane."

"Besides, the kid is right," Nicky said. "If your only objection was needing someone else to get pregnant, it would solve the problem." He was watching me, and something about the way he was doing it let me know that he was feeling exactly what I was feeling. I couldn't feel his emotions the way I could if I dropped my psychic shielding with Jean-Claude, or even Cynric, but I also couldn't keep Nicky from sensing my emotions the way I could the others. As my Bride, Nicky was compelled to keep me happy. It literally seemed to cause him discomfort if not pain to feel me unhappy. He never seemed to share what he sensed from me with any of the other people in our lives, but the look in his eyes said that he, of all of them, knew exactly why I was upset.

"It's really hard to get in the mood sometimes when this kind of topic comes up," I said, and my voice still held an edge of anger, but mostly I sounded peevish and whiny, and I hated hearing that in my own voice. I could do better than this. I had told Nathaniel that if he could get pregnant we could talk about babies more seriously. It had been my way of dropping the topic, but one thing I hadn't considered when we added other women to our poly group was that I wasn't the only one who could get pregnant now. I also hadn't expected how bad it made me feel to think of someone else carrying Nathaniel's child. I still didn't want to be pregnant, but I didn't want him to do it with anyone else, which made no sense at all. But one thing I'd learned in therapy was that just because a feeling made no sense didn't make you stop feeling it.

"I didn't mean to make things harder, or weirder," Cynric said.

Nicky gave him a look that said he doubted that last part. He didn't give Cynric looks like that much, so something was up. "Go ahead, kid. Tell them what you want that doesn't make things harder, or weirder."

"You make it sound like I'm wrong."

"I didn't say you were wrong. I just didn't say you were right."

"I have to be one or the other," Cynric said.

"No, you can be wrong and right at the same time."

"No, you can't," Cynric said.

"As much as I'd prefer the world to be black and white, yes or no, right or wrong, Nicky's right: Sometimes you can be both," I said.

"Ah, *ma petite*, you have grown in wisdom since first we met, for then you believed the world was black and white without gray in between."

"What's that mean?" Cynric asked.

"It means that once upon a time I would have agreed with you, that there was no way to be right and wrong at the same time."

"I still don't understand," he said.

"Tell them your plan and then they'll explain it to you," Nicky said.

Cynric got a stubborn look on his face. "It's logical," he said.

"I didn't argue logic with you, kid."

"Please, stop calling me *kid*. It doesn't really help me make my point."

"Not my job to help you make your point," Nicky said.

I frowned at both of them. "Why are you guys almost fighting?"

"The kid—oh, sorry, Sin—is trying to cockblock me."

Cynric rolled his eyes. "Thanks for that elegant introduction to the conversation, Nicky."

"You're welcome," he said with a smile that looked real, as if he didn't get the joke. I knew he got it, but I also knew he was a wonderful actor when he wanted or needed to be. A lot of sociopaths are.

"Enough conversation, Cynric," I said. "Just tell us what's going on."

"Anita, please use my name."

"That is your name."

"Then use the nickname I prefer."

I sighed and made it a big one, but finally said, "Fine, Sin. I wish you at least spelled it *C-Y-N*."

"You know that everyone mispronounced it that way."

"I know, I know. They kept calling you Cindy, Sidney, or Sid."

"Or Carol, Karen, Carl, or Candy—that was my favorite when I was spelling it *C-Y-N*."

"Fine. Sin, spelled just like it sounds. What's up?" I said, but didn't try to keep the crankiness out of my voice.

His expression went from stubborn to his own version of cranky. He was a very handsome guy, but not in this mood. A lot of men in my life, and women, would have given it up by now, but Cynric—sorry, Sin—had a streak of stubbornness and determination that gave mine a run for its money, which was saying something.

"Nicky is going with Anita to Ireland along with three vampires. If he donates blood to Jean-Claude now, he won't be able to donate again for a couple of days. The same for Anita and the *ardeur*, but I can feed her and donate blood to Jean-Claude now and leave Nicky fresh for later."

"You make Nicky sound like a tomato that'll spoil if we squeeze it too much," I said.

Sin shrugged. "Isn't that pretty accurate?"

Nicky chuckled low and deep in his chest.

I looked at him. "Is that how we make you feel, like an object?"

The smile was still showing in his face as he said, "No, but then, we're in love with each other, and when you feed, the sex is part of our relationship."

Jean-Claude said, "And do I make you feel like a piece of food rather than a person?"

Nicky shook his head. "You make me feel like prey sometimes, but never just food."

"I do not see you as prey, Nicky."

"Maybe *prey* is the wrong word. What do you call someone that you're trying to seduce?"

Jean-Claude looked surprised, which could have been totally pretend, but I didn't think so, or maybe I didn't want to think so.

"I swear to you, Nicky, that I have not tried to seduce you when you allowed me to feed."

Nicky studied the vampire's face for a minute, then turned to me. "Has he been trying?"

"To seduce you?"

He nodded.

"No. I mean, not really. Jean-Claude is very sensual in almost everything he does, and he treats taking blood as important. He never makes it fast food, if you know what I mean."

"You donate your life's blood to keep me alive and well. How can I treat it as anything but a sacred sharing?"

"Sacred sharing, I like it," I said.

"Are you just going to ignore my suggestion?" Sin asked.

"I think we were hoping you'd rethink it," I said.

"Why?"

"I have never taken blood from you, *neveu*, and I would not start now."

"Why not?"

"You do not understand what you are asking of me."

"I've donated blood to Echo."

"You are her lover and her wife's lover. I call you *neveu*. It means 'nephew' and I use the word very deliberately, Sin."

Sin nodded. "I know, you use it to remind yourself that I am your beloved nephew, the prince to your king, not a romantic partner."

"If you know all that, then how can you offer yourself to me like this?"

"I'm not offering to have sex with you, Jean-Claude, just give blood."

"It's never just blood with Jean-Claude," I said, studying his face. I could have lowered my shields and understood what he was actually feeling, or even thinking, because I could share both with my animals to call, but I didn't try to get emotionally closer. Until I found out where this was going and why, I wasn't sure I wanted Sin inside my head that far.

"I know he can take blood without messing with my head; any vampire can."

"But then it is just pain," Jean-Claude said.

"I'm okay with that," Sin said.

"I am not."

Sin looked at the vampire then. "What do you mean?"

"I have worked long and hard to bring myself to a point where I have so many people in my life that I care for who willingly give their life's blood to me. I do not have to take blood where I can find it, Sin, but where I want it."

"I want to be seriously considered for the commitment ceremony."

"We are aware of that, *neveu*."

"I kept asking why I wasn't being seriously considered, and finally someone told me it was because you saw me as a beloved nephew and you don't marry your nephew."

Jean-Claude gave that wonderful Gallic shrug, though it's more graceful than that sounds. It was a gesture that meant everything and nothing, but he looked good doing it. It seemed a very French gesture.

"It's not just Jean-Claude, Sin," I said. "Micah doesn't know what to do with you either."

"But he sleeps in the bed with you, Nathaniel, and me. We've all had sex with you in bed at the same time."

"That's true, but he still doesn't call you a brother-husband."

"I asked Micah before he left town, and he said if everyone else agreed, he wouldn't fight it."

"You have been a busy bee, haven't you?" I said, and again the crankiness was back. I tried not to have issues with Sin, but I did.

"I am sorry, *neveu*, but I will not agree to putting a ring on your finger. That is not the relationship we have, or want."

"Nicky donates blood to you and he's not your lover."

"That is true, but you have already heard him accuse me of attempting to seduce him when I have not tried. I am of a line of vampires that takes power from sensual things, sexual things, and the emotions that such things engender in people. I am proud of you as an uncle or even a father might be. I cannot think of you as that and then hold you in my arms while I sink fangs into your flesh and suck a little piece of your life away."

A moment of doubt crossed Sin's face, but he shook his

head. "I value our relationship, Jean-Claude. I like being the young prince to your king, but I don't want to lose my place with Anita and the others."

"Nothing is threatening your place with us," I said.

He shook his head again. "You've already cut some of your other tigers out of your life as lovers and food for the *ardeur*, Anita."

"If I tried to sleep regularly with everyone I was connected to metaphysically, the people at the core of my life wouldn't see much of me."

"Am I a part of that core, Anita?"

I took a breath and wanted to say something else, but I said the truth. "Yes."

"Then why do you keep pulling away from me?"

"We talked about this, Sin."

"I can't change the fact that I'm only nineteen, or that you're twelve years older than I am."

"I know that," I said.

"Do you?"

"Yes, I do."

"Then why do you punish me for it?"

"I don't punish you for it."

"Even I'm going to agree with the kid on this one, Anita," Nicky said.

I glared at him. "I thought you were designed to keep me happy, especially with you. Just so we're clear, this is not me being happy with you."

He looked at me. "I'm supposed to help keep you happy."

"That would be my point."

"When you're not all weird about Sin, he's part of what keeps you happy. Do you know why he was with me when they gave me Jean-Claude's message?"

It felt like Nicky had changed topics, but I said, "Of course I don't know that. Are you changing topics?"

"Sin and I were talking about what he'll be making for dinner since Nathaniel will be in Ireland tonight and he's the main cook for our poly group. Sin thought that through and came to me with a plan."

I looked from one to the other of them. "That's great," I said.

"Sin and I sous chef for Nathaniel most of the time, or cook some of the dishes."

"I know that."

"Then why do you seem so surprised that we're talking about meal planning while Nathaniel is out of town?"

"I guess we're taking most of the people you cook for."

"It's our night at the Jefferson County house with Zeke, Gina, and Chance. They'll be expecting us and we always cook when we're there."

I was embarrassed to have forgotten all about the little family that was now spending more time in my house than I was. "I wouldn't have even thought to phone them. I'm sorry."

"We have it covered, Anita, but we have it covered because I'm getting on the plane along with Nathaniel."

"I'm sorry, Sin. I didn't even think about the fact that Nathaniel does most of the cooking and meal planning."

"Nathaniel and Nicky both told me as soon as they found out so I could start planning. Nathaniel seems a little caught up with Damian, so Nicky's been helping me plan."

"But I didn't tell you, which was shitty of me."

He nodded, shrugged, and then said, "Shitty will about cover it, yeah."

"Sin and I started out talking meals, but he had a new idea that was more about the personal stuff."

"Do I want to know?" I asked.

"I think it explains some things," Nicky said.

I took a deep breath, let it out slow, and looked at Sin. "Okay, I'm listening."

"We are listening," Jean-Claude said.

Sin swallowed and suddenly looked younger than nineteen, almost as young as the teenager I'd first met. "We all share each other's emotions, thoughts, feelings. I know that how we met and the age difference bother Anita, but I wondered if maybe the fact that Jean-Claude has kept me at arm's length emotionally is impacting how she feels about me."

"What are you saying?" I asked.

"Jean-Claude works really hard to be a good guardian for me. He's started calling me *nephew* as my nickname to emphasize that I'm not his boyfriend, or boy toy, or sexual anything. I appreciate the effort he's made, but what if his working so hard to keep me in the 'child' box, the 'son' box, has made it harder for you to feel romantically toward me?"

I shook my head. "I came into our relationship having these issues, before Jean-Claude ever met you."

"We were both pretty traumatized by the Mother of All Darkness, Anita."

"You didn't seem traumatized. You seemed . . . besotted with me," I said.

"You were the first sex I'd ever had. That can be pretty overwhelming."

I thought about the discovery, just minutes before, of Asher being Jean-Claude's first male lover. It explained so much about why he'd put up with so much bad behavior from Asher for so long.

"You're saying that the 'oh boy it's sex' made you seem less traumatized to me."

"Something like that."

I looked at Jean-Claude. "Could Sin be right? Could your trying so hard to keep him in the 'child/nephew' box impact how I feel about him?"

"Perhaps."

Nicky asked, "How does it make you feel when you catch some of Anita's sexual attraction to Sin?"

Jean-Claude had gone very still, his face an almost unreadable mask, beautiful to look at it, but distant. He was trying very hard not to share anything he was feeling or thinking. "I distance myself from it when she is feeling amorous toward our young prince."

"Sin's right: You have started calling him *the young prince* or *nephew*, all terms to help remind you that he's so young and that you think of him as a younger relative, so the incest taboo attaches to him."

"You know, this much therapy is really not making me want to feed the *ardeur* on anyone right now," I said.

"You must feed before you get on the plane, *ma petite*. Your fear of flying could weaken your control over it, and that would be regrettable in the airplane."

I stared at him. "How regrettable?" I asked.

"If you lost control completely, the pilot could be involved, and how regrettable would depend on where in the flight you were when it happened, *ma petite*."

I swallowed but seemed to have a lump in my throat that wouldn't go down. I had to cough to clear it.

"You're actually pale," Sin said.

"I don't like to fly," I said.

"You're afraid to fly," Nicky said.

"Stop helping me," I said.

He smiled, but it was gentle. "I am trying to help you."

I looked into that one clear blue eye and held my hand out to him. "I know you are."

He came and took my hand in his. "You are Jean-Claude's human servant, Anita. That means his attitudes and emotions affect you."

"Our moods can affect each other," I said.

He squeezed my hand and said, "Then maybe Sin is right."

I looked at Jean-Claude, who was standing close to us. He was still giving a polite blank face, which meant he was hiding his feelings and thoughts as hard as he could. I looked at him. "You agreed with me, Jean-Claude, that the fact that the Mother of All Darkness mind-fucked Sin and me that first time together was what made me not be in love with him."

"Of course that impacted how you would think of him, *ma petite*. How could it not?"

"Yes, but is your putting him in the 'son I never had' box making it worse?"

"I do not know, and that is the truth."

"Then why are you hiding what you're feeling so hard right now?"

"Because it had not occurred to me that my effort to treat Cynric as a good legal guardian should have stopped your ability to love him as you might have."

"You feel stupid for having missed the possibility," Nicky said.

"I would not have put it that way, Nicky, but yes."

"So am I right?" Sin asked.

"I cannot tell you that you are wrong," Jean-Claude said.

"See?" Nicky said. "You're right and you're wrong."

"It's like Schrödinger's cat," I said, "alive and dead at the same time until someone opens the box."

"And what determines if the cat is alive or dead?" Sin asked.

"Leave the metaphors behind, *neveu*. It is my attitude that may have killed the cat."

"For it to affect Anita this much, you must have been fighting pretty hard to keep Sin in the 'young nephew' box," Nicky said.

"I am his legal guardian. Bibiana and Max trusted me with Cynric's well-being. I have tried to do what is right by him."

"You've been wonderful, Jean-Claude," Sin said, moving toward the three of us.

"I have done my best."

"No one could have done better," Cynric said.

"Agreed," I said.

"Agreed," Nicky said.

"But did my efforts cost Cynric Anita's love?"

"Let us worry about that," I said.

"No, Anita. Jean-Claude needs to help us see if this is really the problem," Sin said.

"How?" I asked.

"How can I remedy this harm I may have caused?"

"I'm right about saving Nicky as food for the trip."

"The reasoning is sound," Jean-Claude said.

"Feed on me tonight. If your putting me in the 'nephew' box is really hurting Anita's ability to love me, then it should help change that. If it doesn't change anything, then that's not it."

"It is a dangerous experiment, nephew."

"If it doesn't change her feelings toward me, then you don't have to take blood from me again."

"It may not be that simple, Cynric," Jean-Claude said.

"You've called me Cynric at least three times. You never forget that I prefer to be called Sin."

"Perhaps I am trying to distance myself even more? *Sin* is a rather provocative word to use as a name."

Sin frowned. "Have I missed something here?"

"What do you mean?" Jean-Claude asked.

Nicky shook my hand in his. "I think I got this one."

I glanced up at him, because I was still a step behind.

"Sin was only seventeen when he came to live here. He's grown over half a foot taller, hit the gym, and started filling out all that height."

"What's your point?" I asked.

"He's not just handsome. He's borderline pretty, a beautiful man who is over six feet tall, and athletic."

I wasn't following for a second, and then I caught up all at once. "Oh . . . crap," I said.

"Exactly."

"I'm still lost," Sin said.

"Jean-Claude only started calling you his nephew in the last year or so, right?" Nicky said.

"I guess so."

"Until about a year ago you hadn't gotten that secondary muscle development or filled out your face and the rest of you."

Sin blinked and then the light dawned all across his face. He looked surprised, then went pale, and then he blushed. He got control of himself and finally was able to look at Jean-Claude, who was wearing as careful an expression as I'd ever seen on him. "You've been so good, honorable, and I come in here and step all over it. God, Jean-Claude, I'm sorry for that."

"And if my efforts to be honorable have kept Anita from giving you her heart, then I am sorry for that."

"Now that we're all sorry, do I stay, or do I go?" Nicky asked.

I kept holding his hand, but I narrowed my eyes at him.

"Don't give me the look, Anita. You need to feed before you get on the plane and we are running out of time." He squeezed my hand to take some of the seriousness out of his words.

"Practical and correct, as usual, Nicky," Jean-Claude said, "and I may have a compromise."

"What kind of compromise?" Sin asked, and sounded positively suspicious. It sounded like my tone of voice. Had he learned it from me, or had he inherited it through the metaphysics between us? We'd never really know, but it made me wonder what else he might have picked up from me, or me from him. Maybe I'd finally be able to throw a decent spiral football since Sin was Mr. Quarterback.

"I would like you to see me take blood from Nicky, before I do so from you, Sin."

"Sometimes it's good to see what you're asking for beforehand," Nicky said.

"Are you saying that it weirds you out to donate blood?" Sin asked.

"If I didn't have qualms about it, I'd have done it sooner."

Qualms so didn't sound like a word that Nicky would have chosen to use when he first came to us. I guess we were all learning from one another.

"So you take blood from Nicky, and then what?" Sin asked; those big dark blue eyes were narrowed and again it was my expression on his face.

"If *ma petite* approves, then she will feed the *ardeur* from you, and we will share her as you have with the other men." Jean-Claude met that suspicious expression with one that was elegant, calm, and as unreadable as the dark side of the moon.

They both looked at me. Nicky squeezed my hand gently. I glanced up at him and then back at the other two men. "So it's going to be a foursome?" I asked.

"It would seem so," Jean-Claude said, still in that careful, pleasant voice.

"Just so you know, Sin, normally you'd want to make sure you negotiated how much the other two men touch you while everyone's touching the girl," Nicky said.

"You and I already had this talk."

"But you didn't have it with Jean-Claude yet."

Sin looked at the vampire and there was no suspicion on his face now; in fact, he looked very certain, almost arrogant. In that moment I realized that he was a handsome man who knew he was handsome. That was a change from when he first came to us, and maybe not a change for the better, but there it was on his face in the way he stood so tall and strong. There was suddenly a nearly touchable sense of physicality around him. It was part natural athlete and part his inner beast peeking out.

"I don't have to have the talk with Jean-Claude. He's more nervous of me than I am of him." The look he gave the other

man then was pure predator, and suddenly I wasn't so worried
about Sin's delicate sensibilities.

"Then perhaps we should discuss my boundaries, rather
than yours," Jean-Claude said.

"Perhaps we should," Sin said, and walked toward us all
like he walked onto the football field, or went up to a starting
block for track, like he owned it, and he knew he would win.
Victory wasn't a question; it was a given. When I'd met Cynric
he'd been a shy, uncertain sixteen-year-old boy, but he had
survived the Mother of All Darkness trying to do the darkest
of magic on us. He hadn't just survived physically, but mentally, and emotionally he seemed to have come out of it better
than some of the other, older weretigers. I should have understood that kind of strength grows into more. Watching him
walk toward us, toward Jean-Claude, I finally realized that the
scared boy I remembered wasn't Cynric anymore. He was Sin,
and he'd chosen the name. It had been another clue about who
he had become. You have to have a certain level of machismo
to choose and carry a name like that. Looking at him now, I
realized it suited him. How had I missed it?

29

NICKY STRIPPED HIS shirt off first. He wasn't much for a
slow reveal when he was in the room with me and other men.
I wasn't sure if it was that he didn't want to compete with men
who took their clothes off onstage professionally, or if once he
revealed that massive, muscular upper body he didn't feel like
he had to compete with anyone. I'd seen men move or stop
lifting weights next to him in the gym when he was working
out. Anyone who wouldn't even lift next to him was never
going to get naked in bed with him, but lucky for us none of
those men was in the bedroom with us. Nicky had helped

teach Sin how to lift weights and Jean-Claude had no desire to
bulk up as much as the werelion.

In fact, Jean-Claude came up behind him and trailed his
hand across those muscular shoulders and made an appreciative sound, something he'd never done before with Nicky. In
fact, he put his arm around the other man's shoulders and
neck; the inches of extra height allowed him to lean his face
against the side of Nicky's head, black curls against the straight
blond hair. They were opposites in almost every way, which
wasn't a bad thing, just a thing.

Nicky stiffened, and Jean-Claude leaned in and whispered
something in his ear; as his lips moved the werelion relaxed.
Whatever Jean-Claude was telling him reassured him, or
pleased him, because he smiled.

Jean-Claude laid the softest of kisses against the other
man's cheek.

"You don't have to put on a show for me," Sin said.

"I am not putting on a show for you, Sin. I am admiring
what I will be plunging my . . ." And he hesitated just long
enough to let Nicky's mind fill in the blank before saying,
"Fangs into tonight."

Sin looked at them, eyes narrowing.

Jean-Claude wrapped both arms around those oh-so-broad
shoulders. Nicky gripped the vampire's arm and rubbed his
face against Jean-Claude's hair as if he were scent-marking.
The vampire laid his lips against Nicky's cheek even more
delicately than before so that he put a line of the gentlest of
kisses from cheek to neck. Nicky closed his eyes and turned
his head to the other side so that the strong line of his neck was
stretched bare and waiting. All that strength of that muscular
upper body was suddenly turned in Jean-Claude's arms into
something submissive, takeable. I'd never seen anything like
that between them before.

Sin looked at me, and again it was my suspicion on his face,
or maybe now it was his own. "They're trying to scare me off.
It's not going to work."

"I don't know what you're talking about," I said, and
walked to the other men. It wasn't that the two men didn't
touch when Jean-Claude fed on Nicky, but they didn't touch

quite like this, so it was a show for Sin, but if the men were willing to do it I wasn't going to ruin it for them. Besides, I was sleeping with all of them and I liked to see my men enjoying one another. I slid my hands around Nicky's bare waist. The touch made him open his eye, and I was gazing up into their faces as I caressed the narrowness of his waist until I touched Jean-Claude's shirt and the firmness of his body underneath it. I rose up on tiptoes to offer a kiss. Nicky's arm pressed against my back, and Jean-Claude unfolded one arm from around his shoulders to push his hand underneath my hair to caress the back of my neck so that when I kissed Nicky it was his hand pressing my chest against Nicky's naked upper body, but it was Jean-Claude's hand that pressed my face tighter into the kiss.

I kissed him until my pulse was in my throat, and I drew back, breathless, to turn to Jean-Claude, who bent over Nicky's shoulder. I had to stretch to meet him with Nicky's body between us, but his height in the boots and me going nearly on pointe let us kiss. Nicky put his hands around my waist. I felt him dip like he'd bent his knees a little, and then he lifted me up so that Jean-Claude and I could kiss more. Either my feet could dangle in the air or I could do the airborne version of popping one foot up behind me, which was what I did. Jean-Claude kept his hand at the back of my neck, but this time he pressed me in against his own lips. I wrapped one arm around the vampire and the other one around the werelion. My tongue slid between his fangs, and he kissed me harder. Nicky put one arm around my waist and held me pinned against his chest, freeing up his other hand to grab my ass.

"I've shared Anita with Nathaniel and Micah at the same time. Unless Jean-Claude is planning to mouth-kiss Nicky next, I've seen the show."

Jean-Claude and I pulled back, looked at each other, then at Nicky. Nicky turned his head not to me, but to the other man, offering a kiss, which he'd never done before with any of the other men in my life. Jean-Claude looked at him, smiled, and then leaned into the kiss. I was still in their arms held close and tight, so that I got to watch the kiss so close that I could have joined it, if I could have figured out where my lips would go.

Nicky's mouth worked, putting more into the kiss than just a touching of lips. Jean-Claude responded to the eagerness, his other hand playing in the blond hair as he kissed him back. Seeing them kiss excited me, but being this close to it tensed things low in my body so hard and so tight it was a pleasure bordering on pain. It stole my breath, parted my lips as if I'd drawn a breath to blow out a candle.

Another hand touched my face, made me turn to find Sin there. He kissed me while the two men were still kissing each other. Sin's kiss was as eager as ever; if he was bothered by anything the others were doing it didn't show, as he wrapped his arms around the three of us. I didn't fight the eagerness of his mouth on mine as Jean-Claude transferred his hand from the back of my neck to wrap around Sin and draw him in tighter against the side of Nicky's body and me. Nicky flexed his arm around my waist, almost crushing me against his chest, and the extra force was enough to draw eager noises from me that Sin licked and finally bit gently away.

I felt Jean-Claude's power like an early-spring wind with that edge of winter's cold still riding it, but the promise of warmth and flowers to come. Once, it would have been only the chill of the grave, but the more wereanimals I connected to, the warmer his energy had become. I drew back from Sin, and the other two men had drawn back from each other. There was a crimson dot on the edge of Nicky's lower lip. Jean-Claude's eyes had bled to solid shining blue.

My voice sounded breathy as I said, "You have to be careful French-kissing vampires, Nicky."

He licked the fresh blood from his lip and said, "I'm not used to the fangs yet."

"Bloody kisses like sweet copper pennies in my mouth," Jean-Claude said.

"Pretty talk," Nicky said.

"Jean-Claude always knows just what to say. I think it's something about being French," I said.

"*Non, ma petite, mon lionne*, I am inspired by such bounty before my eyes."

"You know that Nathaniel likes to bite, right?" Sin asked.

We all looked at him.

"I've seen kisses that ended with lips bleeding a lot more than this."

"Then we will have to do better, won't we, Nicky?" Jean-Claude said.

"Yeah, we wouldn't want the kid disappointed."

"Don't call me *kid*."

"Prove that you aren't one and I'll stop."

"How do I prove it?"

Nicky smiled, a damn-near-evil smile. "I've got a few ideas."

30

NICKY TRIED, BUT in the end Sin saw it all as a sort of competitive dare, so nothing that Jean-Claude was willing to do was enough to scare him off. I think Nicky would have been willing to personally do things that would have freaked Sin out, not because he wanted to have sex with him, because I was pretty sure he didn't, but because Nicky was just that competitive. If it was a game of chicken, Nicky was not going to be the one who flinched. Once, I would have said the same of Jean-Claude, but something about Sin hit issues for him that I didn't even know he had. Maybe the idea that his issues were part of what had kept me from being in love with Cynric was true, but if so, how the hell did we prove it, or fix it? Hell, did we want to fix it?

All the clothes were gone, the four of us nude in the newly delivered double king-size bed with the red silk sheets from the even bigger bed tucked in and around the bed, so that we were still on top of the sheets rather than fighting to get them free. Jean-Claude's skin was so white against the crimson sheets. Sin's summer tan looked even darker against them. Nicky looked paler when his skin was next to Sin's tan, but he didn't look pale at all next to the nearly pure white of Jean-

Claude's body. Nicky's eye seemed like an even brighter blue no matter if his face was next to Jean-Claude's midnight blue or Sin's blue tiger's eyes.

I kissed Nicky's face, laying my lips over the scar where his other eye would have been, and he put his arms around me as I lay on top of him and took my kisses to the scars, the same as my lips touching the closed lid of his other eye. I'd convinced him a while back that to me the scar was just another texture of his body to kiss and caress.

Someone started kissing along my back while I was kissing Nicky, and I wondered for a moment, but I didn't have to look to know the feel of Jean-Claude's lips against my skin. He spoke with his mouth against my lower back, his hands smoothing over my hips so that I writhed against the front of Nicky's body. "I need you on top, Nicky."

"All you have to do is ask," he said, and he rolled us over so fast that I made that high-pitched "eep" sound that was such a girl sound. I was just suddenly staring up at Nicky above me. I laughed a little nervously, because I could feel his weight above me. Muscle weighs more, and so did Nicky. We weren't having intercourse yet, so it was just all that heaviness pressing me against the bed. I had a moment of realizing that if he wanted to trap me, I was trapped. It sped my heart, raced my pulse, and made me swallow hard. If Nicky hadn't topped me in the bedroom, would that moment have scared me for real? I don't know, because he did and I let that little flash of fear grow, because I knew he'd like it.

He leaned over my face, sniffing loudly along my skin. "Fear makes the meat taste better," he said in a voice that held an edge of growl. When he raised his face, his eye had changed to lion amber. He let a trickle of growl slide out from between his human lips. I trusted him utterly, but the game was to be afraid in that safe roller-coaster-ride way, so I didn't fight that moment of terror that thrilled through my body. It was instinctive, hardwired into that primitive part of the brain that remembered what a growl like that meant against the skin of your throat.

Sin crawled across the bed from the right side of us. He lowered his head and sniffed the air near me. "She's never afraid of me like this."

"You don't know how to be scary yet," Nicky said.

The weight was suddenly crushing and I said, "Too heavy."

Jean-Claude appeared over Nicky's shoulder and I realized I was pinned under their combined weight. If Nicky hadn't been raised just a little above my chest, they might have been heavy enough to keep me from breathing. I managed to say, "If we were fucking this would be fun, but it's just heavy now."

Jean-Claude laid his head on Nicky's shoulder, settling even more of his weight on top of the other man and on me. "Nicky, do you want to be inside her when I feed?"

"Yes, let me make her come at least once before you feed, because once you do I won't last."

"As you like," Jean-Claude said; he smiled down at me and then slid out of sight, but I could tell by the weight that he wasn't on top of Nicky anymore. Nicky was free to move his body enough for me to feel that he could pretend for Cynric that he was into sex with Jean-Claude, but some things couldn't be faked. He wasn't completely soft, but he wasn't that eager hardness that he usually was when we got to this point. I expected him to change positions, or ask for a hand or maybe a mouth from me, but he didn't. He moved his hips so that I had the choice of spreading my legs or him grinding himself into my pelvis. I wanted to make love to him, so I helped. By the time he'd settled himself between my legs, he was harder than he had been just seconds before, but still not hard enough. With most men, if they weren't hard when they started, you needed to back up and do some more foreplay, but Nicky raised himself on those amazing arms, his upper body rising above me so that I caressed my hands along all that hard work in the gym carved into the body above me. I gazed down the line of his body past the ridged hardness of his stomach until I could see that part of him that he was pushing against me. Even only partially erect, the sight of it tightened my body, and I threw my head back with a small cry so that I was suddenly staring up into his face.

His hair had spilled forward so I could see all of his face. There was no way for him to hide. The first time I'd seen him like this he'd ducked his head and let his hair fall back in front of his scars, but now he just looked at me bold as brass, his face and that one blue eye so confident, so Nicky, now that he knew that I wouldn't look away or flinch. He wasn't going to see anything in my face except how much I wanted him.

He smiled down at me and began to push his hips as if he were already inside me. It made that part of his body rub against my opening and other things. I could feel him growing harder, bigger, and the sensation of it drew small, eager sounds from me, so that I raised my hips to meet him, but he was still not quite hard enough. He put all his weight on one arm and reached down to use his hand to angle the crown inside me. I almost protested, but as soon as the head penetrated I couldn't speak for just a second and he was already pushing himself in and out of me. With every thrust he grew firmer, longer, until he was as hard as he needed to be to start fucking me. We made love, but I made love with all my men. Nicky liked to fuck; there was no other word for what we both enjoyed together. He drove himself in and out of me fast and faster, driving himself deep so that he hit every sweet spot inside me over and over and over again. If Jean-Claude hadn't been with us Nicky would have pinned my wrists and made it rougher, but that didn't work for my raven-haired fiancé. So I got to look down the long line of Nicky's body and watch his body work in and out of mine, until in between one stroke and another I orgasmed, screaming my pleasure into his face. It startled him, I think, but he kept his rhythm so the orgasm built and fed into another one and another. I gripped his arms where he held himself above me, and if it had been most of my other lovers I would have raked my nails down his arms, but we'd had this discussion before so that even while I screamed my pleasure I didn't forget that some night soon he'd be in charge of me and if I bled him now he'd bleed me later. I didn't like being bled during sex any more than he did. Well, except for one type of bloodletting.

Nicky's voice was clear, but full of the effort he was putting into fucking me and not going himself. "Jean-Claude, feed now. I'm not going to last much longer."

Jean-Claude came up behind him again, but this time their combined weight only pushed against Nicky's hips, burying him deeper inside me, which made me cry out again. Nicky shuddered above me, eye closing for a moment, and then he said, "Do it, Jean-Claude."

Jean-Claude smoothed Nicky's yellow hair to one side to bare the strong, thick line of his neck. He whispered in French against Nicky's hair, and I felt some tension go out of Nicky. He was still thick and hard inside me, still holding that impossibly muscular chest up off me on the swell and curve of his arms, but I knew the vampire was inside his head now. Jean-Claude raised his head. "Are you ready, *mon lionne*?" he whispered.

"Yes, Jean-Claude, do it. Just do it!"

Jean-Claude opened his mouth wide, so that I caught a flash of fangs, his eyes a solid burning blue, as if the night sky had caught fire, and then he struck. I could see his mouth locked on the side of Nicky's neck, watch his throat swallowing, his mouth sucking. Nicky's body reacted, beginning to pump inside me again. He was already buried as deep inside me as he could go, and Jean-Claude's body pinned his hips so he didn't have much movement, but what he had was enough. He began to move faster in and out, in and out, hitting deep and hard, so that I screamed out again for him, fighting not to close my eyes so that I could see Jean-Claude drinking him down, Nicky's eye closed, face almost slack as if he'd already gone, but I could feel him harder than ever, so hard, so thick, so . . . He brought me screaming again, and this time he yelled with me, his body shoving one more time deep inside me. I could feel him quivering inside me as he came, and his body shuddered above me as the vampire rode him.

Nicky finally collapsed, throwing his chest to one side so that he didn't bury my face against his pecs. I appreciated it, not just because I didn't have to eat my way to freedom through his chest, but because I could still see Jean-Claude at his throat. I was looking at him with my body still thrumming with all those orgasms as the vampire rose up. His mouth was still open wide enough that I saw him lick along his fangs; his face for that instant was as bestial as any wereanimal's and then it was gone, hidden behind that beautiful face. Only the eyes shining with blue-black fire showed what was inside and had gotten to come out for a few minutes.

He helped Nicky roll to one side where he just lay there, eye closed; only the rise and fall of his chest let me know he was alive. A thin line of blood trickled from the neat fang marks in the side of his neck. For them to bleed that much meant Jean-Claude had gotten a little carried away. We'd all enjoyed ourselves.

Jean-Claude was on all fours above me, his body hard and ready, and just the sight of him above me like that made me cry out again. I reached for him, but he caught my hands and said, "Sin, help me move her to the edge of the bed."

"Why?"

"So you can join us. You need a little encouragement to be able to feed the *ardeur* for Anita."

I didn't know what he meant at first, but Sin pulled-half-carried me to the edge of the bed and I could suddenly see what Jean-Claude meant. Sin wasn't hard, or ready. He was soft, hanging loose against the front of his body. He hadn't enjoyed watching the three of us together. I didn't know what about it had bothered him, but something had——his body told me that.

Jean-Claude moved me to the edge until my head spilled over the side and I was looking at Sin's body upside down. It wasn't one of my favorite positions for giving oral, but with him still soft, it would be good. I'd change positions when he got hard enough, or that was my plan. Sin was almost too tall for the lower bed, all that long leg so that he had to lean in, so he was almost doing a standing push-up just so I could reach him. Jean-Claude's hands cupped my hips, and I cupped the backs of Sin's thighs and sucked him down, so soft and warm. I loved sucking on a man when he was this soft. There was no fight to breathe, no choking, just the sensation of him in my mouth. Jean-Claude's hands caressed my hips and I felt the tip of him brush my opening. It made me pause with my mouth buried as tight to Sin's body as I could get. Jean-Claude entered me and I was so wet, so ready from everything that Nicky and I had done. It was amazing feeling Jean-Claude's body slide inside me. It made me moan with Sin's body in my mouth. He was already growing harder. Jean-Claude found his rhythm quickly and brought me to climax with Sin still inside my mouth, so I screamed my orgasm around him. He shuddered and when I came up shallow on him he was thicker and he started moving himself inside my mouth with me sucking him, so that we started to find a rhythm of him inside my mouth as Jean-Claude found one between my legs.

"Unleash the *ardeur, ma petite*; unleash it so you will feed on both of us when we go."

I called the *ardeur*, unleashed it, uncaged it, and let it roar over all three of us so that the two men both cried out. Jean-Claude brought me again with the feel of him inside me, sliding over and over on that sweet spot just inside. It made me scream around Sin's body as he thrust deeper inside my throat. I didn't have to fight my gag reflex now, because with the *ardeur* I didn't have one; it was great and made oral sex even more amazing than it was. I used my hands on Sin's body to urge him to fuck me harder and faster, shoving all that hard length down my throat deeper than I could ever take it without the *ardeur* riding me, riding all of us.

"Close," Sin gasped out.

"Hold until I bring her one more time." And he caressed himself over that spot three more times to match those three words. The weight grew and spread and I was nothing but pleasure, shaking and shrieking between the two of them.

"Oh, God, please," Sin yelled.

"Almost!" Jean-Claude answered him and shoved himself faster and faster inside me, not trying to caress that spot near my opening, but places deeper inside me.

Sin had stopped moving; I think he was afraid to keep fucking my throat or he'd go before Jean-Claude, so he stayed almost frozen above me. I started sucking on him again since he wasn't moving for me. He said, "Anita, please, I'll . . ."

Jean-Claude said, "In three."

"God, you're joking," Sin said, but he thrust himself in my mouth and down my throat, once. Jean-Claude shoved between my legs. Twice inside my throat. A second time deep inside me. The third time Sin thrust down my throat, and Jean-Claude said, "Now, now!" Sin buried himself as deep inside my throat as he could; I drove my nails into his thigh and his ass and would have screamed as Jean-Claude thrust himself as deep inside me as he could go and they both poured

themselves inside me at the same time. I could feel Sin pulsing, spilling the heat of him down my throat, and Jean-Claude
pouring warm between my legs, and I fed on them. I fed on the
seed of them spilling inside me. I fed on the feel of their bodies plunged inside me. I fed on my nails digging into Sin's
body, on Jean-Claude's hands on me. I fed on them everywhere they touched me, and when I got Sin's blood under my
nails, it seemed to absorb up through my fingertips.

He cried out above me, and then he screamed. I always
valued when the men screamed for me. It was so damn rare.
It all felt so good, so right, and then I felt power rushing over
me, through me, and it wasn't coming from Jean-Claude. It
was Sin. I couldn't see what was happening, because my
face was still buried upside down against his body, but that
body was doing some kind of magic that I'd never felt before. I had a moment to start to pull away from him, so I
wouldn't be choking on him when the *ardeur* left me and
whatever this power was happened, but I was still blind
against his body when the room started to shake and all I
could think was *Earthquake . . . St. Louis doesn't have
earthquakes*, and then we were all scrambling to untangle
ourselves and try to find cover, but how do you hide from an
earthquake when you're in a cave?

31

IT WASN'T AN earthquake, but the lump under the rug that
Sin tripped over turned out to be the floor. It had cracked and
buckled as if something had torn through the rock. All the
floors in the underground were solid rock, some with flooring
over it, but it was basically bedrock, or close to it.

"What the hell did that?" I asked, staring down at the rip
in the solid rock. It wasn't deep, just baring more rock under-

neath, but it was a nearly straight line about five feet long and maybe six inches wide. The rock stuck up on either side of it like a miniature mountain range just brought to life with a valley in between, waiting for grass to fill it.

I hugged myself, but the black silk robe wasn't much for warmth. Jean-Claude was back in his much thicker black robe with the fur collar and cuffs. We'd put on the robes because the guards on the door had come into the room when they heard the noise of the floor cracking. It had sounded like an explosion, and the guards had hit their general alarm button before they came into the room pale and ready to defend us from the danger, except that there hadn't been anything to attack. How can you protect your charges from something that can split the floor open without leaving a trace?

Nicky had gone to get some of the guards with the most experience with magic and metaphysics—the Harlequin. They'd spent centuries dealing with the Mother of All Darkness and the vampire council, who were all heavy hitters for stuff like this.

"If we had not killed him I would wonder if it was the Earthmover warning us," Jean-Claude said.

"He could level a city with a real earthquake, but I didn't know he could do things like this," I said.

"I honestly do not know, but it has the appearance of his sort of power."

I nodded. "Agreed, but I cut his heart out personally, so it's not him."

"Who's the Earthmover?" Sin asked from the chair by the fireplace. He didn't have a robe here, so he'd put his jeans back on and was sort of huddling in the chair. He'd managed to pull those long legs up so that he was hugging his knees. He reminded me more of the teenager I'd first met now than the confidently arrogant lover of earlier. It was almost comforting to see the younger Cynric peeking out of that handsome, muscular body.

"He was one of the vampire council, and one of the oldest vampires I'd ever met until Marmee Noir. He came to town to try to kill Jean-Claude and take over St. Louis."

"I thought the old council members gave up any chance at their own territories when they took a council seat," Sin said, looking at us over his knees, so that his dark blue eyes glittered in the artificial firelight.

"That's true," I said.

"The Earthmover did not come to rule St. Louis," Jean-Claude said. "He came to take over here and use my vampires as his tools to cause a vampire incident so terrible it would repeal the new laws and make us illegal monsters again."

"Why would a vampire want to go back to having no rights?" he asked.

I answered, "He thought that legal vampires would eventually spread across the earth and turn so many humans into vampires that they'd basically run out of food, and thus they'd die out along with the humans. Mutually assured destruction for humans and vampires."

"The Earthmover sought to make vampires illegal again, so we would go back to the shadows where he thought we belonged. He thought the old system guaranteed that vampire numbers would stay smaller, because we had to stay hidden, and thus we would not overpopulate and depopulate our only food source."

"Humans and wereanimals," Sin said.

Jean-Claude nodded. "He talked only of humans, but yes."

"I've listened to the Harlequin and most of the older vamps see us, all of us shapeshifters, as lesser."

"It is a sadly common attitude among the oldest of us."

"Well, it sucks," he said.

"Yes, it does, which is why I am doing my best to promote newer and more progressive attitudes among them."

One of the guards by the door cleared his throat. We looked at him. It was Emmanuel, one of Rafael's wererats; his hair was pale brown, cut short, and his pale gray eyes looked paler in the permanent tan of his face. He wasn't the tallest or the most muscled, but he excelled at everything physical: hand-to-hand, blade work, shooting; he was even good at undercover work. He was also handsome in that clean-cut sort of way. He looked like he should be walking around a college campus somewhere worrying about passing algebra and how it would affect his athletic scholarship, but he was actually a lot more deadly than some of the guards who walked around throwing attitude all over the place.

"Yes, Emmanuel?" Jean-Claude said.

"Some of us really appreciate how hard you try to make the older vampires treat us like we're people."

"Yeah, we do," said the second guard, and I realized it was the new guard, Harris, from yesterday, or was it the day before? Though he was all white-bread as far as I knew, his hair was almost the same shade of brown as Emmanuel's, and Harris was the one with brown eyes.

"It is good to know that our efforts are appreciated," Jean-Claude said with a graceful incline of his head.

"I know that some of the older vamps here in this country and in Europe aren't too happy about it, so I just wanted to say *thank you*."

Jean-Claude smiled. "You are most welcome, Emmanuel, and . . . Harry, is it?"

"Harris, sir."

"Harris."

"I see your pal Barry isn't with you tonight," I said.

He made a face and then fought back to bodyguard neutral. "He's not my friend."

"We let Barry and another guard go," Emmanuel said.

"I've got one more chance to prove I'm not like Barry," Harris said.

"Claudia and Fredo have decided to pair the new guards with more experienced guards—no newbies teamed up together."

I looked at Emmanuel and nodded. "Agreed."

There was a knock on the door, but it opened before we could say anything. It was Nicky with Magda and her master, Giacomo. He was taller than anyone else in the room except Sin. His shoulders were as broad as Nicky's, or damn close, but whereas Nicky had that upside-down triangle that bodybuilders had, Giacomo was built like an old-time refrigerator, a big rectangle of muscle. You wouldn't think he had the same kind of muscle that Nicky did, because his was hidden under an extra layer of flesh, but it was under there. I'd seen them lift weights in friendly competitions in the gym. The other guards would place bets on who could lift more, or do the most reps. It was like the room had shrunk around them.

Giacomo went to one knee in front of Jean-Claude. "My King, how may we serve you?"

Magda had gone to one knee beside him, though she almost never did it when Giacomo wasn't with her. If she thought it was excessive she kept her head lowered so it didn't show on her face. Giacomo was her master metaphysically, and that would be true until one of them died. Marriage had nothing on magic for longevity.

"Rise, Giacomo. I've told you such displays are not necessary in private."

He raised the nearly perfect roundness of his face, the dark brown of one eye and the pale milky blue of the other set in tight folds. The scar that bisected his right eye curved through his eyebrow and onto his cheek. I'd thought he was blind in the eye, and so had some of the other guards in fight practice. They'd tried to go for his blind side and he'd kicked their asses, because the eye worked, not as well as the other one, but he could see out of it.

Giacomo rose as he was bid and gave that nearly infectious smile of his. Nicky was just behind him and Magda. He still had his hair swept to one side so that the scars over his right eye were visible. The two big men stood there with their different scars over the same eye, and it was striking. Two such men with similar injuries on the same eye—what were the odds?

Nicky led Magda and Giacomo to where the floor was broken. They stared down at it and then Giacomo leaned into Nicky and whispered something. Nicky told Emmanuel and Harris to man the door from the other side, and they did it, though Emmanuel looked back as he closed the door.

"Why did we need privacy?" I asked.

"Because I know who did this," Giacomo said.

"Who?" Sin said, coming to stand beside Jean-Claude and me.

"You."

Sin blinked at him. "I don't know what you're talking about. I don't have any ability to do . . . whatever this is," he said, waving vaguely in the floor's direction.

Magda said, "Did you feel a rush of power just before it happened?"

"We were having sex. I wasn't thinking about anything else."

"Actually, there *was* a rush of power from him," I said.

"It was just my beast, Anita. You know that orgasm is one of the times that the inner beast comes closest to the surface."

"I know. That's why all the good little boy and girl shapeshifters get chained up for their first orgasms so they don't kill anyone by accident."

"You were sensing that," he said.

"Did you change shape?" Magda asked.

He shook his head.

Giacomo looked at us. "My King, did you sense anything from him?"

"As he said, we were having sex with Anita between us. It is always magical to be with her when she feeds the *ardeur*. It tends to blind you to any other power."

"It can be quite overwhelming," Magda said.

"Then perhaps the young prince did not understand what was happening."

"I did not do that," Sin said, pointing at the floor.

"You are a pureblooded blue clan tiger."

"I know that."

"Earth is what your clan controlled."

"I know blue tiger is earth, red is fire, white is metal, black is water, and gold is sun, or controls all the other clans," Sin said, repeating it the way you'd say something you were forced to memorize in school but didn't really want to.

"Have you seen Crispin call the small lightning to his hands?"

"It's like super static electricity, is all," Sin said.

"But it is still the power of his clan manifesting since he became Anita's white tiger to call, and the prince of the red clan can now call fire to his hands after becoming Anita's red tiger."

"A little super static electricity and fire like a match appearing in your hand is not the same thing as cracking the floor open," Sin said, pointing at the damage again. I could feel his fear bubbling along my own stomach.

"Our new Queen has not seen the red prince in over a year,

and Crispin is no longer blessed to be among her lovers, but you are much admired by her," Giacomo said, being so polite about it that it sounded like he wasn't talking about sex at all.

"Wait," I said. "Are you saying that Sin's power is more because I'm sleeping with him regularly?"

"Yes, because it is the coin of your vampire line. If you had been descended from a different bloodline, then other types of proximity would have had a similar effect."

"So if Anita slept more often with the other two, then their power would grow?" Magda asked.

"I believe so."

"So why hasn't Dev's power grown? She and Jean-Claude are sleeping with him regularly," Sin asked.

"He has the ability to shapeshift into a lion, as well as a gold tiger, and he has gifted Micah with a second beast shape as well; I would say that Dev's powers are growing."

"Crispin and the red tiger both showed their powers years ago. I've never had anything like this happen before," Sin said.

"Some things take time," Giacomo said.

"Domino and I slept with Anita the same night, a few months after Crispin. Are you saying that we'll both get powers?"

"I have never heard of someone who had mixed clan blood exhibiting their bloodlines' powers."

"So because Domino is half white clan and half black, you think he won't exhibit any of the clan magic?" I asked.

"I have seen the tiger clans when they were at their most powerful, and only the pureblooded among them could work their most powerful spells."

"So why did it take this long for Sin? He's pureblooded blue tiger," I asked.

"He was too young."

"He's been legally an adult for a couple of years," I said.

"Legal adulthood by modern standards is merely an agreed-upon number. Some teenagers I see in this country are very grown-up years before they are eighteen, and others seem to be stuck in a perpetual childhood," Giacomo said.

"Are you saying this proves I'm an adult blue tiger?"

"Yes, Cynric, that is exactly what I am saying."

"Sin, not Cynric," he said automatically.

"It is your choice, but *Prince Cynric* seems to roll off the tongue a little more sweetly than *Prince Sin*."

"*Prince Sin* sounds like a rock star name," I said, smiling and taking his hand to take the sting out of it.

"Nah," Nicky said, "it's a porn star name."

"I'm not *Prince* anything. It's just *Sin*."

"Legally it's still *Cynric*," Jean-Claude said.

Sin frowned at him; again there was that echo of the younger Cynric when sullen was more his style. It was not a style that was going to win him the brass ring—oh, my bad, the gold ring. Jean-Claude would never do anything as inexpensive as brass.

"By any name, you have grown into your powers of earth," Giacomo said.

"Or perhaps it is that this is the first time he has been intimate with both Anita and me?"

"Perhaps," Giacomo said.

"You said yourself that Dev has gained power and he is lover to us both."

"So is Fortune, and she hasn't manifested earth powers, and she's older than me by centuries, so she was old enough."

"But she is not Anita's blue tiger to call. You are," Giacomo said.

"If I did tear up the floor, I didn't do it on purpose and I don't know how to do it again."

"It is like your inner beast, Cynric—Sin—you will learn how to control it and how to use it more knowledgeably as you have more practice," Giacomo said.

"If this is my power, then how dangerous is it going to be? I mean, my tiger form could kill people if I weren't in control of it. Legends say that the blue tigers could cause earthquakes and destroy entire armies. That's an exaggeration, right?"

"No, it is not an exaggeration. I have stood upon a mountain and watched ten of your clan call their magic together and raise the earth itself against an enemy army. You on your own, even with more training, could not wreak such havoc. I am glad to see that the clan that raised you told you the history of your people, but do not fear your powers."

"Queen Bibiana made certain that I knew the history of all

the clans. We thought the gold tigers were extinct centuries ago, so Bibiana wanted the white clan, her clan, to be up to speed on all the legends and history so they could lead if it was needed."

"I'm not sure the other remaining clans would allow that," Giacomo said.

Sin shrugged. "Bibi wanted us ready, just in case. She knew the red tigers' queen wasn't teaching anyone the legends, because she'd asked. Their queen thought the legends were done, because the gold tigers were gone, and the only known blue tigers and black tigers left were enslaved to the Harlequin, who served the Mother of All Darkness, our greatest enemy. No offense on the enslaved part."

"None taken. When our Dark Mother was still alive we were all slave to her plans and wishes," Giacomo said.

"We have all been slaves to one vampire or another in our time," Jean-Claude said.

Giacomo bowed to him. "True and wise words, Your Highness."

"The main reason she has agents looking at foundlings across the world is to find any survivors of the lost clans," Sin said.

"I would have said there would be no survivors, but here you are, my prince. The new genetic tests have proven that you are as pure of blood as Fortune, who is the last of the blue clan that I knew to be alive," Giacomo said. There was something about the way he looked at Sin that I didn't like. He was centuries older than Jean-Claude, so he should have been even better at hiding his expressions, but I'd noticed that a lot of the Harlequin weren't that good at schooling their faces. I'd asked Echo about it and been told, *We wore masks almost all the time; no one saw our faces except when we played a part to gather information, and then we were playing human. We needed our faces to show emotions.* It was as good an explanation as any.

"I was nearly two when someone left me at a church. I was well fed, well clothed, a happy well-adjusted toddler. Someone took care of me for all that time and then just left me."

"There were rumors of clan tigers here in this country, but we were not the ones sent to investigate," Magda said.

"Bibi figured that either my parents had left me to save me from what was hunting them, or they had died and whoever they left me with didn't want to deal with a baby."

I put my arms around his bare waist and hugged him. He looked down at me, but his face still held that edge of anger, sullenness, and deeper in those rich blue eyes was the uncertainty of it. *How could they leave me? Why would they leave me? Was it something I did? Why didn't they want me?* All the questions that children who are lost ask about their past.

Jean-Claude gripped Sin's shoulder tight. I expected him to hug us, but he didn't. He kept that almost-artificial distance from us. I put an arm around both their waists and tried to draw us into a group hug, but Jean-Claude resisted.

Sin looked at him then. "You're afraid to hug me now. Why?"

"Let us say that I am no longer certain of how to interact with you."

A look of absolute pain came over his face, and the emotion of it crashed the shields between us. He was sad and scared that he'd screwed up a relationship that he valued. He suddenly felt very young in my head, because it hadn't occurred to him that sleeping together even just this much would change things between them.

Nicky came over and wrapped us all in one huge group hug. "Don't get weird about it, Jean-Claude."

Jean-Claude hesitated for a minute and then finally hugged us all, so that we were entwined, and it wasn't sexual. It was comforting. It was . . . family. Sin's muscled shoulders began to shake, and it took me a second to realize he was crying. Jean-Claude touched his face and dried the tears away with his hands. The look he gave Sin wasn't romantic; it was very much Uncle Jean-Claude to his beloved nephew, and that was why he wouldn't be able to put a ring on it. Sin had to decide if he was willing to lose Jean-Claude as his "uncle," his father figure, to make him a romantic partner, but he had to decide, because he and Jean-Claude couldn't do both.

32

WE SAID GOOD-BYE to everyone at the Circus rather than at the airport for a lot of reasons. One, it made more sense from a security point of view. Two, we were already needing two large SUVs to get the luggage and us to the airport; it would have taken even more to get everyone to the airport who wanted to say good-bye. Three, we could say good-bye as enthusiastically as we wanted to without someone snapping a picture with their cell phone and posting it on the Internet. Jean-Claude was the vampire of everyone's dreams, which meant that just snapping a good picture with your phone could get you money from some gossip sites.

The luggage had been carried up the long steps by other guards like overly muscled ants trip after trip. They'd loaded everything into the cars outside, and it was time to go. Jean-Claude and I had kissed good-bye in private, but seeing him standing there made me want to do it again. He broke from the kiss to touch the ring on my left hand. It was platinum, white gold, channel-set with white diamonds and one large oval dark blue sapphire. All the stones were set into the metal and, it was all smooth so that it wouldn't catch on anything, including the rubber gloves that I wore at crime scenes. The ring was still shining and beautiful, but it was practical, and I needed that for my job. Most cops wore plain bands or nothing to work, but Jean-Claude had wanted me to wear his promise ring always, and his promise would never be just a plain band of gold. No, he was all about the shiny.

"Ma petite," he said as he turned the ring on my finger, "I never thought to see my ring upon your finger, and now all I can think of is how much I want to add a wedding ring to it."

"We're working on it," I said, looking up into that almost painfully beautiful face.

"Yes. Yes, we are," he said, smiling down at me. I'd shared enough of his thoughts to know that he thought I was beautiful and sexy and utterly desirable, but I didn't understand it. I was good at sex, so maybe the sexy part, but I was also a royal pain in the ass in other areas. He had been one of the most beautiful men in the world for centuries. How does one mortal woman, any woman, compare to that?

Nathaniel put his hand over ours, wrapping his hand so that we were all touching the ring, or maybe the ring was touching us. "It's a promise ring not just for you and Anita, but for all of us." He raised his face for a kiss, and who would be able to turn Nathaniel down? They kissed, and just watching them so close, while we all held hands, made things low in my body tighten. It was a less chaste kiss than the one they'd had in the bedroom when Damian was with us. I realized that both times it had been Nathaniel who upped the ante, not Jean-Claude. Was the great seducer being seduced? I didn't have a problem with it. The men in my life being closer to each other usually worked in my favor. Micah might feel differently, but he wasn't here right now, so I just enjoyed touching them both and having my ringside seat for their kiss.

"Jean-Claude, you cannot allow them to go to her island," said a voice from behind us. It was Asher. He was tall, pale, handsome, with long golden hair spilling around his shoulders. Nothing would ever make Asher physically less than gorgeous, but physical wasn't everything.

The bodyguards around the room came to attention, because the last time we'd interacted with Asher it had gotten nasty. I knew they were under orders to not let us be alone with him. His emotional instability made him dangerous, and sometimes that danger wasn't just to your heart.

"This is for my job, Asher. Jean-Claude doesn't control that." My voice was as angry as I felt. Nathaniel was right—we missed Asher topping us in the dungeon. I missed him being part of a threesome with Jean-Claude and me. I hated that I hadn't found anyone to replace Asher in those two places in my life. The opposite of love isn't hate; it's indifference, and I wasn't indifferent to him yet. Which pissed me off, because I knew better.

Asher had spilled his hair across half his face like a golden veil, and like most veils, it was hiding things. His eyes were as pale a blue as Jean-Claude's were dark, a brilliant, icy blue. I caught the gleam of one through the lace of his hair, but the other eye was bright and visible, set in a face that was so gorgeous that he'd been the artists' model for paintings of angels and gods. "I have always respected your job, Anita. Whatever mistakes I have made in the past, I never presumed to tell you your job, and I am not now, but do not take Damian back to his old master and do not give her Nathaniel."

"We aren't taking him back to his old master, and we sure as hell aren't giving her anyone, let alone Nathaniel."

Asher held his hand out toward us, but it was to Jean-Claude he was giving the weight of those eyes, that face. "Jean-Claude, you have been at her mercy as well as I. You know what she is and what she is capable of. Please, by all that is holy, all that is left us, do not put our flower-eyed boy within her grasp."

"I'm not your flower-eyed boy anymore, Asher," Nathaniel said.

Asher's eyes glittered and I realized it was unshed tears. "And that is my fault, my flaw that drove you away. You have no idea how much I regret what I have done in the past few months. Only Julianna's death is a greater regret to me."

We all stared at him. Julianna's death had been the great tragedy that had driven a wedge between him and Jean-Claude. She had been their heart, and when she'd died it died with them.

"That is a bold statement, *mon ami*, if only you meant it."

"I swear to you, Jean-Claude, that I mean every word."

"Your word of honor?"

"Yes."

Asher was an old enough vampire that his word of honor meant something. An oath breaker was not trusted among the older vampires, and for some broken oaths it was a death sentence.

"Sudden contrition does not seem like something you would feel," Jean-Claude said.

"I have been full of regret for weeks, but I could not . . . decide . . . create . . . a way to convince you of my deep regret until I heard what you are planning, and then I did not care if you believed. I would rather give up Nathaniel forever than let him go to that cursed . . . beast."

That was the first thing he'd said that I was really interested in. I asked, "Do you mean that literally? Is She-Who-Made-Damian old enough to be a lycanthrope and a vampire like the Mother of All Darkness was? And do you mean a real curse, or are you just being dramatic?"

Asher shook his head so that his hair swung just enough to give a glimpse of the scars that he was using it to hide. He used his hair a lot like Nicky did, except Asher simply let the long waves spill down over his scars; of course, he had more of them to cover. He had two good eyes, but an inch or two out from the corner of his kissable mouth were burn scars. They trailed down his cheek and skipped his neck, but the right side of his chest looked like it had melted and re-formed. Holy water acts like acid on vampire flesh, and that was what the Church had used to try to burn the devil out of Asher centuries ago.

"She is a beast in the old sense of being a monster, but she cannot transform her physical body. She is a vampire and we are all cursed, but beyond that I am being dramatic, as you say."

"We were with her a few centuries ago. You are being overly dramatic," Jean-Claude said.

"I was with her longer than you, Jean-Claude."

Jean-Claude drew Nathaniel and me into his arms so he could hug us both. I don't know if it was to comfort himself or to rub Asher's losses in his face. I didn't care. I was good with both. Asher deserved to be reminded that he'd behaved so badly he'd lost all of us and more in one fell swoop.

"After you fled to the New World, Belle had less use for me. She could not use me to torment you anymore."

"We have been through this," Jean-Claude said, his voice very serious and very unhappy, but his arms tightened around us, so that we both curled an arm around his waist to let us be as close as he seemed to want. He could look and sound calm, justified, but he didn't feel it.

"I am not saying you were to blame. I am merely explaining that she was less careful of me after she could not use me against you."

"You know I am sorry for everything that happened between us back then."

"I know, and I am sorry that I blamed you for so many years, but that is beside the point tonight, Jean-Claude. I was not traded for Damian for a few hours a night as you and I were, but given to her for months. Damian was there while I was her prisoner."

"Neither of you has ever spoken of this to me."

"We vowed we would not speak of it even to each other. Do you remember how frightening she was when we were with her for only a few hours at a time in Belle's court?"

Jean-Claude lowered his face against Nathaniel's hair, as if he were smelling the vanilla of his hair to comfort himself. I did it sometimes, too. "That I remember those terrible hours is why I bargained for Damian's freedom from her and brought him here." He almost managed to keep his voice even—almost.

"Then imagine being with her for months."

Jean-Claude just shook his head. "I cannot. I do not wish to dwell on the horrors that did not happen to me, for there are enough that did."

"Three months was my sentence to serve as part of her entourage in Ireland. I was warned that I might die at my first dawn there and not wake again. That frightened me until I had been there a few weeks, and then I began to half-hope I would not wake again."

"We've shared some of Damian's memories, and they're pretty terrible, but wait. . . . Why wouldn't you wake at dusk? Did they tell you that just to scare you?" I asked.

"Not every vampire that traveled to Ireland woke the first night they slept there. No one knows why, but it's as if the land itself is not friendly to our kind."

"People keep telling me that my necromancy may not work in Ireland, or it's not supposed to, and that vampirism isn't as contagious there."

"I do not know about zombies. If anyone could call them from the grave there, it would be you, but they are right about vampires. Even if you give the three bites over the three different nights and drain them dry on the third, it does not guarantee they will rise as one of us. I saw half a dozen humans who should have risen as vampires there that did not."

"Did their bodies start to rot?" I asked.

He had to think about that for a minute. "I know that she kept two of the bodies for quite some time and they did rot. The others were discarded sooner."

"Why did she keep the bodies until they rotted?" I asked.

The look on his face was all for Jean-Claude, as if the look should be enough without words. It wasn't for me. "What are you trying to tell each other?"

"Did she hope that the bodies would rise as something?" Jean-Claude asked.

"One of the reasons she wanted me, other than the obvious one, was to have a vampire that wasn't of her making. She had hoped that I would be able to make more vampires for her, but it worked no better for me than it did for her own vampires."

"Did you ever see her try to bring over a vampire herself?" I asked.

"I did. She was able to create one of us, but the second one did not rise for her any more than the others."

"You know, you being in Ireland might have been good information for Damian to share with me."

"He and I were never friends, but we vowed that each of us would tell our halves of the story but not mention the other if we ever spoke of it at all."

Nathaniel said, "I think Damian's fighting his own fears so hard that he's not thinking clearly about what information might be helpful to you and the police."

I glanced at him and felt the beginnings of my irritation fall away. If Asher was this scared of the Wicked Bitch of Ireland, then Damian must have been petrified. "He's hiding it really well, then, even metaphysically," I said.

"He's being very brave," Nathaniel said.

"Yeah, he is," I said. I added, *Damn it*, to myself.

"So are we risking Echo and Giacomo by taking them to Ireland?" Nathaniel asked.

"Shit," I said.

"I do not believe so," Jean-Claude said.

"How do we know they'll be okay?"

"The reason I was at risk was that I was not a master vampire," Asher said, "but the Harlequin are all masters who gave up their rights to territories of their own to become permanently part of the royal guard."

"Of course they are," I said. "They all have animals to call, and you only get that as a master." I wanted to slap my forehead in a *"coulda had a V8"* moment.

"Except for Damian, you are taking only masters," Jean-Claude said.

"Okay, good to know I'm not risking anyone else like that."

"But if I understand what is happening, there is a plague of vampires in Ireland."

"There's a bunch of them in Dublin, and more people coming up missing every night."

"But the newly risen are never masters," Asher said.

"So there shouldn't be a lot of them in Ireland," I said.

"No, there should not be."

"Did anyone ever say why the vampires didn't rise the way they were supposed to?" I asked.

He thought about it, looking at the floor, frowning, but finally shook his head. "No, just that it was something to do with the land. That the land didn't like our kind."

"The Harlequin told us that the land is more alive because it has such a high concentration of Fey magic and that's why the dead don't rise there."

"Then why are they rising now?" Asher asked.

"One theory is that the wild magic is fading in Ireland finally, like it has throughout the world. It would fade in the cities first, and that's where all the new vamps have appeared so far."

"I cannot speak to any of that, but I know that what you are describing would never have happened with M'Lady at her full strength. Something must be wrong."

I almost asked if she had forced him to call her that, but I didn't. If she had, she had; no need for me to rub it in. "We're going to Ireland to try to fix what's wrong."

"Do you know why she wanted me in Ireland with her, Anita?"

I shrugged. "You're beautiful and great in bed."

Normally that would have made him smile, but not tonight. He swept his hair aside so that all his face was visible. He did that so rarely that it was almost startling. The scars really didn't cover that much of his face. We all found him still beautiful, but for him the scars were nearly everything.

He dropped his hair but didn't try to hide behind it again. "She wanted this, my beauty marred." He lifted the edge of the oversize dress shirt up so that he exposed the much more serious scars that covered him from chest to belt on that one side. The scars were deep runnels in the roughened skin over almost every inch of that side of his upper body, but the other side was still smooth and perfect as it was the day that Jean-Claude met him. I'd shared some of those memories, so I knew what Asher had looked like before the Church had tried to burn the devil out of him.

"That is her great pleasure, to see beauty that is spoiled in some way. She whispered to both Jean-Claude and me what she would do to us if she could. After seeing what the inquisitors had done to me, M'Lady said she could not have done better herself, that it was perfect."

Jean-Claude reached out toward him. "Do not torment yourself, *mon ami*."

Asher let his shirt fall back into place. "Some think her kind, because she will collect those who are marred as her lovers. Many of us think we will never be loved again after we are deformed, so it is a miracle to some. I saw her collect a woman who had lost a limb in an accident. She was not a lover of women; she brought her to be the lover for others of us. But she grew bored easily with most of them and if there was not someone who had met some horrible fate as I had, or the woman had, then M'Lady would create her own."

"What do you mean, create her own?" Nathaniel asked.

"She found another young woman, a dark beauty who would have been worthy of Belle's court. She was not when M'Lady finished with her. She kept her as a servant. The torture was sexual for her, but she seemed to enjoy just having the woman near her with that great beauty ruined."

"Damian said that she couldn't bear anyone being more beautiful than she was," I said.

"And you would take yourself, Nathaniel, Mephistopheles, and Damian to her. Even Echo should go nowhere near

M'Lady. All of you would tempt her to create her ideal of marred beauty. Nicky would be perfect with his missing eye and scars. He would at least be safe from her adding to his injuries."

"Wait. She had Damian with her for centuries and didn't do this to him and he's beautiful."

"He was handsome enough, but not beautiful as you have made him, Anita. His nose had been broken before he came to her, and even that imperfection was enough to quiet her urges toward him, but your magic has straightened his nose and changed the very bone structure of his face. He is beautiful now, Anita. Do you not understand what she would do to him now if he ever comes into her power again?"

"We will be with the police the whole time," I said.

Asher shook his head. "She thought I was even more beautiful like this, and the woman she scarred was one of the few vampires we managed to make while I was there."

"Are you saying you brought over the woman she'd scarred?" I asked.

"I thought she would die like the others. I thought it was mercy to end her life and free her from M'Lady, but she rose. She lived when I wanted her, and she wanted herself, to die. Ironic, isn't it? God's little sense of humor, or perhaps the Devil's. I no longer know who rules in some places on earth. If God is a god of love, then He cannot rule over the evil that is M'Lady, and if the Devil rules her, he must pray that she never dies in truth because she would rule his kingdom in a hundred years."

"Now you are just being overly dramatic," I said.

He went down on his knees in front of us, raising his hands upward as if beseeching us. "I beg of you, Anita, do not take Nathaniel's beauty to Ireland."

"I am standing right here," Nathaniel said, and he was angry.

"I see you, my flower-eyed boy."

"I am not a boy. I am a man, and you do not get to talk around me as if I'm not standing right in front of you."

"Please, Nathaniel, I could not bear it if she destroyed your beauty. Please, do not go."

"We're going to be late for the plane," he said, and his voice was cold with anger. He started to walk away, but Asher grabbed his hand and mine.

The bodyguards were moving in, and one was touching his ear mic, which meant backup would be coming. There were four of them and four of us; if we needed backup from Asher, then things would have gone horribly wrong. I didn't think they'd go that pear-shaped, so I held up my free hand and waved them back. He hadn't hurt us . . . yet. If we were this afraid of him, then no apology in the world would matter, so I waved them back and hoped I didn't regret it later.

"Let go of me," Nathaniel said.

"What he said." I didn't try to tug my hand free, because I knew better than to try to outmuscle a vampire, but I wanted to pull a little. It was just automatic.

"I love you. I love you both. I could not bear either of you being at her mercy. The thought of it sickens me." The tears that had glittered in his eyes earlier were back, but this time they began to slide down his cheeks. The tears were tinged pink with blood like all vampire tears. The color was faint enough that if I hadn't known to look for it I might not have seen it, but I knew to look and so there it was. It took a little of the pitiful out of him crying to know that his tears were stained with the blood of whoever he'd fed off tonight. Yeah, they'd been a willing victim, but still.

"Don't make me use my safeword," Nathaniel said.

Asher let go of his hand but clung to mine with both of his. "Please, Anita."

"What Nathaniel said."

Asher hesitated and then dropped his hands to his side, still on his knees with tears flowing faster down his face. They were leaving little pinkish trails down his skin so that I could see where every single one of them had fallen.

Jean-Claude couldn't stand it and reached out for him. Asher took his hands in his and started speaking rapid French. Jean-Claude shook his head. *"Non, mon ami,* they must understand your apology. I am weak when it comes to you, so it is them that you must win back. I will not come to your bed again unless they do, for they see you more clearly than I do."

I felt Nathaniel startle beside me. I glanced at him and he was already looking at me. The love of several lifetimes was holding Jean-Claude's hands, but it was up to us whether they ever got back together. No pressure.

Asher kept Jean-Claude's hands but turned to us. "I miss you both."

"You said that already," Nathaniel said. I realized that he was angrier than I was at Asher, which meant that the other man was, or had been, more important to him than he had been to me. I knew part of it was that I liked bondage and submission, but it wasn't the serious need to me that it was to Nathaniel. Asher had been an almost-perfect top for him in the dungeon. Apparently, Nathaniel missed it more than I'd realized, which was probably a relationship dropped ball on my part, or Micah's and my part?

He let go of Jean-Claude's hands and knelt in front of us. We were left staring down into those perfectly pale eyes like winter skies are supposed to be and almost never are; his lashes were darker than his hair, as were his eyebrows, so that the eyes were framed dramatically as if he'd used makeup to emphasize them, but I knew it was just natural coloring. He and Jean-Claude were both just that gorgeous; it was what had made Belle Morte collect them in the first place.

He lifted those large, long-fingered hands, thicker than Jean-Claude's through the fingers, and I'd thought for a while that Asher would bulk up more in the gym if he was willing to put the work into weights, but since he wasn't it didn't really matter. He wasn't a weight-lifting kind of guy. He spread those pale hands upward, let all those golden waves fall back so that his whole face was visible, both the beauty of it and the scars that he thought marred it.

"I miss you bound and waiting for me to cause you pleasure and pain. I miss the sounds that Nathaniel makes when I am flogging him, the way his skin parts underneath a whip and how he heals magically from it and asks for more. I miss the sounds Anita makes when we make love to her together. I miss the feel of our bodies piercing her at the same time. I miss sharing Anita with Jean-Claude in that way that we have done for centuries. I miss the feel and smell of your skin, Nathaniel, Anita. I miss plunging my tongue between her legs, and taking you in my mouth. I love the way you want me to use my fangs at the end and bleed you so that I drink you down twice."

I felt Nathaniel give a little shudder beside me. I was pretty sure it wasn't a bad shudder. My own heart was beating faster. Damn it.

"If you miss me at all, then I beg you to give me one more chance. I know I do not deserve it."

"How are we ever going to trust you again?" Nathaniel asked, and his voice was a lot more even than the pulse in the side of his throat. I gave him points for that. I was pretty sure that my own voice would shake if I tried right now.

"I do not know."

"How will we ever trust you to tie us up and hurt us, if we can't trust you to value us at all?" His voice was part anger and part loss, which pretty much summed up being in a relationship with Asher.

"I do not know, but I want more than anything else in the world to win back your trust. What can I do to prove my sincerity to you both?"

Nathaniel and I exchanged glances. He said, "I'm not sure."

I looked down at Asher. Those eyes, those lips, that face, that hair, the hands reaching out to me that knew so many secrets about what I enjoyed. "I don't know, Asher. Every time I think we've found a way for all of us to be together, you manage to find a new way to screw things up."

"I know it is me. My need to have Jean-Claude put me above all others continues to destroy my own happiness. I also know that is never going to happen, not only because he needs a woman in his life, but because neither of us is content with only each other. I am no more happy being with only one person than Jean-Claude is. I thought that if I could have one person put me above all others, then this continuous need inside me would be filled and I would be happy, content at last, but I have had that for months and I am miserable."

"Maybe that's who you're with," I said.

"I thought that at first, but I understand now that no one person meets all the needs and demands I put upon them. I am too much for one person to bear, like a weight that needs more hands to carry."

I wasn't sure what to say to that, because it sounded damned accurate.

"You really are working your therapy," Nathaniel said, and his face showed how surprised he was; me, too.

"I resented you forcing me to go away at first, but as I became less happy with Kane I finally realized that I was with a man who was as needy and jealous as I was; it was a taste of my own medicine, as they say. It was a very bitter pill. Kane was as obsessed with me as I had thought I wanted first Belle Morte, and then Jean-Claude, and finally Julianna to be with me, but obsession is not love. It is insecurity, possession, and it leads to misery."

It was the dream apology that you always sort of want, but you never get. It was like a Hallmark moment, or maybe a Dr. Phil moment. The kind that never really happens, but here he was, our problem child, offering up everything we could have wanted in an apology. It was great and unsettling as hell, like there should be cameras rolling and someone to jump out and say *Just kidding*.

"I love you, Anita Blake. I love you, Nathaniel Graison. I miss making love to you both. I miss fucking you. I miss chaining you up and doing nefarious things to you until you beg me to stop, or until I make the decision that all dominants must make with such charming pain sluts, though Anita will safeword when needed, but you, my . . . Nathaniel, you do not know when to say when, and I love that about you."

Nathaniel held out his hand, and after a moment so did I. We let him wrap his hands around us and pulled him to his feet. I don't know what I would have said, but it was Nathaniel who spoke first. "Are you going to apologize to Dev, too?"

"God, yes. I have treated him the worst of the three of you, I think. Jean-Claude, having put up with me for centuries, is ahead in needing me to apologize for so many things, but I owe Mephistopheles something truly . . . I do not know how to apologize to him. I was so cruel, and I let Kane be cruel to him as well."

"Are you just apologizing to him, or are you wanting him back in your life, too?" I asked.

"I did not appreciate how easy Mephistopheles made the

relationship. I thought love had to come with fights and drama, so what I had with him couldn't be love."

"And now?" Nathaniel asked it ahead of me.

"Now I see him in Jean-Claude's bed, all smiles and a very content cat, and it hurts me."

"Does it hurt you to see Jean-Claude with another man, or to see Dev happy with someone else?" Nathaniel asked.

Asher sighed, and it was for effect, but he was always going to be a bit of a drama queen. It was just part of who he was as a person. You can modify yourself and learn to do better, but your basic personality remains.

"I am not sorry to see Mephistopheles happy with someone else. He deserves that. I have seen him walking hand in hand with you as well, Nathaniel. I was jealous that all of you had picked up that which I threw away and found it gold where I had seen only dross, but that was at first. I began to see more and more how much Kane had poisoned me against our handsome devil, but it was I who had listened to the poison and let it take root."

"You're taking responsibility for everything. What the hell? Did they put you on antidepressants?" I asked.

"Antianxiety medication, yes."

All three of us stared at him. *"Mon ami,"* Jean-Claude said, and the surprise showed in his voice.

Asher started to look embarrassed, but I squeezed his hand and said, "I'm proud of you."

It was Asher's turn to look surprised.

"Very proud of you," Nathaniel said.

"I honestly didn't expect you to get that much use out of the therapist we made you go see," I said.

"I, too, thought you were going because we said you must," Jean-Claude said, moving up beside us.

"I admit that at first it was just as you feared, but I was so unhappy without all of you. So many needs, not just wants, but needs that you had all filled for me and now I had nothing. Even Narcissus, in the dungeon and the bedroom he likes a level of humiliation that none of you would tolerate, let alone desire."

"If you're going to apologize to Narcissus, you might want

to do it in a neutral setting with bodyguards to protect you," I said.

"Surely not bodyguards."

"Asher," Nathaniel said, "we've all been going to therapy, too; Narcissus hasn't."

"He is dangerous, *mon ami*."

"Very dangerous," I said. "You hurt his ego and you damaged his reputation. He's still fighting to regain the respect of his own hyenas."

"Kane says that the hyenas have gone back to their old ways and it is business as usual."

"If Kane truly believes that, then he's delusional in more than one way," I said.

"How is he delusional?" Asher asked.

"That someone as vindictive as Narcissus won't get his revenge on Kane and you. That obsession is the same thing as love. That if you're possessive enough and want it badly enough, the person you love will love you as much as you love them. That any one person could keep you content."

"Even I thought that the right person could do the last part."

I shook his hand where he still held mine. "You were delusional, too, remember?"

He smiled. "Yes, I do."

"We really do need to get going, Anita," Nathaniel said. I looked at him and there was a new, more serious person looking back at me. He'd probably been stronger and more sure of himself for a few months, but I hadn't quite realized it until this moment when he stood there holding someone he'd been in love with enough to want to offer a ring, and he was ready to leave him and the apology of epicness behind.

"My words have not moved you," Asher said.

"The apology is great, almost perfect, and if you can do the same for Dev, then we can all sit down when we come home and talk about being together again, but I'm still going to Ireland."

"Do you think I am lying?"

"No, but we will be with the police and one of the good things about vampires being known under the law is that they have to obey the law, too, so if she tries to harm Damian, or me, or Anita, the human authorities can come down on her."

"What can they possibly do to her?"

I said, "I keep hearing about her castle by the sea. I wonder what would happen with a few well-placed bombs, or even missiles. We are going to be playing with military friends."

"Blowing her lair up would not rescue Damian, or Nathaniel, or you, but only make you die with her."

"I'm just explaining that once we can bring the full weight of human intervention into vampire hunting, the options get really fun."

"*Mon ami*, the Harlequin and other bodyguards are also going with them. It is not merely human police and soldiers who will be protecting them."

"Then I must be content with that."

"Yeah, you must," Nathaniel said.

Asher looked at him. "You are very angry with me."

"Yes, I am. Did you expect that I would accept your apology and everything would just go back to the way it was?"

Asher did that long blink that meant he was thinking. "Perhaps."

"I've had months of you not with me. I didn't just curl up into a corner and wait for you. I never dreamed you'd work through your issues and be willing to get on medication." Nathaniel let go of Asher's hand. "None of us expected that from you."

"It is a sign of how much I want to be well enough to be with you again."

"It's a sign of how unhappy you are with just Kane," Nathaniel said.

As if his name had conjured him, Kane swept the drapes aside and strode into the room. If I could see him objectively, he was tall, dark, and sort of handsome. Okay, maybe he was handsome, but the scowl on his face and the sourness of his energy just sort of ruined the packaging for me. His hair was almost black, but cut short and styled close to his head so that the hairdo looked like a hundred you see every day. He was attractive but in a totally mundane sort of way. He looked like someone that my college roommate might have wanted to date, but not someone that should have been Asher's main squeeze. Maybe it was having so many memories of him with Jean-Claude; after that, everyone else looked sort of ordinary. Okay, not everyone. Nathaniel wasn't, or Micah, or . . . maybe it was love that made people more than ordinary, and I so did not love Kane.

"I knew it. You are poisoning him against me!" was Kane's opening remark.

"You do your own poisoning," I said.

"What's that supposed to mean?" he asked as he came farther into the room.

One of the guards moved in front of him. Kane snarled at him, the echo of his beast trickling through it so the hairs on the back of my neck rose. "Are you so afraid of me that you have to use bodyguards?"

"Last time you took a swing at me, I bloodied you and put a gun to your head, Kane. I think the guards are to protect you, not me."

The snarl turned into a growl that reverberated through the room. The guard said, "You start to shift and I'll hurt you."

"Asher, are you going to let them talk to me this way?"

"We have a plane to catch, Anita," Nathaniel said, and this time he meant it because he went for the far drapes that led to the door up and out.

I started to follow him and then looked back at Jean-Claude. "Let's say good-bye some more on the way up the stairs."

"I think that is an excellent idea, *ma petite*." Acknowledging it was his way of admitting that he didn't trust himself alone with this new contrite Asher either.

I held my hand out to him and he came to take it.

Asher said, "Am I forgiven anything?"

Nathaniel swept the drapes to one side to hold them for us. "You still have to apologize to Dev, remember?"

"But you are taking Mephistopheles with you to Ireland, and you are leaving now."

"I guess you'll have to apologize to him when we get back," Nathaniel said.

"Jean-Claude," he said, and reached for the other man.

I grabbed Jean-Claude's hand and kept him moving with us. "We're not saying no, Asher, but you need to talk to everyone in our lives who stayed and worked through their issues."

"The people who helped us mourn you when you left deserve to know that you want back in, before we decide anything," Nathaniel said, and his voice was cold with anger. I wasn't angry, just had this weird desire to kiss him good-bye. I looked at Jean-Claude as I practically dragged him through the drapes toward the door. It wasn't my thought; it was his. Damn it, Asher had such a hold on him. What would happen if we left him alone with none of us here to balance it?

Kane yelled, "Asher, what have you done?"

"I told you that I would ask their forgiveness."

"I told you that you don't need them, any of them. We only need each other."

"I wanted that to be true," Asher said.

Kane was trying to get past the guard who was blocking him. "What are you saying, Asher?"

"I need more."

"More than me?"

I'd heard this argument before and recently, except it had been Cardinale talking to Damian. What was with all the obsessive jealousy? It was like a theme.

"We really do have to go. The plane's waiting," I said.

Jean-Claude held back against my hand. It made me turn and look at him. I don't know if I'd have had the courage to say what needed to be said, but Nathaniel did.

"If you take Asher back without him apologizing to Dev first it would crush Dev, and he deserves better than that."

Jean-Claude looked at him, then stopped tugging against my hand. "I am sorry, *ma petite*, *mon minou*. I do not mean to be weak."

The three of us stepped closer together to hear one another over Kane's yelling. "If we leave you alone like this, are you going to do something stupid with Asher?" I asked. The moment I said it, I knew it was harsh, but we really did need to leave. There wasn't time to ease into it.

He raised one graceful eyebrow at me.

"We really do need to catch the ride to the airport and head for Ireland, Jean-Claude. I don't have time to figure out how to talk to you about this. I'm sorry if that was blunt."

He shook himself, like a bird settling its feathers. I felt the energy change down his hand, which I was still holding as if I were afraid he'd run to Asher like in some old romantic movie. He was calmer, and it was real, not just him hiding his feelings.

"I am not planning to be stupid, *ma petite*. I've tried to avoid that for centuries."

"We all try to avoid it," Nathaniel said, "but we all have people and issues that make us stupid. We need to know that you won't let Asher upset our poly group."

I put my arm around Jean-Claude's waist and gazed up at him. "I didn't think until just minutes ago that I'm taking all of your lovers with me. Even your regular blood donors are coming with us. I'd realized it was sort of a shitty thing to do even without Asher coming up like this. I'm sorry I didn't think about what it might mean for you sooner."

"I called Jason. He's coming in to visit for a couple of days," Nathaniel said.

We both looked at him. Jason was my wolf to call, though we'd both been so worried that we'd be tied too closely together that a certain distance had gone into our bonding. He'd been another emergency tie for me. He was Nathaniel's best friend and one of my best friends. Until he'd gone to New York with his girlfriend J.J., who was a ballet dancer there, he'd been the manager at Guilty Pleasures and one of the headline dancers. Technically he hadn't moved permanently, but he was about to do a dance tryout for the dance troupe she was a part of, if they could get around him being a werewolf and not just human. If he got the job he'd be the first paranormal American to dance with an all-human troupe. We all missed Jason, but J.J. was the love of his life and we wanted him to have a chance at that, and her job couldn't move here. "You'd already realized we were leaving Jean-Claude on his own, hadn't you?"

"Yes, but when I realized that Micah was going to be gone longer than he'd thought, that's when I realized it might be a problem."

"Do you think I am incapable of being on my own for a few days?" Jean-Claude asked.

Nathaniel smiled at him. "Your power is based on lust and love, Jean-Claude."

"I have been alone before, Nathaniel. I am not a child." He almost never called him by his real name anymore; not a good sign.

"I've been addicted to sex. I will always be a recovering sex addict, Jean-Claude. I'm not saying you're addicted to sex, or romance, or relationships, but if sex were actually what I ate and the only other food I could have was something as intimate as taking blood, I know I couldn't be anything but addicted to all of it. If I projected that onto you and it's not true, then I'm sorry. Jason will be here tomorrow so you'll at least have a blood donor and someone to sleep in the bed with you."

"I am fine alone, Nathaniel."

"Good for you; I'm not."

Asher was finally yelling back at Kane behind us. The bodyguards were moving in to help contain them since their fights sometimes erupted into real violence. I looked at Asher, and touching Jean-Claude, I saw him through more years than I'd been alive. I saw him through true love and romance and loss and so much, but all I could think was, did we really want to hit this mess again? The answer from Jean-Claude's emotions was a resounding yes!

Nathaniel touched us both, hugging us close. "I miss him, too, Jean-Claude. I can't find anyone else who can do what he does for me in the dungeon, but look at him with Kane. Asher chose to tie himself to Kane for all eternity as master and animal to call. Kane isn't that powerful. He isn't the head of an animal group. What kind of master vampire would tie themselves to Kane?"

"I tied you and Damian to me by accident, so I don't have many stones to throw on that one."

"You were brand-new to the power. Asher isn't."

"I have never said that Asher was wise," Jean-Claude said.

"Well, that's true," I said.

Nathaniel looked back at the fight. "I was addicted to sex. Asher is addicted to the idea of true love. Addictions never end in anything but misery."

"Do you not believe that Asher could break his addiction as you did yours?" Jean-Claude asked.

"The apology was epic, but the fight with Kane is just the same old shit."

I looked at Nathaniel as if I'd never seen him before. "That was like a mix of me and you talking," I said out loud.

"We all gain something from our metaphysical ties. Maybe I gained a little more toughness."

"What did I gain?"

"You're picking up too much of Jean-Claude's emotions to think clearly," Nathaniel said.

I gazed up at the vampire in my arms. "Yeah, I guess I am."

"Jean-Claude, Jason will be in from New York tomorrow. Micah's hoping to be home in a couple of days."

"You talked to Micah about this?" I asked.

"Of course I did." Nathaniel looked surprised that I hadn't thought he would.

"I guess I thought you were mad at him."

"He didn't say no, Anita. He just never saw himself married to another man, so he's working his way through it."

Jean-Claude hugged Nathaniel. "We all have our drama, do we not, pussycat?"

Nathaniel smiled. "Yeah." He hugged him back and nestled his head against the taller man's shoulder. Again, it was an escalation of physicality between them, and it was Nathaniel who was pushing the envelope again. I was beginning to think that Micah wasn't the only long game he was playing. Hell, Nathaniel had pursued me for years before I finally realized I loved him. He didn't catch me. I just stopped fighting what was already true. My issues had nearly cost me one of the loves of my own life.

Nathaniel was a submissive personality, but I was learning slowly that submissive didn't mean weak, and that really all the power is with the sub, because once they safeword, then everything stops. I watched him cuddling with Jean-Claude and realized that it might not just be the dungeon where Nathaniel had power.

"By tomorrow night you won't be alone," he said. "Can you resist Asher for that long?"

"Do you really think I am that weak around him?"

"Do you?" Nathaniel asked him back.

I watched the two men, the demand in Nathaniel's face and the doubt in Jean-Claude's. "I will not be that weak."

"Just hold out until Jason gets here tomorrow. He'll help you."

Jean-Claude's phone rang. He was going to ignore it, but the ringtone was the one we both had for Richard Zeeman, our almost long-lost third. We hadn't seen him in weeks. He'd been off on some trip for the college he taught at. Jean-Claude hit the button with the sounds of the fight behind us escalating, so there was no way Richard wouldn't hear it over the phone. It made us walk out from the curtained living room, and when Nathaniel opened the big dungeon-looking door to the bottom of the stairs we all went through, so that Jean-Claude could hear.

He made small noises, mostly *yes* and *hmm* sounds. He hung up and looked at me. "Richard is coming to spend the night and help me talk to Asher and Kane."

"I didn't call Richard," Nathaniel said.

"Me either."

"He says that Rafael called him after he heard the news from Micah. Apparently, our pussycat is not the only one who does not trust me alone with Asher, even for a night." Jean-Claude stared at the phone in his hand and then looked up at us. "Richard has not stayed overnight in the same bed with me in nearly a year. Apparently no one trusts my judgment about this."

"You were in love with Asher for centuries, and your happiest memories were the twenty years you and he had with Julianna. Jean-Claude, that much history is hard for anyone to resist," I said.

Jean-Claude glanced back at the door. We couldn't hear the fight through the dungeon door. It was nearly soundproof. "I will walk up with you. Richard should be here soon after that." And just like that he acknowledged that he didn't trust his judgment around Asher either.

33

I USED TO think that my fear of flying was based on not knowing the pilot. Had he been drug-tested recently? Was he well rested? Trustworthy? How about the plane? Was it flight-worthy? Was the maintenance crew that last looked at it competent? Were the parts going to fall off if everything shook too much? I mean, how well-made was this plane? But I knew Jean-Claude's pilot. I knew he was drug-free, well rested, trustworthy, and had a wife and two kids to come home to, so he wanted to live as much as any of us. I knew the jet was well serviced and well maintained, because Jean-Claude saw to it. Micah double-checked it since he used the plane more than anyone. I trusted both of them to value us enough to make sure it all worked. I'd had to own that my phobia wasn't based on any of those things. It was a phobia from a commercial airline flight that had gone dangerously wrong but hadn't quite crashed, and ever since then I'd hated flying. Okay, since then I'd been terrified of flying and hated it.

Jean-Claude's new plane seated fifteen and even had a section that could be curtained off, in case someone wanted some privacy, though since everyone I was traveling with had super-hearing, the privacy was very illusionary. There was a mini-bar and food on board. If we crashed in the Andes—not that we were going anywhere near them on this flight, but if we did—we wouldn't have to resort to cannibalism for at least a couple of weeks.

The seats were comfortable and swiveled so that you only sat two by two, but the seats faced each other in four-person conversation groups, or you could swivel and talk to the people on the other side of the narrow aisle without having to turn your head. I mean, why make that much effort, right? I'd been on one flight years ago that had probably been the victim of a micro burst, which you actually couldn't control at all. You could be properly maintained, mechanically sound, with the best crew in the world, and micro bursts didn't care, which led me all the way back to—how was I possibly going to do eight and a half hours on a plane without running screaming up and down the tiny aisle?

I texted all the people that I was metaphysically connected to who weren't on the plane with me and told them, *Shields up.* I'd started doing that after Sin had requested I always tell them when I was about to fly. Apparently he'd been in the middle of his driving lesson when I took off and it had not gone well. All strong emotions were potentially shareable, and I really was afraid to fly. It was a scheduled, knowable moment when my emotions were going to run amok, so I group-texted everyone. Yay technology, making polyamorous relationships better since the iPhone was invented.

Nathaniel sat beside me, holding my hand. I had a death grip on the armrest as the jet began to taxi down the runway. I was seriously working on controlling my breathing, because to panic, at least to have a full-blown panic attack, you had to lose control of your breathing first. If I controlled my breathing I could control my heart rate, my pulse, and keep myself from spilling over the edge into hysterics. I hadn't actually cried on a plane in a few years, but I had bloodied Micah's leg through a pair of jeans once when he was my plane buddy. At least if I bloodied Nathaniel's hand he'd enjoy it; Micah not so much.

"Anita, look at me."

I swallowed hard, still fighting to keep my pulse from trying to jump out of my throat, and turned to look at him. I was suddenly staring into those big lavender eyes from inches away. I was just suddenly calmer. I wasn't sure if it was the fact that I loved him, or that he was sharing his own calm with me. Maybe it was both?

"We're going to Ireland to catch the bad guys, and then we get to see Ireland together." He squeezed my hand and I realized that he was excited about the trip. It was one of those moments when I felt the age difference, or the experience difference, between us. I'd never brought him on a police investigation trip on purpose. He'd been with me when crimes happened

and we were suddenly ass-deep in alligators, but I'd never deliberately taken him into the lion's den before. I suddenly remembered why. I was going to spend most of the trip looking at
dead bodies and hunting rogue vampires through the city. It was
like we were going on two very different trips.

Nicky leaned across from the seats in front of us and put
his big hand over mine. "We've got this, Anita."

I looked at him and felt that sense of calmness that he usually made me feel. He'd fixed his hair back so that improbable
fall of bangs hid his right eye again. I looked at that one blue
eye and wished I'd had a hand free to touch that long fall of
bangs and let him know how much I valued that he let me see
all of him.

The plane was gaining speed. I started to tense up even
with both of them touching me, but Damian leaned forward
and wrapped his hand over Nathaniel's hand where he held
mine so that he was touching both of us and I was suddenly
calm. I looked into those grass-green eyes and did a slow
blink. Calm became something solid and sure. I felt the plane
leave the ground and that spurt of fear shot through me, but
Damian leaned in closer and the green of his eyes seemed to
fill my vision. I was calm again, so calm.

I could feel the plane climbing, but it didn't seem to matter.
It would be fine. We would be fine. It was fine. I was fine. I did
a long blink and took a deep, slow breath.

"How do you feel?" Damian asked in a low, even voice.

"Fine, good," I said, and my voice was low and even, too.

He smiled at me and I smiled back.

"We need to bring him on all of our out-of-town trips," Dev
said from the seat behind us.

"I thought you were all upset that you didn't get his seat,"
Domino said.

"I was," Dev said, "but I couldn't have calmed Anita down
like that, so I take it back. Damian can have my seat on the
plane if he can do that every time."

I blinked past Damian's red hair to Dev's white-blond, but
whereas Damian's fell down well past his shoulders, Dev's
barely touched his shoulders, and those shoulders were almost
twice the width of the vampire's. Mephistopheles—our Devil,
as Asher had called him—was a big guy, and would have

looked bigger if he hadn't been sitting so close behind Nicky, who made everyone on the plane except for Giacomo look smaller. Dev would probably have seemed bigger as well if he hadn't been sitting beside his cousin, Pride, who was almost as broad through the shoulders and as wide through the chest. Pride's eyes were rings that managed to be both pale and bright at the same time. Dev's eyes were pale blue with a ring of golden brown around the pupils so that it was as if his eyes were hazel, if blue eyes could be hazel. Most people looked into those pretty eyes and that was all they saw, but if you knew what you were looking at you knew they were tiger eyes. It was the eyes they'd been born with, because all the pure-blooded clan tigers had the eyes of their beast half permanently in their human faces. Both those faces were model handsome, Dev's a little more square jawed than Pride's, but all the gold clan tigers were handsome, or beautiful, as if they'd been bred for height, athletic ability, and beauty. The other tiger clans had some people who were pretty, but it wasn't all of them; of course the two largest clans had three to four times as many members as the gold clan, so maybe it was what happened when your genetic pool was too small—everyone started to look alike. You'd think that would give you deformity or physical weakness, but sometimes it's like breeding for the best racehorses. They're all beautiful, athletic, fast as fuck, and a little high-strung. That about covered it. Dev and Pride were two of the calmest and most even-tempered, which was why they were the only two on regular guard duty with me or Micah.

We hadn't told Dev yet that Asher wanted to apologize to him, too. There hadn't been time, and now didn't seem to be the time either. I was feeling calmer than I'd ever been on a plane. Talking about Asher would upset me, and talking to Dev about Asher would probably upset me more, so fuck it. I'd keep this strange new calm as long as I could. There'd be time to discuss the vampire who broke Dev's heart and then tap-danced on the pieces later, when we were safe on the ground. Just thinking that much started the fear bubbling up again.

Damian said, "Anita."

His saying my name made me look at him and into those impossibly green eyes. The fear receded again like waves pulling back from the sea, and I was back to walking on that calm metaphorical beach. It was better than any meditation I'd ever managed to do.

Socrates asked, "Anita, how do you feel?"

It made me turn and look at him sitting across the aisle from Damian. Socrates' newly short hair was almost shaved so that the tight curl of his hair was completely gone. His face seemed bare, shorn, which would have robbed most men of some of their beauty; I was a big one for nice hair, but his face could carry it. It made his brown eyes look larger, and the dark planes of his face seemed more prominent so that an attractive face had become handsome. Which meant he'd always been handsome. I just hadn't noticed.

"Anita, can you hear me?" he asked.

I nodded. "I hear you."

"Okay, how do you feel?"

"I feel . . . fine, good, though every time I think that part I know I shouldn't be fine on an airplane, and that makes me poke at it and realize that it's not me."

Magda spoke from the seat behind him. "Please leave well enough alone, Socrates. Anita is happy enough. Aren't you?"

I nodded.

"Fine. I'll leave it alone while we're in the air, but I have some questions when we land."

"When we land," she said.

Socrates looked back at her. "You're okay with this?"

"Have you ever flown with Anita before?" Dev asked.

"No."

"I have; trust me, this is good."

Nathaniel said, "She's fine, Socrates, I promise."

"Please don't make me overthink this," I said.

Socrates held his hands up as if to say *okay*, and settled back in his chair. Domino was sitting beside him, watching me with his red-and-yellow fire-colored eyes. They were so much more exotic than the golden tigers' eyes, even Dev's blue-brown ones. The black clan could never pass for human with those blaze-colored eyes.

Ethan, sitting just behind Domino, looked at me with soft gray eyes. They were tiger eyes in a human face, too, but the color, like the golden tigers, helped him pass for human.

Though I'd learned that they looked like tiger eyes, all the clan tigers' eyes that they had from birth functioned more like human eyes for seeing. It meant they didn't need prescription glasses to read, or see far off the way that Micah did with his permanent cat eyes. They looked like tiger eyes, but they functioned more like exotic human ones. Until Micah had admitted his need for glasses, I'd never asked the clan tigers how it worked. Unless you ask, you never know. Ethan's hair was white-blond with gray highlights, or I guess gray lowlights, but there was a streak of dark red that ran from the curls at the front to the back of his head. It wasn't a talented dye job, just natural coloring. He was part white tiger, which gave him the white-blond hair and the paler skin tone, but blue tiger had mixed with the white to make gray in his hair, and the red streak was red tiger clan. What didn't show physically was that he also had gold tiger inside him. He'd gained that as a form after he met me, but he'd always been able to change into three forms; now he had four. If he'd been black tiger clan he'd have been a clean sweep of all of them. His mother had been red tiger clan, his father white, but where the blue and gold had snuck in, no one knew. Both parents were supposed to be pure red clan and white clan, respectively. Guess not.

Ethan looked back at me. "Anita, is there something you wanted?"

I blinked at him and said, very calmly, "A lot of the clan tigers were pushing me to date you more seriously because you have most of the bloodlines."

Damian's hand tightened a little around my and Nathaniel's hands as if he were afraid I'd say the wrong thing. I didn't plan on it. Nicky's hand stayed neutral on my leg as if he knew better, or didn't care about Ethan's feelings; it could go either way with him.

Ethan nodded. "I remember; it was a way for you to not choose among the clans but marry most of them. My mixed heritage that had made none of the red clan want to mate with me was suddenly an asset."

"I know the clan that raised you treated you like shit," I said.

"You rescued me," he said with a smile.

"I'm sorry that after I rescued you my dance card was too

full for the romance you wanted, but I saw Nilda kissing you good-bye in the parking lot. I didn't know she had that kind of happiness in her. I really thought she was too crazy to date. I'm glad I was wrong and that you found each other," I said.

Ethan smiled that smile you get when you're first in love. "All the ancient werebears are a little crazy, but Nilda just needed love and couples therapy."

"You went to couples therapy when you'd just started dating each other?" Socrates asked, turning in his seat to look at the other man.

"She was on the list for mandatory therapy or she'd be fired from the guard. It scared her to go, so I told her I'd go with her if it would help, and it turned into couples therapy after a while."

Socrates shook his head. "You must have wanted to be with her bad, or you're just a better person than I am. When my wife asked for therapy, I said no."

"She was in the parking lot kissing you good-bye. Did she forgive you?"

"No, she left me. I think I wanted her to leave when I first became a shapeshifter. I thought I was a danger to her and our son, and then the hyena group in L.A. was crazy violent. It wasn't until I came out here that I thought I had a job and a life that wouldn't endanger them."

"You're lucky she waited for you to come to your senses," Kaazim said.

"Very lucky," Jake said from the seat beside him.

"She didn't wait for me. I mean, she was dating. In fact, she was dating one guy seriously when I asked her to try again."

"Then you are doubly lucky," Kaazim said. Jake just nodded.

"I am. You saw her: She's beautiful and could have anyone she wanted. I so don't deserve her after all I put her through."

"I'm glad you felt safe enough to bring her and your son to St. Louis," I said.

Socrates smiled at me. "Me, too."

"When is the baby due?" I asked.

"Soon, and we just found out it's a girl."

Appreciative noises were made. Fortune called from the

backseats that she and Echo were sharing, "That's wonderful to feel safe enough to have a family." I remembered what Sin had said, that Fortune had talked to Nathaniel about being his baby momma. There was a spurt of jealousy, which wasn't an emotion I felt much.

The jealousy went straight to anger, which was usually my default for any negative emotion. Damian's hand squeezed, but this time Nicky leaned in closer, running his hand up my thigh. It wasn't sexual, more comforting, but he'd unbuckled his seat belt to do it so that I was suddenly looking into his face almost close enough to kiss. I knew he felt my emotions, but not my thoughts. What did he think had made me feel jealous?

The peacefulness began to seep away on the conflicting emotions. I was suddenly anxious and afraid and . . . Damn it, if I felt that way about Nathaniel having a baby with someone else, what did that say about me, about us? Fortune was even our shared lover. It was a nice, practical solution for everyone, so why didn't it feel nice or practical inside my head and heart?

Nathaniel leaned in and kissed me gently on the cheek. It made me turn and look at him. I realized that he didn't get just my emotions, but sometimes my thoughts. How much had he gotten just now? My pulse was suddenly in my throat and my chest was a little bit tight, but it wasn't fear of being on the plane. Nope, relationship baby panic and not the kind I'd always feared. I'd sat in the bathroom and stared at a pregnancy test and prayed for it to be negative. I'd even had one false positive when I first got all my inner beasts. But staring into Nathaniel's eyes from inches away, I suddenly realized something. I did want to have a baby with him and with Micah. It wasn't a possibility with Micah—he'd had a vasectomy years before we met—but Nathaniel and I could. I just hadn't known until that second that I wanted to do it. Fuck, it was such a bad idea.

Nathaniel gave me a smile that lit his whole face up. He just glowed with happiness, which meant he knew exactly what I was thinking and feeling. Fuck, fuck, fuck.

"Why do you think it's such a bad idea?" Damian asked,

and I realized that the three of us were all too interconnected in that moment for him to be left out.

Dev leaned over the back of Damian's seat and asked, "What is a bad idea?"

Nathaniel looked up at Dev with that shining, happy face. "Anita wants to have a baby with me."

Dev let the surprise show on his face. "Wow, that's . . . un-expected. Great, but . . . wow."

"Wanting to have a baby with someone doesn't mean you do it," I said, a little desperately.

"I thought that's how it worked," Fortune said.

I was suddenly angry with her, because her willingness to get pregnant had made me think too hard about it. I was furious with her in that moment.

"That's not fair, Anita," Nathaniel said.

"Would you really get pregnant with someone else?"

"I want to have a baby with you, but you told me that wasn't ever going to happen and I want children."

"You're not even twenty-five yet. What's the rush?" I asked.

"It doesn't have to be now, but I thought you'd feel differently if it was a woman in our poly group."

"So did I," I said.

Fortune said, "If this is what I think it is, it's about Nathaniel and me. We weren't seriously talking about him and me, but more that I could stop using birth control and keep having sex with everyone. As Harlequin we were not allowed to breed unless the Mother chose us for it, and then, like Socrates, we did not feel safe enough to have me incapacitated by carrying a child."

Echo took her hand and said, "We felt safe enough to contemplate it, but it is not Nathaniel's child we seek, but our own."

I nodded. "I get that—I really do—and you totally don't deserve my anger, but it's just thrown me that I feel this way at all. I mean, you said it: Incapacitated is how pregnancy would be. I wouldn't be able to do my job."

"Nor I, late in pregnancy," Fortune said.

"But the baby will be born and you can both get back into warrior condition," Echo said.

"But then we'd have a baby that would be like the greatest hostage ever," I said.

"To take the child of Jean-Claude and Anita Blake would be suicidal," Echo said.

"It's really unlikely that Jean-Claude would be the bio-dad. He's over six hundred years old. Most vampires aren't fertile after a hundred or so," I said.

"Legally you will be marrying only Jean-Claude, so in the eyes of the world, it will be his," she said.

I glanced at Nathaniel. "You okay with that?"

He grinned at me. "Of course, the baby will call all of us *Daddy*."

I said, "Jean-Claude would probably be *Père*," which was French for "Father," and thanks to channeling him I even pronounced it correctly, which I could never have done on my own.

"Probably we'd have different dad-isms for all of us," Nathaniel said.

"What do you mean, dad-isms?"

"Jean-Claude could be *Père*, but we could use *Dad, Daddy, Dada, Papa, Pa, Pop, Poppy*, all the slang for *Father*."

"You've really thought about this," I said, and not like I was happy about it.

"Anita, I've been trying to think of all the arguments against it so that when we finally talked for real I'd be prepared. I never thought it would come up like this."

"It doesn't matter who's *Dad*, or *Poppy*, or whatever; the kid would still have a sign around its neck saying, *Kidnap me and use me against my parents, please*."

"Echo already said it would be suicide," Giacomo said.

"Yeah, but people do stupid things all the damn time."

"Anita," Nicky said.

I looked at him so close to me, felt the weight of his hand on my thigh, the nearness of all that muscled willpower. "For your baby to be taken they'd have to get through me first."

"And me," said Dev.

"And me," Pride said.

The plane filled with the sounds of all of them saying the same thing.

"Yes, the baby would be a hostage if it could be taken," Echo said, "but the likelihood of anyone, or any group, slaying all of us and taking the child is almost zero."

"And when Echo says that, she means only those of us on this plane," Jake said. "If you add all the rest at home, then there are few children on earth safer than one you would have."

I shook my head, afraid but not of being on the plane.

"All children of powerful people are potentially at risk," Magda said, "but few are as well protected as any we might have."

I looked at her. "We?"

"I do not think I wish to have one, but if Fortune can get with child I think more of the female Harlequin would consider it."

"There is no guarantee that I can get pregnant at all. I mean, I'm over a thousand years old. My body looks like I haven't seen thirty, but I've seen so many more years than that. Now that I have people who can help me not shift form for the time it would take me to get pregnant, which is what lets the clans breed at all, and a safe place, it still may be impossible," Fortune said.

"One of the best things about having the tiger clans come to stay in St. Louis is them helping the other wereanimals through pregnancies," Nathaniel said.

"I'm not sure I'd put that in the *best thing* category," I said.

"But I would. It's made so many people so happy."

I smiled at him. "We both want that."

"Everyone to be happy," he said.

I nodded and couldn't stop from smiling more. Then I frowned.

"What's wrong?" Nicky asked.

I looked out the window of the plane. The sky was still black and star-filled, but I felt the press of dawn. It was the same way I could feel it deep underground in the Circus, or in the pitch-black of a cave when I knew that if I could just fight until dawn the vampires would collapse where they were and we could kill them. Of course, now I knew that if the vampire was old enough, strong enough, and underground far enough they might not "die" at dawn. Damian wasn't the only vampire I knew that could daywalk either. If you read the original book *Dracula* by Bram Stoker, he has Drac walking around in the daylight, only adding a pair of darkened glasses, so dawn isn't a guarantee of safety from vampires and it does nothing to protect you from their servants and allies, but dawn still meant good things to me. It didn't to Giacomo and Echo, though. Damian didn't burn in the sunlight anymore, but the light still frightened him.

Damian said, "Anita is feeling the sun start to rise."

Fortune and Magda started closing all the blinds over the windows. Ethan started to help. Since one of my issues with planes is that I'm claustrophobic on top of being afraid to fly, it didn't make me happy. In fact, my pulse started to speed up, the first beginnings of panic pumping through my veins.

"Look at me, Anita," Damian said.

I looked into his green eyes, but I didn't fall into a peaceful place again. The fear continued to bubble through me. My breath started to get too fast. "It isn't working this time," I said.

"I'm sorry. I'm afraid of the dawn too."

"Sunlight doesn't hurt you," Nathaniel said.

"But that's a new power for me, Nathaniel. I spent centuries terrified of the light; that kind of fear doesn't just go away."

"You can walk in daylight now. It should make you brave," Giacomo said.

Damian looked up at the other vampire. "It should, but right now it doesn't."

Ethan had stopped closing the blinds and was looking at me. "I understand Damian being afraid, but you're afraid, really afraid."

I nodded. "I don't know if I can ride in the plane with the windows shut."

Giacomo said, "I cannot ride with them open, nor can your beautiful Echo." He had finished closing the windows just behind me, so that the only window left open was the one by me. I was leaning toward it like a flower anticipating the sunrise.

"I know we have to close them. I'm just saying that my claustrophobia is kicking in, that's all."

"We could strap Giacomo, Damian, and me into seats in

the back of the plane and you could have your window open," Echo said.

I looked up into that delicate triangle of a face, those blue eyes that could look as light as cornflowers, a blue that was so rich it was almost violet. I unbuckled and all the men let go of me so I could move out into the narrow aisle and reach her. She took my offered hand. The plane wavered slightly in the air, and I had to swallow and clutch a little tighter at her small hand, almost as small as mine. Nathaniel steadied me with a hand on my hip. I patted his hand and then put my hand against the soft paleness of Echo's cheek and kissed the small bow of her mouth. She hesitated and then wrapped her arms around me and kissed me back. I thought, as I always did when I kissed her, how small her mouth was; only Jade's had been smaller, but it may have been the difference in how they reacted to a kiss. Jade had kissed like she did most bedroom things, tentatively, waiting for me to take the lead. Once I made my intention clear, Echo melded her body against mine and didn't need to be led anywhere.

We broke from the kiss at almost the same time, so that we were staring into each other's eyes from inches away. I wondered if I looked as startled as she did. I studied her face and the feel of us holding each other, arms still wrapped around each other's backs. In my high-heeled boots I was almost the same height as she was, and I liked that, too. I had enough tall in my life.

"I value this face more than I fear the window being closed," I said.

She gave me the smile that seemed shy but managed to fill her eyes with pleasure. I was never sure if it was a real smile or one that she thought would please without committing too much emotion. A lot of the older vamps got to a point where they had very few natural facial expressions, because raw emotion had been punished out of them. Jean-Claude had been cautious around me at the beginning, too. I wanted someday to get a smile from Echo that made me sure it was really what she was feeling.

"We should be perfectly safe in the back of the plane," she said.

I shook my head. "Accidents happen, so not worth it."

"So, you do not admire my beauty, too," Giacomo said, and struck a pose, tilting his face up and to the side to show off the scar that cut across his eye.

I laughed, like he meant me to, and said, "You are quite lovely, but I'm not sleeping with you, so I don't care as much."

He looked at me and grinned, and again I wasn't sure if it was all he was feeling, or the expression that was expected. But he could keep his emotional secrets; I'd worry about the people I was trying to have relationships with first.

Fortune came over and wrapped her arms around both of us, so it turned into a group hug. She kissed me, and her mouth was wider than Echo's, the lips a little less full, so that it was more like kissing one of the men once my eyes were closed. Though the breasts pushed in against my shoulder reminded me she so wasn't one of the guys.

"Am I the only one having trouble not making girl-on-girl jokes?" Dev asked.

"No," Nathaniel said.

"Yes," Pride said.

"I enjoy the sight of three beautiful women together as much as any man, but dawn is near," Kaazim said.

Fortune turned to him, still hugging both of us, and said, "You aren't moved by the three of us together. I honestly don't know what moves you, Kaazim."

"To serve my queen and her kings to the best of my abilities."

"Bullshit," I said.

Fortune grinned down at me, then said, "I agree with Anita: bullshit."

"Jake, is that not what moves me?"

The other man grinned, but it was more a baring of teeth, as if he were snarling more than smiling. "I think I would like to be left out of this discussion."

"Do you not know me after all this time, old friend?"

"I know your innermost desires, as much as you know mine, Kaazim, old friend."

"Translation: You don't know," I said.

Jake looked at me. "That is not what I said."

It was Damian who touched my arm and made me look down at him. "I know I would be perfectly safe here even with the window open, and I may not die at dawn, but I would move to the back of the plane with the other vampires if that is all right."

I leaned down and kissed him. "Of course, sit where you feel safest."

Pilot Jeff came over the intercom. "Sunrise is almost here. Is the cabin secure?"

"Nicky, close the window," I said.

He leaned over Damian and patted my hip—okay, my ass—and closed the window. I swear that the lights in the plane dimmed; I knew they hadn't, but it just seemed darker. Crap.

Echo kissed my cheek. "Thank you, Anita."

"I'm a big, grown-up necromancer. I can do this."

She smiled and went to find a seat to strap herself into, because once the sun rose she would drop like the corpse she almost was; Giacomo joined her in moving toward the back of the plane. Damian unbuckled and stood up. Nathaniel reached up and drew him down into a kiss, which he gave without any hesitation. Whatever magic Nathaniel had worked on the vampire, it was still working. He went back to join the other vampires while everyone else rearranged their seats so the vamps could have the seats farthest to the back of the plane where it was a little bit dimmer, just in case.

Fortune hugged me, just the two of us; I had to look quite a bit farther up to meet her pale blue eyes with their almost bright blue eyelashes like the coolest mascara ever to frame the forget-me-not blue of her eyes. It had been her eyes that had made me take Sin to the side and stand him in bright light to discover that his eyelashes weren't black like I'd always thought, but an incredibly dark navy blue. It was a very small sampling, but so far only the blue tigers all had eyelashes the same color as their clan name. The gold tigers certainly didn't all have golden eyelashes, or even eyebrows.

"Thank you for taking care of her," Fortune said.

"You're supposed to take care of your lovers, aren't you?"

She smiled down at me from a face that looked about twenty-five and would look that way forever, but she suddenly looked beyond cynical, as if the years that didn't show on her face were still there in the depths of her blue eyes.

"Yes," she said, "you are, but a tremendous number of people don't seem to know that. Thank you for not being one of them." She kissed my forehead as if I were a child, and then kissed my mouth like a lover. She left me to go give Echo a good-bye kiss, before the sunrise stole her master and lover away. We had coffins packed in the belly of the plane for the vampires traveling with us, and I knew that Fortune and Magda both had duffel bags big enough to put their masters in and carry them out on their backs if they had to, but that was for short periods of time or if something went horribly wrong. There was a third duffel bag in the cabin for Damian, just in case he died at dawn again. If he did we'd treat him like all the other vampires, though neither Nathaniel nor I had had time to practice carrying him like that. Damian wasn't a big guy, but he was tall, so Nathaniel would probably do the carrying just because he was taller and broader than me.

I took my seat beside Nathaniel again. I could see Magda checking Giacomo's seat belt as he reclined the seat back so he was lying down. She wouldn't be giving him a good-bye kiss, because they didn't kiss, so far as I knew. They weren't lovers. They were fellow warriors, battle buddies, partners in that police way, maybe even best friends, but there was nothing romantic between them. Magda had proved with us that she was bisexual, so I wasn't sure why they hadn't added fuck buddies to their list, but with them it seemed to be strictly mutual respect and a partnership somewhere between the ones I had with Edward and Sergeant Zerbrowski, who was my partner when I worked with the Regional Preternatural Investigation Team back home. Edward and I were about to be best "men" for each other. Zerbrowski had put me and Nathaniel on the short list of people who could come get his kids from school in case of emergency. It would never have occurred to me to cross the line romantically with Zerbrowski. Edward and I had decided long ago that our friendship meant more to us than any friendship with benefits could gain us. You can be friends with your sexual partners, but you can't be best friends, because the sex gets in the way, and if you're trying for a romantic relationship, that means regular friendship is almost impossible. I'm told there are people who can pull off both, but I've never met them. Maybe Magda and Giacomo had done the same relationship math and partnership won, too. Or maybe I didn't understand either of them well enough to hazard a guess yet.

I watched the two *moitié bêtes* tuck their vampire masters in, in very different ways. Damian buckled himself in and started lowering the seat back. I guess if he died at dawn, it would be less disturbing than watching his body slump sitting up. Fortune and Echo were each other's primaries, but Magda didn't seem to have a serious lover outside of us, and none of us was very serious with her. Did she want to be serious with someone?

Nathaniel got up to see if Damian wanted him to hold his hand the way that Fortune was doing for Echo. I remembered Jean-Claude asking me years ago to be with him at dawn. Watching him "die" as the sun rose outside the hotel room had been my first confirmation that vampires really did die at dawn. I'd heard his breath rattle out and felt his energy change from alive to not. I knew from medical write-ups that vampires' brain activity didn't go dead like true death and in fact didn't even go as low as most coma patients', but when you were just watching it happen without monitors to tell you different, it looked the same as anyone else dying in front of you. I'd seen people die for real and I'd seen vampires die at dawn, and I'd killed vampires for good. It all looked pretty much the same.

Nathaniel came back to his seat. "Damian's afraid that if he holds my hand he won't die at dawn."

"Why would he want to die at dawn?" Socrates asked from across the aisle.

"When he sleeps like a regular person he has nightmares," I said.

"I can understand wanting to skip that," he said.

I felt the sun rise on the other side of the closed windows, and I felt Damian die. Nathaniel grabbed my hand tight. He'd felt it, too. I heard the curtain close behind us and didn't blame whoever had done it because one window wasn't perfectly set and there was a thinnest of golden lines that slid along the inside of the plane. Domino was closest and he tried to force it down that last fraction. "It's not square in the window. It won't close more."

We got napkins from the bar and wedged them in the crack of the "closed" window. "Good thing none of the vampires stayed up here," he said.

We all agreed. "Someone make a note to get this window fixed. Blackout shades aren't a luxury for us."

"Done," Nicky said, and he was making a note in his smartphone.

We all sat back in our seats, though Dev moved up to sit across from Nathaniel where Damian had been. There was barely room for his shoulders next to Nicky's even in the comfy swivel seats. I wasn't sure they would have fit next to each other in coach seats on a regular airplane.

"What do you guys do on commercial airlines? I mean, how do you fit into the seats?"

They looked at each other and then Nicky answered, "I ride first class."

Dev grinned. "Not fit."

I smiled back. I couldn't help it. "Okay, ask a silly question."

Nathaniel put an arm across my shoulders and said, "We should tell Dev about Asher."

The smile faded on Dev's face. "I don't need to know anything about him."

"This, you actually do," I said.

We told him, and Nicky, and anyone else on the plane who wanted to hear. It wasn't big enough to really keep secrets, especially not when the people in question had super-hearing. It was like trying to keep secrets around Superman: just not happening.

Dev was frowning and rubbing his temples by the time we were finished.

"I'm sorry," I said.

He opened his eyes and looked at me. "You didn't break my heart. Why are you sorry?"

"I guess I'm sorry Asher is such a shit."

"He was a shit to you, too."

"But I didn't want to marry him, so it didn't break my heart as much," I said.

Dev smiled, more chagrined than happy. "Yeah, well, I'm not twenty-five yet, so I get to make stupid choices."

"At least he didn't say yes," Nicky said.

Dev looked at him and it was not a friendly look. "I wanted him to say yes, or I wouldn't have asked him."

"If he'd said yes, then you would just be fucking Asher and no one else; is that really what you want?"

"He was never monogamous for you, but he expected you to be for him," I said.

"Cousin," Pride said, leaning in between Dev's and Nicky's seats, "Asher is one of the most selfish people I've ever met. I don't know how you dated him as long as you did."

"He's the most beautiful man I've ever met," Dev said.

"No one is beautiful enough to make up for being that much of a selfish bastard."

"The sex was amazing."

Pride shrugged, his hands making a push-away gesture. "We'll all stay with the crazy ones longer than we should for the sex."

"I hate the idea that only the crazy ones are great in bed, because it's not true," I said.

They all looked at me.

"What? I'm having great sex and I'm not dating crazy."

They looked at one another now, and then Nicky said, "Anita, I'm a sociopath who tried to kill you and almost everyone you loved when we first met. How is that not the most crazy boyfriend ever?"

"Okay, I'll give you that one," I said, smiling and patting his knee.

Nathaniel said, "I was the crazy boyfriend for years, but I went to therapy and worked through my issues."

"But you still do sex like you're the crazy boyfriend," Dev said, leaning forward and kissing Nathaniel. He parted from the kiss, his hand playing with the thick braid of Nathaniel's hair.

Nathaniel ran his hand along the other man's thigh as he said, "You fuck pretty good for not being the crazy one."

It made Dev laugh and lean in for another kiss. This one lasted a little longer, and I watched sort of fascinated. I'd been with them together more than once and knew they were doing more just the two of them, but that just made them better together and I was good with that.

Dev drew back and said, "I'm so vanilla compared to you."

"Everyone is vanilla compared to Nathaniel," Pride said.

We all shook our heads. Ethan spoke up from across the aisle. "Not anyone else sitting over there with you."

"What do you mean?" Pride asked.

"It's one of the reasons that Anita and I didn't work out as regular lovers. I am vanilla and she isn't, and she's not attracted to straight vanilla men."

"I won't apologize for what I like," I said.

"I'm not asking you to, but I'm trying to explain to Pride that he doesn't understand that Nathaniel isn't the only nonvanilla here."

"Me, too," Domino said. "I'm too vanilla to be part of Anita's harem. I'll do group sex if there are enough women involved, but other than that I'm not oriented the same way that the rest of Anita's men are."

"I thought Nathaniel was the only . . . I don't want to be insulting," Pride said.

"I'm the biggest pain slut of anyone in Anita's life, if that's what you mean."

Pride looked relieved. "Yes, that's what I mean."

"Nathaniel isn't the only one of us who likes pain; he just goes further than the rest of us," I said.

"I guess I consider Dev vanilla except for being bisexual," Pride said.

"I do group sex and you know I'm an exhibitionist," Dev said.

"I guess I was just counting bondage as not vanilla."

"Sorry, Pride, but vanilla sex is narrower than just not doing bondage," I said.

Dev said, "The first time I was with Asher was with Nathaniel, Micah, and Anita. A four-way doesn't count as vanilla."

"Okay, I get that I'm wrong on my definition of vanilla, and if you were as into bondage as Anita, or Nathaniel, I could see you missing Asher. Apparently, he's a talented top in the dungeon, but you and he never did the dominant-submissive thing together."

"No." All the smiles were gone from Dev now. He'd sat back in his seat, not trying to touch anyone.

"If you don't like pain, then a vampire can't go down on you that well, because of the fangs, so was the sex really that good, or was it just the being-in-love-with-him part?" Pride asked.

"He really is good at sex. Anita can back me up on that," Dev said.

They looked at me, even Pride.

"Yeah, he's good in bed, but he's not better than Jean-Claude, or Nathaniel, and you're getting to sleep with both of them," I said.

"You're getting to fuck women again, and that's worth getting rid of Asher right there," Nicky said.

"I love women, but I was willing to give them up for him," Dev said.

"I don't see how you agreed to give up women," Pride said.

"You don't like men at all, cousin. Of course you wouldn't understand it. I saw it as the same as being monogamous for marriage."

"But most monogamous people are just into the sex of the person they married, so they give up everyone else, but if they like men they still have a man to sleep with, and same if they love women. You agreed to give up half the human race that you loved having sex with, and Asher was still getting to sleep with Anita, so only you gave up women. It was totally shitty of him to ask you to do that," Pride said.

"I didn't realize you disliked him that much," Dev said.

"He treated my cousin like shit. He's hurt my friends. He's injured people I'm supposed to be protecting as my job. Why wouldn't I dislike him?"

"Why wouldn't you hate him?" Nicky asked.

"He's not worth that much emotion," Pride said.

"If you liked men, you'd understand."

"No, Dev, I wouldn't. I don't have any crazy exes. I don't do the bad girl or boy. I like nice, kind, and the sex can be just as hot."

"How do you know that nice sex is as hot as bad-girl sex if you've never had bad-girl sex?" Nicky asked.

Pride opened his mouth to say something, then closed it, looked puzzled, and finally laughed. "Okay, okay, I guess I don't, but I have great sex and she's not crazy."

"Who are you having sex with?" Dev asked.

Pride shook his head. "None of your business."

"Hey, you brought it up."

"I did not bring it up. In fact, I'm sorry I said anything."

"Are you dating someone and I didn't know about it?" Dev asked.

"We're not eight anymore, Dev. We all have grown-up secrets."

"If Pride is dating someone, then no one knows about it," Nicky said.

I shook my head. "News to me."

"Who is it?" Nicky asked.

"Why do you care?" he asked.

Nicky grinned. "Because you want to keep it a secret."

"That's Dev's kind of reasoning," Pride said.

"I'm actually with Nicky on this one, because I'm reviewing every interaction with any woman I've seen you with, trying to figure out who it is," I said.

"And why you'd want to keep it a secret," Dev said.

"Married?" Nicky asked.

"No, I would never help anyone cheat on their vows."

"So if she's not married, then why the deep, dark secret?" I asked.

He shook his head. "No, I'm done, because if I keep answering questions you may figure it out and she would be pissed at me. I'm not screwing this up."

I narrowed my eyes at him as if I were trying to bring him into better focus. It would bug me, but more because most shapeshifters are incredibly open about sex and relationships to other people they consider part of their community. There just wasn't the taboo among them that some normal humans had.

"Is she human, like mundane human?" I asked.

He shook his head. "No, I am done talking about this. She's too important to me for me to mess up because I'm trapped on a plane and we have nothing better to do than talk."

The plane swayed in the air, as if it had heard him talk about it. I clutched the armrest and Nathaniel's hand. "Talking about something would be good," I said, my voice a little strained.

"I'm sorry, Anita, but even to distract you while you're being all brave about your fears, I'm not blowing this relationship. It's too important."

Dev looked at his cousin. "You're serious about whoever it is."

Pride nodded.

He stared at the other man and finally clasped his shoulder, so that Pride looked at him. "Would you marry her?"

Pride shook his head, then said, "I mean, yes, if she'd have me, but right now she doesn't want to marry anyone."

"How long are you willing to wait?" I asked, because getting all up in Pride's personal business was better than worrying about how aerodynamics worked.

"As long as it takes," he said.

"Depending on who or what she is, that could be a really long time," I said.

"She's worth it."

"Wow," Dev said, "I haven't heard you this serious since we were thirteen and you wanted to marry the little girl next door."

"I was thirteen, and you and your sister both broke my heart with the little girl next door."

"We played 'show me yours and I'll show you mine' with her. You could have come and played with us."

"I was as serious as a thirteen-year-old boy could be about her. I didn't want to play with her. I wanted to profess my first true love." Pride laughed at himself, I think.

"She grew up way too kinky for you, Pride."

Pride looked at the other man. "How do you know?"

Dev grinned. "Angel went to the same college."

"Do I want to know?"

Dev grinned wider. "Probably not."

Pride shook his head and rolled his eyes. "I'll keep my illusions about my first serious crush, thank you."

"If Angel decides to bring her home to visit, I'll warn you first."

"Wait. What?" Pride asked.

"Could we really get to meet the little girl you guys first played house with?" I asked.

Dev grinned at me. "Angel and she kept in touch after college. They're both bi, so they got a place together with some other recent graduates trying to make it in the big city."

"We don't bring roommates home," Pride said.

"When Angel came home this last time, she said they were dating and have been for most of the time she's been out on her own. She's pretty pissed that she got called to the bosom of her family after establishing a successful life outside the clan."

"Is that why she's so cranky all the time?" I asked.

"Partly, but she's always been the less friendly of the two of us. She blames being named *Good Angel*. Names like that just make you want to rebel against them."

"So, Mephistopheles, why didn't you rebel and become the perfect little angel?" I asked.

He grinned again, and then his eyes filled with a heat that changed the grin to something more primal that made me shiver a little as he stared at me. "I went the other way," he said, in a voice that almost purred. "I decided to be my name."

"Mephistopheles," I said.

"Devil," he said.

The plane lurched again, and I fought not to dig my nails into Nathaniel's hand but just the chair arm. "I try to be on the side of the angels, but I play like I'm for the other team," I said, my voice a little strained.

"You make us all play for the angels, but you recruit from the other side," Nicky said.

"You're not a devil," I said, looking up at him.

"I'm not an angel, either."

"You like reformed sinners, Anita," Fortune said, leaning on the side of Pride's chair.

"You make me sound like the Salvation Army."

"I'm not reformed," Nicky said.

"Me either," Dev said.

"I guess to be reformed you have to be repentant, and neither of you are that," I said.

Fortune laughed. "They are so not that."

"We'll be getting food soon."

"I don't know if I can eat," I said.

"You have to eat, Anita. It helps quiet all the other hungers."

"You have to eat real food, Anita," Nicky said.

"If you don't eat actual food, you'll have to feed the *ardeur* before we land," Nathaniel said.

"Which could spread to the pilot. Yeah, Jean-Claude explained that," I said. I looked up at Fortune. "So what's for dinner?"

34

I WAS FINE until we started to land, and then having the windows closed became a problem again. Landing scared me anyway, but apparently being able to see out while it was happening made it less scary for me, because being trapped in a narrow metal tube with the sensation of it hurtling toward the ground, but not being able to see the ground, so I couldn't tell if we were actually landing, or crashing . . . I started to have a panic attack, fought through it, and held on to Nathaniel and Nicky for dear life. Dev reached across and put a hand on the one thigh that didn't have a hand on it already, and said, "It's okay, Anita."

I wanted to say, *You can't promise that*, but I was afraid if I said anything I'd either start screaming or throw up, so it was better to keep my mouth shut. I felt the bump as the plane landed. I closed my eyes and tried to be relieved, and I was, but I was also almost faint with the desire to get off this fucking metal tube of death!

The door was open and fresh air actually came into the plane. Something tight and unhappy in my chest and stomach loosened. I could breathe again without fighting the urge to scream.

The pilot said, "Everyone needs to show their medical alert cards, and allow customs on board to compare the vampires' faces to their passports, since it is daylight and we cannot bring the vampires to them."

The medical alert cards were the same kind of thing you'd

carry if you had severe allergies or other medical conditions that if you happened to be unconscious doctors would need to know about, except that these cards said we had, or carried, lycanthropy. Ireland and most of the rest of the European Union demanded that lycanthropes carry medical alerts. It could be a bracelet, a necklace, a card, an insert in your clothing, but you had to have something. If a lycanthrope tried to simply enter Ireland, England, or much of the EU as a normal human and then got found out, it was cause for automatic deportation with the possibility of jail time. The people who traveled with Micah already had theirs, and he was able to help us rush the paperwork for the rest of us. Apparently, there's a lot of controversy about it, so the powers that be had made it easier and quicker to get the cards, so that they didn't get sued again for civil rights violations and other similar things. England had originally wanted to force lycanthropes to be tattooed, but not all tattoos remained on all shapeshifters' skin. They then suggested forced branding, and lawyers, the press, and people in general began to make comparisons to the Nazis and how the Jews were permanently marked. So we just needed the cards, but if a government official, like a police officer, asked to see our cards and we failed to produce them, it could be grounds for deportation. You were encouraged to have more than one type of card on you at any given time. I felt a little funny with my card, because technically I wasn't a lycanthrope, but my official paperwork said that I carried lycanthropy, so for government work I needed a card.

I wanted to leave the plane desperately, but I didn't want to leave Damian behind. I'd never had to travel with a vampire that I was responsible for, and during the daylight dead-as-a-doornail time, Nathaniel and I were his only protection.

Magda spoke from the other side of the curtain where she was standing between the two "sleeping" vampires. "Go. I will wait with our masters, and Damian."

That seemed to be good enough for Fortune, because she exited the plane with the others. Nicky, Nathaniel, and Dev were still with me. "I thought you'd be the first one out the door," Dev said with a smile.

"I think I just needed a minute to get myself ready to meet the Irish authorities," I said.

Socrates poked his head through the open door. "We need you and your passports and cards out here."

I tried to stand up, and I say *tried*, because my seat belt was still fastened, and I damn near bisected myself trying to stand. It was the little things that kept me humble.

35

I STEPPED OFF the plane onto the tarmac, or asphalt, or whatever you call the artificial covering of every major airport in the world, and fought off an urge to go down on my knees and hug that rocklike surface. I often felt this way when I got off a plane and back to terra firma, but the urge wasn't usually this strong. Nathaniel took my hand as I got off the little folding steps from the plane. He looked around us and said, "It doesn't look very Irish."

The building and surrounding area were just an airport like almost every other private area of every other airport that I'd ever been to, so it wasn't that it wasn't Irish; it wasn't anything. If you traveled and only saw airports and hotels, then every place was the same. Even internationally, if you stayed in a chain hotel and people spoke English around you, it was like you never left home, except you were away from your actual house, your stuff, and the people you loved. Of course, this time that last part wasn't true.

I looked at Nathaniel with his auburn hair looking surprisingly red in the watery sunlight. The sky was gray with clouds and there was the feel of rain in the air. We had packed rain gear for all of us who already had some. We'd have to buy some for Nathaniel and Damian, but most of the rest of us had some. Mine had the U.S. Marshal logo all over it, so if the local police wanted me to wear something more neutral I'd go shopping, but until they made me I'd wear what I had. At that moment I was wearing a light leather jacket that probably wouldn't like being rained on any more than the one that Nathaniel was wearing. Most everyone else either was wearing leather or already had their raincoats on. Most of the coats were lined, so they were probably better for the temperature than the leather jackets and would definitely be winners when the rain started. Though they wouldn't be nearly as fun to cuddle. I ran my hand down Nathaniel's back and the leather was soft and pettable. Of course, I could feel the firm line of his shoulders and back under the leather, so that might have made me lean toward leather as opposed to raincoats. I looked around at everyone as they unloaded the luggage from the belly of the plane and thought I'd have to touch Nicky and see if I had the same reaction. Maybe it was just the person and not the coat, or maybe it was both?

A uniformed official came out of the building with Socrates, who said, "Which of you has Damian's passport?"

"I do," Nathaniel said, and he went back to the airplane with them so the uniform could look at the "sleeping" vampire and make sure we weren't trying to pull a switch. Since people look different awake and alive, I wondered how hard it was to be sure the pictures matched the vampires. I could do it, because I looked at people alive and dead a lot, but I let it go and moved into the building with the others. I had my own passport and the card that matched the necklace tucked under my shirt against my skin that said I carried lycanthropy. The last time I'd traveled out of the country I hadn't needed anything but my passport. I wasn't really wild about the change.

It wasn't until the uniformed officials inside the building spoke in an Irish accent that it suddenly seemed like we might be in Ireland. It was perfectly understandable, but it gave me the feeling I'd stepped into a movie, because that was the only place I'd ever heard the real accent up until that moment. Damian and others could sort of do one on command, but it wasn't the same. I don't know if the other felt like an act, or if the lilt and rhythm of the customs people were a slightly different accent. Either way, standing there while they inspected everyone's passports and the medical alert cards was less real somehow. I don't think I ever thought I'd see Ireland in person. I sure as hell never thought I'd see it with over a dozen people who included three vampires and ten lycanthropes. Once, I'd thought I was the scourge of bad little vampires and rogue shapeshifters everywhere, and now here I was, one of them. Or that's what my own medical alert card said. *Lycanthrope carrier*, like I was something hauling dangerous freight across the world.

A uniformed woman said, "Congratulations, it's a beautiful ring."

I looked down at my left hand and the platinum ring with its channel-set white diamonds and big sapphire: my work ring. It was all I could do not to say, *You should see the other ring.* That one lived in a safe at the Circus of the Damned while we waited for yet another compromise engagement ring to be finished that would be the one that went with the wedding ring that was also still being handcrafted. The one in the safe was the ring Jean-Claude had given to me for the video proposal. It was all white diamonds, really big white diamonds. The center stone was so many carats that rabbits should have followed me everywhere I went. I always felt like I had a sign over my head when I wore it: *Please mug me.* If I ever forgot myself and punched someone in the face while wearing it, I'd scar them for life. It was a very big ring, very flashy, incredibly expensive, and theatrical. It had looked great in the video and pictures that the engagement coordinator had had taken for us. Yes, there really are engagement coordinators, because asking someone to marry you has to be almost as big a production as the wedding now, or it does when you're the King. The video had gone viral on YouTube and outed me in a major way as Jean-Claude's fiancée. At least the woman hadn't seen the video and didn't ask me where that ring had gone, or if I had broken up with that beautiful vampire, and who this ring was from—I'd had all those reactions to the work ring.

"Thank you," I said, smiling like I meant it.

The gentleman working with her leaned over from looking at Dev's medical alert card and double-checking that it matched his bracelet to say, "Which of them is the lucky man?"

My smile widened. "He's at home."

The woman looked up at the men with me, hesitating here and there in a more lingering way than she had before. I guess

I couldn't blame her; after all, if you don't meet people at work, where do you meet them?

"Very sad he couldn't come with us. It would have been so much more romantic," Dev said.

I wasn't sure exactly where we were going, but I played along. "It would have been."

"Now, Marshal Blake, you know the romance has to wait until the work is done," said a man's voice with a thick American Western drawl.

I turned to find Edward in full U.S. Marshal Ted Forrester guise walking toward us. He tipped his white cowboy hat back on his head and grinned at me. I probably looked surprised. I would never get used to how completely Edward could vanish into Ted Forrester. I'd only learned recently that Theodore Forrester was his legal birth name. He'd always just been Edward to me. Ted was a good ol' boy. Edward was not. They were the same person, so they were both five-eight, though he always seemed taller, yellow-blond hair cut short, mostly hidden under the hat, pale blue eyes, a lean, in-shape body that didn't look as strong as he actually was; I could never decide if it was genetic and he couldn't bulk up, or if he thought lifting was too boring and didn't bother. He pushed away from the wall and walked toward us in his jeans, which fit tight over the cowboy boots. He was wearing a white button-up shirt over a black T-shirt. The smile on his face was Ted's smile, so it was all for the customs officials. He knew he didn't have to waste his good-ol'-boy act on me and my people; we knew his true identity, and Ted wasn't it.

"Hey, Ted, I was beginning to wonder when you'd show up," I said, smiling my real smile, because I really was happy to see him.

"If you'd come in on a commercial flight I'd have been able to check a timetable, but the fancy private jets are harder to time." He tipped his hat at the lady customs official, and she was flustered by it. Edward was so solidly in the "best friend" box for me that I had trouble seeing him as this handsome, flirtatious man, but other women seemed to see it just fine.

He looked at some of the people with me. "This isn't who we discussed," he said, and the real Edward had eased into his Ted voice, just a little.

"Long story," I said.

He let it go, because he knew that meant I couldn't tell him in front of strangers. He eyed them all, and it wasn't Ted looking out of his face now. Even Ted's slightly rounded shoulders were gone, replaced by Edward's upright, shoulders-back, I-was-in-the-military stance. The customs official who had been flattered was looking at him warily now. She'd been on the job long enough to know trouble when she saw it; good on her.

Edward looked at me when he got to Dev and Domino, because he'd been there to see Dev have his moment under fire, when he'd broken down completely. In his defense, the zombie fight in the basement of the hospital had been one of the worst things I'd ever done, even by my standards. It had been a really harsh introduction to my job for Dev. He flat-out told me he didn't want to go zombie fighting with me again. Domino hadn't liked a homegrown zombie of mine that we'd had to burn in a cemetery, and I'd told Edward about it, so he knew neither of them were my top choices. He'd tell me which of the others he didn't like later.

"Later," I said.

"Can't wait," he said with a smile as he crawled back into his Ted skin and just folded back into the charming cowboy act. To her credit the customs official didn't buy it now; she knew something odd was happening and she wanted no part of the blond man with his identity crisis.

We were joined by another man; he was taller than Edward, though not as tall as Dev. It was nice when I had a variety of heights that I actually knew to compare new people to, so the new guy was five-eleven, or six feet tops. I was never good at subtracting the inch or more that even work boots could give a person, and he was wearing the kind of boots that SWAT wore in the field. The kind that I had in my luggage. His uniform was black, from the tac pants to the long-sleeved button-up shirt. It bulked out from the body armor underneath it, but I didn't need that hint; the sidearm worn out where we could all see it was clue enough.

His dark brown eyes scanned the room and us. His hair was a rich brown that was almost a dark auburn, and might be under the right light. Nathaniel's hair was solidly on the red side of auburn, but most people with the hair color leaned more to brown. He had a good face, but the level of energy and edge of threat he brought into the room took away all my interest in him as a man. He raised my hackles, and the energy in the room from the real wereanimals told me that it wasn't just me.

He stared back and didn't try to hide his own hostility, and in fact . . . he added his own energy to the room. Edward went up to him, and I knew before he introduced Captain Nolan that this would be his work acquaintance, Brian. I also knew that he wasn't plain-vanilla human before Edward called me up to introduce us.

"So you're Anita Blake," he said, his Irish accent softening the near-hostility in his voice.

"And you must be Brian," I said, smiling sweetly. I even worked to push it up into my own brown eyes. If I could do it for clients at Animators Inc., I could do it to piss off the cranky Irishman.

He raised his eyebrows at me, then glanced back at Ted/ Edward. "Well, Forrester, are we all going to be on a first-name basis?"

"I call Anita by her first name and she calls me Ted."

"And the rest of . . . her crew?"

"First-name basis," I said.

Captain Brian Nolan shook his head. "I can use your call sign if you prefer, Forrester, but I just can't call you Ted."

"Theodore," I suggested, doing my best innocent face.

Nolan frowned at me. "No."

Edward smiled at both of us. I think he was genuinely enjoying introducing us. His eyes were bluer than normal, and his breathing had sped up a little. I think he liked the energy rising in the room, and the sense of potential carnage.

"Have it your way," Edward said, and turned to me. "Anita Blake, this is Brian Nolan. Nolan, Blake."

"Captain Nolan," he said, narrowing his brown eyes.

"Fine, then it's Marshal Blake," I said, but I was smiling.

"Am I amusing the two of you?" Nolan asked.

"A little bit," I said.

"You always amused me," Edward said, smiling his Ted smile.

Nolan scowled at us. "I don't think I like your attitude, Blake."

"I'm not thrilled with yours either, Nolan, but we don't have to like each other to work together."

He frowned harder, putting deep lines in his forehead and between his eyebrows. It made me add a few more years onto his age, which I'd have called at early thirties; now maybe forty wasn't out of the question. Once people got to a certain age I just sucked at guessing.

"It would make things easier, though, if we liked each other, at least a little bit," Dev said, coming up smiling and just giving off this vibe of being happy to be there, happy to meet Nolan, and just doing his best to turn the energy in a friendlier direction.

He held out his hand and said, "I'm Mephistopheles."

Nolan didn't shake his hand. "What the fuck did you do to earn that as a nickname?"

Dev made a sad face and said, "Sadly, it's not a nickname." He held up his passport so the other man could see it clearly. It read, "Mephistopheles Devlin Devereux."

Nolan actually stopped being angry; his face folded into something human and much more attractive. "That's a hell of a name, Devereux."

"I go by Dev."

"I don't blame you," he said with the Irish thicker in his voice. He almost smiled at the thought of going through life with such a name.

The first and last names were his parents' fault, but I knew that he'd chosen Devlin as his middle name himself. When the gold tigers reached age ten, they got to choose that part of their name. Most chose very simple names, or normal-sounding ones, but little Mephistopheles had chosen the name that sounded most like the nickname he'd already earned, Devil.

"*Devereux* is French," Nolan said, and started speaking in fluent and very rapid French.

Dev shook his head, smiling. "Most Americans don't speak the language of their ancestral country; sorry."

Nolan turned to Pride, who had moved up beside his cousin. "And you are?"

"Pride Christensen."

"Is Pride a nickname?"

He just held his passport out for Nolan. It read, *Pride Christensen*. No middle name, because he had never chosen one.

"If you had the same last names, I'd ask if you were brothers."

"Cousins," Dev said, smiling and clapping Pride on the back.

Pride raised an eyebrow at him and frowned. "Will you ever grow up?"

"Will you ever get the stick out of your ass and learn to have fun?" Dev countered.

Pride rolled his eyes and moved away from his smiling cousin.

Nolan actually did smile, so there was a human being in there somewhere. Good to know. He turned to Fortune, who was next closest. "And you are?"

"Sofie Fortunada," she said, smiling.

Edward interrupted, "Captain Nolan wants to see everyone's passports and get names, which he'll run through every database he can find." We'd already been warned this was not just likely, but a given, which was why everyone had chosen identities that had nothing questionable attached to them. It would so have ruined the trip if someone's name came up on an Interpol list for something. But there would be no issue with Magda Sanderson, Jacob Pennyfeather, Ethan Flynn, Domino Santana, Kaazim Fath, Russell Jones, or Nicky Murdoch.

Everyone just lined up and showed him their passports, much as they had for the nicer and more polite customs officials. In fact, the woman said, "We've already checked their passports and their cards."

"I don't need to see their cards to know they're shifters," Nolan said, and he made the last word sound like it was something nasty. He was rapidly losing all his brownie points with me.

He looked at the passports as if he expected some of them to be fake. The customs officials were all getting a little in-

sulted, because he made it obvious that he didn't trust them to
have checked the documents sufficiently. That extra energy
that rode around him was beginning to prickle along my skin
like insects marching. It was almost like some lycanthrope
energy I'd felt before I carried my own flavor of it, but if he'd
been a shapeshifter himself, why would he need us to bring
our own to play with his team?

"I guess you'll do. Grab your other gear off the plane and
let's go," he said at last.

The female customs official said, "If there's more luggage
coming off that plane, we have to inspect it."

Nolan turned back to her, took an ID out of one of the
Velcro pockets on his pants, and showed it to her.

She scowled at him, very unhappy. "You can't keep doing
this."

"This says I can," he said, and put the ID back in his pocket.
He smoothed his hand over the closure as if to make doubly
sure it was secure. I wondered what kind of ID it was, and
thought it was very interesting that the woman had said, *You
can't keep doing this*, which implied we weren't the first special guests of Captain Brian Nolan.

"Get your bags and follow me," he said.

"To someplace where we can change into something less
comfortable?" I said.

Nolan frowned at me, and again the lines in his forehead
looked almost painful, like scars instead of frown lines. How
many years had he been this unhappy to mark his own face up
like that?

"Just grab your gear, darlin'; you can suit up later." He
turned and started walking toward the plane as if it were all
settled.

"I thought I left Bobby Lee at home. He's the only one who
gets away with calling me that."

Nolan turned around and stared at me. That more-than-
normal energy that I'd felt when he hit the room spiked and
danced along my skin. I had to fight not to shiver like someone
had walked across my grave. It didn't mean that his psychic
gift was death related, or even scary per se; it just meant he
was really powerful.

"Grab your gear, and we'll talk in private," he said, his voice proving that any accent, no matter how lyrical and movielike, could thin down to serious and threatening.

"Will do," I said. Edward, Pride, Dev, and I followed in Nolan's wake. When we got outside I went for the steps leading up into the plane to check on Nathaniel and Damian. I got there in time to see them zip the bag up over Damian's face. He was so still, so . . . dead that it was like watching them put him in a body bag. I think I stopped breathing for a second, my heart just sitting in my chest waiting for the rest of me to tell it to catch up, so that when I breathed again it was a gasp.

Magda glanced at me, but Nathaniel stayed focused on getting Damian safely zipped up. "Are you all right, Anita?" Magda asked. Her eyes looked very gray in the dimness of the plane, as if all the blue had been sucked away.

I nodded, not trusting that my voice wouldn't shake. What the fuck? I'd seen so much worse; why had that small moment bothered me? Or why this much?

Nicky spoke from behind me. "Come outside for a minute."

I shook my head. "I'm fine."

"Don't give me fine. I feel what you're feeling no matter how much you shield from the others." He held his hand out to me, and after a second I took it. He led me a little away from everyone else and looked at me, still holding my hand. "What made you feel that way?" he asked.

I told him.

"You think it's a preview of what could happen?"

"Yes," I said.

"Don't borrow trouble, Anita."

"We're hunting monsters. People die doing that."

"You knew all that when you let them get on the plane."

"You know, you're not always that comforting," I said.

He smiled. "But you're less scared now and more irritated. My job is to make you feel better; sometimes that's just choosing which emotion you like better. You'd way rather be irritated with me than scared and worried."

I frowned at him harder, but I couldn't argue with him. In the end I squeezed his hand tight and we went to get the rest of our bags. Normally I'd have kissed him for that, but Nolan was watching me and he was going to have enough issues with me bringing so many "boyfriends" and "girlfriends"; I didn't need to add fuel to the fire.

We grabbed our bags, full of all sorts of things that would never have made it through normal inspection. Echo and Giacomo went in large lightproof duffel bags just like Damian had. Fortune and Magda strapped their masters across their bodies and helped Nathaniel get his own balance with Damian. Watching them balance the full literally dead body weight of their masters along with both sets of weapons in other bags made me realize why most vampires chose bigger people for human servants. You needed the size just to carry everything. I wasn't sure I could have toted Damian and the rest of my gear. Once Nathaniel got the bag balanced he moved easily. Of course, he wasn't carrying and wearing as many weapons as I was.

Jake and Kaazim offered to carry some of the weapons bags for Magda and Fortune, and the women let them take some of them. Neither man offered to carry the vampires, though Giacomo was a big guy even for someone Magda's size. She was strong enough, but it was more height and breadth for toting someone else who was as tall, but wider, and heavier. I was beginning to see why Magda hit the weights heavier than Fortune did; it wasn't just personal preference— she needed the bulk to lift Giacomo.

Socrates said, "I'd offer to carry him for you, but I think you do a better job of it."

"Thank you for the compliment," she said, and checked the huge duffel on her back one more time, to make sure the smaller bags were tucked up tight so that they helped hold Giacomo's body in place. It's not always how much you're carrying, but how it moves, how it sits on your body, or how it moves with you.

Nolan didn't offer to carry anything, just waited with those frown lines furrowing deeper into his forehead. If he had a single smile line on his face I hadn't seen it yet. I mean, he smiled, but it was as if his face did it so seldom that there was no mark around his mouth of it. There were plenty of frown lines, though. I'd never seen anyone mark themselves up so badly, as if facial lines could be scars.

Nolan led us off across the tarmac with Edward beside

him; they were talking in low, serious voices. The rest of us fanned out behind them. Nathaniel fell into step at my side. It actually seemed odd to walk beside him and not hold hands, but I was carrying too much and I needed to focus on work. Nicky was on one side of us, Dev on the other. Domino walked in front of us and Ethan was behind us. They'd put us in the bodyguard box, as I'd started calling it. I realized that Jake, Pride, Socrates, and Kaazim were carrying a little bit more than the other four men. They'd divided it up without a word, so that the four guards directly around us would have more hands free to go for weapons, if needed. Magda and Fortune's main allegiance was to the safety of their unconscious masters, so they weren't part of the bodyguard equation in that moment. I understood that; if I'd had Jean-Claude in a duffel bag in full daylight, I'd have been worried as hell that some ray of sunlight would get through. I was worried enough with Damian on Nathaniel's back, and I knew that sunlight didn't burn him.

Though, as I glanced up at the overcast sky, thick and gray with the promise of rain, maybe the famous Irish weather would be more vampire friendly than other places. You could get sunburned on a cloudy day if you were pale enough, so did cloud cover really matter to a vampire? In all the years I'd been intimate with vampires, first hunting them and then sleeping with them, I'd never asked about cloud cover. I mean, if your skin fried in the sunlight, was a cloudy day worth the risk?

There were three black vehicles waiting for us that I'd just started thinking of as the police version of the military Humvee, though not all of them were Humvees, and I knew that, but whether it was one of SWAT's BearCats or an armored military transport, they all looked vaguely the same, like a Jeep, an SUV, and a small tank had gotten together and had one hell of a night, and this was the result. Military would be painted in the camouflage of the area, or the current military fashion. The police were very fond of basic black for them.

There were three soldiers standing in a little cluster by the three black vehicles, dressed in the same all-black that Nolan was; between the outfits and the "SUVs," it reminded me a lot of working with SWAT, except I'd earned my place with our local cops, and here the hostility and doubt poured off all of them in waves. It wasn't aimed just at me; we were all unknowns. The three soldiers had no way of knowing how well we were trained, or how our training would complement or conflict with theirs. When you're about to trust your life to someone, you want to know that they're worthy of that trust.

Brennan was tall, dark, and handsome except for the hair being buzzed so close to his head it made me want to pet it to see if it was soft like baby duck feathers or bristly like beard stubble. The face was nice enough to carry the lack of hair, but it still made him seem unfinished to me. Griffin was also tall, not so dark, with a few curls escaping the beretlike hat he had on his short hair, which meant his hair might be as curly as mine if he didn't keep it so short. His eyes dominated his face, huge blue-green orbs with thick, dark lashes. He'd probably spent his whole life having women tell him he had beautiful eyes, and since he'd gone military, he'd probably gotten tired of the compliment before he hit high school. No matter how much he lifted in the gym, or how good he was on the range or on the field, the eyes would make the other men give him grief and the women pester him. Donahue was shorter, but still about five-eight, which made her taller than me by five inches. She was built leaner than me; even under the body armor you could tell the hips and chest were more boyish than my curves. Her hair was brown, straight, and cut short enough that it tried to undercut the whole girl thing, but her face was too feminine to pass for male. She was pretty without a drop of makeup on, which meant she'd have to work even harder to prove that she was really just one of the boys. Her handshake was firm, though her hands weren't much bigger than mine. She smiled when she was introduced to the rest of the gang.

"More women than you've ever worked with on any of the special-operations stuff, isn't it?" I said.

"It is," she said, and like everything she'd said, it was lyrical, and just sounded better than a straight American accent.

Nolan said, "Forrester didn't tell me we'd have this many women in your group." He made no pretense that he was happy about it, and implied in his tone that he would be asking Ted to explain once he had him in private. Nolan was starting not to sound charming even with the Irish accent.

"Is this private enough to talk about the name Anita mentioned earlier?" Edward asked in his Ted voice.

"If the rest of her people step away, yes."

"They all know the person in question," I said.

Nolan looked at me and then at the people around me. "All of them know him, including Mr. Long Hair here?"

"Yes, Mr. Graison knows him," I said, hoping that if I kept repeating everyone's names he'd remember them. I did nicknames when I met a lot of people all at once, too. *Mr. Long Hair* sounded like something I'd use on a stranger, so it really shouldn't have bugged me, but it still did.

"We all know him," Edward said.

Nolan turned to him. "She said my *darlin'* reminded her of Bobby Lee."

Brennan's dark brown eyes went a little wide, then looked at me. He looked me up and down, but not like a man looks at a woman he thinks is attractive, more like he would have looked at me if I'd been a man about my height and size. Shorter men have to work harder to earn their stripes in this kind of fraternity, too.

"How do you know Bobby Lee?" he asked.

"I'll answer you in the car once we get moving," I said.

"Why are you in such a hurry?" Brennan asked.

I looked at Edward, who gave a tiny nod. It was his go-ahead nod. "Because we are wasting daylight and one thing you learn quick about hunting vampires is you want to use every bit of daylight you can."

"We know the job," Brennan said.

"Then let's get moving to Dublin, or are we not hooking up with the local police right away?"

"We need to talk about Bobby Lee before we decide where we're going, Blake," Nolan said.

I looked at Edward. "How honest can I be with him?"

"I'd like to know how he knows Bobby Lee before I answer that question," he said.

I put down the bags I was holding; no reason to hold everything if we were going to be there for a while. Most of the guards followed suit. "Fine. We play twenty questions and then we get our asses moving." I turned to the men. "How do you know Bobby Lee?"

Brennan narrowed his dark eyes and went from speculative to nearly hostile. "We don't owe you an explanation."

"Then we're at an impasse," I said.

"Impasse?" Brennan said.

Griffin said, "It means the situation can't progress, that we're stuck where we are until we agree to move forward." He was fighting not to smile at me or at Brennan's discomfort, one or the other. I'd take any lightening of the mood.

"I know what it means," Brennan snapped at him.

Griffin just smiled pleasantly at him. He was teasing the other man and not in a buddy kind of way, more an "I almost don't like you" kind of way.

"You aren't going to share information until we do, are you?" Edward said.

Nolan just stared at him, which was answer enough.

Edward smiled his Ted smile at me. "Anita, you be the grown-up and tell the captain how you know Bobby Lee."

"Me the grown-up, that's different," I said.

"Answer the question, Anita, please." He didn't say *please* for much of anyone, not when he meant it, so I did what he asked.

"Bobby Lee is one of our bodyguards."

"Our?" Brennan said.

"Jean-Claude's bodyguards," I said.

Edward said, "We all look for work once we get out of the service, Nolan. Now, your turn: How do you know Bobby Lee?"

"We met someplace warmer, and a hell of a lot drier," Nolan said.

"Once you've gone private contractor the military won't take you back," Edward said.

"Bobby Lee can't go back, even if he wanted to," Nolan said.

"I meant you."

"I've never left the military."

Edward looked at him like he didn't believe him, but finally said, "Did you move back to mainstream military?" There was very little Ted in his voice when he asked.

"I put together teams for special assignments."

"You mean like the teams we were assigned to back in the day?"

"Yes."

"If I tell Anita she can trust you, am I going to regret that?"

"Why did it bother both of you that we all know Bobby Lee?" I asked.

"Regular military doesn't work with shapeshifters, not even as private contractors," Edward said.

"Then how did Nolan and Brennan get to work with Bobby Lee?" I asked.

"That is the question, isn't it?" Edward said in a voice that was cold and almost threatening. Ted wasn't going to last as a disguise if he couldn't do better than this.

"What are you afraid of, Forrester?" Nolan asked.

"Regular military doesn't play with shapeshifters, but there are other people who wear the uniform. People I don't want Anita involved with."

I had a thought. "You mean Van Cleef, don't you?"

They both looked at me as if I'd said too much. Nolan looked shocked and walked the two of us out away from the rest of the group. The guards on their four-point formation tried to follow me, but I shook my head and let Nolan lead Edward and me a more private distance up to the front of the Humvee line. When Nolan thought we were far enough away, he turned on us angrily. That otherworldly energy danced in the air and around my skin. I had to swallow past it and tell my inner beasts to stay put and not react to it.

"Forrester, I heard the rumor that you and she were . . . Pillow talk like that will get you in jail for treason."

"She knows the name because I brought her to his attention, or her hanging around with me did. I don't want her to ever meet him, or be involved in anything he's doing, and I need to know right now, Nolan: Is he involved with your unit?"

He looked at me. "Why does Van Cleef want to meet you?"

"I'm not sure he wants to meet me, but I've heard from more than just Ted that he's interested in the fact that I carry lycanthropy but I don't shift."

"She heals almost as well as a lycanthrope, is almost as fast, and has their heightened senses, but she never changes shape," Edward said.

Nolan looked from him to me. "If that's true, then you'd be right up Van Cleef's alley."

"You see why I want to keep her away from him," Edward said.

"You aren't denying that you're a couple with her, then?"

"Couple?" He looked at me. "Anita, are we a couple?"

"Not last I checked."

"Fine. You want blunt. Are you lovers?" Nolan asked.

"No," we said together.

"Why don't I believe that?"

"Because no one wants to believe that a man and a woman can be best friends without sex being involved somewhere," I said.

"A lot of the men in our line of work hate the fact that she and I are better at the job than they are, so it makes them feel superior to spread the rumors."

"It makes me Ted's girlfriend, not an equal, I think."

"What does it give them over Ted?"

I looked at Ted. "Good question."

"You're out of step with the younger set, Nolan. Men can be sluts, too. If I'm sleeping with Anita, then I'm getting supernatural help from her, and I'm cheating on my fiancée, which gives some of the jealous bastards a sense of superiority."

"It's a way of explaining why you're better than they are," Nolan said.

"And then Anita isn't good in her own right; she's my protégée, or trainee, or some bullshit."

"To be fair, you did help train me to be a better hunter," I said.

"Monster hunting has always been an apprentice system, Anita, no shame in that," Edward said.

"Who'd you apprentice to?" I asked, because it just occurred to me.

"Van Cleef," he and Nolan both said, at the same damn time. They stared at each other, and it was only partly friendly.

"Are you still his boy?" Edward asked.

"That summer was a long time ago, Ted."

"Answer the question."

"This isn't one of his projects. I swear that."

"But you are in touch with him."

"And you called him in for help just a few years ago, and

he came. He sent people to rain hell down on your enemies, helped you save your fiancée and her kids." It was the first time I'd met Donna and the kids; bad guys had kidnapped them, and Edward had turned to the mysterious Van Cleef for help, because the bad guys had known the name, and Edward, too.

"Because some of the men involved were old friends of ours, and of his," Edward said.

"They weren't military anymore; they'd gone more rogue than you have," Nolan said.

"I cannot believe I did not ask you if you were still in his fucking pocket before I got Anita on the plane."

"You call him in when you need him . . . Ted." And there was something about the way he hesitated on the name, as if there were another name he was almost saying. I knew that Van Cleef knew Edward was Edward, and not just Ted. I wondered if he'd shared that with Nolan.

"If you want a call sign for me, Nolan, just call me Death."

"Yeah, I know the other Marshals nicknamed you after one of the Four Horsemen."

"Yeah, he's Death, and I'm War, and why does Van Cleef scare both of you so much?"

"I'm not scared of him. That's Ted's issue. I stayed in when he got out; this isn't one of Van Cleef's pet projects, but I've worked with him over the years, while Ted here was trying to hide from him."

"If you didn't hide from him, Nolan, then you must have said yes when I told him to go fuck himself."

"And yet you called for his help in New Mexico to save your family, and he sent the help you needed, ungrateful bastard that you are."

"Bootlicking toady," Edward said.

"Put the weapons back on the plane, Forrester. I'm not letting you into my country with an arsenal."

"Stop it, both of you. I don't know what sort of pissing contest we walked into, but I will not let your history together hurt this investigation."

"You're free to join the investigation and let your pet vampire give all the information he has on the locals, but not with the weapons in those bags, because without my help they're illegal as hell."

"You haven't changed a bit, Nolan," Edward said, and it wasn't a compliment.

"You have, Forrester, but not for the better."

"Guys, guys." I finally waved my hand at them and they both gave me unfriendly stares. I didn't care if they got mad at me. "I thought vampires were killing people in Dublin."

"They are," Ted said.

Nolan nodded.

"Ted said that there are new missing people almost every night now—is that correct, Captain Nolan?"

"That's correct."

"Then why the hell are we not on our way to Dublin? We can help you find the rogue vampires. We can help you kill them."

"Not without your weapons, you can't."

"Are you really willing to have more people die because you and Ted are old friends turned old enemies? Or because you're both being horses' asses?"

"He's still working with Van Cleef, Anita. Don't you understand what that means for not just you, but all the people with you? Once you come up on his radar, you never really get off it."

I looked back at the men and women with me, then called them over to us.

"What are you doing?" Nolan asked.

"Unlike the military, I run a more democratic house," I said.

"What the fuck does that mean?"

When everybody was there, I looked from Nathaniel to Nicky, and then the others, and did what I thought was right. "You all know the name Van Cleef," I said.

"Sweet Mary, Mother of God, Forrester, did you tell all of them?"

"His name came up in another case," I said.

"What case?" Nolan asked.

"We'll talk in detail later, promise, but right now we need this settled." I turned to my people, looked at them one by one.

"There's a chance that this assignment could bring us up on Van Cleef's radar again. He is one of the few men that I've ever seen spook . . . Ted, so if you want to get back on the plane and go home, I won't hold it against you."

"Are you coming home with us?" Magda asked.

"No. I came to save lives and hunt vampires. I'm going to stay and do that."

"Then I will stay, too," she said.

"None of us will leave you unguarded," Kaazim said. The rest of the Harlequin shook their heads.

"I know you think I failed you once," Domino said. "I won't make it twice."

Nicky said, "You know it's not an option for me, Anita."

"I'm making it an option."

He gave me the look, and I moved on. "Dev, Ethan?"

Dev grinned at me. "Even if I were willing to leave you here, how would I ever explain it to the rest of the men back home? No, I'd rather take my beatings here than explain to Jean-Claude and Micah that I left you and Nathaniel here facing some scary top secret spook without me."

"Do you really think I would run away and save myself but leave you in danger?" Ethan asked.

"No, but I wanted you to know that I wouldn't hold it against you."

"You say that, but you don't mean it," Domino said.

"He's right," Dev said. "You say you don't hold it against us if we aren't as brave as you are, but you do. I panicked a little in Colorado with all the zombies, and you decided I wasn't as strong and brave as you needed me to be."

"I asked you to come this time, didn't I?"

"Only because some of your favorites couldn't come along, like Bobby Lee."

I didn't know what to say to that, because he was right.

"We're staying," Dev said.

"We're all staying," Fortune said.

"Nolan says that Van Cleef isn't directly involved in this one; do you believe him?" I directed this question at Edward.

"Yes, I do," he said, but not like he was happy about it.

"Then we stay, solve the vampire problem, and we help

Nolan work the kinks out of his new unit, and then we go home."

"You don't understand, Anita. Just because this isn't Van Cleef's unit doesn't mean it's not his handiwork."

"What difference does that make?" I asked.

"It means nothing is simple, nothing is what it seems, and the monsters won't be the only ones we're fighting against."

"Come on . . . Ted, you know I bring my own monsters to the party."

"If half of what I read in your file is true, Blake, you are one of the monsters."

"Don't believe everything you read, Nolan."

"I thought monsters were taller," Donahue said, smiling at me.

"The rest of us are all taller than Anita," Dev said, smiling back at her.

Donahue frowned, then looked at all of them. "So you're all monsters?"

"Oh, yes," Kaazim said, "we are all monsters."

Everyone nodded, including me, and finally Edward joined us. "There's only one way to find out if your new unit is good enough to fight monsters, Nolan, and that's to fight some."

Nolan stopped arguing with Edward and with us. I wasn't even sure what had convinced him to stop being pissy, but I didn't care. If we were going to hunt vampires here, I wanted the guns, and that meant we needed Nolan and his weird clout. Thanks to Nolan and maybe even the mysterious Van Cleef, we were allowed to load our potentially illegal firepower into the vehicles, and divided our people up between the three vans. We were in Ireland; we had the firepower we needed to hunt vampires and win. Winning meant saving lives. Winning meant we survived. Winning meant the monsters died. It was simple math and anyone who didn't understand that vampire hunting was just that simple wasn't going to be very good at the job. Not being good at most jobs meant you got fired; not being good at my job meant you died. I hadn't come to Ireland to die or get any of my people killed; I'd come to win.

36

BRENNAN DROVE OUR van but didn't like the fact that Nolan got in back with Edward, me, and some of our people. He pushed the point up to arguing with Nolan about it, but one of the pluses to being military is that when your captain tells you to do something, eventually you just do it. Period.

"What's his problem?" Dev asked, as he settled down on the other side of Nathaniel, who was snuggled up against me. Damian was at our feet, still curled up in the lightproof bag. It felt almost like there was more than just him in the bag, as if Nathaniel had stuffed in padding. I'd ask later when we were more alone. Right now we were about as not alone as we could possibly be. Nicky sat on the other side of me, so that I was snuggled between him and Nathaniel, something I normally enjoyed, but not at work, and not with Dev on the other side of Nathaniel. It was the broadness of the shoulders of all three of them that made us all have to sit very close to one another. I didn't mind, though it probably would have made more sense to have either Nicky or Dev change places with Kaazim or Jake, who were slender in comparison. Pride was on their side of the van, too, but his shoulders wouldn't help the issue. I wanted Nathaniel beside me and I knew that Dev preferred to sit beside either me or Nathaniel. Nolan was watching me too closely for me to want to get into an explaining match with Dev about why he couldn't sit beside either of his sweeties.

Dev repeated, "What is Brennan's problem?"

"He is afraid we'll lose control of our beasts," Kaazim said as he found a seat beside Jake.

The van doors were closed from the outside and I heard a click, almost like we'd been locked inside. If Nolan hadn't been inside with us, I'd have been more suspicious. Apparently, I should have been, because Edward looked at Nolan.

"And you're back here with us, because . . ." Edward said.

"To let you know I trust you."

"But you still locked us in."

The energy in the van flared. I was suddenly sitting in the middle of Nicky's beast. I could smell heat and sun and that heavy musk that meant male lion. My lioness lifted her head in the dark and gazed up the long tunnel of my body with eyes that were so dark an amber they were almost orange. I started doing my deep, even breathing exercises, because the last thing I needed was to have an issue with my own inner beasts with Nolan right there. Nathaniel's energy rose, but not like Nicky's did, but then, if it came to fighting our way out only one of them would be helping do that. Dev's lion responded to Nicky's, not just because they both held lion in them, but because Nicky was his Rex, his king. They were pride together, and that meant a lot to the two of them.

My lioness started padding up that long, dark corridor inside me, attracted to all the male lion energy. Damn it.

Pride's energy flared from across the small space and his gold tiger spoke to me and Dev, because that was still his original beast. The wash of gold tiger helped slow down my lioness but woke up the shadow of gold inside me. Her base color was white with pale golden stripes, but I knew she wasn't a white tiger, because when that rose inside me she was almost completely white with few, if any, stripes. It was like snow with muscles and teeth. Gold was like honey that could bite.

"Guys, tone it down until we need the muscle," I said, and my voice was breathy.

Jake and Kaazim didn't flare any more than Nathaniel did. His regular job was stripping onstage and shapeshifting onstage. He had to have nearly perfect control of his inner leopard to be safe around the customers at Guilty Pleasures. The other two were just older than dirt and had the control of millennia of practice.

I smelled other tigers and knew it was either Domino or Ethan in the other vehicles thinking at me, asking what to do. I lowered my shields so that I could hear better. I saw the other interior from a higher height than I had, and it was only the more dominant thinking that let me know it was Domino until he moved his hand enough for me to see it, too. I'd never tried this much mind-to-mind with him, and it wasn't a perfect match yet. Mind-to-mind takes practice, and we hadn't. Ethan was looking at Fortune, and I knew her blue tiger had triggered his, so she wasn't trying to be as calm as her Harlequin counterparts here. I thought soothing thoughts at both of them. Nathaniel sighed beside me and said, "God, I can't keep fighting," and his inner beast spiraled upward like sweet smoke to join the rest. I managed to say, out loud, "Unless you want these expensive rides torn apart, start explaining why you locked us in, Nolan."

I smelled wolf, but it wasn't my wolf. It didn't smell right and it didn't smell like Jake, because I knew his scent. I opened my eyes and hadn't even realized I'd closed them and looked around the van until I was looking at Nolan. His brown eyes were paler, almost wolf amber, which isn't the same shade of amber as lion.

"We need to talk," he said.

"Not while my people are locked in," I said, and I could feel the men in the other trucks waiting for me to give the word.

"We're moving, Blake. I can't unlock anything until we stop."

"Why lock us in at all?" Nathaniel asked that.

"Because the government thinks that the wereanimals contained in these three trucks are the most that have been in Ireland in decades. The plan is to take you to our base and meet the rest of my team."

"And then what?" I asked, in a careful voice, because I was really close to just telling Nicky to make a hole. We were done.

"We're supposed to use some of our own people to test and see if you're what Forrester said you would be."

"And if we don't pass your tests, what then?" Nicky asked.

"We'd put you back on the plane and send you home as too dangerous to deal with."

"But instead you're going to share your secret with us, because the government doesn't know what you are, do they?" I said.

"Yes, and no, they don't."

I thought at Domino and Ethan to wait. We were all right; just be calm.

Edward was leaning away from Nolan as far as the seats would allow. "When did you get attacked?"

"I didn't," he said in a voice that was more bass than it had been before.

"I can feel it."

"You weren't this sensitive to it when we first met."

"I know what I'm feeling now," Edward said, staring at his old friend.

More wolf filled the room, so that thick, almost sour smell started to override the other beasts. Jake's eyes were wolf amber. "Brother," he growled.

"We are not pack," Nolan said.

"Are you saying you were a werewolf when we met?"

"Yes."

"Son of a bitch."

"Accurate," he said.

"What are you talking about?" Edward asked.

"You are a born wolf," Jake said.

Nolan looked at the other werewolf and said, "Yes."

"What are you talking about?" I asked.

"Werewolves are the only native lycanthropes in Ireland," Jake said.

"They pride themselves on being lycanthropy free," I said.

"You can't catch what I have," Nolan said. "You have to be born to it."

Everyone's animal had calmed, because we were all surprised, and shapeshifters were willing to give one another more credit, or so I'd noticed. "Explain," Edward said, and he wasn't happy at all.

"My mother's maiden name is MacTire, MacIntire."

"What the hell does that have to do with this?" Edward said, staring at him.

"It means *wolf*," Jake said.

Edward stared at him. "Are you saying your mother was a werewolf?"

"She was a born wolf and so was I."

"Your da? Your gran-da?" Edward asked.

"No, just my ma."

"You must have cut off your tail," Jake said.

"I had to."

"Then you are tailless in wolf form, too."

"Yes."

"That throws off your balance."

"Yes, but my ma urged me to do it as I got older and it was harder to hide."

"I met your family. They were normal."

Nolan looked at Edward. "They still are."

"Wait," I said. "What do you mean, you had to remove your tail when you got older? If you spent that much time in animal form you'd have other secondary characteristics that were permanent. You'd never pass for human again once you got far enough to have a tail in human form."

Jake said, "As with the eyes for the clan tigers that are their beast halves at birth, so with the werewolves of Ireland."

"You mean wolf tails, or is it ears sometimes?"

"Always tails, though there are stories of some of us born with ears, but people thought we were part of the gentle folk, not werewolves."

"I've read stories of Fey with animal ears; are you saying those were types of lycanthropes?"

"Not all wolves, but many of them, yes."

"How did you pass the blood test for the army?" Edward asked, and he'd sort of recovered himself, or at least his voice was cold and distant. It was a voice that told you nothing except that you should be wary of him.

"My blood work comes up human." He looked at the other men in the van as we picked up speed. We were on a highway, I thought, but in the enclosed vehicle we really couldn't tell. "Devereux, Christensen, your card says that your type of lycanthropy is tiger. Blake's file says she runs with clan tigers—is that what you both are?"

They looked at each other—and then both of them looked at Jake. He gave a small nod. "Yes," Pride said. Dev just nodded.

"You said *their card*. Didn't you smell their beasts just a few seconds ago?" I asked.

"Normally, I wouldn't answer that, because it would be letting you know what I'm capable of, and what I'm not, but I knew I couldn't hide from this many of you, so no, I didn't smell the type of beast. In human form my nose isn't nearly as sensitive as a more standard werewolf."

"How do you know that?" Jake asked.

"I've had to trust other shapeshifters with my secret before."

"But you didn't trust me," Edward said, and his voice wasn't cold now. There was too much emotion in it for coldness.

"Are you bothered that I didn't tell you my secret, or bothered that I'm a werewolf?"

"The first part, and that I didn't spot it. I pride myself on being able to spot the monsters. It's part of what keeps me alive in this business, and you totally got by my radar."

"It was a genetic condition that I could ignore most of the time. I didn't tell anyone."

"A lycanthrope could have smoked me on the PT tests, but you and I were always neck and neck for the top time, number, whatever. Did you hold back so I wouldn't guess you weren't human?"

"No, you pushed me to work as hard as I could to keep up with your arse. Being a born wolf doesn't give you much more than human physical abilities. I'm in the top percentage of most PT and I'm not aging out of it yet, but you pushed me, Forrester, which means you're in the top percentage, too. I'm part wolf—what's your secret?"

Edward tried to keep frowning, and then smiled and stared at the floor as we slowed down. Either we were in traffic or we'd turned onto a smaller road.

"Do I say, *No secret, I am just that good*, or do I say, *Lying bastard*? Every type of lycanthrope I've met is better than human-normal, like superhero better. I'm good, really good, but I'm not superhero good and you should be."

Nolan shook his head. "I swear to you, I did my best to beat you, or at least keep up with you. I'm too damned competitive for anything else."

Edward gave a small smile. "You seemed to be."

Nolan looked at the two weretigers. "Are you both that much above human-normal physically?"

They both said yes, and then Pride added, "Are you saying that your type of lycanthropy doesn't show up on a blood test that's specifically looking for it?"

"That's right."

Dev and Pride looked at each other and then back at Nolan. "If we could pass the physical, some of us would have tried for the military," Dev said.

"I can't picture you in the military," Nathaniel said.

Dev turned to him with a grin. "Not me, but some of my other cousins would have."

"Military service would have divided you from your other loyalties," Jake said.

Pride asked, "Are you saying that even if we could pass the physical, we wouldn't have been allowed to join?"

"It wasn't possible," Kaazim said, touching Jake's arm, "so it does not matter; it is moot."

Nolan was watching the interchange. He was trusting us with his secret, but we didn't have to trust him with any of ours, not until I'd had time to talk to Edward in private. "It sounds like the born wolf is different from the clan tigers in more than just flavor of inner beast."

"It would seem so, but these are the first clan tigers I've ever met, and since I'm almost certain Devereux and Christensen are the same clan, maybe other clans will be closer to my people," Nolan said.

"To our knowledge none of the clan tigers can pass a blood test for lycanthropy," Kaazim said.

"Which means," I said, "maybe what you have isn't lycanthropy. Are you tied to the moon at all?"

He shook his head. "No, we aren't forced to change with the full moon, or forced at all. Once we gain control of the power we can go years without changing form."

All of us who fought against our inner beasts exchanged looks. It was Dev who asked, "Don't you miss it?"

"Miss what?"

"Your beast."

"I do, but it's a preference. I could choose to be fully human and never become the other again."

"Do you know any werewolves who have chosen to do that?" Pride asked.

Nolan nodded. "My mother, for one."

"I'd have never guessed she was anything but human," Edward said.

"The less you change form, the less you give off the energy. It's said that if you go too many years you can lose the ability to slip from human to animal, but I don't think my ma would care. She helped teach me how to control my wolf and how to shift form, but once that was done I'm not sure she ever changed again. I'd come home for visits and ask her to come run with me, but she would never do it again. It was like her being a wolf like me was a dream."

"Did you have other family that went into the woods with you?" Jake asked.

"Cousins, but there are fewer and fewer of us every generation. Unless we start marrying closer into the family line again, there may come a day when there are no MacIntires or MacTires worthy of the name."

"I seem to remember a second cousin of yours that you told me to stay away from," Edward said.

Nolan smiled. "She's married now and has three kids."

"Are any of them werewolves?" Jake asked.

"No."

"Would she tell you if they were, or would she just have the tail removed in the hospital and hide it from everyone?" Edward asked.

"Some have tried, but you can't ignore your shadow from birth. If they take after our ancestors and are not taught control, the inner beast will come out in other ways. The last of my cousins that were treated that way ended up in prison. He nearly beat someone to death in a bar fight. Part of what we learn to control as children is the amoral part of ourselves. The wolf sees nothing wrong with fighting for what is his, or when threatened."

"Wolves in nature seldom fight to the death," Jake said.

"And they aren't put into situations like school, or bars where they can drink until they lose all sense of themselves," Nolan said.

"Very true," Jake said.

"Wolves are not dogs," Nolan said, "and they do not behave like dogs when you put a collar and leash on them."

"True again."

Nolan looked at Edward. "I didn't think it would bother you this much. Makes me think if I'd told you years ago we wouldn't have been friends."

"Honestly, I don't know. I wasn't as comfortable with shapeshifters back then, but you'll always be Wee Brian to me." He said the last with a perfect Irish accent, as far as I could tell.

Nolan sighed and shook his head.

"Wait. Wee Brian," Dev said, "for real?"

"I'm named after my father, who's named after his father, and further back. I hated being Wee Brian."

"*Little Brian* would be bad enough, but even with an Irish accent *Wee Brian* would be hard as a kid," I said.

He smiled and looked up. "My da is Little Brian, my grandfather is Young Brian, and my great-grandfather was Old Brian, because that's what Great-Grandma Helen insisted on calling him after she named their son Brian Junior."

"Both you and your father are taller than your grandfather, so it just made it funnier," Edward said.

Nolan laughed. "You were so confused when I introduced you to my gran-da, Young Brian, after meeting my da, Little Brian."

I perked up; if Edward had met Nolan's family, maybe Nolan had met his. Edward said, "Let it go, Anita."

"How do you know what I was going to say?" I asked.

He smiled at me, the smile that let me know he'd not only seen through me but out the other side, and knew exactly how eager I was to solve the mystery of Ted Forrester alias Edward.

"Aww," I said.

Edward let his smile get a little bigger.

Nolan was looking from one to the other of us. "Either you've gotten much more comfortable with women, or she really is your comrade in arms."

"I'm much better with women than I was that summer, but Anita is going to be my best man at my wedding."

"And you're going to be mine," I said.

"Yeah," he said, slipping back into his Ted voice. "I'll be standing up with you, before you stand up with me."

"Yep," I said, trying for a down-home drawl.

"You really shouldn't try to do accents, Anita; you suck at it," he said in that middle-of-America, not-from-anywhere accent, the Texas/Oklahoma/Wyoming drawl of a second ago gone, and his voice crawling down into the cold-as-ice tones of the Edward I'd come to know and love.

"He always picked up accents like that; within a week of going home with me he sounded like he was a local. If he hadn't been so blue-eyed and fair-haired, he'd have been so much more useful as a covert operative," Nolan said.

"Contacts and hair dye fix a lot of problems," Edward said, still in his own voice, and still crawling around the tones that would tickle along your neck and make you realize just how dangerous he might be.

"You didn't go into military covert ops," Nolan said.

"I didn't say I did."

They had another moment of looking at each other. I couldn't tell if they were best buds or hated each other. It was like it switched back and forth depending on what they were talking about, or their moods. Edward was usually pretty even-tempered, but Nolan seemed to bring out his moody-bastard side. It was like visiting family; the walk down memory lane could bring out the worst in all of us.

"Does Van Cleef know your secret?" Edward asked.

"Not twenty years ago."

"Now?"

"He does."

"He must have given you hell for hiding it."

"I was attacked a few years back by a werewolf. I let everyone think that's what did it."

"If he ever finds out you hid something he wants so badly . . . He's disappeared people for less than this, Nolan."

"What do you mean, disappeared people?" Nathaniel asked.

I patted his thigh. "Think the government safe houses for new lycanthropes, but more secret and probably more permanent than just a cell."

"That's not far off," Nolan said.

"Have you helped disappear other shapeshifters?" Nathaniel asked.

Nolan just looked at him, and it was my boy who looked

away first. He looked at me with those beautiful eyes and he didn't like this one little bit. Me either. It was like lately no matter where I went Van Cleef's name kept coming up.

"I've hunted rogues all over Europe. We were able to capture some of them alive," Nolan said at last.

"Is Van Cleef still chasing the same goal?"

"If you mean super-soldiers, yes. That's why he collected both of us."

"I remember," Edward said.

"I swear to you that he is not directly involved in this; it's the Irish government wanting their own special-forces team."

"You know what I'll do if you're lying to me."

"The same thing I'd do."

Nathaniel said, "Did you both just threaten to kill each other?"

I patted his leg again. "Let it go," I said.

"I'm not going to understand a lot of this, am I?"

"No," I said.

"No," Nicky said.

Dev patted his other thigh. "Don't feel too bad, Nathaniel. I'm more guy-guy than you are and I don't understand it."

"But you understand, don't you?" he asked me.

"Yeah."

"Nicky?"

"Yeah."

He looked across at the others. Pride shook his head. Jake and Kaazim understood.

"We all give up pieces of ourselves to do the job," Edward said.

"Some of us give up more pieces of ourselves than others," Nolan said, and it sounded almost accusatory.

They looked at each other and you could just feel the years between them. Here was someone who had known Edward just as Van Cleef found him, found them both for some mysterious top secret assignment. What had he done to them? What had been so bad that it had made Edward leave the military? What had carved those lines on Nolan's face? Had it been twenty years of working with Van Cleef? I didn't know, but I would find out. I had the keys to Edward's true past; I wasn't going to let them go, as long as I didn't have to meet

Van Cleef to answer the riddle. Anyone who scared Edward that much was someone to avoid.

"You have no idea how much I gave up to leave," Edward said.

"And you have no idea what I gave up to stay."

They looked at each other for another minute, and then Edward held out his hand. Nolan took it, and then he pulled Edward into a hug, and they held each other, not like lovers, but like friends, the kind of friends that you make while the bullets are flying and the enemy is anyone who is trying to kill you and the man beside you. Outside of combat you may not have a damned thing in common, but these are the friends who become family who can call you twenty years later and say, "I need your help," and you help. Brothers in arms are brothers of blood, too; it's just not always their own blood that gets spilled to cement the bond.

37

EDWARD'S CELL PHONE sounded. "Police," he said, and answered it. He listened and finally said, "We'll be there as soon as we can, if Captain Nolan will act as transport." He handed the phone to Nolan. "They want to talk to you."

Nolan took the phone and spent his own time going *Uh-huh*, and *Yes, sir, No, sir*, and finally, "I don't disagree, sir." He handed the phone back to Edward, but apparently whoever it had been had hung up.

Nolan said, "Change of plans. I'll call ahead and let the rest of my team know we'll be late."

"What happened?" I asked.

"New crime scene," Edward said.

"They want him at the scene and, if I feel like you and your people will be assets, you as well."

"They know you haven't gotten to test us yet?" Dev asked.

"They're aware."

"What changed their minds on testing us first?" I asked.

"I believe the phrase was 'I'd take help from the devil himself.'"

"It must be bad, whatever it is," Edward said.

Nolan nodded. "They're more afraid of whatever has happened than of all shapeshifters and necromancers on Irish soil. It's going to be more than bad."

"You always invite me to the best places, Ted," I said.

"You might want to phone your people and prep them. They aren't the hardened campaigners I was hoping you'd bring."

"I won't take everyone into an active crime scene," I said.

"Good, because you're going to be limited and everyone you take in has to be justified."

"Justified to whom?" I asked.

"Me."

"Why you?"

"Because I've talked to you the longest of any of the Irish uniformed officers."

"You aren't a cop," I said.

"No, I'm not."

"What kind of scene is it, other than awful?" I asked.

Edward answered, "They think they found some of their missing Dubliners."

"What do you mean, they *think* they found them?" Dev asked.

"Do you mean the bodies are so messed up they can't tell?" Nathaniel asked.

I leaned my head against his. "I'm sorry that you even know to think that part."

"I'm not. I want to be okay with what you do for a living, and that means being okay with the disturbing stuff."

I just looked at Nolan and said, "I'm going to kiss him now, because that deserves a kiss. Don't give me grief about it."

Nolan held his hands up. "Wouldn't dream of it. I read your file, Blake. I'd be shocked if you didn't have some of your boy toys with you."

"Nathaniel and I live together and we're engaged. He's not a boy toy."

"My apologies; I thought you were engaged to the head vampire of your country, Jean-Claude."

"I am, but if the laws let us, the wedding would be at least four people."

"I can't make a one-on-one relationship work. If you can do four people in a relationship, then you're the better man."

"I don't know about that, but I'm definitely the better woman."

He laughed then. "I'll give you that one."

I turned my head and Nathaniel turned his, and we kissed, because we were sitting that close to each other. I drew back enough to look him in those flower-colored eyes and say, "Thank you for trying to understand my job."

"Thank you for trying to understand me," he said.

That made me smile, because that was probably the biggest part of being a successful couple in two sentences.

"Where's my kiss?" Dev said, smiling.

I rolled my eyes at him, but Nathaniel just turned his head the other way and offered up a kiss. Dev leaned over and took it.

"Don't ask," Edward said.

"Don't tell," Nolan said.

Dev leaned around Nathaniel to me, and I gazed up into that earnest face. "What did you do to deserve a kiss?" I asked, my voice mild.

"I'm going to go into the crime scene with you. Whether it's zombies, or vampires, or whatever, I'm with you until you tell me to stay with the car."

"Good point," I said, and kissed him, too.

I turned and kissed Nicky last. He kissed me back, then said, "What did I do to earn a kiss in front of the police?"

"I'm taking you into the crime scene with me. Think of it as an apology."

"I'm okay with blood and gore—you know that."

"It's one of the things I love about you," I said.

He smiled at me. "And that fact is one of the reasons I love you."

"And the fact that I'm not as good with the gory stuff is why you're not in love with me," Dev said.

I looked back at him and wasn't sure what I would have

said, but Nolan asked, "Now, I'm confused. Why does he get a kiss if you're not in love with him, but you are with the other two?"

"Do you just kiss people you're in love with?" I asked.

He looked surprised and then sort of laughed. "No. No, Blake, I definitely kiss women I am not in love with. If I could have given that habit up, I might still be married to wife number two."

"Two divorces? Your ma must have made your life hell," Edward said.

"She thought I married too young the first time, and she was right. She's upset about the second one, though. She liked Kathleen. Everyone likes her. She's just that kind of person."

"I'm sorry that it didn't work," Edward said.

"Me, too." He looked at me. "How many other people did you bring with you that you'll be kissing on, Blake?"

"At a crime scene, none, but three, four more."

"Every time I tried dating that many women at once, they found out and I was in fear of me life."

"Maybe that was your problem," I said.

"What was my problem?"

"You said they found out, which meant you were cheating on them. Everyone in my life knows about everyone else."

"I've never met two women in my life who wouldn't have killed me, or left me, for sleeping with the other one."

"Oh, Captain, you have been dating the wrong women."

"At least two of Anita's other people are women," Edward added.

"Nope, that settles it. Blake, you really are the better man."

That time I didn't argue with him. I seemed to be winning Nolan over; never argue when you're winning.

38

MY FIRST SIGHT of Dublin was the sea. Nicky had gotten out first along with Kaazim because they were bodyguards and they were in the seats closest to the doors. I guess technically my first sight of Dublin was the paved road that I stepped out on, but I could see that at home. The first thing that let me know that I wasn't home was looking past Nicky's broad shoulders and seeing the gray rolling expanse of the Irish Sea. Nathaniel stepped out beside me and took my hand, and I let him, because I never expected to be standing in Ireland looking out at the Irish Sea; just saying it in my head sounded impossible, or exotic, or cool, or something. I let myself take a few seconds to appreciate the good stuff, before I turned to the bad stuff.

Edward whispered, "Hold hands later."

Nathaniel let go of me first and turned to say, "Sorry. Is it bad that I'm enjoying being in Ireland with Anita when the crime scene is right here?"

"It's not bad," Edward said. "You have to take the moments where you can with our job, or you start believing that the bad stuff is all there is in the world."

I turned and looked up the gentle slope toward the long line of cars and emergency vehicles that had pretty much blocked the street. The uniforms and crime scene tape were different, but a crime scene is a crime scene is a crime scene. Just by the number of people at the scene I knew either it was a murder, it was something important other than a murder, or the town I was in was small and didn't get much crime. I was betting that the last one wasn't true. Dublin was a major city and all major cities have enough crime to keep their police busy.

We were looking at the sea in between a series of houses that weren't so much perched at the edge of the sea as perched on the edge of the cliffs above the waves. A lot of the houses seemed to have glass-enclosed solariums, or just enclosed porches. It wasn't much over fifty degrees Fahrenheit and the rain picked up as we stood there so that it went from a light sprinkle to a drizzle.

"Welcome to Ireland," Donahue said, "and before you ask, yes, it rains every day."

"Decide who's going and who's staying with the trucks," Edward said, and his voice was all business Edward. Ted's down-home drawl was totally gone. I wondered what in the last few minutes had made him give up on it.

I left pretty much everyone at the trucks, except for Nicky, Dev, Jake, and Kaazim. We had an understanding that I wasn't taking all four of them into the crime scene, but four seemed to be the bodyguard minimum for foreign soil, so rather than arguing I just told them not to get in the way of anyone else, and we followed Edward up the hill. He'd pulled his cowboy hat down snug to keep the rain off his face. I had pulled up my hood, though pulling it up far enough to keep the rain off my face meant I was limiting my peripheral vision, and the movement of my hair inside the hood would even mess with my hearing. Not great.

Nicky had pulled out a billed cap and put it under his hood. It seemed to keep the rain off without him pulling the hood up as snug, which meant he didn't have to compromise his side vision or hearing as much. He'd done this before. He'd done most things before when it came to crime and violence; he was just used to being on the other side of the equation.

Kaazim just pulled his shemagh around his head and pulled his rain hood up over it; Jake did what Nicky had done with a ball cap. Dev had pulled up his hood and then slid it off again. I think he'd decided to get wet rather than compromise vision and hearing. Since he was supposed to be my bodyguard, I was okay with that. I was really wishing I'd put my hair in a braid, or at least a ponytail, before I shoved it all under the hood as I followed Edward and Nolan up the hill.

People started to stare at us, and for once I didn't think it was my fault. Nolan was in full tactical gear. It wasn't just the civilian gawkers staring either. Apparently even the other police weren't used to someone dressed in full battle rattle showing up at a crime scene. Nolan got stopped by a man in a suit who turned out to be a police bureaucrat. I would have said a detective—I never got a clear introduction and he talked like a paper pusher, not a policeman, because he seemed more interested in the fact that Nolan showing up in full gear was sending the wrong idea. People would think someone was armed inside the house, or holding hostages, or both, because that was the only reason to have someone like Nolan here. The suit never questioned the rest of us, so Edward kept moving and we moved with him. I hated leaving a man behind, but if Edward was okay with leaving his old frenemy behind, then who was I to question it? Besides, we hadn't gotten me inside the actual crime scene yet and I was still expecting another suit to protest me, or the men with me. Until that happened we kept moving up the road in the persistent soft fall of rain. It felt like autumn though I knew it was still July here, just like back home. The air was damp and chilly, fresh with rain, and the constant murmur of the sea was like background music to the crackle of the police radios and the noise that always happens around a major crime scene. It was like we'd changed seasons along with countries. I'd have liked to ask someone if it was always like this in July, but I didn't want anyone to hear my accent or figure out that I was new to the investigation. If I kept my mouth shut and just stayed at Edward's side, I might finally get to help investigate something.

Dev's blond hair looked almost luminescent with rain by the time we got up to the top of the hill. Nicky's and Jake's hat brims were beaded with water, but it wasn't heavy enough to actually drip off. Water was beaded all over Edward's white cowboy hat, too. It was the same hat he'd had as Ted since I'd first met him as his alter ego, so the brim was worked well up with his hands and it fit his head just right. It still bothered me that he had a white hat. It just seemed like false advertising. In the rain the hat looked like old ivory, off-white, and that made more sense. Edward wasn't a bad guy, a black hat, but he wasn't exactly a white hat either; off-white would do.

The neighborhood at the top of the hill was very different from the stretch of houses perched by the beach; though some of them on this side of the street probably had a great view of the sea, that wasn't the main selling point. I think the point was more security, because almost all the houses up here had stone walls around them. The walls were all taller than I was, so they were like stone versions of the wooden security fences back home. The yards behind the fences were invisible from the road, or from the lower floors of their neighbors' houses. The houses were close enough together on the sides that seeing over the fences and into the yards might happen depending on the height of the houses involved. The gates that I could see were mostly metal and looked as security-serious as the stone-walled fences themselves. From what few glimpses inside through the gates I got, the yards looked well planted and thick with lush vegetation. I didn't know if it grew that way or if gardeners helped it along. Back in Missouri either you hired someone for that much nice yard, or you worked at it on the weekends yourself. It didn't just magically grow that way.

"I'm counting three ambulances," Edward said.

"Isn't that a lot?" Dev asked.

"Yes," we answered in unison.

"Does it mean there are survivors?"

"Maybe," I said.

The house that was the focus of all the cars was tucked in behind one of the stone walls with only the top of its roof showing, or at least it was all I could see. I'd have liked to ask Nicky—or Dev, who was even taller—if he could see more, but one, I try not to point out how short I am, and two, it wasn't a police officer kind of question. Men did not ask other men who were taller if they could see better over a wall, unless actual enemies were hiding behind the wall to maybe shoot them. Short of emergencies involving death, men did not admit to certain things and that was one of them. I'd been working in male-dominated fields for too long not to understand the rules. If you wanted to play with the boys, you needed to know how to play like one.

There was a uniformed officer in front of the metal gates leading inside. He stopped us, because now that we didn't have Nolan with us none of us actually had credentials for this country. We needed an Irish cop to get us inside. Edward flashed his Marshal credentials, and the uniform didn't react badly to them. It meant even if he didn't know Ted on sight, he knew he was around and helping with the case. He still wouldn't let us inside the gate.

In his best Ted cowboy drawl, he said, "I appreciate that you've heard of me, pardner. Could you locate Superintendent Pearson or Inspector Sheridan to escort us inside?"

"Who are they?" he asked, and nodded at us.

I flashed my credentials, and the fact that they matched Edward's seemed to reassure the officer. "We heard more of you were coming from the States."

I smiled and tried to look helpful, encouraging even. "We just landed at the airport and came straight here," I said.

The officer glanced at the other four men. I expected him to ask for their badges, too, but he didn't. He glanced behind him at the gate and the house beyond, and then he shivered. You didn't see that often in cops that have been on the job long. Either he was younger than he looked, or something in the house behind him had seriously unnerved him.

"I know we're supposed to think of them as citizens with a disease and they can't help what's happening to them, but . . . this isn't a disease."

"We're here to find them and stop them," Edward said.

"I hope you do . . . stop them, I mean. I hope you stop them all." And there was anger in his voice now.

"Let us inside, pardner, and we'll start hunting 'em down."

He reached toward the gate. He wanted to let us inside, but we hadn't been cleared. What's a cop to do? I was sort of wishing him to let us in but wasn't sure how much trouble he'd be in if he did it.

Edward's phone rang. "Inspector Sheridan, I'm at the gate trying to get inside now. Yes, Marshal Blake is standing right beside me." He listened for a second and then said to the officer, "The inspector would like to speak with you."

The officer hesitated and then took the phone. He did a lot of *Yes, ma'am, No, ma'am*, and finally handed the phone back to Edward, who was smiling warmly at him, doing his best Ted impression.

"You can go inside. Inspector Sheridan will meet you at the front door." He opened the gate for us and in we all went, all six of us.

39

INSPECTOR RACHEL SHERIDAN was tall, slender, with nearly black hair falling in glossy straightness to her shoulders. She'd turned the ends under with a curling iron, or maybe curlers. My hair was so curly that I didn't really use either, but whatever she'd done it looked good. She managed to be both pale and dark complexioned, like someone who would tan if she ever got enough sun. The white button-up shirt may have helped her face look darker. The black pantsuit didn't fit her well, as if she'd lost weight recently. Her face was a soft triangle, and the bones of her face and even her hands were delicate; *elfin* was the word that came to mind, even though she had to be five inches taller than me, or maybe more. But despite the height she was delicate looking and very pretty. If she'd been just a little curvier I'd have said she was beautiful, but I'd have had to know if she was naturally that thin or starved herself. If the first, we could talk; if the second, I didn't have patience for women who ate lettuce leaves or less to keep some mysterious perfect size.

She let us step inside enough to get out of the rain, but then stopped us because there were four more of us than she was expecting. "I'm glad you're here, Ted, and Marshal Blake. I will be happy to have your expertise today, but I don't know these other men."

We did quick introductions. She couldn't even shake hands, because she was wearing the rubber gloves that she'd already walked through the crime scene wearing. She was also wearing the little booties over her shoes. She wasted a nicer-than-work smile on Edward, but as I introduced the rest she smiled a little more than typical at a crime scene at Nicky and Dev. I guess everyone has a type and, apparently, Sheridan had a thing for blue-eyed blond men. She wasn't unprofessional, but

I could just tell that she was a little more happy to see them than Jake and Kaazim. I filed it away for later to make sure she didn't waste too much time flirting with men who were taken. I'd run afoul of one female detective back in St. Louis who still held a grudge because I had "pretended" that Nathaniel wasn't my boyfriend, so she felt she'd made a fool of herself over him. Women puzzle me. Sheridan motioned all of us to the box of gloves. "Even if you don't all get to walk through the house, I don't want to waste our time eliminating any of your fingerprints from the investigation."

None of us argued; we just slipped the little plastic-bootie things over our shoes and then gloved ourselves. Now whoever was walking through the crime scene wouldn't accidentally track in evidence, or step on evidence in the house, and we wouldn't be getting forensics excited about a fingerprint that didn't match the family.

A tall man, as in taller than Dev, walked into the room. He was almost completely bald with just an edge of dark hair trimmed short. His jacket was a subdued gray check, pants solid gray; he wore a white button-down shirt that seemed to be handed out to all detectives in America, and here, bisected by a tie that almost matched the jacket. Once, I would have thought it matched, but I'd been dating Jean-Claude and Nathaniel too long, and it had made me pickier.

"Forrester, good that you're here, and you as well, Marshal Blake." He was wearing gloves, so there were no handshakes with this inspector, who was introduced as Superintendent Pearson, either. He glanced at the men around us. "And who are these gentlemen?"

Names weren't what Pearson wanted to know. He wanted to know what good they were going to be inside his crime scene. How could they help the investigation? The four of them stayed silent and let Edward and me do the talking. They probably didn't know what to say either.

Edward said, "It depends on what kind of scene we have here. Everyone has their specialties."

Pearson nodded, as if that made sense. "Currently, we're trying to decide if it's safe to move the vampires out of the house. Do you remember the vampire that burned up on us before you came in on the investigation?"

Edward turned to me. "Paramedics got called to an unconscious victim, but when they tried to take him out of the house
on a stretcher the sun was up."

I gave him wide eyes. "He burst into flames?"

Edward and both of the inspectors nodded.

"Wow, that must have been quite the surprise for the paramedics."

"According to witnesses the vampire woke up as it was
burning to death and started screaming. The paramedics
weren't prepared and didn't know what to do to help the victim . . . the vampire."

"Once they go up in flames from sunlight there isn't always
a way to put out the fire," I said.

"May I interject?" Jake asked.

"If you have something useful to add," Pearson said.

"Once a vampire is out of direct sunlight, you simply ex-
tinguish the flames as you would on anyone, though admittedly some types of vampires burn more violently than
others."

"Marshal Forrester has been trying to enlighten us on the
variety of vampirekind," Pearson said.

Sheridan asked, "If the paramedics had put the vampire in
the ambulance, would they have been able to put out the fire,
or would the entire ambulance have gone up in flames?"

"I'd have rushed him back to the house—more room to
work with and less likely that you'll burn down an entire
house. I am not certain I would want to take a combusting
vampire into the back of an ambulance. You say this one was
screaming and thrashing around?"

"Witnesses say he was," Pearson said.

"The vampire was panicking at that point and might have
reached out for the medics. If the vampire had grabbed hold
of them in his panic he could have burned them, too, and the
interior of the ambulance could have gone up with them inside it."

"They attempted to douse the flames but didn't think to try
to get him out of the sunlight," Pearson said.

"I told them that the only thing I'd ever used sunlight for
was to burn vampires. I'd never tried to save one, so I didn't
know if it was possible," Edward said.

"I've never tried to save one from sunlight, not once they caught fire anyway," I said.

"I am glad that I could add something to the conversation," Jake said.

Pearson was looking at him closely. "We have a house full of paramedics who are wanting more information on how to treat vampires medically."

"I will be happy to lend what knowledge I possess."

"Is that why you have so many ambulances out front, because you're treating the vampires and the victims both?" I asked.

"We transported everyone in the house that didn't have fangs as victims found unresponsive at the scene," he said.

"I told them that fangs were one way they could tell vampire from victim," Edward said.

"The not breathing is a clue, too," I said.

"But some coma patients have respiration so shallow that it can barely be detected, Marshal Blake. A doctor with better equipment needs to make that decision."

"That's fair. So how many . . . victims with fangs do we have left, and are they what the three ambulances are waiting for?"

"We have three possible vampires on-site," Pearson said.

"How many nonvamps did you transport?" I asked.

"Four."

"What are you doing with them?" I asked.

Sheridan answered, "The hospital is trying to figure out if they are alive, dead, or other, and if there's anything they can do to bring them back."

"I just read a new study on brain activity in vampires. It turns out that unlike the true dead, bodies that are going to rise as vampires don't go completely brain-dead," I said.

"Does that mean that vampires aren't the walking dead?" Dev asked. "I mean, brain death is one of the ways they decide whether to pull the plug on life support, so does that mean vampires don't really die?"

"It's cute when you try to be deep," Nicky said.

"Actually it's a good point, but for right now if the hospital looks for brain activity on the victims and doesn't find any, then they're probably dead," I said.

Dev gave Nicky a look that said, *See, I was right.* Nicky frowned back at him. I noticed that Sheridan was watching the interchange more than Pearson.

"Where did you read this new study?" Kaazim asked.

"I'm on a list for science and medical articles about vampires, zombies, wereanimals, and preternatural research in general. It's like an old-fashioned clipping service except it comes on the computer and doesn't kill trees unless I print something."

"That's my partner, always trying to improve herself," Edward said, so dryly that I couldn't tell if he meant it or was wanting to be far more sarcastic than Ted would be.

"I talked to the couple that owns this house personally, Marshals. Less than two weeks ago they were in wanting—no, demanding—that we work harder to help locate their missing daughter." Pearson's pleasant but unreadable cop face crumbled around the edges, and I got a glimpse in his brown eyes of how much pain this was causing him. It was just a moment, but it was enough to let me sympathize.

"Are the parents at the hospital, or here?" I asked.

"Mr. Brady is at the hospital along with his parents and the youngest daughter. Mrs. Brady is here along with the daughter we couldn't find and the daughter's best friend."

"It's always hard when you knew them before they became vampires."

"Have you known people before and after?" he asked.

I nodded.

"It's always harder to kill someone that you knew," Edward said, and there was none of Ted's happy down-home charm in that sentence.

Pearson looked at him. "Have you killed all the people you knew once they became vampires?"

"They were trying to kill me at the time," Edward said.

"When people first become vampires, the bloodlust is so powerful that they will attack anyone. They just want food, and that means fresh blood," I said.

"Is that why we found the daughter here with her family?" Sheridan asked.

"No," Edward said, "you found her here because some of them remember enough of their humanity to go home. They can be drawn to places they knew well in life, and it's easier to persuade family to get close so they can feed."

"Also they can enter their own homes without being invited in first," I said.

Edward nodded. "I told them that vampires can't enter a private residence unless invited."

I added, "So any private house or building that they were invited into when alive they can still enter as a vampire, unless someone who owns the building revokes the invitation."

"How do you revoke an invitation?" Sheridan asked.

"You say, 'I revoke my invitation.'"

"Really, that formal?"

"I don't know. I've literally only done it by saying those words." I looked at Jake and Kaazim. "Gentlemen, does it work without the phrase?"

"Telling them to get out and that they are no longer welcome in your home would work," Jake said.

"Simply telling them, 'You are no longer welcome,' or 'You are no longer my guest,' works as well," Kaazim said.

"Unless they lived in the house in life," Jake added.

Kaazim agreed. "That does make it more complicated."

"It seems like there are a lot more rules to vampires than we knew," Sheridan said.

"Yeah, there are rules," I said.

"We need to know all the rules," Pearson said, "but right now I would like the Marshals to accompany us to look at the victims."

"If they have fangs, Superintendent, they aren't victims. They're vampires," I said.

"I talked to Helena Brady for the first time a month ago, and then two weeks ago. I've been looking at the picture of her daughter Katie for weeks hoping we'd find her alive. Her best friend is Sinead Royce. When she went missing just after Katie, we didn't think it was vampires; we thought we had a child abductor that knew the girls. We thought it was a child molester, or a stalker, or anything but vampires, and now they're all lying in there dead, or undead, but whatever they are, something did that to them. Something drank Katie Brady's blood and turned her into this, and that makes her a victim, Marshal Blake."

"Yes, of course it does, but . . ." Edward grabbed my arm and stopped me. He was one of the handful of people on the planet who could grab me and tell me to stop, and I'd stop. I looked up at him, waiting for an explanation.

"One step at a time; let's see what there is to see first."

"Sure, Ted, whatever you say."

Kaazim and Jake had been so helpful that Pearson let all four of them stay by the door with only one uniformed officer standing by to make sure they didn't touch anything. We were all inside the crime scene, which was more than I thought we'd get, and if the vampires in the next room rose early we had at least four people within earshot who would be more than just humanly helpful. If I didn't piss Pearson off completely, we were part of the investigation at last. I didn't want to piss the Irish detectives off so badly that I got put back on a plane for home, but I had a bad feeling that they were going to try to treat the vampires like people with fangs. That would be a mistake; eventually it would be a fatal mistake for someone.

40

THE ROOM WAS done in bright colors. One half of the room was a circus theme complete with a cartoon-circus-parade wall mural and a clown lamp beside the twin bed. The other half of the room was covered in posters of boy bands I didn't know, some actors that I did know, and a rugby poster that seemed to be mostly a shot of buff men in small shorts fighting in mud. I'd never really thought of rugby as the male equivalent of women wrestling in oil, but suddenly I could see the analogy, because I was trying to see anything but the bodies in the room.

Helena Brady lay on the twin bed underneath the rugby poster with her daughter curled beside her. She had a protective arm around the girl, and if they'd been breathing, it would have been a charming example of mother-daughter love. The only positive was that Katie Brady looked to be about fifteen or sixteen years old. If we could keep Katie from killing anyone else and the Irish legal system didn't want to execute her for anything she'd already done, then as the years passed and she grew older in her mind and emotions, she'd have a body that would be adult enough to have a grown-up life.

Sinead Royce lay on the other bed underneath the circus parade. She looked older than Katie and could have easily passed for eighteen. "How old is this one?" I asked.

"Sixteen. They're both sixteen," Pearson said.

"How old is the younger sister that's at the hospital?"

"Eight."

"That's a big age gap to share a room," I said.

"They moved Michael Brady's mother in with them after his grandfather died, and then moved her mother in when she had a bad fall, so the girls had to share a room."

"The dutiful son and daughter," Edward said.

"They were, or are, good people," Pearson said.

I stared down at the bodies on the bed and was angry. "This isn't right."

"No," Edward said, "it's not."

I shook my head. "One of the few taboos that all vampires have is you don't bring over children. The two teenagers you could make a case for, because if the vampire is old enough they may think of sixteen as an adult, because for centuries it was, but whoever made Katie Brady a vampire let her loose on her family. Whoever made her had an obligation to keep track of her until she was able to think for herself, because like Ted says, one of the first things vampires do is go home. The vampire creator is supposed to keep that from happening."

"Why?" Pearson asked.

"One, it's morally questionable, but two, it's bad for business. One of the ways that vampires got discovered back in the old days was that one person would die from some unknown disease, a wasting disease they used to call it, and then one by one the rest of the family would die, so someone would get the bright idea to dig up the first family member that died, and voilà, there's the vampire. Most of the old vamps liked to stay in their coffins during the day, because it was the most sun-lightproof place they knew, and some believed that they needed to sleep in their original coffin at night or they'd die at dawn and not rise again."

"Are you saying that vampires are superstitious?" Sheridan asked.

"People are superstitious. Why not vampires?"

"Katie didn't have a funeral. She went missing," Pearson said.

"Modern burial techniques like embalming, or organ donation, will kill a vampire before it can rise the first time. If creator vampires want their offspring to rise from the dead, they'll take the body with them and hide it."

"You said *if*. Some vampires do not care if their—what did you call it—offspring rise?" Sheridan asked.

"You know how some people are crazy, or mean, or just careless?"

"Yes."

"Vampires can be all those things, too."

"What can we do for them?" Pearson asked.

"They're all new enough that once darkness falls they will have to feed. If this is Mrs. Brady's first night as a vampire, she will be uncontrollable, or at least not controllable by a baby vampire like Katie, or Sinead. I don't mean baby vampire because they're teenagers. I mean they're less than a month dead. Whoever made Katie should still have her with them at night and be controlling how she feeds. There were rules against shit like this before vampires were legal."

"In America, would you execute Katie?" Pearson asked.

"It depends on whether she's outright killed someone that we can prove; for all we know some of the bodies with their throats torn out are hers."

"I hope not," he said.

"Me, too, but she had to be getting her blood somewhere besides her family."

"Why do you say that?"

"Because she needs to feed every night, and she hasn't been feeding on her family long enough to have them be her only food source."

"How do you know that?"

"The parents wouldn't have come to you two weeks ago

demanding more action on her disappearance if she'd already started feeding on them."

"She fed on Sinead."

"Is her family still alive and well?"

"To our knowledge."

"Do they live close to here?" I asked.

"Yes."

"You might want to check on Sinead's family, then."

Pearson cursed as he walked out of the room, already on his phone. He was sending officers to the other home. I hoped the other family was okay. I didn't really want this kind of moral dilemma twice in one day.

"What can we do for them when they wake for the night?" Sheridan asked.

"There are only three options," I said.

"Kill them," Edward said.

"Yep, that's option one."

"What's option two?" Sheridan asked.

"Lock them in a coffin or cell with holy items all over it and contain them. Though you need to make sure that whoever guards them is religious and wearing their holy item of choice, because even baby vamps can capture you with their gaze and make you their bitch."

"And the third option?" she asked.

"Do nothing and let them keep attacking people," Edward said.

"Okay, four options, then," I said.

He looked at me. "What fourth option?"

"You get a vampire strong enough to control them."

"I don't think we want to give the Brady family over to Damian's creator," Edward said.

"No," I said.

"She's the only master vampire in Ireland."

"Not anymore, she's not," I said.

We looked at each other. "Shouldn't you talk to your vampires before you volunteer them for babysitting duty?"

"Yes, but I can't talk to them until after dark and by that time the vampires in this room will rise, too, and it'll be too late to ask."

"Catch-22," he said.

"Yeah," I said.

"I don't understand," Sheridan said.

"Anita brought more than one vampire with her."

"Are you saying your vampires might be able to control the new ones?"

"The three in this room maybe, but since they didn't make them, and they aren't related to the vampire that did make them, I'm not sure how much control they'll have over them."

"Then we're back to three options," he said.

"We won't let you execute them," Sheridan said.

"Two options," he said.

"We can't let them feed on whoever they want," she said.

"Option number two, it is."

"How strong are your holding cells and do they all have windows?" I asked.

41

I DON'T KNOW who had Nolan's back in the government, but whoever it was had clout, because the police gave the three sleeping vampires over to him. Pearson and Sheridan didn't like it. In fact, we got to hear Pearson yelling on the phone that it wasn't right, that Helena and Katie Brady and Sinead Royce were still Irish citizens and deserved better than this. He said other things, but that was the big part he kept repeating in different ways. None of it made any difference. Nolan, Brennan, and Donahue—Donnie—put the three women into body bags like the corpses they almost were and loaded one vampire per vehicle, which meant there were two vampires per, because we'd brought our own. Edward told Nolan that if he valued his expensive toys he shouldn't lock us in the back once we were inside them. I was glad he'd said it, because it saved me having to threaten his old friend. Admittedly, it would have been Nicky or one of the other wereanimals that actually tore the door off, but I'd have given the order.

Dev was soaked by the time we walked back down to the trucks so that when he got inside water streamed from his hair down inside his rain jacket. He was so wet that Nathaniel kissed him but asked him to sit on the other side with Kaazim and Jake. It also gave us enough room on our side to not be quite so cramped. We still had Damian in his duffel bag at our feet, but now Nolan and Edward had a body bag full of vampire at their feet, too. They'd tagged the vamps on the outside of the bags, so we knew it was Helena Brady with us.

Nolan's phone sounded and he looked at the screen. The lines in his face seemed to deepen as if some extra burden had been added. "What's wrong?" I asked.

"Pearson sent me baby pictures."

"Of his kids?" Dev made it a question.

"No, of the vampires."

"He sent you baby pictures of Katie and Sinead?" I asked. Nolan nodded. "Want to see them?"

"No," I said.

Edward just shook his head.

"Why would he send you baby pictures of them?" Dev asked.

"The text with the pictures says, 'Whatever you do to them, remember they're someone's babies.'"

"Pearson thinks it will make it harder for us to kill them," I said.

"Harder for me," Nolan said. "He didn't send the pictures to you."

"He doesn't have my phone number," I said.

Edward's phone sounded. He shook his head but got it out and checked. "Pearson," he said, but put the phone away without swiping it open.

"You're not even going to look at it?" Dev asked.

"No."

"It doesn't matter if they were adorable babies if they wake up trying to tear people's faces off," I said.

"Maybe it does," he said.

"Are you saying that if someone's cute as a baby, we shouldn't kill them?" Nicky asked.

"I'd rather not kill anyone," Dev said.

We all looked at him, even Nathaniel. Edward said, "You do know why we're here, right?"

"To figure out why vampires are suddenly able to spread in Ireland as fast as anywhere else in the world, and to stop it if we can."

"How do you think we're going to stop this, Dev?" I asked.

"Solve the mystery and fix what's gone wrong."

I exchanged a look with Edward, who without saying a word let me know that this was why Dev hadn't been on his list of who to bring to Ireland.

It was Nathaniel who said, "Dev, honey, do you understand what fixing means for Anita and . . . Ted?"

"I'm not stupid, Nathaniel. I know. I didn't say I wouldn't do what's necessary. I just said I'd rather not kill people. Why is that a bad thing?"

"Because it makes us all wonder if you're a shooter," Edward said.

"My scores are good at the range."

Edward looked at me, as if to say, *Explain it to him.*

"You know that's not what we mean when we say someone is a shooter, Dev."

"I know what it means, Anita. I know you pride yourself on your kill count being higher than any other vampire hunter in the U.S."

"I may have the highest legal count worldwide, not just in America."

He frowned at me. "And that's great, but even you prefer not to kill when you don't have to, or did I miss something?"

"Would I prefer not to have to kill people while we're in Ireland? Yes, but I'll still do it."

"And if you need me to pull the trigger, I will, but why did I lose guy points from everybody in this truck because I said I'd prefer not to?"

"It makes us wonder if you'll hesitate when the time comes," I said.

"I didn't hesitate in Colorado," he said.

"No, you didn't." In my head I added, *That wasn't the prob-lem.*

"Those were zombies," Edward said. "It's easier to kill them, because they look like corpses."

"You're saying that I'll hesitate because the vampires look like people."

"No, I'm saying that I'm concerned you might hesitate when I need you, or Anita needs you, or Nolan needs you."

"And you're more worried because I said I didn't want to kill people if I didn't have to?"

"Yes."

"Don't most people prefer not to kill other people?"

"Yes," Edward said.

"So what did I say wrong?"

We all exchanged a look, and I mean all of us. Nathaniel understood something that Dev still didn't seem to get, but then, Nathaniel had picked up a gun and killed to save our lives before. The guard that had dropped the gun had been shot to death at our feet, but Nathaniel hadn't frozen; he'd picked up the gun and used it. He'd never been one of the armed guards, but he'd proven everything he needed to prove to me that day. Dev still hadn't. Though come to think of it, I wasn't sure that Nathaniel would have been as cool under fire with the zombies in the hospital. It had been one of the worst things I'd had to do, and that was saying something. Maybe I wasn't being fair to my golden tiger?

Dev looked at Jake sitting beside him, as if for help. "You must stop looking to me for help, Mephistopheles," he said.

"Why would he look to you?" Nolan asked.

"I am older and more experienced," Jake said, his face and voice utterly bland. He was smiling slightly, and I realized that his pleasant face, which was one of his versions of blank cop face, was very similar to Dev's; was that where my golden tiger had learned it? I knew that Jake had helped raise and keep safe generations of golden tigers. He'd been one of the Harlequin who had hidden the entire clan bloodline from the Mother of All Darkness when she'd declared that it needed to be destroyed. Legend handed down for thousands of years said that the clan tigers were the key to defeating her, but in particular the gold tigers, because they were supposed to rule over all the rest. Jake and others had rescued a few gold tigers, and that was Dev's family line.

"I thought Devereux was an athletic pretty boy who wouldn't look up to anyone like that," Nolan said.

"Why is being athletic and pretty bad?" Dev said.

"It's not, if you have more going for you than just muscle and looks," Nolan said.

"I don't know if I have much more going for me than that." It was a remarkably self-deprecating comment coming from someone who had been handsome, athletic, and charming all his life, as far as I knew. People like that don't do self-deprecating very well.

"It's too late to play humble, Devereux," Nolan said.

"Am I playing?" Dev looked at him, and suddenly there was confusion on his face, and he looked younger, as young as he was, I guess, since he was still a few years under twenty-five. Nathaniel was only a little older, but he never seemed as young as Dev did from time to time.

"Every man I've ever met who was as big and handsome as you was anything but humble."

Dev flashed him a smile. "Don't hate me because I'm beautiful."

"You're too young to know that commercial," Nolan said.

"There are whole websites dedicated to old commercials," Dev said. "My first serious girlfriend showed it to me, because she agreed with you. She also didn't like the fact that I got more attention than she did when we went out to the clubs."

"Beautiful women are used to being the center of attention," Kaazim said.

"A woman won't date someone she thinks is prettier than she is," Nolan said.

"I'm dating a lot of men who are prettier than me," I said.

Nolan frowned at me, and the lines in his face folded into the frown like it was his natural look. He really needed more reasons to smile soon. "Who?" he asked.

I took Nathaniel's hand in mine, and nodded at Dev across the van. I laid my head against Nicky's shoulder. He said, "Don't include me in the prettier club, Anita. I know I'm attractive, but not in the same way that Dev is, and I'll never be as beautiful as Nathaniel, but that's okay. You don't have to protect my ego on this one."

I wasn't sure what to say to that, so I said, "It feels mean to say they're pretty and not include you, because you're hot, too."

"I didn't say I wasn't hot. I said I wasn't as beautiful as they are, and I'm sure as hell not as beautiful a man as you are a woman. I'm dating out of my league and I know it."

"I think you're ballparking my league just fine." I smiled at him and offered up a kiss, which he took with a smile of his own.

"It's like we're not even here," Nolan said.

"You haven't seen anything yet," Edward said.

I gave him a frown. "Are you saying we overshare with you?"

"Not with me, but Nolan isn't me and he's not used to this much honest communication."

"The only way to have this many relationships is to talk honestly."

"But not in front of strangers," he said.

"So it's okay to stand shoulder to shoulder with Nolan and kill vampires, but we're not supposed to talk about emotional stuff?"

"Yeah, that's what I'm saying."

"Well, fuck that. Nolan started it by making a statement that isn't true, and I could prove it, so I did."

"You didn't prove anything, Blake."

"Dev and Nathaniel are prettier than I am, but I'm in relationships with both of them. That proves that women, or at least this woman, will date people prettier than they are, so I've disproved your blanket statement."

Nolan frowned harder so that the lines on his forehead looked like they'd been carved into his flesh with a dull knife. It looked almost painful and made me want to touch his face and try to smooth them out. I wouldn't do it, but the more he made his face look like that, the more I wanted to do it.

He looked at Edward and whatever look they exchanged, Edward understood it. "She's being honest."

"She thinks she's being honest," Nathaniel said.

I looked at him sitting beside me, still holding hands with me. "What's that supposed to mean?"

"I've never known a beautiful woman who didn't know exactly how beautiful she was," Nolan said.

"Now you do," Edward said.

I was pretty sure I understood what he was saying, but it made me uncomfortable, so I said, "How far to your head-quarters?"

"Are you changing the subject?" Nolan asked.

"Yes."

He frowned harder yet, and the lines looked almost artificial. I didn't even usually notice things like this, but Nolan's face seemed etched with some grief that had spent too many years fashioning itself a home on his face. It was like he needed a hug.

"We're not that far outside Dublin," he said.

"Don't I get any points for the fact that if I pull my holy item out it will glow?" Dev asked; apparently we weren't done with the conversation.

"That will be more helpful when we don't have vampires fighting on our side," I said.

"The first time I pulled out my cross it didn't glow," Nolan said.

"Are you saying now it does?" Edward asked.

He nodded. "You might say that watching all the other holy objects glow in the face of evil was a conversion experience."

"Were you not raised Christian?" Kaazim asked.

"No, my father is actually an atheist. He said he couldn't believe in anything that caused so much pain, when it was supposed to be a benevolent god."

"I've got some close friends who aren't religious for similar reasons," I said. Nathaniel had dutifully gone to church with me, but Micah had refused. He said that he couldn't reconcile a loving God with some of the things he'd seen in his life. Since he'd spent years being at the mercy of one of the most twisted sexual sadists I'd ever met, I understood his confusion, but I did not share it. It had actually bothered me that if it had been Micah I planned to marry instead of Jean-

Claude, I still couldn't have married in the Episcopal Church. Jean-Claude couldn't step into the church, but Micah wouldn't step into one.

"It bothers you that they don't believe," Nolan said.

"Yeah, it does."

"Sorry, Anita, but sociopaths aren't big on God and the angels," Nicky said.

"My only problem with so many of you not believing is that we're hunting vampires, and holy objects only work if you believe, so yes, Dev, you get brownie points that you believe."

"Blessed objects work regardless," Jake said.

"Yeah, because they're empowered by the belief of the holy person who blessed them, not by the belief of the person wielding them," I said.

"I guess I need one of those before we meet any more vamps in person," Nicky said.

"I can lend you a blessed object, Murdock—though you admitting that you're a sociopath . . . does that mean I shouldn't trust you at my back?" Nolan said.

"As long as we're on the same side with the same goals, I'll have your six."

"And if our goals aren't the same?"

Nicky looked at him, and that one blue eye looked colder, like spring skies when there's a sudden frost and all the flowers die. "Then I won't have your six."

"So if our goals diverge, I shouldn't trust you?"

"You've been in this business longer than I have; trusting anyone is for suckers."

"You trust Anita."

"If I couldn't trust her I don't think I would be in love with her."

The van went around a bend of the road a little fast, and we all reached for things to hold on to. Nathaniel held my hand tighter, and I reached for Nicky's arm; it was like holding on to a warm, flesh-covered tree, or maybe a rock. His biceps were sort of epic.

"I'll never have arms half as good as this, no matter how much I lift," I said.

"You'd look silly with arms as big as Nicky's," Dev said.

I smiled. "I know, but it's still unfair that the men have the edge in the gym."

"You can have babies," Nolan said.

"That is so not a good trade-off," I said, but I let myself lean my head against Nicky's shoulder, my hand still around his arm.

"You know I'd have the baby for us if I could," Nathaniel said.

I rose up from leaning against Nicky and fought not to give an unhappy face to Nathaniel. "I know, and I wish you could, because I so am not looking forward to being pregnant."

"It might be nice to have babies underfoot again," Jake said, looking at Dev.

"Don't look at me. I'm still trying to figure out the romance part. I think babies are a step above that."

"Sharing a baby can be romantic in a way," Nolan said.

"I have a story or two about babies; one of them is even about this one," Jake said.

Dev smiled and patted his arm. "There's nothing romantic about changing diapers; I remember that story."

"I am a very old friend of the family, enough that I babysat on occasion," Jake said, to Nolan's look.

"What story?" I asked.

Dev shook his head. "I'm armed to the teeth and about to help you hunt big bad vampires. I would like to do that without Jake telling any stories that include me in diapers or in elementary school."

"I bet you were an adorable baby," Nathaniel said, smiling.

Dev smiled back. "I was, but I don't need to be reminded that I'm the youngest one here."

"You don't mind that sort of thing normally," I said.

"Maybe I want to be a grown-up."

I remembered being his age and having things to prove. "Okay, you're a grown-up. We can save the embarrassing stories for later."

"I think I may even have pictures on my phone of him as a baby," Jake said.

"You're just teasing me now. You do not have my baby pictures on your phone."

Jake got his phone out without a word and pulled up the

pictures. He swiped though until he came to one and showed it to Dev, who got a strange look on his face. He wasn't unhappy, but he was deeply surprised.

"I didn't think you kept pictures of us," Dev said as he handed back the phone.

"I know," Jake said.

"Wait. I want to see," Nathaniel said.

He looked at Dev, who shook his head. "Later," Jake said, and put the phone away.

"Old family friend, is it?" Nolan said.

Jake looked at him. "I never had children of my own."

Dev put his arm around the older man and said, "Sentimental bastard," and kissed his forehead. Jake pushed him away, smiling, calling him a cheeky child or something, but Dev was smiling more like his old self again. When people ask if love can last they always seem to mean romantic love, but there are all kinds of love, and they can all last.

42

THE ENCLOSED VANS were opened inside a garage that looked as if it had been emptied of its contents just minutes before we arrived. There were two new people already in civilian clothes waiting for us; the clothes might have looked street normal, but if you knew what to look for, you could see where the dangerous toys were hiding. They stayed with us while Nolan and the others went to change, because one thing Nolan had to agree to was more civilian clothing and less looking like a soldier. He had enough clout that we had the vampires with us, but not enough to let him run around Dublin looking like a paramilitary bad guy from the latest action flick. Nolan requested that Edward come with them. He told me he'd be right back, I said fine, and we were down a man just like that, but they were down two, so I guess we were still ahead.

Flannery was as tall as Nolan, Brennan, and Griffin, like they were the beginnings of a sports team; even Donnie was almost as tall as the men and had that same easy physicality that only those who have been gifted athletes, or at least incredibly physical, their whole lives seem to have. Flannery was dark like Brennan, not as handsome, but his smile was bright and made you smile back before you thought about it. I'd take a little less attractive in exchange for pleasant. I'd had my fill of beautiful but moody men, or women for that matter.

Flannery's jacket fit too tight across his shoulders, so his shoulder holster printed, worse on his left side where the gun sat. It looked like either the jacket was borrowed or he'd gained body mass since he bought it. I caught a glimpse of the extra ammo magazine under his right arm held in a leather pocket. Most people wouldn't realize what that glimpse of dark leather was, but then, we weren't most people.

Mortimer—Mort—was the shortest of the team at five-six, but he moved like he had springs that propelled him forward, energy contained in a body that was honed down to muscle and compact flesh. In a jacket bulky enough to hide the guns, he looked delicate the way that Micah did in sloppy clothes, but I knew physical potential too well to believe that he was as dainty as he looked; I was betting that a lot of bigger men had underestimated him, and regretted it.

I knew this wasn't all Nolan's team; Donahue had said she was Donnie because there was a second Donahue on the team. Flannery explained that they would be accompanying us pretty much everywhere from this point on. "One of us for every two of you," he said, still smiling, but his brown eyes were smiling with him, as if he couldn't think of anything he'd rather do than babysit armed strangers while they hunted vampires in his city. Of course, maybe Nolan hadn't shared all the intel he had, and there might be more going on than he was sharing with us. Military who have worked black ops for too long not only know how to keep a secret but start doing it even when they don't have to, or maybe that was just how it had affected Edward. My experience with people in this line of work was actually pretty limited when I thought about it. I just felt I knew more of them, because the ones I did know I knew so damn well.

Griffin had thrown one of the body bags over his shoulder, and Donnie had the other one. I didn't know which teenage vampire was which, but it didn't really matter. They were both going to the same place: a cell here at the "warehouse" that was apparently the headquarters for Nolan's new group. The fact that we hadn't seen any of the drive here meant that we didn't know where the hell we were, or how to get here, or how to leave. I mean, we knew to go out one of the doors, but beyond that we didn't know which way Dublin was, or the airport we'd landed at, or anything really. I'd seen so little of the country that it was like any other business trip out of town. Throw in the hotel later, and add a cemetery, and me being able to actually hunt vampires, and it would be like Old Home Week. Nathaniel was still hoping to have a few days at the end of everything to actually play tourist; me, too.

Nolan had left the last body bag behind when he took Edward off for their secret squirrel talk. The body bag lay on the concrete floor where Nolan had left it after he and Brennan dragged it out. They had treated it like you treat the dead, like they had no feelings to worry about and no flesh to bruise. Come nightfall the vampire in the bag might have both. It depended on how long she'd been undead and how much control she had. Whoever had made their daughter a vampire should have been able to call all of them out into the night to do his or her bidding, but it was like the "master vampire" was just making vampires sort of willy-nilly. If there was a plan, then neither the police nor Nolan and his people could figure out the logic of it. Maybe there was no plan; maybe it was just a vampire that was doing whatever the hell they wanted to do in Dublin.

"Nolan said to secure the prisoners," Griffin said.

Brennan grabbed one end of the body bag. Jake grabbed the other end and helped him lift. "Allow me to help you."

"I can carry it."

"Of that, I have no doubt, but it is the heaviest bag and we are here to help you."

"Are we putting vampires in the cells without testing them first?" Donnie said.

"We're following orders," Brennan said.

"Are you saying that Nolan pushed to have you guys take the vampires as prisoners, or whatever, but you've never actually had a supernatural anything in a cell to see if it will hold them?" I asked.

Brennan scowled at me. He really wasn't handsome enough for the sour disposition, but then, I didn't think anyone was worth it anymore. "We know our job, Blake."

Fortune flashed him her best smile, which was a pretty good smile. "But isn't part of why we're here to help you test things out?"

His face had started to soften as he looked into her blue eyes, but he fought it off and scowled even harder. I wondered if he'd learned the technique from Nolan.

"They were supposed to help us test the cells before we used them for actual prisoners," Donnie said. If she was having any trouble holding the body in its bag, it didn't show. I realized she was built a lot like Magda and Fortune, tall and athletic-looking. Even with more women on the "team," I was still the short, delicate-looking one. Even Echo was inches taller than me, so having all our vampires up and running wouldn't change that I was sort of the runt of the group. I didn't normally worry about it that much, but I suddenly realized that this was the most women I'd ever worked with at one time and I was still the short one.

"Then maybe we should do that before nightfall," Nicky said.

"They feel like dead bodies now," I said, "but once the sun goes down they won't be."

"What am I supposed to do? Say *Oh my* and drop the bag because it's supposed to be full of scary vampire?" Donnie asked.

"No, I'm just saying that it'd be good to know your cells will hold before the 'prisoners'"—and I made little air quotes around the word—"wake up and start looking for food."

Griffin and Donnie exchanged a look. Brennan scowled harder. Mort joined him in the scowling, though he wasn't as good at it yet. I wasn't sure if he was just more pleasant than he was pretending to be, or if he hadn't been around Nolan as long. Flannery stepped up, smiling.

"I think it's a good idea to test the cells before we lose the sun," he said, still smiling.

"Great. Then let's do it," I said.

"Which of your people gets locked into the cell to try to break out?" Brennan asked; he'd taken the bag from Jake and hefted it over his shoulder.

"Let me do it," Nicky said.

They all looked at him. "No," said Brennan.

"We want a fair test for the vampires that will be in the cells tonight. I don't think you, Mr. Murdock, are going to be an equivalent for a mother and two teenage girls," Flannery said.

Nicky gave them a grin that was more a snarl. "You're just afraid it won't hold me."

"I will do it," Magda said, "if someone will watch over my master."

"I will be honored to bear his burden, and treat him as if he were my own master," Jake said. It sounded more formal than they usually talked to each other, and maybe it was a type of prepared speech, but regardless Magda lifted the duffel bag holding Giacomo and started to hand it to Jake.

"You really call the vampire in that bag *master*?" Donnie asked.

Magda looked at her. "Yes."

"I don't," Nathaniel said.

"Is it like a bondage thing?" Mort asked.

"No," Magda said.

"Why don't you call yours *master*? Is it a guy-girl thing? Please tell me it's not some kind of male-versus-female thing," Donnie said.

Nathaniel smiled at her. "No, of course not. Damian just isn't my master."

"Then why are you carrying him?" she asked.

"Because I needed my hands free for weapons," I said.

"Is he your master?"

"No."

Griffin said, "What do Ms. Fortunada and Ms. Sanderson mean when they call their vampires *master*? If it's not a bondage thing, is it like a real slave thing?"

"It's more the old idea of fidelity to the Lord of the Manor," I said.

"Some vampires demand to be called *master* by all of their underlings," Fortune said.

"Do your masters demand that?" Donnie asked.

"No," most of us said together. Then we all looked at one another, and Nolan's people looked at us, too.

Donnie said, "That was a little disturbing that all of you said that."

I shrugged. "You asked the question."

"I didn't think you had a master in that way, Marshal Blake," Flannery said.

"Jean-Claude gets the title so the other vampires don't get all weird about him marrying the Executioner."

"But when you call him *master*, do you mean it?"

I looked into Flannery's brown eyes and told the truth. "No."

"Does that bother Jean-Claude?"

"Sometimes he says it does, but honestly, I think it's one of the things he likes about me."

"That you will never call him *master* and mean it?" Flannery asked.

I nodded.

"I think you're right," Fortune said. "He wants partners, not servants, in his romantic life. I've never known a man centuries old who wanted to be in less control of women."

"Jean-Claude is a modern kind of guy," I said.

"Maybe," she said, and there was something in her look that let me know had we been alone there would have been more to say. But it wasn't the kind of information you shared in front of strangers. I didn't poke at it, because Fortune was a good judge for what was public-speak and what wasn't. I trusted her judgment and I let it go. I could be taught.

"Show us the cell you want Magda to try to smash her way out of," I said.

Flannery and most of the others were watching the exchange between Fortune and me. He, Donnie, and Griffin all seemed to understand that the conversation had stopped for a reason, but they didn't push at it. Apparently, they'd come knowing when to back off a topic. It had taken me years to learn that particular lesson.

Flannery led the way to a door in the far wall. It was a different door from the one that Nolan and Edward had vanished through. Wherever they had gone, it wasn't to the cell block. I'd love to think that Edward would tell me later exactly where they had gone, but I knew better. No one alive kept a secret better than Edward.

43

WE DIVIDED UP into two groups. One went to the control room, where all their security cameras would be recording things and they could look into the cell as well as the hallway outside the cell. The second group went to the hallway with Magda. I sent Nathaniel with Damian up to the control room, because I was pretty sure that Magda was going to get out, and violence of some kind seemed likely. I wanted both of them safe and out of it. Since Jake was keeping Giacomo safe he stayed with them, and Fortune stayed there for the same reason. If we didn't have to leave the vampires unguarded, then why do it? In fact, there was really not a good reason for most of us to go down to the cells, so in the end it was just Magda, me, Nicky, and Socrates. He wanted to see the state-of-the-art cells and he could talk police with Flannery, and Griffin, who had actually been in the Garda Emergency Response Unit, before Nolan recruited them. They were both former military, too, but their civilian jobs had been as cops. Donnie, Mort, and Brennan had always been military. One of them had even been military police, an MP, so they'd handled detainees before. Socrates got more information out of everyone in a shorter time than I ever could have. I had a badge and was technically a real cop, but because I'd never been military and I hadn't come up through the ranks like a regular cop, I just didn't know how to talk like all the other cops. Socrates was great at it. They liked that he'd been a detective in Los Angeles, a real cop, before his "accident." They'd gotten to the point of finding out that he was in a traditional marriage with nothing that made them uncomfortable or forced them to think outside the box. It made it all so much easier for him to find out that Flannery was married, too, and everyone else was single; beyond that I don't know because we got to the cell block.

There were two cells finished on one side of a corridor that was empty and smooth, as if it had been started and never finished. There were two more cells roughed out on the other side. Everything was painted white from ceiling to floor, so the hallway had a science fiction feel to it, complete with cameras near the ceiling inside clear bubbles that were supposed to be bulletproof. I was pretty sure that I knew a caliber big enough to make bulletproof into bullet resistant, but I let it go. We weren't here to test the cameras out; we were here to test the cells.

The doors were oversize, like they were expecting small giants. The hinges were large but strangely flat to the wall. There were two small windows in each door, one in the upper part and one in the lower part. Both had small bars in them and were covered by sliding metal panels. When the panels were closed the doors were solid metal.

Donnie used her earpiece to signal for the doors to be opened. "We can't open the doors from down here," she said.

"What if you have a medical emergency with one of the prisoners?" Socrates asked.

They exchanged a look between all of them who weren't us. "Like what kind of medical emergency could a shapeshifter or a vampire have?" Brennan asked.

"If you put more than one new shapeshifter in a cell together, they will tear each other up," he said.

"I thought they wouldn't attack each other," Donnie said.

"Whoever told you that was wrong," I said.

Socrates added, "We're less likely to attack each other, because humans smell more like food, but if a brand-new shapeshifter can't get to anyone else it will turn on another of its own kind."

"What about vampires?" Donnie asked.

"They can't feed on one another, so I don't think they'll try to hurt one another." But I was frowning as I said it. I looked at the others. "You know, I've never seen new vampires that didn't have an older one around somewhere. Will the newly vamped attack each other if there's no other food around? I mean, they don't know that they can't feed on each other unless someone tells them, right?"

"Giacomo says that other vampires smell bitter. They don't smell like something edible," Magda said.

"Okay, then probably you can house multiple vampires together and they won't eat each other, but that doesn't mean they won't be violent to each other. I mean, I've seen vampires kill each other."

"We don't have enough cells," Donnie said.

"I think these three will be fine together," Flannery said, and turned to me. "What do you think, Marshal?"

"I think you're probably right, but we should put vampires in separate holding areas if possible, or have them chained up so there's no chance of them hurting each other, or themselves."

"What are your cells for them like, then?" Griffin asked.

"They aren't held long enough for it to be pertinent," I said.

"What does that mean?" Donnie asked.

"It means she executes them," Brennan said.

"Well, not just me, but yeah, usually they're executed too quickly for special cells to be needed."

"You think they can't be held safely, don't you?" Flannery said.

"I think we tried it in the States and ended up with a lot of dead correctional officers and fellow prisoners trying to be fair to vampires, shapeshifters, and even human sorcerers."

"But you've fought to get more lenient legislation on the books in your country so that execution isn't the only answer," he said.

I nodded. "When the vampires are being controlled by a powerful enough master, they literally have no will of their own. They can be forced to kill and do other terrible things totally against their will. I fought to have the law reflect that. Because once I realized they really had no choice, killing them for it seemed worse, but the law didn't give me another option, so I worked to give myself another option."

"Then you would rather not have to execute them?" Flannery said.

I thought about my answer and finally said, "If I think the person I'm about to kill was innocent, then yes, I want an option, but don't mistake me for someone who's against the death penalty. Most of the people I've executed have taken multiple lives, and I believe that ending their lives saved others."

"We may have to agree to disagree," he said, smiling, but his eyes stayed serious.

"We may," I said.

The doors to the cells opened and one was as white as the hallway, but the other one was shiny. "Silver-infused paint," Nicky said.

"Maybe one is just a glossier paint than the other one," Donnie said.

He shook his head.

"How did you know that quickly?" she asked.

"Being around this much silver . . . you know."

"Then it will limit what you can do inside the cell," Flannery said.

He shook his head.

"Magda is not getting in a silver-lined cell," I said.

"I am wearing good boots and I can use my clothes to protect my hands," she said.

"No."

She looked at the others and asked, "Do you want me to destroy the most expensive cell or the one that is the most useful?"

"Destroy away, as long as you can't get out," Brennan said.

"Destroying it means I will break out of it."

"The silver will sap your abilities and you'll be just as human as we are," he said.

She and Nicky both laughed. Socrates didn't. "That's not what silver does to us."

"I will be just as strong inside either cell. All you need to tell me is which cell you prefer I break out of, and which you want to keep for the vampire prisoners."

"You haven't even touched the door or walls yet," Mort said.

"I do not have to."

He looked puzzled and almost frowned, but mostly just puzzled. "How can you be that certain you can break out without trying first?"

"I know my capabilities," she said, giving him that calm face she did so well. I knew from experience that she could hide almost any thought behind that placid mask. It wasn't the pleasant smiling face that Fortune did; in fact, it unnerved some people because Magda looked almost totally unemotional when she did it. But I knew that she could be feeling anything, everything, behind that look, just like Fortune's one smile. It was a different way of hiding in plain sight.

Mort shook his head. "I thought I was arrogant."

"It is not arrogance. It is self-knowledge."

Mort stared up at her, studying her face and trying to see behind it, I think. He finally laughed. "That makes perfect sense to me."

"Are you saying your bragging is because you really are that good?" Donnie asked, smiling.

He gave her a look that was a little too direct, but she had started it. "Have I ever said I can do something and not been able to do it?"

She had to think about that for a second or two, and then her smile faded around the edges. She gave a much more considering look. "No, you always do what you say you'll do."

"Self-knowledge," Magda said.

Mort nodded. "Self-knowledge."

Flannery touched his ear and said, "We have a decision. If it won't harm Sanderson, we'd prefer she try to break out of the silver-lined one."

"I'll leave the choice up to her, as long as we are clear that it's not an order," I said.

"I understand it is my choice," she said, still giving me that blank look that I knew could be hiding almost any thought or feeling. I knew one thing: Whatever was going on behind her blue-gray eyes, if she said she could break out of both cells, then she could.

"Is there anything in the cells that will hurt Magda other than the silver in the paint?" Socrates asked.

"What do you mean?" Flannery asked.

"Is anything booby-trapped?"

It was an excellent question. "I knew I brought you along for a reason, because you ask better questions than I do."

He smiled at the compliment but gave serious eyes back to the other man. "Is there anything in the cell that we need to know about before we put one of our people inside it?"

"What Socrates said," I said.

"We are trying to create a jail that will hold the supernatural. A regular jail cell would not be booby-trapped, and neither is this one," Flannery said.

"Promise?" I said.

He gave a small smile. "Promise."

I looked at Magda. "It's up to you."

She smiled then, and just walked into the silver-coated cell.

"You can't use any of your weapons to break out, because we'd confiscate them from a real prisoner," Mort said.

"Understood," she said. She just stood there calmly, waiting for them to close the door.

Flannery gave the signal and the door started to swing shut. I watched her as long as I could, but her expression never changed. The door closed with a *whoosh* instead of a *clang*. I didn't understand exactly how the door worked, or where the lock was, but I didn't like having one of my people on the wrong side of it.

I leaned into Nicky and asked, "Would just standing surrounded by that much silver hurt?"

"Not unless it touches our skin," he whispered back.

Socrates leaned in close and said, "It would still be unnerving as hell."

"Nothing unnerves Magda," Nicky said.

I agreed, but I still stared at the door and prayed, *Don't let her get hurt proving this point.*

44

THE HALLWAY SEEMED very quiet after the door shut. It was almost like that hush before a storm, or like that moment when you close the door to the gun room behind you and you're in that little air lock room between the gun shop and the firing range where both doors must be closed before you can open the one that leads to the actual firing line. At the gun range you can hear the gunshots from the next room, but they're muffled both from the door and the room's sound-proofing and the ear protection you're already wearing, but you know that on the other side of that last door it's going to be loud and full of potentially deadly things.

It was quiet for several minutes, so that Brennan said, "She's not getting out of there."

Something hit the door so hard the metal rang. Brennan jumped, and he wasn't the only one. "Magda was looking the door over, figuring out where best to apply force," Socrates said.

The metal rang again, and there was an almost whining sound with the next blow. "What is that?" I asked.

"The metal protesting," Nicky said.

A spot in the door began to bow outward. I realized that Magda was kicking the door over and over again in the exact same spot. Had she figured out the lock mechanism? Had she spotted the weakest point on the metal? Or had she just chosen a spot and started pounding at it? I'd ask her later.

Nicky looked at our three hosts and asked, "What are you going to do when she gets out?"

Donnie showed a Taser in her hand. I shook my head. "Nope, we didn't negotiate for you hitting Magda with a Taser."

The door began to crumple outward where she was kicking it. Mort asked, "Would a Taser slow her down?"

"Do they affect us? Yes. But not through a heavy jacket and sweater," Nicky said.

"And if the Taser just causes them pain but doesn't stop them, you better have another idea," I said.

"Pepper spray," Donnie said.

"If it wouldn't work on a bear, don't try it on a lycanthrope," I said.

"We don't have bears in Ireland."

"America has bears and it's not that pepper spray in their eyes might not work, but your chances of getting it in their eyes before they claw you badly are pretty small. Same goes for wereanimals—you'll never make it."

The metal door looked like a bubble was growing in it, a rapidly thinning bubble. It wasn't a question of if, but when she'd break through, and they still didn't have a secondary plan. Lucky it wasn't a real bad guy busting the door.

"What are you going to do?" Nicky asked.

"Flash-bang," Mort said.

"It would disorient her, but then what?" Nicky asked.

"We subdue her," he said.

"How?" Socrates asked.

Mort pulled out what looked like a small black stick in his hand; one sharp movement downward and the "stick" telescoped out into a baton. It was an ASP, which was like a thin club and you could use it like one; it was good for pressure points and just a policeman's little helper.

"Are you seriously going to try to subdue Magda with an ASP?" Socrates asked.

"Yes."

The door shuddered.

"You haven't tried hand-to-hand with one of us yet."

"No. Why?"

"When she comes through the door, if Nicky or Anita tells her to put on a show . . . you'll have your answer." Socrates said it and started moving back down the hallway. He was right. If they were really going to be swinging at her and she was going to be dodging and maybe swinging back, farther away was going to be better.

Nicky took my arm and started backing us both away from the door. The door didn't fall down like it would in the movies.

It bowed outward and I think she peeled it partway out of the doorframe, because I got a glimpse of her hair and face, a shoulder through the opening. I was strong, but not strong enough to look at that door and think, *I'll just kick it until it breaks*. That was like superhero strong, supernatural strong.

Donnie, Brennan, and Mort had their ASPs out and ready. Flannery had backed down the hallway in the other direction. Since I couldn't see a door on that side, he was still trapped with a potentially pissed werelion.

Magda shoved her shoulder into the opening she'd made at the edge of the door and wall, braced her hand on the doorframe, and just shoved. If I'd been either of the three waiting humans I might have jumped the gun and tried to hit her then, but they didn't, because we were all on the same side, or they were just too amazed at what she was doing to move. Either way, she was about to come out.

Nicky called out, "Magda, don't hurt them much!"

Her eyes flicked up to see more of the hallway. She shoved one last time hard, the metal screaming with the force of it, electronics sparking around her. Mort braced and did a little bounce on the balls of his feet, some kind of martial arts training. Brennan looked like he was about to box, and Donnie was just ready. I don't know how much of it Magda actually saw, but she gave that snarling smile that I'd started thinking of as a werelion kind of thing. She looked like she was going to push at the door again, but instead she ducked back into the room.

Mort stayed ready, so did Brennan, so did Donnie, but nothing happened. The hallway and the cell with its peeled-open door were quiet except for the sparking of the electronics that Magda had damaged when she opened the door.

Flannery yelled, "She's coming!"

If I'd done the math, I'd have said that Magda couldn't have leaped through the narrow opening she'd made, but I wasn't doing the math. She came through that improbable opening in a blur that even I couldn't follow. It was more a sense of movement like I saw her behind my eyes where you see dreams . . . or nightmares.

45

THE BLUR THAT was Magda hit the wall opposite the door and bounced back. Mort was the only one fast enough to hit the floor, so she went over him, but she hit Donnie and Brennan both. If we hadn't told her not to hurt them, they'd have been done, but not hurting someone in a fight is harder than it sounds. Pulling your punch takes more skill than landing one, but even pulled they both went flying. Brennan hit the wall beside the other cell. Donnie slid across the floor and caught herself against the wall, but rolled to her feet and was in a fighting stance before Magda was on her again, which was pretty damn impressive.

Mort actually hit Magda as she came over him to go for Donnie again. It didn't hurt her, but it threw off her leap and made her use the wall to turn and come back for him. I could see Mort as he fought with the blur that I knew was Magda. He was trying to land a blow, any blow, with the baton in his hand. I didn't understand how he was avoiding her blows, but I knew he was, because his other arm was coming up and he was moving like he was fighting. I started to be able to see her moving, but it was still like watching the afterimage as if you saw where she'd been, not where she was, because your eye just couldn't comprehend the speed. Mort had to be seeing her better than I did, because he was blocking her blows. It was like they were sparring, but it was movie-special-effects sparring, because no one moved like this in real life. It was like watching magic.

Donnie tried to back Mort up, and she got a few hits with her baton, but she seemed to have more trouble timing her blows with Magda's movements. Twice she almost hit Mort, because he moved with Magda and by the time Donnie swung she had a different target, one she didn't want to hit. It was like Mort and Magda were dancing and Donnie was trying to cut in.

Brennan staggered as he got up off the floor from where he'd fallen. He was shaken, maybe hurt. If you don't know how to fall, you shouldn't spar. Magda hadn't meant to hurt him, but she'd trusted that he knew how to keep himself safe.

Mort bent backward at the waist, so Magda swept over him. Donnie tried to come from the other side and Magda reacted to it, but Donnie was immediately on the defensive. "Don't try to see her. Feel it," Mort said, as he avoided Magda's blows and Donnie waded in and got shoved out of the way again.

Donnie said, "What do you mean, don't see her?"

Brennan tried to join the fight, but whatever had happened in the initial rush made him too slow. His baton vanished from his hand in a movement so quick that he was left staring at his empty hand as if it had literally vanished instead of Magda grabbing it and spinning away with it.

Mort finally hit her and he didn't expect to, so he connected harder than he'd planned. Magda slowed down enough that I saw her face clearly and the bright red at her cheek. He'd bled her. There was a second where he saw it, too, and his face showed that he was sorry, but she touched the blood on her face and then spun toward him with that blurring speed, and if I'd thought the fight was furiously fast before, I'd been wrong. Mort could not keep her from hitting him; no human could have.

Donnie moved in to help but was sent staggering back with blood on her own face. This had gone far enough. Apparently Brennan thought so, too, because he drew his sidearm and pointed it at the fight. Magda was moving too fast for him to be certain of hitting her and not Mort, and we were standing on the other side of the fight. There were too many friendly targets in the hallway. Fuck.

46

DONNIE YELLED, "BRENNAN, stand down!"

I had my gun in my hand and hadn't meant to draw it. Brennan couldn't get a solid target on the moving fight, but all I had to do was hit him. I yelled, "Brennan, down, put it down, now!"

Donnie stood up taller and was suddenly all I could see down the barrel of the gun. I lowered it and aimed at the ruined cell. "Donnie, down, floor!"

"Don't shoot him," she said.

"Disarm him, Donnie, or we will," Socrates said.

Flannery moved at the other end of the hallway. "Brennan, holster your weapon."

"It's the only way to stop it," Brennan said.

Mort fell to the floor and Magda knelt over him, the baton coming down. Nicky yelled, "Magda!" and his beast's energy filled the hallway in a skin-trembling rush. She hesitated, looking at him with eyes gone to lion orange. Socrates was already moving down the hallway in his own dark blur of speed, but he wasn't as fast as Magda. Nicky had chosen not to rush the fight, afraid he'd spook Brennan more. Nicky put his body in front of mine to shield me, so that I didn't see what happened next. The gunshot was thunderous in the hallway. You forget how loud it is without ear protection.

I tried to move around Nicky, but he kept his body firm in front of mine. Damn it! "What's happening?"

He moved enough that I could see around him, but he kept one arm sort of back so that he kept me swept mostly behind him. But I could see Magda helping Mort to his feet. Donnie was holding a gun in her hand, but I could still see her own gun in its holster at her side. Maybe she had a backup, but I was betting it was Brennan's gun. Had she disarmed him before Socrates could?

Flannery had Brennan up against the wall, talking low and urgently to him. The younger man wasn't fighting to get away, but he wasn't happy either. Socrates was standing beside Donnie and Flannery.

"What the fuck just happened?" I asked.

"Donnie and Flannery disarmed him before Socrates got there," Nicky said.

I still had my own gun out. I let out the last of a breath I hadn't even realized I was holding and holstered it.

The door behind us opened and I almost went for my gun again, but it was Edward and Nolan. I started to breathe again and tried to relax, but that wasn't happening completely. We needed out of this hallway, or I did.

"I thought Forrester had trained you up better than that, Blake," Nolan said; he was angry and looking for a target. I wasn't sure why that target wasn't Brennan, but if he wanted to fight, that was fine with me.

"I don't know what you're talking about, Nolan. It wasn't me who broke training."

"First your wereanimal goes berserk and then you draw your gun and threaten a target you had no intention of shooting. Didn't anyone teach you that you don't draw your gun unless you mean to use it?"

"Magda did exactly what you said you wanted. She tested your fancy jail cell and your people."

"Bollocks, she wasn't good enough to get past Mort." He yelled it, pushing past Edward to advance on me. Edward didn't try to stop him. He knew I could take care of myself, and part of him was going to enjoy the show.

"She could have had me a dozen times, Captain. She was incredibly controlled," Mort said.

"You fought well," Magda said.

He grinned at her, pleased.

"If you can't control your animals, then you need to go back to America!" Nolan was looming over me as he yelled.

I stepped closer to him, invading his personal space. I yelled back, "Don't you ever call my people animals again, when it was your man who pulled his weapon on us!"

He stepped into me and screamed, "I'll discipline my man, but who disciplines you for pulling yours?"

I realized I wanted to fight, because part of me knew that I would have shot Brennan. I don't shoot to wound, so I stepped into Nolan. I moved forward into the fight instead of trying to calm it down, because I didn't feel calm. Brennan didn't need killing, but I knew that was exactly what I would have done if Donnie hadn't stopped me. I stepped into Nolan until only the smallest fraction of space was left between us. It was aggressive and designed to make the fight worse. I was afraid of what I'd almost done, and fear has always translated into anger for me. My beasts came with my anger in a rush of energy that fueled the aggression. We could fight; oh yes, we could. I felt Nolan's beast flickering inside him, rising toward the surface of him in his own rush of confused emotions turned to rage. It wasn't the same kind of wolf as the one inside me, but they recognized each other. Bow-fucking-wow.

"Your man lost his nerve and pulled his gun, because he didn't know what else to do, Nolan! This is why you can't jail the monsters! This is why you kill them, because you can't do anything else!"

He snarled into my face. "You pointed your weapon at a friendly that you had no intention of shooting; if you were my man I would take your sidearm and you would not get it back!"

"I pointed my gun at an armed threat, and I don't shoot to wound!"

He almost snarled the next words into my face. "Brennan was pointing his gun at the threat he saw in this hallway."

Was there an edge of growl in my own voice as I spoke? "He staggered away from that wall. He wasn't steady enough to fire into a fight. He was a danger to your own man."

"My men are trained to fire during a fight!"

"I'm trained to end the fight!"

"What the fuck does that mean?"

I was damn near on tiptoes putting my face up into his, as I said, "I'm an executioner, Nolan!"

"You wouldn't have shot him!"

"The fuck I wouldn't! Donnie blocked my shot."

"I did, sir," Donnie called.

My wolf with her mostly white fur was just suddenly clear

inside me. I could see her standing with the black saddle mark across her, the slight darkening around her eyes that was the beginning of the marks around a husky's or malamute's face. She looked up into his brown eyes with her gold ones and his energy rose to hers. His eyes changed to amber.

Nolan looked down at the floor, blinking, then leaned back from me. He took a step back, and in a much calmer voice he said, "Your woman still lost control."

"No, Captain Nolan, she did not, because if she had, there'd be fresh bodies." My voice was calmer, too.

When he looked at me again, his eyes were back to human brown. "If Donahue hadn't spoiled your aim on Brennan, would you have shot him?"

"I was taught that you don't draw your gun unless you mean to use it, and if you start shooting, then you shoot until the target is stopped. Dead is stopped."

Nolan looked at me. "I don't want to lose men to friendly fire."

"Then you need to train them not to lose their nerve the first time they realize just what they're up against."

"I did not mean for him to hit his head," Magda said. "I overestimated his ability to fight, as I underestimated this one." She clapped Mort on the shoulder. He winced. "Did I hurt you?"

"I'll be bruised, but so will you."

"No, I will heal any damage before bruises form."

"That must be nice," he said.

"Yes, it is," she said.

"I've never met anyone that much faster than me," he said.

"You are very fast for someone who is only human."

He took the compliment, and I realized that in that weird guy/warrior way Mort and Magda were now friends. It had sort of been how Edward and I first bonded, too, so I understood how it worked, but I was just girl enough to know it was a little crazy.

Edward stepped up beside Nolan. "You thought your cell would hold up."

"I did."

"You thought your people would stand a better chance at subduing a shapeshifter."

Nolan nodded. "I did."

"Don't take it out on Anita or any of her people."

"He just did take it out on me," I said.

Edward smiled at me. "Yeah, but I wanted to see who would get the most riled."

"You wanted to see which of us would get angrier?" I asked, raising an eyebrow at him.

He smiled at me, and it was all Ted charm, but the glint in his eyes was all Edward—that part of him that liked to know everyone's weaknesses, like an out-of-control temper that you aimed at the wrong person. I understood why Nolan was still only a captain at forty; with that kind of temper I was amazed he'd made captain. Of course, he had just watched us prove that his unit wasn't even close to prepared for the monsters. That was worth a temper tantrum or two, just not this public.

"Are the vampires going to be that strong and that fast when they wake up?" Donnie asked, nodding toward the cell where they'd stowed the body bags while we tested the other cell.

Nolan looked at me. "Well, Blake?"

I appreciated that he asked my opinion and not Edward's. I think he was trying to make up for the yelling match. "Not as fast, and the newly dead won't know how to harness all that superstrength yet. Magda has had years of training and practice. She's not only stronger and faster than human-normal, but she knows how to use all of it. You've got a suburban mom and two teenage girls. Just being vampires won't make them instant martial arts experts or give them washboard abs; that takes work whether you're dead or alive."

"So will the other cell hold the new vampires?" he asked.

I looked at Magda. "Will it?"

She nodded. "For a few nights, yes, but they will learn how strong they are, and they will begin to use that strength. They will also learn how to use the other things they have gained from becoming vampire."

"You mean mind tricks," Nolan said.

"Their gaze can trap you and make you into their slave. It can turn a man against his friends and family."

"It doesn't work over cameras. As long as we don't open the door and look them in the eye, we'll be fine."

"You'll have to feed them," I said.

"We'll shove in some bags of plasma," he said.

I shook my head. "They can't feed on old blood, only fresh."

"We can get rats to put in the cell."

"First, the vampires are still at some level going to be who they were in life, so I don't think that shoving live rats in a room with a mother and two kids is the best idea."

"You mean they'll be afraid of the rats?" Donnie asked.

I nodded.

"I know where we can buy rabbits," Flannery said.

"They would drink the blood of animals, but it won't sustain them."

"What does that mean, it won't sustain them?"

"It means that animal blood fills their stomachs, but it's missing some ingredient that keeps the bodies from rotting. The brain stays intact and working, but the body starts to rot like a zombie's does. They still have eternal life unless they're killed, but the looking-just-like-they-did-at-death rots away."

"How do you know that?" Donnie asked.

"I've seen a master vampire that tried to give up feeding on people. It was pretty horrible."

"Is there any way to reverse the process?" Flannery asked.

"Yes, but not without literally sacrificing other people's lives to replace the energy the vampire has lost through trying to go their version of vegetarian."

"You mean they have to consume enough blood to kill people?"

"No, literally the ritual that might fix the damage requires human sacrifice. I've never heard of it being done successfully, but I was approached by someone who wanted me to help them do it."

"They wanted you to perform the ritual?" Flannery asked.

"No, they wanted me to be one of the human sacrifices."

His eyes went wide. "Cheeky buggers."

"I thought so."

"What did you do to stop them?" Nolan asked.

"I've already told you what *stop* means to me, Nolan."

We looked at each other for a long minute, and then he nodded. "Yes, you have."

I felt Magda move beside me, and something about it made me turn and look. She was watching Brennan walk up the hallway toward us. We were also standing in the way of the only exit from the cell block, so he had to come this way to leave, but it had still put Magda on alert. I didn't blame her.

Mort stepped a little in front of her, so that Brennan would have to pass in front of him and not Magda. I had a moment to see how much smaller Mort was than the werelion. He wasn't just shorter; he also was one of those men who muscled but didn't bulk up much, so that he looked almost delicate standing in front of her. Since Mort was three inches taller than me, it let me understand just how tiny I must appear to everyone else.

Brennan stopped his six feet of tall, dark, and brooding handsome in front of Mort. "Would you actually protect her against me?"

"Magda did what we asked her to do: point out the flaws in our system."

"Would you stand with her against me?"

"She didn't point a gun at me, Brennan. You did."

"I wasn't aiming at you. I was aiming at her." And he pointed a finger at Magda as he said it.

"Do you really think that you could have hit her without hitting me?"

"Yes," he replied, but he was a little too defensive about it. He'd gotten spooked by Magda and he'd let his fear make him foolish.

Magda took a step forward and Brennan took one back; even with Mort between them he didn't want to be closer to the werelion. Crap, we might have broken him for this duty; if he couldn't get over being this afraid of wereanimals, not only couldn't he work with us but he'd be a deficit working with any of the preternaturals.

"Donnie, escort Brennan to medical. I want him checked out."

"I'm fine, sir."

"I didn't ask your opinion, Brennan. I gave Donnie an order," Nolan said.

"Do you actually believe that I would do anything to endanger a member of my own team?"

"I'll review the recording and then we'll revisit this topic. For now, I want you to go with Donahue to medical."

"Sir . . ."

"I gave you an order, Brennan."

"I didn't do anything wrong."

"Are you going to make me repeat myself again?"

Brennan took a deep breath and stood up a little straighter. "No, sir."

Donnie was standing up with us now. "I'll see he gets to medical, sir."

"Go with her to medical now."

"Yes, sir." He saluted, and after a moment's hesitation, Nolan saluted him back. Donnie saluted him and then herded Brennan toward the door. He looked back and it was almost hate. I wasn't sure if it was aimed at Magda or all of us, but either way it wasn't a good look.

When the door closed behind them, Nolan went closer to inspect the door of the cell that Magda had torn open. "If this had been a real prisoner escaping, could we have used Tasers effectively?"

"They would work, but their effectiveness would depend on the type of lycanthrope," I said.

"Why does it depend on that?" he asked.

I shrugged. "It's just like how some humans go down instantly and some need a second or third hit of electricity to stop coming at you."

"But if a wereanimal keeps coming, you won't have time to squeeze off three Taser hits," Edward said.

"What about tranquilizer darts?"

"It might work short-term if you could get the right dosage, but all drugs work through their system a lot faster than they do through a human, or the real-animal equivalent. If the lycanthrope is already starting to shift, then their metabolism works even faster, so once they go down you have no way to judge how long until they wake up."

"Have you ever used tranquilizers on them in your job?"

Edward and I both shook our heads. I said, "The dose needed to make it work also runs the risk of stopping their heart. Heart damage is one of the few ways to kill almost everything, and you don't want to be in the middle of giving a were-anything CPR when it wakes up angry with you."

Flannery laughed, but it was more nerves than humor, I think.

"You have something to add?" Nolan asked.

"No, sir . . . I mean, yes, sir."

"Talk."

"Maybe there's a way to use magic to slow down or even contain the supernatural beings."

"You mean casting spells?" I asked.

He smiled. "Something like that, yes."

"The witches I know in the United States might be able to do something to help strengthen the door, and I guess you could work a containment spell on vampires not being able to cross the threshold, but it wouldn't help you against lycanthropes," I said.

"The more powerful the vampire, the fewer spells that will contain them," Magda said.

"True," I said.

"I would like to sit down with all of you who know magic and discuss possibilities," Flannery said.

"Are you a witch?"

"No."

"Are you a practitioner of the occult arts?" Edward asked.

Flannery looked at him and smiled. "Yes."

I looked at Edward. "I've never heard anyone call it that outside of books."

"You haven't traveled in Europe as much as I have."

I nodded. "Okay, Flannery, if you aren't a witch, but you are a practitioner, then what kind of practitioner are you?"

"Here they would call me a Fairy Doctor."

"You get your power from the Fey, the little people," I said.

He nodded, smiling wider. "I'm impressed, Marshal. Outside of Ireland, most people don't know the term."

"Someone who visited your country explained it to me."

"Would I recognize the name?"

"I don't think so."

"Outside of Ireland, what would they call you?" Socrates asked. It was a good question.

"Not much. My powers are tied to the gentle folk of this

land, literally this soil. I have to be in a country long enough to persuade what few Fey remain there to help me. All the local nature spirits are very leery of strangers and strange magic."

"Have you ever persuaded foreign . . . gentle folk to work with you?" I asked.

"I have, but even with them it didn't work as well as it does here with my more familiar friends."

Edward said, "Let's discuss ways to contain the vampires before they wake up for the night."

"Good idea," Nolan said, "though I think, Mort, you should report to medical, too, just in case some of those bruises and scrapes are more serious than you think."

"I'm fine, sir."

Nolan just looked at him. Mort grinned. "Yes, sir."

"The gentle folk may be able to help us contain the vampires," Flannery said.

"They haven't helped much up to this point," Nolan said.

Flannery smiled. "I hadn't met Marshal Blake and her people. I've told my friends enough that they would like to meet face-to-face."

"What does meeting us have to do with the . . . gentle folk helping with the vampire problem?" I asked.

"If the Fey like you, they may agree to helping more," Flannery said.

"Do you mean they could have been helping this whole time and have refused?" Edward asked.

"Don't judge them by human motives. It will just frustrate you," Nolan said.

Edward frowned. "I think Marshal Forrester should not come to the meeting," Flannery said.

"Where Anita goes, I go."

"You're not magical enough, Forrester. I'm sorry, but the wee folk prefer different energy."

"If they don't like you, they won't meet with you," Nolan said.

"I don't want Anita going alone," Edward said.

"You and I can wait in the car, but we can't go in if the Fey say no. If we try to crash the meeting, they won't help us."

"Anita is not going alone," Edward repeated.

"Oh, she won't be alone. They want to meet some of the people she brought to our shores," Flannery said.

"Like who?" I asked.

Flannery flashed me a bright smile. "I'll give you a list."

"Jake needs to be on that list," Edward said.

That surprised me. I'd have thought he'd say Nicky.

We finally got to leave the hallway. Mort went to medical, though I was pretty sure he was fine. It wasn't until Edward wanted to include Jake in our meeting that I began to think we were going to talk about more than just containing the prisoners. I was pretty sure I knew why he wanted to include the only werewolf we had brought with us. Edward had noticed Nolan losing control for that moment in the hallway. If anyone in the group knew Nolan's secret, I was betting it was Flannery. When you work with what amounts to nature spirits, it's hard to miss a werewolf. If he had missed it, then my opinion of Flannery's magical abilities was going to be low before we ever started comparing notes.

47

WE SETTLED IN the back of the truck, which was beginning to feel like our home away from home, for privacy, and I put Domino up front with the driver. Flannery told me that not everyone could go in to meet and greet, but I was free to bring more people, so I did.

"Safety tip: Don't admit to being able to see the gentle folk unless Flannery asks a direct question," Nolan said.

"Why not?" Nicky asked.

"Because not all of them like being spied on, and back in the old days, they'd ask which eye you could see them with and blind you in that eye."

"I'm already down an eye," he said.

"We'll talk about what we saw and didn't see when we're all alone and inside somewhere in the city," I said.

"That would be best," Nolan said. We'd already asked Nolan, and Flannery was the only one of his people who knew his secret, so we could talk freely about that, at least.

I wasn't sure how to start the talk, but Flannery was. "Before we talk other magic, we should discuss what happened with Captain Nolan in the hallway."

Nolan startled badly enough I could tell from the back. "I don't know what you mean, Flannery."

"Captain, please, I felt your wolf stronger than I've felt it in months."

"No one else noticed."

"I did," I said.

"You felt my beast, because you have your own."

"I saw your eyes change, Brian," Edward said.

Nolan looked at him. "You did not."

"You were so busy trying not to flash the color change down the hall toward your people that you didn't think I was standing beside you. I saw your eyes change, but I felt the energy roll off you, too."

"You never felt it when we worked together in the past."

"I didn't know what I was feeling back then. I'd barely started working with preternatural stuff. I have years more practice under my belt, and I know what I felt."

"How could you differentiate between me, Blake, Sanderson, Murdock, or Jones?"

"I've worked with Anita too long not to know what her energy feels like; same for Murdock. The others not as much, but I still knew how many shapeshifters were in that hallway from the feel of their energy. I'll be honest: If I hadn't seen your eyes I wouldn't have been sure it was you, but I would have known it had to be either you or Mortimer, because that's the direction I was sensing it from."

"All right, so you sensed me."

"Is it just being around so many other people with similar gifts that roused your wolf?" Flannery asked.

"No." This from Jake.

"What was it, then?" Nolan asked, and he was a little defensive like Brennan had been inside.

"When is the last time you were around a woman of your kind?" Jake asked.

"I see my mother at least once a month."

Jake smiled, gently, as if he were trying to lead him through something hard. "No, I mean a woman who is someone you could have a romantic relationship with, Captain Nolan."

"Years."

"Have you been around any female werewolves that are like me?"

"Only to fight them in other countries."

"So, again, no chance for romance."

"I suppose not."

"Then Anita is the first she-wolf you have met in years who isn't trying to kill you, or isn't closely related to you."

"Are you saying that my wolf reacted that strongly just because she's a female wolf?"

"Something like that."

He shook his head. "I'm not saying you're wrong, Pennyfeather, but I haven't reacted that way to a she-wolf since I was a teenager. Why now?"

It took me a second to remember that Jake was Pennyfeather. Jake asked, "When is the last time you let yourself become a wolf?"

Nolan took in a lot of the damp, fresh-smelling air, and then let it out in a rush. "I don't remember."

"Your people may be able to go for years without changing form, but your other half is still in there with all the same needs and wants of any creature."

"How long since you had a date?" Edward asked.

Nolan frowned, and again I had the urge to smooth his forehead and see if the lines would soften. I didn't act on the impulse, but it was an unusual thought for me with a stranger. I wondered if my inner wolf was behind it.

"I don't really date anymore."

"How long since you had sex with someone else?" Edward asked.

Nolan scowled, hands going into fists. I thought for a second we might get to see another fight, but he controlled everything but his voice, which was dark and low with suppressed anger. "That is not your business."

"That's answer enough, so that long," Edward said.

I think Nolan started counting to twenty, very slowly, in his head so he didn't take a swing at Edward. Since I had on occasion done the same thing with him, I really couldn't throw stones.

"That will make it harder to be around Anita," Jake said.

"Why?" Nolan asked.

"Because she's a she-wolf and your wolf recognizes that." He stared at Jake for a second. "You're joking."

"We are all attracted to those who carry similar energy, Captain."

"So is it hard for you to be around Anita?"

"No, but I've had far more practice interacting with other female werewolves than you have. Also, I become my other form at least once a month. I feed my body's needs and wants, Captain. You, it seems, do not."

"I told you, we're dying out, and those of us who are left don't want their children to be wolves. I can't tell you about a single child of people who kept their tail into adulthood. In the seventeen and eighteen hundreds the British used the tails on our soldiers as propaganda to prove that the Irish weren't human, that all of us were just animals, so it didn't matter if they slaughtered us or starved us. We went from being a people proud of their heritage to one that began to believe the lies. What if we were just animals, not the Irish, but us, the wolves of Ireland?"

"That was not true then, and it is not true now," Jake said.

"I reacted to Blake's wolf like I was in heat; that's not human."

"You've never been a pretty girl at a bar on a Saturday night. Trust me, Nolan, men behave a lot more animalistic than you did in the hallway," I said.

"That has been true of men and pretty girls for forever and a day," Magda said.

"On behalf of all my sex, my deepest apologies," Jake said. The rest of the men wisely said nothing.

"You just need a woman in your life," Edward said.

"You sound like my ma."

Edward grinned at him. "I hope we can visit before we leave. She hears that I'm married with two kids, she'll give you even more grief about it."

"If I understand it, you're not married yet, and if Ma finds out you're living in sin with kids in the house, you're the one that will get the grief."

Edward gave a smile that gave me a sudden glimpse of what he might have been at twenty when he met Nolan. I'd never met anyone who had known him this long. I so needed to ask questions of him when Edward wasn't around.

As if he read my mind, Edward said, "I think Anita is hoping to see some of the countryside with her lovers before we all go home."

"My ma wouldn't know what to do with you, Blake. Too much sin for any one woman, is likely what she'd say."

"I think I'm offended," I said.

"I think we all are," Dev said.

"It's nothing personal. My ma is a big one for finding sin in people."

"Nolan's mother didn't like me much either. She doesn't hold with folks that work with the Fey," Flannery said.

He grinned at me, his teeth strong and so white that I was beginning to think he'd had them bleached, which didn't fit with his messy hair, which couldn't seem to decide if it was wavy or curly, and he kept running his hands through it and trying to push it back away from his ears. It was longer than regulation for any army or police force I was familiar with, but the rest of him screamed someone who had been in a uniform most of his adult life. I wondered if the longer hair was an effort to look less like a uniformed officer; if so, he'd been in Nolan's unit awhile.

"What's wrong with working with the Fey?" Dev asked.

"My ma doesn't like anything that makes a person stand out as different," Nolan said.

"Because she's hiding her differences?" I asked.

He nodded.

"I asked to meet her," Flannery said. "There are so few native wolves left in Ireland, I wanted to meet Captain Nolan's family."

"Ma was right mad when she figured out he was a Fairy Doctor."

"She got more worried when she found out I had never married."

Nolan laughed. "She was torn between fixing you up with a local girl and keeping the Fey away from her friends."

"So she'd want all of us to be married?" Nathaniel asked.

"Oh yes."

"Could you tell she was a wolf when you met her?" Jake asked.

Flannery shook his head. "I could tell there was something Fey about her, but not what."

"Is it Fey to be an Irish wolf?" I asked.

"It's why they don't like any of the wolves that cut off their tails. They love their own deformities, but they would see it as a betrayal of their heritage," Nolan said.

"Your tail was not a deformity," Flannery said.

"You tell that to the other lads in school and their families," Nolan said.

We were all quiet for a few minutes as the truck whirred along the road.

"Being different is always hard," I said. "You know that vampire that tried to use me as a human sacrifice?"

"I remember the story," Flannery said.

"His friend was a necromancer, too. They approached me initially to combine our powers and help heal the vampire."

"Ah, well, I'm sorry for that, but I assure you that I only want to do positive magic. Human sacrifice does not qualify as positive magic."

"Is that what they call it now?" Jake asked.

"Call what?" he asked him.

"Is it positive magic instead of white magic now?"

"Yes, actually that is the new, more politically correct phrase."

"I guess black magic being bad and white magic being good doesn't match the new social justice climate," I said.

"The last necromancer we dealt with felt like her magic should wither the grass as she walked," Flannery said, and that memory stole the smile from his face and made his eyes look haunted. It was the kind of look that combat gave you, or working violent crimes too long. You were haunted not by real ghosts, but by the ghosts of memory. Real ghosts were sort of boring, and not really a problem if you ignored them and didn't feed them power by paying attention to them. The ghosts of the past didn't go away because you ignored them.

"Some of the people with my psychic ability give the rest of us a bad name."

He looked startled. "You think it's a psychic ability?"

"Yeah."

"But you do magical rituals to raise the dead. If it were purely a psychic ability, there'd be no ritual needed."

I opened my mouth, closed it, and finally said, "I raised my first zombie spontaneously when I was a child. I didn't do a damn bit of ritual for it."

"Who was it?" he asked.

"What, not who. It was my dog. She came home and crawled into bed with me. I thought she was alive again, at first."

"That should make your power metaphysical, not mystical, but . . ." And it was his turn to hesitate, as if he were trying to pick his words more carefully.

"But what?" I asked.

"Maybe you are a psychic just like a natural witch, but I've never known a necromancer who didn't need magic ritual to raise the dead."

"I'm a special little snowflake," I said.

"Maybe, or maybe you're the kind of necromancer that the legends tell about."

"What legends?"

Nolan said, "Please, Blake, don't play stupid."

"Yeah, yeah, raise an army of the dead and conquer the world. Legends and myths say that witch kings and voodoo queens keep trying it, and keep failing at it."

"I saw some of the films from Colorado last year," Flannery said.

"You raised an army of the dead," Nolan said.

"Only to combat the one that the bad guy had already raised," I said.

"But you still raised all the dead for miles around the city of Boulder, Colorado," Flannery said.

I shrugged, not sure what to say.

"That is legendary magic, Blake," Flannery said.

"Do I blush and say *Aw shucks*?"

"If the land and the gentle folk like you, Blake, then that's good enough for me."

Nolan said, "Flannery is my expert on magic, so if he likes you, then that's good enough for me, too."

"When did you fight this other necromancer?" Jake asked.

"Just a few months ago. I'd never seen anything like it, until I saw the videos from Colorado and what Blake did there."

"Was she human?" Jake asked. "The necromancer, I mean."

Flannery nodded. "As far as we could tell, yes."

"You've thought of something," Nolan said.

Jake smiled and looked so friendly, so open. "Anita fought a vampire that could raise zombies just last year, and you fought a human necromancer within the same year. I just find that an interesting coincidence."

"You don't think it's a coincidence any more than we do," Nolan said.

"I don't know what you mean," Jake said.

"People hadn't seen a real necromancer in living memory, and now suddenly we've got three," Nolan said.

"We killed the one in Colorado," I said.

"We had to kill the one in—"

"Flannery!" Nolan snapped, and stopped him from saying the location.

"I'm betting it wasn't in Ireland, was it?" I asked.

"That's classified," Nolan said.

"And now we've got vampires spreading in Ireland, which your gentle friends should have helped prevent," Jake said. He looked at me and there was something in that look. Were we to blame for all of this? Had killing the Mother of All Darkness unleashed some of her power to spread through the world? Or had fear of her power kept other necromancers in check, since she had given standing orders to the Harlequin to kill all necromancers on sight?

Flannery nodded, solemn, almost sad. "Here in the countryside the land is still alive in the way it's always been, but something is wrong in Dublin. Parts of the city are losing their . . . for lack of a better word, magic."

"Do your friends know what's happening?" I asked.

"No, only that unnatural death is spreading through the city. Corpses become part of the earth here, Marshal. They do not rise and walk as the undead."

"They do now," I said.

He nodded.

"That's why you didn't want Anita to come over, because you didn't want to bring more death magic here," Edward said.

"Yes, and if she had felt like the other one that we killed elsewhere, I'd have done everything in my power to send her back on the next plane. We don't need more death here, Marshal Forrester."

"What if the only way to stop the vampires from spreading is to kill them?" I asked.

Flannery looked solemn, but said, "Whatever is happening in the city, I don't want it to spread further. If it's not stopped, then Ireland will cease to be Ireland."

"Let's start with Anita looking over the crime scene photos and forensics," Edward said.

"You really think I'm going to see something you missed?"

"You're the only one I trust to know more about the undead than I do."

"That's high praise," I said.

"I'm not a necromancer, and I'm not about to marry the head vampire of America. I also don't have another vampire at my feet in a bag who will wake up and answer questions for the police."

"Your intimate knowledge of the vampires was a point in your favor for being involved in this investigation, Marshal Blake," Flannery said.

"And a point against you," Nolan said.

"I know, I know. How can I keep being the scourge of vampirekind if I'm sleeping with the enemy?"

"Something like that," Flannery said, trying to take the sting out of it with a smile.

"Funny how so many people hate the fact that I'm . . . intimate with the monsters, but they're all willing to have me use that intimate knowledge to help their asses out of trouble." It came out a little more bitter than I'd planned, but I really was tired of it.

"I'm sorry for the hypocrisy," Flannery said.

"Me, too."

"I think my friends will like your magic, Blake. They don't share the same prejudices as humans."

"No, they have their own," Nolan said.

I expected Flannery to argue the point, but he didn't. He just let it go. Truth is truth, I guess, and the truth is everyone everywhere is prejudiced about something. Why should the Fey be any different?

48

WHERE DO YOU go to meet Fey in Dublin, Ireland? A pub, of course. Somewhere in the back of my head I was wanting to see Irish countryside, maybe a moor, or a bog, or something that didn't look like a street in most older cities. Yeah, Dublin is centuries older than our entire country, but that just meant the streets were narrower and they reminded me of parts of New York and Boston, except different. Dublin was different and not like any city I'd been in before, but it wasn't different enough to conquer all my movie, book, anthropology, and folklore dreams of Ireland. So when Flannery walked us up to a small, narrow-fronted pub, I had to fight off my disappointment. I wanted some greenery, damn it.

Nathaniel was with me, Damian still strapped to his back. Flannery had been very particular about who was invited to this little shindig. He had picked out all the people that I was metaphysically connected to, as in all my animals to call. I didn't like that he had been able to pick them out of the group so easily, but it boded well for his magic. If he hadn't been able to pick them out, I'd have thought less of his mystical abilities; sometimes there was just no satisfying me.

Edward had liked it a lot less than I had, because he and Nolan had to stay with the car. Jake and Kaazim stayed with

the car, too. The rest of my people went on to the hotel to
check us in, but they, like Edward, wanted to be nearby just in
case. I didn't argue; they were supposed to be my bodyguards,
which meant I needed to let them do their jobs until we
stepped inside the police station. Once inside there, we'd rene-
gotiate, but that was later. Right now we were inside a pub.

It was like a lot of older bars with the entryway a little
raised so that you stood exposed in the dark atmosphere, waiting for your eyes to adjust, while everyone else in the bar
could see you perfectly. I'd seen it in so many older bars that
I suspected it had a purpose other than making me feel insanely exposed. Maybe it gave anyone in the bar who wanted
to duck out the back time to run and hide? It always made me
feel like a target, but maybe that was just me.

Flannery walked down the few shallow steps as if he
owned the place. He didn't feel like a target. He led us to the
long, curving sweep of the bar, which was made of dark, well-
varnished wood that gleamed in the low light. He didn't make
us sit at the bar, thank goodness. Sitting with my back to an
entire room of strangers just didn't work for me. Flannery got
the attention of the bartender and motioned to some empty
tables farther into the room. The bartender nodded an acknowledgment and went back to serving the men at the bar. I
couldn't remember what time it was there, but they seemed
busy, even though it felt early in the day to me. Hello, jet lag.

My eyes had adjusted, so I could see the people at the tables look at us as we followed Flannery through the big open
room. Most of the tables were full, but there was a lot more
room between tables than I was used to seeing in bars back
home. They weren't trying to pack in as many customers as
possible, which seemed like bad business, but it wasn't my pub
or my area of expertise. I actually liked the more open seating
plan, but it seemed odd all the same. The looks as we passed
between the tables were a little odd, too. It wasn't the normal
way people look at a girl or even at strangers; it was almost
hostile. I tried to see our group from an outsider's perspective.
Seven tall, athletic-looking men and me. Even Flannery
moved like someone who'd had training. It's hard to explain,
but if you know what you're looking for, you can usually spot
a police officer, soldier, or just someone who is comfortable

with organized violence. Hell, sometimes you can spot people comfortable with disorganized violence. Either way, if you know what you're looking at, having this many of us in your local pub might make you unhappy. Of course, most civilians wouldn't see the potential in all of us, but the looks we were getting from the tables said that most of these men did. And it was mostly men; the waitress running food out to the tables and I seemed to be the only women in the place. In St. Louis, that would have been unusual, but it was my first trip to Dublin, so I didn't know if maybe the Irishwomen didn't like this pub. Or maybe there was something else going on and the male customers didn't want women in the way.

I had Nathaniel with me, and he had Damian still unconscious in the duffel bag on his back. If we got into a real fight, I was going to be seriously pissed that they were getting endangered. Flannery and I would have words if this went pearshaped.

In order for us to all sit down at the table, I was way too close to Nicky's shoulder, so he kindly put it across the back of my chair and part of Nathaniel's because his arm span was just that wide. Damian was still safely tucked in Nathaniel's bag at our feet, so if we had to get out fast, it was going to make it harder. We'd already discussed that Nathaniel's only job was getting Damian out safely, if we needed to move with a capital "M." We hadn't expected trouble, but planning for it was automatic.

Nicky cuddled closer to me and, I realized, closer to Nathaniel on the other side of me. He was sitting like that so I wasn't squished against his shoulders, but it was also a way of showing that we were both under his protection. For Nathaniel I liked the extra help; for me I'd have preferred to not need it, but in a normal bar, having a man show you were part of a couple with him could short-circuit a lot of misunderstandings. My ego could take being seen as under Nicky's protection if it would keep us from having trouble with Nathaniel and Damian beside us. Dev was at the end of the table, which put his back to the main door, which he hadn't liked, but he'd wanted to sit beside Nathaniel and I'd wanted him beside me, so . . . He could have made Ethan sit with his back to the door, but then Dev couldn't have held hands with either of us and he wanted to touch more than to be safe, which was one reason Dev wasn't one of my main guards when I could help it. Maybe there was more than one reason why he had fallen for Asher; he'd have made the same trade-off between public affection and safety.

I leaned over the table toward Flannery's smiling face and whispered, "Why don't the locals seem to like us very much?"

"Some of them don't like that I'm working with a unit that's supposed to help control them."

"You didn't think to mention that before you had me bring Nathaniel and Damian?"

Domino leaned in on one side of Flannery and gave a low growl. Ethan leaned in on the other side and did the same. Flannery's eyebrows went up a little bit, but he kept smiling. "We aren't in danger, Marshal Blake. They just aren't all in favor of putting together a human paramilitary group to police supernatural beings on Irish soil. Surely, you can understand their issue with it."

"Sure, so long as that issue doesn't rain all over me and mine."

Ethan and Domino leaned in a little closer to him. Domino sniffed along his face a little more noisily than was needed, but sometimes it's about the effect on the person you're trying to intimidate. I was unhappy enough with Flannery that I sort of enjoyed seeing his pulse beating faster in the side of his neck.

"Are you actually threatening me, Marshal?" Flannery wasn't smiling when he said it. I couldn't blame him, but I was pissed.

Nathaniel leaned in and spoke low. "Don't piss off the local police because you're worried about me, Anita."

"Just for future reference, Flannery, I'm seriously protective of Nathaniel."

"I understand that you and Devereux are both dating him," he said, looking at the two men holding hands, "but I didn't realize that all your men felt the same way."

"I just like being scary," Domino said.

"Peer pressure," Ethan said. "I never could resist peer pressure." He said it flat with no hint that he was kidding.

Flannery looked at him, obviously trying to figure out if he was kidding. He didn't look at Domino; I think he just believed him. Sometimes I forgot that Domino had started life working for the old-fashioned mob. He had no police record from it, or he couldn't have come on this trip, but the lack of record was probably not due to him never having done anything worth getting arrested for, rather to him just never getting caught. As he leaned into Flannery, invading the hell out of his personal space, and implying, though not stating, that he'd hurt him if he made me unhappy, Domino seemed very comfortable. Maybe I was wasting his talents on bodyguard and police work; too bad I didn't have need for a leg-breaker, and if I did, I had Nicky. Or me, for that matter. I tried to never give an order that I wasn't willing to follow personally—lead from the front and all that.

Nicky spoke low to me. "We're all picking up your anger and your worry for Nathaniel. Tone it down."

I took a deep breath and let it out slow, counting the seconds as I did it. My worry for Nathaniel was at the base of all of it. Fear so often leads to anger. I was better than this. I could do better than this, so I did my deep breathing, my slow count, and finally had to close my eyes with Nathaniel's hand still in mine, and the solidity of Nicky's arm across both our shoulders. It didn't help all that much. I had to let go of Nathaniel's hand and sit forward enough that I couldn't touch Nicky's arm, and try to find just me in the metaphysical mix. I had to find my quiet center devoid of anyone else, which was a lot harder than it sounded with them all sitting so close to me.

I opened my eyes slowly and was able to look at Flannery without that spurt of fear and anger. I felt almost nothing as I looked at him across the table. I'd told my metaphysical mentor, Marianne, that the quiet peace of meditation was similar to the quiet before I shot someone. She hadn't liked that much, but one kind of emotional calm is very like another. Sociopaths must be some of the calmest people on the planet.

Both Ethan and Domino had eased back from Flannery, giving him elbow room at the table again. "That was intense," Domino said.

"I don't normally pick up your emotions that strongly," Ethan said.

"My apologies to everyone on that side of the table," I said.

"We'll forgive you almost anything," Domino said. "It's our host you need to convince."

I looked into Flannery's brown eyes. "Do you forgive me, or am I on your shit list for letting my anger leak all over everything?"

"As the person being threatened, no, but as a practitioner of the arts, that was fascinating."

"I'll take halfway forgiven," I said. "It's probably more than I deserve after that. I really am better at control than this, normally."

"Jet lag can affect a lot of things, Blake."

"Are you worse at controlling your powers when you travel internationally?" I asked.

"Yes, but I have to convince the local Fey to cooperate with me before I'm dangerous, so it's not as large an issue for me." He glanced at the two weretigers still sitting on either side of him. "Would you have really hurt me here in the pub, in front of witnesses?"

"I'd prefer no witnesses, but if Anita said go, then yeah," Domino said.

Ethan shrugged, and said, "You seem like a nice person, but she's the boss."

A voice from behind them said, "She's a great deal more than that to you."

We looked up and an elderly woman was just standing there, only a few feet behind Ethan. I'd have sworn that she hadn't been there before, and because the room was too open and not that crowded, there was nowhere for her to have come from. If she'd been a vampire, I'd have said she'd mind-fucked us, but she so was not the walking dead. In fact, I don't know if I'd ever felt so much life. It was the way I'd felt a few times in the forest or in the mountains—those moments when you just suddenly feel how alive everything around you is, and you can almost breathe in the energy of every humming insect, flying bird, windblown tree, or silent, heated moment of sunlight.

The woman was shorter than me, a little bent forward over a cane. Her dress was long enough to touch the floor and covered in small blue flowers over a lighter blue background. A red shawl that looked soft and hand-knitted covered most of her upper body. Her skin was browned from years of being outdoors, so her face reminded me of a dark brown walnut. A cheerful, smiling walnut with eyes that were a rich blue and seemed to belong to a much younger face. She leaned heavily on the dark wood of her cane as she moved smoothly toward us, with only the slightest hint of a limp. It was obvious that whatever had caused her to need the cane had happened long ago since she used the cane so expertly.

Flannery got up, smiling, and went to meet her partway. "Auntie Nim," he said, and kissed her on her cheek. She laughed when he kissed her, and for just a moment, I thought I heard birdsong.

Flannery's auntie Nim made me want to smile, but I didn't know why, which made me suspicious and not want to smile at all. He offered her his arm, which she took with more bubbling laughter. It made me think of a burbling stream in some pristine forest with birds singing, so why didn't I just give in to the good feelings and enjoy them? It was me and I was wearing a badge. I was on the clock to try to save lives in Dublin. I'd give in to euphoric magic and happy little old ladies after we'd accomplished something. Besides, it was magic that I didn't understand, but it seemed like it was trying to cloud my mind, and that wasn't cool.

Domino and Ethan were watching her come this way, and they seemed to be fighting not to smile.

"It's okay, Anita," Dev said.

"How do you know that?" I asked.

He smiled. "I'm not just here because I'm pretty."

"What?" I asked, because the comment made no sense to me.

He reached his free hand across the table to me. I didn't want to compromise my gun hand in a strange bar in an alien city with known magic walking this way. Did I think I'd need to shoot our way out? No, but . . . holding hands with both hands right that moment would make me feel less relaxed, not more.

I shook my head.

"Does he mean so little to you, Anita Blake?" the woman asked as Flannery pulled a chair out for her and helped her settle herself with the shawl and long skirt.

"It's not that," I said.

Flannery made Ethan move a chair down so he could sit beside his aunt, which put her closest to Nicky on the other side. If he was fazed by our new tablemate it didn't show, not even in so much as a twitch of the arm he had across our shoulders.

Auntie Nim smiled at us, and it was as if the sun had come out from behind the ever-present clouds. I felt like a flower that had to turn toward her. It was as if the air in the pub was suddenly fresher and easier to breathe. Her eyes, which were like the rich blue of autumn skies or like cornflowers, were startling in the dark brown of her face. Had they been that color a moment before? Surely I'd have noticed eyes that blue even from a distance? I couldn't remember.

Dev stood up and moved around behind Nathaniel and me. His hand was incredibly warm against the side of my face. I started to ask him to sit back down, because no matter how good it felt, it seemed inappropriate for a business meeting, but then he touched Nathaniel's face, too. It was like Dev's touch was a key inserting itself in the lock of us. He turned that key with the near fever heat of his skin against ours, and suddenly things looked different.

Now Auntie Nim's eyes weren't the blue of sky and flowers, but gray like clouds and rain. Her face stayed the same, as if the lines of age in her face and the weathered tan of her skin didn't bother her enough to use illusion to change it. I liked that, or she didn't have enough magic to hide that part of her appearance, but I hoped it was the first, and not the second. She seemed tireder, and less bursting with sunlight and birdsong.

"What are you doing, Devereux?" Flannery asked.

Dev leaned in and whispered to us both, "Remember, you have magic, too."

With him touching me, I could remember that, and I could feel more of Nathaniel through our entwined hands. It was as if something about her magic had dampened our own. Why would it work like that? I didn't know how to ask Flannery without giving away that it had, and if it was accidental, I didn't want to give his aunt any ideas.

I looked at Domino and Ethan on the other side of the

table, trying to judge how much they were being affected by Auntie Nim without Dev to protect them with his touch. I could have just asked, but that seemed like giving away too much, so I dropped just a tiny bit of my shields, which kept them from invading too far inside me. With Dev touching me, I could feel that I kept the walls between myself and the two men across the table higher and thicker than with Nathaniel or even Dev. I wasn't sure what it was about being hooked up to our Devil that made me suddenly aware of how differently I shielded with them, but it was there like a thought, or maybe knowledge, that I hadn't wanted to really understand before. I filed it away for later, because right now we had other problems. Yeah, I was aware that was how I ran a lot of my life, one emergency to another, so I didn't have to dig too deep at other issues. My therapist and I were working on it.

Domino and Ethan both startled as if I'd touched them for real and they hadn't known I was behind them. Domino shook his head as if he was trying to clear his ears after a loud noise. Ethan shivered from the top of his head down the rest of his body that I could see above the table. They glanced at me in turns, and then went back to paying attention to the possible threat in front of us all.

Auntie Nim narrowed her eyes at us. I didn't feel like a flower with the sun overhead now, not unless the flower was trapped in an ice field and the weak winter sun was too far away. She didn't like that we'd seen through her illusions.

"You missed this one, nephew," she said in a voice that was as cold as her attitude and didn't hold a single note of birdsong in it.

"I told you what he was, what they all were."

"You said he was a tiger in man form, and golden, but you did not tell me he was a witch."

"I've been called a lot of things, but never a witch," Dev said, trying for light and cheery in the face of her disapproval.

"Dev . . . Devereux isn't a witch," I said.

"If you believe that, then you do not know his worth, Anita."

"Maybe we're defining the term witch differently," I said.

"What do you see when you look at me, Devereux?" Nim said.

"What there is to see," Dev said with a smile, but his hands stroked against our faces. It was a reassuring gesture; I just wasn't sure if he was reassuring himself, us, or both.

I raised my hand up to touch his hand where he cupped my cheek. It looked loving and gentle, and it was, but what I said next was neither of those things. "What does it matter what he sees or doesn't see? I thought we were here to discuss your vampire problem and why the metaphysics in Dublin have changed after a thousand years."

She sat up a little straighter, using her cane to push herself forward. She was wearing black lace gloves on her hands, so I couldn't see if her hands matched her face. I'd never seen anyone wear gloves like those outside of a historical drama. "What do you mean, my vampire problem, Anita?"

"I meant Dublin's vampire problem. Since you live here, it's sort of your problem, too, right?"

Was it my imagination or did she relax when I said it that way? What was it about what I'd said first that had bothered her so much? I made a mental note to ask the men later if they could figure it out, because it had bothered her. I just had no idea why.

"I was a part of this place before the humans named it Black Pool."

Flannery added, "That's basically what Dublin means, Black Pool."

"Then do you know why vampires are suddenly rising in such numbers here?"

She put both hands on the head of her cane, flexing them around the well-worn wood of it. Her gray eyes darkened to a dark charcoal gray like the sky before a rainstorm. "Death magic."

"It was one reason that we didn't want another necromancer here," Flannery said.

"So you think that a necromancer is behind your vampires?" I asked.

Auntie Nim turned those storm-colored eyes to me. It made me sit back a little and involuntarily clutch Nathaniel's hand harder and press Dev's hand tighter against my face. He responded by rubbing along the line of my jaw, which felt great, but also felt a little too touchy-feely for a meeting that had anything remotely police oriented about it. I still didn't make him stop touching me; there was something about it that helped keep my head clear.

"If it is not true necromancy, then it is a type of vampire we have never seen. It is as if whoever is behind all our troubles is drinking far more than mere blood. It is drinking the life, the magic, from the very earth of Dublin." Auntie Nim's face was grim, her eyes full of a fierceness that would probably have been hidden behind sunshine and birdsong if Dev hadn't been touching us. She didn't look like your favorite grandma now. She looked predatory, like something that would hurt you. The charcoal gray of her eyes was almost black with anger, or fear, or some emotion I couldn't understand.

"I'm a necromancer and I'm pretty up close and personal with the vampires, but I don't know any of them that could do what you're describing," I said.

"The vampire that was mistress of Ireland before she lost control can feed upon fear," Nim said.

I nodded. "Yeah, I've met other vampires that could do it, but no one as good as she was once."

"Do you know for certain that she lost power? Why couldn't she be the one behind all these new vampires?" Nathaniel asked.

It was a little odd for him to be asking the crime-busting questions, but they were good questions, so I just waited for some good answers to match them.

"Moroven was never a necromancer. It is not her magic."

"Did you know her before she became a vampire?" I asked.

"I did, and she was never a necromancer, a fearful thing in her way, but she never possessed power over the dead."

"What made her fearful in her way?"

"You know she is a night hag who can feed upon fear."

"Yes, but that's a power she gained after she became a vampire."

"No, she was always able to feed on nightmares and terror."

"Really?" I said. "I've never met a person who could do that unless it was a talent they acquired after they became a master vampire."

"Is night hag what you call those once human who can feed on fear in vampire form?"

"Yes."

"Then she is more than that and we must add new words to her power. She can cause terror in others so that she may feed upon it."

"Damian has memories of her doing terrible things," Nathaniel said. "Anyone would be afraid after that."

The old woman shook her head. "No, Graison, I do not mean she frightened people with torture and then fed upon their emotion. I mean she could cause fear in someone with a touch, or less, and feed upon that."

"You're saying that the fear she was able to cause in Damian wasn't just from his memories of her?"

"I am saying that she was a *mara*, a nightmare, able to create fear so she could feast upon it."

"Wait. You mean she could feed on people in their dreams, not just when they were awake?"

"She began as something that fed on bad dreams, took them away from the sleepers, helped take away their night terrors, but over the long years, she turned her gift into something less gentle. If there were not enough nightmares to feed upon, she would enter people's sleep and give them bad dreams so she could feed."

"Are you saying she was supposed to be a sort of dream keeper and help people have fewer nightmares?" I asked.

"In the beginning."

Flannery added, "The authorities here have seen a few night hags over the years: people who fed on bad dreams, but the more they fed, the worse the dreams got and they drained the person's life away through the nightmares."

"You have people in Ireland that are that good at feeding through dreams?" I asked.

"It's common enough here to be classed as a psychic ability."

"Not magic," I said.

"No, because the ability can be stopped with modern drugs. When Auntie Nim told me that the master vampire of Ireland was a type of night hag, I went back through the files of other cases. In most of them, the people exhibiting the behavior say they aren't doing it on purpose. It's like they sleepwalk, except that they're sleepwalking through other people's dreams."

"Are you saying, that if modern antipsychotics or antidepressants can stop a person's abilities, then it gets classified as psychic, but if drugs don't work, then it's classified as magic here in Ireland?" I asked.

Flannery said, "That's one of the ways we differentiate between the two, yes. You don't do it that way in America?"

"No, we don't give meds like that to people unless they're really depressed or psychotic."

"How do you stop people who are using their abilities for evil purposes?"

"If we can prove someone has deliberately harmed another person via magic, it's an automatic prison term or death sentence."

The look on Flannery's face showed clearly what he thought of our idea of justice. "That's barbaric," he said.

"Can your night hags drain a person to death?"

"Yes, but we spot them before it gets that far."

"If they've already drained someone to death, what do you do with them? How do you keep the rest of your law-abiding citizens safe?"

"Appropriate drugs and treatment until they're no longer a danger to others."

"How many drugs do you have to give them to make them safe?" Nathaniel asked.

Flannery looked down and then back up, but he had trouble meeting Nathaniel's eyes. Maybe it was the weight of my gaze right next to his, or maybe it was just the weight of innocence in his. I'd found that Nathaniel had that almost childlike belief in what the right thing should be; it didn't mean he believed people would always do the right thing, but he had a way of making you want to live up to his better ideals.

"Go on, nephew, answer him."

Flannery looked at her, but not like he was happy with her either. "The dosage is appropriate to render them harmless to others."

"That's a way of not answering the question," I said.

"Do you honestly think that killing them is better?"

"Than drugging them into a coma, or frying a brain that works just fine until it stops working? Yeah, I think death might be preferable to that."

"Once, we were not afraid to kill when it was needed," Nim said.

Flannery frowned at his aunt. "There has been too much bloodshed over the years here. We don't need more of it."

"If you gave the night hags the choice between your drugs and a clean death, many of them would choose the latter. You know that, Flannery?" I said.

"I do not know that, and neither do you."

"You know it in your bones, nephew, or you would not be angry with us now," Auntie Nim said.

"If you knew she was a night hag, why didn't you treat her with the force of the laws you already have?" I asked.

"To our knowledge she's never killed anyone, so she doesn't come under our laws."

"Did you even know she existed?" I asked.

"Are you asking if I knew there were vampires here and didn't tell anyone?"

"I asked what I wanted to know."

"I didn't know she existed. I didn't know there were vampires here until you told the other officers. They told me, and I asked Auntie Nim. She told me the truth then."

"I didn't withhold anything from you, nephew," Auntie Nim said. "You had never asked me if there were vampires in Ireland."

"You listened to me talk for weeks about the vampires and how there are none here, but you said nothing."

"With that level of condemnation, you are lucky that you truly are my nephew, for if you were not, such criticism of our ways might leave you defenseless when you need your magic most."

"Is that a threat, Auntie Nim?"

"It is the truth, nephew."

"Does Nolan know that you're actually part Fey?" I asked.

"He does," Flannery said.

"But the rest of the team doesn't, do they?"

"Do the other Marshals you work with know all your secrets, Blake?"

Flannery and I looked at each other for a long moment and then I shook my head.

"I would ask that you keep mine," Flannery said.

"I'm honored that you trusted us with it."

"Auntie said that you needed to know. She's like most of the Fey. They'll keep a secret until they want to share it, but if she says that something needs doing, then it's usually important."

"I needed to see you, Anita, you and all your . . . men," Auntie Nim said.

I wasn't sure I liked that she'd hesitated before the last word, but I let it go. I wasn't going to push, because I wasn't sure what word she'd almost said, and I still had some secrets from Flannery and all the police that I worked with, except maybe Edward. I wasn't sure I had any secrets left from him, or anything important.

"Why was it important to see us?" I asked.

"You felt the anger when you entered our pub."

"Yeah."

"Look around you now and feel."

I thought it was an odd set of directions, but I looked around the pub and tried to sense the hostility, but it wasn't there. The people at the tables were more relaxed; a couple of them even smiled at me. I nodded and smiled back, because we were here to get information. People were more likely to do that if they liked you, or at least if they didn't dislike you. A smile could go a long way toward that.

Auntie Nim called out to one of the smiling men. He came over to our table with his hat in his hands, literally. He had dark, almost black hair, brown eyes, and skin that would tan if it was given a chance. He looked a lot like Flannery and Mort, though his hair was shoulder length, much longer than either of their hair.

"This is Slane. He may come to you with messages, or aid from me."

The man smiled again and gave a little bob of his head. His hair swung forward with it and I glimpsed something underneath all that hair. I blinked and didn't say anything, because one, I wasn't sure, and two, it wasn't any of my business to remark on someone's ears. We all had our physical imperfections. Besides, my father didn't raise me to point and say, *You have ears like a hound's.*

"It's all right," he said in a voice that was the thickest accent we'd heard yet. "Auntie Nim says trusting you we are." Or I was pretty certain that was what he said. I'd double-check with Flannery later.

Slane swept back his hair on one side and showed that his ears really were like long, silky dog ears. They were colored like a beagle's ears, brown and white, but they were longer and looked more like a coonhound's, or a shorter-eared basset hound's maybe.

"Nifty," I said.

"I don't know that word," he said.

"Cool, or nice, or interesting. They look silky," I said finally, because I was suddenly having a socially awkward moment. Slang travels badly from one country or language to another. I'd have to remember that nifty wasn't that common here; hell, it wasn't that common back home.

He smiled wider, pleased at the compliment. "They're why I wear my hat inside most times. Helps keep my hair down over them, because most women don't think they're . . . nifty."

"Their loss," I said, and seeing the puzzlement on his face, I added, "If they can't see that different is interesting and not bad, then it's their loss for letting differences keep them from getting to know you." Again I got that I was verbally digging out of the hole I'd just dug my way into with my feelings, but at least I was digging out and not in deeper.

"A lovely thought," Nim said, "but you are no more human than some of my descendants, so I would expect you to be more open-minded than most."

"Thank—"

"Don't finish that," Flannery said. "Don't say that phrase to my auntie, or to any of the older Fey. It's an insult."

"Okay, I'll try to remember that."

Nim put back her shawl enough to show off her dark auburn hair. It was almost the same color as Nathaniel's. "You look like you could be one of my get, Nathaniel Graison."

"Get? You mean descendant?" he asked.

"I do."

"I don't know much about my family. I don't know if any of them were Irish or not."

"Are you an orphan?"

"Something like that," he said. He squeezed my hand as he said it. Dev petted his face and the side of his neck more, picking up on his need for more touch. I hadn't thought that it might bother Nathaniel that he didn't know his ancestry.

"A lot of us don't know much about our families," Domino said.

"You and Mr. Flynn could pass for Fey here, with your hair and eyes, for most of us bear something that sets us apart, but your energy is not ours." Nim pointed a black-gloved finger at Nathaniel. "But that one, that one feels more like home."

"I honestly don't know if I'm Irish in any way," he said.

"Those eyes could be our mark upon you."

"You get eyes like that and I get dog ears," Slane said, smiling so that I couldn't tell if he was actually complaining or just remarking.

"I do want to find out more about my family," Nathaniel said, "but we came to find out what you know about the vampires and the magic being damaged here in Dublin."

"You don't know what's doing it, do you?" I asked.

"I hate to admit it, but I do not."

"This meeting was mostly so they could see you and feel your magic, Blake, and all of you," Flannery said.

"It's been interesting, but if you knew they couldn't help us solve the case, then wasn't this a waste of daylight?" I asked.

"Many of my people did not believe that a necromancer, especially one about to be wed to a vampire, would be someone we wanted here in Ireland," Nim said. "They did not believe you would help us. We all feared you would make things worse, but my nephew here said he would bring you to meet us if he thought your power was positive magic and not negative."

"Cousin said you were life energy, fertility, not death," Slane said.

"Well, I do my best, but I do raise the dead. I won't hide that I am a necromancer."

"I saw some of the stuff on YouTube from Colorado last year," Slane said. "You are the stuff of legends, Ms. Blake."

"I never know what to say when people use words like legend," I said.

"It is just the truth," Nim said. "Accept it and stop being embarrassed by it."

"I'll try," I said.

She smiled. "Since we can be of so little help, we will let you go so that you do not waste all your daylight, for I fear for our city once night falls again."

I nodded. "Me, too."

She got to her feet and both Slane and Flannery moved to help her up. I wasn't sure if it was a sign of respect, or if she really needed the help, but Nicky stood up as if he'd help, too, and we all stood up then, though I put Dev's hand in mine, along with Nathaniel's on the other side. My gun wasn't going to help me as much in here as whatever Dev was able to do. I'd be asking him in private exactly what he had done and how he'd known to do it, but not yet.

Auntie Nim leaned more heavily on her cane than she had before, and I realized that part of what her glamour had done was to give her that smooth gait. Now I saw how much she needed the cane. Her skirt had caught on itself, and I had a glimpse of her feet. One old-fashioned black shoe and one black hoof, split like the hoof of a goat. No wonder she needed the cane.

I watched her walk back to the table with Slane at her side. Flannery went ahead of us, leading us toward the outside door. I couldn't help looking at him harder than I had before. He looked like a normal human, but there was always something to mark us, Nim had said. For the first time I was wondering what a man was hiding under his clothes and it had absolutely nothing to do with sex.

49

FLANNERY GOT CALLED back into the pub for one more private word with his aunt, so he sent us ahead to the car. Fine with me, because that meant we could talk in private, too.

"What did you do in there, Devereux?" Nicky asked from behind us. I was holding Nathaniel's hand and Dev was holding his other one. The three of us abreast were taking up all the sidewalk and then some. The world really wasn't made for walking in threes; hell, twos were hard on some streets. We were getting some glances, which we could have avoided if I'd been in the middle of our hand-holding, but the two men were lovers, so screw it.

"What did you do that made her call you a witch?" Domino asked.

Dev laughed. "I added power and clarity to Anita and Nathaniel, that's all."

"But how did you do it?" Ethan asked.

Dev looked across at the other man. "I've been trained since birth like all of us in our clan."

"But trained to do what? I mean, what did you do today, just now, that was part of your training?" Ethan asked.

"To be whatever my master needed me to be."

"We know that," I said, "but what did you do in there?"

He looked at me, his face serious. "I was trained as if I was going to be one of the Harlequin in a lot of ways. They couldn't be the spies and executioners of all vampirekind if they couldn't keep clean of other people's psychic abilities."

"The Harlequin are either master vampires themselves or their animals to call are protected by their own masters against crap like this, but I'm your master and I was caught. How did you help break us free of the illusions?"

"Did you see through her illusions from the beginning?" Nicky asked.

"Yes," Dev said.

"How?" he asked.

Dev seemed to think about that as we walked. A light pole came up and we had to decide who was letting go of whom so we didn't walk into it. Dev let go and walked wide, dipping down into the brick-lined street, before rejoining us on the sidewalk. "Would it make sense if I said we were all raised to be a sort of living talisman?"

"I heard the sentence and all the words are English, but I still don't understand," I said.

"Jake will probably explain it better, but they used magic on us from the time we were babies. They sort of forged us into . . . talismans. All of us see through illusion and magic better than anyone but a true adept of the mystical arts. We can act as a sort of familiar to add to our masters when they perform or fight magical energies."

"All of us can act as power boosts and familiars for Anita," Nicky said.

"We can?" Ethan said.

"News to me," Domino said.

"She's done it with me, Micah, and Nathaniel, and I think with one of the vampires that's out of town now."

"Requiem," I said. "I may be able to use any undead for a power boost, or it may need to be one that's bloodbound to Jean-Claude and me."

"I didn't know that," Dev said. "That does give you more options."

"So you're almost proof against certain kinds of magic?" I said.

"Yeah. If you want details on how it was done and how it works, ask Jake and Kaazim."

"Could any of us do it with training?" Domino asked.

"I think you have to be gold tiger."

"Could I do it, then?" Ethan asked.

"You're part gold tiger, so maybe. Ask Jake, though you may need to have started from a baby. That's what they did with us."

"What if someone evil and crazy had won, like the Lover

of Death we defeated last year in Colorado? Would you have served him, too, just like you serve me?"

Dev wasted a very nice smile on me. "I don't think I was his type."

"It's a serious question," I said.

The smile slipped away until he was almost as solemn as I ever saw him. "We were raised to serve whoever killed the Mother of All Darkness and became the new King of Tigers. They trained us to serve all the vampire bloodlines, so I guess in the end, I'm supposed to say yes."

Nathaniel stopped and turned to look up into Dev's eyes. "The Lover of Death drew power from causing death by violence or disease. The only way for him to grow strong enough to rule would have been to constantly slaughter people. Would you really have helped him do that?"

"I don't think I could have done that, but I have cousins who could have and maybe would have. Literally, Jake went through us like a litter of kittens, or puppies, and periodically made us into smaller groups that concentrated on one set of skills over another. Pride, Envy, and I were in the group that was more schooled in Belle Morte's bloodline, which is one of the reasons that we were offered to Jean-Claude and you."

"Who was in the Lover of Death's box?" I asked.

"It doesn't matter, Anita. He's dead. No one has to serve him now."

"You don't want to tell me, because you're afraid I'll hold it against the ones who would have gone to him."

"I know you'll hold it against them. I can feel it just standing here with Nathaniel between us."

I sighed and let my breath out slowly. "Is it really the jet lag that's making me so emotional?"

"You need real food and a couple of hours of sleep in the hotel, and then we need to do something outside in the sunlight," Nicky said.

"Will that help me stop losing control like this?"

"Sleep will help everybody feel better."

"Why the sunlight?" Nathaniel asked.

"Because the more daylight you get in the time zone you're in, the faster you adjust to it."

"Fine. Let's get to the car and either get food or a nap," I said. "I need to feel more like myself."

"Necromancy doesn't work here the way it does anywhere else in the world, so they keep saying. Could that be affecting you?" Nathaniel asked.

I looked at him. "I don't know, maybe."

"That's an excellent point, though," Ethan said.

"We still don't know if my necromancy will work at all here."

"We can't find out until full dark," Nicky said.

"And by then we'll be ass deep in newly risen vampires," I said.

"Yeah."

"You should try to raise a zombie while you're here in Dublin, just in case," Nathaniel said.

"In case of what?" I asked.

"To see if you can raise the other kind of undead to help us."

"You mean use zombies to help us fight the new vampires?" I asked.

"Why not?"

"If Ireland doesn't know what to do with vampires, they sure as hell aren't going to know what to do with zombies."

"They go back in their graves," he said.

"If I can raise them at all."

"I just think it would be a good idea to find out just how much necromancy works in Ireland."

"We are not going to have a zombie-versus-vampire war through the streets of Dublin, Nathaniel."

"I'm not saying it's a good idea. I'm just saying that it's good to know what our resources are, that's all."

"You mean like extra weapons," Nicky said.

"Yes."

"I like it," Nicky said.

"Well, I don't," I said. "I don't raise zombies without a good reason, and just seeing if I can do it isn't good enough."

"Nap, food, and sunshine, and then we'll see how you're feeling," Nicky said.

"I am not going to raise a zombie in Ireland just to see if I can do it."

"It's hours until dark, Anita. We'll revisit the topic later."

"No, we won't," I said very firmly.

Nicky leaned in and whispered, "You want to know if you can raise the dead here. You want to know if you can be the first necromancer to ever raise the dead in Ireland. I can feel what you want, Anita."

What could I say to that? I didn't want to raise the dead there, and I tried to never raise zombies without a reason. I'd raised them to answer historical questions, to tell which will was the real one, or to finish giving court testimony, but to just raise one to see if I could didn't seem to qualify as a good reason, but . . . Nicky was right: There was a part of me that wanted to know if I could do what I'd been told was impossible there. Was it ego to want to see if I was really legendary enough to raise zombies in Ireland? Yes. Was I going to give in to that much ego? No. No, really, I wasn't. No raising zombies in Ireland. I'd gone there to help with the vampire problem. I wasn't going to make a second undead problem for them. Nope, not going to do it, but part of me was really wondering if I could.

50

AS WE ROUNDED the corner and were finally in sight of the car, Nathaniel jiggled my hand in his and said, "If you tell me that Ted is good at undercover work, I'll believe you, but wow."

I looked down the brick-lined street to where Edward and Nolan were waiting beside the truck, car, vehicle. Edward was leaning against it with his cream-colored cowboy hat pulled low over his face as if he were napping. He'd bent one leg so that the bottom of his black cowboy boot was against the side of the truck. He'd opened his Marshal coat enough that you could glimpse his white button-up shirt. Normally he'd have been in tactical pants and boots made for fieldwork that didn't involve horses, but except for the jacket, he looked like he'd come from central casting for a Western movie.

"He is undercover," I said. "He's pretending to be Ted Forrester, good ol' boy."

Nicky added, "He's being what most foreigners want Americans to be: cowboys. They'll see the stereotype and not look as closely at the reality of him."

Nathaniel looked from one to the other of us. "So you're saying he's hiding by not hiding?"

"Something like that," I said.

Nolan stepped out from behind the vehicle and he was all in black. He'd gotten out of his special teams battle rattle like the powers that be had strongly suggested, but he was still wearing tactical pants, boots, and a black Windbreaker, and well, he just looked so damn military. It was partially his choice of civilian clothes, but it was also the attitude. He was so on alert, while Edward looked almost asleep.

"Nolan is the same no matter what he wears," Nathaniel said.

"Ted changes like a chameleon. You just haven't seen him do it much, because he gets to be himself around me."

"Where are Jake and Kaazim?" Dev asked.

"We'll ask Ted and Nolan," I said.

When we were close enough, Ted folded himself off the car and came toward us. He was smiling his best happy-to-see-you smile. Even his blue eyes seemed a warmer shade of color, as if he believed the smile all the way up and through. The world had lost a scarily good character actor when Edward went into covert ops.

"Jacob is saving us a table at a restaurant that Nolan says will give us a good opinion of Irish cuisine."

"Sounds good," Nicky said without missing a beat. I looked from one to the other of them.

"Maybe I'll learn a new recipe we can use at home," Nathaniel said.

"Sure, but after food, Nicky says a couple of hours' nap will help me deal with the jet lag."

"You having a problem with it?" Nolan asked.

"She's crankier than normal," Dev said.

Edward laughed out loud, his head back, his whole face shining. "Crankier, and no one's bleeding or dead yet?" He laughed some more. I was beginning to think it wasn't his Ted act, but just him being genuinely amused. Nolan was starting to chuckle along.

I looked at them, my face totally deadpan, and said, "Flannery isn't with us anymore, is he?"

Nolan stopped laughing and looked at me. Edward laughed harder. The other men with me managed to look solemn. Nicky said, "It was him or us."

Edward laughed so hard, he was starting to cry as Nolan said, "Where's Flannery?"

It would have been even funnier if Flannery hadn't cleared the corner behind us just then. Nolan scowled at all of us. "That wasn't funny."

"Yeah, it was," I said.

Edward just nodded, laughing so hard, he had to lean against the car. The other men held out until Flannery came up and said, "What's so funny?" Then we all lost it.

51

WHEN EDWARD HAD finished laughing his ass off, he came over and hugged me, which he almost never did. He even apologized for laughing at me, which he did even less often. During all the unheard-of hugging and apologizing he managed to whisper, "Local informant wants to talk."

I pulled back as if everything was normal and said, "So, where is this amazing Irish food?"

He grinned, very Ted, and said, "Pub."

I gave him a look, suspecting this was the Irish version of his cowboy act. Pubs and drinking, very Irish, right? God, I hoped not, because as a teetotaler, I'd learned years ago that people are far less interesting drunk than they think they are, and they don't have nearly as good a time as they remember. I drank occasionally for Jean-Claude, because he could taste solid food, wine, and liquor through me. It was one of the common benefits of having a human servant: You could taste food that you hadn't tasted in centuries. I'd never be the wine snob that he was, but I was learning to appreciate a few vintages.

The pub was full of dark wood just like the last one, but this one had more tables placed closer together so it was more like those back home. It seemed the owner of the place planned on making money from all the crowded tables. It was so crowded in fact that if Jake and Kaazim hadn't already been there holding tables in the corner, we'd have never gotten seats together and maybe not at all.

Normally I wouldn't have liked the level of noise and crowd, but today it was a nice change from the strangely empty pub where Flannery had taken us. This one felt like a real business; the other one had felt like a front where you did things that didn't really have to do with drinking or food.

There is always that moment when you have police officers or combat vets when no one wants to sit with his back to the door, but there's usually no way to avoid it for a large party. Jake and Kaazim had gotten there first, so they had seats with a good view of the room and a solid wall at their backs. I expected them to offer me a seat beside them—I was Queen and all, or was going to be—but Jake stood up and did the air-kiss thing as a greeting, which he'd never, ever done, but he used it to whisper, "You need to sit where you can get up easily."

I was already tired of the whole clandestine thing, but I nodded, smiled and went along with it. I ended up sitting at the end of the table with my back to part of the room, but at least I could see the main door from the corner of my eye, and the bar with the door to the kitchen area was straight in front of me. Nathaniel sat by me, but at the corner of the table so his back was to the main door. He was used to sitting that way most of the time when we went out with enough of the guards. Damian was tucked under the table at our feet again. Dev didn't fight that his back was to the door here any more than he had at the last pub, because he could hold Nathaniel's hand. But he looked at the mirror above our table and I realized he could see the whole room in it, including the door. I tried to remember if there had been a mirror in the last place, but if there'd been one, it had been too small for me to notice. Ethan drew the short straw and had to sit beside Dev, but he was using the mirror, too. Really, there were no terrible seats here. Jake and Kaazim had done well. Edward sat beside Kaazim so he'd be closer to our conversation, with Nicky and Domino beside him. Nolan and Flannery were actually on the other end, opposite me. I thought at first their seats were bad because they had their backs to the bar and kitchen entrance, but there was another large mirror on the wall in front of them. Either through reflections or direct line of sight, we all had pretty good seats.

The waitress got our drink orders. I asked for a Coke and a glass of water, because apparently hydration helped with jet lag, so part of my problem was I hadn't had enough water, or so Edward told me. At Nolan's suggestion, most of us ordered the Guinness beef stew. Most of the men ordered either Guinness to go with the stew or another local beer or ale. Nathaniel was the only one who got just water; even Edward indulged in a local stout that Flannery recommended.

The waitress set a couple small, useless napkins down in front of me before she set my water on one, but she hesitated before putting the Coke on the other napkin, and I realized there was writing on the napkin. In neat block letters, the message read, "Ladies' room, five minutes."

I fought not to look up at the waitress in any way that wasn't perfectly normal. She had medium brown hair pulled back in a loose ponytail, dark brown eyes, and a pale face, so either she needed just a little makeup or she was pale for other reasons. Was she going to be meeting me in the bathroom? Was she the informant? Was she scared? Was that why she was pale?

Nathaniel and Dev both noticed the napkin. Jake probably did, too, but he didn't show it. I tried to act as normal as Jake and Kaazim, but I knew I failed. I wasn't sure I was even as smooth as Nathaniel. Dev was strangely good at it, too.

The waitress set the drink down on the napkin, and the moisture began to smear the writing almost immediately. She didn't look at me again, just handed out the other drinks. I checked my watch for the time and started keeping track of it. Was I supposed to go alone, or were there other people getting messages with their drinks? I was bad at undercover work for more than one reason. It made me antsy and gave me a huge urge to poke at things.

Edward got up first, though he had to make people move for him to get out. He didn't announce he was going to the bathroom, but it seemed logical. If I'd had Magda or Fortune with me, we could have done the girl thing of never going to the bathroom alone and I'd have had bodyguards with me, but being the only girl made it sort of awkward. Flannery got up next.

At four minutes, I made my apologies and got up from the table to meet our mystery woman. Dev started to rise, but Nicky beat him to it. He followed at my back like a shadow with no apologies that he was doing anything but guarding me. So much for clandestine.

The bathrooms were in a narrow hallway of their own that had another exit at the end of it. Nicky and I started to have a discussion on him checking the room first, but the door opened enough that Edward was able to motion us both inside. Flannery was already leaning against the sinks, looking unhappy. Once the door closed behind us, he let me know why he was unhappy.

"You cannot trust them, Forrester. It's why they weren't at the other meeting."

"If they are her animals to call, then they should know more about the local vampires than anyone we've interviewed so far," Edward said.

"Who are we talking about?" I asked.

"The local Selkies."

"Roanes for Ireland," Flannery said.

"Roanes, Selkies, whatever—who are they?" Nicky asked.

"Seal people," I said.

"You mean wereseals?" he asked.

"No, they're more like the clan tigers, born seals, not made by an attack," I said.

"They are also the animals tied to the vampire master of Ireland," Flannery said. "They may give us information, or they may spy for her. Until we know for certain that she isn't behind the vampires spreading through Dublin, we have to treat her as our major suspect for the mastermind behind all of it."

"Why are you suddenly so reluctant to talk to another supernatural being?" I asked.

"Because Auntie Nim warned me that the Roane are so terrified of their mistress, they will do anything she commands. If they fail her, she tortures or kills them. If that was the price for disobeying her, then they cannot be trusted, Blake."

"Or maybe that gives them the best reason to be trustworthy," I said.

There was a soft knock at the door, and our brown-haired waitress stuck her head in, as if checking that we were all there. She looked even paler than she had before; she was scared. Was she a seal maiden like in the old stories? The next person through the door was a man. He was only a little taller than me, about Mort's height, but he was more obviously muscled, as if he'd bulk up if he tried harder. His hair was black, straight, and long enough that he ran a hand through it to tuck it behind his ears. He had large, dark eyes so truly black that the color of his iris made it impossible to tell that he even had a pupil in the middle of that perfect liquid blackness. The eyes dominated his face the way that Nathaniel's could, and he was almost as fair of face as my fiancé.

"My girl has put a closed sign outside the door, so we won't be disturbed, but we still must be quick." His voice held an accent that I hadn't heard before, smoother or heavier. I wanted to hear him say something else, just so I could hear the cadence of it.

Edward made the introductions. "Riley, this is Anita Blake, Nicky Murdock, and you know Flannery, I think."

"Not personally, but of him. Tell your aunt that we have nothing to do with this plague of the dead here in Dublin."

"You as in your people, or you as in your master?" Flannery asked.

"I speak for myself and no one else, but my people are not involved. I do not believe our mistress has done this, but I stay as far away from her as allowed. I am not part of her inner circle, but one of many of us who work here and other cities to bring in money for our people and for her. Other than some rents from properties she brings in nothing, like some great bloodsucking parasite."

"If neither you nor the Wicked Bitch of Ireland is behind the vampires in Dublin, then who is?" I asked.

"I don't know."

I frowned at him.

Edward saved me from asking, "Then why so much secrecy if you don't know anything?"

"I knew that you were Anita Blake's partner in the United States Marshal program. It's her that I wanted to meet."

"Why?" Edward said, and there was almost no happy Ted in that one word, just cold suspicion.

"We hear that Jean-Claude is fair and just, that he's forcing the vampires to treat their animals with fairness. We also hear good things about Micah Callahan and the Coalition he runs. We need help."

"What kind of help?" I asked.

"Our mistress has always been harsh, but lately she seems to have grown both in power and in cruelty. She is punishing us as never before. I fear—we all fear—what she will do next."

"Is she breaking the law?"

"Human law, yes. Vampire law that says we are her animals to use and abuse as she sees fit, no."

"That second part isn't as true as it was," I said.

"Can we appeal to Jean-Claude or Callahan for help?"

"The Coalition mostly handles disputes between animal groups, not vampires and the groups."

"Then as the new King, can Jean-Claude intercede for us with our mistress, before she destroys us as a people?"

"Is it that bad?"

"We are told you brought Damian back to Ireland with you. Is that true?"

"And if it is, what of it?" Nicky said.

Riley looked at the big man, but he wasn't afraid of him. "Ask him what she is capable of, and tell him when he wakes for the night that she has grown worse. She tortures those we love so she can feed on both their terror and ours for them. Those of us allowed to go out for work can never take all our families with us, so she has a hostage in case we try to leave her territory. We all know what will happen to those left behind if we try to escape, but many of us want to leave her."

"I can talk to Jean-Claude, but I can't promise anything," I said.

He started to take my hand, but Nicky got in the way so Riley had to just drop his hands to his side and plead just with his eyes. They were good at being sad, those eyes. "Tell him we would do anything to be free of her."

"Anything is a big offer," I said. "Do you understand what it could mean?"

"I know that we will never be truly safe until she's dead, truly dead."

"I'm not an assassin, Mr. Riley."

"I know you kill vampires in America."

"When I have a legal order of execution on a vampire who's killed people, yes."

"She's killed hundreds over the centuries."

"I can't convict her for centuries-old crimes. No one can," I said.

"She is hurting, torturing, maiming people here and now, in this time."

"If you can prove that, then the Irish police may be able to help you."

"If she finds out that I spoke against her to you, she will kill me or have me killed. You'll never find the body either, for the sea does not give up its dead."

"What do you want me to do for you, Mr. Riley? What can I do for you that's worth that risk?"

"There is a new vampire ruler for the first time in thousands of years. He seems to believe in equality for all preternatural beings. I ask—no, I beg—for his aid against the abusive monster that creates and feeds upon my people."

"I'll talk to him, but the original deal with the European vampires was that Jean-Claude just rules America."

"Maybe that's why she's gotten worse: She doesn't think anyone can touch her now." He shuddered, pulling his coat a little tighter around himself.

"You could probably have gotten the same response in an email to him or Micah," I said.

He looked at me then, with sorrow in his face. It was the

kind of look you see on the news when people stagger out of natural disasters or war zones. "Some things you can't put in an email," he said, and raised his shirt. His stomach was covered in scars. I'd seen worse, but not many.

Flannery made a sharp hiss between his teeth before he could stop himself. Edward showed nothing. Nicky was very still beside me. What did you say in the face of torture like that?

"She did this to me, because I was too afraid of her to want to bed her. She started cutting me and told me if I didn't find my desire that she'd cut lower and make certain I never desired anyone ever again. Somehow I found a way to . . . do what she demanded." He slid his shirt back in place, covering up the wounds.

"Evil bitch," Nicky said low and with feeling. It had to hit some of the issues from his own abuse.

"She is that," Riley said.

"You're proof, Riley," Flannery said. "Come to the police station. I'll help you fill out a complaint."

"My mother and sister are still back there with the evil bitch. I can't go to the police unless I can free my family first."

"We can't arrest her without a charge."

"And you can't rescue my family before you arrest her, I know. Don't you think we've thought about going to the human police before?"

"If your family is being held against their will, then that's kidnapping or something, right?" I asked.

"Yes," Flannery said; his whole attitude had changed once he saw the scars.

"She is inside a fortress that has stood for centuries. You cannot rescue all her hostages before you enter her den, and she will kill them."

"I'll find out what we can do," Flannery said.

"No, you must give me your word of honor that you will not tell the other officers."

"You've reported a crime to me, to all of us, and we all have badges."

"I did not come to you as U.S. Marshals and Irish Garda. I came to you as a Fairy Doctor, a vampire queen, and Death, because that is what the vampires call you, Marshal Forrester. If I wanted to sign the death warrant for my mother and sister, I would have walked into a Dublin police station years ago."

Riley finally got Flannery's word of honor that he wouldn't tell any other officers or Gardai but only other Fey. If they could help the Roane, then the Roane would take the help. "I have been too long. I must go," he said, and he left with our cell phone numbers memorized, but he wouldn't give us a number at which to contact him. He was too afraid that his phone could be taken and my name would be found in the contacts list.

The waitress shooed the men out and finally me, and started mopping the floor, because that was the story she'd told her boss: Someone had made such a mess, she had to mop the floor. She didn't want to talk to us anymore, so we went back to the table. The food was waiting for us. The stew was amazing, served with dark, sweet bread. I had three glasses of water, along with two Cokes, so I was hydrated and caffeinated. Life was good.

Edward dropped us all at the hotel to meet up with the others, because we all needed to catch a couple of hours of sleep while we could. "The local police have gotten cold feet about you again, Anita. They seem to think if they let you see all their evidence, you'll use it to go off and start killing vampires."

"Why are they more afraid of my level of violence than yours?" I asked.

"You have a higher kill count."

I leaned in and whispered, "Only legal kills."

He smiled and then chuckled. He'd always be ahead of me if we counted illegal kills, but that wasn't something to share with the Irish cops.

"Are you saying they may not let me help tonight?"

"Get some sleep, Anita."

"Damn it . . . Ted."

"By the time you've had a nap, your fiancé may be awake for a phone call."

"Yeah, I'll be talking to Jean-Claude."

He watched Nathaniel and Dev walk past with some of the

luggage. The other guard who had checked us in had just dumped the luggage in one room to be sorted later. "And, Anita, actually sleep."

"I'm finally exhausted from the time change. Trust me, I'll sleep."

Nicky went past with more luggage. "Dev is making noises about wanting to bunk with you and Nathaniel for today. I think you'll sleep better if I'm the one with you and Nathaniel."

"I'll agree with that," Edward said, smiling.

I frowned at both of them. "I plan on sleeping, nothing else, for the next couple of hours."

"Scout's honor?" Edward asked.

"Yes!"

"Can you give the Scout's honor if you've never been a Boy Scout?" Nicky asked.

"Enough, let's go to bed and sleep."

In the end it was Dev who bunked with us, because Nathaniel voted that way. We really did sleep, but we put Nathaniel in the middle of Dev and me; that wouldn't have worked if it had been Nicky. We got Damian out of his bag, and he fell into our arms with the limp, heavy roll of a dead body. The new technology could say that vampires' brain activity didn't go down to true dead like that of a corpse, but when you were holding them in your arms they felt dead. Maybe if I hadn't had a job where I saw so many people die, it wouldn't have haunted me so much when it was someone I cared for and it was only temporary for the day. We put Damian into the closet for extra sunlight safety. We had to balance him right and keep shoving in arms and legs to keep him from getting caught in the door. It didn't feel like we were tucking our lover in for the night or the day; it felt like we were hiding a body that we didn't want the maid to find.

I cuddled down on the far side of the bed with Nathaniel tucked in at my back, one arm holding me tight to the front of his body like I was his favorite comfort object. His naked body touched as much of mine as possible like we always slept when we were next to each other. Dev's arm came across Nathaniel so that he cupped his bigger hand around my body, tracing Nathaniel's arm so that they both held me as we began to drift off to sleep.

I dreamed about Riley the Roane, though I kept calling him a Selkie in the dream. It was the word I was more familiar with, but he kept correcting me as we walked down one of the streets of Dublin with the tight, neat brick sidewalks and the rougher stones of the road itself. We were walking in the middle of the road at one point; cars had to stop so they wouldn't hit us. I kept saying, "We need to get out of the street or we'll get hit."

"It doesn't matter," he said, and held out his hand to me. I took his hand and the dream changed. We were someplace dark, and he was chained with manacles at his wrists. Even in the dream, I realized they were manacles, not cuffs, because there was no lock, just that metal piece that slipped in and twisted to the side. If you could reach it, you could free yourself, but Riley couldn't.

There was a beam of sunlight coming from somewhere above us like a natural spotlight that showed his face and upper body. The light was bright enough that I could finally see a clear line between his pupils and the black irises of his eyes. He blinked those large, beautiful and strangely inhuman eyes at me. They were human eyes, but the color echoed his seal, and the dream changed again. I was standing beside the Irish Sea at the crime scene, except I had walked down between the narrow houses and was on the rocky shore. The sea was gray and whitecapped, the air cold and smelling of rain and storm. There were seals in the water, riding like surfers waiting for that perfect wave. They looked at me with huge black eyes. I'd always thought that seals were cute, but when one of them looked up at me through the water, it looked like a drowning victim, dead in the water but moving, still looking at me with huge dead eyes. I stared through the cold water into those dead eyes with the wind whipping my hair across my face as the rain started to fall in cold, wet drops. The wind picked up the water, and suddenly I couldn't tell if it was rain or seawater that was drenching me.

The sea was empty except for the storm. Where had the seals gone? And I was back looking down at Riley chained to the floor of that cave with its beam of sunlight that should have been cheerful but wasn't. There was a hand with a long, thin, slightly curved blade cutting through his clothes and baring the pale skin of his untouched stomach. I thought, *That's not right. Where are the scars?* Then it was like a video that kept jumping from one scene to another—scars, untouched skin, scars, untouched skin. The blade sliced that flawless skin, bright red blood following the line of the blade like a red-ink pen drawing lines across his skin, except it was the "paper" that held the ink, not the "pen." The crimson ink began to spill out of the lines that she carved in his skin, trickling and chasing down his skin while he told her that she was beautiful, that he wanted her, wanted her so much!

She cut his clothes off him until his body lay pale and strangely beautiful against the dark rock with that splash of sunlight. The cuts on his stomach looked like lines leaking bright red ink to spill down the sides of his body and onto the floor. She caressed his body where he lay limp and small, too afraid and in too much pain to hide that he didn't want her, that he didn't want anyone like this. The video jumped again. His body was covered in old scars, but this time the knife moved down lower; this time she would not stop.

I tried to scream, *No, don't!* But it was my hand holding the knife covered in his blood. Nathaniel's screams woke me.

52

I WASN'T THE only one who had heard Nathaniel's screams, because Nicky damn near took the door off, before Dev could open it. All the guards tried to be in the room at the same time, but it wasn't big enough. We finally had to decide who to kick out and who to keep. Nathaniel and I had had a version of the same dream, except that where my dream had switched between Riley scarred and Riley getting the wounds the first time, Nathaniel's had switched between Riley getting cut up and Nathaniel being the one chained and tortured. There was another knock, and it took us a second to realize the knock came from the closet door. Dev opened the closet door and Damian half fell out into his arms. I thought at first that Damian had shared our nightmare, but he hadn't dreamed anything. He'd been dead to the world until something about Nathaniel and me freaking out had woken him early.

"I woke in the dark and I didn't know where I was, but I could feel Nathaniel's fear and yours, and . . ." He reached out to us through the crowd of too many bodies in too small a space. Nathaniel went to that outstretched hand, and the moment they touched, I couldn't taste my pulse on my tongue anymore. Even letting Nicky hold me with all that strength hadn't calmed me this much, so I pushed away from him and went for them. I took Damian's other hand and was calmer yet, but when Nathaniel's other hand was in mine so I was touching both of them at the same time, I was almost eerily calm. It was like on the plane flying to Ireland, calm beyond all reason.

"How do they do that for you?" Dev asked.

Nathaniel turned to him. "I can help Damian do this, but I couldn't help us with Flannery's aunt and her mind games."

"We all have our talents," I said, my voice calm, because with the two men holding me, I was about as calm as I got outside of special circumstances.

"But mine never seem to be exactly what you need," Dev said.

"Your talents were exactly what I needed in the first pub with the Fey."

He smiled for me, but not like he believed it. Normally I'd have tried to figure out how to make him feel better, but confusing relationship issues would have to wait. "Riley said that she would kill his sister and mother if she found out what he'd done."

Nathaniel shook his head. "No, she's going to cut him again and this time she won't stop." Even with the three of us held in that unnatural calm, the fear of that shared nightmare thrilled through us and into Damian. He'd been dead to the world while we dreamed, but now he saw what we'd seen and felt, and it was pretty awful even secondhand.

"She'd never touched Riley when I left, but it's been five years. I guess he's old enough for her now," Damian said, his hands clutching ours so tight, it almost hurt.

"Do you know him personally?" I asked.

"I know most of the Roane around her, at least by sight."

"Do you have a phone number for Riley? We need to warn him."

"It was just a nightmare," Dev said.

"No," Damian said, "I never had a number for him. He was a teenager, eighteen or nineteen at most. His mother helps take care of the fortress, so Riley was just Isabel's son."

"Neither of you does dream magic," Kaazim said. "Could you both be panicking over a shared nightmare?"

We both shook our heads. "I wish, but no, somehow she was in our dreams, or we were in hers," I said.

Nathaniel looked at me, his eyes as pale as I'd ever seen them, lavender gray. "She knows that we saw his scars, Anita."

"Yeah, because when she showed us the nightmare, I wondered where his scars were."

"I wondered the same thing, Anita. It was like we were remembering him from today, but it was mixed up with her memory of hurting him."

I nodded. "Yes."

"We have to warn him," Nathaniel said.

"How? He has our phone numbers, but we don't have his."

"Flannery's aunt might know how to contact him," Dev said.

"Do you have a number for his mother?" I asked Damian.

"No, there's no phone at the castle, and She-Who-Made-Me doesn't like cell phones. She doesn't like most of the new technology."

I realized that I was still nude, so were Nathaniel and Dev, but their nudity didn't bother me. I squeezed Damian's and Nathaniel's hands once more for luck and let go so I could start getting dressed. The calmness that had been keeping my emotions in check faded when I stopped touching them. I'd known it would, but it was still a shock to taste my pulse in my throat again. It was as if the calmness had stopped the panic but not helped me process it. Just one minute calm, and the next I was back to having woken from a gruesome nightmare. The calm that the three of us shared didn't allow us to skip the bad stuff; it merely delayed us having to deal with it.

Nathaniel clutched at Damian and reached for me again. "I love you, but we have to get dressed and find him before she does."

"Riley said that he was in Dublin for work, but that the Wicked Bitch isn't here. We'll find him," Nicky said.

"If she sends one of the other Roane into the town to call Riley home, he will have to go to her," Damian said.

"Why does he have to go?" Dev asked.

"Because his mother and his sister are both still at the castle with She-Who-Made-Me."

"She uses family members as hostages to make sure the Selkie who travel outside for work obey her," I said.

"Riley's sister can't be more than sixteen now. She was just a little girl when I left."

"This is not your fault, Damian," I said. I had underwear and a bra on, but I was struggling with the jeans. I'd picked out a pair of date jeans, not work jeans. Skinny date jeans weren't good for wearing weapons. I stripped the jeans off and started pulling clothes out of my open suitcase.

"Anita, Anita, let me help," Nathaniel said, and knelt beside me to reach into the part that was still packed and magically got out a pair of black tactical pants and a fresh T-shirt. He'd packed the suitcase, so he knew where everything was; even if I had packed it, I still wouldn't have remembered it all.

He got his own clothes out before he stood back up. I had the pants on by the time he'd chosen his outfit.

Nicky turned to Dev. "If you're coming with us, get dressed fast."

"Do I have time to just change into fresh clothes?" Damian asked.

"I don't know. Do you?" Nicky asked.

Damian stripped off his shirt in one smooth motion and went for his own suitcase.

"Why doesn't someone call Flannery and ask if his aunt Nim knows how to contact Riley?" Dev asked.

I stopped in my frantic scramble for clothes. "That was smart, but I don't have a number for him either."

"I'll call Edward," Nicky said.

"Since when do you have his cell phone?" I asked.

Nicky just smiled at me and started to punch in buttons on his phone.

Dev started getting dressed. I had everything on but my boots and weapons. He'd never be dressed in time to go with us.

Dev's voice was muffled as he pulled his shirt on over his head and asked, "Where are we going if we don't know where Riley is now?"

"Girlfriend's work," I said as I got my first gun settled on my belt.

Nicky got off the phone. "Edward is calling Nolan to contact Flannery."

"Great," I said.

Damian was dressed in fresh clothes, including a coat that I'd never seen before and a pair of nice but utilitarian-looking boots. His jeans were tucked into the boots. His crimson hair fell loose around the shoulders of the warm, weather-resistant coat so that he looked like a male model in an outdoorsy-clothes commercial. The clothes were right, but he was too pretty to actually hike in them.

Nicky waved his hand in front of my face. It startled me. "Do you have all the weapons you need?"

"Sorry. It's not like me to get that distracted in an emergency." I checked the two wrist-sheath knives with their high silver content and the big blade down my spine in its custom-made holster, which attached to the shoulder rig. It held mostly extra ammo now, and it attached to the gun belt where my main handgun sat in an inner pants holster. If I could have figured out a different way to carry the big knife, I'd have gotten rid of the custom-made shoulder holster, but it was great for extra ammo and a smaller backup gun. I put the AR-15 on its tactical sling across my body over the T-shirt and sweatshirt I was going to wear under my coat. I'd have to leave the coat unfastened to be able to get to the AR, but I couldn't open-carry, not in Ireland. Hell, back home in the States, it would have freaked people out, even with the words *U.S. Marshal* emblazoned on the back of my Windbreaker.

I was already missing my Bantam shotgun, which was back in the armory at Nolan's compound along with a few other things, but there was just no way to keep all our dangerous stuff at the hotel. They'd offer you a safe if you had expensive jewelry, but I'd never seen a hotel, no matter how nice, that offered you a secure weapon locker. It was always a problem when traveling for business.

My phone rang and it was Edward's ringtone, so I picked up. "Wait for Nolan's people to get there before you go out, Anita."

"We're big boys and girls. I don't think we need to wait for a babysitter."

"You don't have Irish credentials, and neither do I. We need someone with us who has credentials. That's part of the deal I made for all of you when you came into the country, remember?"

"I remember something vague about Nolan's people being with us when we were out in the city."

"I won't make you wait for me, but don't leave the hotel without at least one of Nolan's people with you. Promise me, Anita."

"Damn it, Edward, did Flannery have a way of contacting Riley?"

"Flannery is trying to get hold of his aunt now."

"Then we need to get to the restaurant before his girlfriend is off shift for the day."

"I know that, Anita."

"What's the worst that could happen if we get caught in Dublin without proper ID?" I asked.

"You could be deported or even jailed if you get the wrong Garda and the wrong judge."

Oh. "Okay, good point. How long until Nolan's people arrive, and where the hell are you that someone else will get to the hotel first?"

"I'm trying to convince the police that you won't start slaughtering people in the streets and you really will be useful to the investigation."

"I thought we'd settled all that before I got on the plane."

"So did I," he said, and he sounded tired and frustrated, and underneath that was anger. Eventually, if they kept pushing him, they'd get to his anger and stay there.

Nicky's phone rang. He listened and then hung up. "Donahue and Brennan are downstairs to escort us where we need to go."

"How did they get your number?"

"I told Edward to give it to whoever needed it."

"Good thinking." I looked around the room. Everyone looked dressed and ready to go. Jake, Kaazim, Ethan, and Domino were waiting out in the hallway for us. Fortune stuck her head out of her room long enough to kiss Nathaniel and me good-bye, and then she went back to sleep. She had Echo in her room still waiting for nightfall. She couldn't leave Echo unprotected, and we didn't need the whole crew for this. Magda and Socrates were still at Nolan's compound trying to make friends with the rest of his people. After what she'd done to one of their new superstrong cells, I really hoped Nolan had a plan B.

Donnie met us in the lobby, smiling. Brennan, a lot less happy, was behind her. Honestly, I was surprised to see him, but I did my best to just take it in stride. Apparently, medical had cleared him, and Nolan thought he could handle the assignment. "Forrester says you need an escort," he said.

"Actually, he said *babysitter*," Donnie said, grinning.

"I appreciate you keeping us legal," I said, and kept walking toward the door. They fell in behind and to the side of me.

"What's the emergency?" she asked.

"We may have inadvertently let the bad guy know we were contacted by a local today." Jake and Kaazim did the bodyguard thing at the door, checking for safety and holding the door for me.

"Unless you know something we don't, we don't know who the villain of the piece is yet," Brennan said.

"Let me rephrase, then: the suspected bad guy."

"Who do you suspect?" he asked.

"Where are you parked, and will it hold all of us?" I asked.

"Not far and yes," Donnie said.

"Lead us to the car."

"You do know that you don't outrank us, right?" Brennan said.

Donnie went to the left and kept walking. We followed her with Brennan keeping up, but not happy about it. "Are you deliberately ignoring my questions?" he asked.

"I'll answer them in the car on the way, Brennan, but I'd really like to find our local informant before he ends up tortured and killed."

"Tortured and killed? What are you talking about, Blake? You're here to help us with our vampire problem, not to get involved in another crime."

"I'm hoping to stop another crime from happening—if that's okay with you?" I walked past him with Nicky at my back. Brennan stopped asking questions and just caught up with Donnie. I fought the urge to start jogging down the sidewalk. We didn't need to attract that much attention yet. It was still daylight. Riley would probably be safe until nightfall. Of course, Damian was awake already, and about the time I had decided to jog, Donnie had stopped at a van. I could save the running for later.

53

WE COULDN'T FIND Riley. We couldn't find his girlfriend. It was like the harder we tried to locate them, the more lost they became. Our last hope was that Flannery's aunt would come through, but the last info from him was that Auntie Nim didn't have much to do with the Roanes, because they weren't her creatures. It was as if people refused to do business with the werewolves in St. Louis because wolf was Jean-Claude's animal to call, and their Ulfric was his *moitié bête*. I still thought it was interesting that Flannery's Fey relatives had known about the vampires in Ireland all this time, but they hadn't shared the news with him, not even after vampires had started showing up in Dublin. I actually asked him why they didn't tell him sooner. His answer: "I asked them if they knew anything about the new vampires in Dublin. I didn't ask them if there were other vampires in Ireland outside the city." Apparently the Irish Fey answered direct questions, but what you didn't ask, they didn't answer, even if logically it was connected. An important safety tip to remember if I had to question any of them on this trip.

I'd set my phone alarm to the time when Jean-Claude typically woke for the night in St. Louis, but I didn't need an alarm. I felt him wake for the night, thousands of miles away. I knew when his eyes opened for the first time to stare at the ceiling, felt the warmth of the body curled beside him, one arm flung across his stomach. I knew by the size and weight of the arm that it was Richard, because I had the only other men in his life who had that kind of size and muscle. He knew I was sitting in the back of the van with Nathaniel beside me. I saw, felt, smelled the warm darkness of his bed and Richard's body fever warm beside him. His shoulder-length hair in a wild tangle hiding the handsome face. I couldn't remember the last time Richard had slept over with any of us. Jean-Claude's voice whispered through my head, *"Ma petite,* what have you been doing while I slept?"

Just hearing him, feeling him inside me like that, felt as if I could finally take a deep breath and let go of some tension that I hadn't known I was holding. Nathaniel gripped my hand tighter. I knew he felt it, too, because we were touching when it happened. Damian reached from the seat behind me, where he'd been out of direct sunlight in the more enclosed depths of the van, but now he reached into the sunlight from the windows so he could touch my shoulder, and there was that jump of connection from him to me, to Nathaniel, and to Jean-Claude, and then Richard stirred in the bed. I knew he was awake, had a moment of seeing the darkened room through his eyes and Jean-Claude's so that it was almost dizzying. I was glad I wasn't driving when it happened. Damian squeezed my shoulder as his other hand found Nathaniel's arm, and the world steadied again. I could still see the ceiling above the temporary bed and missed the old canopy, could feel my head resting on Jean-Claude's shoulder and arm while my other arm was across his body and my only view was silk sheets and the white gleam of the vampire's body. I knew they were both nude, and the moment I thought it, I realized that I had thought it too loudly and that they'd both heard me, and suddenly there was awkwardness in the nudity that hadn't been there before.

Why? Because I hadn't just thought nude; I'd thought about the possibilities of them in the bed, wrapped in silk, naked. That was all me, and I tried to make that thought loud, too.

Richard started to get up, spilling the sheets down his chest, baring his upper body, opening up the cocoon of warmth his body had made beside Jean-Claude. Then a sense of calm washed over all of us, as in all five of us. The beginnings of unease in Richard quieted. He lay back down in the sheets, finding the warmth his body had made for him overnight. It put him back beside Jean-Claude, who lay very still, waiting for the other man to decide what he was doing. I could feel everyone more clearly in my head in that moment than Jean-Claude. He was very carefully neutral, though I could feel the tension in his body through the connection to Richard.

Nathaniel leaned back toward Damian, who leaned forward, his long hair sliding forward like a veil to cover the sides of his face from the sunlight. His hair wasn't much of a barrier, but it was better than bare skin in bare light. He'd kept the sunglasses on; they wouldn't come off until we were in a dark room or night fell. Nathaniel stroked that red hair and then rubbed his cheek along Damian's face like a cat scent-marking. Damian laughed and leaned his face against the other man's so that Nathaniel could hold him as much as the seat belts would allow.

I felt Richard's surprise at the interaction. It was a big change in Damian's comfort level about touching other men. Richard moved up higher on the pillows so that he was taller than Jean-Claude, but he didn't move away from him, just moved his arm so that it lay across his chest and not his stomach. It left Jean-Claude's arm around Richard so that they held each other, though I knew that if Jean-Claude were more certain of his welcome, he'd have held him differently.

Richard said out loud, "Relax, Jean-Claude. Just relax. Cuddle if you want to cuddle, but don't lie here feeling this tense. It's not a trap, I promise," because we'd all heard Jean-Claude's thought, because it was too loud to hide. "It's a trap, a girl trap." Girl traps aren't about genitalia; they're about that more feminine habit of saying, *Do this* or *Don't do that*, and punishing the masculine half of the couple for doing what the feminine half asked/told him to do in the first place. There are girl traps and boy stupid, but it's not always women who set the traps, and it's not always men who are stupid. We all take turns.

Jean-Claude relaxed slowly, inch by cautious inch. The way that Richard was lying across his arm, it was more comfortable and natural for him to curl his arm around the other man's back and turn a little into Richard. They were only an inch apart in height, but the way Richard had fixed himself on the bed made him seem much taller, except that I could feel where everyone's legs were, and it was an illusion. An illusion of dominance, and I had a moment to hear, feel, realize that part of the two men's problem with each other was that they were both dominant. I don't mean in a bondage-and-submission way, but just big, athletic, dominant men who were both used to winning. Jean-Claude had spent too many centuries at the mercy of other masters to be as obvious about it as Richard could be, but it was there as they lay as entwined as I'd seen them in a very long time. Who would submit? Who would bend first? Without me there to help them bridge that decision, they were stalemated. Asher helped them, too, sometimes, but if he hadn't been in the doghouse, Richard wouldn't have been there at all.

The sorrow among us all, the almost possibilities stretched among us like a light going out. Nathaniel said, "No, not this time." He kissed me, and with Jean-Claude and Richard so deep in my head and heart, it startled me, as if the bedroom in St. Louis was more real than the van and the men touching me here. It was what the three of us could have been and never were. I let myself fall into Nathaniel's kiss, fall into the total abandon of his love, his desire. He had no stop, held nothing back. It had scared the hell out of me at first, but now I realized that was why he was in my life, why he was my leopard to call, why we wore each other's rings.

The sorrow from Richard was drowning deep, like the ocean had suddenly poured over us to dampen our spirits and drown us in "what might have beens." Damian's own sorrow spilled like blood into the ocean of Richard's regrets. Nathaniel drew back from our kiss, and his eyes were solid, glowing lavender like flower petals with the summer sun behind them.

I whispered, "No."

"Yes," he said. "Say yes."

"To what?" Richard asked all the way from St. Louis.

"Happiness, just be happy," Nathaniel said, and he turned those glowing eyes to Damian.

The vampire looked at him for a long moment, and then he leaned into Nathaniel's need and they kissed. It was gentle, almost chaste, but watching them kiss from inches away thrilled through me like it always did. Two men, both my lovers, kissing right there in front of me—what was not to love?

Richard felt my body react to that kiss, and his regret swept up and over the excitement in my body and the lightness in my heart and drowned them both.

"What the hell are you doing back there?" Brennan said from the front seat beside Donnie.

Kaazim said, "We need to park and give them some privacy, or at least distance from this level of metaphysics."

"What?" Brennan asked.

"They're doing magic," Dev said.

"In the van?" Donnie asked.

"Yes," Kaazim said.

"God, Richard, just enjoy being in the moment," I said.

"You're not in the moment," he said to the air, as if I was in the room.

I would never have said so out loud, but we were too far into one another's heads, so the thought came crystal clear. "And whose fault is that?"

"Mine," he said, "yours, his." He kissed Jean-Claude on the head the way you'd kiss a child, affectionately, but it meant nothing. I didn't understand how it could mean nothing, when he was naked in bed with Jean-Claude. The possibilities for me were almost endless.

"Who's Richard?" Brennan asked.

"Park," Nicky said.

When Damian and Nathaniel pulled back from the kiss, Damian slid his sunglasses off, and the vampire's eyes were shining green fire. Green and lavender eyes turned to me aglow with power and peaceful happiness. Even here in the country where Damian had known so much pain and after the nightmare Nathaniel and I had just shared, we were still happier than Richard. We were scrambling to find someone to keep them from being victims again, and I couldn't stop the memory of Riley's scars from crossing from my mind to theirs. Once that memory crossed, everything followed in seconds; minutes later they both knew why we were searching for him, the nightmare that was half memory, just not our memory.

"Park soon," Nicky said.

Richard held Jean-Claude closer, but again it was for comfort and not for romance. "Well, that's awful," Richard said.

"*Ma petite*, if we interfere to save the Selkie and his people, it will be war between us and Ireland, for she is master of that country. She is the vampire queen of Ireland."

"She's lost control, Jean-Claude."

"And some new vampire has smelled the weakness," Richard said.

"Yes."

Damian leaned closer to my face, until the green of his eyes seemed to fill my vision. He thought about memories of her torturing the Selkie like the CliffsNotes version of horrors. Richard pushed us away from him, but he could only push so far, because he wasn't comfortable enough with himself to have all the power at his command.

"I don't want that in my head," he said out loud.

"I left them behind, Richard," Damian said out loud in the van. "I thought I was helpless to save anyone but myself, but now I know differently. I know I am not powerless or weak. I have returned with a queen and her princes at my side."

"You speak of war," Jean-Claude said.

"How can you show us all those terrible things and then expect us to agree to you risking Anita falling into her hands?" Richard asked.

"I'm not a victim, Richard, no matter what happens. That doesn't change," I said.

Donnie found a parking spot. She turned the engine off, and we were suddenly sitting in silence that was too thick, like the way the air gets heavy before a storm. Damian leaned in even closer so that all I could see was green, and whispered, "I haven't fed yet today."

My stomach was suddenly cramping with hunger. Nathaniel grabbed my arm and the back of a chair. We were suddenly starving. I saw Jean-Claude's eyes spring to life in the nearly dark bedroom, blue, as if the midnight sky had caught fire. Richard's hands convulsed as he hugged the vampire to him.

"*Ma petite*, tell me you fed the *ardeur* since arriving in Ireland."

"We took a nap for the jet lag," I said.

"We haven't fed the *ardeur* today," Nathaniel said.

"And everybody out," Domino said, opening the door. All our people got out without any other prompting; they knew the drill. If you didn't donate blood and there was a hungry vampire in a van, you got out. If you weren't into group sex in a van on the streets of a foreign city, and the *ardeur* might rise, you got out.

Brennan couldn't get out fast enough, but Donnie wanted to know what was happening. Kaazim got her out of the van and called to Jake. They were like most of the Harlequin; they only donated blood to their masters, but Jake turned to us. "Tell Jean-Claude that there is a reason that vampires treat their *moitié bêtes* as lesser, because in the end there can only be one."

"One what?" I asked.

"King." Jake said, and closed the door to the van behind him.

54

NICKY STAYED, BECAUSE he wouldn't leave me, even if that meant he had to open a vein for a new vampire. Dev stayed, because he didn't have a problem with donating blood to the right vampire. I hadn't known that Damian qualified as the right vamp for him, especially with the *ardeur* as a possibility, but strange things had already happened in the last few days, so what was one more?

"I must close the ties between us more than this, *ma petite*, or one hunger could feed into another."

"Understood," I said.

"Why is the hunger so much worse?" Richard asked.

"Jet lag can make such things worse," Jean-Claude said.

"Now you tell me," I said.

"I did not dream you would leave your hotel room without feeding Damian."

I couldn't argue that; it had been careless, even stupid.

"I will think upon what you have shown me, *ma petite*. I will talk to Pierette and Pierrot since they traveled to the Emerald Isle more than any of the other Harlequin. Perhaps they will have more insight to share."

"Have Sin help you. Pierette talked to him a lot easier than I thought she would talk to anyone."

"I will include our young prince."

Damian pulled me out of my seat and drew me back into the dimness of the rear of the van. His eyes glowed brighter without the sunlight to compete with them. Nathaniel came with us.

After pushing Richard back onto the bed, Jean-Claude stroked the thickness of his hair to one side, so he could see the strong, clean line of his neck. In the van we didn't have enough room for even two of us to kneel comfortably. Nicky helped us fold up some of the seats, as if we were making room for getting a delivery.

I, we, felt Jean-Claude's bloodlust and underneath that, or entwined with it, was another kind of lust. It was as if something about my triumvirate powering up was affecting how much feedback we got between both groups.

Richard rose and glared at the other man. "No," he said, as if we couldn't all feel exactly how negative his reaction was to Jean-Claude seeing him as a lust object.

Dev touched my arm, which made me look at him. "I need to know if it's as bad as the glimpses I'm feeling," he said as if that explained anything.

"If what is that bad?" I asked.

"Richard and Jean-Claude." He held on to my arm, and I could suddenly feel his energy like warm sunlight. It seemed to chase away the anxiety that had automatically attached to

Richard's attitude. I realized it was just that: automatic. He behaved a certain way, and I felt a certain way. Jean-Claude had similar problems with him. It was as if he'd conditioned all three of us, himself included, to function badly together. I'd always assumed that Dev being so easy to deal with meant he wasn't a deep thinker, or a deep feeler, or somehow by being easy and fun, he was less. In that moment of warm clarity, I realized that Dev was easier because he simply had fewer hang-ups than the rest of us.

Richard snarled, "Get out of our heads, Devereux!" The moment he used the last name, I realized that bit of knowledge had to have come from my memories in Ireland. I hadn't shared that specifically with Richard, which raised the question of how much had just quietly been transferred between us all without anyone knowing.

"No," Dev said, "don't you go all serious, too."

"The serious tones down the *ardeur*," I said.

"But it will need to be fed today," Nicky said, "and you need to pick the time, not get surprised by it in the middle of a police investigation."

He had a point.

"Everyone has a point, but me," Richard said, and just like that, he wasn't pretty enough to overcome his deficits. I wasn't perfect, God knew, but I tried harder than this. That thought went through everyone's head, which didn't help anything.

Dev stopped touching me, and things were a little less bright. It felt depressing, like Jean-Claude, Richard, and I were just trapped on the hamster wheel of the same damn issues we'd been working on forever. I did my best to think how much I appreciated Richard working through his issues in therapy, but underlying all of it was the pattern the three of us had set up, a pattern that didn't work.

Dev was texting someone on his phone, which made me want to grab his phone and throw it. This was not the time or place, damn it! We were having a crisis.

"*Ma petite*, you must find a way to be less loud in our heads."

"I'm sorry. I don't mean . . ."

"It's the truth, Jean-Claude. It's just the truth. No amount of therapy is going to fix the three of us," Richard said. He was sitting up in bed now, with the sheet tucked around his waist, and all that muscled beauty as useless to Jean-Claude as it was to me even though one of us was sitting right next to him and the other was half a world away.

Tired of waiting for our impromptu therapy moment, Damian had pulled Nathaniel to him. They kissed, but Nathaniel turned his face to the side and offered his neck. The fang marks on it from yesterday showed against his skin.

"Nathaniel can't donate blood today after all you took yesterday," I said.

Nathaniel's eyes sprang back to life like a lilac spark. I felt a spurt of anger from him. It reminded me of the anger he'd shown to Bobby Lee back in St. Louis. I did not want a repeat of that. Damian kissed the side of his neck just over the unhealed bite mark, and then raised his head to say, "She's right, Nathaniel. I took blood from you four times yesterday. You must rest."

"Four times?" Nicky said. "He needs red meat and lots of it."

"They both do," Damian said.

Nicky looked at him and quirked an eyebrow. "How many times?"

"Anita has two bites."

"Six times, impressive."

"It's all about blood pressure," I said, "more blood, more pressure."

"No," Nicky said, "six times is impressive for any man, dead or alive, Anita."

Dev joined in with "You get rubby spots after a while, if nothing else."

"If Anita and I can't donate, then who can?" Nathaniel asked.

Jean-Claude in my, our, head said, "Damian and I need to feed, whomever that may be with."

Richard turned and glared at him. "I am going to donate blood to you this morning."

Jean-Claude was finally angry. "I do not go where I am not wanted, and I do not beg for blood or sex."

Richard's anger flared to answer, but there was a knock on

their door. "Who is it?" Jean-Claude snapped, his voice hot with anger.

"It's Angel, Jean-Claude. I was told you might need me."

The two men on the bed exchanged a look, and then Jean-Claude said, "Who told you that?"

"My brother."

"Mephistopheles?" Jean-Claude made a question of the name.

"He's the only brother I have," she said through the door.

All of us in the van were looking at Dev. "They need someone to help them bridge their issues, and everyone else who could help is here in Ireland." He said it as if it were the most natural thing in the world to have texted his twin sister to get out of bed and show up at the door of two men she'd never slept with for morning sex and blood donation.

Jean-Claude said, "Mephistopheles, what have you done?"

"I told Anita that all the gold tigers were raised to meet the needs of the new Father of Tigers, whatever those needs might be."

From the door, Angel said, "May I come in?"

"She's your sister," Richard said, and since he had one of his own, the comment held the confusion and creep factor of it.

"Enter," Jean-Claude said.

The door to the room opened, and Angel walked in barefoot, a short black robe showing off miles of long, bare legs. She was only four inches shorter than her brother, and five-eleven was plenty tall enough to give you legs. I'd forgotten that she cut her hair so short. It was almost shaved on the sides, where it still showed the black dye, but the roots growing in at the top of her hair were yellow blond. It would take months for her natural color to grow back out. The shorter hair made her face look more square, more like Dev's face. Until she'd cut her hair, I hadn't thought they looked that much alike, but nothing made her any less feminine. She'd been the Goth girl for years, thus the hair, but the mix of hair color seemed to play to the fact that her eyes were a mix of blue and brown just like Dev's, except his was a pale blue with a line of pale tan/gold and Angel's eyes were a brighter blue with a brown that looked black from where the men watched her from the bed. The black hair helped the illusion of the eyes, which was probably one of the reasons she'd done it. The robe was open just enough to show a glimpse of breasts that moved under the silk of her robe as she strode toward the bed.

I felt Richard's reaction to her, so tight and hard that it made me gasp. It fed into Damian's blood hunger and hit the *ardeur* like an appetizer before the meal. "Shit," I said out loud.

"Lovely as always, Angel, but why are you here?" Jean-Claude asked.

"I heard that you were one girl short this morning."

"If Devereux can't hear me, Anita, tell him that brothers don't send their sisters to other men for fucking," Richard said, and he meant it, even with his body telling all of us just how much he enjoyed seeing her. Richard would stand on his principles over his desires almost every time, which was admirable but not helpful.

Angel and Dev started talking at the same time, and they were almost word for word, one in the bedroom in St. Louis and the other in the van in Dublin. "We used to go out clubbing together in our teens. We're both tall, and that makes people think you're older. We would pick out couples to see if we could seduce both of them or take turns picking out a woman or a man to take home or at least to a motel. We got so many people to do their first girl on girl, or boy on boy, or threesome."

"He's your brother," Richard said. "How could you have sex in the same room with him?"

"We were the only two bisexual people we knew," Angel said. "It was just sort of part of who we were as twins."

Richard was shaking his head.

"Until Angel decided she didn't want to be part of the grand plan to be the perfect golden tiger for the next Father of Tigers, she was my best friend. We did almost everything together. I went shopping with her so much that some of her friends thought I was gay, until they found out I wasn't." Dev grinned as he said the last. Words like *incorrigible* came to mind.

Angel went to Jean-Claude, untying her robe so that it hung open as she came to the edge of the bed. "When they first demanded I give up my life and come serve you, I was so angry, and I still resent that, but I've watched you, both of you, and I'm intrigued. I'd like a chance to find out if you're as good as you look."

Jean-Claude smiled. "A charming offer." He held his reaction in utter control, as if afraid to react even in the depths of his head, because I was there listening. I decided to help, by letting him know that I wasn't bothered by it.

"Let her be the bridge you and Richard need."

"How can you be okay with this, Anita?" Richard asked.

"I'm out of country with half a dozen lovers of my own. It would be ridiculous of me to get pissed because you have a chance to sleep with Angel." I couldn't quite hide the next thought, or maybe reaction, of my own. I was intrigued by her, too. There was that little spark of interest in her that still surprised me when it was about another woman.

Richard said, "I'm still not used to you liking women."

"Me, either," I said.

Angel smiled, and said, "Let's see how this goes. Maybe we can all play together when Anita gets home?" And that was enough to tip the balance for Richard. I think Jean-Claude was just trying to stay out of the pitfalls of the situation until Richard and I decided it for us all.

Angel then said, "Dev asked if it would be possible for you to feed some of Anita's *ardeur* needs because they're trying to find a missing person before he gets hurt."

"Are you offering to feed the *ardeur* for me?" Jean-Claude asked.

"I'd like to know for myself if it's as amazing a fuck as the stories claim," she said.

He laughed, an abrupt, pleased sound. She'd do fine.

She looked past Jean-Claude to Richard and said, "You are both very different people. If we were one-on-one, I'd approach you both very differently, so I will want a little guidance as to how to be with you both."

He looked at her for a long, serious moment and then said, "We can do that."

"*Ma petite*, I will close the links down low between us, if you will do the same on your end?" Jean-Claude asked.

"We will." And we did. I left them to their blood and sex, and they left us to ours.

55

THERE WAS A knock on the van door. I called, "Who is it?"

"It's Domino. Auntie Nim's friend Slane is here with the information we wanted."

Dev said, "You go. I'll feed Damian, if he's okay with that."

I could feel that Damian wanted to sink his fangs into Nathaniel and me more, but a lot of the heat had dissipated. I was pretty sure it was in St. Louis with Richard, Jean-Claude, and Angel. I was careful not to think too hard about that, just in case it reopened the marks too wide between us. I did not want to suddenly be in their heads in the middle of sex, or worse yet in the middle of Jean-Claude feeding the *ardeur* for both of us.

"If you let me capture you with my gaze, it won't hurt. It will just feel good," Damian said.

"I'm all for feeling good, but now that you've come to the Dark Side, I'm sure you could make it feel even better."

"Dev," I said.

He grinned at me.

"I'll stay and make sure that he behaves," Nicky said.

"I plan on being the perfect gentleman," Damian said.

"I wasn't talking about you," Nicky said.

Nathaniel and I left them to it, and got out of the van into a fresh bout of drizzling rain. Slane had his hat pulled down low against the wet; with the long hair, his puppy dog ears were completely hidden. "My mistress is impressed with the effort that you have put into searching for the missing Roane and his lady."

"I'm glad to hear that, but do you know where they are?"

"Nay, but if there comes a time when we could lend a hand to you and yours, we will."

I looked at him for a second. "That's great, but I'm a little confused. I thought you had information that would help us find the Roane and his girlfriend."

"No, but there is a Roane who has come forward. He would meet with you."

"After what happened to Riley, I'm not sure that's a good idea," I said.

"He understands the danger, but he wishes to talk to you and especially the red-haired vampire you have brought back with you."

"Why does he want to talk especially to Damian?"

"He knew the vampire before he left Ireland."

"Okay. Where do we meet him and how do we keep him from being disappeared on us like the last Roane?"

"We will use our magic to keep him hidden. Young Riley should not have tried to sneak behind his master's back without magic to hide him from her eyes."

"I understood that Nim and all of you wouldn't have anything to do with the Roane, because you didn't want to be on the Wicked Bitch's shit list."

"I'm not sure I understand what that means."

Nathaniel said, "Being on someone's shit list means they're mad at you and hold a grudge."

"Then yes, we did not want to be on the shit list."

"What changed your mind?" I asked.

"You have shamed us, and not much will do that," he said with a smile, but his eyes didn't look happy.

I wasn't sure if I was supposed to apologize for making them feel bad or celebrate that they were going to help the Selkies now. We seemed to be ahead, so I just said, "Where and when is the meeting?"

"Now and not far."

"How did you know that Damian was awake for the day? Most vampires wouldn't be."

"Our magic is fading here in Dublin, but we still have our ways."

"Is that a polite way of telling me you won't answer the question?"

He looked surprised. "I gave you an answer."

I had a moment of wanting Flannery here to do cultural translation, but just let it go. I might ask him later. Right now I'd make sure our vampire had finished his snack, and then we'd go meet the new Roane. I hoped this one had better luck afterward than Riley had.

56

THE FIRST MEETING had seemed pretty secret to me, and yet Riley and his girlfriend were both missing. This time we met in a churchyard at the edge of an ancient-looking cemetery. Compared to last time, it was out in the damn open, and that had gotten two people kidnapped. I didn't understand why we were meeting here until Damian hesitated at the edge of the stone wall. He had the hood on his coat up, his hands plunged into the pockets, sunglasses back in place. Honestly, with the hood up, there was almost none of him in the sunlight.

"I can't step on holy ground," Damian said.

I had a "duh" moment. "Crap, of course you can't. Some vampire expert I am."

He smiled. "Trust me, I won't forget that stepping on holy ground could make me burst into flames."

"Wait. I've had vampires with me in graveyards before, and they didn't burst into flame."

"This is a graveyard inside a church wall. It's potentially part of the church itself, and I can't enter a church."

Nathaniel said, "You're not sure if you can step on the grass inside the wall or not, are you?"

"No, but it's not worth the risk to me."

I hugged him and said, "Totally not worth it. You stay here, and I'll go find our mystery guest."

Slane watched us waiting on the other side of the little metal gate, and I asked him, "Why did you choose this location when you knew we had a vampire with us?"

"I did not choose it," he said, which answered and didn't answer the question all at the same time. Nathaniel stayed with Damian, along with Donnie and Brennan, at Slane's request: "Humans make some of us nervous."

It was interesting that none of the rest of us counted as human. Not bad or good, just interesting. Dev was happy to stay with Nathaniel and Damian. Nicky went where I went, but after that, everyone let Jake be senior guard and send himself and Kaazim with me, while everyone else waited outside the wall with our nervous vampire.

Slane left us waiting among the weathered tombstones, while he checked that there was no one inside the church that we'd want to avoid. I was right there waiting on the edge of the graves, and I just couldn't help myself. I lowered my shields just a little, and there was nothing. It was like standing in the middle of a meadow or a garden. There was no sense of the dead under the ground. It was just living ground. Had the bodies been moved but the grave markers left in place? That happened in the States sometimes. Hell, in St. Louis, if a company had permission to build on an old graveyard, they only had to move a spadeful of dirt from each grave and the tombstones, but weren't forced to move the actual bodies. Was that what had happened here?

Nicky leaned in and whispered, "What's wrong?"

"I can't feel the dead. I can't feel anything except the ground, which is fertile and alive."

Slane came back out of the church. "Is this the first Irish graveyard you've visited, Ms. Blake?"

"Yes."

"Does it feel any different from the ones back in America?"

I frowned at him. "Is this a trick question?"

"It's not meant to be."

"Have the bodies been moved?"

He looked out over the graves. "To my knowledge what was buried here is still here."

"If this Roane wants to meet with a vampire, why meet inside a church? He knows that the vampires can't go in there."

"Once he feels reassured, then he will come out to Damian."

"What will reassure him?" I asked.

"Come inside the church and ask him yourself."

I stared back over the graveyard and its strangely alive ground. As a teenager, I'd have given anything to be able to walk through a cemetery and feel nothing, but now . . . I wasn't afraid of graveyards, but I was a little afraid of this one. Why couldn't I sense anything?

"You are unsettled, Ms. Blake. I thought it was tradition that necromancy doesn't work in daylight."

"You can't raise the dead in daylight, but I can sense the dead."

"What of ghosts? Do you sense them, as well?"

"I try not to see ghosts."

"How can you not see them?" he asked.

"The same way I don't go around raising the dead willy-nilly: by controlling my natural gifts."

"So, without control, you can cause the dead to rise spontaneously?"

"No, not exactly. Let's meet this mystery man, Slane. I have to meet up with the local police later."

He led the way into the church without another word. The church smelled old, like mildew and water and . . . weariness. I'd never thought a church could have a feel to it like a person who had seen too much and needed to rest. How did you let a church rest? I genuflected and crossed myself automatically and then I went up the church aisle.

Slane led us to a man sitting in one of the pews. He had long black hair shot through with silver and white, not gray, so that the contrast in colors didn't look so much like age as just the way his hair was colored. I knew plenty of people who would have loved to have the color combo as a dye job, but nothing was going to look quite like the real thing. Slane moved past the man so that I could sit next to him. Nicky sat on the other side of me; Kaazim and Jake sat in the pew behind us.

The stranger looked at me with huge black eyes, so like Riley's that it startled me for a second, like looking into the eyes of the dead. Was it a premonition or just a family likeness?

"I was told you wanted to meet with me," I said.

"And Damian," the man said, and his voice was a deep bass. You didn't meet many men with voices that low.

"He can't come inside a church," I said.

"I wasn't certain that you would be able to walk inside a church," the man said.

"Yeah, yeah, I'm a necromancer, all evil and ungodly. That's me."

He blinked those huge liquid eyes at me. I didn't think he'd gotten the sarcasm. Apparently neither had Nicky, because he added, "Anita's joking. She gets tired of people assuming that she's evil just because she can raise the dead."

"My apologies, then, miss, but I had to be certain you weren't in league with her."

"How does the fact that I can enter a church prove that I'm not?"

"Do you believe in God, miss?"

"Yes."

He smiled. "I have prayed for God to send us someone to help destroy the mad creature that rules us. I believe that person may be you, miss."

I shook my head. "I'm no one's savior. That job belongs to the man hanging on the cross over there."

"Don't you believe that we can all be instruments of God's will?" he said.

"I believe that God calls us to do His will, but free will means we can say no."

"Saying no did not work out so well for Jonah," he said, smiling that gentle smile of his.

"I don't think there's a lot of whales in Dublin," I said.

He smiled wider. "We are a seaport, miss. You would be surprised what swims in the waters here."

I smiled, realizing that I'd treated him as if he didn't turn into a seal part of the time. "I'm Anita Blake. What's your name?"

"Moran."

"Well, Moran, are you ready to go outside and talk to Damian?"

"Not yet. I need to know if it is true that you freed Rafael and his wererats from the Master of St. Louis, who had enslaved them."

I licked my lips and thought about what to say, because I had freed the wererats by killing the old Master of St. Louis. I hadn't had a warrant of execution for her, but I'd killed her to keep her from enslaving me like the wererats. I didn't regret killing her, but I didn't want to confess to murder to a stranger either.

"I don't know you well enough to answer certain questions."

"Can you free us, Anita Blake, like you did the wererats?"

"I might be able to free individual Roane, but to free all of you would mean your mistress would have to be dead."

He nodded very solemnly. "Yes, that would be the only way."

We sat there and stared at each other. "Why does everyone in Ireland think that I'll just kill people here?"

"Perhaps your reputation precedes you," Slane said, peering around Moran. I frowned at him. He shrugged and leaned back so I couldn't see him around the other man.

"Would you be willing to tell the police what she's done to you and your people? Would you be able to help me prove her crimes to the police?" I asked.

"There is no death penalty in Ireland," Moran said.

"So I keep being told," I said.

We looked at each other for another long moment.

"I'm not an assassin," I said.

"Of course not," he said, but he looked at me with Riley's eyes, and there was a silent demand in them: Help us, save us, kill the monster for us. "Will you help us, Miss Blake?"

"It's Marshal Blake. I have a badge. I'm a police officer. I cannot assassinate someone for you."

"She is evil, Marshal Blake."

"I understand that, but it doesn't change the fact that Ireland doesn't have a death penalty, and if it did, you'd need a trial to get to it."

"We cannot afford the time a trial would take, Marshal Blake. You know that for something like M'Lady you either kill it or you leave it alone. You do not try and put it on trial."

"I'm not arguing with your reasoning."

"But you will not help us?"

"I can't agree to assassinate her for you. I'm sorry, truly sorry, but I can't tell you, 'Yes, I'll do it,' because if I said that, you might count on it. You might make plans based on her being dead."

"We would."

"And if she didn't get dead, then those plans would get you killed. I won't be responsible for that."

"I am told that if you slay the animal to call of a master vampire their death can drag the vampire down to true death at last. Is that true, Marshal?"

"It can be," I said, and I didn't like where this conversation was going.

"I thought that the death of their animal or their human servant was a guarantee of their destruction."

"Most of the time the death of one causes the death of the other, but I've known vampires powerful enough that it didn't work that way."

"You give me no hope, Marshal Blake."

"I thought you were going to give us some hope about Riley and his girlfriend," I said.

"If someone told you that, then I truly am sorry, for I have no hope to offer for Riley and his lady. He was young and foolish, but a good boy."

"He seemed like a nice person," I said.

"He was."

I didn't like that he used the past tense. "Do you know where Riley and his lady friend are?"

"I do not."

"Do you know what happened to them?"

"Not precisely, but he will be tortured to death. It is the penalty for disloyalty, or sometimes it is the penalty for catching her attention. She has always been unstable, but the last two years, she has become much worse."

The timing was after we'd killed the Mother of All Darkness. Was this our fault, my fault? "I'm sorry, Moran, truly."

"I believe you, Marshal Blake. If you had not been able to enter the church, then I would not have helped you. I did one deal with the devil centuries ago. I thought it would keep my people safe, but I was wrong."

Kaazim leaned into us from the pew behind. "Is Moran your real name?"

"One of them."

"What is the name that most know you by?" Kaazim said.

"Roarke," he said.

Kaazim's gun was suddenly pointed at Roarke's head. "If you move, I will kill you," he said in a low, careful voice.

Nicky had grabbed me and was moving me backward, away from the man.

Slane said, "I was told he was just one of Roarke's seals. I did not know he was Roarke himself."

"We will discuss your potential treachery later," Kaazim said.

"Who is this guy?" I asked.

"He's her *moitié bête*, and the king of the Roanes," Jake said, as he moved into the pew we'd just left.

"Fuck," I said.

"Do not curse in the church, Marshal," Roarke said.

"Why did you want this meeting?" Jake asked.

"Inside the church, she cannot see into my heart and mind. I had to arrange the meeting as she ordered, but I have carefully kept my mind blank of the details. I told her I was going to church to pray here so she would not be alarmed when I vanished from her mind. I also knew it would prevent Damian from recognizing me too soon."

"What do you want, Roarke?" Kaazim asked.

"I want M'Lady to die and my people to be free."

"What are you supposed to be setting us up for? What does the Wicked Bitch want to happen here today?" I asked.

"She wants Damian back, and she would like your *moitié bête* at her mercy. God forgive me, she would like all your pretty men at her mercy."

I just dropped the shields that were keeping out Damian and Nathaniel, and Dev, and Domino and Ethan. I just let them know what I knew. If Damian hadn't been with them they could have come into the church to use it as a sanctuary, but the vampire couldn't enter it and we couldn't leave him alone. Damn it!

"If anyone attacks our people outside this church, I will kill you," Kaazim said.

"But don't you understand? That is exactly what I want you to do," Roarke said.

"What are you saying?" I said.

"I believe in God, Marshal Blake. I cannot take my own life, but if I am killed, then it may drag her down to death with me."

"Your death might just kill her human servant and not her. She might sacrifice the servant to save herself," I said.

"But if she is bereft of both her animal and her servant, then she will be far less powerful, true?"

I didn't know what to say, because he was right, but it wasn't a guarantee. "It would hurt her power base, but maybe not enough to free all your people."

"If she is no longer my master, then she can no longer draw on all the other Roane through me. She will have to wait for my people to elect a new king, and that will take enough time for Damian to lead you to her stronghold and help you kill her."

Jake said, "If someone is killed inside a church, it ceases to be consecrated ground until the rituals are performed again."

"But I will already be dead, and she will be weakened."

"I did free Rafael and his wererats. I freed them by killing the old master of the city that could call rats. Once she was dead, they were free."

"All I want is for my people to be free of the monster that I let into our peaceable kingdom," Roarke said.

"Are there other Roane waiting outside to attack us?" Jake asked.

"There are, but they are waiting for me to signal them."

"I thought you said the signal was you leaving the church," I said.

"That is for attacking you. She wants to capture you, too. Didn't I mention that?"

"No, you left that part out." I wanted Nathaniel in the

church with me, but if he came inside, that might alert the waiting bad guys.

"Why does she want Anita?" Nicky asked.

"She wants to kill you as you killed the Mother of All Darkness, so she can drink the power inside you, as you drank the Mother."

"So she needs me alive to kill me in person," I said.

"Yes, but she wants Damian back to be her slave again, and she wants to use those you love to make you afraid. She will feast on your fear, Marshal."

"How many people are hiding out there, waiting to attack us?" I asked.

"Enough that you should call more Gardai now while you can," he said, and he was so calm. He shouldn't have been this calm.

I didn't argue with him. Edward answered on the second ring. "Anita, I still haven't convinced everyone here to include you completely."

"It doesn't matter," I said, and I told him what was happening.

"We'll be there in fifteen minutes, maybe less." He didn't even ask any questions before he hung up.

"Kill me, Anita. Kill me and maybe you will kill her, too."

"Maybe no one has to die today," Kaazim said.

"I'm afraid that someone will die today, and I've decided it will be me," Roarke said in that strangely peaceful voice.

"Anita has inherited the Mother's ability to cut servants and animals to call free of their masters."

"That is not possible. You are lying to trick me."

Nicky said, "Can the seal people smell a lie like a were-animal can?"

"We can tell if someone is afraid or nervous, but that does not make them liars."

"I give you my word of honor that Anita has broken the bonds of animals to call from their vampire masters without killing either of them," Kaazim said.

"Your word of honor?" Roarke made it a question.

"Yes," Kaazim said.

Jake said, "Anita could try to break you free of your mistress. No one need die here today."

"It is too late, for once I fail her today, she will torture those I love, because to torture me harms her."

"Is her human servant like you? Does he want her dead?" I asked.

"No, he loves her. He enjoys what they do together and what they do to others."

"Then maybe you can help us trap him, too. If we kill both of you together, then her chances of survival are much lower than if we just kill you today," I said.

"She will know what I have done. I cannot keep her out of my memories."

"If you're trying to shield from her, can you?"

"For a time, but only from a distance. If she is before me, then I am weak. If she touches me with her pale hands, then I cannot keep any secrets from her."

"What if we arrest you?" I asked.

"What are you thinking, Anita?" Jake asked.

"What if we arrest him on assault or attempted murder, something, and put him in a cell? What if we keep him away from her and it's not his fault?"

"You are only delaying the inevitable, Marshal."

"Who would she send to break you out of jail?" Jake asked.

"You think she would send her servant, that she would send Keegan."

"Would she?" Jake asked.

"She might. She just might."

"Let us take you into custody, Roarke," I said. "Let's try to keep everyone alive for a little bit longer."

"If I agree to this, I need your word, all your words of honor."

"What do you need us to swear to?" Jake asked.

"That if Keegan and I are in one place at one time, you will kill us both to kill her."

"Can I try breaking you free of her power before we put a bullet in your brain?" I asked.

"I am not eager to die, Marshal, so if you wish to try such magic on me, I give you permission. I pray that it works, but if it does not work, then I want your word that you will kill me before you let me go back to her."

Kaazim and Jake gave their words without hesitation. I

think Nicky only hesitated because he could feel how conflicted I was about it, but in the end, he gave his. And in the
very end, as we heard sirens in the distance coming closer, I
promised Roarke that if we couldn't figure out another way, I'd
kill him.

57

THE IRISH POLICE were happy to put Roarke in a cell. They
were thrilled that I hadn't shot him. There was one drawback
to not shooting him or not trying to break him free of the
Wicked Bitch while he was still inside the church: Once he
was outside of consecrated ground, she could contact him
again, just like I'd been able to contact Jean-Claude and Richard all the way in St. Louis. So as the police escorted him to
the truck that would take him to jail, he started to struggle. I
don't know if he was struggling because she controlled him or
if it was to make sure any Roane in the area reported that he
had tried to escape, but one of the officers escorting him went
flying into one of the police cars. The other police dog-piled
him, or tried to, but he kept his feet and kept moving forward,
as if he just planned on walking down the street and away.

Donnie, Brennan, Edward, and Nolan jumped on the pile,
and their weight made Roarke stagger, but he didn't go down.
Edward did something with his right hand, and Roarke's right
leg collapsed, but he got back up. Tough motherfucker. "May
I aid them?" Kaazim asked.

"Yes," Jake said. "I will stay with our principals, but we
must have the Roane in a cell before full dark." I realized that
he meant me and Nathaniel, and maybe Damian, and he was
right about the timing. The sky was growing dim; it was dusk.

Kaazim joined the crowd trying to control Roarke, and it
was enough to swing the difference. Edward and Nolan would
have gotten it eventually, but with Kaazim helping them and

the police, they managed to get the prisoner in the transport. The officer who had been flung into the car was sitting beside it with another officer giving him first aid. I could hear an ambulance in the distance, which meant he was hurt even worse than I'd thought. Roarke wasn't as strong as Magda, so the cells at Nolan's headquarters might actually hold him. The truck went screeching off down the road with the prisoner in it.

Edward came back up the steps with Kaazim a little behind him. Nolan was talking to one of the cops he seemed to know personally. "What did you tell them to get them to drive like that?" Ethan asked.

"That he'd get even stronger once night fell."

"That may be true," I said.

"Either way we want him in a cell before the vampires are up for the night," Edward said. He looked at Damian, who was standing beside me. "Can She-Who-Made-You walk around during the day?"

"Yes."

"Lucky she's not here in Dublin, then," he said.

"You have no idea how lucky," Damian said.

Nolan came up the steps scowling so hard, the lines in his forehead looked like they'd been cut in with fresh knives.

"What's wrong?" Edward asked.

"They won't let us have Roarke. They're taking him to regular lockup."

"You don't have an extra cell anyway," I said.

"I guess we don't, thanks to your werelion."

"Magda did exactly what you asked her to do. It's not her fault that your cell couldn't hold up."

Nolan nodded, gave a small laugh, and said, "Fair. My people aren't even as strong as the Roane, but neither of us is as strong as your lioness. The combination of strength and her training made a joke out of all our preparations."

Dev patted his shoulder. "There, there, it wasn't a joke. It just wasn't as useful as you'd hoped."

Night fell, and it was like something inside me that had been closed tight all day opened. I took in a deep breath of the rain-damp air. My phone rang, and it was Magda.

"The new vampires have risen here," she said. "They were

completely out of their minds until they took blood, but then they seemed very calm and much more sensible than most new vampires that I've seen over the centuries."

"That's good, right?"

"It is, though Nolan's people did not like having to donate blood. Giacomo and I were there to hold them and make sure the first feeding was controlled. Otherwise they would have torn open their victims in search of blood."

"Are they coherent enough to answer questions?" I asked.

"I believe so. Giacomo is talking to them now with some of Nolan's people helping guard the little vampires. The daughter and mother are asking about the rest of the family. Did they rise as vampires, too?"

"Oh, shit," I said softly, but with real feeling. "I'll call you back." I yelled for Nolan. "Who's watching the vampire victims from earlier today?"

"They're at the hospital," he said.

"What hospital?"

"What's wrong?" Edward asked.

"The others woke savage until they'd fed. Where are the rest of their families?"

Nolan cursed under his breath and was already on his cell phone and moving toward the cars. We all divided up between the two cars, but I kept Nathaniel and Damian with me, though maybe putting all three of us in one car wasn't my best idea, not if the Wicked Bitch wanted to take all of us, but the thought of being separated from them, especially Nathaniel, made my throat tight. I still remembered all the panic I hadn't let myself feel when Roarke told us that the plan was to kidnap him, because the Bitch wanted all my pretty men, but especially Nathaniel. Good idea, bad idea, I kept him with me, and Damian stayed with both of us. We weren't alone, by any means, but it was still like triple-baiting one car. I tried not to think of it that way as Donnie kicked the van into high gear and screeched out after Nolan's car.

I prayed that we'd get there before any of them injured, or killed, someone at the hospital. Magda had said that once they fed, the Irish vampires were lucid. How terrible would it be to wake up to yourself covered in someone else's blood, maybe sitting beside the body? I prayed not just to get there in time to save the victims, but to save the new vampires from truly becoming monsters.

58

BY THE TIME we got to the hospital, it was all over but the crying. I'd executed more vampires than anyone else, and killed more than I could actually keep track of some days, but I'd never had to sit across a table from one who was crying hysterically because she was covered in her victim's blood. If I hadn't seen the delicate fangs as the grandmother wailed her distress, I wouldn't have known she wasn't human. The newly dead either looked almost alive and became less human as time went on or they were more inhuman at the beginning of their existence and learned how to be more human as time went on; it all depended on the bloodline they descended from. Whatever vampire was creating these was unlike any bloodline I'd ever seen.

Except for the hospital gown covered in fresh blood and the fact that her hands were restrained behind her, Mrs. Edna Brady looked like what she had been: a seventy-something grandmother who had been a regular churchgoer and the matriarch of a loving family. She'd managed to wipe most of the blood off her face before she'd been restrained. There was one smear in her short white hair that nothing but a shower was going to get rid of. I knew that from experience. Once you got blood in your hair . . . I looked at her and didn't know where to start. I hunted vampires. I didn't hold their hands and explain to them how to be the best bloodsucker they could be.

Lucky for both of us, Damian and Jake were with me. "Edna," Damian said in a soothing voice. "Edna, can you hear me?"

She continued to wail, and I mean wail; terms like crying

and hysterics didn't cover it. Edward and Nolan were dealing with Edna's son, who had also risen as a vampire. Kaazim was helping them out. The father had been utterly calm. In fact, he didn't remember how he got so much blood on him or why he was in the hospital. Amnesia for the first few nights is a blessing apparently, because we were staring at the impact of remembering everything.

Nathaniel was in the hallway outside the room they'd given us. Dev and Nicky were permanently attached to him by my orders. Ethan and Domino along with Donnie had gone to the hotel to pick up Fortune and Echo. Echo would go in and try to talk vampire to vampire with the male vamp Edward and Nolan were trying to question.

I was so ready to trade vampires with Edward. I was sympathetic, but I just simply didn't know what to do with Edna Brady. I don't know if she couldn't hear us or if she just didn't care. Damian had been gentle, patient, and charming, and nothing had stopped the awful screaming or taken one shade of panic out of her eyes. I was starting to get a headache just from the noise.

I finally screamed her name at her. At first I didn't think she heard me, but her eyes started to focus as if she finally saw us and the room we were in rather than being trapped in that moment when she'd come to herself, cradling the unconscious body of her first victim.

"Edna! Edna! Edddnaaaa!" I screamed at her, and the wailing slowed. She blinked and looked at us again. She was in there; behind all the noise and terror, she was still in there. That was good, I thought.

"Edna, can you hear me?"

She blinked at me. She looked scared and confused, but at least she stopped wailing.

Damian tried. "Edna, can you hear us?"

"Nod if you can hear us?" I asked, and she nodded. Yay, progress! "Do you know where you are, Edna?"

"Hospital," she said in a voice that sounded raw from screaming.

"That's good, Edna," Damian said. "Do you remember why you're in the hospital?"

She seemed to think really seriously and finally said, "My

granddaughter disappeared. . . . She came home. She wasn't dead."

I let the whole definition of life and death go for now. "Something like that, yes."

"Voices, shining eyes, they promised me something. They promised me . . . I looked in the mirror and I looked the same. I thought I'd be young again, but I looked just the same. It didn't work the way they said it would."

"What was supposed to happen, Edna?" Damian asked.

"Vampires are young and beautiful. I thought I would be twenty again, or thirty, but there was a mirror in my room, and I looked as old as ever. I hadn't changed, and then a doctor came in happy that I was awake, and . . ." Horror filled her eyes up one memory at a time. "Oh, my God, I tore open her arm. I drank her blood!" She started to retch as if she was going to throw up.

"It's okay, Edna. It's okay," I said, though that was a lie, such a lie.

"Is the doctor all right?"

"She's in surgery," I said.

"Did I tear her arm almost off? I wouldn't do that. I would never hurt someone like that, but I remember the blood and . . . and voices promising me . . . I'd be young again."

"I'm sorry, Edna," Damian said.

She stared at him. "You're young and beautiful. You both are. That's the way it's supposed to be. That's why you give up everything, to be young forever."

I started to explain to her that vampires are the age they die at forever. That they don't grow older, but they don't become younger either. But Damian stopped me from explaining it to her. He whispered, "Later. Give her some time."

"Where's Frankie?"

"Your son?"

"My husband. Where's Frankie?"

I looked at Damian, because Frankie hadn't made it. He'd had a bad heart for years, and the doctors theorized that the shock of being drained of blood, or maybe seeing his granddaughter as a vampire, had been too much for him. Who the hell knew? If you had a bad ticker, how the hell would you ever survive the horrorfest that had befallen this family?

The youngest daughter hadn't made it either. Her throat had been so small that the fangs had pierced too much and collapsed her windpipe. She'd suffocated before she could bleed out, so no vampirism for her.

"Who did this to you, Edna?" I asked, and my voice was gentler than it had been. It was all just so awful.

"Who did the voices belong to," Damian asked, "the ones that promised you eternal youth? Who told you that?"

"He did."

"Who is he?" I asked.

"He came with Katie. She brought him home. He found her when she was lost and he brought her back to us."

"What was his name, this Good Samaritan?" I asked.

She smiled at me. "Yes, he was a Good Samaritan. He found Katie and brought her back to us. He told us that we could all be together forever and never grow old, never die. I remember his eyes . . ." She frowned. "Or I don't remember his eyes. I don't know if I remember what color his eyes were, but they were like stars."

We questioned her for a while longer, but all we learned was that the man had short, dark hair, maybe black, maybe brown. He was Caucasian. He was young, but since she was in her early seventies, that could have meant anything from teens to fifties. His eyes had glowed like stars, which could have meant they were paler colored, gray, or pale blue, or it could just have meant that she remembered them glowing, but not the color.

Edna's son, Katie's father, remembered even less. His memory seemed to stop with Katie at the door. She'd come home. She wasn't dead. That's where he stopped. It was more merciful than what Edna remembered.

In the hallway Nolan asked, "Will they remember more as time passes?"

"Yes," Damian said.

"Yes," Echo said.

"Why do neither of you sound happy about that?" I asked.

"Would you want to remember any of this?" Echo asked.

I looked into her lovely blue eyes, and said, "Hell, no."

"Some people don't ever remember their first night," Fortune said. "Maybe they won't either."

"Edna Brady already remembers most of it."

"The man doesn't."

"The best chance we have of finding the vampire that is doing this is to start with the teenage girls. One of them was the first victim. She'll remember the most about the one that created her," Echo said.

"They found Sinead Royce's family," Superintendent Pearson said. He'd come in late and mostly just monitored us. He didn't want to see either of the victims in person. He was having a lot of trouble coping with them as vampires when he'd seen them alive and looking for their daughter just days ago.

"Your face says it's not good news," I said.

He shook his head. "The whole family was so brutally attacked that none of them rose as vampires."

"How can you be sure?" Echo asked.

"They're starting to rot."

"Sinead had two younger brothers, as well as the parents," Pearson said.

"Where were the bodies found?" Edward asked.

"In a shed three houses over. The smell alerted the neighbors."

"Where were the owners of the house?" I asked.

"In the shed," he said.

"I take it that they won't be rising as vamps either."

"No."

"Is this the most victims that were torn up too badly to rise as the undead?" Echo asked.

"That we've found, yes."

"Maybe it's a clue," I said.

"A clue to what?" Edward asked.

"I have no fucking idea, but it's something different in the pattern and different is something."

"Do you want to go look at the shed?" he asked.

"No."

He smiled. "Want to go look for clues in a shed that was full of decomposing bodies?"

"When you put it that way, how can I resist?"

59

WE NEVER GOT to investigate the shed. Some of the neighbors decided that it must be evil, or full of some disease that was ravaging their town, so they set it on fire. We got to watch the fire department do its job, but that didn't help us find a clue to what, or who, was spreading vampirism like a summer cold through Dublin.

In fact, everywhere we went that night, there were no clues, only more victims. Either the victims that the newly risen had attacked or the new vampires themselves, who weren't much better at being vampires than Edna and Michael Brady. One thing was different about almost all of the newly risen, though: Once they took blood, they stopped being dangerous. They couldn't always remember anything, but they were more coherent than any newbie vampires I'd ever met. They also looked more normally human.

"What bloodline is this?" I asked Echo and Fortune.

"I do not know," Echo said, and Fortune just shook her head.

Kaazim and Jake didn't know either. Since between the four of them they'd seen thousands of years of vampires, we were well and truly clueless. Eventually we got sent back to our hotel for sleep and food, but I was too tired to eat. The jet lag had finally caught up with me in a major way. As Nicky opened the door, I leaned beside it and stared at the opposite wall as Domino and Ethan opened the next door. Magda and Giacomo were on the other side of them. They'd left the three vampires at Nolan's compound with its one working cell. Magda made a comment about the three new vamps tearing up the cell they were in the way she had done to the other one: "They have not the will, nor the training yet. The cell will be sufficient for the newly risen who are untrained in combat."

I thought that was interesting wording and texted Edward to tell Nolan that they might need special accommodations for any vamps who had military, martial arts, or other physically trained backgrounds. He was staying at the compound with Nolan. Apparently there were living quarters there, though Magda said calling them apartments would be too much; they were more like barracks. Since I'd never been in the real military before, I didn't actually understand the difference, but I was too tired to ask for an explanation. No, I was so tired, I didn't care what the explanation was; that was the truth.

Fortune and Echo were beside us on this side of the hallway. Socrates had decided to stay at Nolan's in the barracks, to continue to foster goodwill and to learn as much as he could about what the plans were for the paramilitary group. That left Pride in a room by himself, or sharing with Dev. Jake and Kaazim were bunkmates, but somehow if Socrates had been there, we'd have been short a bed. Nicky had bunked next door with Pride for the nap earlier, but I didn't want to give up Nicky for the whole trip. I just didn't. I was in love with him, and other than Nathaniel, that wasn't true of anyone else on the trip with me. I liked some of my people very much, and was wildly attracted to others, but it wasn't "in love." This tired after the night we'd just had, being held by people you truly loved sounded just about perfect.

My phone rang as Nicky got the door open. It was Jean-Claude's ringtone, so I answered as Nicky held the door for me. "Hey, tall, pale, and handsome, what's up?"

"*Ma petite*, I will soon be down for the day."

"The time difference is going to take some getting used to," I said as I sat on the edge of the king-size bed.

"Yes, but I cannot take the *ardeur* for you while I sleep. You may wake for the morning before I do, and if so, then you will need to feed the *ardeur* when you wake. You must also eat a real breakfast, not just coffee. I need you to take care of your physical needs so that me being unable to take your other hunger will not get out of hand for you."

"Crap," I said, and the wave of tiredness washed over me.

"*Ma petite*, what is wrong?"

I didn't try to explain, just thought about the last few hours. He got the shorthand version, all the awful in a fraction of the time. His comment was "That is truly terrible, *ma petite*. I am so sorry that you are having to deal with such things."

"It's my job," I said.

"Actually, it is not, but I understand that you feel that way."

Opening to him enough to share the memories let me know that he was alone in the bedroom sitting on the edge of the bed as I was. "Has Richard gone back home?"

"*Oui*, Jason has arrived from New York."

"Tell him hi for me and give him a hug. I miss him."

"As do I, *ma petite*. If you are still away by the next weekend, his J.J. will be joining him here in St. Louis for a few days."

I thought about the blond ballerina who had finally won Jason's heart. They were very warm thoughts on my part. She was probably my favorite female lover after Echo. I wasn't sure why Fortune and Magda were third and fourth on that list respectively, but I could honor the truth of it without overanalyzing it. Fortune was committed to Echo and liked men a lot. Magda seemed content to treat all of us as fuck buddies.

"Have fun," I said.

"I hope that you are home by then, *ma petite*."

"Me, too. Hey, ask him if I am home next weekend, could he and J.J. stay over anyway?"

"I will happily do so," he said.

I smiled. "That would be great."

"I have spoken with Micah on the phone about the Roane and their plight with She-Who-Must-Not-Be-Named."

"Edward's calling her that, too. I'd really prefer not to mix Harry Potter with this awfulness."

"As you like, *ma petite*. Micah will be speaking with Rafael at more length since they are both still on the West Coast trying to prevent a shapeshifter war."

"I'd have thought the negotiations would be done by now, or they'd have picked who to fight and kicked their asses."

"I do not have all the details, but it seems more complex than first explained."

I thought about calling Micah, but it seemed too complicated, especially if I still had to feed the *ardeur*. Why was I this discouraged? Was it the jet lag? Edna Brady's screams? The fact that two entire families had been wiped out by this new vampire? Or the thought that something we had done to the Mother of All Darkness had weakened Damian's old master enough to allow the new vampires to get a foothold here in Dublin? I kept coming back to that: Somehow this was our fault for not taking charge of things. We'd just wanted to run America and trust the rest of the world's vampires to take care of business. I was beginning to realize how naïve that may have been.

"*Ma petite*, this is not our doing. Do not take on the guilt of it."

"Was I thinking that loud?"

"Yes," Nathaniel said as he went into the bathroom and closed the door. I realized that Nicky, Dev, and Damian were all in the room. There was no way that all of us were going to be able to sleep in one king-size bed.

"They are a bounty, *ma petite*, not a burden. Please remember that."

"I will, but thanks for the reminder."

"Time is growing short here, *ma petite*. I must sleep and the demon we share must come home to you."

"The *ardeur* isn't a real demon, Jean-Claude. It isn't even evil, just occasionally inconvenient."

"It is still the power that has earned me the title of incubus, and you that of succubus."

"Fine, but I've dealt with real demons, Jean-Claude, and it's a whole new level of bad."

"That I believe, *ma petite*, but dawn is almost upon me. Are you prepared for the *ardeur* to be returned?"

"You fed it well today, right?"

"*Oui.*"

"Then it shouldn't need feeding again that soon. I can control it better than that now."

"Tonight, yes, but I can feel that you have donated too much blood and not eaten enough real food, plus the jet lag and the stress of your job. You underestimate how much energy it all takes."

"I promise that I will eat breakfast tomorrow morning, and I will feed the *ardeur* without it forcing me to feed it."

"Thank you, *ma petite*."

"You're welcome. I'm just exhausted. We're all tired."

The four men looked at one another and then at me. "You just need to pick your bedmates so we can all get some sleep," Nathaniel said, smiling.

"*Ma petite*, they are all handsome, all good lovers, and you are in love with two of them. Do not allow the ugliness of the night to paint this moment as anything less than beautiful."

I sighed and knew he was right. I really did. My therapist would have agreed with him, but I was still exhausted and discouraged, and I felt vaguely like everything going wrong was my fault somehow, so why did I deserve such happiness after what had happened to the Bradys and the Royces?

"It is not an exchange of blessings, *ma petite*, not an either/or. You did not create the vampire who is haunting Dublin, nor did you cause the families to fall into his clutches."

"I'm beginning to believe that something about killing the Mother of All Darkness weakened Damian's old master and gave this new monster an opening here in Ireland."

"If that is true, then we will deal with it. We will fix any problems we have inadvertently created, but we will not take the guilt of it to heart. That we will not do, and you must not. You are the Queen. It is your choice whether you are going to be a queen of joy or sorrow. I have been ruled by both, and I much prefer joy."

"So do I," I said.

"Then prove it to me, to yourself, to the men in the room with you or to the women next door to you. You have many blessings with you. Please, please, *ma petite*, treat them, and yourself, as such."

"I will try," I said.

I could almost feel him smile, not through vampire powers, but just knowing him, knowing us. "Thank you, *ma petite*. That is all I can ask. Now I must get to bed. Jason will be out of the bathroom in time to tuck us both in for the day."

"Have fun," I said.

"He is not bisexual enough for much fun, nor do we have time before sunrise."

"Just enjoy having Jason home for cuddles and blood, then," I said.

"That I will do. *Je t'aime, ma petite*."

"I love you, too."

60

I WOKE CURLED between the warmth of Nathaniel and the cooling skin of Damian. The vampire was dead to the world, but there'd been no more nightmares. Something about all three of us touching kept the Wicked Bitch out of all our dreams, and us out of hers. It had been what made me choose Damian to be on the other side of me from Nathaniel, but the vampire had grown cool overnight and woken me. I was about to marry Jean-Claude, and I wasn't sure I'd ever be able to sleep comfortably beside him or any vampire. The thought slid into the down mood that I'd gone to sleep with and that was apparently still with me.

Nathaniel made small protesting noises and snuggled closer to me. He was almost fever warm. Damian was growing cold on the other side of me, but worse than that, he felt dead. He had that loose, heavy feel to him that only dead bodies had. I moved away from him, but his body slid into the space so that he was still touching me, so still, so dead. I started to get out from between them, but Nathaniel turned and wrapped his arms around me, trapping me between the two of them, pressing me more in against Damian's cold body. Not icy cold, but that bloodless, lifeless . . . My heart was speeding up; my pulse started to beat in my throat so that it felt like I was choking. I had to get out of this bed and away from the vampire.

I pushed against Nathaniel's arm, trying to get him to let go enough so that I could get up, but he did what he normally did. The more I struggled, the tighter he held on, making little protesting noises about warm, and sleepy, and not getting up. Normally it was cute, but not today.

"Nathaniel, let go!"

"Warm," he muttered, snuggling so tightly against me that I couldn't move, but me struggling to get away had made Da-

mian's body slide heavier against me so that he was literally
deadweight trapping me in the sheets. It threw me back to
waking in a coffin with a vampire who planned on making me
her servant when she rose for the night. I felt the bubbling
weight of a scream. The fear was choking thick.

There was a knock on the door, and I screamed, a small yip
of a scream but a scream. It startled Nathaniel enough that he
let me go and rose to look at me. "What's wrong?"

"It's Nicky, Anita. Open the door now!"

He was picking up my fear. "I'm okay, Nicky. I'm just
spooked."

"Let me in the room, or we'll be paying for a door."

"We're getting up," Nathaniel called, but he was looking at
me. He whispered, "What's wrong?"

I shook my head and slid out of the bed. I was opening the
door buck naked, when I realized there might be more people
than just Nicky in the hallway. I was scared enough that I
wasn't thinking clearly. What the hell was wrong with me?

"I need a robe," I said, moving back so that no one could
see me at the door. I started to close it, but a hand stopped the
door. "Everyone out here has seen you naked," Nicky said.

Dev said, "We have breakfast."

"And coffee," Domino said.

"Hell, why didn't you say so?" I tried for light, but it wasn't
real. I was still scared as if we'd had another nightmare, but I
didn't remember dreaming anything last night. I stepped back
and let them into the room, using the door for my modesty, at
least until the men had trooped inside. Then I had to close the
door, and modesty wasn't actually possible.

Ethan managed not to stare at me at all, but he was the only
one of the four men who managed it. Domino stared but managed not to ogle me. He was carrying the coffee, so I was all
right with being stared at. Dev was cheerfully lecherous about
it; his hands were full of trays of food. Nicky had more food
in his hands, but he wasn't cheerful about it. He gave me a
look that was so intense, it stripped his feelings as naked as
my body. It made me go to him and try for a good morning
kiss, but his hands were too full and I was too short.

Nathaniel got out of bed to help set up the food. Dev leered as cheerfully at Nathaniel as he had at me. They grinned at each other. I shook my head and rolled my eyes at them both.

I grabbed the hotel robe that was on the back of the bathroom door for our use, while the men set up breakfast on any flat surface they could find. "Boo on the robe," Dev said. "I wanted to leer at you both while we ate breakfast."

"Nothing personal to Nathaniel, but he can get dressed as far as I'm concerned," Domino said, smiling.

Nathaniel stuck his tongue out at him as he walked past them all for the bathroom. We had just woken up, but there were some things that I still didn't like to do as a couple, and one of them was bathroom stuff. I still preferred that to be private. I was pretty sure I always would.

"Where is everybody else?" I asked.

"Eating in the other rooms. There wasn't room for all of us to eat room service in any one room," Domino said.

"Did you have more bad dreams?" Ethan asked.

"You felt me be all scaredy-cat, too?"

"I don't pick up your emotions as strongly as Nicky does, or some of the other men, but I felt it this morning."

"No bad dreams. All of us sleeping together took care of it, but I just can't wake up beside one of my lovers feeling that much like a real corpse." I looked at Damian, who had collapsed into a still heap of paper white skin and crimson hair.

"You flash back on waking up in the coffin with the one vampire?" Nicky asked.

I nodded, shivering even in the thick white robe. Domino held out coffee to me. It made me smile. "Thanks."

He took his own coffee and let the others get their own. They'd wait on me, but not on one another, at least not outside of helping Nathaniel in the kitchen, but that was more family chores, not small romantic gestures. Bringing me coffee in the morning definitely got you a brownie point in my book.

My phone sounded with Edward's ringtone. I hurried, glad the coffee had a lid, as I went for my phone, which was still plugged into the wall. "Hey, Edward, what's up?"

"Roarke broke out of jail last night."

"How?"

"No one knows. He was just gone this morning."

"So he didn't break out. He walked out," I said.

"Security footage showed him mind-fucking one of the guards. Nothing in the research says that Selkies can do that."

"They can't, but I know that some animals to call and some human servants of a powerful enough vampire can capture someone with their gaze just like a vampire," I said.

He lowered his voice. "Speaking from experience?"

"Yeah."

"I'll tell the local guards and the Gardai," he said.

"I didn't know that Roarke could use his gaze like that, or I'd have warned someone. It's a really rare ability in an animal to call."

"I'll make sure that they know that," he said.

"Is there anything we can do to help? Do you need us at the jail?"

"Do you know how to track a Selkie? I guess Roane here."

"I don't have any seal lycanthropy in me or in anyone with me. It's not even lycanthropy. It's just what they are."

"They've got a BOLO out on Roarke with his picture to every Gardai in the area. If he's still in Dublin, maybe someone will see him and report it."

"You don't sound too optimistic."

"He mind-fucked personnel here at the jail like a master vampire, Anita. The Wicked Bitch didn't make him do all that without a plan to keep him hidden from us. She'll keep him close to her now."

"That's what you would do," I said, "but you're not crazy. She might do things differently."

"She might, but crazy doesn't always mean stupid or even careless."

"No arguments," I said, and sipped my coffee. It was just like I preferred it, which meant Nicky had ordered it, no matter who had carried it in the door. "So what do you want us to do today?"

"Come to the station, ASAP. You were helpful enough last night that they're willing to let you see more of the evidence finally."

"Yay!" I didn't sound truly enthusiastic.

"Are you okay?"

"I woke spooked. Something about dealing with the family

members last night tanked my mood, and I just can't seem to let it go."

"It was bad, Anita. You and I don't usually have to deal with the victims, except to avenge them."

"I hate thinking of the vampires who kill people as victims," I said.

"Me, too. It makes our job back in the States harder."

"Yeah," I said, and again there was that melancholy.

"You need more sunlight if you can get it today. It'll help with the jet lag and time-change adjustment. How soon can you get here? I want us to have a strategy by the time the vampires rise for the night."

"Were there more deaths last night?"

"Yes."

I sighed. "I can be there in twenty minutes."

"No," Nicky said, "you need to eat first."

I frowned at him. "I've been informed that I have to eat breakfast. Jean-Claude made me promise that I'd eat solid food and not just coffee before I went vampire hunting today."

"Sounds like Donna."

"They worry about us," I said.

He gave a small laugh. "Yeah, they do."

"Why is that funny?"

"You and me with domestic lives."

I laughed and sipped my coffee. "Yeah, we were both such loners when we met. Now look at us."

"I'm about to be married with children, and you have more domestic partners and fiancés than most old-school Mormons."

"I'm not a polygamist, Edward."

"Oh, really?"

"I'm into polyandry, not polygamy."

"Polyandry means multiple men, I know, but I've met the three women you're traveling with, and I think they put plenty of 'ygamy' into your 'andry.'"

I laughed, and some tightness in my heart eased. "Thanks for that. I'll see you soon."

Nathaniel said, "You also promised Jean-Claude that you'd feed the *ardeur* before you went out today."

"Let's eat and get dressed and see how long that takes," I

said. I looked at Damian. "We have to dress him, too, before he goes in the duffel bag to carry for the day."

"Dressing a dead body is a lot harder than it sounds," Domino said.

"It's not that hard," Nicky said.

I looked from one to the other of them. Nathaniel said, "You aren't talking about dressing vampires, are you?"

They looked at each other, then back at us, and said in unison, "No."

"Then the two of you get to dress Damian, while Nathaniel and I dress ourselves."

"I'll let the others know that we'll be moving out sooner than we'd planned," Ethan said.

"Tell them that Roarke escaped and how," I said.

Ethan nodded. "Of course." He went out and left us to dress and get ready for a day of crime fighting. I was really glad that Nicky and Domino were going to be dressing the vampire. I didn't want to touch him right now; the thought of it made my skin creep. Some big, tough vampire slayer I turned out to be.

"You really should feed the *ardeur* before we leave the room," Nicky said. Domino and he were laying Damian out on his back on the bed. It was the way you laid a corpse before you bagged it.

I shook my head. "I promise to feed later, but right now let's see if we can catch some bad guys." They stopped trying to argue with me. One of the good things about them all being able to feel varying degrees of what I was truly feeling and thinking was that they knew when I was done. As I watched them start to dress the corpse in my bed, I was done. Fortune would be packing Echo into the big duffel bag, too. It was like body disposal, except we kept the bodies.

61

SOMEONE WHO KNEW more about jet lag than I did put us in a room with a window. Apparently, as much sunlight as possible even the second day you land in a different time zone helped you not get so much lag in your jet-set lifestyle. Natural sunlight on your skin outside was better, but we'd take what we could get while we looked at the crime scene photos. Nathaniel, Dev, Fortune, Pride, Donnie, and Griffin all went out to sightsee in the sunshine. Nathaniel kissed me good-bye, and I wrapped the feel of him around me like you'd wrap your favorite robe, a comfort object that just happened to be the man I loved. As we drew apart, Dev stepped up and said, "Me next." I frowned at him, because it was sort of presumptuous and we were in the hallway with police persons watching. I tried not to be too kissy-face at work, because it played hell with your reputation. It wasn't the brilliant smile that made me not be cranky; it was the uncertainty in his eyes that let me know he wasn't sure of his welcome. The handsome, confident Mephistopheles wouldn't have gotten cuddles from me in front of the other officers, but the less confident Dev got more play with me. He wrapped one arm around me and the other around Nathaniel. I had a moment of hugging them both, and it was good, but I suddenly missed Micah. It was like a wave of homesickness for the feel of him in our arms. I tried wrapping my arms around both of the men with me, but when I tried to cuddle between them, my spot on Nathaniel's chest didn't have the curve of Micah's neck on the other side of me. Dev was so tall that my face was pressed even lower on his chest than on Nathaniel's so that I could hear the thick beat of his heart against my ear. Sometimes when Jean-Claude was in high enough boots, I could rest my head over his heart, but the vampire's heart didn't always beat, so I wasn't used to this thick, constant beat against my ear. It was both reassuring and unnerving, because I wasn't accustomed to it.

Nathaniel stepped back so that Dev could wrap his arms around just me. It left me cuddled against his chest with the sound of his heartbeat thick and sure against my ear. He touched my hair with his fingers, which made me raise my head so I could look up all that tall, broad upper body to meet his eyes. He was watching me watching him, and I realized that I'd taken too long. I should have offered a kiss and let him go off with Nathaniel for their sightseeing. Now it had gone on too long and the sounds around us were growing quiet as the police and other personnel were slowly stopping what they were doing to watch. I didn't look around to see if I was right, or if I was just being self-conscious, because I'd learned that if people were watching, you didn't want to make eye contact, and if they weren't watching, you felt silly for looking.

"What are you thinking?" he asked softly.

"That I can never decide what color your eyes are."

He smiled, and said, "My driver's license says blue."

"So does Nathaniel's, but his really aren't blue," I said, smiling back.

"I like that you think about my eyes that much."

I didn't tell him that it was partly because the rest of him puzzled me almost as much as his eyes. I hugged him more tightly around the waist, pressing our bodies even closer together. Close enough that I could feel that he was beginning to be happy to be there, which meant I needed to kiss him and send him on his way before he got to the point where walking was uncomfortable without adjusting things.

I moved minutely so we had a little more room so that I could go up on tiptoe and he could bend down. He brought his hand up to cradle one side of my face, while his other arm stayed behind me to steady me as I rose to meet his lips. The kiss was soft, but with more lips moving than that sounds like, a tender kiss, with just an edge of tongue like a promise for later. Things low in my body responded to him so that I was breathless when he broke the kiss and pulled back to look into my eyes. If I'd been a man, Devereux wouldn't have been the only one who needed to adjust things before we walked away.

"Wow," I said softly.

His smile, his eyes, his whole face was shining with happiness. He liked that he'd gotten that much reaction from me. Part of me was happy, and part of me was confused. I kept thinking I knew how many people I had in my life, how many I wanted in my life, and how many were occasional fun and food, and then one of them would do something like this, and I'd want more than just fun and games. Damn it.

Nathaniel took him by the arm and pulled him away. "We'll do more kissing later. I want to see Ireland."

Dev laughed and let himself be pulled away. I saw Detective Sheridan watching us and knew that there'd be no misunderstandings now about her attraction to this particular tall, blond man. Good. Fortune came up to me, smiling and shaking her head. "I can't follow that. Let's just shake." She meant it, but she also had come up to get her kiss. She was one of the women in our lives and in our beds, so . . . I rolled my eyes at her, but offered her a kiss. I had to go up on tiptoe for her like I did the men, but our kiss was light and not serious by comparison. Fortune's heart belonged to Echo, whom she was leaving in my care while she saw Dublin for the first time and helped guard the others. But she had asked for a kiss goodbye, which meant the acknowledgment of the relationship mattered to her. Sometimes it's not about romance; it's about belonging, about knowing that someone cares for you enough to kiss you in public and say, *This is mine*. Or at least *I'm thinking of making it mine*. Acknowledgment was important to Fortune and to Dev, to Devereux. Wasn't it weird that I liked him better with that name attached to him? *Dev* seemed unfinished, like a nickname for something longer, and since it was short for *Devil*, which I was never going to cry out in a moment of passion, *Devereux* made me happier. Maybe Shakespeare had been wrong, and a rose by any other name wouldn't be as sweet?

I was actually sad to see Nathaniel and Dev go without me. It would have been nice to go out holding hands and being all romantic tourist with them. But I had a job to do, so I joined Edward in the room where we'd look for clues. Nicky helped me place Echo and Damian in their lightproof bags at the sides of my chair and then he went out into the hallway with Domino, Kaazim, and Jake to be good bodyguards. Socrates and

Ethan had stayed with Magda at headquarters. Socrates thought it would be a good idea to show some of Nolan's people the speed of a regular lycanthrope. He and Ethan were good, but they were slower than Magda because they weren't Harlequin or sleeping with me and Jean-Claude. Though they were going to leave that part out and just say it was age and practice that made her even faster than them.

Flannery got to wait out in the hallway with my guards, because he was there to partner, or back up, or even keep an eye on his boss. Nolan got to join us in the room this time; whoever had his back was pushing hard that he get involved in things. Pearson and Sheridan didn't like it, but they took it like the professionals they were when the top brass above you force people into your investigation. We settled down with pictures of horrors spread on the table, a fresh map of Dublin on the corkboard, and people bringing in actual paper for us since I didn't have an iPad or a computer with me to read things on-screen. My iPhone was good for a lot of things, but reading detailed forensics wasn't one of them. I looked at the first victim with their throat torn open and thought, *I really don't want to be here.* I wanted to be out in the sunshine with Nathaniel and Dev and Fortune and even Donnie and Griffin. They both seemed pleasant and would probably be good tour guides for the city. I promised myself that I would get a few days of vacation in here with my people before we flew home. I would, damn it, but first we had a mystery to solve. Why were vampires spreading through Dublin for the first time in their history? Why was the fairy magic of the city's land fading? Why wasn't Damian's old master policing the new vampires or destroying them? Had she really lost that much power, and had she lost it because we'd killed the Mother of All Darkness? How did we find the vampire who had started all this in the city, if it wasn't M'Lady? How did we find the vampire that seemed to be enjoying tearing people's throats out? How did we keep more of the families of Dublin from joining the Brady family as the new undead? We had so many questions; what we needed were answers, and that was why I didn't get to play tourist. If we solved the mystery, caught all the bad guys and girls, and saved Ireland from its first-ever plague of vampires, then I could be a tourist; until then it had to be all business for me, because if I didn't do my job more people would die. Was it weird that I still thought of the Brady family as having died, even though they were vampires now? I was in love and engaged to Jean-Claude, but looking down at the new vampires in the children's room today, I'd still thought, dead, murdered, not undead, and alive. Even when your murder victims can come back to "life" at sunset, it doesn't always change the fact that they had their lives taken from them. Being made a vampire against your will was still murder in the United States; it'd be interesting to see how Irish law handled it. It takes a while to get used to the thought that your victim can give testimony in their own murder trial. It would be up to Irish courts and politicians to decide if being turned against your will was considered murder here; all I knew was that back home Edward and I would have had warrants of execution on the asses of every vampire involved in this, as I looked at the photos of fang marks, torn throats, and a few bodies just torn apart— killing whoever had done this totally worked for me.

62

HOURS LATER WE had the map covered in crime scenes and locations. Sheridan had stayed to help us color-code everything, though I was certain they had a map somewhere that had all of this already marked. I'd actually asked, "Aren't we duplicating something you've got in your murder room?"

"We don't call it that," she'd said.

"Sorry, but whatever you call it, haven't you done this already?"

"They want to see if you find a pattern they've missed," Edward said. "If they give you their map, then you'll be looking at what they think is important."

I gave him the look that deserved. "We're wasting time duplicating effort."

"No, truly, Marshal Blake, we want your opinion without our bias."

I'd let it go, but I didn't buy it. I was pretty sure they just didn't want me to see all their evidence, just in case I turned out to be an evil necromancer after all.

They even let me pick the colors that went with each thing I wanted to mark. Fine, whatever. A color of flag for the homes of bite victims that had survived and were still not vampires, plus the places they were attacked if it was known in a different color. Flags for victims that hadn't survived but didn't rise as vampires. Flags for people who did rise as vampires. Flags for bodies that were so dismembered that even the police weren't sure if they were vampire victims, or if they had a serial killer on their hands. They were pretty sure it was just vampires indulging in their newfound strength, because of the timing and the fact that you had to be more than human-strong to tear a body apart like that.

Those were the pictures I looked at the longest, because it was rare for vamps to tear a body apart like this. Even as I was looking at them in pictures, my mind refused to "see" them for what they were at first. It was the mind's way of protecting itself, of protecting us from seeing something so horrible that it would leave a psychic wound, almost literally. But it was part of my job to look at things that most people never had to see. I couldn't afford to look away, because there was something wrong with the scene. Something just didn't ring true for a vampire-related crime scene.

I spread the pictures out on my part of the table and forced myself to try to make sense of them. I'd really started to want to listen to my brain when it said, *Don't look. We don't need another nightmare in here*, but I knew that if I flinched I might miss something, and part of me would always believe that something I missed would be *the* clue that would solve the case. Solving the case meant saving lives, so I looked down at the pictures. I wasn't sure at first if it was one body or two. I saw one shoulder with an intact arm, but no hand. A hand with no arm, so probably a match. Even through all the blood, I could see that the fingers were thick and the hand big enough that I was pretty certain it was a man's hand. The arm looked big enough that it helped me feel fairly confident that it was male. There was a lower half of a body near it that seemed intact and to match in size, so one dead male. I looked at the other bits in the blood, trying to make them into the missing parts of the upper body, but I couldn't do it. I wasn't sure if the parts were just so torn up that I couldn't put them back together from just pictures, or if there were parts missing. If there were missing bits, then this wasn't just vampires, because the one thing they couldn't do was eat solid food. The man's body was one of three that looked like they'd been torn apart. None of the bodies had a visible head in the mess, but there were enough pieces scattered that the head could have been crushed and scattered among all the other gory bits.

"You seem fascinated, Marshal Blake," Pearson said.

I glanced up at him. "I'm trying to do the serial killer math, and I can't get the body parts to match up. Did you find all the parts to the man's body at the scene?"

Pearson did a look with everyone in the room, including Edward and Inspector Luke Logan. Inspector Logan was medium height, dark, and average looking. He paced a lot, and the room wasn't big enough for it. He'd joined our merry little band a couple of hours into it all. There was already a good-size table covered with pictures and reports, with chairs for five, and the board on its stand with the map. Plus the bags with Echo and Damian in them were tucked up beside my outside leg and the back of my chair. A sixth person would have been a tight fit for the room, but a sixth person who paced energetically and liked to talk with his hands . . . I was rapidly understanding why no one else liked him.

"What was the look for?" Nolan asked from the other side of Edward, which put him at the end of the table. I guess I wasn't the only one on the outside of that knowing look. It pissed me off that Edward was hiding things from me, but when didn't he? He liked his secrets too damned much. He and I would talk about it later, in private.

"I told you she'd spot it," Edward said.

"Spot what? Why is it important that Blake can't find all the body parts?" Nolan asked. He looked at the pictures in front of me.

"Can you find all the body parts in those pictures?" Edward asked, looking at Nolan.

The Captain was quiet for a moment, watching everyone's face. Only Logan had looked away, arms crossed over his chest, as if he were trying not to give anything away. Finally, Nolan said, "No, but you could have stray dogs, or crows that picked up some pieces."

"Do you see animal footprints in the blood?" Pearson asked.

Nolan leaned over Edward farther, looking at the pictures. I pushed them closer toward him, but he finally shook his head. "No."

"We don't rule out crows, or other birds flying in and grabbing some of the body before we found it, but there's no bird native to the area that could carry off enough of the body to explain the missing pieces."

"What do you think happened to the missing body parts?" I asked.

"I don't know," Nolan said.

"I was actually addressing everyone in the room with the question, not just you, Nolan. You're as late to this party as I am."

"We'd like to hear your theories first," Sheridan said.

"Why?"

"Forrester had his theories, but I requested he not share them with you until you had your own opportunity to view the evidence yourself," Pearson said.

"Why withhold information from me?"

"Because Ted here has been bragging about you for days, and we wanted to see if you're as good as he said," Logan said, his arm flung out from his body and half-pointed and half-flapped toward Edward.

"That is not it," Pearson said, frowning at Logan.

Sheridan stepped away from the map to say, "Ted had some . . . interesting insights about this particular series of photos. We wanted to see if another vampire hunter would come to the same . . . insights."

They were all being so careful about their word choices; even Logan had been less obvious and that seemed like something he found difficult. I sighed and gave Edward a look. He gave me a steady look back. "I'd have told you, because I know you'll see it."

I gathered the pictures back from Nolan and spread them out in front of me again. "Did you put these pictures in here to trip me up?" I asked.

"What do you mean, trip you up?" Sheridan asked.

"Trick me."

"No. I mean, no." She looked puzzled enough that I believed her.

"Are these photos from another case?" I asked.

"Why would you ask that, Marshal?" Pearson said.

"They don't match. Not just this man, but any of the dismembered bodies."

"We only have three," Sheridan said.

I looked at her to see if she was kidding, but she looked totally serious. "Does Dublin get enough dismembered bodies that three new ones are no big deal?"

"No, of course not," she said.

"It's as rare a crime here as it is back in your city," Pearson said.

I looked at Nolan and Edward. The first looked puzzled, and the second inscrutable. No one kept a secret like him, no one alive anyway.

"This doesn't look like the work of a vampire," I said.

"We thought they were strong enough to do it," Pearson said.

"They are, but they don't usually go in for this kind of display of pure visceral violence."

"Why not?" Pearson asked, and he was looking at me as if he wanted to see inside my head to exactly what I was thinking.

"It wastes blood and it's messy. Once you tear into a fresh body like this, you are going to be covered in blood and gore. No way could you walk the streets after that and not have someone call the police."

"Except for the wasting blood part, what you just said could apply to anyone," Pearson said.

"A human being couldn't rip a body apart like that," Logan

said, flailing his arm nearly into Sheridan's shoulder. He stepped away from her as if she were hot to the touch and went around to the other side of the room near the door.

"It doesn't look like a blade was used to dismember the bodies; am I wrong? Did you find tool marks?"

"No, no tool marks," Pearson said.

"Then I don't think a human being did it."

"Then what are you talking about, Blake?" Logan said.

"I'm saying you might have a vampire crime spree and something else has moved into the city, too. I agree it's supernatural, but the one thing vampires can't do is eat solid food. A human serial killer could take souvenirs to eat later but isn't strong enough to tear the bodies apart. A vampire could tear the bodies up but would have no reason to take meat away from the scene."

"Did you just call the victims' body parts *meat*?" Logan demanded, striding into the room and trying to fill more space than he could. Pearson and Nolan were taller, and almost everyone in the room lifted more weights than showed on their frame, and that included Sheridan now that I'd seen her arms in the short sleeves of her white blouse. She was built like a taller version of Mort, all sinew and muscle except with more curves. She might work at being thin, but she worked out, too. I liked that I wasn't the only woman in the room with perceivable biceps.

"That's what I think our killer thinks."

"What do you mean, Blake?" Pearson asked.

I fought a sudden urge to look at Nolan. "A shapeshifter could dismember the body without tools and could have just eaten part of the body."

"But wouldn't a shapeshifter be covered in blood and unable to hide from the police just like a vampire or a human?" Nolan asked; if he felt weird taking part in the conversation, it didn't show. If I hadn't known his secret, I wouldn't have thought a thing about it.

"Yes, but a shapeshifter can literally change not just their clothes but their skin, so that the beast form could be covered in blood, but once they shift to human form again they're blood free and clean."

"But we should have still found a nude human passed out near the crime scene, and we didn't."

"I told them that not all lycanthropes have to fall into a comalike sleep after they switch back to human form, but they didn't want to believe me," Edward said.

"Why not? You're right," I said.

"Because all the literature says that they fall into a deep, almost comalike sleep after they shift from animal to human form," Pearson said.

"Unless you think you two boyos know more than all the other experts combined?"

"On this, yes, because the books you're reading are from people who studied lycanthropes, interviewed them. I live with them," I said.

"I'm just good friends with them," Edward said in his Ted voice, "but that's still more personal than the book experts."

"How can you be so certain of that?" Sheridan asked.

"Because we read the same books you're reading," I said, "and I read them before I was close to any shapeshifter. Most of them do have to sleep it off, almost like a blackout drunk. In fact, a lot of the ones that sleep hard like that don't remember most of their night in animal form."

"But you're saying that some of them just change to human form and can walk away from a scene like this?" Sheridan asked.

"Absolutely."

"Is this the point where I say *I told you so*?" Edward asked in a heavy down-home accent.

"Only if you're not the gentleman I know you are," Sheridan said with a smile.

Edward gave her a smile and a little nod. If his hat had still been on his head he'd have tipped it at her. I couldn't tell if he was flirting with her, or he was so far into his part as Ted that he couldn't react any other way.

"So you were right about her, Forrester," Logan said as he continued to pace the wall by the door. "You trained her. You taught her everything she knows."

"Oh no, Logan. I trained Anita to be better at killing the monsters. She taught me how to understand them better."

"Thanks, Ted, and thanks for nothing, Logan. Just love it when men assume that because there's a man in a woman's life they teach us everything we know."

He scowled at me, but he was an amateur compared to Nolan. "It's just a figure of speech, Blake."

"You just keep telling yourself that, Logan, while the rest of us try to catch the bad guys."

"What do you mean, bad guys, Blake? You're here to help us find the vampire that's behind all this, so it's just one bad guy."

"Someone is also killing people by tearing them apart, and that's probably not a vampire, and there are a couple of neck wounds that don't show any fangs."

Edward picked them out of the pile of photos without me needing to point them out. He handed them to me and I held them up to Logan, Pearson, and Sheridan like I was doing show-and-tell. If Nolan wanted to see them better he would have to move his chair. "Did your medical examiner find any marks that couldn't have been made by human teeth?"

"No," Pearson said, "but a savage bite like that where the vampire worries at the wound like a terrier with a rat can mask precise dentation."

I had a moment of doing the long blink while I fought not to remember a vampire doing just that to me. "Anita is very aware of that, Superintendent Pearson." I looked at Edward. I was trying to ask with my eyes how much show-and-tell he wanted me to do. I had scars that showed exactly the kind of vampire attack that Pearson was talking about.

"Are you trying to tell us we have three different crime sprees in Dublin, including a human serial killer that's using their teeth to tear out throats?" Logan demanded, stopping in his pacing long enough to look at me.

"No, I'm saying that might be what's happening. Just because you have vampires and violent crimes in the same city doesn't mean that all the violence is vampire related."

"We aren't trying to blame all our violent crimes on the vampires, Marshal Blake," Sheridan said. She was standing beside the corkboard. I think she'd gotten up in hopes that Logan would use her chair; no such luck.

"I know that, Inspector Sheridan, but this is a lot of victims to come from just one vampire."

"We aren't stupid, Blake. We know that no single vampire could do all this," Logan said, motioning at the map with a gesture so wide that he almost hit Pearson in the top of the head. Logan either didn't notice or ignored it, because he didn't apologize. In fact, he paced around the table again, going behind Nolan—again.

Nolan stood up and went to the far corner of the wall with the window. He put his back in the corner so that there was no possible way for Logan to walk behind him again. He'd told Logan at one point that if he walked behind his chair again he'd put him on the floor, but Pearson had taken offense. He didn't like Logan either, but Nolan had been forced into his investigation from on high, so Nolan wasn't his favorite person either. He'd told Nolan, "If you try to put one of my men on the floor, you and I will have words and you will not like them."

Nolan stood in the corner, glaring at Logan, who walked around the whole table again, crossing behind Edward and me—again. Like I said, the room wasn't big enough to pace, especially with this many adults already in it.

"Anita doesn't mean that one vampire did all the victims," Edward said.

"That's what she said."

"No, it's not. I—"

"It's what you said."

"But it doesn't mean—"

"How can it mean anything else?" he demanded, in a voice that seemed stuck between angry and whining. The tone was not user friendly to his listeners. In fact, I was beginning to have to fight not to grit my teeth.

"If you'd stop interrupting me, I could explain."

"You think you're an expert on vampires, so that makes you a better cop than us. Is that it?"

He paced toward Nolan, who said, "Don't pace in front of me, Logan."

Logan turned and came back toward the table and me. He tried to pace between Echo's bag and the corkboard, but he was moving faster than he could negotiate the space, and he tripped on the bag. I'd have let that go, except after he tripped, he kicked the bag.

I stood up and stepped over Echo's bag, driving my shoulder into Logan as I moved. He stumbled back even though he was at least five inches taller and nearly a hundred pounds heavier.

"What the hell, Blake?" he nearly shouted.

"You kicked one of my people."

"They can't feel anything. It's daylight."

"Who made you the vampire expert, Logan?" I asked, and stepped in close to him again. He had to step back or I'd have stepped into him again.

"I'm not fucking enough of them to be an expert," he said.

"Logan!" Sheridan said.

"I bet vampires aren't the only thing you're not fucking," I said.

"Marshal Blake!" Pearson said; I heard his chair go back and moved so I could see him standing up. I knew he wasn't a real danger; it was just automatic.

"What the fuck does that mean?" Logan asked, his face darkening; either he was getting angry or he was blushing.

"It means anytime someone starts accusing me of using sex to get good at my job, it usually means either they want to fuck me and I said no, and you and I haven't known each other that long, or it means that they aren't getting any, so they're just pissy because I'm having more sex than they are."

His face was starting to go purple; it wasn't a blush; it was blood pressure. Inspector Logan had a temper, great; maybe I could goad him into doing something stupid enough that Pearson would send him home.

Edward got out of his chair, but not to come to my aid. He knew I didn't need it, but I also knew he wasn't getting up for nothing. He moved around the table, talking as he moved. "Rachel, I don't think you need to hear all this," he said in his best down-home Ted accent. "Why don't you take me out for that tea you were bragging about at that hotel?"

Oh, goody, Edward had the same idea I did. We were going to make Logan lose his shit.

"Oh, Ted . . ." Sheridan began; I was pretty sure she'd say

something like she wasn't hearing anything she couldn't handle, but Logan never gave her a chance to answer.

"You are not taking him to tea at a hotel," Logan yelled, or maybe almost yelled. I was just close enough to him that it was that loud.

"I will take who I want, where I want," Sheridan said, her voice rising.

"No!" he yelled.

I kept looking at him and resisted the urge to turn and look at Sheridan behind me. I was the closest to him and if he lost his shit badly enough I wanted a chance to pour gasoline on the flames, and not get hit or trampled in the process. His face was almost purplish with temper. He was too young, early forties tops, and not nearly overweight enough to turn this kind of color from anger. He made an inarticulate noise low in his throat. I wanted him to leave the room, not have a stroke, and I suddenly didn't know which was more likely. He was literally inarticulate with rage. Wow.

"Inspector Logan, you will refrain from personal remarks to Inspector Sheridan. You have been warned more than once about this kind of thing," Pearson said in a voice that was deep and projected well, so that it carried over whatever anyone else was going to say. It made me wonder if Pearson had theater training.

A tic started to pulse just under Logan's right eye. His hands were in fists at his sides. It was like he was afraid to move, or even speak, because he didn't trust himself to do anything. I had a temper, but this was a new level of problem. I wondered if they'd forced him to take anger management classes yet. Or maybe I didn't, because if this was the after, then I was glad I had missed the before.

He was staring past me at Sheridan, I was pretty sure, but I was looking at Logan. He was so angry. I wondered if his skin would be hot to the touch with it. My stomach cramped as if I were hungry. I'd eaten at breakfast. Then I realized that it had to have been at least five hours since then, probably more. I was overdue for food. Fuck. I stared at the skin jumping just under his eye. He was so angry, so rage-filled. I swallowed hard, fighting the urge to sniff near his skin and see if he smelled like food. I didn't just feed off lust, or love; I could feed on someone's anger. I could touch Logan's arm, his face, and drain all that rage away. If I was careful he'd just be calm. If I wasn't careful he could be disoriented, or even forget the last few minutes and what had happened. It wasn't that dissimilar from vampire mind tricks. If I was careful, I could just take a little and no one would ever know. It would calm things down. It would help. The moment I thought that, I stepped back from him. I could not feed on one of the Irish cops with witnesses. Being a necromancer made them think I was evil; if I sucked energy out of one of them, they'd be sure of it.

"Are you all right, Anita?" Edward asked, because he'd seen me take that step back. I would never have backed up from Logan, not normally.

"No, I don't think I ate enough today. I appreciate everyone bringing me coffee when you have all the great tea, but I think I need real food." I emphasized that last word a little, hoping he'd understand what I meant.

"When you don't think coffee is enough, something really is wrong with you, pardner." He made a drawling joke of it, but he'd understood me. He'd seen me feed before.

"We can have food brought in," Pearson said.

"I think I may need some air, too," I said. I had to get away from Logan, who was still almost shaking with his anger. I resisted the urge to tell him he needed to learn to meditate or take a yoga class, just to see how angry I could make him. He'd make such a good snack.

"I apologize for Inspector Logan," Sheridan said.

That was it for Logan. He backed up and marched out of the room without a word. I was pretty sure he didn't trust himself, so leaving was his only option. When the door shut carefully behind him, Pearson said, "Don't judge us by Logan."

"What's his problem?" I asked, taking deep, even breaths.

Pearson looked at Sheridan, and she looked embarrassed. "I made the mistake of dating a fellow officer, and when I broke it off—" She shook her head. "It was a grave misjudgment on my part."

"I'm going to go check on Logan. I think it was my misjudgment thinking the two of you could work a case together again." Pearson left, closing the door behind him.

"If you don't meet people at work, where do you meet them?" I said. Now that Logan was gone, I could breathe a little easier.

"Exactly," she said, and then her pretty face looked very unhappy, "but it was still a mistake."

"Dating Logan? Oh yeah."

"He wasn't always like this. I swear he wasn't. I mean, he had a temper, but not like this."

"You don't have to apologize for Logan," Nolan said from the wall where he was still standing.

"But I feel like I should, like it's somehow my fault," she said.

"You don't have to date a man just because he's upset that you stopped dating him," I said.

"There are a lot of fish in the sea, Inspector; you need to fish a little farther out into the ocean, that's all," Edward said.

"But all the good fish are taken," she said, looking at him.

"Not all of them," I said.

She looked at me then, and gave me wide eyes. "Well, you certainly have caught your limit."

"Or a little over," I said.

She smiled. "Well, let me know if you're going to throw one of them back. I might want to be there with a net."

"I'll keep that in mind," I said, smiling.

"I think Anita and her men in the hallway still need food," Edward said.

"We can have food brought in for everyone," Sheridan said, "unless you think that eating and looking at the photos will be a problem?"

I looked down at the torn throats, the mangled bodies, and then had another thought. "I let myself get distracted; are any of the skull, brain, head parts in the debris I'm seeing in the pictures?"

"What do you mean, Blake?"

"I mean, did they crush the head and mix it up with the other small bits, or did the killer take the heads?"

"We haven't found any brain matter at the crime scenes," she said.

"So whoever is killing them is taking souvenirs after all."

"Why wouldn't they eat the head?" Sheridan asked.

"It's like all animal heads, not great eating raw, though I'm told that brains mixed with eggs make really fluffy scrambled eggs."

Sheridan made a face at me. "Have you eaten brains?"

"No, but I went to college with a girl whose family owned a cow farm, and her mom mixed the brains into her scrambled eggs without telling the kids. They thought it was delicious and didn't know, until they got out on their own and tried to make eggs like Mom did, and couldn't get the fluffy, creamy texture."

Edward gave a low chuckle as Sheridan's face paled. Nolan joined him in the chuckle and tried to turn it into a cough. Edward apologized. "I'm not laughing at you, Rachel. I'm laughing at Anita telling that story when we're thinking about getting food."

"We're going to be looking at crime scene photos while we eat. I didn't think the egg story would be a problem."

He laughed again and patted my shoulder. "You just keep thinking there, Butch. That's what you're good at."

I rolled my eyes at him and wished I could remember a movie-line comeback, but nothing sprang to mind.

Pearson stuck his head back in the room. "What does everyone want for lunch?"

"Not eggs," Sheridan said.

63

THE SANDWICHES WEREN'T Irish; they were just food. When you're ordering sandwiches that can be eaten while you look at paperwork and photos on a crowded table, a sandwich is a sandwich is a sandwich. It wasn't a bad sandwich, but it wasn't great, either. It really was just another work trip for me except that I was the only one who got a Coke to drink; even Edward got bottled water. He told me if I behaved myself today maybe the detectives would let us all eat in the big room with desks so we weren't all having to share the little kids' table.

"I don't know what you mean by that, Ted," Sheridan had said. Pearson apparently had decided to eat elsewhere, or was skipping lunch and holding Logan's hand, or maybe beating the shit out of him. I really didn't care which, as long as Logan was somewhere else. I knew I'd have to deal with him again, but later was better than now.

"It'd be much more comfortable sharing this meal at your desk like we normally do," he said with that Ted smile that seemed to melt women into their socks but had never worked on me, because I'd met him when he was being just Edward. His cold-blooded-killer mode was far less charming than good ol' boy Ted.

She actually got a little flustered, spilling bits of her sandwich on one of the photos. Thanks to modern technology, we could print more almost instantly, but still you tried not to get the evidence messy. While Sheridan grabbed for napkins I gave Edward a raised-eyebrow look. He smiled innocently back at me as if butter wouldn't have melted in his mouth, then went to help her clean up, which made her start to drop things again. I didn't know what game he was playing, only that he was playing one. I was so bad at being devious that I didn't try, but he was really good at it. I just didn't know why he was being devious in Inspector Rachel Sheridan's direction. Maybe it amused him? I wouldn't know unless he told me, and if I asked outright, he wouldn't, so I just watched the show.

Nolan, who was sitting at the end of the table again, caught my eye, and just the look let me know that he was wondering what game Edward was playing, too. I gave a small shrug and took another bite of my sandwich.

"I wonder if Jacob Pennyfeather would have any insight into these crimes," he said as he helped Sheridan pick up the papers she'd managed to knock off the table.

She looked up at him, brown eyes wide and a little startled. "I don't know."

"He knew more about saving vampires than we did at the last crime scene. Anita and I know more about killing them than healing them."

She stood up with the papers clasped to her chest. "I don't think this case is about saving vampires."

Was Edward flirting with her because he saw an opening to manipulate her? Nothing specific, but just a possible way to gain an edge if he needed it. Was that it? If so, it was very calculating. He was my best friend; sometimes I forgot how cold-blooded he could be dealing with other people. Would he talk Sheridan into doing things we wanted and risk damaging her career? Would he care? He told me once that he'd tried manipulating me like a girl—i.e., flirting—and I'd been so oblivious to it that he'd stopped trying. I watched him with the detective and wondered how different things would have been if I'd been more susceptible to his manly wiles.

Nolan shook his head, so I looked at him, giving him encouragement to explain his expression if he wanted to. "Good to know that one of us has gotten better at it." His smile was a little ironic, but not unhappy. He just seemed amused.

Edward turned and gave that version of a younger smile again. "That's not the only thing I've gotten better at."

Nolan laughed out loud, which startled me and Sheridan. We exchanged one of those looks that women have probably been exchanging around men since cave painting was the new thing. I shrugged, because in this instance I really had no clue. I watched the two men, their eyes sparkling with laughter and some secret adventure that their long-ago selves had had together.

"If I ask what's so funny, would you tell me?" I asked.

They did another of those looks that meant more to them than it did to us. Nolan shook his head. Edward said, "You wouldn't think it was funny."

I said, "You know, a few years back, I'd have said, *Try me*," which made Nolan laugh again and he hid his face with his hand. I frowned at him, but continued. "Now I'll just trust you that it won't amuse me."

"Thank you," Edward said, his face still shiny with suppressed humor. "I know that's high praise from you, because you like to know everything that's going on around you."

"What if I want to know what it is?" Sheridan asked.

The two men looked at her, looked at each other, and then cracked up like a pair of twelve-year-olds. I'd never seen Edward like this; I liked it and found it unsettling at the same time.

"Trust me on this, Sheridan. If Ted doesn't think I'd find it funny, you won't either."

"Is this a male-bonding type of thing?" she asked.

I nodded. "Oh, yeah."

She shook her head, and we got to have one of those shared moments when women shake their heads at the men in their lives. I was usually all alone when these moments happened, so it was nice to have someone to roll my eyes with and feel vaguely superior because we weren't men. Men get to do it in reverse.

I finished my sandwich while they continued to do the straight-guy version of giggling. The flirting with Sheridan for whatever purpose was put on hold while the men bonded, or maybe rebonded. Between the flirting and this, my bestie was just surprising the heck out of me this trip.

We'd all finished our lunch, and Pearson rejoined us without Logan. I was okay with that. Sheridan actually did talk to Pearson about getting Jake's input on the case. He didn't say yes, but Edward's little bit of flirting had paid off. It made me wonder, if he actually took her to dinner, how much more cooperative she'd be with us, but that seemed a slippery slope since I was going to be best "man" at his wedding.

"Mr. Pennyfeather and his partner aren't in the hallway to invite inside even if I were so inclined, Sheridan. It's only Murdock and Santana on post currently."

"They were going to take turns grabbing sandwiches," I said. "It's hard to eat standing up in a hallway. An international flight takes a lot out of you, so we're still a little beat."

"We could have offered your men a desk or something to eat their lunch at," Pearson said.

"That would have been nice," I said.

Pearson got up and started for the door. "I can see what I can find for them to use."

"Thank you, Inspector, but I'm pretty sure that at least two of them will stay on the door."

"I know you're implying they're standing guard, but we are inside a police station."

"True, but until they have more of a role in the case, they're going to do the only job they have."

"The men with you don't even have badges in your own country. I can't justify letting them see evidence in an ongoing investigation."

"Totally reasonable," I said.

Pearson gave me a narrow look. "Why does that sound like a criticism?"

"It's not meant as one," I said.

He looked from me to Edward and back. He looked downright suspicious. People usually had to know me longer before I got that look. I did my best to give inoffensive and pleasant back. I used to try looking innocent, but I really wasn't good at it, even when I *was* innocent.

Pearson looked even harder at me. It wasn't his hardest look—I gave him the benefit of the doubt that he hadn't made detective without being able to stare the socks off a suspect—but he was still trying to give me a "hard" look. I smiled at him. I'd found it an effective way to either irritate people or win them over. It could go either way when they were already trying to intimidate me by being a hard-ass.

"Now, Anita, I'm sure Superintendent Pearson is just doing his job," Edward said in his drawling Ted voice, which managed to be pleasant and theatrical. I wondered if the Irish police were disappointed that my accent wasn't the same as his.

I started to say, *I never said he wasn't*, but one minute we were doing some mild double-team manipulation and the next minute the hair at the back of my neck rose and goose bumps ran down my arms. I think I stopped breathing, my throat tight with the power that was reaching out.

"Anita," Edward said, "what's wrong?"

"You're pale," Sheridan said.

Nolan had grabbed the back of a chair. He was fighting to stand upright and not show that he was sensing it, too.

I held up a hand, and Edward understood that I wanted them to be quiet for a second. He made everyone else stop talking. I needed to listen. Listen to what? There was a voice on the air, or in it, and the voice was saying something, wanting something.

There was a sharp double knock on the door. Pearson said, "Who is it?"

"Nicky Murdock," he announced, but didn't wait for an invitation before opening the door. "Anita, what the hell is that?"

I held up my hand and waved it at him, and he went quiet. I listened, reached out toward that skin-prickling rush of energy, and found . . . "Come out," I said.

"What does she mean, come out?" Sheridan asked.

I repeated it. "*Come out.* That's what it's saying, over and over. It's wanting . . . us to come out. Them to come out."

"Who is *them*?" Edward asked.

I felt Damian take his first breath for the day inside the bag at my feet, felt him startle before the bag moved. Edward actually jumped as the bag bumped his chair.

I knelt beside Damian's bag. He was afraid of the small space and of the power that had jarred him awake. "Close the shades," I said.

Nolan was closest, but I think it was taking all he had to simply try to stand there, gripping the back of the chair, and not show the reaction that all the other preternaturals were having. Nicky walked across the room to do what I asked. The weak sunshine was suddenly plunged into gray twilight. Pearson didn't complain or tell Nicky to get out of the room because of evidence. No, Pearson was staring at the bag on the floor as it struggled. It was his turn to look pale. I saw Domino in the doorway; he was still watching the hall like a good bodyguard.

I unzipped the duffel bag. One long pale arm shot out, grabbing for air. Damian forced the zipper down before I could get to it, pulling his upper body free of it like a butterfly emerging from its chrysalis. His hair spilled out around him like liquid fire, so perfectly red in a stray line of sunlight that managed to get through the draped window.

He grabbed my hand in his, green eyes wide with the fear I could already feel. "It can't be," he whispered.

"It can't be who?" I asked.

"Her."

"Who is *her*?" Sheridan asked.

"It's a compulsion spell," Jake said from the open door, where he and Kaazim had just run up.

"A what spell?" Pearson asked.

"A compulsion spell, a magical way of ordering or commanding people," Jake said.

"I have not felt one so strong in many, many years," Kaazim said.

Damian wrapped both his hands around mine. "It's her. It's her, Anita. It's her."

"Who?" Sheridan asked.

"She-Who-Made-Me."

"Who made you? What are you talking about?" Pearson said.

"She was always able to call her vampires from their coffins in daylight. She could wake us early."

"The vampire that made him," I said.

"She's calling all her vampires to her," Damian whispered, "and I still answered her." He clung to my hands. "I'm yours, yours now; why did I answer to her?"

"I don't know. I don't know why I'm hearing it, too." I looked up at Jake and Kaazim. "Can you hear it, too?"

"Yes," Jake said.

"We can," Kaazim said.

I looked down at the bag that still held Echo. "She's not waking up."

"She was not created here," Kaazim said.

"Neither was I, or the two of you."

"I can't hear it," Nicky said. "I just feel you."

"I can hear something," Domino said. "It's like a whisper in the next room, just noise, but it's still there."

I wanted to ask if Nolan could hear it more clearly, since he had been born here in Ireland, but he was trying to play human. He was grim-faced, fingers turning white as he gripped the chair, but he wasn't going to admit he could hear anything.

"So why are the three of us hearing it?"

"And why is Domino hearing it more than I am?" Nicky asked.

"I don't know," I said. Damian was getting a little frantic

to get out of the bag, but he'd gotten a piece of his shirt caught in the zipper. Nicky knelt to help me with it.

"I smell fresh blood," Domino said from the door.

I didn't smell it, but I trusted that he did.

All the wereanimals except for Nolan sniffed the air. "What are they, scent hounds?" Pearson asked.

"Better than that. They can smell a scent and then tell us about it," I said.

"A lot of blood," Nicky said, and he started tugging at the stuck zipper a little harder.

"It's close to us," Kaazim said.

"How close?" I asked.

"It's in the building, on this floor. I'm sure of that," Domino said.

"No, no," Pearson said softly, but there was a lot of feeling in those two words. He smelled scared.

"What did you do, Pearson?" Edward asked.

He didn't answer, just took off and pushed his way past Domino and running down the hallway. Sheridan followed him, and so did Edward and Nolan.

I yelled, "Edward!"

He ignored it, because it wasn't his name. Damn it. "Go with them," I said.

Domino did what I asked, but Jake and Kaazim stayed in the doorway. "Our loyalty is to you."

"Damn it, then carry Echo!" Jake came to do what I'd ordered. Nice to know he listened to some of what I said. Nicky tore the zipper away from Damian's bag so that he was finally free; we helped him to his feet and started running out of the room. Kaazim was still helping Jake get Echo settled on his back. They yelled for us to wait. I listened to them as well as they'd listened to me: selectively.

64

THERE WAS NOBODY in the hallway except for a few uniformed officers, but Nicky started jogging down the hallway without hesitating on a direction. I stayed with him, trusting his nose to lead us to the blood. I had to drop back a little behind him to keep from running into people as I ran and he jogged. Damian came up beside me, both of us at Nicky's broad back. We got some puzzled looks from the officers and personnel in the halls. Surely if it had been a serious emergency they'd have been running with us, but it seemed like business as usual except for us. Kaazim and Jake had caught up with us by the time we went around the second corner. No one was acting alarmed, so we'd slowed to a fast walk. Where were Edward and Domino? I wanted to find everyone, but I wasn't emotionally attached to anyone else.

Sheridan was standing outside a closed door. She was so pale her brown eyes looked black and stranded in her face like islands in the middle of a milk-white ocean. Even her lips were bloodless; the light lipstick she'd had on in the other room was gone. She raised one hand up to push at her hair, and I saw the pinkish shine of it as if she'd rubbed her lips a lot in the few minutes since we'd seen her. What the hell had happened?

"It's in the room," Nicky said.

"What is?" I asked.

"The blood."

Sheridan looked at us then, her eyes looking like burned-out holes in her head. I'd thought she was beautiful and now she looked haggard, as if every hour of sleep she'd ever lost had all caught up with her at once.

"Sheridan," I said.

She looked at me but didn't see me, not really.

"Rachel, can you hear me?"

She nodded. "I'm keeping the crime scene intact until forensics gets here."

"Where are the others?" Jake asked.

"Looking for him."

I grabbed her upper arms and gave her a little shake. Her eyes focused on me; she even blinked. "Inspector Sheridan, I need you to focus. Report, damn it."

She jerked away from me. "We found another vampire after Nolan got the others. Pearson . . . all of us wanted to keep this one. They were fixing up a cell that wouldn't expose it to light. It's just a dead body until dark. It should have been safe."

"Inspector Sheridan, what happened?"

She looked at me as if she didn't like me much, but I didn't care. "The storage room had a lock on it. It was supposed to keep people from walking in on the body, not to keep it in, but Logan must have come to check on it, and it woke up early and it killed him."

"Jesus," I said.

"They're tracking it. Santana could smell the vampire, so they went that way." She pointed down the hall away from us. Her gaze had slid to the side again, as if she couldn't bear to focus on anything for too long. Her reaction could have been from just the violence of it to someone she knew, but I didn't think it was just that. Yeah, Logan had been an ass, and it had been a mistake to date, but she'd cared for him. I wondered if she'd known just how much she cared for him until now. Fuck.

"Anita, we need to move," Nicky said.

I nodded. "Can you track them?"

"Yes," Jake said. We'd worked it out that whichever were-animal had the best nose was just supposed to take the lead on things like this, rather than debate it. Wolf beat tiger and apparently jackal, and we hadn't brought any wererats, which actually had one of the best noses in the wereanimal kingdom.

"Do it," I said. Jake moved a little ahead of us with Echo still strapped in her bag to his back. Kaazim dropped back to the rear, putting Damian and me in the middle with Nicky and Jake ahead. I glanced behind us at Sheridan leaning against the wall by the door where maybe the off-again, on-again almost-love-of-her-life was lying dead. I'd give her a hug later, if she'd let me, but right now we had to find Domino and Ed-

ward and the vampire that had already killed one Garda. I
prayed that it wouldn't kill anyone else before we found it, and
then I realized that Edward was ahead of us on the hunt. As I
followed Jake and Nicky, I kept waiting to hear gunfire. If I
were the vampire, I'd have been running.

65

"THERE'S A MAN screaming up ahead," Jake said.

"Stack and move," I said.

We stacked up on Jake, one hand on the shoulder of the
person in front of us, gun in the other hand ready but pointed
down. Except for Damian, who hadn't trained with us; the rule
was if you didn't train for stacking and moving, then you kept
your gun holstered until we weren't standing on top of one another. I put my hand against Nicky's back, because his shoulder
was a little high to hold and move at the shuffle-jog. Damian
didn't have any trouble putting his hand on my shoulder. Getting the rhythm of the shuffle step was a little harder for him,
but he was more graceful than I would ever be, so he managed
not to step on me. It was a formation that worked well in crowds,
and if we were going into a dangerous situation. Logan was
dead, so dangerous it was.

I was pretty certain that the screaming man wasn't Edward, and it was unlikely to be Domino, but it was somebody. Saving somebody would be good. We came out into a
larger opening; it wasn't exactly a room, but it seemed too
big to call it a hallway. Did police stations have entryways
like a house? I just didn't know enough about architecture to
know what to call it. But whatever it was, I heard Edward's
voice ahead.

"Don't do it, pardner."

"She's calling," a man's voice said.

"If you step out there you will burn," Pearson said.

Damian whispered to me, "She is calling. She wants us to come to her."

"Why? Why would she want all her vampires to go out into the sunlight?"

"Maybe it amuses her," he said.

"Is she really that crazy?" I asked.

"Maybe."

We widened our formation to something that looked like the point of a spear, with Jake still at the head of it. Now we all had better views of what was happening at the door, and if we had to use our guns we wouldn't shoot one another. Pearson, Edward, and Domino were near the outer door with a small group of other police persons. I could only glimpse the vampire by the door around everyone in front of us. He was tall, dark-haired, and had dark eyes. His face was almost pink with the rush of the blood he'd drunk. If we didn't want to be shooting into someone's back we needed to move up closer; of course, if we did that the vampire might move out into the daylight. The crowd moved enough for me to see that the vampire was clutching Logan's suit jacket to himself like he was cold. I knew just how to warm him up.

"Move up. We don't want to risk being friendly fire," I said.

"He may be afraid of us," Damian said.

"He should be," I said.

No one else questioned it. We moved up so we'd have a clean shot if it came to that. The vampire did look at us. The fear showed on his face. Apparently, we looked more threatening than anyone nearer to him. Since one of those was Edward, the vampire just didn't know how to do a good threat assessment.

Pearson turned enough to see us, but not enough to give the vampire his back. Good for him. "Marshal Blake, please stay back."

"We talked to Sheridan," I said.

"This is still a citizen of Ireland who deserves a chance at a trial."

"Logan was one of your men. How can you say his murderer deserves anything?"

"Anita's right. In America we'd have a warrant of execution for all the vampires involved in these crimes," Edward said.

"We do not execute people in Ireland," Pearson said, his voice rising.

"I have to go to her," the vampire said.

Damian called out to him, "Brother, don't do it. Do not listen to that evil voice in your head."

The vampire looked at him, and for a minute there was someone in there looking out at him like an echo of who the man had once been. "I wish I could shut out the voice, but she is all I hear. I must go."

"If you go, you will burn alive. I have seen it before."

"I'm sorry, brother. I'm sorry for the policeman I killed. I don't even remember doing it. I came to myself with my mouth at his throat and his blood everywhere. I would never have hurt anyone like that, but I know I did." He reached behind him for the doorknob. If they'd let him go, that might have been all except for the barbecue outside.

Some of the uniformed officers jumped him as if he were just human, like you'd tackle any would-be suicide, but he wasn't human. He smashed one man's head open against the wall in a smear of crimson, and grabbed another one. He was slow by comparison to the vampires I was used to—the newly dead are slower—but he was faster than they were expecting. Fast enough to grab one of them and tear out his throat so the arterial spray showered over his face, the walls, other officers, over Logan's jacket. Fast enough to grab another officer before they could all scatter and hold him in front of his body like a shield. Seeing all that, a female officer still crawled up, grabbed the fallen man's arm, and started trying to pull him to safety. Another officer came and took the other arm and they pulled him away from the door and the vampire. I watched them start to try to stanch the blood, but unless they had an emergency room trauma surgeon hiding in the building, it was already too late. It didn't make the effort a bad one, and it didn't change that they'd been brave to pull him to safety.

I kept waiting for a holy object to flare to life, holy fire to help save them, but there was nothing. It was as if the vampire didn't trigger the holy objects even while he was going all vampire on their asses.

Edward and Domino had their custom AR-15 rifles

snugged against their shoulders. Nolan had his sidearm out and aimed. We moved up to join them. The vampire's bloody face didn't look human or sympathetic anymore. He hissed at us and then his eyes filled with blue light.

"Welcome home, Damian." It was the man's mouth moving, but it didn't sound like the same voice of a minute ago. It wasn't a woman's voice, but there was something about the cadence of it that made me think feminine.

"This is not home. This was never my home," Damian said from beside me.

The vampire gave one of those wild laughs that rise and fall up the scale like something on a Halloween haunted house sound track, except this was real. It raised the hair at the back of my neck and made my gut tense with the madness in it.

He took one step back and a little behind me. "She can't hurt you, Damian," I said.

"Are you sure of that, Anita Blake?" the vampire said.

I snugged my own custom AR-15 rifle to my shoulder. "Yeah, pretty sure."

Edward said, "Can we shoot it now?"

The vampire twisted the officer's head around. Their eyes locked for a moment. I checked and the officer didn't have a visible gun. It was the only saving grace as the vampire bespelled him with his gaze and sent him to run straight at us, while he opened the door behind him and stepped out into the thick summer sunshine.

Edward switched his rifle around and smashed it into the officer's face. He fell to the floor, out cold, and the first screams outside rose to shrieks. The sunlight would do our job for us; all we had to do was wait for the screaming to stop, and then put out what was left.

66

PEARSON WOULDN'T LET the vampire burn. He grabbed a fire extinguisher and went outside. Edward followed him with his rifle still at his shoulder. The rest of us did the same, except for Damian. I told him to stay inside. He wouldn't burn in the sunlight, but he'd watched his best friend and shield brother burn to death because the Wicked Bitch of Ireland had forced him into the sunshine. I'd shared the memory with Damian and could still hear the evil melodious voice: *One to keep, and one to burn.*

I wasn't going to let her add to the trauma she'd already caused him. The vampire was completely engulfed in flames; only Logan's jacket was slow to burn so that it was almost like a movie effect for the Human Torch, but the body standing screaming in the middle of the street wasn't fireproof. Pearson had to get right up on the figure to use the extinguisher. Edward and Domino stayed right with him, rifles to their shoulders, just in case. Vampires burn hot enough to melt human flesh and rupture bones from the heat. I didn't agree with what Pearson was doing, but that close to the flames it was like standing near the door to hell. It was incredibly brave, and I didn't understand why he was risking his life to try to save someone who had killed one and probably three of his officers. I'd have let the bastard burn. Logan could have been bloodlust, but the others at the door weren't.

The rest of us stayed out of the way. If they needed backup, we were there. A police officer came out with a second extinguisher and moved to help Pearson in his humanitarian effort. The fire did go out, but a few seconds later the flames started again, because the vampire was still in the middle of the sunlit street.

Jake leaned in to me and whispered, "Do you want us to help get the vampire out of the sunlight so he'll stop burning?"

"No."

"As our queen wishes," he said, and straightened back up to stand at my side and watch the flames flare back to life as new sunlight hit vampiric flesh.

I heard Nicky whisper behind me, "Burn, baby, burn."

The vampire started to flail its arms as if it were fighting things that we couldn't see. The shrieking started again; it was a bad sound, the kind you'd hear in your dreams later. Vampires burn well once they ignite, but it's not quick. A human being would be so hurt and in such shock that they'd pass out, or at least lose the ability to keep screaming, but vampires are tougher, a lot tougher.

Movement behind us, and it was Damian with a borrowed coat held like a sunshade over his head and upper body. He knew sunshine didn't burn him anymore, but even if he had to go out in it he wore a hat, sunglasses, gloves. It was more phobia than fact, but the fear was real. Everybody was being brave today.

Pearson emptied his extinguisher and could only stand there and watch. The second officer that had come out was still trying to keep the flames from reigniting. The vampire fell forward to its knees and reached out like a drowning person grabbing that last handhold. He grabbed the officer's arm and the man's yells joined the screams of the vampire, because the hand was on fire that had wrapped around the police officer's arm. The hand would keep burning until it burned through the man's arm.

"Shit." I reached back under my hair for the big blade that was in a spine sheath, but Kaazim touched my elbow. "Allow me." He unsheathed a long, curved blade and moved forward in a graceful line of robes. The blade flashed in the sun and then came down on the vampire's wrist, severing it. The small spurt of blood heated to steam and the wound cauterized itself, but the hand continued to burn around the officer's wrist.

Kaazim sheathed his blade and threw the man on his shoulder, running in a blur of speed back inside the building. Once the vampire's hand was out of direct sunlight he'd be able to put the flame out and have it stay out until they could pry it off the officer's arm.

The vampire grabbed at Pearson with his remaining hand; Edward pulled the detective out of reach and Domino stepped up closer, his rifle aimed at the burning vampire. I'd seen Domino flinch around zombies, but apparently vampires didn't bother him even when they were *en flambé*. I wouldn't have wanted to get that close, but then, maybe he hadn't ever seen a flaming vampire hold on to a person until they melted through their waist and bi-fucking-sected them. I had, so I stayed standing on the edge of it all with Damian, Jake, and Nicky. Jake would have helped if I'd told him to, but if he couldn't put out the fire I didn't want him close to it either.

Damian huddled near my left side; I'd pretty much broken all my people from clutching at my main gun hand when I was on the job. To use the AR I'd need both hands, but it wasn't his fault that I'd trained him up for handgun cuddling. Besides, he'd been brave enough to come out into the sunlight and watch one of his worst nightmares; I gave brownie points for effort. I let the AR hang from its tactical sling, and I drew my sidearm so it was ready to go in my right hand, just in case, and put my left arm around his waist, pulling him in against me. He actually put his arm around my shoulders, collapsing the coat around us a little, because he was only holding it up with one hand. Normally I wouldn't have let him compromise my vision on one side and maybe even my hearing through the thick cloth, but Jake and Nicky were on that side. If they couldn't warn me in time, or take out the threat, realistically I was dead anyway, so I cuddled with Damian closer than I'd ever cuddled with anyone at a crime scene.

He pressed his face against the top of my hair, and I realized he was hiding his eyes. He'd watched for a while, but it takes a long time for an adult human being to burn, a lot longer than you think it would. If it had been human, then it would have passed out, and at least have been unconscious toward the end. It also wouldn't have been able to keep screaming. There are all sorts of screams, but these were some of the worst I'd heard. They were higher and more piteous. I wasn't sure how much longer I could listen to it without offering to put a bullet in its head to finish things.

The body was blackened sticks licked with flame, but even with most of the muscle and ligaments burned down to strings it still hadn't curled up against the heat the way a human body would, and it was still able to move. It opened its mouth wide enough to show the still-white fangs and teeth as if the fire wouldn't touch there. Swallowing fire and smoke is one of the ways that people die quicker in fire. It should have worked the same with vampires, because the mechanics of their bodies were still human-ish, but something worked differently for the vampire. Whatever it was, it wasn't a kindness.

Edward spoke to Pearson, but he shook his head. I was betting he'd offered to put the vampire out of its misery just like I was thinking of doing. I didn't understand why he'd refused it until I heard the sirens and realized it was an ambulance. They were going to try to save the vampire. Fuck, there wasn't enough left to save; even if they could do it, they didn't want to.

I kissed Damian and said, "Go back inside. I've got to try to stop this."

He shook his head. "She's feeding on his terror."

"The Wicked Bitch?"

"Yes."

"You're out here so you can sense her better," I said.

"We need to know what she's doing."

"I'm sorry to interrupt," Jake said, "but this needs to stop."

The ambulance had pulled up and they had a stretcher on wheels coming with equipment and two paramedics. They didn't look as surprised as they should have, so they'd been warned ahead of time. One of them had a fire extinguisher, but the other one had a pile of smooth-filament fire blankets piled on top of the gurney he was pushing. It was like the information that Jake had shared with Pearson and Sheridan had been disseminated to the first responders, or at least the ones riding in the ambulances, but it was too late to try.

I went to Pearson. "You can't do this," I said.

"We have to help him if we can, Blake."

"It's too late, Pearson. Even if they can put the fire out and put him on fluids or whatever and keep him from dying, he won't heal. He won't even heal as well as a human being. Fire is one of the few things that a vampire cannot heal from, at all."

Pearson frowned at me. "What are you saying, Blake?"

"I'm saying that the vampire will be trapped in that body as it is now, but maybe not die ever. Eternity like this is not mercy."

Pearson looked at me for a second, then blinked and blinked again. "I don't know what to say to that, other than the ambulance is here. Once the medical personnel get on site they are in charge."

"Pearson, even if they can do this, don't let them."

"It's out of my hands, Blake."

"Fuck," I said.

One of the medics was putting out the fire, and the other one was putting a blanket over the flesh that had stopped burning. I knew that normally they would not have let anything touch third degree, or whatever degree the vampire had burned to, but keeping the fire from reigniting in the sunlight was more important than anything else if they meant to actually save him.

They covered him in a layer of blankets. They got him on the gurney and because they kept him out of direct light they were able to get him in the ambulance. I saw them start an IV before the door closed them inside with the vampire.

Jake and Nicky came up to me, and Jake said, "They need an armed guard."

"Are you kidding me?" I asked.

"I wish I were."

"That man is too hurt to do anything to anyone," Pearson said.

"He is not a man, Superintendent. He is a vampire," Jake said.

Pearson shook his head. "No, no. If you had wanted to help, the time to do it was before the ambulance got here."

"In the future we will offer more aid. We did not dream that you would try to save what was left," he said.

Domino, Edward, and Nolan were running toward the closed ambulance. I don't know what had alerted them, but I'd

learned if Edward was running to run with him. Jake and
Nicky came with me, and the distance was short enough that
Pearson was beside us when Edward reached the doors. Dom-
ino and Nolan faced them, rifle and handgun at the ready.
Edward didn't wait for us to clear the last few feet, but opened
the doors, as if even one more second was too long.

67

I SKIDDED TO a stop on the other side of Nolan, bringing
my gun up before I even looked inside the dimness of the
ambulance. It took a second for my eyes to adjust from the
sunlight to the shadows. Domino yelled, "No shot, no shot!"

Nolan echoed him. "No shot, no shot!"

"No shot!" Edward yelled from the far side of Domino.

I was left staring into the back of the ambulance to see the
nightmare of blackened flesh and bone that was the vampire
curled around the paramedic like he'd used the officer inside
to shield himself. He was feeding at his neck. It was a normal
feed; the man would survive if we could get him out in time.
I didn't have the angle, but Edward had a head shot; I knew he
did and then I realized the second paramedic was behind the
struggling pair. There was no shot that wouldn't hit him. Fuck!

The paramedic yelled, "Get us out of here!"

I hopped up into the ambulance as Nolan climbed inside.
There wasn't room for anyone else. I heard someone shout my
name, probably telling me not to be stupid, but it was too late.
I was committed. Nolan put his gun against the vampire's
forehead, but the other medic was still in the way. It would go
through the vampire and into his chest. The vampire's victim's
eyes were unfocused. He'd stopped fighting, because the vampire had mind-fucked him. At least he wasn't scared anymore.
The other paramedic was scared shitless and I didn't blame
him.

I tried to ease farther in so I'd have a shot from the side, but the vampire growled at me and his eyes flared blue again. The color looked too alive in the blackened skull-like head. The vampire bit harder into the neck, tearing at the flesh just a little bit too much like a warning. If he worried at the side of the man's neck like a dog with a toy, he'd take out his jugular vein and that might be all she wrote.

"Don't hurt him," I said.

"He's already eating him!" the paramedic hugging the back of the ambulance yelled.

"No, he's just feeding on the blood. If that's all he does, your friend will be fine. I'm going to have the other medic get out of the ambulance," I said.

"What?" he asked.

"I'm talking to the vampire."

The vampire bit deeper at the man's neck.

I changed my grip on my gun, slowly, carefully, so that I was holding it left-handed and pointed at the vampire. I didn't have a killing shot for sure, but if it started to tear out his throat I'd shoot regardless. I spoke to the paramedic. "What's your name?"

"What?"

"Who are you?" I asked.

"Gerald, Gerry."

"Okay, Gerry, here's what we're going to do. You are slowly going to move toward my hand and you're going to stay at my back, between me and the wall, and you are going to get out."

If the Wicked Bitch or the vampire she was using knew anything about guns, they wouldn't let him get out, but I was betting that she was like a lot of the really old vamps. Modern firearms weren't their thing. I flexed my free hand at the paramedic like I was trying to get a child to take my hand to cross the street. Gerry the paramedic moved toward me.

The vampire made a low, evil sound in its chest.

"You've got one hostage. You don't need two."

He shook his head, burying his mouth deeper into the neck. Blood was beginning to spill out around the vampire's mouth. He wasn't drinking anymore; he was bleeding him. Fuck. I held my other hand up to stop Gerry from moving closer. He stopped moving. I stared at that shining blue eye and started sinking into that quiet center where I went when I had time to line up my shot and aim into the living eyes of someone else, because those blue eyes were full of so much life. I'd never felt the energy of any vampire burn so—alive.

Nolan's voice came low and even as he said, "If you tear his throat out we will shoot."

"If he keeps bleeding like that he'll die anyway," Gerry said.

"Don't help, Gerry," I said, keeping my eyes on the vampire and his victim.

There was movement near the door of the ambulance, and it took everything I had not to look in that direction, but Edward was there, Kaazim was there, Jake was there, Domino was there, and Nicky was there. They would have it covered. I had to trust that they would, because I didn't dare look away from the vampire and that one shining blue eye, which was the most I could see of its face as it tried to keep hidden from Nolan and me behind the man's throat and head.

"She's telling him to fight." Damian's voice.

"Get out of here," I told him, but I forgot one important thing: his name. Gerry thought I was talking to him, because he came toward me scrambling as fast as he could, but he was only human-fast and that wasn't fast enough. The vampire tore out the side of the victim's throat, pushing him toward Nolan, spoiling his shot. I had time to move in front of Gerry before the vampire slammed into me and drove us both back against the side of the ambulance. The vampire was snapping its teeth at my face as I shoved my empty right hand into its chest and shoulder to keep it off me as I fired point-blank into where its heart should have been. The sound of the gunfire in such a small space was thunderous, and deafened me. The vampire kept coming, screaming soundlessly now into my face as it tried to eat me. I got one knee up enough to help my arm hold it off us, and fired a second shot into the chest. It seemed to hesitate as if that one had hurt more, and then I caught movement out of the corner of my eye. It was Edward. I had a split second to decide. I stopped trying to push the vampire off me with my arm and moved it up to protect my face and eyes. It meant I was blind as I felt the vampire move forward; my knee wasn't enough to keep it away, but another shot echoed. I felt things scattering over my arm and the rest of me, but I kept my eyes closed. I trusted Edward. The vampire wasn't pushing so hard against my knee. The man behind me was grabbing my shoulders and I think screaming. Another shot rang out and I was deaf except for the reverb of the shot echoing inside the metal so that it felt like my bones were reverberating with it. My head was full of a high-pitched, echoing buzz that had nothing to do with any sound outside my head now.

Someone was pushing my gun hand and gun down, but it wasn't an attack; it was just safety. I lowered my arm and realized that it hurt, but I was looking into Edward's face. I'd known it would be him. He said something, but I just shook my head. He seemed to understand, because he stopped trying to talk to me and touched my arm, gently. There was a large bone splinter sticking out of it; some piece of the vampire was stuck in me. If I hadn't put my arm up, it would have been stuck in my face, but I'd been this close to a head shot before; I knew that blowback could be a lot more than just brains and blood. Nothing like experience to help keep you safe; if it had been anyone but Edward I don't know if I would have trusted enough to block my eyes.

Gerry the paramedic was pushing out from behind me and fell out the open door of the ambulance. I thought he was running away, but when Edward helped me out of the ambulance Gerry was kneeling beside his friend, taking over first aid from Nolan, who'd been trying to stop the blood from pouring out quite as fast. Gerry had bits of burned flesh and small bits of bone sticking out of his face like shrapnel, but he did his job. He stayed with it. I wasn't sure I had enough brownie points to give him for that. He didn't seem to have any bone fragments as long as the one in my arm, so we let him do his job. I saw the flashing lights before I realized a second ambulance was pulling up. I hadn't really heard it, or if I had, the ringing in my ears kept me from understanding what I was hearing.

Nicky pulled the body of the vampire out into the light. It started to combust on the street almost immediately. This time when someone suggested putting extra bullets into the body to put it out of its misery, or to keep it from attacking anyone else—I honestly couldn't hear which was offered, but whichever—Pearson let it happen. Nicky shot until what was left of the vampire's head was gone and the burned rib cage splintered into pieces, spilling the still red and bloody heart out into the street, where it pulsed for a second and then burst into flames.

68

NEW AMBULANCES AND new paramedics arrived at the scene. They triaged the injuries, and I was happy not to be in the front of the line. It meant I wasn't dying. They had taken both the men who'd had their throats torn open; I hoped that meant that they would make it, but I knew that in America the ambulance crews in some states are not allowed to declare someone dead at a scene, especially if lifesaving measures have already been started. I prayed that they would be all right, but it really depended on if the vampire had gotten the jugular vein, and then whether he'd just nicked it or torn it wide-open. The last possibility was that they were transporting corpses but weren't willing to admit it, but the first two left hope. I prayed for that hope. I prayed even though the memory of the spray of blood inside the station house made me worry the most about the first man. I didn't know what else would make that amount of blood pour from the neck that fast except for the jugular to be torn wide-open. You didn't live long once that happened.

I did want to pray for them, but concentrating on almost anything else beat the hell out of looking at my own injury. The blackened bone splinter hurt, but mostly it looked alarming. It's just not okay to look down at your arm and see something foreign sticking out of it. If I thought about exactly what was sticking out of my arm—a piece of someone's skull, okay; a piece of a vampire's blackened and burned skull—then it got a little creepy. The sensation of something stuck in your body that is big enough to move around in a sort of painful wriggly feeling if you move too much went way beyond just the pain of it. Or maybe the sensation made it hurt more?

I started to get queasy as I tried to hold my arm absolutely still, waiting for the medics to get around to me. Edward was talking to the police that he'd made work friends with in the days he'd been here ahead of me. He'd been wearing the super-duper earplugs that he'd recommended to me, and I had a pair, but I had been in a police station. I had thought we were safe and I didn't put hearing protection in, so although my head was still ringing from the noise of the shots inside the ambulance so that I couldn't really hear what people were saying, or a lot of other sounds, Edward was fine. Later, I'd ask him if he just lived in the damn earplugs. Knowing Edward, he probably did. The ringing in my head had stopped, and my hearing was returning faster than I'd thought it would. Yay for super-healing ability!

Nolan was staying with him, though I wasn't sure he was helping with the making-friends part. Jake and Kaazim were searching the crowd for threats, or old friends. I wasn't exactly sure which, and not sure I cared as much as I should have, because I was fighting not to throw up. One, it would make the Irish cops think less of me, and two, there was no way to throw up without moving more of my body than I'd want to move, like my arm.

Domino, Nicky, and Damian were with me at the ambulance full of exploded bits of vampire like the one in my arm. It was considered unsanitary now, so until they cleaned it up, no one would be using it unless they ran out of supplies in the other ambulances, or got desperate to transport someone. There really weren't messy bits until farther into the ambulance, so Damian was sitting just inside it out of direct sunlight. I sat on the edge of the open back of it with my feet swinging so that I felt like I was five again. Damian had his hand resting against my back. He wasn't rubbing it, or petting me, because that had made my body move minutely, which wasn't good right now. The doors of the ambulance were still open, so we were blocked from sight of most of the crowd that had gathered outside the police tape and barriers. Nice to see some things were the same as back home; if there was a crime scene, you always got a crowd.

I could look up at Domino standing in front of me like a living shield, blocking me and Damian from sight of pretty much anyone. Nicky had been doing the same on the other side of the door, but now he was kneeling in front of me, helping me hold my arm very still. It wasn't bleeding much, which was both good and bad. The bad was that it meant the bone shard was probably in deep and tight, so that it acted like a cork in the wound stopping me from bleeding much at all, which was good, but it also might mean that they'd want a surgeon to help them take it out of my arm.

Nicky waved his hand in front of my face, so I'd look at him. He directed my line of sight to his face. I looked into that one blue eye with the fall of his blond hair hiding the other one, if it had been there. I did the long blink, which usually meant I was a little shocky.

"Is she okay?" Domino asked.

Nicky didn't answer him, just kept staring at me, so I could keep my focus on his face, on the blue of his eye. Damian answered, "She's a little in shock, but her hearing has come back better than I'd feared."

I blinked at Nicky and turned my head back to look at Damian, which made my arm move just a fraction too much. My stomach tightened and the wave of nausea rolled up my throat and over me. I felt the sick sweat starting as I swallowed hard.

Domino touched his own stomach and said, "I felt that one even through shielding. If she throws up, I'm not sure I can keep from joining her."

"Don't you start," I said; my voice sounded normal in my head, which it shouldn't have, not that soon after all the shooting in the confined space of the ambulance. When Nathaniel had called on my phone earlier I hadn't heard it. Damian had taken it and talked to him. Apparently Nathaniel and Dev—Devereux—had both felt the shadow of the sound concussion and the wound in my arm. At that point, I couldn't hear well enough to talk on the phone; now I was hearing just fine. What the hell? My ears should still have been ringing with it, at the very least. The thought helped chase back the nausea.

I looked at Nicky where he was kneeling in front of me. "Can you hear me?"

He smiled and nodded.

"Say something to me," I said.

"I'm fine," he said.

I narrowed my eyes at him, because I didn't believe him. I turned my head again to look at Damian. Nicky tightened his grip on my arm just a little to help steady me. It was exactly what I needed in that moment, which he managed to do most of the time. I said to Damian, "My hearing shouldn't be this good yet. I think Nicky's taken the damage for me like a good cannon-fodder Bride."

Damian looked past me at Nicky. "It is his job metaphysically as your Bride."

I sat there with Nicky's hands so firm and steady on my arm, and he didn't feel like expendable cannon fodder. It felt like his hands on me helped me breathe a little better. "Yeah, but now I'm in love with him and that seems shitty. Okay, that seemed shitty once the system was explained to me."

Damian smiled at me and touched his fingertips to the edge of my face. "You can be so harsh, but you are also one of the most genuinely caring people I've ever met."

The compliment embarrassed me. I wasn't sure why, but it did. "I don't know what to say to that."

"You don't have to say anything."

Domino said, "If Nicky really can't hear well, we need to know that if he's going to keep being one of your bodyguards today."

"Good point," I said, glancing at him. The sunlight was touching the top of his hair, making the few white curls in all the black almost iridescent, as if the thick Irish sunlight brought out the shine in his hair.

"He'll feel me talking, because he's touching me. One of you say something where he can't see you talking."

Damian bent down to kiss me so that his face was hidden from Nicky's view. He kissed me, soft and gentle, but as he drew back, he said, "Can you hear me, Nicky?"

There was no answer from the man holding my arm. I had to fight an urge not to turn and look at his face, because that would be enough to give him a clue. "Try again," I told Damian.

He bent down and got another kiss, but he kept our foreheads touching so that his long hair fell forward, and even if you'd been standing, you couldn't have seen our faces, let alone our lips. It probably looked very intimate, but Damian spoke like that, hidden from sight. "Nicky, if you can't answer my question, then you have to step down as Anita's bodyguard."

We waited a second with our faces touching, but Nicky didn't answer the question. Crap. "Nicky, can you really not hear us at all?"

"That would be a no," Domino said.

Damian sat back up and looked at Nicky. I turned around and looked at him. I looked into that face, which seemed to steady me just by being here. Not everyone I loved made me feel that way, so maybe it wasn't our special love, but the fact that he was my Bride. I hated thinking that, but it was a type of hiding from the truth not to think it. "Nicky, can you hear anything we're saying?"

"Yes," he said.

Domino was standing a little behind him, so that he couldn't see him as he asked, "How much can you hear?"

Nicky turned and looked at him. "Some."

"How much is some?" Domino asked.

"My ears are ringing, and I'm hearing everything down that long tunnel that happens without ear protection."

I touched his face with my free hand, turning him to look at me. "Why didn't you tell me?"

"You can hear, right?"

I nodded.

He smiled. "Then I'm doing my job."

"If you shift to lion, will that fix it?" I asked.

He frowned, which probably meant he didn't understand everything I'd said. I tried again with fewer words and enunciating carefully. "Shapeshifting will heal you?"

"Yes."

"But he needs to shift soon," Domino said. "The longer you go without shifting to heal, the greater the chance that you'll have some damage left over. It works that way more with some things than others, but hearing can be one of them."

"You could change in the ambulance," I said.

Nicky frowned at me.

Domino said, "He'll have to stay in beast form for a few hours to make sure it heals completely. He can't just shift back and forth even if he's able to do that without risking permanent damage to his hearing."

"He can't run around Dublin in lion form, Anita," Damian said.

"Especially not one the size of a small horse. We're all bigger than the regular version of our animal side. A lion that big would attract a lot of attention," Domino said.

"I'd think any lion loose in Dublin would attract attention," I said.

"True, but our normal beast size is huge. It won't pass for a natural animal."

"I've seen shapeshifters that were the normal size of their animal," Damian said.

"I haven't."

"I think it may be an older type of lycanthropy," he said.

"That would explain it, and be weird. Why would older lycanthropy strains make their beast half look like a regular animal?" Domino asked.

"Maybe it's camouflage," I said. "Back when there were more real lions, tigers, and bears running around, if you could pass for a real animal I'd think you'd go undetected longer."

"So why did that strain die out and ours with the really unnatural-looking beasts survive?" Domino asked.

Nicky was watching the conversation, but unless he read lips he couldn't follow it. I felt guilty about the fact that it was my damage he was suffering through. I hadn't consciously given him the hearing damage. I touched his face, which earned me a smile. I wanted to give him a kiss but was afraid that leaning that far forward would make my arm move too much. My stomach had settled down, and I wanted to keep it that way, because there was nothing romantic about throwing up on someone.

"I know that the shapeshifters that looked like normal

beasts didn't hide in their animal form as stringently as those who couldn't pass for ordinary," Damian said.

"That led to many of my brethren being hunted like common wolves," Jake said. He'd apparently walked up while we were talking.

"Are you saying that the fact that they could pass for a normal wolf meant they let themselves be seen, and that led to them being hunted?" I asked.

He nodded.

"But ordinary weapons couldn't harm them," Domino said.

"Once the hunters knew it was no ordinary beast, other weapons and magic were brought to bear," Kaazim said.

"Wait," Domino said. "Are you saying that your wolf and your jackal look like the natural counterpart?"

"Mine does," Jake said.

"So your lycanthropy is old-school," I said.

"Very old-school," he said with a small smile. He still had the pack with Echo inside it on his back. I wasn't sure I could carry her like that at all, but wounded I knew I shouldn't try.

"My jackal does not, but that is neither here nor there," Kaazim said.

"There are reports from all over the city about people being on fire," Jake said.

"People?" I made it a question with the upward lilt at the end.

Nicky asked, "Did you say people are on fire?"

"Vampires. I believe all reports are of vampires."

"Nicky, can you hear us?"

"Some," he said.

"I'm sorry," I said.

"My job," he said.

"I'm still sorry."

"I'm not."

"Are you sure all the victims are vampires?" Damian asked.

"The news and social media are speculating, especially the latter. They are saying anything from religious zealots burning themselves alive in protest to a serial arsonist setting helpless victims on fire with some unknown combustive agent that cannot be extinguished by normal means."

"The police don't realize how good your hearing is," I said.

Jake smiled. "No, but I can also hear the crowd that has gathered, as well as the police."

Kaazim added, "They are talking about the book of faces and other Internet sources. The police are trying to decide what they can reveal to calm the rumors."

"If the vampires tore into people like this one did, then that should be in the media, too. They'd know at least some of the other victims are vampires," I said.

"If what we are hearing is to be trusted, then the other vampires have not attacked the people that tried to help them," Kaazim said.

"Why did this one attack, then?" I asked.

"Vampires are driven by bloodlust, but underneath that is the person they were before the attack. Some remember themselves sooner, and if they were a good person before they became a vampire, they do not cease to be good."

"A few people would be able to fight the craving for blood," Damian said, "but not many. No matter how good a person you think you are when you first rise from the grave and seek blood, there is no pity, no humanity left."

"Once they have fed for the night, sanity can return," Jake said.

"But that first feeding is often vicious enough to kill, like what happened to Detective Logan. Have there been reports of more victims like that?" Damian asked.

"You are very right, Damian. There should be more. Even a good man rises the first few nights as a crazed beast," Kaazim said.

The air whispered along my skin, heavy with power. It made my skin run in goose bumps again, and that made me shiver, which moved my arm. The pain was sharp and the sensation of the shard moving in my arm made my stomach roll again. I took a deep breath and let it out slow.

Domino was holding his stomach. "You know, you've been hurt worse than this. Why does this make you nauseous?"

I took a few more calming breaths, then said, "I don't know."

"Do you hear it?" Damian said, and even those few words were full of fear.

I concentrated on that whisper of power, tried to listen, and just like before I could hear the words, "Come out, come outside." I nodded. "I hear it."

"It's just noise to me again," Domino said.

"Come out," Jake said.

"She is compelling more of her creations to come out into the light," Kaazim said.

"Then she's limited on how many she can control at one time. Not that that really helps us stop her," I said.

"Can we stop her this time?" Domino asked.

"I don't know, but I'm open to ideas," I said.

"We need to get this wound treated, before you do any more vampire hunting," Nicky said.

"Is your hearing back completely?" Jake asked.

"No," Nicky said. "I won't hear everything that's coming."

"I'd have tagged you for being too manly to admit it," Domino said.

"If I can't hear everything, and I lie about it, it could endanger Anita."

"Good man," Jake said, and patted Nicky on the shoulder the way he patted Dev and Pride.

Damian's phone rang. He answered it by saying, "It's Nathaniel."

"Is he all right?" I asked, my pulse speeding up just thinking about possibilities.

"He says he's fine." Then he was quiet, listening, but his hand came back to rest on my shoulder as if something about talking to the other third of our triumvirate made him want to touch me more. I didn't mind as long as he didn't push on me.

The evil energy faded away—no, not faded. It was like it was muffled, and there was music in its place. I couldn't hear the tune, or the words, only that there was a tune and someone was singing—something was singing.

"Do you hear music?" I asked.

"No," Jake and Kaazim said together. They exchanged a look at each other and then Kaazim said, "But the compulsion is quieter, not gone, but as if its power has been dimmed."

"I hear music," Domino said.

"Can you make out the words?" I asked.

"No."

"Me, either."

"I don't hear it, but Anita feels calmer," Nicky said.

"What the hell is it? The music, I mean."

"Whatever it is seems to be on our side, or at least not on hers," Jake said.

Damian said, "Nathaniel says it's Flannery's friends."

"You mean the fa . . . little gentle folk?" I finally managed to get out something that wasn't going to insult every Fey within earshot.

"Flannery has them dimming her magic with their own, but it's a temporary fix," Damian said, and he was listening as he talked, as if he were repeating things.

"How temporary?" Domino asked.

"How much time do we have?" I asked.

"They aren't certain since they've never done anything like this," Damian said, "but they think maybe until dark."

Jake was looking off in the distance, but whatever had caught his attention was hidden from the rest of us by the open ambulance door. "Nolan and Forrester are coming this way."

Kaazim looked that way, too. "They are moving with purpose."

"Ed . . . Ted always moves with purpose, and probably so does Nolan," I said.

Domino moved so he could see around the door. "You know how Ted is Clark Kent?" he asked.

"Yeah," I said.

"It's serious Superman face coming this way."

"If Superman needs me to play Batman for him, then I'm going old-school Bat."

"What does that mean?" Domino asked.

Jake answered, "Batman originally used a gun and shot people rather than using gadgets and kung fu. I would have thought you would be too young to know that, Anita."

"My dad had a comic book collection, and he liked Batman," I said.

"Ah, of course."

I looked down at my arm. "Good thing I practice shooting with my left arm."

"This is why we practice with our off hands," Kaazim said.

"Your groupings on the range are as good left-handed as they are right-handed," Nicky said.

"Yeah, but my speed for drawing and finding my target in a dynamic training exercise is a little slower," I said.

"It's our job to shoot the bad guys and protect you," Domino said.

"Not when I'm working with the police," I said.

"You have your own version of Clark Kent, Anita. It complicates things," Jake said.

I didn't even try to argue, because he was right. "If I had shot the vampire inside the building as soon as I saw him, there'd be two less wounded, and one less dead police officer."

"But Superman wouldn't have done that anyway," Domino said.

"That is so not my superhero alter ego."

"You and Ted are both more Batman than Superman," Nicky said.

"Agreed." And then Edward and Nolan were with us, and since it was just my people we didn't have to pretend we were mild-mannered anything; we could just be what we were, which was the good guys who worked like bad guys, because to catch the villains sometimes squeaky-clean doesn't do it. Sometimes to clean up the dirt, you have to get dirty yourself. If I'd shot when I first wanted to, I wouldn't be hurt. If I'd shot then, I know that Edward and my people would have joined me. There might have been only two casualties today, Logan and the vampire. I'd have been good with that. I was pretty sure the families of the injured and fallen officers would have been good with that, too.

69

FOUR HOURS LATER my arm was wrapped in bandages, and they'd even insisted on putting it in a sling. Since it was my right arm, I'd had to have Edward help me adjust where all my weapons were so I could get to them with my left arm. This was why I practiced off-hand weapons practice, from guns to blades and hand-to-hand. I couldn't remember the last time I'd hurt my right arm this badly, maybe never. If it had been a wound caused by almost anything else, I'd have already been healed, or at least starting to heal without a trip to the emergency room, but a wound caused by something preternatural or magical healed slower. Now that the piece of vampire was out of my flesh I would start to heal faster than human-normal, but because of what made the injury I probably wouldn't heal like I normally did. In fact, what I really needed was to find someplace private and use some of my metaphysical healing abilities, but since almost all of them either were sex based or looked like they were sex based, it didn't seem like the thing to do when I was surrounded by the Irish police and medical personnel. Saying, "Excuse me while I take my lover off for a quickie. No, really, it'll help me heal"? Nope, just nope.

Besides, the local painkillers they'd given me had stopped working before the doctor finished sewing up the wound. Only pride had kept me from throwing up, and if it hadn't been Edward holding my hand my pride might have lost. One of the reasons he had been holding my hand was his insistence that I'd be tougher with him than with one of my lovers. He'd been right, and it had freed Nicky up to get a ride back to Nolan's headquarters, where he could change into his lion form and heal the damage to his hearing that he'd taken for me. I was still determined to keep Domino off the menu for me, so that had left me with Damian for sexual healing, but I was still surrounded by police and doctors. Besides, my stomach hadn't settled completely, so sex didn't seem like the best idea. Nausea was one of the few things that ruined even my mood for sexy naked time. Nathaniel, Dev, and the rest of our party hadn't gotten back to us until all the cursing at Edward and the hazmat-suited doctor and nurses was over. Yes, the doctor and nurses who actually helped treat me had taken one look at my medical alert card and treated me like a contagious plague victim. It had been like being sewn up by an astronaut, or abducted by bulky aliens.

Now I was standing in a large, long room that had its lights so dim it was almost dark, but when they raised the light levels, the unconscious vampires had squirmed, or even cried out, though the monitors hadn't registered any more brain activity, as if whatever made them react to the brightness wasn't them. Did the Wicked Bitch of Ireland dislike light? She could walk out into full sunlight, so why did the hospital's indoor lighting bother her puppets?

Nathaniel squeezed my other hand; normally I wouldn't have let him hold my only working hand in a room full of potentially hostile vampires, but he had bandages on both his wrists where he'd voluntarily helped feed some of the undead in this room. We'd already had our fight that had been all about my fear for his safety and nothing to do with logic, or the fact that I was hurt far worse than he had been. I wanted to feel the solid reality of his hand in mine more than I wanted to keep my hand free for weapons; besides, all the vamps in this room had calmed after they'd taken blood. They'd calmed enough that Fortune and Flannery had been able to reason with them. Some of them had been burned in the sunlight, but none as badly as the one that had left his bone in my arm, because Fortune had grabbed a heavy tablecloth and put out the fire on the first one that staggered out into the light near their sightseeing. She'd let that one feed on her own wrist, and it had come back to itself. Maybe it wasn't the exact person it had been before someone made it into a vampire, but it was still a reasoning, thinking person once it fed. Most of the vampires that they'd either saved from the sun or found before they staggered out into it had been reasonable after they took blood, but not all of them. Griffin was in surgery now because one of the vampires had damn near torn through his wrist. The vampire had taken Griffin's blood and still tried to kill him, and when the others had gotten him to safety the vampire had attacked them, too. It just wanted to hurt people like the one at the police station had. They had had to kill three vampires but had managed to save dozens.

Some of them were lying in the beds now with IVs sending fluids to their burned, or just undead, flesh. Others in the room had called ambulances when they "woke" to themselves and found that they'd tried to rip out a friend's or family member's throat. Others had turned themselves in to the police after waking up covered in blood, with no memory of what was happening. If other of the new Irish undead had hidden after their first murder of the day, then we'd find them later by the bodies they left behind. They'd given drugs to the vampires to put them out of their pain, and some just a sedative in case the craving for blood returned. Most of them had volunteered for anything that would keep others safe.

Nathaniel's bandaged wrists had been the hospital's insistence. He hadn't thought either vampire bite needed the attention. To me later he'd whispered, "I get more hurt at home from sex with Asher than this." Wisely, he hadn't tried explaining that to the doctors.

Devereux and Damian stood behind us. Fortune and Jake were off with Nolan's people to try to answer more questions about vampires and how to take care of them. Edward and Nolan himself were off trying to get their/our group more powers of authority. There was some talk that killing the two vampires we had was going to get us kicked out of Ireland, but there were too many dead people and too many vampires waiting for nightfall for most of those in power to want to lose their experts on the undead. They'd keep us around until the crisis was over, but after that I wasn't sure. I'd hoped to sightsee around Ireland for a few days when it was all done, but I was beginning to wonder if they were just going to escort us to the airplane and tell us, *Don't ever come back.* Yeah, they were scared and they had a right to be scared, but fear makes people look for someone to blame. I was a necromancer and sleeping with the monsters; it made me an easy target for hate-mongers.

The room was very quiet with just the rush and whir of the machinery and monitors to break the silence. That, combined with the dimness, made it all unreal, or like a scene from a bad dream. They'd isolated all the vampires in their own area; even the burn victims weren't being taken to the burn unit. The doctors had cut away the tissue that had to be excised, but they would heal even less than a human patient would. Fire was one of the few things that the supernatural could not heal from. I knew that burns from holy water scarred over eventually, but I didn't even know if burns from actual fire would do that much. Would the open skin, so raw and painful, be where they were trapped for all eternity? God, I hoped not.

"There are other rooms full of vampires; how did just your group give enough blood for all of them?" I asked. It was something I hadn't thought to ask before. My stomach was settling down and the pain in my arm was just a dull ache, so I was thinking better.

"People started coming up to us and offering themselves for feedings," Dev said.

I looked back at him. "You're joking."

"He's not joking," Nathaniel said. "At first we thought the Irish were some of the bravest people on the planet, and some ordinary citizens did help us put out the flames, and even donated a wrist or two."

"We stopped letting civilians help once Griffin got hurt," Dev said.

"You said *at first*. What did you mean?"

"I guess technically they're Irish, too, like the original Irish, but they were Flannery's friends."

"You mean Fey?"

He nodded and squeezed my hand a little tighter. "What's wrong?"

"Some of them were too beautiful to be real, like they'd walked out of a wet dream," Dev said.

"Others looked ordinary," Nathaniel said, "but there was always something about them that wasn't quite . . . human normal."

"Auntie Nim came and offered her own blood," said Dev.

"Really?" I said.

"Her and her people," Nathaniel said.

"They made you nervous," I said, shaking Nathaniel's hand.

He nodded without looking at me.

"What's wrong?"

"They liked us, me because I had blond hair and him because his was dark red. When I said, 'Where are all the Irish redheads you see in movies?' they said, 'In fairyland, because we stole them away.'"

"Nathaniel, are you worried they'll steal you away?"

He shook his head. "I don't know, Anita. It's the first magic that's really . . . unnerved me, I guess."

"They kept asking him if he was one of theirs, like his ancestors had gone to America or something," Dev said.

"They said that only one of them would have flower-colored eyes."

"You're wondering if they're right," I said.

He looked at me with those lilac-colored eyes. "I don't know anything about my family really, Anita; for all I know, one of my ancestors could be from here."

"Why does that bother you? Most people would love to have some fairy blood in them, or royalty."

"I don't know, but it's like I can feel something inside me that isn't my leopard now. It's like something's awake that I didn't even know was asleep."

"Flannery says that his magic only works really well here; if you have blood ties to Ireland maybe that's true for you, too," I said.

He looked at me, startled. "You mean I could be a . . . what, a Fairy Doctor?"

"Maybe," I said.

"They liked Nathaniel," Dev said. "They kept touching his hair, his arm, the way people do when they're flirting."

"You like flirting," I said.

"Normally, but this felt more . . . It wasn't flirting, Anita, not the way we think of it, but we couldn't have saved nearly the vampires we did if they hadn't come to help."

"One of them called it a debt of honor," Dev said.

"What does that mean?" I asked.

Damian moved up closer behind us, hugging us both lightly around the shoulders. "It means that something about what's happened makes them feel they owe the help to the city, or to Flannery, or to the victims themselves."

"Why would they feel that?" I asked.

"I don't know. The few that I met over the centuries were very mysterious and kept their secrets better than most vampires."

"Why did She-Who-Made-You do this? What did it gain her?" Nathaniel asked, in a whisper. It was that kind of room; you just couldn't raise your voice.

"She's a night hag; they feed on terror the way that Jean-Claude feeds on lust. She has feasted on the fear of her victims and the entire city's panic," Damian said.

"I knew some master vamps could feed on fear, but let me just say, I'm happy to be on Jean-Claude's team. I'd rather be with a vampire that feeds on blood and lust than terror, or anger, or violence and death like some of the other blood-lines," Dev said. He was standing a little to one side, behind Nathaniel. Everyone else who wasn't either talking to the Irish about helping vampires, killing vampires, or our political future here, or healing themselves, was outside in the corridor waiting to come rushing in if we yelled for reinforcements.

Nathaniel leaned back and offered a kiss, which Dev happily took, though he was careful not to touch Damian's hand where it curled around Nathaniel's shoulder. Honestly, I'd expected Damian to move out of the way; the fact that he didn't was interesting, but not as interesting as the problem in front of us, which was the Irish vampires.

"What can we do to help them and stop her?" I said.

"Let us go somewhere else for this discussion. They seem unconscious, but they're still her vampires," Damian said.

"You think she could use them to eavesdrop," I said.

"I do," he said, and turned for the door behind us, turning us because he still had his hands on our shoulders. We didn't argue with the movement. I think we were all ready to get out of this room, but as Damian herded us toward the door he stumbled. Dev caught his arm and we turned to help. It was hard to tell in the dim light with someone as pale as Damian, but he looked especially pale. My stomach cramped suddenly so hard it almost doubled me over. Nathaniel's breath was coming too fast as he said, "What was that?"

"Shit, he hasn't fed."

"How have you not fed and not tried to tear anyone up?" Dev asked.

"Centuries of practice," our vampire said.

"Could you teach them that kind of control?" Dev asked.

"In time, some of them, but not everyone wants to control their lust for blood, or is capable of doing so. There was one of her other vampires that specialized in the most violent feedings I've ever seen. He literally tore his food apart, limb from limb. He didn't want to control the violence inside him. He wanted to let it out every night if she would allow it." He swayed in place. Dev tightened his grip on his arm. I tightened mine on the other. Nathaniel squeezed his hand tighter.

"We need to get him somewhere and get him some food," Nathaniel said.

None of us argued. We just moved toward the door, getting in one another's way as we tried to open the door and move ourselves through it. Dev finally let go so he could open the door and usher us through, which saved us from having a Three Stooges moment in the doorway. Damian leaned against the wall in the hallway and started to slide to the floor. Nathaniel and I caught him and other hands came to keep him upright, but we needed a room and privacy with our shared vampire—now.

70

NATHANIEL FELL TO his knees beside Damian and a wave of dizziness took my vision in a stomach-turning swirl. I caught myself on my one good arm and felt other hands on us. I had a moment of not being able to tell if I was watching

Domino holding Nathaniel, or if I could feel him cradling me. Was I leaning against the wall with Kaazim holding me in place, or was I kneeling with Dev's hands on my shoulders? I forced myself back into my body and my mind, but it meant that I had to shield hard from everyone.

Nathaniel gasped, "Anita, you can't take that much from us."

Damian's eyes rolled back into his head and he went completely limp. Kaazim said, "My Queen, you must not cut them off, or one could die."

I wasted breath cursing, but I lowered my shields. The wave of dizziness and nausea made me collapse, and only Dev's arm kept me from hitting the floor; unfortunately he was on the side of the injured arm. The pain of it being pressed between his body and mine brought me out of the faint but didn't do anything for my stomach. I fought to breathe and not throw up as I tried to even out the power between the three of us. Damian had hidden how much energy he'd been using up, but now he couldn't hide it any longer. He should not have been able to die from not eating. Vampires couldn't starve to death; they could rot, or go mad from it, but they couldn't fade like this, like a person who was slipping away for real.

I was looking up into Dev's face, and his eyes looked almost entirely pale blue; the brown was lost in them from this angle, or in this light. Pride was standing over his shoulder, looking down at me with a worried expression on his face. I smelled heat, hot, as if temperature could have a scent. Heat and dirt, as if ground could be pounded by the sun until it changed the smell of it, the feel of it beneath our feet, and beneath the delicate paws . . . I smelled spices, exotic, unnameable, or unnameable by me. I saw a fox, a wolf, no, no, a jackal. She was delicate and dainty, a beautiful golden-eyed lover both in this form and the other. I had a glimpse of a dark-skinned woman with pale brown eyes, smiling, welcoming . . . and then she was gone.

"No," a voice said. "No, I will not remember things that have been lost for so long. It is torment and you are not queen enough to force that upon me yet. I pray to my old gods that you never grow to such power, or such evil."

I realized it was Kaazim, and when I moved my head

enough to look he was holding his wrist, putting pressure on it. Damian was sitting against the wall unaided and looking alive again, so to speak. He smiled and licked a minute drop of blood from the edge of his mouth, content as the cat that had eaten the delicious canary.

"Kaazim, your blood is yummy," Nathaniel said, and it made me turn my head enough to see him cradled in Domino's arms more on his side than I was, because he didn't have an injured arm to work around. Ethan was standing over them both, uncertain whom to help, or how. I couldn't blame him on that one; I wasn't sure what was happening either.

"That should not have happened," Kaazim said, his voice shaking a little around the edges.

"No," I managed to say, "it shouldn't. You're not one of my animals to call, or Jean-Claude's. Your memories shouldn't come across like that."

He cradled his arm as if it were more hurt than just a simple wrist feeding. I wondered for a second if Damian had bitten him more than he needed to just to take blood, but discarded the idea. I'd have felt it if Damian were losing that kind of control. No, Kaazim wasn't cradling a physical wound, or not one that we'd given him. It was almost as if it were a remembered injury to match the memory we'd seen.

"Only my master should be able to draw such things from me, and she would not need to, for she was there." His voice was grim, and matched the bleakness of the look in his dark brown eyes.

"I am sorry, Kaazim. I did not mean to make you sad," Nathaniel said.

The werejackal looked at him, but his eyes didn't soften. He looked at Nathaniel as if he hated him. "You did not, but the vampire did."

Damian's voice came thick and slow like he'd been woken from a wonderful nap that might have included a sweet dream or two. "I did not mean to make you sad either, Kaazim."

"I do not believe you."

"I remember what it was like to lose everything to a vampire, Kaazim. I would not willingly draw such a memory from your mind to mine."

"It did not seem to make you or Nathaniel sad."

"The energy was amazing, like being drunk on strong spirits, but your downer was not lost in our high. I promise you that." Damian reached out and touched the other man's shoulder, but he jerked back and got to his feet in one smooth motion that ended in the slightest of sways.

"Are you all right, Kaazim?" I asked.

Nathaniel moved out of Domino's arms and motioned him toward the other man, but Ethan had gotten to him first. Kaazim stood very straight and firm, but he was leaning just a bit against the wall. Ethan reached out toward his arm, but stopped when Kaazim glared at him. "May I take your arm, just to steady you?"

"I would like to tell you no, but it is as if the vampire took more than just the small amount of blood. I should not feel like this unless I have fed several vampires in a very short space of time."

Ethan reached out slowly and took the other man's elbow; when he didn't protest he took a more solid grip. "I have you," he said.

"It is not you having me that I fear," he said, and looked not at Damian, but at me.

"Why do I get that look? I didn't do anything to you."

"Damian is your creature, Anita. What he does is your doing."

"You know that's not as true as what the council and Mommy Noir convinced people of, right?"

"I know that Damian has never had this kind of power, but Jean-Claude does, and through him . . . you."

The look he gave me was chilling, so much so that I struggled to my feet, and Dev helped me, moving me farther away from one of my own bodyguards. Pride moved in front of us, closer to the werejackal.

"That small extra space will not save you if I deem it otherwise."

"I know," I said, and fought not to just pull a gun while I had the chance. It shouldn't come to that, so I made the choice not to draw a weapon. If he crossed those few feet and killed me I was going to feel really stupid.

"Then why move away from me, my Queen?" His voice was icy with his anger, like the desert in the grip of winter's cold.

"You know you'd have to get through all of us before you hurt Anita," Dev said; he'd already moved himself a little in front of me so that I was partially behind that big upper body of his. Pride said nothing, just took a fight stance. It telegraphed his move, but they all practiced together. They knew each other's moves; there would be no surprises during the fighting, only that there was a fight at all.

Ethan said, "Kaazim, do not threaten to break your oath to Jean-Claude and Anita." He was standing nearest to him, but his voice was calmest, his energy gentle, even soothing. I began to see why he'd been able to establish a relationship with the volatile werebear Nilda.

"Do you think that I will not hurt you because you have brought happiness to one of us?"

Apparently, I wasn't the only one who was thinking of Nilda. "No, Kaazim, I think you could kill me, but not out of fear."

"I am not afraid of you, boy."

"No one is," he said with a smile.

The comment made Kaazim think harder, because it was a puzzling comment, which was probably what Ethan was aiming for, because Kaazim would calm down if he could think long enough to not just lash out. I was 99.9 percent sure of that; the fraction of uncertainty was because I didn't know why getting those memories had scared him this badly.

"I'm sorry for whatever just happened, Kaazim," I said.

"I meant only to take blood from your wrist, Kaazim. I give you my oath that I intended nothing more." Damian had stayed sitting against the wall. I think he could have stood, but he didn't want to appear more threatening to the other man, and since he was so much taller, sitting was definitely less threatening.

"You smell like you tell the truth, but I have never had a vampire siphon off my energy like that without centuries of practice at doing it on purpose."

I tried to move around Dev and Pride and have more direct eye contact with him, but the two men were too in the way. "You told me yourself, Kaazim, that you wonder how much of the Mother's power went into me when I drank her down. This feels more like her than us."

He looked at me, and it wasn't a good look. "Is that supposed to make me feel better, my Queen?"

I held the weight of his dark brown eyes with my own. "I was hoping, yeah."

"So either you are lying to me, or you have power inside you that you can neither control nor know when it will surface. Which of these is a comfort?"

"Put that way, it sounds sort of bad, but I meant it to be comforting."

He shook his head and sighed. "I am well enough to stand now, weretiger."

Ethan hesitated and then moved his hand slowly from the other man's arm. Kaazim stayed standing nice and steady. He even moved away from the wall so he wasn't leaning against anything.

"Your naïveté is one of your charms, Anita, but it is also a weakness, because it speaks to a lack of experience with the amount of power you now have inside you."

"Then perhaps, old friend, it is time to realize that everyone here is a child, except us, and to give them the understanding and teaching that requires," Jake said. He and Fortune came around the corner and seemed to know everything that had just happened, which made me wonder how long they'd been listening just out of sight.

"Nice of you to join the party," I said.

"Do you not understand, Jake? These children were able to get through my defenses."

"Were you shielding as hard as you could when you let Damian feed?" Fortune asked.

Kaazim didn't look surprised, exactly, but he stiffened, flinched maybe.

"You weren't, were you?" she said.

"I did not think it was necessary."

"You were arrogant," she said, smiling to take some of the sting out of her words.

"As Jake said, they are children compared to us."

"Children grow up, my friend."

"Jake, Jacob, you cannot tell me you would not be equally upset."

"They drew forth what you loved and miss most; if it had

been the Mother she would have brought it forward and forced you to live through the loss of that love. When they realized something was wrong, they did not hold you tight and force themselves on you further."

"I did not plot behind her back for thousands of years to end up back where I started only with a new face to wear the same power."

"You really are afraid that I'll turn into her, aren't you?"

"No, Anita, I am afraid that she is already inside you, and will control all of us again while wearing your face, but it will still be her."

"Maybe what keeps me from becoming the monster is the fact that I give a damn about the people around me, and I like someone who makes me smile."

"That would explain you picking Dev over me," Pride said.

"That would explain you picking him over all of our tigers," Kaazim said.

"I know I'm not the king you would have chosen," Dev said.

"You are not king, Mephistopheles. You were too busy chasing after Asher like a lovesick kitten to win either Anita or Jean-Claude to your cause."

Dev's face darkened. "I am trying to make up for that now with Jean-Claude and Anita, and Nathaniel."

"No one matters in this but Anita, Mephistopheles. Do you not understand that the Master or Mistress of Tigers must love one of our tigers, must wed them to keep us all safe? It is the last piece of magic that will keep Anita free of being possessed by the Mother's power, and the rest of us free of what will happen if this last stone is not firmly in place."

"I'm working on picking a tiger for the commitment ceremony with Nathaniel and Micah," I said.

"Yes, but you do not want to commit to them. Mephistopheles had a chance to win your heart, but he did not pursue it."

"I'm pursuing it," Fortune said.

Kaazim shook his head. "You are committed to Echo, as you must be to your master; your heart is not free to give."

"We tried and failed," Domino said, motioning at Ethan.

"Our fate hangs with two boys," Kaazim said.

"What two boys?" I asked.

"The blue tiger back in St. Louis that truly is a child, and this one who only behaves as one."

Dev's hands rolled into fists and he actually took a step toward the other man. I touched his arm, because I knew that would go badly. I'd seen them both in practice and Kaazim would kick his ass.

Nathaniel said, "Dev isn't just one of your tigers now. He's a lion, too. The golden tigers are supposed to rule all the other colors, but he's beginning to rule other groups as well; isn't that part of your legend, too?"

"And Sin literally made the earth move just before we got on the plane," I said. "Just because people are younger than you are doesn't make them children, just young."

"We don't have time for this; night is coming," Damian said.

"You are right," Jake said.

"We don't have time to admit aloud that the Mother's energy is waiting inside Anita like a coiled snake in the dark ready to strike? We don't have time to say that if she does not pick a tiger to love and marry, all we do here in Ireland is useless, because the Mother's power will consume the world and all of us with it?"

"She will not consume us today, but once night falls Damian's old master will do her best to destroy more of Dublin's people," Fortune said.

"You are letting your fears get in the way of our mission," Jake said, gently.

"No, Jacob, I am not. You and Fortune are allowing all this to interfere with our first and most important mission. What does it matter to us if all of Dublin burns tonight, if we do not prevent the evil from rising again?"

"Are you saying that it doesn't move you at all to see all those people in the beds there?"

"I am sorry that she has done this to them, she and her people, but if Jean-Claude and you had been able to contain the power it would not have come to her. They might not be hurt if you had chosen a tiger to call your own."

"Are you saying that somehow by marrying one of the tigers, magically all the scattered bits of the Mother's energy would be chased out of everyone else, or that Jean-Claude would suddenly be powerful enough to keep this kind of shit from happening?"

"That is what legend tells us."

"I think you're whistling in the dark, Kaazim."

"What does that mean?"

"I think you don't know how to put the genie back in the bottle."

"If you could call the djinn as the old Master of Tigers could do, we would have a formidable weapon against our enemies."

"Sorry that I didn't inherit anything but his ability to control the tigers, but I still think you worked all those centuries to kill the evil queen and didn't think what might happen afterward."

There was a moment when he glanced at Jake and Fortune but tried not to, and that was enough. "It is hard to plan for all eventualities," Jake said.

"You saw the defeat of your tyrant, but not what would happen to her vacant throne," Damian said.

"We thought that the one who defeated her would take her throne by right of conquest," Kaazim said.

"But by the time you won the war, the vampire council had imploded and there wasn't a European throne to take," I said.

"We did not anticipate an American king," Jake said.

"Echo says what we really didn't anticipate is that it took centuries to build the council's power base, and we expected it to transfer seamlessly to the next ruler, the next council," Fortune said.

"A little naïve of you all, wasn't it?" I asked.

Kaazim gave me a sour look. "Perhaps in retrospect," Jake said, smiling, but not like he was entirely happy with it all.

"Kaazim, I'm sorry we got through your shields further than you wanted, or we wanted, but can you get past it to do your job here and now?"

"We can put out this fire tonight, Anita, but it is like a house fire when the world is about to burn."

"Can you follow orders and do your job to help us save Dublin, or not?"

"What does one city matter if you carry the seeds of the apocalypse inside you?"

"I'll take that as a no," I said, and looked to Jake and Fortune. "All right, tell us what you've learned, because we need a plan before nightfall that doesn't need Kaazim to work."

"I will do my part of any plan," he said.

I shook my head. "You had your chance, Kaazim. You said you'd let Dublin burn, let Ireland be destroyed tonight, because you're worried about a disaster that's not here yet."

"You feel her power inside you. You must," he said.

"Power is not destiny," Jake said.

"I'm a big believer in free will," I said.

"And I have seen too many centuries not to believe in fate," Kaazim said.

I turned to the rest of them. "Let's find Edward and get our plans off the ground without gloomy puss here."

"I am not a puss," he said.

"Fine. Without gloomy dog here—no, that doesn't work, does it?"

"Gloomy puppy?" Nathaniel offered.

"Gloomy pup?" Pride suggested.

"I expected better of you," Kaazim said.

"Dev isn't perfect, Uncle Chaz, but he's trying, and you really are a gloomy hound and always have been."

"Uncle Chaz?" I said.

"When we were little, they were Uncle Jake and Uncle Chaz," Pride said.

Kaazim ignored the old nickname; too angry to care, I think. Then he said, "You are right." He turned to me. "And you are right, as well. I have made the mistake of a soldier: letting the fear of defeat in war steal my courage for fighting today's battle. Thank you for reminding me that if we do not win today's battle, then we will never survive to win the war."

"I was thinking more, you win the war one battle at a time, but okay, let's go find Edward and get our well-armed ducks in a row."

"How do you know what ducks you need, our Queen?" Jake asked.

"We'll figure that out as we go," I said.

He looked at me for a moment, then threw back his head and laughed. "Just like that."

"It's Edward. It's me. It's all of you, Nolan, and his people.

It's the gentle folk of Ireland singing sweet songs in our ears. With all that on our side, Jake, we'll figure out which ducks we need."

"Before nightfall?" Kaazim asked.

"Yes."

"There is no doubt in you," he said.

"I don't have time for it."

Fortune came up to me and Dev because he was so close, throwing an arm around us both. "We'll find gigantic carnivorous ducks," she said, and kissed us both one right after the other so that I tasted the echo of his mouth on hers. Nathaniel came over and added his kisses to ours, and Damian came to kiss two out of the four of us. Kaazim made an impatient sound that we were wasting time, but I've gone into a lot of fights now, and starting with a kiss beat the hell out of starting with a punch.

71

DAMIAN GAVE ADDRESSES of the old lairs that his old master and cronies had used five years ago; since they'd been using some of them for centuries it was a good bet they were still using some of them. You'd expect that once we knew possible places to go we'd suit up and bust down some doors, but it didn't work that way in America or in Ireland. The police would be gathering information on the addresses: public records, blueprints, find out if they were owned and lived in by human beings we could verify, because some of the addresses hadn't been used by M'Lady and her crew in a while, like decades. He made a list of centuries-old lairs. Not because they had been used recently, but because she owned them and she gave up nothing. Some of the buildings probably didn't even exist anymore. Those would be weeded out first and then they'd gather as much intel as possible. I'd worked with enough tactical units to know that the information gathering saved time and possibly lives later, but it was still a delay that always drove me a little crazy. It wasn't as bad this time because we didn't know which address we needed to hit, and the info would help us narrow the choices.

What to do while we waited? Edward and I both had some ideas; they just weren't the same ones. "If we can figure out why the holy objects didn't work at the police station and get them working before we send people into battle again, it will give us an advantage. It will give an advantage to the newbies who have never fought vamps before."

"How do you know the newbies will have that much faith?"

"They're fresh out of the packaging when we all believe in right and wrong, and that we can save the world. Your faith is always shinier before it gets a good test run."

"But not stronger," he said.

The comment surprised me from Edward, but I nodded and said, "No, not stronger, just newer."

"Your cross didn't go off either, you know."

"When no one's cross worked at the door to the station, I didn't think to draw mine. I might have, but about then he went out the door into the sunlight. I've never tried to trap a vampire between a cross's glow or burning to death in sunlight. I think I'd go for the cross first, if it were me, but once it gets dark the crosses will be the only glow they need to fear. Besides, Damian was right beside me; when some of the vampires are on our side, holy objects are a mixed blessing."

"If I'd brought my flamethrower, that wouldn't be true about the glow."

"You've almost burned one house down around us. It's left me not a fan of your flamethrower."

"You're never going to let me forget that, are you?"

"Nope." I smiled when I said it, but I meant it.

Edward wanted me to go off with one of my people and try to heal my wounds with a little sexual healing before I did anything else. "It will take time for Pearson to get permission for you to do a demonstration to peacekeepers he doesn't have under his direct charge."

"How much time?" I asked.

"Make it a quickie, thirty minutes or so; they won't have everything organized before that."

"I knew there was a reason we were friends; I like a man who considers thirty minutes a quickie."

He grinned. "Twenty minutes in a pinch, but you're not just having sex; you're trying to heal a wound made by something supernatural. That might take more time."

I double-checked with Pearson, but Edward was right; it was going to take time to get all the Gardai's ducks in a row. Apparently someone had recorded us shooting the burned vampire to pieces in the street with a smartphone. It was all over the Internet and it looked pretty brutal, so the upper management of the local constabulary wasn't sure how much more help they wanted from the Americans. When I pointed out that they'd probably want the Americans on their side come nightfall, he'd said, "No one making this decision saw the vampires in person today. None of them have even walked into a crime scene or seen a victim in person. They don't want to believe what's happening to our city."

"They better believe and fast, Pearson, because we all need to make plans to try to keep Dublin from going up in blood and vampires tonight."

"I know that, Blake, but I'm not the one ultimately in charge."

"Are you actually saying that the powers that be may send me and my people home tonight rather than let us stay and help you fight?"

"It's not a fight, Blake. It's a crime to solve."

"We know who's behind it, Pearson. We just need to find her and make sure she can't do this again."

"We only have your vampire's word that it's his old master, Blake. We have no proof that we can take into court. We can't arrest her unless we catch her hurting people personally."

"Are you honestly saying, with Flannery and his people telling you the same thing that Damian and I are telling you, that it's not enough to convince your boss's boss that we just need to find her before nightfall and end her ass?"

"They aren't comfortable with the American solution."

"American solution . . . Shit, Pearson, you saw what just one vampire did to your . . . peacekeepers today. What do you think is going to happen when night falls and she can control that many vampires?"

"I can't prove that will happen, Blake, and neither can you."

"If they wait until tonight to plan a response, it's going to be a bloodbath. You know that."

"I have been very clear about what I believe is happening and will happen tonight, but you have to understand we have never had vampires here. We're Irish; we can usually make friends with any supernatural element that comes our way."

"Yeah, just a magical minority. I get it, but, Pearson, the Fey are scared, too. They don't know what's happening to Dublin, and they're worried it's going to spread from here to other cities."

"The gentle folk are part of the discussion with my superiors."

"And they still won't budge?"

"They're budging, but not as fast as you are wanting."

"It's not what I want, Pearson. It's what's needed."

"Perhaps, but I have to go through channels, Blake, and if you, or any of your people, act without clearance from us, then your likelihood of being escorted out of Dublin and to the airport when we need you most is almost a given."

"I'd like to say you're joking, but I know you're not."

"We do things differently over here, Blake."

"All bureaucracies are the same, Pearson. We've just had longer to deal with the problem in my country."

"No, Blake, one of the reasons that we preferred Forrester to you is that even your own FBI hasn't invited you to lecture and help train their agents. Even your own countrymen consider you more likely to resort to violence. Plus, you are a beautiful woman who is completely comfortable with violence. That unnerves some people almost more than the necromancy."

"Are you saying this comes down to some kind of weird sexism?"

"Publicly I will say no, but privately, a little bit."

"So if I were less attractive, this would go over better?"

"Even taller and more physically formidable would help, but you're this petite, attractive woman and it seems to bother some of my superiors that you're so comfortable with violence."

"That is ridiculous," I said.

"A little bit," he said.

"I can't grow taller in the next few hours, Pearson."

"I know that."

"Is there anything I can do to help them like me and my people better?"

"Stay out of trouble, and by trouble, I mean don't shoot anyone. Don't do anything violent until I've talked them through this."

"And if I'm attacked, can I defend myself?"

"Of course, you can defend yourself, but if you are attacked, making sure there are witnesses to them throwing the first punch, so to speak, would be helpful."

"So you're saying that even if I defend myself, any violence will count against me, us?"

"Just don't shoot anyone, please."

"I really don't want to get close enough to use a blade, Pearson. That's a good way to get even more hurt than I am."

"No, Blake, no blades either. Don't shoot anyone. Don't cut anyone with a knife."

"These are vampires, Pearson. What am I supposed to do, arm-wrestle them?"

"I know this sounds unreasonable to you, Blake."

"Damn straight, it does."

"But we don't resort to guns as soon as you do in your country. We call ourselves peacekeepers for a reason, because we see keeping the peace as our primary task."

"If you and your superiors don't have a battle plan before dark tonight, there won't be any peace in Dublin. As soon as Flannery's friends' magic fades enough, the Wicked Bitch of Ireland is going to call all her vampires to her. She has created an army here; don't you understand that?"

"We're hoping that most of the vampires are in the hospitals, currently under sedation."

"The drugs won't keep them unconscious once night falls," I said.

"The doctors think differently," he said.

"Because they think the vampires are people with a disease, and they aren't."

"Vampirism is a disease, just like cancer," he said.

"Yes, but cancer patients don't crave human blood, or become stronger and faster. They can't capture people with their gaze and force them to turn on their own people."

"The doctors in charge of the patients think the drugs will keep them comatose tonight."

"Fine, but what about the other vampires in the city?"

"We're hoping that most of them are either dead or in the hospital wards."

"Oh my God, are you telling me that they, that you, really believe that we have most of the vampires in the city contained?"

He cleared his throat and said, "That is the prevailing theory."

"Theories are great in the laboratory, or in the boardroom, but out on the streets your theory is going to meet reality tonight."

"If you don't shoot or stab anyone between now and nightfall, I may be able to get them to agree to you and your people being part of the watch groups that will be patrolling the city."

"If we help patrol the city we will be cleared to shoot in self-defense, at least?"

"I won't ask that question and neither should you, Blake."

"Why not?"

"Because sometimes it's better to beg forgiveness than ask permission and be denied."

"Jesus, Pearson, you're setting your fellow Gardai up to be slaughtered."

"I'm doing the best I can; just stay out of trouble for a few hours. We have time before dark, if nothing else goes wrong and ends up on YouTube."

"We have no control over who has a phone and records what," I said.

"Stay out of sight, then, just until I can talk them through this, and then you can show us how a holy item is supposed to work."

"Fine, fine, but . . . fine," I said, and hung up because I didn't trust myself to say more. Apparently I had time for more than just a quickie.

72

MY FIRST CHOICE would have been Nathaniel, or Nathaniel and Damian, but I'd fed the *ardeur* on them recently and I needed to give them another day of rest. Maybe more now that Nathaniel had donated blood to multiple vampires today. I actually asked Dev to go with me, but Jake stepped in, saying, "He has donated much blood today and should rest before he feeds anyone else again."

Dev had protested, but in the end we'd listened to the older and more experienced voice, which left me with a quandary. Fortune had also donated to multiple vampires, Magda was thirty minutes or more away with traffic, and honestly girl-on-girl sex took longer, because it was girl foreplay for two, instead of just one. Yes, some men need more foreplay than others and a lot more men enjoy foreplay than will admit it, but I was out of women and almost out of men. Just when you think you've overpacked, you realize you didn't bring enough of something.

I'd done my best to get both Ethan and Domino off my list of lovers, because they both wanted more emotional commitment than I could offer. I was so over my limit for emotional caretaking, but I needed to use the only healing ability I had, which like so many of the abilities I had inherited was sexual in nature. As Dev had said earlier, lust was better than fear, or death, or violence, and I could feed off anger, but I couldn't heal with anger and that was what I needed.

"You could look a little less unhappy about this," Domino said.

"I'm sorry, really," I said, and I included Ethan in the apology. "It's just that I keep trying to trim my list of lovers and make a big deal out of the trimming, and now here we are again."

Ethan smiled. "Your dance card was beyond full by the

time I came into your life; I figured that out once I got to St. Louis, and yes, I was disappointed, but now I'm with Nilda, and I'm happier than I've ever been. That wouldn't have happened if you hadn't met me in Washington."

I patted his arm. "Thanks, Ethan, but will Nilda have a problem with us sleeping together again?"

He shook his head. "She knows I'm one of your *moitié bêtes*, and to a member of the Harlequin that means I belong to you first and everyone else second."

"Good to know," I said, and turned to Domino, who was not smiling.

"Will Jade be okay with us doing this?"

"Jade wants to fuck you, too, Anita. She'll be fine."

That made me frown, because I'd just gotten free of a relationship with Jade that had been unsatisfactory on my part and frustrating for her. I didn't want to get dragged back into it when we got back home.

"Is it really that bad a choice, the two of us?" Domino asked.

I smiled, but looked down because I knew it wasn't going to make it all the way up into my eyes. "No, of course not. You are both lovely in bed."

"*Lovely* sounds like girl-speak for *good, but not great*," he said.

"Why are you making this difficult?" I asked.

"Because if I'm going to get a chance to have sex with you again, I want you to treat it less like a chore you have to do, and more like something fun. I know you're only doing it to try to heal, but still, sex is supposed to be fun, Anita."

That made me smile all the way up, so I let him see it. "Thanks for the reminder, because you're right. I was treating it like a chore, and I'm sorry for that. I'm just worried about what the Irish police are going to do, or what they're going to allow us to do tonight."

Edward said, "Nolan and I will help Pearson persuade the upper management."

"I hate it when police are run like a corporation. It just doesn't work that way," I said.

"That's still how most of them are run, especially in the larger cities."

"It still doesn't make it right," I said.

He agreed with me but sent me off with the two weretigers, saying, "Have fun."

I looked at the two men who were waiting for me a little down the hallway. They were almost the same height, just under six feet. Domino's shoulders were broader and he just bulked up a little more when he worked out. Ethan was even more slender than when I'd met him, honed down from the workouts and training that our guards did. Both of them were in better shape than when I found them. Domino had been muscle for the mobster who was also master vamp of Las Vegas. Being mob muscle didn't come with a set exercise routine. Ethan had been a bodyguard for the queen of the red tiger clan. I looked at him, realizing just how much thinner he was now, and he'd been thin to begin with; either he wasn't eating enough or he'd leaned down through all the exercise with us. Once I got him out of his clothes, either he'd have more visible muscle or he'd have less muscle mass in general from poor nutrition. Either way, once we got to our hotel room I'd find out.

73

I DIDN'T FIND out if Ethan was starving himself or had just carved himself down to lean muscle, because Domino won the toss, or rather threw down with "I am more dominant than you are, so unless you want to fight about it . . ." which Ethan didn't. It was sort of my fault, because I was having trouble choosing and had made some noise about why not make it a threesome? Neither of them wanted to do that, but they took my suggestion as meaning I had no preference between the two of them, so they decided for me. Normally, I might not have been okay with that, but there was nothing normal about our trip to Ireland. My arm was aching by the time we walked to the hotel, so I was good with someone else taking the initiative.

Ethan went into the connecting room and shut the door between us. I sat down on the edge of the king-size bed, my arm in the sling, and hugged it a little closer to me, carefully.

"How much pain are you in?" Domino asked.

"Enough. I want this healed."

He came to stand near me. "I mean, are you in so much pain that it's going to interfere with the sex?"

"My concentration may not be what it's supposed to be," I said.

He knelt in front of me. I was suddenly looking into those red-and-orange eyes. They so looked like tiger's eyes in his human face, but strangers would ask where he got the cool contacts. Very few people saw the reality of him. I wasn't sure if they lied to themselves, or if other people were just that blind to anything outside the ordinary. Micah's leopard eyes didn't have clean circles of color between his gold and yellow. It was more an intermingling of the two colors, but Domino's red and orange were separate, not perfect circles, but the imperfections of it made the two colors bleed over just a little here and there, so the illusion was less fire and more water, as if his eyes held both heat and cool, flame and liquid. I touched his face, laying my fingers beside those eyes and tracing downward along his cheek to find the softness of his lips with just the tips of my fingers. The movement made him close his eyes for a moment and let his breath out in a long sigh that seemed to hold months of stress and tension, just blown away with one breath.

I caressed his hair next, playing with the scattering of white curls as if someone had spilled white rose petals into all that raven-black hair. He was watching me now, the tiger eyes full of so many emotions that no real tiger would ever feel, because they couldn't possibly overcomplicate their lives as much as humans did.

He touched my face and his hand was big enough to cup the entire side of it, so that I laid my cheek in his hand as if it were a pillow and let myself relax into the nearly fevered warmth of his skin.

I said, out loud, "So warm."

"I have warmer places on my body."

"Show me," I said.

74

ONCE HE WAS nude, I could see the play of new muscles under his skin; he was beginning to bulk up and I could trace the shadow lines of a six-pack across his stomach just hidden below a layer of warm, soft, kissable skin. He was only a few pounds from having that cut fierceness that graced the cover of so many magazines, but he looked beautiful just as he was, and I knew through dating so many dancers and weight lifters that a true six-pack is either a very clean diet, or genetic luck, or a combination. We all hit the gym to stay in shape for our jobs whether it was stripping onstage, performing in ballet, fighting monsters, or guarding other people's bodies, but for that fitness-model look you had to spend almost more time in the gym than with the people you loved, and it just wasn't worth it to me.

Domino had to help me off with my clothes; getting the sling off had been almost the most painful part. First it was straightening the arm, which hurt, and then letting the arm hang hurt. We ended up putting the sling back on once I was nude. That way I wasn't wincing every time I moved.

"Why does this hurt so much?"

"You had a piece of someone driven into your arm so deep that you almost had to have surgery to have it removed," he said.

"Oh," I said, and after that, I stopped asking stupid questions, or tried to; I sometimes say what I'm thinking too much when foreplay is just starting. I did my best not to ask anything else that obvious. Either I managed it, or Domino didn't care enough to comment. He just ran those warm hands over my body, and he was right; other parts of him were even warmer.

I tried oral sex on him in one of my two favorite positions, with him lying flat on the bed and me kneeling over him, but I couldn't bear for my arm to hang at the angle I needed. I straightened up with him firmer than when I'd started, but not to my usual level of happy. I knelt beside him and said, "I'm sorry my arm is in the way."

"I would love for you to go down on me later when you're feeling better, but I understand that you're hurting. Let's fix that."

"Sounds good. How?" I was cradling my arm now. It wasn't aching anymore; it was just hurting. Waves of pain were radiating from my arm, up my shoulder, down the side of my body. It was not as bad as when they'd cleaned and treated the wound, but it was bad enough that I was beginning to wonder how I was going to get past it for sex. I liked a little pain with my sex sometimes, but this was not the right kind of pain. This just fucking hurt.

"I can feel the echo of how much you're hurting," he said.

"I'm sorry for that," I said.

He touched my good arm. "You don't have to be. It's part of my job as your beast half to feel what you're feeling and help you heal it."

"Domino, I'm not sure if I can do this hurting this much."

"You've just gotten spoiled sharing our healing abilities," he said, smiling and trying to make light of it.

"Yes, I have gotten spoiled. I'd forgotten what a bitch it was to get hurt during an investigation and still have to keep going."

"I have an idea," he said.

"I'm all ears."

He looked me up and down, lingering on my breasts. "I wouldn't say that," he said, and he touched where he'd looked the longest, and it felt nice to have him caress my breasts, but the pain overwhelmed it.

He finally propped pillows up against the headboard and helped me recline with pillows helping to hold my arm in place, so I didn't keep having to use my good arm to hold it.

He started caressing my thighs and passing that warm hand over the front of my body. He didn't try to go for the gold, didn't try to play with me, but just kept petting me with those big, warm hands of his, and I started to relax into the pillows and his touch. He finally started touching more to the point, helping me spread my legs wider so he could lie between them tracing the edges of me, petting me and finally laying one big hand over the front of me so that he cupped all of me in the fevered warmth of his hand, pressing the palm of it against me, so that it was almost like being held, but just there. It was so gentle and I felt myself growing wet and tension trying to leave. I wanted what went with that tenderness.

He began to play with me, tracing over that sweet spot that had swollen at all that gentle foreplay. I couldn't have handled rough tonight. Domino ran his fingers over and around, and then over, caressing, teasing, until my breath came faster and my body felt eager for more. I expected the orgasm to come, but I stayed on that edge. The pain wouldn't let me release myself to the pleasure.

"It feels good," I said in a breathless voice.

"But you're not going to come, are you?"

"The pain keeps getting in the way." I looked down at him lying between my legs, his hand on my thigh now. "I'm sorry."

"Don't apologize, Anita. We've all been hurt."

"But you can shift and heal."

"Not everything," he said. He kissed my thigh, and then again a little higher up.

"I couldn't bear it if you went down on me and I couldn't go; that would almost be too much frustration for me."

He rose up from kissing his way down my thigh. "You turning down oral sex means you're hurting even more than you're letting me feel."

"One of us hurting this much is enough."

He laid his cheek on my thigh and gazed up at me with those startling eyes of his. Maybe if he'd been a more consistent lover for me, I would have gotten used to them by now, but we'd never made a habit of each other, so every time I looked into his eyes like this, the alien beauty of them in his face thrilled through me. If I'd been a different kind of person it would have thrilled me and frightened me, because the eyes screamed different, not one of us, not like me, so hard, but differences weren't bad to me, so the thrill turned to seeing it as beautiful like a rare orchid, or like a painting that was all bold colors and movement, so that even if you didn't know what the artist meant you still liked the energy and color of the art.

"There, that's better," he said, and he was right. Something about staring into his eyes had calmed me, and once I calmed down the arm didn't hurt so much.

"I've lost the knack of coping with injuries like this. I'm like a pain wimp now."

He laughed, softly. "You will never be a wimp about anything, Anita, but you are out of practice coping with injuries."

"It hurt more because I wasn't expecting it to hurt this much."

"And now?" he asked.

"Better, as long as I don't abuse it too much."

"I think we can find something to do that won't abuse your arm." He kissed the top of my thigh, then rubbed his cheek lower on my thigh.

"Whatever could you have in mind?" I asked.

He grinned up at me as he kissed his way lower on my thigh. "I've been practicing more since we did this last."

"Have you, now?"

He nodded, rubbing his face against the inside of my thigh as he did it.

"Show me what you've learned."

He smiled with his lips against my thigh. "I learned part of it watching you go down on Jade with Jason's girlfriend helping."

"J.J. was a very good teacher," I said, and felt the heat start to rise up my face, as I thought about the blond ballerina.

He gave a low chuckle that ended in a rolling bass purr. That last sound made me shiver in a good way, but it shivered the muscles where I'd been stitched up, too, which wasn't nearly as fun.

"I'm not sure if I can translate this pain into pleasure."

"You'll just have to hold still when you orgasm," he said.

"I don't know if I can."

"I've heard stories about you holding still when you have to for it."

I frowned at him. "Who's been talking?"

"Hmm-hmm," he said, lips against my thigh, "no kissing and telling." He kissed my thigh again, this time just at the edge of that deep curve on the inside of the very upper part of the thigh. He laid the next kiss inside it, letting his breath come out warm and soft against my skin. I fought not to shiver again, or at least to keep my arm still. I sort of succeeded.

He kissed my mound, and blew another soft breath. It was so warm, it was almost hot against my skin. It sent my breath out in a long sigh, eyes closing, and he chose that moment to lick between my legs, one quick teasing line.

It made me look at him, half laughing.

The look in his eyes stole the laughter away and left me breathless, my body already tightening. Every man has that predatory look in him somewhere, but this one was coming from a pair of eyes that belonged in the striped face of a real predator. His tiger gazed up at me, and the thought of him putting his mouth on such intimate bits of my body made me shiver for more than one reason. I'd almost made peace with the fact that a little fear with my sex, a little danger with those I trusted, just flipped my switch. As he began to lick around the edges of me, careful to take his time and warm me up for what would come next, I admitted that part of the thrill was not the gentleness, but the thought that even human teeth could do damage. When you think about it, oral sex is one of the most trusting things we do with a lover. If that lover is a shapeshifter who has real fangs and claws inside him, it's even more about trust.

I let myself relax into the feel of his tongue circling around the edges of me, licking in long strokes on either side, coming closer, but never quite touching me where I wanted it most. I finally asked, "Please, please."

He rose up enough to ask, "Please what?" but the look in his eyes let me know that he knew exactly what, but I played the game.

"This all feels wonderful, but please make me come, no more prep work, no more teasing."

"It's called foreplay, Anita, not teasing." He licked to either side, but purposely avoided the one last spot I wanted him to touch.

"Domino, you're driving me crazy. Just do it."

"You mean this?" He licked a quick line from my opening up, and barely touched the one spot I wanted him to touch the most.

I laughed half in pleasure, half exasperation. "Domino!"

"When I make you come, I want you to say my name."

I almost said out loud that I tried not to use anyone's name, because I didn't want to cry out the wrong name. I'd done it a few times, and so far everyone had been a good sport, but it wasn't flattering to have your lover call out someone else's name in the middle of sex. It just wasn't, but as I stared down the line of my body into those flame-and-sunset eyes, what else could I say but yes?

He brought me with his tongue, his lips, his mouth, licking and sucking over that one sweet point, and because he'd done so much foreplay the orgasm was bigger, more all-consuming, so the orgasm washed over me in wave after wave that left me quivering and screaming, my hands trying to find something, anything to dig my nails into, to hold on to as one orgasm spilled into the next, or maybe it was the same one over and over like waves against the shore; it's all the same ocean, but not the same wave.

I screamed his name with my head thrown back, eyes closed, his name like a frantic prayer spilling over and over from my lips, "Domino, Domino, Domino!"

His face was suddenly above me. "Your arm seems better."

I blinked up at him. I'd slid down the pillows and buried myself deeper into them as I thrashed around. The sling was loose around my neck, because my arm wasn't in it anymore. I managed to gasp, "Yes."

"Good, because I want to fuck you now."

"Yes, God, yes."

He smiled, and my mind could almost process that he was on all fours above me, his arms on either side of my upper body, his knees between my legs. He was already wearing a condom like a pale shadow over the hardness of him.

He leaned his lower body on top of me but kept his upper

body propped above me. He tried to slide himself inside me but couldn't quite get the angle. If I could have moved I'd have helped him, but I was still lying there boneless and floating on the afterglow of the sex we'd already had. He used his hand to guide himself inside me. I was so wet, but tight, the way I got after oral sex. He was wide enough that he had to push to work himself inside me, one delicious inch at a time. I was making small, eager noises by the time he got himself as deep inside me as he could, our bodies wedded together as intimately as it was possible to be.

"Look at me, Anita," he said.

I'd been watching his body sliding inside mine, but his words made me look up. He was staring down at me. "I want you to look at me while we make love. I want you to look into my eyes the whole time."

"I don't know if I can."

"I want to watch your eyes while we make love. I want you to watch my eyes and not my body."

The thought of looking him in the eyes the whole time made me uncomfortable, and strangely self-conscious. I might have protested, but I'd been with Jade enough to know why he might be asking this now. She saw too much eye contact during sex as aggression, and that had been with me, another woman; I couldn't imagine how much worse the issue would be between her and a man. Even in the middle of sex Jade seemed to hide; I could understand Domino wanting someone who didn't hide. Someone who saw him, and enjoyed being with him, no flinching, no punishing him for being a man. You could have sympathy for Jade's issues, but her unwillingness to work through them in therapy had limited my sympathy after a while. I didn't ask if Domino was coming to the same conclusions. I just gave him what he wanted. I looked at him as his body began to work in and out of mine. He stopped moving long enough to throw enough pillows off the bed to give himself a firmer surface for his arms to push against. I stared up into eyes that reminded me of fire as he found his rhythm, a little faster now, but not as deep as he could go, seeking for that first spot close to the opening. I knew my breathing changed, but something must have shown on my face, because he smiled and kept sliding himself over and over in that hip-moving rhythm that had quickened my breathing and made me grab onto his arms where they kept his upper body propped above me. I watched the orange of his iris spread until the red was only a thin line around his pupil as his own breathing began to speed up. I could feel the weight between my legs growing, and knew I was close. I told him so, as I stared into his face and let him see every shade of pleasure, every small frown and smile and gasp, and I watched the same from him. It was almost too intimate, as if we were stripping each other bare in a way we'd never done before.

Between one second and the next, one thrust of his body and the next, he brought me screaming wordlessly, too overwhelmed for any words to hold. I spasmed with the orgasm, throwing my head back, closing my eyes.

"Look at me, Anita. Look at me!" His voice was a deep growl, so bass it didn't sound like him at all anymore.

I opened my eyes and looked up to find his lips half-parted, his eyes almost frantic. He fought his body to keep its rhythm so I would scream my pleasure just one more time. I felt my nails dig into his arms where I was still holding on. He stared into my eyes and I stared back, and what I saw just a second before looked almost like fear, as if he were afraid to let himself release. His body shuddered above me, stumbled in that rhythm, and he cried out above me, his eyes wide and frantic as he thrust himself as deep inside me as he could get, which made me scream for him again. I felt him shudder inside me, felt him go inside me, his body pulsing with it, which made me cry out again and rake my nails down his arms.

He finally closed his eyes and bowed his head over me, while his chest rose and fell as if he'd been running. There was a fine sheen of sweat down the middle of his chest. I wanted to touch his curls so close above me, but I couldn't make my arms work. I couldn't make anything work. I was just floating in the afterglow of all of it.

His voice was breathy as he said, "Thank you."

It took me two tries to say, "Oh, Domino."

He raised his head enough to look at me.

I smiled and said in a voice that was almost too breathless to work, "Domino, it was my pleasure. Oh God, it was so my pleasure."

He smiled then and started to pull himself out of me, one hand going to the condom to make sure everything stayed in place. He half collapsed beside me. "I need to clean up."

I patted his chest sort of awkwardly, because it was a bad angle for it. "You do that. I can't move yet."

He got to his feet beside the bed and then staggered into the wall, trying to get into the bathroom. It made me laugh, and he laughed with me. Sex so good you run into walls.

75

I WAS STILL lying on the bed, letting my mind and newly healed body drift, when there was a forceful knock on the door. It was the sort of knock that police give, very authoritative and loud. The adrenaline rush cleared the floating happiness of afterglow. I sat up and called out, "Domino?"

There was a knock at the connecting door, and Ethan said, "Coming through," and opened the door without asking. He had a gun bare in his hand, and I was okay with that. I was scrambling across the bed for the one I'd left handy on the bedside table. Once I had it in one hand and the sheets covering my chest in the other one, I felt a little better. I always needed clothes and weapons to feel really secure.

Domino came out of the bathroom, still nude, but he had a gun in his hand, which meant he'd stashed one in there somewhere and I hadn't known it. I was sort of impressed, or sad with myself. "I heard," he said.

"Who is it?" Ethan asked from the open connecting door.

Domino shook his head and went toward the door. Most people would have put their eye to the peephole, but he didn't. He stood to one side and about a foot from the door, as the knock sounded again, and a man's voice said, "Hotel security!" The voice had that cop sound to it. I was betting he either had been a cop or was one earning extra money on the side.

"I'm sorry. Who did you say you are?" Domino asked, though I knew he'd heard perfectly.

"Hotel security. Is everything all right in there, sir?"

"We're fine."

"Could you open the door and let us verify that everyone in the room is fine?"

"I'm sorry, but I'm not comfortable with opening the door," Domino said.

"Sir, if you don't open the door, we will be forced to unlock the door and enter without your permission."

"The safety bolt is on. You won't get in," Domino said.

"We are just following up on a noise complaint, sir," a second, slightly less authoritative voice said.

Domino turned and looked at me, smiling in that way that men do when they're proud of the noise you've made together. "If you had a noise complaint, I'm sorry. We'll be quieter."

"People said they heard a woman screaming. I'm terribly sorry, sir, but we need to verify that the woman is not in any distress."

Domino smiled broader and shook his head. "Anita, can you tell them you're not in distress?"

I held the sheet a little tighter to my chest as if I needed more cover-up just to talk through the door. "I'm sorry we were loud, but I'm fine."

"I'm sorry, miss. We'd love to be able to take your word through the door, but we need to actually see you face-to-face," the second male voice said; he sounded younger than the other one.

"Is there a law in Ireland against loud sex?" Domino asked.

"No, sir," said the voice through the door, "but there is a law against domestic abuse. If you don't open the door and let us see the lady for ourselves, we will be forced to call the Gardai and report this as a potential assault."

"I didn't think we were that loud," I said.

Ethan said, "You were loud."

"If you didn't know what we were doing, would you think I was screaming for help?"

"Maybe."

"Just a minute. We need to get some clothes on before we open the door," Domino said, and backed away from the door. I'd have liked to say he was being paranoid, but the knock had spooked me, too. Maybe we were all just professionally paranoid.

"Thank you, sir, ma'am, miss." It was the younger security guard again; he sounded uncomfortable even through the door.

It wasn't just clothes we needed. The guns and blades that we'd been wearing were in a pile on either side of the bed. We had no official status in Ireland, so without one of the Gardai that knew us, or Nolan and his people with us, if we opened the door and the security people saw this many weapons, they would call the cops. We could put some of the dangerous stuff under the edge of the bed, but I didn't want to shove them too far under, because then you couldn't reach them, or worse yet I didn't want to spend time searching for a gun that I'd forgotten was under the bed. I'd never done it yet, but I didn't want to break my streak.

"Sir, ma'am?" said the cop voice at the door.

"Just tidying up," I called out, trying to sound like a woman who had rented a hotel room with her lover and was maybe hiding bondage gear or sex toys from sight, not weapons. Nope, no weapons here.

Ethan holstered the gun he'd drawn so he could help us put weapons in the closet. Domino pulled on underwear and jeans. He picked up his holster, but Ethan shook his head.

I whispered to Domino, "We don't have any legal status here. Without Nolan and his crew, we're just armed strangers to these men. I don't know what we were thinking going out without Nolan or someone with credentials to vouch for us."

"We couldn't bring Donnie and Griffin upstairs with us," he said.

"Still should have asked for a card or something from Nolan," I said.

"You were in pain, and we were thinking about sex," Domino said.

"Edward let us walk off alone, too," I said.

"Him, I don't have an excuse for," Domino said.

Neither did I, which meant I'd be talking to him about it later, but first . . . another loud knock. "We've been patient, but either you open this door now, or we call the police, assuming that the lady in question is injured."

Domino put on a T-shirt loose over the top of his jeans and put one handgun at the back of his waistband. It wasn't an ideal place to carry for real, no matter how many times you see it in movies, but for a few minutes to not spook hotel security it would do.

I'd started to put a robe on, but in the end I got one of the few oversize sleep shirts that I'd packed and put it on over jeans. I could have hidden my AR-15 under it without it showing, but I settled for my EMP tucked into the holster I normally carried it in; yay gun belt! I had to put it a little more to the front than I normally carried it, but I wanted concealment more than I wanted a fast draw. We only had to show the hotel security that I wasn't a victim, and then we could call Edward or any of our people still at the police station and get an escort back there. The fact that Domino and I had both taken the time to arm ourselves before we opened the door said we were indeed paranoid.

The last knock shook the door. "This is the last warning, sir. Open the door or the Gardai are being called."

"We're coming," I called.

Ethan went back to the other room, shutting the door between. Domino and I visually checked the room one more time for weapons, and then he opened the door with his body not in line of sight from the door, and me farther behind him. I'd stopped arguing with the bodyguards when they were guarding.

"Sorry, really, but the room was a mess," Domino said in a wonderfully ordinary voice.

The two men in the doorway were both wearing dark suits and white button-up shirts, and they were shorter than Domino. The one in front was older and heavier, carrying enough around his middle that combined with the gray buzz cut of his hair he'd need to worry about cardiac health soon. His white button-up shirt strained across his chest and stomach, showing the undershirt as an imprint because it was all too tight. The second one looked like he should have still been in high school if he'd been in the States. Baby-fine white-blond hair cut short and a spattering of freckles across his cheeks made him look like an extra on a 1950s sitcom, but the black suit fit him well and the shoulder spread looked more grown-up than the face.

I probably looked about the same age in the huge T-shirt and jeans, so I guess I shouldn't throw stones, and God knew what my hair looked like after sex. Yeah, the stone-throwing could wait.

A voice down the hallway asked, "What's wrong?"

"Go back inside, ma'am. Just a noise complaint."

"Miss, could we step inside the room so we don't attract more attention, please?" the older one asked.

I didn't see a problem with it, but the bodyguards and I had a deal: I would remember to let them do their job. So I said, "Domino?"

"Sure," he said, and stepped back, keeping me behind him as they came through the door. Once we were all in the room, it seemed a lot smaller.

"Miss, please step out where we can get a better look at you," the older one asked.

It was reasonable since the lights were dim in the room, so I stepped out from behind Domino. I fought the urge to touch my hair; if I'd been that worried about it, I should have looked in a mirror before we opened the door.

He arched an eyebrow that was still black like his hair had been once. The young one gave me wide dark eyes. Apparently, I wasn't meeting expectations for him either.

"Were you fighting?" the older one asked.

"No," Domino said, "we were—"

"I didn't ask you. I asked her," he said, and even with the Irish accent, it was still a cop voice, abrupt and cutting across any nonsense.

Domino didn't argue, just stepped a little back so I was more to the front. "No, we weren't fighting," I said.

"We had reports of a woman screaming, miss. If you weren't fighting, what were you doing?"

I could have been coy, but I wasn't good at it, so I decided to try the absolute truth. "We were having sex."

He looked startled instead of cynical for the first time. His sidekick looked at the floor as if he suddenly didn't want to look at me or Domino. I don't think they'd expected me to just admit it.

"And that's your story?" the older guy asked.

"It's the truth," I said.

Domino held his arms out so they could see the bloody scratches on them. "The sex got a little rough, but it wasn't my girlfriend who got hurt."

I blushed, didn't mean to, but it helped our story, so it was a well-timed blush. "Sorry about that, Dom, really."

"I'm not complaining, Anita, just explaining to the nice hotel security." We shared one of those couple smiles, one that was actually not real for us, but we both played it for real. I realized that I'd gotten better at undercover work over the years; I'd never be great at it, but I was improving.

The older security person was looking from one to the other of us as if he knew something was off, but not what. If he'd been an on-duty cop he'd have probably found a way to check us out more, but he was hotel security and he'd done his job. We just needed to keep looking pleasant until he left.

The younger guy was so embarrassed that he still couldn't look at either of us. With everything people do in hotel rooms, I wasn't sure he had the nerves for the job. Then he looked up, and there was something in his eyes that didn't match embarrassment and made him look older.

The older guy said, "Well, thank you for letting us in your room, and just keep the noise level down." He started to turn for the door, and his fist lashed out at me as he moved so that it was just a continuation of the movement. I managed to avoid being hit, but the other fist was swinging back at me. The young one had rushed Domino, and we were both suddenly too busy avoiding getting hit to go for the only guns we had within reach.

76

THEY WERE MOVING in a blur of speed; all I could think of was Magda in the hallway with Mort. I remembered what he'd said: *Don't try to see it. Just feel it.* I was faster than human, faster even than Mort, but I wasn't as fast as the big fists that were flying at me. I managed to avoid the blur of his big fists, and blocked a few, but it was a waiting game. Either I was going to find an opening and cripple him, or he'd get through my guard and that would be it. I didn't have time to look for Domino, or wonder where Ethan was, because it was everything I could do just to keep ahead of the fight I was in; I could hear the noises and got the sense of the fight that Domino was having in his part of the room, but that was it. And then there was a sharp pain in my chest. I couldn't breathe. I couldn't raise my arms. I couldn't . . . A fist connected with the side of my face.

The next thing I knew, I was on the floor looking up with the big guy sitting across my waist. I wasn't completely passed out, but I was close, and I couldn't catch my breath. Why did my chest hurt? I was stunned from the blow to my face, which made some things feel distant, but the pain in my chest and the fact that I couldn't catch my breath, that wasn't from this fight. I didn't see the door to the connecting room open, but I saw him look up, saw his eyes react, and then his hand moved. I got a glimpse of a silver blur and thought, *Knife*. It felt like my right shoulder had been hit by a baseball bat and my arm went numb, but I was already numb and distant from the head blow; what was happening to me? I saw the younger guy go past toward the door behind me. I wanted to look for Domino and Ethan, but I still couldn't move enough. It would pass. I knew it would pass, but would it pass in time?

"Don't kill that one," the older guy said. "She's having

trouble breathing." He didn't sound Irish at all now, more Ukrainian, or maybe Russian, or something.

I heard the sounds of fighting and another sound that was wet and not good. Someone was hurt bad. What did he mean, *Don't kill that one*? Why had the young one been able to just walk away from Domino? I heard sounds of struggling behind me. I still couldn't catch my breath. My chest felt like he was sitting on it instead of my waist. There were bad sounds coming from the other side of the room where Domino had been. I could move now, I was pretty sure, but if I turned to look at Domino or Ethan, then the man on top of me would know I could move. I wanted to use that one chance to try to save us, not just look around. Fuck.

The wet, bubbling sounds in the other part of the room sounded more frantic. I sort of knew what they meant, but I didn't want to think it all the way through, not yet. I started gasping for air—couldn't breathe, couldn't breathe . . . couldn't . . .

"Take that thing out of him, before you kill her, too," the older guy said.

I had to look now, but I knew. He was my animal to call, one of my *moitié bêtes*; he gave me some of his healing, speed, strength, stamina, and I gave him more power, but there were downsides.

My chest felt like it was collapsing, I was struggling to breathe, and it fucking hurt to try. I had to see. I turned my head, while I gasped like I was suffocating. Domino was pinned to the closet door with what looked like a sword hilt sticking out of his chest. Blood was bubbling out of his mouth; he coughed on it, choked on it. I had a shadow of the pain he was experiencing and the frantic struggle to breathe, drowning in your own blood while your lungs collapse and your body keeps trying to breathe, because your body keeps trying to work, even when it's too broken to ever work again.

I watched Domino struggle for breath, and knew no matter how much pain I was enduring, it wasn't as bad as what he was feeling. He looked at me with those fire-colored eyes, and what I saw in them was failure. Drowning in his own blood and all he was thinking was that he'd failed me. I did not want that to be his last thought. I tried to tell him with my eyes that he hadn't failed me. I couldn't speak and I didn't want to try to talk to him mind-to-mind; I was afraid it would make everything worse.

The blond stood in front of him, wrapped one hand around the hilt, and braced the other against Domino's chest. He pushed as he pulled on the hilt, and just that extra pressure on his chest made us both start to choke, our bodies shaking and starting to convulse.

The man sitting on me tried to hold me down and keep me from hurting myself, I think. "Get it out of him, now!"

"It's stuck on a bone, or something," the other one growled. "If she dies . . ."

The blond tore it out of Domino's chest, blood gushing around it as his body fell to the floor. It bowed my spine, made me try to breathe and not be able to, and then suddenly I could breathe. My chest still ached, but it wasn't a sharp pain anymore. I breathed and it hurt to do it, but I could do it. Shallow breaths hurt, but . . . I tried a deeper breath and it wasn't painful. Another one and it was better. Other things were better, too. I thought of Nathaniel and knew he was standing with Damian beside him, and Dev was there, too. I could feel them now, and they could feel me. They knew at least some of what was happening to me now. I was afraid to open up the link as completely as I could, because I didn't want the shapeshifter who was touching me to sense what I was doing.

The shapeshifter in question said, "That's it, calm, even breaths. You'll be all right."

I didn't want him to comfort me. I didn't want him being nice even when I knew it was a means to an end. For some reason they didn't want me dead, so he'd work to keep me alive, but that was the only reason I wasn't bleeding out on the floor with Domino. I turned to look at him. He wasn't moving at all now. He just lay there on his side, but he'd fallen at an odd angle, unable to cushion or direct it. His neck was hyper-extended, which would make breathing even harder, or maybe easier. I didn't know anymore. But I could see his face, see his eyes too wide as he struggled to breathe, that awful wet sound coming from his chest, or his throat. Blood coated his chin and mouth. I could still taste his mouth on mine. He shook, or shivered; a gout of blood spilled out of his mouth and the horrible wet rattling breathing stopped. I saw his eyes go, watched him dying inches from me.

I screamed. I screamed for help. I screamed, because there was nothing else I could do. The man on top of me popped me in the side of the face the way you hit a cat that was chewing something, not to hurt, just to startle. It made me look away from Domino to him.

"No screaming," he said, and took a syringe out of his jacket pocket. He removed the plastic that covered the needle.

"After the screaming she already did, they'll just think it's more sex," the other one said.

I didn't look at him but kept my eyes on the man with the needle. I did not want to let him give me whatever was in the syringe. I didn't even have to know what it was, to know that much. I must have telegraphed something, because when I tried to hit him, he blocked me with his arm and settled his weight more solidly on my waist. He had to weigh over two hundred, maybe closer to three; I was pinned unless I moved him. All I could do was try to struggle enough to keep him from using the needle. I'd alerted Nathaniel and the others; they'd tell Edward and Nolan, and the other police. They knew what rooms we were in; if I could delay long enough, maybe help would come.

I still didn't know what they'd done to Ethan, other than that he wasn't supposed to be dead. I wanted to look behind me and see for myself, but the man sitting heavy on my waist leaned down toward me with the needle. I put my arms up the way you did when you sparred except my arms were probably his target, so it was hard to know what part of me to protect.

"I promise you the drugs will just knock you out, nothing else."

"Your word of honor?" I asked.

He looked a little surprised, and then said, "Yes."

"For me to take your word, you'd have to be from a century where that really mattered, and this is not that century."

"My original century was, Miss Blake. I give you my word of honor that this will only make you sleep."

"I believe you," I said.

"Then put down your arms and let me give you the shot."

"Nope, I don't want to be unconscious."

"We can hit you until you're unconscious," the younger one said.

"You don't want to kill me, and hitting someone repeatedly in the head until they're unconscious is a good way to do that by accident."

"But I do want to kill you. I want to kill you so very much," he said, as he walked closer to us so I could look up at both of them.

"But you won't, at least not here and now."

"And why won't I?"

"Because someone else wants me alive, and that someone else has enough power over you to make your friend afraid of me dying here and now."

"You gave away too much," he said to his friend.

"You shouldn't have used the weapon on one of her *moitié bêtes*. It could have killed her."

"He was better than I thought he would be, and the other one was coming through the door."

"So you admit that you couldn't take him without resorting to a magical weapon," the one sitting on me said, and there was derision in his voice. I'd thought they were partners but was beginning to think they didn't really like each other. It didn't mean that they weren't work partners, but it did mean that they weren't a completely united front. Division in the ranks always gave opportunity to find people you could turn; *traitor* was only a bad word if they were betraying you. If they were helping you betray the other side, *traitor* could be a very good word.

The young-looking one snarled at his friend, an edge of growl in it that sounded too deep to come from his thinner chest. He looked in shape, but it was the shape of someone who hadn't hit all their secondary growth spurts yet, and now he never would.

He raised the weapon he'd taken out of Domino's chest, and it didn't look magical. It looked like a short sword, but the blade was almost pyramid shaped and the blade wasn't . . . It seemed heavier and oddly shaped. I tried to look at the blade coldly, trying to see the magic in it and not Domino's blood all over it. If I looked at it clinically I wouldn't start screaming again—maybe.

The one who was sitting on me moved, and I was there to sweep at his hand with the needle in it. "Come help me hold her."

There was a noise behind me. The younger one looked at the source of the noise. "If you don't want me to kill that one, too, we need to get out of here before he comes to."

"Then help me with her."

I wanted to look back for Ethan, but he was only unconscious; they'd said so, and there was no reason for them to lie about it after what they'd just done to Domino. I kept my attention on the two men in the room who could hurt me; the rest would have to wait. I prayed for Ethan and for myself and for Domino, though I knew dead when I saw it. The dead don't need prayers; that's for the living.

"You're not going to win this one, Anita Blake." It was the young guy, standing over me now. There were no extra lines on his face; he still looked about seventeen, but his eyes . . . It was like looking into two dark caves.

There was another small sound behind me. It sounded like a knife moving in flesh, but that couldn't be it. Our attackers were in front of me, and Ethan was alone. Calm, I had to be calm, had to think. "You know my name, but I don't know yours."

He smiled. "I am Rodrigo, and this is Hamish."

"Do not give her our names."

"Why not? She's not going to tell anyone."

That let me know they meant to kill me, not here and now, but I wasn't getting away to share any information. So why not kill me here, and could I reach my gun before they killed me, or knocked me out? The big man settled more solidly against my waist.

"Forget the gun. You can't get to it," he said.

He was right. I hated that he was right, but he was. "What do you want?"

"Aren't you going to ask why?" Rodrigo asked.

"Why what?" I asked.

"Why we're doing this? Why we killed them? Why we haven't killed you?"

"No, I'm not going to ask any of that."

"Why not?" he asked, and smiled, as if he realized the irony.

"Because it won't help."

He looked at me with those cave-dark eyes. I realized the only other person I'd ever seen with eyes like that was a serial killer, and one of the most frightening people I'd ever met. It let me know what I was dealing with, but I bet he hid behind that youthful face and slaughtered people, joyously.

"My, how very practical of you."

"You have no idea how practical I can be, Rodrigo."

Rodrigo laughed, head back and delighted. "Was that a veiled threat? Do you think you will ever be in a position to harm me? Oh, that is optimism such as I have not heard in centuries."

"Don't tease her," Hamish said.

"What does it matter?"

"The look she's giving you matters."

Rodrigo knelt beside us; his knee brushed my arm and I moved away. He tried to pin my arm, but I kept moving it away. He frowned at me like I was a misbehaving child. "Now, Anita, you know you can't possibly elude us. We will pin you and Hamish will give you the shot."

"I know," I said.

"Then it's not very practical for you to struggle against the inevitable, is it?"

"I suppose not."

"But you're going to struggle anyway, aren't you?"

I lay there, looking up at both of them. The big guy was getting sort of heavy on my waist and stomach. Funny how if I was having good sex the man never seemed that heavy, but in other circumstances I realized just how much smaller I was than most men. I wasn't going anywhere with him sitting like that, but I didn't have to move him. I just had to keep him from sticking whatever was in the syringe into me. If I could delay everything long enough I was still hoping that the cavalry would ride to the rescue; I just needed to give them as much time as I could. "Yes, I'm going to struggle anyway."

"We aren't supposed to kill you, but we can hurt you. If you make us hold you down like this, I will use it as an excuse to cause you pain."

"Somehow, that doesn't surprise me," I said.

"He will enjoy hurting you," Hamish said.

"I believe that."

"Do not put yourself at his mercy, Anita Blake."

"I'm not at his mercy. You're here, Hamish."

"Do not look to me for protection from Rodrigo. That would be a grave mistake." He said it and he meant it, but he wasn't happy about it. Again, I smelled division in the ranks.

"Duly noted," I said.

"I like hurting people," Rodrigo said.

"You like killing people," I said.

"That, too, but I really do enjoy a slower death; otherwise I'd have stabbed your lover through the heart, instead of the lungs."

I couldn't keep my eyes neutral. It made him smile wider. "Oh, you didn't like that at all. Let's do this, Hamish. I know what sweet nothings I want to whisper in her ear."

"Then grab her arms and stop talking us both to death."

"Oh, when I do anything involving you, it won't be talk, old friend." I had seldom heard the phrase *old friend* sound so hostile.

"He just threatened you," I said.

"He does that," Hamish said.

"Roddy, I don't think he's afraid of you. Are you, Hamish?"

"I fear no one," he said.

"Not even Roddy, or especially not him?"

"Why are we letting her talk like this?" Hamish asked.

Rodrigo frowned; he looked like a petulant middle schooler, as if he should stamp his foot and complain to his mommy. "I don't know."

"Hold her," Hamish said, and this time he meant it, and so did I. I used my feet and legs and every bit of lower body I had to try to throw him off me. I didn't expect to really move him off me, but it kept him from using the needle on me, and that was my goal. Not to let them put whatever that was in me, and to stay in this room until help came.

"Hold her!" Hamish yelled.

Rodrigo got one of my wrists pinned, but I got a palm strike under his chin that rocked him. He tried to hit me back, and I somehow managed to block him with my one free arm, which pissed him off even more. "Stop squirming!"

"Squirming is one of my best things," I said.

"This is going to happen. Stop fighting it!"

"Fuck you!"

"Only if it would cause you pain."

"I doubt you're that well-endowed."

He snarled at me, sending his beast's energy playing along my skin. I breathed it in like a familiar cologne, but he shut down too fast. I couldn't tell what scent it was; it was a level of control of his energy that was really rare, but then, he was one of the Harlequin. One of the ones who had fled across the world and the ones with us hadn't found yet, or had given up on finding. We'd told them to stay home with us and leave the world alone. If I lived through this we'd be changing that policy.

He pinned one wrist under his knee, making sure to grind it to hurt, but I'd been hurt worse before, even recently, and I knew for a fact that once they got me out of this room unconscious, I'd eventually be hurt a hell of a lot worse. He got a hand on my other arm, and my wrists were pinned under his knee and hand. I knew it was over, but I still moved the rest of me as much as I could. Hamish put his hand on my chest and leaned, and that pretty much ended my upper-body moving, and if he'd pressed long enough, my breathing. He shoved the needle in my arm, and I couldn't stop them. I screamed and Rodrigo slapped me hard enough that I saw stars for a second. When my vision cleared I was already starting to feel warm.

"What did you give me?" My words were clear, but my tongue was starting to feel thick; all of me began to feel like it was getting wrapped in cotton like some breakable object to be wrapped up for shipping. Whatever the stuff was, it was fast acting.

Rodrigo leaned over me, petting my hair, and I couldn't stop him. They still had my arms pinned, but it wouldn't matter for much longer. My body was starting to feel heavy, thick, and distant. "It doesn't matter what we gave you; it's working." He leaned his dark eyes over mine, and it was too close to the intimate eye contact that Domino and I had just shared. It helped me fight clear for a moment. I dropped every metaphysical shield I had and silently broadcast to anyone and everyone, everything, that could hear me, feel me. I needed help and I needed it now!

"What are you doing?" Rodrigo asked, leaning so close that I smelled the soap he'd showered with, and underneath that was heat and fur and . . . leopard.

"Get back, Roddy. Don't touch her now!" I couldn't focus on the man sitting on top of me now, couldn't make my eyes work the way I wanted. I kept watching the blond.

"Why can you touch her and I can't?" he asked.

"Because I'm not one of her animals to call, and you are."

I stared into the wereleopard's cave-dark eyes, and thought, *Mine*. He said, "No."

The drugs hit a new level and my beast quieted. Everything quieted. I couldn't move, almost didn't want to move.

Rodrigo petted my hair again. "That's better." He moved to one side and used my hair to lean my head back so I could see Ethan. I couldn't have moved enough to do it myself now. Ethan dangled from the door, a knife through his shoulder pinning him in place while the rest of his body hung there. He was deeply unconscious or the pain would have revived him.

"I did that," Rodrigo whispered near me, and then rolled my head to look at Domino, "and that, and if we get to kill you, I'll beg to help. I am not your leopard to call. I am something you cannot tame."

It took almost all the effort I had to make my lips move and whisper, "Harlequin."

It startled him, as if he didn't think I'd know what they both were, but what else could they be? Nothing else could have taken out two of my tigers, with all their training, and me this fast. He reached toward Domino and came back with his hand scarlet with fresh blood. He wiped the blood across my lips and I couldn't stop him.

"When she is done with you, I will make you choke on your own blood." He shoved his fingers down my throat, but I didn't choke for him. "Swallow the blood of your tiger, Anita. Swallow him down for the very last time!"

I tried not to, but I couldn't do anything but swallow. All

blood tastes the same, like sweet copper pennies. Darkness was starting to eat my vision. My tongue was almost too thick to use, but I fought to say it, while I stared up into Rodrigo's black eyes: "All the . . . Harlequin . . . belong . . . to me." Then the darkness came and I wasn't sure if it ate me, or I became it, but Rodrigo's black eyes were the last thing I saw.

77

I KNEW I was dreaming, but I knew it wasn't my dream. I was wearing a dress from a century that I'd never lived through. The skirt was heavy with one of those odd hoops, if that's what you call it, that made the dress go out to either side of your hips like you should be able to set plates on the stiff satin cloth. The cloth was red and gold, and the tight cinched waist pushed my breasts up too much so that even I was distracted when I saw myself in the mirror that was leaning up against the stone wall. It was a very realistic dream. I could feel the long skirts brushing against the rough stone floor. I had enough of Jean-Claude's memories to know that there should have been sweet rushes or something on the floor, but it was rough-hewn rock, almost cavelike, except there were windows, long, thin, and reaching almost to the high vaulted ceiling. I could hear the ocean, feel the wind of it. I thought, *But where is the smell of the ocean?* And that was when I knew it was a dream. There's no scent in a dream; that part doesn't work when we sleep, which is why most people don't smell smoke from fire in time. Noises wake us, but not smells.

Whoever had picked the dress had left my hair loose, curling thick and utterly black around the whiteness of my skin. My eyes were dark. Some trick of the light in the room made them look black, but I had Rodrigo's eyes carved into my brain and I knew my eyes were brown, because his were truly black. A natural blond with black eyes, you didn't see that much.

"The Welsh come colored like that from time to time," a woman's voice said.

There was a woman in the mirror now, and it wasn't me. She was taller than me, slender, model thin, but not starved, just built that way. She had long, straight blond hair that fell well past her waist to swirl in the white dress she wore. It was from a much earlier century than mine, loose with long belled sleeves that almost hid her hands. Gold ribbon laced her tight through the bodice so that it showed her small, high breasts to good effect. Her eyes were a clear pale blue, the shade that coloring books tell you is what water looks like, but it almost never does in real life. She was almost everything that I'd ever wanted to be when I was about twelve to sixteen, when I realized I would never be any of it.

"Wishes," she said.

"When I was a child, before I knew my own worth, yes," I said.

She walked closer to her side of the mirror; the room looked identical, as if we were both standing in the same place. She was shining in the sunlight in a way that hair and skin didn't if you were human. She was almost unearthly in her beauty, like a shimmering white goddess.

"Yes, I was a goddess once."

"They worshipped you as one," I said.

"You don't believe I'm a goddess?"

I started walking toward the mirror as I said, "No."

"Could anyone but a goddess build a dream for us to speak in?"

"I've met other people who could create dreams, and they weren't gods."

The shining light of her flickered for a second like a bad connection on a video, and then it steadied to shine and be lovely again. I stood in front of the mirror now. It was a very old mirror, the glass full of imperfections, dark marks in the glass itself, a bubble here and there.

"It was a marvel of craftsmanship in its day," she said.

"I bet it was," I said, and looked at her like a tall, thin, blond reflection in the mirror. I could see that there were flowers and leaves embroidered on the gold ribbon of her dress now. Why had she put me in a dress that was closer to Belle

Morte's taste than hers? Or did she want to wear bright colors, but they washed her out?

"I wear what I wish to wear," she said.

"Pastels look terrible on me, but I bet they look wonderful on you," I said.

The image of her flickered again, the shining white light gone for an eyeblink, replaced with darkness, rough stone, like a cave, or a tomb. Then the white figure was back, shining harder, as if trying to make up for that last glimpse. Take no notice of that man behind the curtain.

I could see that her high cheekbones were paired with a chin that was a little too pointed for my taste, a nose a little sharp; *witchy,* I'd have said once, but I knew too many witches now and none of them looked like that.

I got another glimpse of the dark cave, and her face bare of the light for a moment, and anger in those pale blue eyes. Too pale, not as rich a color as she was pretending to have here in her dream . . . our dream.

"It is not your dream. It is mine!"

"Have it your way," I said. "Why did you bring me to your dream?"

"I thought this would be more pleasant."

"It's not a bad dream, so what do you want in this pleasant dream?"

"You have something I want," the image in the mirror said.

"What's that?" I asked.

"Power."

"Yeah, you and everybody else."

"What?" she asked, as if I'd confused her. If she could read my mind it shouldn't have confused her, which meant she could only read part of my thoughts.

"I am in your mind," she said.

"But you still don't understand everything I'm thinking, or everything I'm feeling, do you?"

"I understand all!" But there was that flicker again, and I saw her standing in the dark place, her thin face closer to mine than it was in the dream.

"I don't remember the early deities claiming omniscience," I said.

The flicker again, because I'd confused her again. She

came back to the mirror in her white dress with its gold and embroidery, but she wasn't shining anymore. She was lovely, but not otherworldly so. Her eyes were blue, but I knew people with bluer ones.

"When I am done with you, I will find your blue-eyed lovers and carve their faces down to ruin!"

That scared me and I couldn't hide it with her inside my head, and she understood the fear. She smiled a thin smile. "I wanted to make this pleasant between us, Anita, but if you are determined to be unpleasant, I know how to do that, too."

Dev lay on the floor beside me. His eyes were gone, just blood and thick bits as he screamed and reached out for me. I grabbed for his hand before I could think, and it felt real enough, but . . . it wasn't. It wasn't and I knew that it wasn't. I'd given her an awful idea to use against me, and she had, but it wasn't real. If she'd wanted to hurt me this wasn't the man to choose. Dev vanished and it was Nicky with both eyes bleeding and gone, but that wasn't right. He only had one eye, and she didn't know that. She wasn't perfect; even this far into my subconscious she couldn't see that clearly.

"I see more clearly than your man will after I take his last eye."

I carefully, very carefully, didn't think of anyone else, just put a blank wall between me and my thoughts. It was like shielding for metaphysics; just think walls. I put up a wall between us and it appeared in the middle of the room, dividing it in half with the mirror on the other side.

She screamed then, and the scream shattered the wall, so that I put up my arms to shield my face, and thought it was like the vampire exploding. I wasn't surprised to find a piece of stone embedded in my arm. I'd given her the image. I had to stop that.

I pictured the wall again, but this time it was smoother, metal, and mine. Her power hit it, but the metal only bent with her efforts; it did not break. Her power beat against my wall, my metaphysical shielding, and she couldn't get through.

"But you are still trapped in my dream, Anita Blake!"

Was I? I wasn't sure how to break the dream without dropping the wall, and I wanted the wall to stay. I'd learned to do lucid dreaming where I could change dreams as I had them, or even break free of bad ones, but holding the wall while she battered it and trying to figure out a way to break the dream was a few more balls to juggle than I could keep in the air.

I started with the dress, and I was suddenly wearing black jeans, a black T-shirt, black boots, and my favorite holster with my favorite gun. I felt more me as I looked up at the metal wall dimpling as she beat on it. It bent here and there, but she couldn't break through. I could hold the wall. I could stand in the dream and be okay. Interesting, and I did my best to stop the thought there, no other memories, nothing. I would give nothing to be used against me here. Nothing but the wall, cool metal, smooth without any handholds for her mind.

She screamed again, the metal of the wall bending as if a giant had hit it, but it held. She couldn't get to me anymore. She couldn't play with me in dreams, and she couldn't make the dream into a nightmare. I could wait her out. She must have realized that, because she decided to let me wake up, or maybe I just woke on my own.

78

I WOKE IN the dark place I'd seen in the moments when the dream wavered. It wasn't completely dark, though; there was natural light coming from somewhere in the wall or ceiling. I was in a thin beam of pale sunlight. I was also almost on my knees, but not quite, because chains at my wrists kept me from my knees, or the stone floor. I'd been hanging there for a while, because my shoulders were aching. I got to my feet slowly, carefully, because I knew it would hurt even more as full circulation came back to my shoulders, arms, and hands. I was wearing a red satin nightie that I'd never owned. For a second I wondered if I'd fallen into another dream, but my arms hurt too much for that. I'd tried to be chained up like this for sexy bondage one time back home and found that I could only have my arms up like this for so long before I started to hurt. I'd done one scene where my legs had gone out from under me, and Asher had let me hang like that for a while. I hadn't said my safeword; if I had he'd have unchained me and taken care of whatever hurt, but once he had unchained me my arms had hurt more and for longer than ever before. If I couldn't hold myself upright when I was bound in some way, then I asked for a new position, or just to be held and loved. Unfortunately, there wasn't a safeword in the world that would get me out of this dungeon.

I stood there and waited for the pain in my shoulders to die down enough for me to feel how many pins and needles were burning through my hands. I flexed them, trying to rush the process, because I'd woken up alone. No one was actually hurting me yet, or even guarding me. Good. First, I needed to be able to feel my hands, because it's hard to fight if you can't. As far as I could see there was no electricity in the room; in fact, there were unlit torches in wall sconces, which meant there were no cameras, no way for them to watch me until they came into the room. Better.

I kept flexing my hands and trying to rotate my shoulders to see if anything was damaged from hanging however long I'd been there. The daylight meant that either it was only a little later the same day, or it was the next day. If the first, then I'd only been out for a couple of hours tops. If the second, then I was lucky I could move my arms, or feel my hands at all. It would also mean that whatever had happened in Dublin that night was over and I'd missed it all. That scared me, tightening my stomach, making me wonder if everyone I cared about was all right. Then I realized I was being stupid. I didn't need a phone to call home.

I reached out to Nathaniel first and there was nothing, just a blankness, which scared me even more. I took a deep breath, let it out slowly, got myself calmer and reached out for Dev . . . and nothing. I tried Jean-Claude, and again, nothing. It wasn't that everyone here in Ireland had died in some horrible vampire debacle; something was preventing me from contacting anyone psychically. I'd had a human witch that was able to do that once, so the fact that the Wicked Bitch of Ireland would have someone powerful enough to do it shouldn't have surprised me.

There was one opening in the room, a rough doorway that seemed to have stairs beyond it that went up; other than that I didn't see any other doors. Unless there was a door at the top of those stairs to keep me prisoner, they were pretty confident they didn't need a door to hold me. I looked at the manacles on my wrists, because that was what they were; they didn't lock with keys but with a metal piece that slid through a hole. If I could have gotten one hand close enough to the other I could have undone them, but the chains were too widely spaced for that. I looked at the chains themselves. They were big links, like the size of a log chain, so they were big and meant for holding things a lot heavier than me. They weren't fastened to the stone ceiling but went through holes in the ceiling, which meant if someone was at the top of the room above me they'd see the chains move and know I was awake. I'd been so busy looking for modern things, I hadn't thought that old-school would work just fine.

I listened for movement that might let me know that they were coming to check on all that chain movement like a fish on a bobber, but it was quiet. I realized I could hear the sea. Dublin was a coastal city, so that shouldn't have surprised me, but somehow I thought of the room in the dream and the fact that the windows had looked out over the sea. It was as if the room in the dream were more real to me than Dublin and that one glimpse of the Irish Sea. I had a second to wonder if this was still a part of that dream, and then I smelled the damp and the mustiness of the room. I breathed deeper and could smell the saltier freshness of the sea air. You couldn't smell things when you were dreaming. I hugged that fact to myself, because it helped me not worry about the whole dream-versus-reality thing. I'd treat it as real until I knew I was wrong.

I heard voices on the stairs. I debated on pretending to still be unconscious, but I'd just gotten the feeling back in all my extremities, and besides, no one coming through the doorway would be human. They'd be able to tell if I was asleep just by my breathing and heart rate. There was really no sense in pretending, so I was standing, waiting, when Hamish came through the doorway, but he wasn't with Rodrigo anymore. The man with him was tall, dark, and not handsome. He wasn't ugly, but he wasn't pretty either. It was like he had several great features, but they didn't all belong on the same face at the same time.

He was definitely not handsome, but something about the way he carried himself as he entered the room made you want to look at him. There was an energy to him that made Hamish easy to overlook, which would have been a mistake, because the flashiest person in the room isn't always the most dangerous.

I caught a glimpse of white behind the second man, and it was the Wicked Bitch herself in person at last. She was wearing the same dress she'd worn in the dream, but it wasn't the shining perfection it had been. The dress had dirt on the hem from the rough stone floor, or maybe she'd gone for a stroll outside. She was still beautiful and sort of exotic, for lack of a better word, but it wasn't heavenly light and fireworks in the real world.

The two men took up posts on either side of her, but a little in front, so they were between her and me. I wasn't sure if they were afraid I'd hurt her, or she'd hurt me, but they were definitely placed so they could keep us apart if need be. Interesting.

"Anita Blake, we meet at last."

"I was thinking almost the same thing, though I don't know what name you prefer," I said.

"*M'Lady* will do."

"You called me by my Christian name and surname. Seems like using a nickname would be too informal after that." I didn't want to call her M'Lady. Maybe just stubbornness on my part, but I didn't want to use the name she forced people to use.

"You are very calm for someone who awoke in chains," she said, searching my face for some hint of what I was really thinking.

I tried to shrug but mainly made the chains rattle. "Not being calm won't change anything."

"Such possession of self is rare."

"Thank you," I said.

"I hope you do not mind the change of clothes, but your others had become quite . . . disheveled."

"I appreciate your thoughtfulness," I said. I'd shared enough of Damian's memories to know that being nice to her was my best chance at not getting hurt. It might also make her more talkative, and I needed more information. Where was I? What day was it?

She watched me with those pale blue eyes that she'd worked so hard to make bluer in our shared dream. "There is no fear in you now. Perhaps I have been too generous and should have hung you up nude."

"I said *Thank you.*"

She frowned.

"Allow me, mistress," the second man said.

"Not yet, Keegan." She walked closer until she was only about two feet in front of me. I could have kicked her, but I didn't see what it would gain me. They hadn't hurt me yet; if I hurt them first that would probably change.

"As my mistress wills," he said, but his face showed a sour disappointment. Whatever he had offered, he enjoyed doing, and I would probably not enjoy it at all.

"The first time I touched your energy through our shared vampire, you were nearly helpless before my terror. Now you stand before me and there is no fear in you. How can this be?"

I just looked at her, willing myself to be calm and patient, and wait. I wasn't sure what I was waiting for, but I was hoping I'd know it when it happened.

"Lay your hands upon her, mistress, and her calm will shatter," Keegan said.

"I would not recommend that, M'Lady," Hamish said.

She turned and looked at Hamish. "Why should I not touch her?"

"You have both drunk deep of the powers of the Queen of All Darkness."

"What of it?"

"Her powers will grow with touch as well. I told you what she did to Rodrigo."

I so wanted to ask what I had done to Roddy, but I didn't. They'd assume I knew exactly what I did, and either they wouldn't believe me or they'd know just how new I was to some of my powers.

"He is weak of will," Keegan said.

"Rodrigo is petty, cruel, and nearly honorless, but he is not weak," Hamish said.

"Are you saying I am no stronger than Rodrigo?" she demanded.

Hamish bowed and said, "I would never say that, M'Lady. We are all your humble servants and pale in comparison to your greatness."

I half-expected her to call bullshit on the pretty speech, but she didn't. She seemed to take it as her proper due. "Then I will put the fear of me into her."

"I advise against it," he said.

"You dare to doubt our Queen," Keegan said.

"I never doubt the Queen of Nightmares, or we would not have come halfway around the world to serve her."

"Then watch and learn," Keegan said.

She reached one pale hand toward me. I waited for her to hesitate at the sunlight, but she didn't. She moved through it as if she'd never seen a vampire go up in flames from it before. She touched my face and it took a lot not to pull away, but I knew that would amuse her and I didn't want to amuse anyone here.

She caressed my cheek and said, "Such a pretty girl. I normally don't think dark hair and eyes are striking, but you are quite lovely."

"Thanks, you too—on the lovely part, I mean. You're as pale as I am dark." I remembered through Damian's memories and Asher's story that she was very insecure, insanely insecure. When dealing with a crazy person, it's always safer to go along with the delusion, as far as you can. If she wanted to be the fairest of them all, I would be her biggest cheerleader.

"We would make a fine pair of opposites for some man's bed, you and I." I didn't like that idea at all; I fought not to show it but apparently failed, because she smiled and said, "That bothers you. I would have thought that sex would not bother you, being of Jean-Claude and Belle Morte's bloodline."

I tried to think of a polite way to put it, still trying not to trip her crazy. "We just met. I like to get to know someone before I have sex with them. You know, at least a coffee date."

"Coffee date," she said. "What is a coffee date?"

A woman's voice from the stairs said, "When people meet online, or in a place where they don't know each other well, they will often make their first private meeting in a public place like a coffee shop or café. They will have coffee, or tea, and talk. If the talk goes well, then they will plan a more traditional date."

The woman was slender, taller than me by a few inches, but still shorter than everyone else in the room. She had soft white-blond curls spilling around her face in an artfully styled cloud that brushed her shoulder. I got to her face and had a moment of wondering if Rodrigo was cross-dressing, because the face looked identical to his, but the body underneath seemed female. Some cross-dressers are better at the switch than others, but still I was betting I was looking at his twin. She was wearing black-on-black clothing top to bottom and it looked a lot like what I normally wore to hunt vampires in, including the boots being more work than club. Her eyes looked as black as the clothing; in this light I couldn't be certain, but I remembered staring up into her brother's eyes and I was betting hers were as black as his. Eyeliner and mascara made her eyes look larger and even more of a contrast with her pale skin with that smattering of freckles.

"Rodina, what are you doing here?" Keegan demanded. He seemed to demand a lot.

"I wanted to see the witch that has made my brother so useless. I would have said that no one could move Rodrigo, not like this, so I had to come see for myself."

"This coffee date, why would they do such a thing?" the Wicked Bitch asked.

"They believe that meeting in public, during the day especially, will keep them from being carried off by people who mean them harm. Dating when you are alone with someone means you have no one to come to your aid if they decide to do terrible things to you." Somehow as Rodina said it, the likelihood of terrible things happening seemed to grow. I wouldn't have wanted to be alone with either her or her brother.

Those black eyes stared straight at me as she came down those last few steps and glided across the floor. She looked past her supposed queen as if she weren't there. I met her bold gaze and said, "I bet you and Rodrigo are killers on a coffee date."

She smiled, pleased with herself. "We like good coffee. Be a shame to waste it on violence; so many things can get spilled."

"So that first date," I said, "must be a lulu."

"*Lulu*. I haven't heard that used in decades," Rodina said, rolling her eyes.

"Do not play the teenager here. You are older than I am," Hamish said.

"But I was a teenager when I stopped aging, when we stopped aging. I'm sorry that your master did not find you sooner, Hamish," she said, trailing her fingers along his arm as she passed him. He turned so that he kept her in view like you did when you sparred. Once the gloves went on, all bets were off.

"You seem not yourself, girl," Keegan said.

"I feel very much myself today," she said, moving past Hamish so that she was closer to their mistress and me than anyone else.

"Perhaps I should remind you that being too much yourself does not meet with my approval."

Rodina gave a small bow. "I am, as always, at your disposal, M'Lady."

"You know I prefer that you curtsy, even when you are dressed like a man."

Rodina dropped into a low, perfect curtsy, even mimicking holding a long skirt out to the sides. "As you wish, M'Lady, so shall it be."

The would-be queen did not offer the other woman a hand up, and by rules of etiquette Rodina was stuck in that very uncomfortable low curtsy until her mistress told her to get up or offered her a hand up. The vampire that didn't look very much like a vampire at all turned back to me.

"Do you know why they all refer to me as M'Lady?"

"An endearing nickname?" I said, trying to sound casual, because I was pretty sure we were getting closer to the painful part of things.

She smiled, looking down demurely, though it looked like a practiced gesture and not a real one. Something you do because it's expected, but you don't mean it. "Because to say my name aloud is considered bad luck. To come to my attention at all is considered ill-fated."

I licked my lips and fought to keep my pulse even. "I heard that," I said.

"Allow me to demonstrate." She offered her hand to Rodina, who raised a slightly startled face, but she had no choice but to take what was offered. M'Lady helped the other woman stand but kept their hands entwined.

"M'Lady, what have I done to offend thee?"

"I do not like your attitude today, and your brother's loyalty is in question. Do I need to question yours, as well?"

"No, M'Lady, you do not."

"We shall see," the vampire said, and one minute Rodina was standing tall and sure of herself, except for a slight uncertainty in her black eyes, and then her knees buckled. My skin ran with goose bumps just being close to whatever was happening.

"Please, mistress," Rodina said through gritted teeth.

"I like my servants humble, Rodina, and you and your brothers never quite get there."

The kneeling woman's face was so pale that her freckles stood out like ink against her skin. She looked as if she might faint. "Please." She hissed it, as if words were about to fail her.

"Say my name, girl."

"M'Lady," she said, sweat breaking out on her face as if she had a sudden fever.

"No, my real name."

"Moroven."

"No, my *real* name."

"Nemhain," the kneeling girl said in a voice that was strained as if she were in pain.

"Scream my name, girl."

"Do not . . . make me . . . do this, please!" Her words were pulled from between her teeth as if she were afraid to open her mouth too wide, for fear she'd throw up. I could feel the power rolling off Nemhain, but I still didn't know what she was doing to the woman on the floor.

"I will pull every horrible moment in your long life from your mind and make you relive the terror of it. All you have to do to stop me is to do what I ask. Is that so harsh a burden, Rodina?"

The girl shook her head, lips tightly closed. She was swaying on her knees now. She kept shaking her head as tears started to roll down her cheeks. "Nemhain! Neeemhaaainn!" She screamed the name until it echoed against the stone walls.

The vampire let go of her hand and Rodina fell to the floor, one shaking arm catching her just before she would have lain on her side. She looked like what she really wanted was to curl up in a fetal position and weep, or throw up, or all three, but she fought to stay upright. She fought not to faint; she fought to save as much of herself as she could from what had just happened.

Nemhain turned to me with a smile, most unpleasant. "Now, it's your turn, Anita. I suggest you call out my name much sooner than she did; after all, you are merely human and do not have the reserves of strength that a shapeshifter does."

I tried not to tense up, but I couldn't help it. I breathed out fast and tried to relax into it. It helped with a beating sometimes, and this was just another type of beating.

She reached out that pale hand, and I couldn't help but jerk back from it. She laughed, high and wild, the kind of laugh that only comes out of supervillains and the truly insane. "Keegan would enjoy holding you for me, Anita, or you can take your medicine like a big girl like Rodina did."

Keegan came up behind her, and there was something in his brown eyes that made me not want him to touch me, ever. Rodina's voice came shaking and weak sounding, but she still said it. "Just take it. Don't make it worse."

Strangely, in that moment I trusted the crazy bitch on the floor more than the one standing in front of me. I looked into Nemhain's pale blue eyes and said, "Just do it."

"So brave. I will break you of that before I am done."

"Talk is cheap, girlfriend. Do it, or don't."

She frowned at me as if it wasn't the reaction she wanted, but she laid her hand against my face and called her power. We were both done being nice.

79

MY SKIN RAN in shivering goose bumps with all the power she pushed into me, but it was like standing in the middle of a river that flowed past the rock of me. I could feel the water, knew I was getting wet, but I was still above water, still safe and unmoved by the torrent.

I looked into her blue eyes from inches away, with her hand cupping the side of my face, and all that energy flowing around, but not into me. Just like in the dream, she couldn't get past my shields.

"No." She whispered it.

I looked at her and said, "Do you still want me to say your name?"

"This is not possible," Keegan said behind her.

"I cannot see into your mind. I cannot draw your fears to the surface of it. The chains you wear are like the blade that slew your tiger. They are enchanted to separate you from all your other parts. Jean-Claude cannot help you while you wear them. You are a vessel for power, nothing more. I should be able to do with you as I like once you are shorn of all the other powers that aid you."

"Surprise," I said softly.

She poured more energy down her hand and put a second hand on the other side of my face so it looked like she was moving closer for a kiss. *"No!"* She shouted it, so angry, centuries' worth of rage. I could smell it like something sweet and bitter rising off her skin. She was right on one thing: She had cut me off from all the other people I was connected to meta-physically. It was supposed to make me weaker, but in that moment, I realized I was like a loaded gun, and whatever she had done to me had taken off my safety. For the first time, I had the ability to feed on anger, thousands of years of untapped rage, and had no one in my head or heart with more practice at controlling their hungers.

I didn't think it was a bad idea, or a good idea. I just fed on her. I fed on her hands as they cupped my face. I fed on the look in her pale eyes as they widened in surprise. I fed skin to skin, draining her down as she held me. So—much—anger. I felt my eyes fill up with my own power. I watched her face grow peaceful as she fell into my gaze, and still I drank her rage. I'd never tried to drain anyone like this, but then, I'd never had anyone who'd offered such a feast of time and ire.

Hands dragged her away from me, but she reached out to me, wanted to keep touching me, like any vampire victim once you mind-fuck them deep enough. Keegan and Hamish held her between them. Her eyes were still unfocused like a sleepwalker's.

"Her eyes," Hamish said, and it took me a second to understand it wasn't Moroven's eyes he was referring to, but mine.

Keegan looked up at me and then at the floor. He wouldn't look me in the eyes while they were glowing. I felt like every inch of my skin should have been glowing with power, not just my eyes. Oh, my God, it felt so good.

The Wicked Bitch, who turned out not to be so wicked after all, took a deep shuddering breath and looked up at me. I'd thought I'd drunk deep of her rage until I looked into her eyes again. Hatred, such burning hatred—it filled her eyes, her face, as if she were formed of it. Something in that one look did what all her power hadn't done before: It scared me. I don't know why, but I couldn't keep my pulse even, couldn't stop that spurt of adrenaline. It's always funny what will scare you and what won't. You never know, not even about yourself.

"That's better," she said in a voice that was icily calm and controlled and didn't match the hatred in her eyes at all.

"Mistress, are you well?" Hamish asked.

"Answer him for us, Keegan," she said.

"The woman is afraid now. We are very well, indeed," the man said, smiling a most unpleasant smile.

"Why would she be afraid now?" Rodina asked, her voice still holding an edge of the fear that Moroven had caused her.

"She sees me now. Don't you, Anita?"

I swallowed past the lump in my throat, my mouth suddenly dry. I couldn't have explained it, but I'd never had anyone look at me with such hatred. I don't know why, but it did frighten me. Damn it.

"I could feed upon your fear now, as you fed upon my anger, but I think I will let your fear grow first. You have so little inside you that it is not a feast for me." She walked closer to me and peered into my face. "Not yet anyway, but it will be, Anita. I promise you that before I kill you and take the power that is rightfully mine, I will create inside you a fear to equal my hatred."

I had to swallow again to say, "I'm not sure there's enough fear to equal your hatred, Moroven."

She smiled and it was a prettier one than Keegan's, but they were still the same smile. It was most unpleasant and promised worse. "See, Anita, I knew you would say my name. In a few hours, you will scream both my names."

I shook my head. "I don't think so." But my heart seemed to be in my throat. Why did the hatred make me more afraid than the anger? Then I realized I had my own anger, but I wasn't sure that I hated anything as much as Moroven hated the world.

"We will leave you to contemplate your fate, Anita, but not alone. No, my Harlequin brought a very special guest to keep you company."

My pulse had been calming down, but now it skyrocketed. Who did she have? Who else had she kidnapped? I tried to think who else had been in the hotel. Nathaniel and Damian had been with the police; they were safe. Who else did that leave? Donnie and Griffin had been in the lobby, but . . . I prayed hard for so many people not to come down those stairs, but Edward wasn't on the list. . . . Somehow the thought of it being Edward didn't seem possible, as if he weren't touchable. I knew that wasn't true, but I was less worried about him than about almost anyone else I loved in Ireland.

She watched my face as she said, "Bring in our other guest."

As if they'd been waiting on the stairs for her order, two

men walked into view carrying a third between them. My heart fell all the way to my feet, my knees went weak, and I had to make my hands into fists to keep myself upright and not show more emotion than I already had. It was Nathaniel. I didn't know how they'd gotten him away from the police and all the people who were supposed to keep him safe, but there he was, the absolute last person I wanted to see dragged in here with me. God help me. God help us.

He was shirtless, with his arms fastened behind his back. I couldn't see any injuries on him, which was a relief. The long braid of his hair was piled on top of his body, as if they'd tripped on it at some point and just gotten it out of the way. They'd tied a piece of gray cloth across his mouth for a gag. I stared into his wide lavender eyes and felt unmanned. To keep him safe, I would do anything; we were both so fucked.

He was in manacles, too, but he had them on his wrists and his ankles, with more chain wrapping around his upper body and his legs. They'd carried him down, because he could barely bend his body in the chains, let alone walk.

"I knew there had to be more fear in you somewhere, Anita, and there it is, and all for this man. Your leopard to call. Your fiancé, so I'm told, though you seem to have promised yourself to more men than you can actually wed. How does Mr. Graison feel about your wedding plans with Jean-Claude?"

I didn't know what to say. I couldn't seem to think of anything useful. I tried to think of anything that wouldn't make this worse or give her the emotions she was wanting to feed on, but nothing constructive came to mind. For once in my life, I was frozen and didn't know what to do. I mentally screamed at myself to get my shit together, to think, but all I could do was look into his eyes and be afraid for him. Fuck, I had to do better than this!

"Speechless with fear already, Anita? Do I need to do something to help loosen your tongue?"

That, I had an answer for. "No, no." Even the extra no was nerves, and she knew it. Damn it!

She went to Nathaniel and stroked the heavy braid, gathering it up in her hands and letting it fall to the floor. He looked at me, ignoring her as if she wasn't there. I stared into those lavender eyes, that face, and tried to sense him. He wasn't just one of my *moitié bêtes*; he was the other third of my own private triumvirate but I couldn't feel him at all, as if he were less present than the other people in the room. Whatever magic was on the chains made Nathaniel almost blank. I couldn't sense his energy at all, but I could sense hers, and Keegan's, and Hamish's, and Rodina's, but not Nathaniel's. The metal didn't keep me from being psychic; it just kept me from being psychic with the people I was metaphysically joined with. That was interesting, maybe even useful. I couldn't think how to use that knowledge yet, but it was something, and I'd take it, because something was better than what I'd had a second ago.

"Such beautiful hair," she said. She stroked down his chest, touching the bare skin between the chains. Nathaniel got touched more than that when he danced onstage at Guilty Pleasures. We were okay. We were okay. I kept repeating that in my head like a mantra. "He's in such good shape, Anita, so much exercise to put all that muscle on his chest and arms. All your men seem to be quite fierce about their gym routines, but then, so are you, aren't you?"

"Yes," I said, because she didn't seem to like silence. "Yeah, we work out."

"The tiger that we left wounded in the hotel killed two of my Roanes before he came to help you. My seal folk are not the Harlequin, but they are well trained. The fact that he slew two of them so quickly is testament to the training of your guard."

"Ethan killed two of your men. I wondered what kept him out of the fight in the other room so long."

She motioned at the two men holding Nathaniel, as if close to two hundred pounds of muscle wasn't heavy at all. "They wish that my Harlequin had brought your wounded warrior here so they could revenge their brethren on him."

I looked at the men more closely. One had black hair with dark brown eyes; the other had paler brown hair with gray eyes. They were handsome in that traditional guy way, but with Nathaniel in the room, they just didn't look that good to me. I was biased, but they were broad through the shoulders and looked like there was the promise of muscle under their clothes. They didn't have the black-on-black eyes that Roarke and Riley had had. I'd started thinking I could spot all the Roane, or Selkies, from their eyes, but apparently not. Good to know.

She came to stand in front of me again. "Do you want to know how we came to have your Mr. Graison in our power?"

"Sure," I said, and my voice was almost as uninterested as I was trying for, and I'd almost gotten my pulse under control. The plan hadn't changed: be nice, be polite, don't trip her crazy, and make her think she is the most beautiful thing in the room. The only thing that had changed was that the stakes had been raised for the moment when I stopped being nice again. I kept my thoughts from going any farther down that track. One moment at a time, just this moment, deal with this moment. The next moment can go fuck itself until we get to it.

"You recover yourself very quickly, Anita. It makes you very interesting to me."

"Maybe we can go shopping sometime and have girl talk," I said, and even managed a smile.

"Are you making fun of me?"

"No. If you wanted to go out shopping, gossiping, and girl bonding, I'd be totally down with that."

She frowned at me. "I do not understand you."

"Just offering to be friendly," I said.

"You cannot be friends with your food, Anita. You have already fed upon me, and I will return the favor soon."

"I'm engaged to be married to a vampire. I can be very friendly to people who feed off of me."

"I, too, feed upon my servants," she said, and motioned at Keegan, "but would never allow them to feed upon me, even were they capable of it." It was really good to know that he was her human servant. I'd thought probably, but it was nice to have it confirmed. If I got a chance to try to kill anyone, other than her, he'd go to the top of the list, because now I knew that killing him might kill her, too. Yippee.

"Most servants of vampires can't feed on their masters," I said.

"Not just most, Anita, all, or all save for Jean-Claude and his new bloodline. There seems much confusion in his new-found power on who is master and who is slave."

"We understand who wears the pants in the family," I said. I could be calm as long as I didn't look at Nathaniel, but just focused on the white bitch in front of me. I was doing my best to sort of pretend he wasn't here. It helped me think better.

"You may find that the pants have changed owners," she said, then called out, "Roarke, bring our other guest."

And just like that my heart was racing, and I looked at Nathaniel. His eyes widened as if to tell me something with a look, but for once I couldn't read his expression. Without our ties open between us, I was head blind and just had to watch as Roarke, King of the Roane, walked down the steps. His dark eyes stared at me as if he'd never begged me to kill him or been anything but tall, imposing, and hers. He came into the room radiating energy much more than he had at the church. He was leading another man by the hand. It took me a second to realize it was Damian. My fear spiked again until I realized Damian wasn't chained or restrained in any way that I could see. He just walked down the stairs with Roarke like they were buddies. What the fuck was going on?

80

MOROVEN WENT TO Roarke and greeted him with a kiss. If he didn't want to kiss her back, it didn't show. Had he lied in the church, or was her control of him just that good outside of the church? If we all survived long enough, I'd ask.

Damian stood beside them, his face almost blank. His eyes were open, but it was as if he didn't see anything in the room. I realized that Roarke wasn't leading him by the hand; he was holding Damian's wrist. It seemed odd, but then Damian just standing there while the two of them kissed was odd.

"Damian!" I called his name, and he jumped as if I'd startled him. "Damian!" He blinked and looked at me then; for a second he was in there looking at me. He said, "Anita!"

Moroven laid her hand beside Roarke's so they were both touching him at the same time, and his eyes went blank again.

"What have you done to him?" I asked.

She looked at me and smiled that unpleasant smile that Keegan shared with her. I wondered if it had started out as his or hers. "Once I separated you from your servants, Damian was mine again, as he has always been. He gave himself and Mr. Graison over to me once your powers were not clouding his mind."

"I don't believe that."

"He betrayed your Nathaniel, as soon as I called to him. He came back to me, because you are not vampire enough to hold him."

There was no way that Edward would have let them just walk out of the police station. It made me want to ask if anyone besides Nathaniel had been betrayed. But there was nothing for me in that line of questioning. Once we got out of here, then I'd ask Damian and Nathaniel all sorts of questions, but not in front of her, not with her making his eyes go dead. I had to believe we would get out of here, because I had too much at stake to think anything else.

Moroven leaned in against Damian's body, raising her face up toward him for a kiss. His eyes were alive again, his again, and he actually flinched away from her. She said, "Kiss me, Damian!" She made it an order, and he bent toward her, but his eyes stayed aware. He did not want to kiss her, and that was enough to bring him partially out of her control, even with her and her animal to call touching him.

"Damian, don't kiss her," I said.

He stood back up straight and tall, too tall for her to reach him. She turned to me with a hiss; her eyes glowed blue. "He is mine!"

"You sent him to Jean-Claude. You were done with him once, Moroven. Why do you want him so badly now?"

"Because he is mine!" She screamed it, the glow fading from her eyes.

"If all you wanted was your lover back, you could have sent a letter," I said.

She moved away from Roarke and Damian, and I expected his eyes to go back to being blank, but they didn't. Something about the interchange between us all was helping him fight it. If I could only figure out what had helped and keep doing it.

"A letter would not have brought me you, Anita, and that is what I wanted. That you brought Damian back to me is a wonderful gift, and I will never give him up again."

"Why did you give him up to Jean-Claude in the first place?" I asked; more information could only help, right?

"Your lord and master wrote to me, said that he had dreamed of Damian's pale flesh for centuries and that he would force Damian to be his catamite. It was something that our crimson-haired vampire had a near . . . mortal terror of," and she laughed at her own wordplay. Most of the people in the room who belonged to her laughed. Rodina and Hamish were the exceptions. Maybe their white bitch of a queen wasn't all she was cracked up to be for them.

"You had men here," I said. "You didn't have to send Damian all the way to America for a little sodomy."

She made an unhappy face. "What good to me is a man who prefers men? I do not collect such men. I gave him up to be tormented by Belle Morte's prize pupil, only to find that when Damian returns home, he has a taste for men now. Jean-Claude must possess some witchery that I did not envision."

I fought to keep my face blank, because I knew it wasn't Jean-Claude's witchery, at all. Nathaniel was two for two, being the only male lover of two heterosexual men. I was pretty sure Jean-Claude and Asher had more to their credit, but no one that I knew.

She tried to walk all the way around Nathaniel and the two Roane, but Rodina was in the way of her skirts. "Oh for Goddess' sake, girl, rise and go stand with Hamish."

Rodina didn't make Moroven order twice, just got to her feet and moved over to stand with her fellow Harlequin. They might not like each other a lot, but neither of them liked Moroven at all. I wasn't sure how I was so positive of that, but I was, and somehow I knew I was right.

"Jean-Claude is one of the most beautiful men on the planet," I said. "I mean, I may be prejudiced in his favor, but he is the king of seduction."

"I know how seductive he can be, Anita, or did he neglect to mention that he was my lover?"

"He told me that Belle Morte and you traded Damian and him for a while."

"I tried to keep him, but Belle would not give up one of her favorite poppets."

"I heard that, too," I said.

"Did they tell you what one of my passions is, Anita?"

"I'm not sure," I said because I wasn't.

"Ruined beauty," she said.

"No," Damian said loud and clear. He actually stepped forward with Roarke still gripping his arm.

She turned and looked at him. "How are you fighting free without her power to bolster you?"

"I am here. I'll stay with you. Just let Anita and Nathaniel go unharmed."

"Tempting but I did not create a near army of vampires in Dublin for fun and frolic, Damian. I was beginning to wonder what horrors I would have to unleash on Dublin before the great vampire expert would finally come to Ireland." She looked at me and smiled.

"Are you saying that you did all that just to get me here?"

"The only power you possess that is more attractive to the Mother of All Darkness is your necromancy. It is also what allows you to control vampires, so I lured you to the only country in the world where your personal magic will not work. Now, when I kill you and take the rest of the Mother's power into myself, it won't linger over your necromancy. The magic will simply come to me, as it was destined to."

"If you kill Anita, I may die with her," Damian said.

Moroven looked back at him. "I do hope not, but even the joy of tormenting you with your new face is not enough to make me forgo collecting all the power that is due me." She came to stand in front of me again. "How ever did you change his face? I thought only Belle Morte could do that."

I tried for the truth. "I'm not really sure."

"Come now, Anita, eventually you will tell me all your truths, so do not bother lying."

I glanced at Hamish and Rodina, because any wereanimal or vampire powerful enough should have been able to tell that I'd just told the truth. Hamish gave a blank face, but Rodina smirked just a little. They knew that their new queen couldn't tell if someone was lying. The only other master vampires that I'd ever met that couldn't act like undead lie detectors had been ones that were so self-delusional that it compromised their ability to tell what was real.

"Since I didn't know that it was possible to make a vampire servant out of anyone, it was all a little accidental."

"Lies, but I know how to get the truth." She motioned for the men with Nathaniel to move over in front of me.

Keegan went just behind the opening to the stairs, but on the opposite side that people seemed to walk down. I saw his arms move, as if he pressed or pulled something in the walls, and a thick chain snaked down from the ceiling. It wasn't a pair of them like the ones on my wrists, but just a single thick line of chain with a large hook on the end of it.

"No!" Damian said. He started to push past Roarke, and then I saw the Roane's eyes glow like black diamonds. Damian's eyes unfocused and he stopped moving forward.

I looked into Nathaniel's eyes just feet in front of me. He was starting to struggle as much as the chains would allow, which wasn't much. Whatever the men were going to do, they didn't want him moving around. My heart was in my throat. I pulled on the chains at my wrists and knew doing so was useless.

"Damian, wake up!"

He startled awake, shoved Roarke, and then hit him solid in the face. Roarke fell to the ground. Rodina and Hamish moved in a blur of speed to catch Damian's arms. Rodina put a blade to his throat.

"This is why we had to gag your Mr. Graison. If you call out to him again, Anita, I will gag you, and I'll cut out your lover's tongue." Rodina's eyes blazed blue as if spring skies could burn. I believed she meant everything she said.

The chain was directly in front of me so that I'd have a good view of whatever the men were planning to do to Nathaniel. Or hell, maybe he'd have a good view for what they were going to do to me. Whichever way the pain went, they meant for us to watch each other endure it. Sadist much?

Keegan hooked the end of the single chain through the chains at Nathaniel's ankles. He tugged the connection, and when he was happy with it, he nodded. The two men holding Nathaniel began to lower him to the floor as Keegan went back to the wall and reached around an outcrop. I could see just the edge of the silver handle as he began to rotate it and the chain started going back up into the ceiling. The two Roane held Nathaniel gently until they were told to let him go. I'd have expected them to use it as an excuse to hurt him, but they didn't.

Keegan moved the chain up until Nathaniel's face was almost perfectly in front of mine so we could look into each other's eyes. He was hanging only about four feet in front of me, out of reach, but not by much. I looked into those lavender eyes, my flower-eyed boy, and my stomach was clenched so tight, I didn't know if I was going to throw up or hyperventilate. There had to be a way to stop this from happening. The thick braid of his hair trailed down from his body like an auburn rope to pool on the floor.

"M'Lady," Damian said, "please do not do this."

"Have pleas for mercy ever moved me, Damian?"

"No," he said, and he tensed in Hamish's and Rodina's grips.

Rodina asked, "Can I slit his throat if he keeps struggling?"

"No, that might kill Anita too soon. I need her terror to open her to me for feeding, and then I will feed on all her power. If she dies before I crack this so-tough nut, then the Mother's power may seek yet another vessel, and that stops here with me."

"If we can't cut him up, how do you want us to subdue him from rescuing his boy toy?" Rodina asked.

"You are the Harlequin. Are you so inadequate that you cannot even control one vampire for a few minutes?" Moroven yelled at them.

"Can we injure him?" Rodina asked.

"No! Now, do your job!" Moroven turned back to us, and I didn't want that, because whatever was about to happen was going to be bad, like, nightmare bad.

"You're the motherfucking Harlequin. Are you going to let her talk to you that way?" I asked.

"She's the boss," Rodina said.

"Only because you follow her."

"We follow the Mother's power," Hamish said, "whatever vessel it chooses."

"Enough!" Moroven screamed. She walked around the edge of the wall just like Keegan had, except she didn't make any more chains appear. She came back with a big knife in her hand. It gleamed silver, and just the way the edge caught the sunlight let me know it was sharp. I didn't know for certain it was a silver blade except in color, but I was betting it was, even as I prayed that it wasn't.

"I want you to look into those big, pretty eyes, at that lovely hair and that fit and strong chest, and think upon this, Anita Blake. I am going to make a nightmare of his beauty, and then I will fuck him in front of you, and when you are filled with terror at what I will do next to your two men, I will drink you down!"

Moroven strode to Nathaniel in a swirl of white skirts. Damian and I both screamed, "No!"

She grabbed the thick braid of Nathaniel's hair like a handle to hold him steady. She moved to the side so we could watch each other. She put the blade against his hair and sawed through it. She could have done so many worse things—I knew that—but watching that long, thick braid of auburn hair fall to the floor took my breath. I sagged in the chains, because my knees didn't hold me in that moment.

We stared into each other's eyes, and I watched one lone tear trail down Nathaniel's face. I screamed, not a scream of terror or sorrow but of rage. I lost my shit and cursed her, threatened her, and finally told her, "Kill me now. Because every minute you leave me alive gives me more chances to kill you first, you evil bitch!"

Moroven laughed in my face, then threw the blade down on the floor between us. "Anger. I cannot eat anger, Anita. But I give you my word, when I come back, I will pick up that blade again and I will carve up that beautiful body, or maybe I will take an eye. I want him to have at least one good eye so he can see the ruin of his beauty and your horror at it, but he doesn't need two for that."

I fed my anger as if it were a real fire. I fed it so that it would blaze higher, because she couldn't feed on me, couldn't

kill us if she couldn't find my fear. I touched that boiling pool
of anger that had been inside me since my mother's death and
been fed by every horror I'd seen since, and I let her see it in
my face.

"If my using the blade upon Nathaniel does not frighten
you, then I will use it on you, but I will find what frightens
you, Anita, and then you are mine." Moroven walked to Damian, who was still held between the two Harlequin. "You
believe me, don't you, Damian? You believe that I will do everything I have promised."

"Yes," he whispered, his eyes wide, showing too much
white around the edges, like those of a horse about to bolt. She
touched his face and his personality just slid away so that his
eyes were like empty windows.

Moroven turned to me with a smile. "He's afraid for you
both. It opened him to me, and now he is mine again." She led
Damian up the stairs as if he were a zombie with no will of his
own. "Enjoy your last view of Nathaniel's beauty, Anita. I give
you my word that the hour I give you now will be the last time
you see him whole."

81

WE WERE ALONE except for the two Roane, who stood to
either side of the doorway like good guards. They were both
armed with handguns, peeking out from underneath their
shirts, which seemed almost un-Irish by this time. In a country where most of the police—excuse me: Gardai—aren't
armed, it seemed wrong for anyone else but us.

Nathaniel and I looked at each other. I concentrated on
those big beautiful eyes of his and did my best not to look at
his hair. It would grow back. It would. But if I paid attention
to it at all, I was either going to start crying or screaming, and
neither was going to help us. We needed to help ourselves, not

hurt ourselves. Moroven was going to do that for us in an hour. I pushed her threats away, shoved the hatred in her eyes out of my head, or as much as I could. None of it helped me. I stared into Nathaniel's eyes and thought how much I loved him. I looked down at the braid of his hair lying underneath him like a promise of things to come, which was exactly what it was. Fuck. I prayed for an idea of how to get us out of here, along with Damian.

Nathaniel rubbed the side of his face against the chain that was across his shoulder; he scraped the gag out of his mouth. He worked his jaws and said softly, "Gag was fastened over my braid."

"Once she cut it, you had slack," I said.

He smiled. "It will grow back."

I nodded and managed to smile back at him.

The guard with the paler brown hair came toward us. "How did you get the gag out?"

Nathaniel answered, "It was tied around my hair, so now the gag is loose."

The answer seemed to make the man uncomfortable. "You should do whatever she wants you to do," he said.

"She's going to kill me anyway," I said.

"There are different ways to die, Anita. Don't let her kill you slowly."

"What's your name?" I asked.

"Barnabas," he said.

The dark-haired guard called, "Don't talk to them."

"If you don't want to watch her kill us slowly, Barnabas, help us get out of here."

He shook his head and started backing away. "I feel sorry for you, but not that sorry."

"Barnabas, get away from them!"

"I'm coming, Tommy." But to us, he said very low, "Don't look to me for help. If she tells me to kill you, I will. I'll make it quick, but I will kill you both if she orders me to."

"Good to know where we stand, Barnabas," I said.

"Stop talking to the prisoners!" Tommy yelled, and started walking toward us.

Barnabas just walked back toward the other man, who continued to berate him for talking too much to us. He made it sound like we were stray puppies that you couldn't get attached to because we were going to be put down anyway. I got the feeling that this wasn't Tommy's and Barnabas's first rodeo that had ended with prisoners dying—fast or slow. There was no help there. We couldn't offer Barnabas enough of anything to get him to betray the Wicked Bitch, and his friend Tommy was even less user friendly.

Nathaniel said, "It would be a shame if you never got to experience just how double-jointed I am again."

It seemed like a nonsensical thing to say, but I knew in a moment like this, it had to be important. I must have looked as confused as I felt, because he whispered, "More double-jointed than Houdini."

I finally realized what he meant: he was almost completely double-jointed. He could rotate his shoulders all the way around and pretty much everything else. It was interesting in the bedroom and when he danced onstage, but in this moment, it might be exactly what we needed. He could get out of the chains, and then he could let me go, if we could distract the guards.

I had to be the distraction, but how? I was wearing lingerie, so sex was an option. It certainly wasn't a fate worse than death or watching while the Wicked Bitch cut pieces off Nathaniel. If I got the guards close enough and raised the *ardeur*, it might work, but I didn't know if Moroven would sense it. The *ardeur* could be a flashy power, and we didn't need more attention.

I looked up at the chains on my own wrists. My one hand was almost small enough to pull through if I was willing to lose some skin and bleed myself. Wait. The guards would notice that.

I looked at Nathaniel. "I love you."

"I love you more."

"I love you most."

"I love you mostest," he said, smiling.

I smiled back, took a deep breath, and started pulling on my loosest wrist, hard.

Tommy of the black hair called out, "What are you doing?"

I ignored him, because what I needed was for both of them to come to me and turn their backs on Nathaniel. I put all my body weight onto my left wrist and pulled! My hand moved a fraction in the cuff. If the guards weren't here, I might actually be able to get one hand free, and that would be all I needed to get my other hand free. If the guards would stand there and let me pull on my wrist for about fifteen to thirty minutes while I scraped myself up, I could get away, but I was betting they wouldn't have the patience for it. I was counting on the fact that they wouldn't just stand by the door and watch me do it.

"What are you trying to do?" Tommy yelled.

"Get away," I finally said.

"You can't get away," he said.

I was going to need some lubrication to work my hand through. Lucky for me, my body made something that would work. If I wanted it badly enough. I stood up and started pulling, tugging, and rubbing my wrist against the manacle.

Barnabas called from the doorway, "You're just going to hurt your wrist."

"If I don't get away, she's going to hurt a lot more than my wrist."

The guards looked at each other and then started walking toward me. "Stop doing that," Tommy said.

"Or what?" I asked.

"Or we'll hurt you."

"Not half as much as the Wicked Bitch of Ireland will when she comes back in here," I said, continuing to tug on my wrist.

"Are you trying to bleed yourself?" Barnabas asked.

"Yes," I said.

"Why?" Tommy asked.

They were both in front of me, between Nathaniel and myself. Barnabas glanced behind at Nathaniel, so I leaned my body weight on the manacle and showed them why I was trying to get blood. "See, it moves a little. I think if I had some lubrication that I could get this hand out. Once I get this hand free, then I can just reach over and free my other hand."

"We're standing right here," Tommy said. "We won't let you do that."

"How are you going to stop me?" I asked, pulling harder on my wrist. I was going to have to be careful or I'd end up spraining my wrist before I got any blood to loosen things. I wanted so badly to look past them to Nathaniel and see if he was getting loose, but I didn't dare.

"Don't make us hurt you," Barnabas said, and he sounded like he didn't want to hurt me, but he would.

Tommy grabbed my arm just below the wrist. I think he thought that would keep me from pulling on it. I heard chains moving, and it wasn't me, so I started pulling wildly on the other wrist, which no one was holding. It made a lot of noise so that even I couldn't hear if Nathaniel was moving his chains.

"Stop it!" Tommy yelled, squeezing my left arm hard enough that it hurt a little, but not as much as the scrapes I'd already put on my wrist. I tucked my legs up and let all my body weight hang from my wrists, which surprised Tommy so that he let go, which let me rattle the chains like a fake ghost at a bogus séance.

Tommy hit me openhanded across the face. It was a good hit; it rocked me a little so that I just hung there in the chains for a second while my head and the rest of me caught up. He grabbed me by the front of the nightie and dragged me upright. The nightie wasn't a shirt; it wasn't even a dress, so he ended up flashing everything below my waist. Women can complain about men staring at their breasts, but trust me, there are worse things to have stared at.

There was that frozen moment when the men looked down and I could almost feel the click in Tommy's head, as he thought of something else he could do to me. I tasted blood when I swallowed. He'd busted my lip a little when he hit me, and the taste of my own blood made the beasts inside me rise like heat over my skin. They didn't like getting hit in the face either. I was alone in my head with all my beasts for the first time ever, with no more experienced lycanthrope inside me to help me. My body felt like it was starting to catch fire, so hot.

"What the hell are you?" Tommy whispered. He was still holding my arm.

I saw Nathaniel between their bodies. He was free and picking up the knife Rodina had dropped. Barnabas started to turn; if I hadn't seen Nathaniel, if there hadn't been two of them, if my beasts had had a few seconds more to rise, if I had had access to anyone's power besides my own, but I didn't. I called the only power I had that would kill and distract while it happened. I'd learned how to drain life energy through the touch of skin to skin from Obsidian Butterfly. She hadn't meant to teach me how to do one of her tricks, but one of my gifts was that if a vampire used a power on or around me often enough, I retained it either temporarily or forever. This one was forever.

It took Tommy a second to realize something was wrong, and then his hand where he touched me started to dry out, as if I'd put an invisible straw in his skin and he was a juice box. He tried to let go of me, but he couldn't. He yelled, "What are you doing?"

"Defending myself," I said, and my voice sounded distant, peaceful, because it felt good to drink him down, so much energy.

"Barnabas, help me!"

Barnabas started to reach out, but Nathaniel leapt onto his back and thrust the knife into his chest. The man made a sound and plunged his elbow back into Nathaniel, trying to get him off his back, which meant Nathaniel had missed the heart. He stabbed him again and this time Barnabas fell to his knees with Nathaniel still riding him.

Tommy was screaming now, and his body was covered in deep lines, as if he was in a desert where the sun was draining him dry, but it wasn't the sun or the heat, it was just me. I had no idea if anyone was close enough to hear the screams, but I couldn't stop even if I wanted to, because the moment I stopped feeding on his energy, he'd be free to turn and help Barnabas fight Nathaniel. He was still stabbing, trying to get a killing blow as the other man struggled. I could not afford for another trained man to join the fight Nathaniel would lose. So I stared into Tommy's eyes and watched his skin run dry until it was like leather, and still he screamed, higher and more piteously but I couldn't afford pity. Pity would kill us.

Nathaniel staggered to his feet covered in blood and breathing hard, but the other man didn't get up. Nathaniel had won. We'd survived because he'd killed Barnabas. I stared at the dried husk that was the man I was slowly killing. The strong hand that had grabbed my arm was just bones covered in dry skin. It didn't even feel like a hand anymore, and still I fed on the very essence of his life. If I stopped now, I could give back the energy I'd stolen and he'd heal, but I didn't want him to heal. We were fighting for our lives. Tommy didn't get to live any longer than Barnabas had.

Nathaniel's voice was hoarse, almost as if he'd been the one screaming. "Can I undo your wrist? Is it safe to touch you?"

"No," I said, and I swallowed all the power I'd gained from the man in front of me. I pushed the urge to feed and feed and feed back in the dark box of my soul, and Tommy fell to the floor like a broken doll.

Nathaniel reached up one hand and undid my right wrist. He still had the completely blood-soaked knife in his other hand. It felt good to have one wrist free, but the magic was still there, still blocking me. I reached over and undid the other wrist myself. The moment that I wasn't touching the chains I could suddenly hear all my people; every metaphysical link was there again. Nathaniel was there again, bright and like another beating heart. I swayed with the fear from Dev, and Damian came back to life inside my head like a piece of myself that I hadn't known was missing.

Nathaniel reached out to me and then dropped his bloody hand before he touched me. "I can feel you again."

"Wipe your hands on his sweater," I said, motioning to the dried husk that was lying at our feet beside the bloody mess that was our other victim.

Nathaniel squatted down and wiped his hands, and the knife on the sweater, and then stood back up. "He's still screaming."

"I can't hear him."

"I can."

"Hand me the knife." He gave it to me without comment. I knelt down, and now I could hear a high-pitched noise. He would stay alive in there, maybe indefinitely. Obsidian Butterfly had used it as punishment for her people, placing them in stone coffins until she wanted to get them back out and forgive them. I plunged the blade through the dry paper skin of the lower chest, turned the blade sharply up and in, until I felt the thicker meat of the heart. Most of the rest of the insides had dried out like the skin, but the heart was still there, almost as thick and alive as normal. I drove the blade up into that beating source of life until the screaming stopped.

I stood up and offered Nathaniel the blade again. He shook his head. "No, you keep it. It took me a lot to kill the other one. You did it in one strike. I'm not good enough with a knife yet."

"It comes with practice," I said.

He nodded. I knelt down and was getting Tommy's gun out of its holster to give to Nathaniel when Rodina came down the stairs so quietly we didn't hear her at all. She had a Glock in her hand pointed nice and steady. Some days you just can't win for losing. Fuck.

82

SHE LOOKED AT us, smiling, and finally laughed, "Here I come to rescue you, and I'm not sure you need it."

"Why would you help us?" Nathaniel asked.

"Because the Lady Bitch is not our Evil Queen."

"And you think I am?"

She looked at us and then to the floor at the bodies. "Maybe I don't know much about being good, but I don't think that's it."

I couldn't argue, so I didn't try. I just stripped the gun off of the body that I had killed, and handed it to Nathaniel along with an extra magazine. If you're going to loot the bodies, take the extra ammo. The gun was a Glock, never my favorite. It just didn't fit my hand right. Nathaniel checked to make sure it was loaded, automatically. It was good to see he'd been paying attention.

"Thank you for letting me see you feed on her, Anita. I have had my fill of that pale bitch."

I gazed into those black eyes so like her brother's and realized, "Somehow, I rolled you when I rolled your brother."

"Yes, the only other one that could ever do that was the Queen of All Darkness herself. I knew we had been following the wrong heir."

I didn't argue with her; I'd been arguing with people for months that I wasn't the heir to the Mother of All Darkness. It was getting silly to keep protesting, so I'd stop. I didn't like it, but I could stop playing the lady who protesteth too much. I got the gun off of the other body, though the grip was slippery with blood. Nathaniel might not have killed the guard with the first blow, but he'd hurt him enough that he didn't go for his gun; that was a serious win in my book.

We needed to move. Rodina had a backpack with tactical boots that fit me if I stuffed them with the thick socks and a black hooded sweatshirt to go over the lingerie. I had done my best to ignore how cold I was until I got the clothes on, and then I could finally shiver. She even had an extra hooded sweatshirt for Nathaniel.

She led us up the stairs with a short sword bare in her hand. She'd holstered her gun. She told us silence was essential and we followed her, but I said, "We need Damian."

"We'll be lucky to get the two of you out of here. He's still with the pale bitch and both her servants."

"We can't leave him," Nathaniel said. He must have thought at Damian, because suddenly the vampire was loud in our heads. *Go,* he thought at us. *I'll join you in Wicklow.*

"He says to leave. He'll catch up with us in Wicklow," Nathaniel said.

Rodina smiled. "Agreed."

I'd managed not to think about Domino until I saw Rodrigo waiting for us in the hallway just off the stairs. Then my careful compartmentalizing fell apart. Rodina stepped between us. "This is Ru, the other third of our triplet."

He looked identical to Rodrigo until I got to his eyes. They didn't look like dark caves or even the teasing hardness of Rodina's. There was something softer about this one. He dropped to one knee. "My Queen."

"Where's Rodrigo?" I asked.

"He is my brother and your man now, as Ru and I are," Rodina said.

"Anita, we have to escape first," Nathaniel said.

I looked at him, and if I hadn't had a bloodied knife in one hand and a gun in the other, I'd have touched his hair. He was right. Domino was dead; we weren't. "Get us out of here. Rodrigo gets a pass until we're safe."

"Your word of honor?" she asked.

"Yes."

He came around the corner like a mirror image of his brother. "I see my death in your eyes."

"You forced my lover's blood down my throat after you killed him."

She looked at her brother. "Rodrigo, really?"

He looked strangely embarrassed and shrugged. "It seemed fun at the time."

"Fun!" I said, and took a step toward him.

Nathaniel grabbed my arm, "Anita, we need out first." He looked at Rodrigo and said, "And you, stop saying stupid things like that."

Rodrigo looked at me; his cave-dark eyes held more thought than cruelty in that moment. "If I had not done that one stupid, cruel thing, we would not be standing here now, Anita Blake."

"Out first, Roddy," Rodina said. She led the way and we followed, because what else could we do for now? I had to put the gun in the pocket of the sweatshirt to take the flashlight they gave me. The knife stayed out, because I had nowhere to put it. Rodina led the way down a tunnel that opened in the rock. It was narrow and hit my claustrophobia so that I swear I could feel the rock beginning to close around me. I put the blade against one wall and the flashlight against the other so that my hands would let me know that the walls weren't really narrowing around me. It was just my phobia. It wasn't real. I could smell fresh air. I could smell the sea. There was gray light ahead. Rodrigo vanished out of the opening, and when I got to the end of the tunnel, it was a black rock overlooking a sheer drop to the sea below.

Rodrigo was standing to the left on the rock, offering me his hand. I so did not want to take it, but the light was dying and I couldn't see what he was even standing on or why he wasn't tumbling down onto the rocks below us, so I took his hand. He helped me up shallow stairs that were literally carved into the rock face. I'd have never even seen them, let alone been able to navigate them. Rodina was guiding Nathaniel up the steps behind us. Ru brought up the rear.

Rodrigo hunkered down behind a rise of thick grass and flowers at the top of the cliff. He motioned for me to stay low, so I did. There was the wind blowing the grass, making the flowers nod, and there was a ruin of black stones toward the end of the highest point of the cliff. "The Black Castle," he said. "Everyone thinks the only thing left is the ruin, but the fortress is inside the cliff. Her hiding place has always been here, as the castles above her have risen and burned, but always she has been the puppet master to the men above."

When he was sure the coast was clear, he led us through the grass and wind. There was a couple taking pictures of themselves straddling a rusted cannon that looked out over a harbor. There were more tourists or maybe locals picnicking or taking pictures of the sea as the light began to fade to twilight.

"And no one knows she's here?" I asked.

"No," Rodrigo said.

"One of her great strengths is that she hides in plain sight," Rodina said. She opened her backpack and said, "You can't walk around with a bloody knife in daylight, Anita."

I didn't like it, but I gave up one weapon, because she was right. We'd been fighting for our lives, but everyone up here was having a great day by the sea.

Rodina pulled up her hood to hide her hair and said, "We're tourists. We're going to blend in." She took Nathaniel's hand in hers and hung on his arm as if she'd always been there. Rodrigo apologized but said, "It is for safety's sake."

"Fine." I took his arm with one hand and put the other hand inside my pocket, where the gun was weighing it down. The gun made me feel better, though I admit it was tempting with him on my arm to just turn and kill him where he stood. If Nathaniel hadn't been with me, I might have, but he was, and we were outside. We were escaping. I'd kill him later.

The triplets led us down the grassy headland, across a parking lot that still had plenty of cars in it, and toward the town that lay spread out before us. It was still daylight and the only daywalking vampires behind us were Moroven and Da-

mian. The Roane were the greatest danger as long as the sun
was up. I felt like I had a target between my shoulder blades,
and it took everything I had not to look back, but with my
hood up, I actually did blend in. There were even a couple of
other women with skirts as short as mine, though they were
wearing tights under theirs. My legs were still so cold that I
could barely feel them. It was like I'd been able to ignore the
cold until I got outside in the wind. Nathaniel's new haircut
helped us blend in, but every time I saw him without all his
hair it was like a little punch in the gut. He'd wiped most of
the blood that was visible off on a cloth that Rodina had given
him, and the sweatshirt hid the rest. He was much better at
playacting than I was, so they looked much more like a couple
than Rodrigo and I did. Rodrigo was probably better at pretending to be a couple, but he was worried what I'd do if he
did. Ru had separated from us to walk ahead through the tourists. I'd catch a glimpse of him here and there, which probably
meant he wasn't hiding that hard from us.

We were crossing a stone bridge over a river that flowed
into the sea. It was all really pretty, but it was moments from
full dark. We needed cover before that happened. "We need to
not be out in the open," I said.

Rodina leaned in against Nathaniel, smiling as if I'd said
the best thing. "We'll head for one of the churches that will
keep the vampires out."

"What about the Roanes?" I asked.

"You and your men have killed four of them already today."

"How many more are there here?" I asked.

"Dozens," she said, still smiling.

"We need a plan," I said.

"Where're Dev and Edward?" Nathaniel asked.

He was right. I wasn't thinking clearly. I didn't know what
was wrong with me, and then I did. Damian was fighting to
stay with us, and not let her take him again, but he had all
three of them touching his skin: Moroven, Keegan, and
Roarke. He could fight off one of them, even two, but three . . .
It was like they were trying to steal a piece of us. I stumbled
and had to clutch at Rodrigo. "What's wrong?" he asked.

Nathaniel answered, "Damian." He'd thrown his arms
around Rodina as if he were hugging her, which looked less

suspicious than me clutching at just Rodrigo's arm. Then Damian was gone, vanished from my mind, my heart. Moroven had captured him again. Damn it!

Rodrigo said, "Are you all right?" He was holding me around the waist; apparently I was closer to falling down than I'd realized. My skirt was not long enough for around-the-waist holding. He helped me stand up and pull everything back into place.

"She's got Damian again," I said.

Ru suddenly appeared beside us. "We need to keep moving."

He was right. Nathaniel asked, "Did she take Damian over again because she knows what we've done or just because?"

I shook my head. "I don't know."

"There's no general alarm yet," Rodina said.

"How do you know?" I asked.

"We aren't running," she said.

"Good point," I said.

We were walking like two ordinary couples with Ru as our third wheel on yet another quiet, picturesque street. There was a line of boats bobbing in the water along the quay with a blue building on the other side of the road that was apparently a seafood restaurant and a shop called the Lighthouse and the Fishman, respectively. There was fresh Irish seafood, or so the signs said. We walked without running. Rodina managed to giggle at something Nathaniel said.

Rodrigo said, "Do you want me to do the girlish laughter, while you pretend to be clever?"

I fought not to glare at him, which would have ruined the whole "touristy couple" camouflage. The best I could do was lean in and say, "Fuck you."

He smiled as if I'd said something wonderful. I actually saw an older couple across the street smile at him. I lowered my face against his shoulder to hide the fact that my expression didn't match. It made it look like I was cuddling against him. Great.

Ru had stopped walking and was staring down into the dark water. There was a seal in the dark water; you could just see it. It stared up at us with huge black eyes that reminded me of Roarke's, except under the water like this it looked like a drowning victim. I whispered against Rodrigo's neck, "Is it just a seal?"

"When they're in seal form, you can't always tell them apart," he whispered back.

Ru knelt by the water and made soft sounds somewhere between growls, grunts, and purrs. The seal ducked underwater and vanished. Ru got to his feet fast. "That wasn't a seal." He was backing away from the water.

"Fuck," Rodina said. She let go of Nathaniel's hand and faced the water.

"What do we do?" Nathaniel asked.

The water, which had been quietly sloshing between the boats, began to boil with whitecaps, but there was nothing visible agitating the water. "Run!" Rodina said, and grabbed Nathaniel by the arm and started down the street. The rest of us followed. We got stared at by the few people still on the quiet street, but it didn't matter anymore. It was too late to pretend. The seals threw themselves out of the water onto the street behind us. I saw one shiver, and it stood up a man, fully clothed and pointing at us. Fuck!

Rodrigo dragged me around the side of a building. In the distance, I saw a church. It would keep out the vampires when it got dark, but it wouldn't keep out the Selkies now.

We had to scramble over a wall to get into the churchyard, and suddenly we were surrounded by tombstones. It was a graveyard. Nathaniel grabbed my arm. "Raise the dead. Raise zombies, Anita."

"I'm not sure zombies will rise here."

"Try," he said.

"I'd rather not die with our new queen, not just yet," Rodina said. "Try."

"If they find us, we'll hold them off," Rodrigo said.

"We are your Brides now, Anita Blake. We must keep you safe and happy," Ru said, and he moved into the darkness, vanishing into the shadows as if by magic.

Rodina moved the two of us into the shadows on the edge of the gravestones. "Do what only you can do, Anita. We'll do what we are good at and protect our Queen."

"We need a knife," Nathaniel said.

I'd thought she'd dig out the blade we'd used to kill the

Roane in the Black Castle, but she handed me a clean blade from a sheath at her side. "And the one we used in the castle," I said.

Rodina didn't question it, just fished it out of her backpack. I heard a noise at the wall. "Do magic, Anita. Do it for the man beside you." Then she ran for the wall and the quiet sounds of struggle.

I stood in that peaceful green space and realized it wasn't dark yet; almost no one could perform necromancy before dark. Necromancers were like vampires; we didn't function well in daylight. It was dark on the streets, but there was still light up there in the sky. I could feel it. I reached into the ground underneath our feet and searched for the dead. It was dirt, living earth.

"I can't feel the dead, Nathaniel."

He used the clean knife to slice across his palm and offered it to me. "Help me walk the circle with you." I saw Rodrigo or Ru throw someone back over the wall.

Nathaniel touched my face. "Anita, I need you."

I looked up into his eyes and thought about what would happen if they captured us again. I sliced my hand open, which startled him, but I clasped our hands together, blood to blood, and said, "We walk the circle together."

I visualized it like a line of white light shining down as we walked. I ignored the sounds of fighting, because I had to trust the three Harlequin to protect us long enough for me to do this. The dead would not rise here, but there was power here that I could use all the same. I prayed for protection and guidance. Nathaniel was an extra kick of energy, but I was already heavy with energy from having drained the Roane in the castle. I heard the circle close with an almost audible pop and felt a pressure change that made us both have to swallow as if we'd changed elevations. I took the knife with the Roane blood still on it, not even dried completely, and I pushed it into the ground. I hoped it would do what we needed.

The three Harlequin were backing toward us with a crowd three deep surrounding us. How many seal guards did Moroven have? Shit. They rushed us, and the triplets did their best. Rodina threw one over her shoulder and it fell through the circle. That could have been accidental, but then he stood up and stepped back through the circle to draw a sword almost as tall as I was, but half his body went through the circle.

"It'll keep out vampires, but not these guys," I said. Then full dark came. I felt it in my bones like an echo. The triplets all backed up through the circle and to us so that we were standing almost back to back. There was a solid wall of the Roane in human form waiting outside the circle, which I knew they could cross.

"Not that I'm complaining, but what are they waiting for?" I asked.

"The vampires to arrive," Rodrigo said. "She's told them to wait."

"I won't be captured," Rodina said.

"Nor I," Ru said.

"Crap," I said, and looked around for something, anything to help us. I saw something not that far away that gleamed in the dark. When I looked at it straight on, it wasn't there, but out of the corner of my eye, it was like a white phosphorous glow, a ghostly glow.

"The prophecy says that to guarantee our dark mistress will be lost and the Master of Tigers triumphant, they must marry one of the clan tigers," Rodrigo said.

"Is this really the time for a history lesson, Roddy?" Rodina said.

"If I die here, I need someone else to understand what's happened."

"What are you babbling about now?" she asked.

"What's in that direction that would be really haunted?" I asked, motioning.

There was a moment where the three of them sort of shifted and thought, and then Ru said, "Wicklow Gaol."

"It's just a historic site now," Rodina said.

A wind blew high and shivering through the trees overhead. It didn't smell of rain, but it felt like a storm was coming. There was a black cloud boiling in the sky toward the sea. "What is that?" Nathaniel asked.

"It's her," Rodina said, "her and all her dark court."

"We will give our lives for you," Ru said.

The black "cloud" began to separate into individual shapes. It was vampires flying in a mass like some Halloween witch poster. I leaned into Rodina. "Can you fight your way free to the gaol?"

"I cannot promise."

"Is it important enough for us to die for?" Rodrigo asked.

"There are dead there that will rise," I said.

"You won't have to kill me for what I did to your lover, Anita. The sea folk will do it for you." He gave a battle cry, which was the only term I had for the sound, and leapt into the mass of enemies.

83

IT WAS SUDDENLY a hand-to-hand fight, and we were outnumbered. It was Nathaniel who used a gun first, the sound thunderous even outside. It startled the man in front of me so that I stabbed him through the heart and was able to throw him back into the mass of his friends. And then suddenly, they stopped fighting. They cried out in confusion, almost in pain. I had no idea what had happened. I knew it wasn't any magic of mine.

Rodrigo and Rodina grabbed us and started running while Ru guarded our backs, but none of the others chased us. We ran. I tapped that part of me that was my beasts, that part that helped me work out with real lycanthropes in the gym, and I ran so that the streets were a black blur. I ran until the evil wind at our backs wasn't fast enough to keep up. Nathaniel stayed at my side easily, and so did Rodina and Rodrigo, but Ru stumbled and his sister had to grab him to keep him with us. I raced toward the white light shining as if the full moon had fallen to earth. I could see it more in front of my eyes the closer we got to it.

The triplets were actually behind us as we ran through the entrance to the huge stone building. If we survived, I'd make them do more cardio. A white-haired woman dressed in a long skirt and what was supposed to be authentic clothing but wasn't quite said, "We're closing for the day."

Rodrigo pulled a gun and showed it to her. "Run away now. Bad things are coming."

She ran away, yelling for help. She went through a side door into a café that was apparently still open. I hoped no one got brave. I wanted to use the ghosts, not make new ones.

Damian was suddenly loud in our heads again. He wanted to know where we were, and we thought it at him. He was above us in the night sky, and he thought of the gaol as old hunting grounds.

Two dark shapes appeared in the doorway. They were dark-haired, pale-skinned, dressed in black as if they'd come from central casting for vampires, one male, one female, but they were the real deal. They stalked in through the doors because they didn't need anyone's permission to get inside a public building. They looked at the people huddling in the café. They grinned wide enough to flash fangs.

"We will feast tonight, as of old," the man said.

The woman said, "They've seen us. We have to kill them now."

"No," I said, "you will not harm these people."

"You have no power over the dead in Ireland, necromancer," the woman said.

"You will not harm anyone in this building tonight," I said. I heard a whisper in the hallway and felt a cold wind down my spine. It wasn't vampires. I closed my eyes briefly and the whole building burned with ghosts like white phosphorus, thick with the moving pulse of hundreds, maybe thousands of restless spirits. They were angry. I'd never felt so much anger from ghosts before, and then I realized why. They were angry at the vampires.

"How many people did you kill in here over the centuries?" I asked.

They smirked at each other. "Enough," she said, and he nodded.

I pressed my still bleeding hand against the stone wall and felt the power shivering through the building, just waiting. Nathaniel put his hand over mine, and you could feel the building's bones shift and surge.

"What was that?" the male vampire asked.

Damian ran through the doorway, shoving past the two vampires. He joined us, breathing as if he'd run a race. He held his hand out to me. I cut his hand, and he reached out toward ours as we touched the stones.

"What is it?" he asked, as he placed his bleeding hand over ours against the stones.

"Vengeance."

The building shuddered around us, and a wind started down the hallway at our backs, not from the outside, but from inside the building. The two vampires went for the door, but a new vampire was there to stop them. He was huge by any standard, a giant of a man who had to stoop through the door and straighten up carefully.

"Damian, you shit bag. You killed Roarke!"

"Bachman, I see she called you back from Dublin."

"It served its purpose, for there stands the power that will make M'Lady into the new Queen of All Darkness."

"This is the one who's been tearing people apart in Dublin," Damian said.

"And now that you've let all these people see us, I'll get to slaughter them all," he growled at us.

"He's always been more beast than vampire," Damian said.

The Harlequin brought up their guns and Bachman did rush into battle, but not with us. He dived through the doorway into the café and screams followed.

"Save them!" I said.

"We can't leave you alone," Rodina said.

The wind spilled our hair around our faces. I could see the light like white fire burning through the building. It shuddered above us, like a giant waking.

"We aren't alone," I said. "Go and save them. That's an order!"

"No more people die here because of us," Damian said. Somewhere in all of it, the two vampires had vanished outside again. If I hadn't known better, I'd have thought they were more afraid of Bachman than us.

The triplets went through the door and toward the sound of screams. We walked forward and the ghosts came with us. The light was so bright that I could see the individual shapes of the vampires in the blackness as they swept toward us. I'd never seen so many that could fly like that. It was a rare gift and I remembered that Damian was amazing at it, too. It was her bloodline; they could all fly.

A vampire had a man in its grasp, feeding at his throat as it rose into the air. A gun exploded near us; the vampire wavered and dropped the man, who fell heavily to the parking lot. A second shot, a heavier boom of a sound, and the vampire exploded in a fine red mist. I knew who it was before I saw Edward step out of cover and say, "Did you forget to invite me to the party?"

"Never. Keep them off of the civilians."

"Who keeps them off of you?"

"They do," I said, motioning at the ghosts.

"You told me ghosts can't hurt people."

"They can't on their own," I said.

The ghosts swarmed around us, formed a pulsing, throbbing cloud as white and shining as Moroven's was black and dark. She stepped out of that cloud of shadows and illusion and called out, "Ghosts cannot harm us!"

"We harmed them!" Damian yelled, and he shared memories of walking into cells where people who could not afford to pay the gaoler starved to death, so the bite was a mercy in the end. Skin fever hot to the touch, vampires feasting on them like vultures at a corpse, draining them dry. The new prisoners, still healthy and beautiful, but Moroven liked beauty and collected them for herself. The victims that were tortured as part of their sentence, and pleased her because of new scars. Children weeping in the dark held, comforted, and killed. So many dead, so much murder. Moroven's kiss of vampires had treated the gaol as their personal grocery store for centuries. It was as if Damian's memories joined with the ghosts, made their stories, their lives, real again. The power of it roared upward like a thunderous waterfall of ghosts. They wailed and began to talk, and a lot them remembered exactly which vampire had killed them.

The townsfolk were screaming and pointing now; even they could see it. The ghosts cried out for vengeance the way a murdered zombie will go after its murderer above all else. Ghosts don't have a physical form that can harm anyone, but

I'd given them blood and I was holding the hand of my vampire servant and my *moitié bête*. We touched our bleeding hands together the way I'd combined power with another necromancer to raise a bigger, older zombie, and the ghosts became a roaring storm of wind and rage that attacked the vampires.

The white-and-black storm rose into the air. Edward, Nolan and his people, Dev, Magda, Socrates, all of my people except for Domino and Ethan, one dead, one injured—so many warriors on our side, but there was nothing to fight on the ground. The battle was in the air, and the only one of us who could fly was holding my hand, mingling his blood with mine.

The window in the side of the café exploded into the street. It was Bachman with the triplets chasing him away from the people inside just like I'd told them to do. They climbed out after him, but the big vampire charged us, grabbing Donnie before she could bring her gun up, and then Giacomo was there as big as Bachman, and the fight was on. Donnie fell free of it, and Dev pulled her to safety. More of the vampires were on the ground and I saw Hamish. The rest of the Harlequin had joined the fight. I saw Nicky wade into him and marveled again at the blur of speed that was my Bride.

"You will not kill us!" Keegan yelled, and he was just there with a shotgun aimed at the three of us. No one was close enough to help us. They were all fighting, as Nathaniel and I tried to get our guns up in time, but I'd been too deep in the magic and neglected the rest. Edward was moving, but he wasn't going to be in time, and suddenly the triplets were there. Rodrigo stepped in front of Keegan and they fired at the same time.

It sounded like thunder as Keegan fell backward and Rodrigo dropped to his knees. Nolan, Donnie, and Brennan surrounded Keegan, but he didn't get back up. Rodrigo had finished him. Moroven screamed out and fell to earth in a shining white light of ghosts, because now with both her servants dead, she didn't have the power to fight the vengeful spirits. I didn't know that ghosts, even ones full of magical blood, could drain the life from a vampire. Maybe I'd shared Obsidian Butterfly's gift with them. Rodina and Ru were still guarding me, so I was the one that knelt beside Rodrigo, along with Nathaniel and Damian.

The shotgun had opened Rodrigo's chest up. His heart was trying to beat in an open wound. "I have been what a Bride is meant to be for their Groom, Anita Blake: cannon fodder." He laughed and spat blood.

"Don't try and talk," I said.

He choked, spat more blood, and said, "The oldest translations of the prophecy talk about joining life forces, mingling souls. They didn't mean marriage." He coughed so much blood, I wanted to tell him to stop talking, but I wasn't sure he could hear me anymore. "It says for life . . . part . . . why some tiger clans are so serious about their monogamy."

There were sirens in the distance; they'd try to save him. Rodina and Ru were kneeling beside their brother now. The fighting was mostly over. Moroven's death had literally killed some of her supporters as she tried to reach out and save herself by stealing from them.

"I killed her clan tiger in front of her. She watched the light go from his eyes and then she drank his blood. Don't you see?" Rodrigo said.

"The King of Tigers wasn't supposed to marry a tiger. He was supposed to sacrifice it and drink its blood," Rodina said.

"Yes," her brother said.

Ru asked, "Would you ever have agreed to a human sacrifice where you drank blood?"

"Never!" I said.

"You certainly wouldn't have agreed to one of your own lovers and *moitié bêtes* being sacrificed so you could watch them die and drink their blood," Ru said, staring down at his brother, whose face looked like a mirror image of his own.

"No," I said, but with less force.

Rodrigo said in a voice that was too thick with wet things that should never have been in a living throat, "I felt the power shift as soon as you swallowed the blood, and then you said, 'All the Harlequin belong to me,' and I knew it was true." He coughed up dark blood in a wave down his face and upper chest. The ambulance came, but there was no one to save.

Epilogue

THE IRISH GOVERNMENT wasn't very happy with Nolan and his crew starting a firefight in the town of Wicklow. The whole paramilitary paranormal squad might be over before they ever got started. If that made the mysterious Van Cleef unhappy, maybe he'd fix it, if he could. Edward went home to visit with Nolan's family. They wouldn't let me come along and pry into the past. I pouted, but I was just glad that they were mending the friendship.

When Moroven died, I didn't feel any energy boost. Either calling the ghosts made me blind to it, or the power that was in She-Who-Made-Him had found another vessel to inhabit. I hope not. Apparently all the Harlequin really do belong to me now, or to Jean-Claude. Or at least they want me to be their Evil Queen. I'm not sure how I feel about that, but I know that we can't keep the Harlequin in St. Louis. They are starting to travel the world and police the preternatural world again. The European vampires are making noises about fighting us; after what just happened in Ireland and some rumors elsewhere, they can go fuck themselves. The vampires are not grown-up enough to be without more adult supervision. I guess that's us for now.

Riley and his girlfriend were imprisoned in the Black Castle, but Moroven had been so busy trying to capture me that she hadn't had time to do much harm to them. It turns out that Riley was Roarke's great-great-great-grandson, and he's now King of the Roane, who are a free people once again. The black-on-black eyes are a sign of kingship for them.

The new vampires in Dublin aren't like any anywhere else in the world. Part of it is the land itself and the magic of it, but part of it is that Moroven was never human. She was one of the Tuatha Du Dannon, the high courts of fairy, who one dark night fell into darkness. She was Fey and that was why her type of vampirism could survive here. It would have been nice if Flannery's auntie Nim had shared that. She said, "What difference would it have made?" I didn't have an answer to that. Maybe she's right, but it seems wrong.

Ireland is treating the vampire outbreak as the largest national health crisis ever, but they are incorporating the newly undead into mainstream life more smoothly than we did in the States. But the vampires here really do seem more like people with fangs, with a few exceptions.

We took Domino's body home. I am the true heir to the Father of the Dawn and the Mother of All Darkness, because I "married" one of my tigers. It means the commitment ceremony is suddenly way less complicated, because we only have to include people we genuinely love, but I'd willingly go back to complicated if it would bring Domino back. Nicky says I'm lying to myself on that one. I told him to keep his sociopathic logic to himself, that even I need some illusions.

Asher cried when he saw Nathaniel's hair. He also apologized to Devereux enough that they're lovers again, though I think it's mostly to torment Kane on Dev's part. We'll see.

Micah said yes to Nathaniel's proposal. So we may have yet another wedding to plan; it seems to be a theme for the year. The first night we were home together the three of us, I agreed to talk seriously about maybe getting pregnant. Petting Nathaniel's new short hairstyle makes me remember what could have happened. Damian has joined us in the bed a lot. Micah is letting him have a spot on the other side of Nathaniel with me in the middle. Jean-Claude isn't sure where to put him yet. We're working on it.

Ru and Rodina joined us at home, but feel totally cheated that Nicky got sex to become my Bride, but they just got a bit of magic. They miss their brother, Rodrigo, and he died well, which is just as well, since otherwise I would have had to kill him. After what he did to Domino, there was no other option. Nicky agrees. Everyone agrees. So why does it feel weird to owe Rodrigo my life, Nathaniel's life, and Damian's life, and still know that I would have killed him if he had survived? Sociopath much? Maybe. Not sure that's a good attitude for a would-be mommy, but it's a great attitude for an Evil Queen.

#1 *New York Times* Bestselling Author
LAURELL K. HAMILTON

Find more books by Laurell K. Hamilton
by visiting prh.com/LaurellKHamilton

"Hamilton remains one of the most inventive and exciting
writers in the paranormal field."—#1 *New York Times*
bestselling author Charlaine Harris

"The master of the most unusual of genres."—*Starburst*

"Number one *New York Times* bestseller Hamilton is still
thrilling fans."—*Library Journal*

laurellkhamilton.com
LaurellKHamiltonOfficial
LKHamilton